W9-BWW-790

THE SOUTHERNERS

The Southerners

by

EDNA LEE

APPLETON-CENTURY-CROFTS, INC.
New York

Copyright, 1953, by

EDNA LEE

All rights reserved. This book, or parts thereof, must not be reproduced in any form without permission of the publisher.

All names, characters, and events in this book are fictional, and any resemblance which may seem to exist to real persons is purely coincidental.

PRINTED IN THE UNITED STATES OF AMERICA

for my son

HARRY LEE

—IN APPRECIATION OF THE INVALUABLE HELP
AND HOURS OF WORK HE CONTRIBUTED
TO THIS BOOK.

THE SOUTHERNERS

The International Cotton Exposition held in Atlanta, Georgia in 1881 . . . drew together the Apostles of a new Industrial Era for the South and it opened the eyes of Northern Industrialists to the field of investment that lay in the South. The Exposition was considered the manifestation and inception of the "Industrial South."

—*American Cotton Handbook*

by Gilbert Merrill
Alfred R. Macormac
Herbert R. Mauersberger

Part 1

I HAVE NO REMEMBRANCE OF WHEN or how I learned I was "alone in the world," as people speak of those, like me, who are alone in a special way. Nor do I recall when I first heard—not my name Jessica but the shortened Jess, and knew that Jess was me.

As far back as I can look into the pale mist of childhood I have been Jess and I have been alone. Both name and aloneness I accepted as absolute and unalterable, as I did the state of being alive, and, as a small child, was affected by one no more than the other. Perhaps discovery of aloneness occurred at too early an age to affect me; or perhaps it did affect me and, in the miraculous way of children, I thrust the knowledge into the limbo reserved for remembrance too perilous to recall.

Who knows how far into the past memory reaches? Are the familiar faces and incidents of our known past all of memory? What of the half-glimpsed, shadowy fragments that hover on the sill of returning; the isolated flashes that angle across consciousness, lighting up briefly scenes and faces placeless and nameless in recollection?

Does memory have its ghosts? Wistful phantoms of reality that once existed? Known and touched and loved when the mind was too young to retain continuity? Now lost . . . But forever lost?

When I was a child such flashes often came to me, as to all children, perhaps as I lay in my small bed, mazed in the drowsiness preceding sleep or, tiring from play in Mitty's yard, cast myself down on the friendly and familiar earth. Drowsing there, my face in cupped arms, aware of insect life stirring the grass and of the mouldering, pungent smell of earth, the alternate waves of fact and fantasy flowed in and out of my mind like a tide bearing upon it the scenes which I called my pictures.

There were many pictures. Some were pure fantasy and inspired, I know now, by stories Mitty told or read to me. I was a fairy queen dancing in a magic circle, ringed by courtiers; I was a snow-white bird flying against the blue arch of sky; I was—but no matter. These fantasies come to every child, part of the secret self held inviolate against a humdrum world.

There were other pictures, inspired by what I do not know and unaccountable, for they had no connection with anything which in remembrance had ever happened to me. Two came more often than the others. One was a room; a vast room and many-windowed with a ruby-colored carpet stretching endlessly into space. Each time it floated across my inner vision its splendor startled me to wonder, yet, for some reason, left me desolate. At whatever age it came—and it came even after I was grown up—against the room's vastness and the ever-stretching glow of carpet, I stood so small and lost. Even when I shut the picture out, the sense of desolation remained.

But the second picture I never shut out, for it brought not desolation but a sort of happiness. It was of—not a man, but the half-materialized impression of a man, never fully resolved. Yet I knew him better than anyone I had ever really known. I knew he was young and, to me, beautiful. His eyes, deep-set and somehow lost, burned with a sort of radiance. I knew his smile, the small, constant cough, the dry, hot touch of his hand when it held mine. Yet even as I say "I knew" I realize that knowledge was only feeling, for he never emerged from his nebulous intangibility. Only one thing emerged clearly: the unfamiliar sense he brought that I was loved and cherished.

He came oftener than the others, oftenest of all, invoked, some would say, by a child's alone and hungry heart, eager for that which life had denied: the feeling of being loved.

Actual memory began with Mitty and her small neat house which stood in a sparse community lying beyond Atlanta's West End. Because a battle had been fought and lost in its pine woods, it was called Battle Hill. But in the days of my childhood the only evidence that on this land men had fought and died were the eroded breastworks of red clay which here and there straggled across it.

Mitty's house stood somewhat apart from the community, separated from it by the road which ran between Atlanta and the big cemetery. On one side of the road were scattered the general store, the marble yard, the unpretentious frame homes that made up the community of Battle Hill. On the other loomed the cemetery, its imposing stone and iron entrance dominating Battle Hill as a castle dominates its peasantry, its sweep of well-kept sward protected from encroaching pine forest by high hedge. Beside it, just outside the hedge, was Mitty's little house. To reach it you went along a small path which led from the car tracks and, twisting through a stretch of pine woods, came at last to the cleared spot where it stood. Beyond it was the house of Mr. Harbuck, caretaker of the cemetery, and his wife. A fact which accounted for Mitty's invariable remark that she lived "over by the Harbucks'." Beyond the Harbucks' the path plunged into deeper woods and ended at the shanty of the Negro woman Janey, and Man, her hunchbacked son.

Mitty's house was small and stood so low beneath the tall pines that only one step separated its veranda from the ground; and it was plain. But I am sure no flowers ever rioted so gloriously as those in Mitty's yard and on Mitty's veranda and on every inch of Mitty's window sills.

Or no bird ever sang so ecstatically as Petey, Mitty's canary. The water that came up from Mitty's well in the cool, dripping bucket has never been equaled, and the odors of her kitchen on baking day occasioned such exquisite agony in my small stomach that Mitty, half laughing, half scolding, would compensate with bread and syrup and shoo me out to play.

The cemetery just beyond the hedge was my play place; and what a wonderful place it was. I was too young to question what lay beneath the stones as I played my games among them. Sometimes I pretended each was a door leading to a secret house. Sometimes they were children with whom I talked, calling them by names I made up. Sometimes I spread my skirts and danced among them, while the tall, aloof angels, trailing forever their marble robes, looked on. One of my earliest recollections is of standing tiptoe at my window at bedtime to look out upon them, and thinking they must miss me. So lonely they seemed in the night.

On fair days when Mitty got her work "in hand," she would walk in the cemetery with me. With my small hand in hers, almost as small, we strolled among the mounds, Mitty stopping now and then to read an epitaph, her lips moving silently as she read. At first, I had no realization of why she stopped or why her lips should move. But there came a day when I was five or so that it occurred to me to wonder. I looked up into her face, curiously.

"What do you see on the stone, Mitty?"

"Why printing, dearie, like in the story books. But cut right into the stone, you know."

"Does it tell a story like the books?"

"Aye." Mitty's voice was solemn. "It tells a story. The beginning and the end too, I'm thinking."

"Read me what it says, Mitty."

She read slowly, "Robert Haynes Humphries, beloved father of—"

A word caught my attention.

"What is a father, Mitty?"

She looked down into my upturned face, her own, usually so twinkling, puzzled. Then as we strolled on she, with several false starts and talking above the subject and below the subject and all around the subject, tried to explain about fathers. But beyond the fact that fathers were invariably men and quite necessary if you wished to be born at all, I gathered scant information about them.

We strolled on, my mind considering what she had told me and in consequence coming up with another question.

"You say everybody has a father, Mitty?" I asked politely.

"And that they do, dearie."

This, naturally, led to the next question.

"Do I have one?"

"Of course, dearie."

"But where is my father, Mitty? I never see him. I haven't ever—have I?"

"Not since you can remember, my blessed. That's a fact."

I trudged beside her, my hand in hers. "Do you know where my father stays, Mitty?"

She didn't answer, and I believed her thoughts, as was often the case, had darted on to something else. When I'd waited for what I considered a reasonable time, I brought her back to the subject in hand.

"If you *do* know, Mitty, I'd like to go see him."

She stopped in her tracks and, facing me, put her arms around me. "He's dead, dearie," she said quietly. Then realizing that the word meant nothing to me, hurried on. "When folks get sick or old, or maybe just tired, they let them rest in beds like these." Her little arm swept the space before us and her eyes looked out over the quiet graves. Suddenly she shivered and, her hand drawing her shawl close, trembled. "It's turning coolish, dearie. We'd best be going in."

We turned back toward home, Mitty not speaking and I pondering on the information I had gleaned. If I had a father, I reasoned—and according to Mitty, that I had been born at all proved beyond doubt that I had—it was inconceivable that I did not know him, even know how he looked. So my practical young mind began to cast about for the figure of a man it would find acceptable as a father. A search—due to the few men I'd known—that was limited. Certainly Mr. Harbuck, the cemetery's lean gray caretaker, offered no possibilities. Neither did Mr. Bratton who ran the general store. And these exhausting my list, I had to draw upon imagination; in consequence coming up with the young man of my "pictures." Recalling the deep-set radiant eyes and the feeling he brought that I was loved, I wished he truly might be my father; and for no more substantial reason than wishing, the wish was suddenly fact. He *was* my father. And I wondered if somewhere in a place like this he slept in his narrow bed; and if the stone above him said *Beloved Father of Jess Kildare*.

I had been brought to stay with her, Mitty said, as if I were a slice of time, "a bit after three." I was twelve when taken away. But the years between three and twelve were not clocked by years but by living. When Mitty's flowers—growing in pots and tin cans and whatever container offered itself—must be moved into the house, where they all but crowded us out, I knew that winter drew near. By the same signs, I knew when spring had come again. The season mattered not at all, for Mitty had a way of bestowing magic on each. In winter when her fires cracked and snapped on the hearth and enfolded the room, the flowers nodding on the window sills, Petey chirping in his cage, how pleasant that room was. As we roasted apples or popped corn and, as Mitty read my story, ate them, I knew I loved winter best. Then spring would come. Out the pots of flowers must go. Mitty's treasured cuttings and seeds must be planted and tended. The days grew longer and warmer, warm enough, at last, to go barefooted. And when I felt the cool moist earth against my small feet, I knew I loved summer best.

In recollection, there is no sense of days or years, of springs or winters. Time is woven into one inseparable pattern and, viewed down the perspective of years, what a satisfying, unchangeable pattern it was. The snug winters in the little house, alive with Mitty's cheerful voice and Mitty's busy feet tapping as she washed and ironed and baked. Summers, running under the trees or playing in the cemetery, perhaps wading in the brook beyond Janey's. Going to Mr. Bratton's store across from the cemetery; waiting while Mitty shopped, my eyes glued to the candy in the fly-specked case and—Mitty telling me I might buy five cents' worth—my soul torn with indecision between the pale candy bananas and coconut strips. Afterward helping Mitty carry the brown bags of groceries back along the little path under the pines; and always, summer or winter, as the house came into view, thinking what a darling little house it was.

Even the incidents that broke into our days were in themselves so familiar they not only failed to disrupt them but in time merged with and became part of the pattern. Mr. Harbuck on his way to or from his work in the cemetery would pause to pass the time of day with Mitty, to relate with cheerful complacency the condition of his wife's diseased kidney; and I wondered if, being responsible for the cemetery, he viewed any possible customer, even his wife, with a businesslike eye. Or colored Janey, delivering her bundles of wash, pulled by Man, her humpbacked boy, in his homemade wagon, would stop in passing to exclaim over Mitty's roses or Mitty's poppies or whatever happened to be in bloom. While she and Mitty hovered over the flowers, Man would wait beside his rickety wagon, his arms looking too short for the squat deformed body, hardly taller than mine though he was half-grown, his big teeth white against his black skin when he grinned. If Janey lingered (and she always did) he'd call, "Cum on, ole lady, fore I'se too ole to pull dis waggin," and his laughter would gurgle like water over stones. Then off they'd go along the little path, Janey pacing her quick steps to his lumbering ones, their honey-sweet voices fading and dying with the creaking wheels, under the pines.

Church played a part in our lives, though too seldom to be familiar. For Battle Hill depended on one of the itinerant preachers with which the Methodist Conference doled out spiritual nourishment to the poor and undistinguished of small communities. However, what this nourishment lacked in quantity was compensated by fervor. The "quarterly" Sunday, when the preacher held all-day meeting, was no mean event. Farmers drove from miles round to attend it, their wagons weighted with families and friends, a huge splint basket of lunch under the wagon seat. And the church ladies of Battle Hill, not to be outdone by "county folk," arrived with hampers, sometimes even small trunks, crammed with fried chicken, layer cakes and deep-dish pies.

Church to me was not an unalloyed pleasure though I liked to walk with Mitty to the tree-shaded hill where it stood. Once, watching the people ascend the steep incline that led to it, I thought God, pleased with their coming, helped them take the hill. After a few of Preacher Cantrell's sermons, however, I discarded that fancy. For his God was too fearful a God and too mighty to pay much mind to a little hill or a little girl. Tall and thin, with a huge nose jutted between his eyes like Mitty's ax blade, Preacher Cantrell directed—or seemed to direct—his rantings of hell-fire and damnation at me; and valiantly as I tried to escape him, counting bluebottle flies in summer, in winter gazing out at the bare trees, my eyes were irresistibly pulled back to his.

On nice Sundays the punishment bestowed on my straying eyes surpassed any he could foretell; for the open windows afforded a view of the picnic tables under the trees. Also of the Battle Hill ladies as they set out the great platters of food, which I would survey with doleful eyes. For I was not allowed to share it. Almost before the notes of the Benediction died away Mitty would lead me up the aisle and out the door and, without stopping, head for home. And my longing backward glances and timidly voiced wish to stay availed nothing. We must get home, she'd say, to freeze the ice cream or make the pie, prepare whatever treat she planned for Sunday dinner.

It was on one of these homeward walks, inspired, no doubt, by Preacher Cantrell's sermon, that I asked Mitty what a "husbing" was. She looked down at me, puzzled. But only for a moment. Then, her eyes twinkling, she laughed. "You mean husband, don't you, blessed?"

I quoted gravely, "Is that what you cleave unto?"

"That's right, dearie."

"But what is a—a husband, Mitty?" I persisted.

"Why a husband—is a—" Mitty groped. "Why, dearie, it's a man."

I considered this and decided it cleared up nothing.

"Every man is a husbing, I take it, Mitty?"

She laughed again. "Lawsy no, dearie! To be one he must stand before the preacher alongside a lady, you know. And promise to love, honor and obey."

"And cleave unto," I quoted.

She nodded. "And cleave unto."

"Until death do us part—" I quoted further.

"Until death do us part."

My mind was immediately faced with making such a promise, and being unable to keep it.

"S'pose you get tired of cleaving, Mitty? Can you stop?"

"No, dearie, and that you can't. For better or worse, the Good Book says. And sickness or health. And let no man put asunder."

Except for the fact that you had to go on cleaving, this was somewhat beyond my comprehension. I shifted my questions to another quarter.

"What happens when you do cleave unto, Mitty?"

"Well, dearie, a lot of things. But mostly children."

This was wholly beyond comprehension. "Children, Mitty?" I was skeptical.

"Aye. The man is the father, you see. And the lady is the mother—"

"But where do they get the children?"

Mitty had to think this one over. But finally she came up with an answer of sorts. "Why, from cleaving unto, blessed."

As this was totally without meaning, I passed over it. "And the children belong to them, the man and the lady?"

"Indeed and that they do," Mitty said firmly.

I was struck by a breath-taking thought. "Mitty," I exclaimed, "did I have a mother?"

"Why—of course, my blessed."

Never before had I heard of a mother, at least in connection with me, and it was an astounding discovery. Yet even in the moment of discovery, I was possessed by the conviction—for whatever reason or no reason—that she, like my father, was dead. Hopefully I asked Mitty if this was true and anxiously waited her answer.

So much time elapsed before it came, I had to remind her. "My mother, Mitty," I said politely. "Is she dead too?"

She held my hand so tight it hurt. "Yes—yes, my blessed."

"But my mother and father cleaved unto, and got me? Didn't they?"

Short of breath from walking too fast, or so I believed, she answered with considerable difficulty. "Yes—my blessed, they did, for a fact."

Encouraged, I asked my next question. "And I was their very own child, wasn't I? And belonged to them?"

Apparently she had lost even more of her breath. But finally she managed to gasp, "Yes—my blessed. Yes, for a fact."

That I had ever belonged to somebody was miraculous news, even if those to whom I'd belonged were dead. I asked Mitty humbly, "I don't belong to anybody now? Do I, Mitty?"

She looked down at me with loving eyes. "Oh, but you do, my blessed. You belong to the Great Father of all children—to God."

If I failed to find God wholly satisfactory as a father, I did not let her know it. I would have preferred one to walk in the cemetery with me on fair Sundays; to buy me candy in Mr. Bratton's store; to toss me high on his shoulder as we started home. Somehow I knew that the young man in my mind, firmly established as the father I'd never known, would have done these things. For only I would have been *his* child. God, I reasoned, had too many children to spare much attention to one.

After that, lying in bed in the dark, I scrunched my eyes tight, hoping, in the pictures this often produced, I'd "see" the mother I had no memory of seeing. I never did. Once, drifting off to sleep, I was suddenly enveloped in a lovely fragrance and I started up, half-believing that she had come to me. Then I knew it to be the honeysuckle in Mitty's yard. Another time I dreamed of her, though even in the dream not seeing her; only hearing her laugh nearby. And waking, heard her laughter echoing in the room. But I never saw her. Sometimes I wondered why. But then I was beginning to wonder about a number of things. For I, Mitty said, was growing up. I was going on six.

Though the expected visits of Mr. Dolphus Queen invariably occurred at an unexpected hour, as if he hoped to take us unaware, they failed to upset the tranquillity of our days. He dashed up on his big black horse and dismounting strode through the door without knocking, then tramped from room to room, his whip swinging over his arm, his eyes darting about Mitty's spotless house as if expecting to unearth guilty secrets. Watching, I would be cold with excitement. Not because he was such a giant of a man and as brown as a gypsy; though he was. But because of the purple wen beneath one eye which pulled the eye out of focus and distorted the eye, until it was not an eye but a living thing, independent of and without regard for Mr. Dolphus Queen.

When convinced that no secrets waited to be dragged into light, he would stride to the hearth and tower straddle-legged before it, the whip swinging from his arm.

"Well, Mrs. McDaniel!" His voice, which matched his body in size, made the flowerpots tremble. "And how are things—in general?"

Mitty, sewing or darning (her hands were never idle), would answer with cheerful unconcern.

"Things in general? Why fine as can be, sir."

Mr. Dolph's eyes would turn toward me as I stood by Mitty's chair. And if the bad eye slid wickedly this way and that and (as if determined to be disagreeable) everywhere except in my direction, the good eye would find and observe me. Then it would travel back to Mitty.

"Things—in general are springing up. Eh, Mrs. McDaniel?"

Imperturbably, Mitty continued to lay neat stitches. "Oh indeed yes, Mr. Dolph."

The good eye sought me again and contemplated me while the bad one danced a gruesome sort of jig.

"Um!" said Mr. Dolph, regarding me thoughtfully. Then, as explosively as if he fired the words from a gun, "School now, Mrs. McDaniel!"

Mitty laid more neat stitches. "Yes sir. I've given the matter considerable thought."

The good eye fixed upon her gravely. "And arrived at a conclusion?"

"And arrived at a conclusion, sir."

"What is that conclusion, ma'am?"

Holding her needle mid-air and with her cheerful face turned up to his brown one, Mitty unhurriedly stated her conclusion. There was, she said, a school in Battle Hill. Oh, not a city school like they had in

Atlanta. Just a county school. Which, she knew, might rate as an objection with some. But if her opinion was worth a toot, said Mitty, the county school would answer well enough for now. And *things in general* would not have to be disrupted and upset, which, in her opinion, would be too bad with *things in general* doing so nicely.

Things in general, invariably the theme of conversation between Mr. Dolph and Mitty, had, from time to time, given me cause for considerable speculation. At one period when I was much younger than going on six, I believed the "General" to be none other than General Lee whose picture hung over Mitty's mantel, and that "things" inside of him—I had some vague impression of a tapeworm—accounted for Mr. Dolph's unfailing "How are things in general?" As time passed I, growing older and wiser, discarded General Lee, decided that I was "things in general," though Mitty, when I hinted as much, was quick to deny it. "Things in general," she explained, meant—well—most anything you might mention, or not anything in particular, or just—things in general. Had I not been convinced they meant me, I would have been thrown into a state of greater confusion. Being convinced, I knew discussion of school meant school for me and was thrown into a state of excitement instead.

Mr. Dolph heard Mitty's conclusions gravely, his good eye as steady and attentive as the bad one was neither. When she finished he took out a prodigious bandana handkerchief and blew his nose so lustily that Petey, silent in his cage before, began to sing as lustily. Which caused Mr. Dolph to send him a look in which the good eye was as ominous as the bad. This was not lost upon Mitty; and quietly she told me to put the cover over Petey's cage. As I obeyed I was conscious of Mr. Dolph's good eye following me and remaining with me until I returned to Mitty's side. Then it went back to Mitty.

"Mrs. McDaniel!" His roar actually made the flowerpots jump.

"Yes, Mr. Dolph."

"You don't figger on—er—complications now? Concerning things—in general and school?"

Mitty's hand held the needle mid-air again while she answered. "Why no sir, I don't. With things in general as good as gold. And smart as a whip. And loving and willing." Her cheerful face was suddenly not so cheerful and the twinkle in her eye flashed almost like lightning. "If there should be er—what you mention, sir, it would be so unchristian, so wanton cruel, and to such a loving heart—I think I'd tear the schoolhouse down, sir, with these two hands."

Mr. Dolph's good eye regarded Mitty with as much surprise as if before that eye she had suddenly sprouted horns, and, taking out the handkerchief again, he gave his nose another lusty blow. This, despite the cover, sent Petey into a fresh burst of song. For the moment, Mr. Dolph ignored it.

"Your sentiments, Mrs. McDaniel," he roared, his voice trying to make itself heard over Petey's, "do you proud. But a word of caution, ma'am. We know the South. We know people. We also know how generally they look on such things—as things—in general—" Then when Petey, as if determined to sing Mr. Dolph down with trills and runs and cadenzas, mounted to ecstasy, Mr. Dolph broke off and spread his hands disgustedly.

Mitty, her placid twinkling self again, bade me take Petey's cage to the kitchen and—her work-roughened hand patted mine—why didn't I have a glass of milk and a few of that fresh batch of teacakes?

So Petey and I withdrew to the kitchen and, with his cage on the table before me, I had milk and teacakes, planning as I fed Petey crumbs through the bars of his shabby old cage how I would study hard at school and learn fast and someday be a fine lady. And oh, what a day that would be! I would buy Mitty a handsome dress and a gold watch and Petey should have his new cage. Not a tacky old cage like this with its bars all bent and rusty. But a handsome cage, painted green and trimmed with gold! And Mitty would never again have to say, as she said every morning, "Just you wait 'til my ship comes in, Petey dear, and you shall have your new cage."

I was pulled back from that day by thudding hooves that receded into distance. They told me Mr. Dolph had taken his leave, and in a moment Mitty came through the door briskly, her eyes bright. "Put Petey back in the sitting room, dearie, and set table for me." Then, as I moved to obey, she looked at me from the old stove into which she fed firewood. "Oh, you are such a help to Mitty. Now"—she turned brisk again—"let's get supper on in a hurry, so I can tell you the fine news."

We got supper on in a hurry; Mitty, as was her custom with tasks, making a game of it. Wagering she could do this before I did that and both of us rushing about with a great number of collisions and a great deal more laughter. But at last the bowl of turnip greens and corn dumplings was borne to the table, the end of cold ham brought from the safe, the blue pitcher of milk flanked by the teacakes. And when we'd pulled up to the table and bowed our heads for the blessing, Mitty told me the grand news. I was to start to school in September, she said. Moreover, Mr. Dolph was sending yard goods from Atlanta for new clothes I'd need. And she was to get Miss Pack, who sewed out by the day, to come in and make them. This threw me into a state of anticipation, particularly the new clothes, that would have been ecstasy except for one lurking doubt. Would Mr. Dolph in selecting my dress goods follow the dictates of his good eye, or the bad?

My imagination had reared such an altogether miraculous picture of school, I was almost afraid to trust it. So while Mitty washed dishes and I dried, I, with innumerable questions, tried to prepare myself for possible disillusionment.

I dried a plate vigorously. "Now tell me, Mitty. Just what do you do at school?"

"Why, dearie, you do learning. Reading like in books, and writing.

So if ever you was away from Mitty you could write me a letter and say, 'Dear Madam'—"

The idea that I would call Mitty "Dear Madam" or ever be away from her, for that matter, was too ridiculous. And I laughed so hard I came near to dropping the plate. But seeing that Mitty didn't laugh, I stopped off short.

"There will be other children at school, I suppose, Mitty?"

Mitty did laugh then. "Other children, dearie? That there will. And such a running and a jumping and a whooping and a playing of games—"

"Will they let me play too, do you think, Mitty?"

"Why of course they will. A nice little girl and sweet as a rose in the clothes Miss Pack will make for you. And as good as gold. And Mitty will put extra cookies in your lunch box to share with your friends—"

I looked at her wide-eyed. "Friends, Mitty? You mean I will have friends?"

"Why of course, my blessed. As easy as falling off a log."

This almost passed believing and opened up such a delightful prospect that I managed to prolong discussion of school right up 'til bedtime. Even after I lay in my bed, the knowledge I'd drawn from Mitty remained with me. I saw myself with real children, playing their games, laughing with them—*belonging*. I would never have to pretend again that the tombstones were children. At that thought I sat up in bed and looked out at them and, feeling their loneliness anew, was swept with remorse. They had been faithful, I thought, and always there when I needed them. And they were lonely too. I must not forget how loneliness hurts.

Miss Pack, the seamstress, arrived on a day arranged by Mitty, an oilcloth bag containing the implements of her trade on her arm. She took off her hat, her eyes taking in the house and me at the same time, and bringing out these implements, ranged them on Mitty's sewing machine. A pair of giant scissors, a limp tape measure and a fat pink pincushion that bristled with pins and needles like a porcupine. Then she produced a black sateen apron with a thimble in its pocket and, tying it about her soft body that bulged here and there like the pincushion, announced she was ready for work.

Mitty laid out the materials Mr. Dolph had sent out from Atlanta and which, for days, I'd hovered over like a mother hen. Nainsook for my small underclothes, lace and embroidery to trim them. Gingham for school dresses, gay and fresh enough, Mitty said, to eat. Most wonderful of all was the red cape Mr. Dolph had included. Already made and warmly lined, with a hat that Mitty called a "tamashanter" to match. When I tried them on, pirouetting and dancing in my delight, Mitty declared I was her own blessed Red Riding Hood, but her face as she fingered the stuff of the cape was thoughtful. It was handsome, she said, and finely made. Now she wondered if Mr. Dolph—

She broke off and it occurred to me that she wondered if Mr. Dolph himself had made the cape. And I had a picture of him at his sewing, hampered by that unreliable eye.

Now she spread the materials before Miss Pack and piece by piece they discussed them, Miss Pack's greasy fingers creeping in and out of the folds like fat worms, as if they must know the exact grade of cotton in every inch. At last she looked across at Mitty and announced darkly that there wasn't a piece but what was the best—the very best—quality. Easy to see, she said, that money had been spent. Now, she had no idea what sort of arrangement Mitty had; but if Mitty was expected to provide this quality out of what she was paid—

Mitty was quick to reassure her. "Oh dear no! Clothes are provided extra."

Miss Pack's forefinger tortured her pimpled chin. "And you mean to say never a word as to whose—?" Her laugh was snickering. "Well—it's a wise child that knows its own father, ain't it? Not that it's the first time money's been paid out to keep a *little secret* under cover. Why, I could tell you of a case right in West End—"

"We'll start on the underclothes." Mitty was firm as she put the nainsook on the table for cutting. And in the pinning of pattern, the snip-snip of scissors, the basting, trying-on and stitching, Miss Pack's case was buried past resurrection.

Waiting in body-waist and drawers to be fitted, I decided I didn't like Miss Pack. Her eyes, boring through thick spectacles, were always prying, her ears always listening. As she stitched, the machine whirring no faster than her tongue, she unearthed, with sly hint and snickering laughter, bits of unwholesome gossip. Did Mitty know that Lena Cathright wasn't at her uncle's in Atlanta like her mother gave out? She was in a *house*. On Collins Street. And had Mitty heard about Mame Dunlap going out back to fetch stovewood and finding a buck nigger crouching behind the woodpile—just waiting for—well a body knew what— The snickering laugh again. Not that he got Mame. Lazy as she was, she went over that cord of wood like a bird. It sure had folks riled up, though, about niggers. And a good thing. Niggers were getting too uppity since they let old Booker Washington speak at the Cotton Exposition. Why, a body could tell the way they looked at a white woman what they had in their evil minds. Well—they'd better mind their P's and Q's in Battle Hill. Battle Hill folks wouldn't stand for any foolishness. No sirree! They still knew where to get tar and feathers. Ropes too—if it came to that.

Listening, I had no understanding of what the avid eyes and snickering laugh implied; but I thought her not unlike the big wood rats that foraged at the trash pile back of the house, filching what unclean bits they could scavenge. Her eyes, boring through thick glasses, took on the sly glisten I'd seen in theirs. Seeing, I would shiver with disgust.

As she stitched and Mitty pulled bastings, she put forth sly questions that fastened like tentacles on unsuspecting Mitty and clung until they drew some sort of answer. It wasn't that she was curious, she said, she was just interested. Such a little dear, *somebody* was; *somebody,* anybody should be proud to claim. And hid away out here as if the somebody who should be proud wasn't proud but ashamed. Now—how did it happen that *somebody* was brought to Mitty? Now—wouldn't Mitty admit she knew who *somebody* belonged to?

Innocently, Mitty exclaimed, Oh dear no! It had all come about through Mr. Dolphus Queen, lifelong friend of her dead husband Charlie, who worked for those lawyers in Atlanta. When they told Mr. Dolph to find a good place, straight off he'd thought of her.

Miss Pack put out another tentacle. "And never a word as to who pays for keep?"

Mitty said firmly, "Never a word."

That, Miss Pack announced darkly, meaning the word that hadn't been said, was all that need be said. It proved that something was rotten in Denmark. Out went another tentacle. Now didn't Mrs. McDaniel agree?

Mitty, her eyes troubled, allowed a half-admission to be drawn from her. "I reckon so," she said. "Not that it makes a speck of difference. My blessed is my blessed, whatsoever."

"You don't agree"—this was another tentacle—"with Dr. Cantrell's text last Sunday? That the sins of the fathers will be visited even to the third and fourth generation?"

Mitty stated in no uncertain tones that she did not agree. With Dr. Cantrell or the Bible either, if it meant such a thing. If God was such a one, she went on, as would punish a loving heart for what that heart couldn't help, God, as far as she was concerned, could go roll his hoop. Then, as if realizing she'd said more than she wished, she suddenly put down her sewing and, with tight-pressed mouth, pattered off to the kitchen. After that she pulled no more bastings for Miss Pack, but busied herself elsewhere. And Miss Pack's prying, deprived of Mitty, turned on me.

Time and time again, as she pinned and fitted a garment, I had to endure the questions—asked quietly lest Mitty hear—for which I had no answer. One such time remains with me to this day. Not because it differed from others, but because years later I was to find in this day explanation for what was to happen.

I would see myself again at the age of six standing before her as she pinned, my awed eyes watching as she plucked pins from her mouth where she invariably held them. Drawing my small body erect at her sharp "Stand straight," holding it stiffly while she pinned and adjusted. A claw of nausea, caused by rigid erectness and humid August heat, but most of all by the odor that rose from Miss Pack, gripped at the pit of my stomach; gripped tighter when the questions began:

"Honey, whereju live 'fore yu come to Mitty's. . . . Whereju get them pretty eyes of your'n, sweety. . . . Bet yu can't tell your pa's name, can yu. . . . Where's your folks live at. . . . Don'tju even know where 'bout yu come from. . . . Cat got yu tongue. . . ?"

I meant no disrespect when I failed to answer. I had no answers. I could only stand shamed, in frozen silence.

Suddenly her voice rapped out, "What yu lookin' at me thataway for?"

"Because your eyes shine just like the wood rat's at the trash pile."

I had answered in childish honesty, not knowing it would anger her. But I saw her face turn sick-white with fury.

She jerked the fitted garment over my head, unmindful of the pins, ignoring the scratch one left on my arm though it was deep enough to draw blood. To keep her from knowing it hurt, I acted as if it was nothing and used my own remedy for wounds. I spit on my finger and pressed it against the scratch.

This would not heal the pain, I knew, but it always stopped the bleeding.

So bright the sky that arched over the world on the day I started to school. So sweet and cool the September woods that early morning as Mitty and I went along the twisting path beneath the pines. In my new flower-spattered gingham, I skipped beside her as excited as if bound for a new land, which, in a way, I was. I hardly heard when she repeated for the hundredth time that I must always wait for her after school at Mr. Bratton's little store. That never, never for any reason whatsoever, must I cross the car tracks or come through the woods alone. Because—she anticipated my unfailing "why"—it was best for her blessed, that way.

The schoolhouse was a longish walk. We had to follow the little path through the pines to the car track, cross the tracks and Gordon Road to the opposite sidewalk, reaching, after a little, Mr. Bratton's store, which stood across from the cemetery. Here we turned down another street lined with small houses not unlike Mitty's, except for one. This, built of brick and having two stories, I considered impressive, and I asked Mitty who lived there. It belonged, she said, to Mr. Stopper, who in his own opinion was top of the Battle Hill barrel. He was not only head of the school board, but with his wife—who put on more airs than Mrs. President Cleveland—ran the Methodist Church as well as Pastor Cantrell. All because—here Mitty sniffed—Mr. Stopper, being "in marble" and handy to the cemetery, had made more money than either had been used to. For both of 'em, she added, had been raised to smell the patching.

Listening as we passed Mr. Stopper's and went on, it did not occur to me, as once it might have, that Mr. Stopper was done in marble like the cemetery angels. I had come to know this was Mitty's way of referring to a man's calling; that just as she put Mr. Stopper "in marble" she put Mr. Bratton "in Groceries & Sundries" and Mr. Boland "in mules."

At the next corner we turned again, this time into an unpaved street that ran downhill to a hollow, then straightway proceeded to run uphill to a crest. And there, said Mitty, pointing to the small frame building perched on the crest, was the schoolhouse. Looking, I saw that children of various sizes ran and jumped before it, just as I'd known they would; and as we went down one hill and up the other, their voices came to meet us.

Hearing them, I hoped we would stop in the schoolyard, but we didn't. Instead we entered the schoolhouse, where—Mitty informed me—I had to "register up." A procedure that sounded more difficult than it turned out to be. It was accomplished, after a considerable wait, in a small room with *Principal's Office* on the door, where Miss Massey, the principal, sat behind a battered desk and interviewed "register-uppers."

While we waited our turn I, fascinated to the point of awe, looked at Miss Massey. For never had I seen a lady—or anything—like her. She was so bony and had skin so yellow and eyes so black, she might have been moulded of yellow wax with shoe buttons stuck in for eyes. Yet I knew by her prissy voice and the way she smiled (with just her mouth) that she was a lady; and I was suitably impressed. I was more impressed by the ring on her pointing finger. For the huge purple stone that would make most hands look prettier seemed to make hers only bonier and yellower. If such a thing was possible.

When my turn came to "register up" I began, in spite of the ring, to lose my awe of Miss Massey. For she talked to Mitty as if Mitty was nothing and she, herself, everything; and questioned Mitty over and over about me, as if there was something she wanted to know that Mitty refused to tell. At Mitty's answers, though her mouth smiled, her eyes didn't believe her. And they looked at me as they would at a dose of castor oil which she hated to take and wouldn't take unless forced to. But after a period of silence, when amethyst finger rubbed waxy nose (as if hoping to rub a decision from it), she added my name to the list before her. I would report on Monday, she said. To Miss Reddy's room.

What a wonderful day that first day of school turned out to be. What new and fascinating perspectives were opened up before me. What an amazing place the schoolhouse was with its blackboards and chalk and its battered desks, one—or more accurately, one-half of one—mine. And the teacher, Miss Reddy! What an altogether perfect creature she was. Where have you seen skin so flowerlike, hair so black, eyes so deeply blue? Where a dress to compare with her serviceable gray serge? And how kind she was. As you turned and twisted in your half of the desk lest you fail to see and hear everything to be seen and heard, how cool the hand that patted your cheek as she paused in the aisle beside you. How warm the smile she bent upon you as she said, "Jessica, try to be less excited, dear." How merry her laugh. "I'm afraid you'll explode."

The first day fades into the second, the second into the third. Routine transforms the new into the familiar and you are less excited but not less happy. Life without school recedes into the limbo of the unbelievable and is not to be imagined. At recess you give Mitty's sandwiches (as well as Mitty's cookies) to Ellen or Mattie-Lou or whoever is attached to the outstretched hand. But you save the best for Janet of the quick brown eyes and flashing dark pigtails. Janet occupies the other half of your desk and you have designs upon her—of which she is unaware. She is to be your best friend. Toward that end you save cookies, sharpen her pencils and compliment her pinafores with equal fervor. When you learn that her last name is Stopper, that her father is none other than the Mr. Stopper "in marble" and head of the school board, that she lives in the big brick house, reverence is added to the total of your love.

Your teacher, Miss Reddy, is already so enshrined in your heart, you know you will never forget her, and you never have. You love her when she is gay, love her equally when she is not gay, but cross. You love her best when she seems worried or has a headache; when she presses her hand against her forehead, you desperately wish for a magic potion (always available in fairy tales) with which to banish her pain.

You start in to learn the alphabet and make the tremendous discovery that C and A and T spell cat. From that moment you tirelessly put letters together. At supper you ask, "Mitty, what does xeb spell?" And are not discouraged to hear it spells exactly nothing.

You try to decide which part of school is best and can arrive at no conclusion because every part seems best. In the morning when the class stands and sings "My Country 'tis of Thee" you are sure that is best. You are equally convinced by every following period. When the first grade, to which you belong, must sit quietly while Miss Reddy devotes herself to the second grade that occupies half of the room, you do not yawn or stretch like other first-graders. You drink in Miss Reddy's teaching without understanding it and your respect for the aged second-graders who do understand it is so overwhelming that to think of yourself as ever attaining their eminence is past believing.

In this new world where everything is strange, nothing strikes you as strange. When Janet's mother, Mrs. Stopper, in silk and beaded cape, visits the classroom and holds a whispered and haughty conversation with Miss Reddy, you accept it as natural though it gives Miss Reddy a headache and she is cross the rest of the day. Next day it seems equally natural, as hand in hand you and Janet march out for recess, that Mrs. Stopper, and a portly gentleman you take for Mr. Stopper, should talk in the hall with waxy Miss Massey. And when you find Mr. Stopper's cold eye fastened upon you, you think it's because you are Janet's friend and you are proud.

When Miss Reddy stops you as you leave for home and, hand gentle on your shoulder, gives you a note for Mitty, it is only a natural incident in this amazing world, so you do not wonder. Neither do you wonder next day when it is Mitty who comes to the schoolhouse, who, like Mrs. Stopper, talks in the hall with Miss Massey. When school lets out and, leaving, you pass Miss Reddy's desk and she reaches and gathers you close and murmurs, "Dear child, dear child," it is only more wonder heaped on the total wonder of wonder. And on dancing feet, with a hop, skip and jump, you make your way to Mr. Bratton's store to meet Mitty.

She waited for you, but not as usual, for her twinkling eyes had lost their twinkle and were red and watery instead from, she explained as she wiped them, the glare of the sun. Holding her hand you crossed Gordon Road and the car track and turned in the little path. Mitty telling, as you followed its twisting way, how it was you wasn't to go back to school. It was, she said, something about the county line. Only those who lived inside the line could attend Battle Hill school. Her house, being across the car track, was outside the line. Which, she said, wiping her eyes again and again, being a stupid old woman she hadn't known; or she'd never, never have sent her blessed to that place. And would her blessed mind, she asked suddenly, her being so aggravated with the water that kept running from her eyes, if we rested on this log a bit.

You sat on the log beside Mitty in the quiet woods where the pines sighed on and on like a hurt that wouldn't stop hurting; and when she felt rested, you went on home. You told Mitty you didn't mind about school or not playing with the children. You could still play in the cemetery and now—Mitty looked so uncheerful, you tried to be extra cheerful—you could give the tombstones real names. You could call the little girl angel Janet. But the most beautiful angel of all you would call Miss Reddy.

That was an unhappy time, a confused time, darkened by a child's bewilderment when the familiar face of life, for reasons she doesn't understand, is distorted and suddenly strange. For I was either old enough or discerning enough to know that Mitty's explanation was not the real one, which left me with no reason at all. I thought back to the days at school, trying to discover if I had been at fault. Had I fidgeted in my desk too much? Worried Miss Reddy? Sung too loud? Bothered Janet? I found no answer. Perhaps there had been a mistake. Perhaps one day Miss Reddy would come to say I could return to school, share Janet's desk again, sing with the others of mornings.

It was a tiny hope and illogical, with nothing to feed on but hope itself, but at least it sent me to my schoolbooks again. If I might go back, I reasoned, the little I'd learned must not escape me.

One afternoon—I think a few days later, though I am not clear about time—perched on Mitty's front step, I studied my letters, thinking how comfortable the C looked, how bossy the T; and so engrossed that when I heard footsteps along the path I only glanced up idly. Then I saw Miss Reddy. She came toward the house exactly as I had imagined so many times that even when she stood at the step before me I didn't believe. Only when I felt her hand on my cheek was I convinced that she was true.

She smiled and her hand patted my cheek. "I've missed you, Jessica."

I looked up at her, but there were no words to tell her what I felt. Perhaps she knew. For she sank to the step beside me and took my hand and held it. "Jessica, do you want to know why I've come today?"

I thought I knew why, but some childish pride held back admission. I looked at her gravely, and waited.

"You see, Jessica, I've thought about you. So much. And I told a friend about you. How smart you are, how dear." She waited, after a little went on. "My friend, her name is Sarah Key, is a teacher too, Jessica, but without regular assignment. She wants to teach you, Jessica, come here and teach you. You'll learn faster than in school—"

At a sound behind us she broke off and, turning, we found Mitty in the doorway, her face not Mitty's face but cold and set like marble. When she said, "Come in the house, Jess," her voice was strange like her face.

I moved to obey, but Miss Reddy's hand stopped me. Rising, she went swiftly to Mitty. "Mrs. McDaniel, I must talk to you."

"I can't see what good talk will do." It still wasn't Mitty's voice. "There's been too much talk already. Unless"—her eyes sharpened—"unless the way folks think is different."

Miss Reddy shook her head. "No." I hardly heard the quiet voice. "No."

"Then there's nothing to talk about—" Mitty began.

Miss Reddy's hand on her arm stopped her. "Oh! But there is—" And when Mitty's face refused to yield, she cried out again, but softly, "I don't come for them. But for myself. I haven't slept for thinking—that eager little face." She broke off, then went on, almost whispering, "It mustn't go to waste."

They looked at each other across the space between them. Then Mitty said, "Maybe we'll have that talk after all. Come in."

They went inside and I went back to my ABC's, their voices as I studied drifting from the house on the quiet day. I didn't try to hear. I didn't want to hear. I heard Mr. Stopper's name and Miss Massey's and, for some reason I could not fathom, Miss Pack's, but I didn't wonder or even care. Without really telling me, Miss Reddy had told me what I wanted to know. And even that didn't matter, I told myself fiercely. I'd learn anyway—somehow, some way. And someday be a fine lady and buy Mitty her silk dress and gold watch, and Petey's new cage. I didn't care about their old school. I didn't care. But even as my childish heart stormed defiance, I heard again the children's voices singing, saw again Janet's dark flying pigtails. And I knew what I said wasn't true—That I did care. It was the first time I'd ever told a lie. Even to myself.

Miss Key, thin and quiet, with eyes too big for her angular face, came and talked with Mitty. And Mitty afterwards, with numerous beginnings and a great deal of wasted paper, wrote to Mr. Dolph to inform him of what had transpired in regard to school and of Miss Key's offer to teach me at Mitty's. Within a few days he answered in person, dashing up on his horse unexpectedly, which we always expected. He found me lying on Mitty's bed beneath her Star and Moon quilt though the September day was unseasonably warm. When Mitty told him I was "under the weather," he was more disturbed than my indisposition warranted. He paced the floor, the unreliable eye darting this way and that, and roared that Mitty must call a doctor, and immejately, and tell him to come on the double-quick.

That, Mitty stated calmly, she would do tomorrow if I wasn't better. Today—she was giving me a course of calomel. No doubt when it "moved" I would be fit as a fiddle.

Lying under Mitty's quilt, alternately hot and cold, I dozed and waked only to doze again, their voices as they talked in the dim room now near, then faraway, as if wafted in and out on a tide. Once when the tide came in it bore Mr. Dolph's voice, held to unbelievable quiet.

"I know how you feel, ma'am"—this was his voice floating in on the tide—"and may their souls roast in hell for it. But mebbe it will comfort you to know their meanness has done *things in general* a favor."

"A favor!" Mitty's voice trembled with indignation. "You call *that* a favor!"

The tide came closer.

"A favor I said, ma'am, and a favor I mean. In this way. 'Til now, 'yon food and clothes and a roof over her head, no concern for *things in general*. No concern atall. But your letter, ma'am, got my dander up. And without consulting certain parties who bear down heavy on being consulted, I skivvied a bit and got your letter to another certain party. And, ma'am, it got *their* dander up too."

"And high time," Mitty sniffed.

"And high time," Mr. Dolph agreed. "But up the dander is, ma'am."

"What will it mean for Jess?" Mitty's voice was trembling again.

The tide turned and began to go out, carrying Mr. Dolph's voice with it.

"What it will mean, ma'am, I don't know. I ain't allowed to know. I do know that where there warn't no concern for *things in general* beyond points mentioned, now—and we can thank those Christers for it—plans are being made."

The tide had receded so far that Mitty's voice came back thin and quavery. "Will they take her away from me, sir?"

So far out the tide now, so small Mr. Dolph's big voice. "That I don't know, Mrs. McDaniel. But depend on it, ma'am, plans are being made. The dander is up."

The tide was all the way out. I slept again.

How long I slept I do not know. Once I fancied that Mr. Dolph leaned over me and laid his huge brown hand gently on my forehead. But when I waked I knew it had been just a dream. The late afternoon shadows lay long across the room and Mitty leaned over me with a cooling drink. Mr. Dolph, she said when I asked, had been gone this long, long time.

Mitty had said time and time again that Janey, the Negro washwoman who lived in the woods beyond us, was the best friend she had in Battle Hill. She was constantly stopping by with a mess of collards or turnip greens from her garden, or a jar of piccalilli she'd put up, or sending Man, her hunchbacked boy, with a loaf of fresh-baked bread. Now, when I lay sick, she gave further proof of friendship. She was in and out of the house day and night, freeing Mitty from tasks to give her time for me; sitting with me while Mitty caught some rest. None of which I noticed. I lay dazed with fever and for the most part sleeping, only waking to scream out in terror at some dream induced by fever. It would take her and Janey both—Mitty said afterwards—to hold me on the bed, little thing though I was. She'd wondered time and time again what her blessed could have dreamed.

I did not tell. I was ashamed to tell. For there was nothing fearful about the dream, nothing to invoke such terror. Just my six-year-old self in the vast high-windowed room where the ruby carpet stretched endlessly into space. And feeling so small in the vastness; and lonely and lost.

Little else, while I lay sick, registered. Sometimes, waking in the night, I'd hear Mitty and Janey rocking and talking on the porch and, turning over contentedly, go back to sleep. But other times, not feeling sleepy, I would lie and listen to Janey's voice, soft and soothing as music as she talked about Man, her boy. She worry about Man, she said, 'til it wuz lak a stone on her breas'. Allus she worry, whut wid de Battle Hill boys chasin' him an' makin' fun of his hump. And now wid all dis ruckus since Miz Dunlap claim she find er nigger behind her woodpile, she worry for sure. White fokes wuz blamin' colored fokes wid all sort of meanness. Making it hard for 'em. Good and bad alike. If Man git out of her sight a minute, she near went out her mind. Particler since he had dat sunstroke. Eber since, iffen he run too fas' or git riled up, he take some kin' of spell. And sit lak a rock and needer see or hear when you talk to 'im. Jus' lak a rock and deef and dum' as one.

This with everything else sank below the rim of consciousness as my fever rose and waned. But on the first day I was allowed to sit up in bed, it drifted up to the surface again. For Man came to stand on the porch outside the window, his dark face one enormous grin. His old gray goose done hatch her aigs, he said, and he brung little missy a baby gosling.

He thrust a small box through the window and I inspected the tiny thing, so cunning in its awkwardness. And I showed it to Petey, chirping in his cage beside me, while Man looked on beaming and so altogether cheerful that what I'd heard Janey say seemed only another dream.

Evidence which proved it to be real was brought to us by Mr. Dolph —and soon. He dashed up a morning or two later with a largish box swung to his saddle. With the box under one arm and the inevitable whip over the other, he strode into Mitty's room where, propped against pillows, I was having a midmorning snack. While his bad eye cavorted uncaring, his good one regarded me with steady kindliness, until Mitty came in from the kitchen and it turned her way.

"Things in general is better, ma'am?"

"Oh yes, sir! She's out of the woods now. A little feeding up and taking it easy and she'll be fit as a fiddle."

He said "Umm" doubtfully and, crossing to my bed, dropped the box upon it and, before I could speak, strode out, calling to Mitty as he went, "A word with you, ma'am, if you please." And while I lifted the lid from the box and dug beneath layers of tissue paper, thrilled by the unexpected present, he and Mitty talked outside on the porch.

I heard nothing they said, for the lifted tissue paper revealed a doll—but oh what a wonderful doll she was! As tall as me, at least almost as tall, with golden hair and big blue eyes, and dressed fine enough for a queen. Holding her close, but not too close, I knew for the first time the joy of belonging. For she was mine and only mine. She belonged only to me.

Gratitude to Mr. Dolph rushed over me and made me feel so weak I might almost have been sick again. And then and there I resolved she should be named for him. And though to stand by the resolution proved not easy, after giving thought to the problem awhile it was settled. "Dolph" I could not call my darling. So with the help of "I Shall Be Queen of the May, Mother," Mitty's favorite poem, I arrived at May Queen. And May Queen she was through all the years she was my comfort and standby.

With this disposed of and feeling tired, I relaxed against my pillows, May Queen in my arms. It was then, as I lay there content and almost dozing, that Mr. Dolph's voice talking to Mitty on the porch outside began to penetrate my consciousness.

"—and Lonzo Wills tells me there's been trouble out this way."

Mitty repeated, "Trouble? What kind of trouble, sir?"

Mr. Dolph's voice sank. "Nigger trouble," he intoned.

Mitty sniffed. "Oh that? It's just a lot of talk."

"You never know, ma'am. And you—and the little one alone with some of 'em living so near—"

But Mitty only laughed. "Why sakes alive, Mr. Dolph! The only colored folks near us are Janey and Man. They wouldn't harm a fly." Her little laugh was scornful. "They leave that to the white folks and churchgoers." She added firmly, "And anybody that tries to tell me different can just go roll their hoop."

I waked in the night, whether the next night or the next I do not know, and stared into the darkness of my little room where, being better, I slept again. Sensing something awesome in the darkness that held everything invisible, the foot of my bed, the chest that held my clothes, where the fireplace stood. From the sitting room came the sound of the clock, its tick-tick-tick going on and on; and I recalled that Mitty had said every tick meant a second of life gone forever, and never to be lived again.

I pulled the quilt over my head to shut out the ticking, but the picture I could not shut out. I saw a long line of seconds; hundreds, thousands, marching relentlessly to nowhere. I brought my head from under the quilt and tried to count as they marched, but it struck me how many had passed before I started to count; that before I was born, or even Mitty, the seconds had marched away to nowhere; and I gave up counting. Yet all the time the clock ticked on.

Then, as I lay staring into the void of dark, other sounds imposed themselves upon the silence. The voice of the clock, as if yielding to an intruder, withdrew. Raising up and leaning on my elbow, I listened, trying to name the sound. At first it seemed only the murmur of the pines. But in the next moment I knew better. Murmuring it undoubtedly was. Not of trees. Voices. Now and then a single voice rising briefly. Then, self-consciously, dropping and merging with the others again.

Now beneath the murmuring I caught another sound. One familiar and easily recognized. The scrunch, scrunch of feet against the pine needles that carpeted the little path. They, like the voice of the clock, made a picture; one actually seen many times as the men and boys of Battle Hill passed on their way to hunt in the woods beyond Janey's. Or with dogs sniffing at their heels, trailed a possum on moonlit nights. Yet now, lying in the dark, the sound of feet stirred a shapeless fear, as if like the seconds they marched to some dark unknown.

Quietly I slipped from my bed and crept to Mitty's in the next room and slid under the covers beside her. Snuggled against her small warm back, my fear of murmuring voices and marching feet was vanquished. Already they came from a distance as if receding down the little path toward Janey's. After a little I could hear nothing, not even the scrunch, scrunch of their feet on the pine needles.

I waked again as daylight's ghostly gray seeped through the windows, to find myself alone in Mitty's bed. But from the kitchen came the smell of boiling coffee and the tap of Mitty's feet; and as I sat up and rubbed my eyes I heard Janey's voice. "I blames myself," it chanted, "I blames myself. 'Til de day I die I blames myself."

Over the tinkle of china Mitty said, "Here, drink this hot coffee, Janey. It'll give you strength."

"Whut use I got for stren'th now? Ever breath I'se drawed since he was born has been for him." The mournful chant followed. "I blames myself. I blames myself."

Mitty pleaded. "Take just a little coffee, Janey."

As if she hadn't spoken the singsong voice went on.

"Yestiddy we delivers fo' bundles of wash an' to save a leetle time I tells him ter leave Miz Stopper's, dat I'll go up de road and leave Miz Billing's. Den cum back fer 'im. Five minutes I'se gone and not a minute more. When I gits back it done happen."

Mitty asked gently, "What did happen, Janey?"

"All I knows is whut she tell de sheriff—Miz Stopper, I'se speakin' 'bout. She say she go in de kitchen and dere he is. Sittin' in a cheer. She ask 'im whut he mean sittin' down in her house. He don' answer she say. Jus' sit dere and look at her strange-like. One of dose fits, Miz Mitty, but she don' know dat. She runs out screamin' and fokes come runnin'! But when dey go in to fotch 'im he ain't dere. When I comes home I find 'im. In de cheer lak a stone. All day he sit dere. Lak a stone and needer speak or hear when I speak. Wedder he eben know what happen I'll never know."

Mitty pled, "Drink your coffee, Janey," but the singsong voice heeded her no more than before. "Las' night I heer 'em comin', down de path, and I runs to 'im and begs 'im slip out back and hide out in de woods. He jus' sit dere lak a rock and look at me. An' dey bust in de door and drag 'im out. 'Til de day I die, I'll see his pore eyes lookin' back." The singsong voice halted; then took up its telling again.

"When I hears dere feet tramp off, I goes out. And looks for 'im. I looks and looks. And wile I looks I pray de good Jesus not let it be whut I feared it wuz. Den I comes to de tree, Miz Mitty. Dat big hickory down in de leetle hollow. And knows Jesus ain't hear my prayer. He was dere, pore thing, he was dere. Wid his pore han's whut dey tied hangin' down afore 'im." Her voice stopped, then took up its old refrain. "I blames myself. To save five minute and not a minute more, I sen' 'im to Miz Stopper's by heself."

Her voice died, and silence, broken only by the tick-tick-tick of the clock, held the house under its spell. Sitting in Mitty's bed, I remembered the seconds that had marched to nothingness in the night, seconds in which had been wrought that which could never be undone. I looked out of the window and up at the sky where the rising sun touched the gray with color. I asked of no one but of *something—somewhere:* Who makes the sun rise and the seconds march to nothing? And who made Man good inside yet gave him black skin and a twisted body and let him march away to nothing, too? And who made me? And what is me? I try to see the *me* of me as something *someone* thought worth making, not—like the seconds and Man—marching forward to nothing. But I know I am only a child important to no one, except Mitty. And sitting there in Mitty's bed, I cry as though my heart is broken. But when Mitty comes running and asks why I cry I cannot tell her.

The transition from the unawareness of childhood into the state of awareness is not always accomplished gradually and so imperceptibly it escapes notice. Often it is a rude awakening; caused by an incident or suddenly acquired knowledge that so shocks the young spirit it is as if Life, grasping the child's shoulders, shakes it to awareness of a world never seen before.

Man's death did that for me. It shocked me to realization of a world —and a life—far different from the one I'd known; and it made me aware of *self;* not merely my own self but the untouchable core of being in all living creatures. And with clearer vision I saw them—no longer meaningless shadows on the perimeter of existence, but each a separate entity possessed of one thing, his and his alone, the hidden being of self. The death of Man made me know that. I was never to escape it.

From Man's death I learned, too, of the significance of death, heretofore a word implying—as Mitty had wished it to imply—an intangible impression of sleep and rest. Now I realized that just as the self in Man was no more, so it was destined for the selves in all. With intense shock —more terrible because I could speak of it to no one—I knew some day I too would die, and cease to be. Lying in bed in the dark I tried to imagine how the state of *not* being could be. How this that was me, with eyes to see, hands to feel, feet to run, could stop being. And my heart would grow big and choked in my breast with fear. Even when I decided I could never know, that no one could ever really know, there were still nights when I lay awake—afraid. But with the passing of time this, too, passed.

Month by month, summer and winter, life with Mitty went on. It differed but little from the years before. Flowerpots in and flowerpots out continued to announce the seasons. Mitty's winter fires snapped as cheerily, Petey in his shabby cage sang as blithely. Mr. Dolph's expected visits managed to be unexpected and his conversation, delivered with the whip on his arm, continued to revolve about *things in general.*

Nevertheless, there were changes. There was Miss Key. Three mornings each week she rode out from Atlanta on the streetcar to teach me. To compel me with conscientious thoroughness to grind at letters until I could read, at words until I could spell, at writing until, in childish, unformed scrawl, I could actually write.

As time and study advanced me to geography and history, I began to have a sense of a widening world. And when, through Miss Key, I came to literature, I was never quite so lonely again. Because of David Copperfield and Maggie Tolliver and Jane Eyre my sense of not belonging seemed easier to bear. They, too, had walked down lonely passages.

As I grew older, the shadow of not belonging, like my actual shadow, loomed at times large beside me, at others shrank almost to nothing, the events of my days affecting one, as the sun affected the other. Busy in the house with Petey's singing and Mitty's cheerful voice about me, the shadow retreated into nothingness. But on balmy Sundays when I strolled in the cemetery with Mitty, and saw other girls with fathers and mothers, perhaps sisters and brothers, it sprang full-bodied from its hiding place to walk beside me. Then more than ever I would cling to Mitty; for only in Mitty's little house and Mitty's love could I shut the door on the vast, shapeless unknown beyond.

To escape it I deserted the actual life of my days for another, the world of illusion. Threaded with fragments of fact and fiction, patterned after my heart's desire, I'd spin my fantasy of life, almost always one in which I found someone to whom I belonged—usually my father. In summer, lying on my stomach beside the little brook in the woods beyond Janey's, watching the water frolic over the rocks and the tadpoles skimming the surface, I lived my dream life.

In the unadorned garb of the missionary, I walk along the narrow streets of a foreign city that is stalked by plague and death and dying, a city from which all living beings have fled—except myself. Alone, I minister to the sick and the dying, soothe their brows, give each a few words of kindly wisdom, and see the light of hope dawn in their fevered eyes. Not until I have helped and saved each suffering soul do I stumble to my feet and, turning, find a stranger, his eyes deep-set and burning with a sort of radiance, standing at my side. He takes my hand, speaks in his vibrant voice: "Who comforts the sick, the starving, and the dying? Tell me who so Pastor Kildare can say—well done."

In winter, closed in the safety of Mitty's little house, I felt less need for my world of illusion. But walking home from Mr. Bratton's store in winter's dusk, I'd glimpse through lighted windows a scene of family life—a father and mother, a brood of merry-faced children—and it awoke in me the desolation of exile, of being so close to the happiness enjoyed by so many I could almost touch it; but knowing the door that led to it was somehow closed to me.

Yet I was neither an unhappy girl nor a solemn one. For whatever Mitty lacked in learning, her understanding of the heart needed no instruction. When I turned moody or kept too close to books, as I often did, she devised tasks to lift me from inactivity and introspection. If I demurred—and sometimes I would—she reminded me, but always with cheerful lovingness, that I must "justify." Her way of saying you must deserve what you receive or share; the golden rule by which she lived.

Wise Mitty! Cheerful Mitty! Loving Mitty! How fortunate as we put up fruit and piccalilli in your small kitchen, or poured glowing jelly into jars, or roasted apples at your heart-warming fires, that the years ahead were not revealed to us. For how could our hearts—yours or mine—have borne it?

I had just passed my twelfth birthday when I was taken away from Mitty. Mr. Dolph, observing my distress when he informed me of the impending change, which he did without warning, was almost as distressed. I must be a sensible gel now, he said, the bad eye going on a rampage, and not take on so. It made him feel like a reg'lar tyron (I think he meant tyrant) which he wasn't atall, having a heart as soft as butter in summertime. But orders was orders. What he had to do he had to do, come hell or high water.

Mitty, her arms about me, patted my shoulder and gave me what comfort she could. "Dearie, dearie! You've no cause to take on so. Why, going to a fine school in Atlanta, Mr. Dolph says. To get the learning Miss Key said you oughter have. It's what we've wanted for my blessed all along."

I knew it. Still I continued to cry brokenheartedly; for I could hardly bear it. And as Mitty packed my clothes in the new trunk that arrived in the buggy with Mr. Dolph, I wandered through the rooms of Mitty's little house and out in Mitty's garden and over in the cemetery, saying good-by to all the dear familiar things: the little brook, the cemetery angels, and to my darling May Queen. Who, lest Mitty be too lonely, I must leave. Not until Mitty called for the third time, did I at last obey.

Good-by to Mitty and Petey I would not, could not say. Even when Mr. Dolph had hoisted my trunk and himself into the buggy and waited, I clung to Mitty and kissed Mitty and Petey, then Mitty again, and promised to write every day and come every week. Then I was on the buggy seat beside Mr. Dolph, gazing through blurred eyes at Mitty on the porch with Petey's cage held high so I could see him 'til the last. Mr. Dolph roared, "Get up," and popped the whip, and we were moving off. I looked back frantically, though able to see but dimly because of my crying; and a moment later, a curve shutting the house from view, able to see nothing and feeling frenziedly that I must go back, must kiss Mitty once more, yet knowing I couldn't and so crying all the harder. And if in recollection I find myself inclined to smile a little, I recall also that I was only twelve; and leaving the one person in the world who loved me.

We turned into Gordon Road, which would eventually lead us to Atlanta, Mr. Dolph popping his whip so often and so vigorously, yet not once touching the horse, it occurred to me it might be his way of expressing sympathy, that if I stopped crying, he might stop the whip. The experiment was not wholly successful. For while I managed to check my crying to an occasional hiccough, he continued to pop that whip. And popped it so often and so vigorously that afterward when I thought of him it was in his whip-popping position, the huge body thrust forward, the long arm sweeping the air.

However, I was calmer; and my mind, temporarily paralyzed by parting with Mitty, began to register again. I saw that the horse clop-clopped along a dirt road bordered by pine woods, so like those around Mitty's I was near to crying again. But I wouldn't; and soon was rewarded by a change of landscape. For when Gordon Road crossed Cascade, it was a road no longer but was transformed into Gordon *Street*. A busy street with its flow of drays and wagons, with streetcars lumbering past, with fine carriages drawn by prancing steeds, linked two and two, their hooves beating a tattoo against the Belgian block pavement. A splendid sight in my opinion. But not in Mr. Dolph's. He recalled the "good old days" when the cars had been mule-drawn, adding somewhat glumly what with 'lectricity and the telyphone and talk of a horseless carriage, the world was moving too fast. And no good would come from it.

He broke off abruptly, and with a movement equally abrupt pulled a small packet from his pocket and dropped it, almost furtively, in my lap. Startled, I picked it up and glanced at him questioningly. His good eye, being next to me, caught that glance, which made him pop the whip and his words with increased vigor.

"For you," he exploded. Then, scowling fiercely, bent his gaze on the road ahead. And I unwrapped the packet and opened the small velvet box it revealed.

It held a watch, the smallest imaginable, hung on a fleur-de-lis pin, and so prettily done in gold and blue enamel forget-me-nots, I was thoroughly enchanted. Nevertheless, I was puzzled. Who, I wondered, would give me this gift which, being of a practical turn of mind, I was sure had cost a great deal. When I asked Mr. Dolph, "But, Mr. Dolph, who would give me this?" my voice was incredulous.

He popped the whip at least six times before he admitted sheepishly, "Me."

I knew my "Oh, Mr. Dolph!" was a feeble expression of the gratitude I felt. But he stared at the road ahead so fiercely and was so altogether unapproachable I dared no more than a timid "Thank you, sir." And we drove on in silence, my hands cupping, my eyes adoring the watch. And wishing—oh how I wished—that Mitty could have seen it.

Mr. Dolph's whip and voice popped together.

"Forget-me-nots," he explained.

I looked up. "Sir?"

He repeated, "For-get-me-not," cracking down on each syllable as if he cracked a nut.

Politely, but with no idea of what he meant, I said, "Yes, sir."

"They means," he still bit his words, "that you must *for-get-me-not.*"

I was surprised and I was pleased, as who wouldn't be? And I hastened to assure him with all earnestness that I could no more forget him than Mitty—or Petey. If I thought at the last name he pulled down his mouth distastefully, perhaps it was only my fancy.

He popped the whip again. "If anybody, man or beast, had told me," he said, "me being a bachelor and not overfond of children at their best, a state, mind you, I ain't ever caught 'em in, that I would come to be so uncommon fond of a little gel"—pop went the whip—"I would have called 'em cutthroat and liar."

Awed by his ferocious speech and the more ferocious cavorting of the bad eye, my "Yes sir" was conciliating.

He popped the whip and went on, "Nigh on to nine years I've sashayed between Certain Parties and a little gel. And seeing what a good gel she is and with what uncommon good sense, fight as I did, I come to be fond of her. And seeing that little gel pulled sharp-like on leaving somebody she loves whups me. Really whups me down. And so, wanting that little gel to know the lay of the land, I say to her—*there are reasons.*"

"Reasons, sir?" I repeated politely.

The whip popped louder, his arm swept a wider circle.

"Reasons," he roared. "What they are I don't know. I ain't allowed to know, seeing as certain parties hires me to deliver papers and fetch papers, and carry summonses, and see to this and report on that, which needs—in certain parties' opinions—no headwork atall. But mark you this, little one. My head tells me the reasons are there, that they have been there, that they will be there. And don't you forget it any more than you forget your Mitty or"—I was sure his mouth pulled down this time—"that fool bird. And when things pull on you sharp-like—as does leaving your Mitty—say to yourself, 'There are reasons.' And let saying it stand you in good stead."

Had I been older, even old enough to perceive the great heart beneath the uncouth exterior, I would have obeyed my half-born impulse and begged him, then and there, to tell me what he knew regarding me. Bound for a strange place where I would live among strangers, I needed that knowledge more than ever in all my life. But the feeble impulse, for lack of courage, died. For I was very young.

By this time, the horse having covered considerable ground as Mr. Dolph talked, we turned into a ramshackle street running parallel with railroad tracks. Lined with dingy stores, grain and feed houses and junk yards, none well kept or even tidy, it was not a pleasant street. And though here and there what once had been a handsome house rose among the derelict buildings, like a gentlewoman fallen on evil days, it had assumed the down-at-heel appearance of its neighbors. Mr. Dolph explained how in early times, Peters Street—Decatur Street too—had been fine residence streets. Now they belonged to the colored folks, as I could see. Looking, I did see. Except for an occasional white person, those who milled along Peters Street were Negroes; and I was puzzled. Why, I wondered, did they choose this sordid down-at-heel neighborhood? The terrible shanties, glimpsed on side streets, for homes?

When I asked Mr. Dolph he said, popping his whip, that colored people lived where they had to live. I looked at him, surprised. "But do they have to live . . . here?"

He explained that they warn't made to live here but, knowing what was good for 'em, it was where they lived. They had to keep their place, he added, or get into trouble.

"But, Mr. Dolph, do you think that is right?"

He "calkerlated" he couldn't say. Many a time he'd tried to figger why white folks believed the Lord had elected them cock o' the walk. Mebbe the strong always kicked the weak around. Time and again he'd heard Pa tell of helping to run the Cherokees from Georgia, of lining 'em up and marching 'em off at gun point. Women and children, too. Mebbe it was "hooman natur" if you was the strong un, to be a bully and pick on those too weak to fight back.

With more informed eyes I looked at Peters Street again. And seeing the sordid squalor in which they were forced to live, felt for them a sort of kinship. They, too, were set apart and held out. Not through any fault of their own but because they were different—and weaker. Who decided these things? I wondered. Who believed themselves wise enough to decide who was worthy? Who unworthy and kept out? Surely someone very wise—someone as wise as God. Yet if God made all in His own image and destined some for unworthiness, was even God wise enough?

The hands of my forget-me-not watch stood almost at noon when we reached the bustling Whitehall Street shopping district, where our progress, impeded by numberless vehicles—drays, wagons and carriages, as well as streetcars—was slowed, often halted, to Mr. Dolph's disgust. But I didn't mind the delay. My incredulous eyes were too engrossed with the dazzling array of shop windows, with the elegant carriages sweeping past us, the lovely languid ladies, poised against their cushions, so beautifully dressed and beplumed they might have been creatures from another world. For this, the bewildering stream of wheels and people, of shops so impressive that their very names—Rich's, High's, Davison-Paxon-Stokes, Regenstein's—took on a sonorous majesty, was a new world to my marveling eyes. And I hardly noticed when Mr. Dolph reined in the horse and, getting out, tethered it to a post.

When I did, I looked at the building that rose before me and was overwhelmed by the idea that this was my destination. It towered so high, its numberless windows appeared so blank and bleak, its exterior so cold and forbidding that instinctively I shrank into my seat when Mr. Dolph would have helped me from the buggy.

The good eye regarded me, perplexed; the bad one with fiendish delight. "What is it, little one?"

Falteringly, I asked if *this* was the school, and he hastened to explain. It was only the building, he said, where Poteat & Whidby, the lawyers who hired his legs, had their offices. He had been ordered, in case of something requiring his legs coming up, to stop by. He would be here no more than a minute.

Holding my hand he led me into the building and down a corridor toward a sign that said *Elevator*. This turned out to be a queer sort of cage that we, with several others, entered. Its door clanging shut, to my horror it started to rise, and rise it did, slowly but surely, though toward what or where I did not know. Nor did I know if it would ever descend again. However, perceiving that others accepted this miracle calmly, I concluded there was nothing to fear. Just the same, when the cage slid to a stop and Mr. Dolph and I stepped out onto a more familiar foundation, I released a big breath in relief.

Another stretch of corridor carried us to a door with POTEAT & WHIDBY lettered on it, big and black, and a small *Attorneys at Law* beneath. It admitted us, when Mr. Dolph opened it, to an office divided by a rail and gate into a fairly large space behind the rail and one very small before it, the latter being occupied by a half-grown boy who paid us no mind as we went through the swinging gate.

Mr. Dolph and I crossed the office, my eyes taking in two young men in eyeshades who read documents from the stack between them with such feverish dispatch that I wondered if, like Mitty and me, they raced to see which would finish first.

At a door in the rear, Mr. Dolph knocked but, not waiting to be admitted, pushed it open and we went in. And I saw that this office was much larger than the other and much more impressive. The floor was carpeted, the huge desk at the other end was handsomely carved, the leather chairs beside it deep and comfortable. Except for a bookcase that held heavy dull-looking books and a straight chair or two, it contained nothing else. It had a muffled churchlike quiet, out of respect, I supposed, for Poteat & Whidby whose names I had seen on the door. I wondered if the two men behind the desk in very black suits and very white linen were Poteat and Whidby; and if the young man who stood between them, like the & on the door, must always keep one from the other.

At our entrance they glanced up and, having seen us, went back to whatever engrossed them, which seemed to be another document. Mr. Dolph, tiptoeing in an effort to preserve the churchlike air, an effort that failed because of his creaking boots, led me to a chair near a small alcove and put me in it. Then, still tiptoeing and still creaking, he returned to stand nearer the desk and, spinning his hat on his huge finger, waited.

I sat in the chair and wondered; about everything I saw, everything I had seen. I wondered if the thin man with the mouth like a ruler-edge was Poteat and the other, who struck me as handsome, was Whidby—or the other way round. I wondered about the young man standing beside them, now and then leaning to murmur in their ear as he pointed to the document; and why he should seem so young when they seemed so old, and he so cheerful and they so sour; which led me to wonder if he was really so cheerful or if his reddish hair and freckled face made his twinkling eyes bluer and cheerfuler than they were.

When the room offered nothing more to wonder about, my wondering turned to Mitty and Petey and what they did at this very minute. And why the time since I left Mitty seemed already longer than all the years I spent with her. And how long would time seem—time being able to shrink or lengthen regardless of clocks—before I saw her again.

Unable to sit still another moment of that time, I quietly left my chair and moved toward the window in the alcove to search for more bearable sources of wonder in the street below. But at the curve of the bay window I stopped. An old man waited on the window seat, his hat on the cushion beside him. A very old man who looked as if, like time, he'd shrunk to nothing and with hands that curled, gnarled and crooked, on the head of his cane like tree roots. But with black eyes sharp and bright as the fox's eyes in my Aesop picture book.

I looked at him, thinking I'd best go back to my chair, yet not going, for the eyes that looked back at me were not unfriendly. They shone as if almost, but not quite, they wanted to smile. I took a tentative step toward him. "Hello," I said.

His voice was sharp like his eyes when he replied, "Hello, young lady," and we stared at each other another moment. Then he rasped, "Got a name, young lady?"

I told him I had a name.

After another interval of looking at each other he barked, "Gonna make me guess it? Named Mary?"

I shook my head.

"Not Mary, eh? Mebbe Sally, Polly, Mattie-Lou?"

When I told him my name was Jessica Kildare, he made no comment. But after a little he asked how old I was, and, moving a step closer, I told him that too. "How old are you, sir?" I asked.

He cackled aloud as, getting up slowly and stiffly, he balanced himself on the cane and reaching, patted my head. Then he left the bay window and advanced into the office, thumping the floor with his cane. "Let's git to business," he barked. "Can't dandle here all day. Trouble with lawyers. Talk talk talk, dandle dandle dandle . . ."

Hobbling and thumping and barking, he seemed a fearful old man to me, and perhaps to others too. For one of the men behind the desk—the handsome one—rose and came down the carpet swiftly to meet him. "We're at your service, sir," he said smoothly. "Our regrets for the—er—delay."

The old man broke in, "Regret, my foot. Let me dandle here all morning." His lifted cane pointed at me. "See to this young lady, Poteat." Then, as the handsome man's eyes turned my way, "Well, gonna keep her dandling all day too?"

When Mr. Poteat's eyes had regarded me briefly, he left the old man and came on to me. "And who is this young lady?" he questioned.

His voice was mellow and beautiful, like the tones of the Battle Hill church organ. And his smile so friendly and warm I forgot to be shy, which no doubt he intended. As I told my name again and answered his questions—How old are you? What grade are you in? Do you like school?—I smiled up at him, not knowing how I answered for gazing at his face. From a distance that face, under its crest of tarnished silver hair, had struck me as handsome. Now, seeing it close, that illusion was shattered. For so many lines were etched up and down that face and across that face and on every inch of that face's surface, I had the impression of seeing it through crumpled cobwebs. But his eyes were quick and alive; and when the old man thumped his cane again and barked, "Well, let's git on with it," they smiled at me as if he and I shared a secret. And with another smooth "Yes sir" he took my hand and the three of us moved toward the desk.

He let the old man wait while he spoke to the two men behind the desk. "You gentlemen must meet this charming young lady." His beautiful voice made it sound true. "Jessica, this"—his hand gestured toward the thin, sour man with the ruler-edge mouth—"this is Mr. Martin Whidby. And this—" The hand moved to the young man with freckles. "Mr. Andrew Hardee. Gentlemen—Miss Jessica Kildare."

Mr. Whidby's "How de do" was as sour as his face, but the young man, Andrew, gave me a smile so cheerful that I liked him at once. Then the old man's cane was thumping again, the sharp voice barking, "Let's git on with it." Mr. Poteat's beautiful voice was saying, "Delighted to have met you, Jessica." Almost before I knew it Mr. Dolph was stepping forward and leading me from the room. Glancing back, I saw that they, the old man too, were hunched over the documents again. Only the young man Andrew remembered to send me a twinkling smile before we went through the door.

It was late afternoon before we found ourselves on the last part of the journey which would end, Mr. Dolph informed me, at Mrs. Plummer's Seminary for Young Ladies. For on leaving Poteat & Whidby Mr. Dolph, declaring he was hungry enough to eat a horse, took me to Folsom's restaurant, where he ate a great quantity of food, washed down with great quantities of beer. And if he was upset by my lack of appetite, and he was, it did not affect his. But eat I could not. My longing for Mitty and Petey and the little house, dormant during the day, now came alive, and ached and throbbed like a bad tooth.

When finally we emerged from Folsom's, the weather had changed and a sad little rain was falling. Peachtree Street, as the horse ambled down it, was almost dark, its gloom intensified by a border of dripping trees. It was not too dark, however, for me to discern the handsome houses that lined it, some of them looming as huge and overpowering as palaces. But having to my homesick eyes so little reality, they might have been pictures seen in a book. And when Mr. Dolph reined in the horse before one rising vast and turreted in wide grounds, I looked at it, not comprehending. Only when I saw the brass plate that embellished the gate and read its inscription did I know. This was my destination.

As Mr. Dolph lifted me from the buggy I wanted to clutch his broad shoulders, to cry out that he must not leave me here, he must take me back to Mitty; wanted to give utterance to at least one of the pleas rocketing through my mind. But instead, walking silently beside him up the path that led to the porch, on the porch standing in silence while he lifted the knocker, I did not think, I would not let myself think. I counted the squares of stained glass outlining the doorframe; noted their shapes and varied colors warmed by inside light. But of the strange new life waiting behind that door I refused to think.

Then the door opened and a Negro girl hardly older than I peered out with a hesitant "Yassah?" On Mr. Dolph's roaring, "Mrs. Plummer, if you please," she looked at him aghast, as if he might be the lion he imitated, and conducted us with wary glances over her shoulder to Mrs. Plummer's parlor. Here she muttered, "I'll tell her," and skittered away.

We waited in the parlor, Mr. Dolph overpowering the slender chair he occupied and humming a small, nonchalant tune as proof that he remained unimpressed. I could manage no such pretense. Some quality of the room awed me. Not the furnishings, though they struck me as elegant. Rather it was the room's correct stiffness and order, its feeling of not being lived in, its silence which no sound penetrated. I knew I would never walk casually across its carpet, but as Mr. Dolph had moved at Poteat & Whidby, on tiptoe as one walks in a church. This plunged me deeper into homesickness.

Then suddenly Mrs. Plummer was in the doorway.

Startled, I straightened, for no footstep, no sound whatever had announced her approach, and this, when you considered her appearance, was extraordinary. For she was a tremendous woman. Not tall or brawny. To the contrary, rather short and small-boned and with hands and feet unbelievably small and graceful. But fat overlaid the delicate bones in such ponderous masses that, defying its corseting and overflowing, it appeared below the waist and above the waist and on shoulders, bust and hips in almost elephantine rolls. Yet it was not the mountainous flesh that made her as she paused in the doorway—to me—so formidable. It was the coldness that robbed her violet eyes of the beauty they might have had, and the unyielding face, which with its delicate features and clear skin might, softer and more yielding, have claimed prettiness.

Standing in the doorway in her severe but fashionably cut black, she was not only an impressive figure, she was one of such inexorable authority my twelve-year-old spirit quailed. When, without speaking, the cold eyes surveyed me, it quailed still more. But without reason. For dismissing me as of no importance, the eyes went back to Mr. Dolph, who had risen at her appearance. Regally she inclined her head in his direction. "Mr. Queen," she intoned.

Mr. Dolph's bow was equally ceremonious. "Ma'am, your servant."

Her dimpled hand waved toward me. "This is the young lady in question?"

On Mr. Dolph's admitting that I was the young lady in question, the regal head inclined again—this time toward me.

"Miss Kildare?"

Not knowing what I should do, but feeling called upon to do something, I inclined my head and echoed, "Mrs. Plummer."

The cold eyes regarded me speculatively before they turned back to Mr. Dolph, who waited, his bad eye darting in frenzy, his big finger spinning his hat.

"It may be well to inform you, Mr. Queen"—Mrs. Plummer's manner implied that she was a woman who would tolerate no dillydallying but went straight to the point—"that in my interviews with Mr. Whidby I stated to Mr. Whidby my opinion on certain aspects of the situation in hand." After a pause she added, "I am gratified to inform you that Mr. Whidby agreed with my opinions—in toto."

Mr. Dolph repeated "in toto" as solemnly as if he knew what it meant, though he knew, I was sure, no more than I.

"I considered it only fair to point out to Mr. Whidby," Mrs. Plummer continued, "in justice to all concerned, that the Seminary for Young Ladies in its entire history—an illustrious one, I may add—has never had to deal with a similar situation. It agrees to do so now only because of my regard for Mr. Whidby's character and Mr. Whidby's position in Atlanta." She paused again, and when Mr. Dolph, his bad eye still darting, the big finger still spinning, said nothing, she inquired, "Do I make myself clear?"

With Mr. Dolph's assurance that she made herself clear, she went on.

"Regardless of my great respect—and no one could have more—for Mr. Whidby's standing and Mr. Whidby's character, the Seminary for Young Ladies must also be considered. Furthermore, its unimpeachable character must not be jeopardized in the slightest iota."

She waited, her eyes fixed upon Mr. Dolph who, realizing it with a start, repeated hastily "slightest iota," and she swept on.

"Bearing the character of the Seminary for Young Ladies in mind, it might be well for you, Mr. Queen, and you, Miss Kildare"—the cold eyes swept my way—"to be enlightened as to my opinions. Opinions, you will please bear in mind, with which Mr. Whidby agrees. In toto."

Mr. Dolph, more alert this time, echoed "in toto" without delay.

"It is my opinion," said Mrs. Plummer, "and Mr. Whidby concurs, that as a resident pupil of the Seminary for Young Ladies, Miss Kildare can expect the following advantages. Her education shall be continued, her comfort provided, her wishes—in reason—permitted. In return, Miss Kildare will accede to certain regulations; imposed, not from any wish to restrict, but for the best interest of all. Regulations, I repeat, with which Mr. Whidby concurs. Miss Kildare will not at any time, or for any purpose, absent herself from the seminary without my knowledge and permission. In the seminary, she will conform to the routine essential to an efficiently run menage. Also, she will cheerfully accept the light duties necessary in the training of one who hopes to become self-sustaining." She paused to inquire gravely, "So far you see eye to eye with me, Mr. Queen?"

He affirmed that he saw eye to eye, his bad eye refusing to see eye to eye with anybody or anything. And Mrs. Plummer rolled on.

"There are also a few minor regulations," she said, "naturally with Mr. Whidby concurring. First, Miss Kildare will refrain from intimacy with the other young ladies. Friendly, she can be; courteous, she must be. But intimate—? No. In young ladies intimacy leads to confidence, confidence to revelation. Revelation, in this case, will not be tolerated. You understand, Mr. Queen?"

Mr. Dolph without missing a twirl said, "In toto." And her eyes circled to me. "Do you understand, Miss Kildare?"

I didn't. I understood nothing, was aware of nothing except being weary and hungry and generally miserable. But, more miserable under her cold waiting gaze, I ventured a timid "In toto."

What she said after that I heard vaguely, though I knew she said a great deal. I had reached the stage where the mind refuses to absorb—in toto—all it hears. I knew the Seminary for Young Ladies shuttled in and out of what Miss Kildare *must do* and *must not* do without one mention of what Miss Kildare might do if she was pleased to do it. Miss Kildare must cooperate with the other young ladies, must obey and respect the teachers, must make herself a contented member of what was—in toto—one big happy family. However, back she went to the *must nots*—Miss Kildare must not expect to enjoy the friendship of the other young ladies outside the seminary, nor join in their outside social activities in which the young ladies—all with enviable family backgrounds—would naturally participate. Moreover, in becoming a member of the seminary, a privilege she was about to be accorded, Miss Kildare entered upon a new life. One on which the old must not intrude, would not be allowed to intrude. To allow it to intrude would be to render a disservice, not only to the Seminary for Young Ladies and the young ladies themselves, but to the enviable family backgrounds which reposed confidence in Mrs. Plummer.

It went on and on but, occupied with the task of keeping awake, I failed to hear. Through eyes that persisted in drooping against my will, I saw that Mr. Dolph leaned first on one foot and then the other and knew he, too, longed for escape. But the stern measured voice, as if it proclaimed the laws of a nation, flowed relentlessly on. Enumerating such a long list of *musts* and *must nots* for Miss Kildare that, half asleep, I began to feel that Miss Kildare wasn't a person at all; that she was only a dummy that must move, even breathe to Mrs. Plummer's ordering.

Already, without realizing, I had accepted her domination. For when her voice finally stopped and Mr. Dolph crossed to bid me good-by, I looked up into his brown and rugged face, and because of her watching eyes dared say none of the things that cried to be said. But he understood. And, squatting Indian-fashion before my chair so he might better look into my eyes, he took my hand and patted it.

"Don't forget, little one"—his voice was gentler than any memory

I had of it—"what I said. *There are reasons.* If things pull on you sharp-like, call it to mind. And let it help you stand up to 'em."

I longed to speak but couldn't, not because of Mrs. Plummer's eyes alone, but because of my quivering lips that warned how close I was to tears. I could only try to smile for Mr. Dolph and press the big hand holding mine. He stood up then and placing his hand on my head faced Mrs. Plummer and spoke, his voice steady and respectful.

"Orders is orders, ma'am, and so I leave this little one in your hands. I hope they're the right hands, ma'am. And kind. I've known her"—the big hand, patting my head, was amazingly light—"since she was but little more than a baby. I knows this, ma'am. She's a good gel. And eager to please. And not needing a tight rein or a touch of the whip. She handles best with a easy hand." He paused, then added humbly, "If you'll be bearing it in mind, ma'am, I'll be thanking you."

He spoke with such sincerity and, for Mr. Dolph, such unaffected simplicity that to this day I marvel that his plea failed to reach the mark for which it was meant, the understanding of a woman's heart. But fail it did. For while Mrs. Plummer heard him with relentless courtesy, her face softened not a jot and the cold blue eyes were no less cold. When he finished he waited, twisting his hat, obviously ill at ease; and as if to prolong his discomfort, she let him wait for what seemed an interminable time. But at last she bestowed another regal bow upon him and her "Mr. Queen, good evening" was unmistakably dismissal.

He patted my head gently again and without returning Mrs. Plummer's "Good evening" stalked out of the room. Stiff and desolate in my chair, I watched him go until all I could see was the tail of the whip that swung back and forth on his arm.

When the front door closed behind him, I looked at Mrs. Plummer almost fearfully. So completely had I resigned myself to her domination, I would have known neither surprise nor the power to resist had she ordered me into chains. Mrs. Plummer, however, ordered no chains. Mrs. Plummer did nothing more alarming than move with incredible ease to a button set in the wall and press it. Then waited with frowning abstraction and impatient toe-tapping, in the manner of one detained by trifles while matters of magnitude loomed.

Her summons was answered by the Negro girl who had answered the door, and the intent, abstracted gaze turned upon her.

"Pearlie, conduct Miss Kildare to her room."

Both Pearlie's voice and face were blank when she echoed "Room?" and Mrs. Plummer's hand was annoyed. "This is Miss Kildare. She will occupy the room next to Miss Mabie, on the third floor."

Trailing Pearlie's scrawny figure along the hall, I glimpsed through open doors that lined it a series of schoolrooms, their scarred desks and dusty blackboards stirring memories of another; and of Miss Reddy and Janet's dark flying pigtails. And it struck me as strange that now

I was to have what so many years I had dreamed of; yet the idea failed to bring pleasure. It had been gained, I reflected somberly, at too great a cost, the pain of leaving Mitty. And if I told myself that in time I would feel differently, I knew that time was not now.

We left the empty schoolrooms behind and at the end of the hall paused in a vestibule that afforded entrance and exit in various directions. On one side wide stairs rose to the upper floors and a narrower flight descended to the basement and, Pearlie informed me, the dining room and kitchen. And this side door—she opened it as she explained—led outside to the grounds. And over yonder across the grounds, her knuckly finger pointed, stood the cottage where Mrs. Plummer lived with her family.

We stepped to the little side porch as she talked, and peering out I tried to get an impression of the place. Except for the bare stark limbs of great trees, I discerned nothing. The light in Mrs. Plummer's cottage shone too distantly to pierce the dark around us. Standing there beside Pearlie, sensing rather than seeing the somber aspect, I was shaken by a spasm of homesickness close to actual illness. I thought of Mitty and the little house as it was at this hour, and my heart cried out, when oh when would I see them again? I heard again Mrs. Plummer's relentless voice, "The old life must not intrude on the new," the words acquiring meaning now which earlier had escaped me. Was Mitty part of the old life that must not intrude, and Mr. Dolph and Petey? If they were, how could I bear it?

At this dreary thought, drearier no doubt because of the dark and the dripping trees, I was seized by the impulse to then and there run away; to dart down the side steps and across the grounds to the street, to flee up the street with, I was sure, the elephantine Mrs. Plummer in pursuit crying "Stop thief" like Tom in the *Water Babies*. I knew that being young and light I could outrun Mrs. Plummer, who being neither probably couldn't run at all. Nevertheless, I abandoned the idea. I was too confirmed in my conviction that what Mrs. Plummer set out to do Mrs. Plummer would do, and hope of escaping her was futile. Since it was, I concluded miserably I might as well go inside. Turning to Pearlie, shivering beside me, I said as much to her.

She said, "Sho, honey, but first I gotta gib yu this." Her hand groped in the dark and, finding mine, pressed a folded slip of paper into it. "He gib me silver half dollar iffen I git it to yu." Then, before I could question, she darted in the door and hissing, "Watch out fur de cat," started up the stairs, not taking them one at a time but hopping and jumping ahead as nimble as a cricket; then waiting until I came up with her and straightway hopping ahead again.

On the second floor, which held nothing but classrooms, we turned up the stairs that led to the third; stairs so narrow and steep and twisting that even Pearlie took them warily and without a single hop. They landed us in another hall neither as long or as wide as those below, its roof sloping sharply to small dormered rooms, one of these mine. And when Pearlie, climbing on a chair, had lighted the gas, I surveyed it, wondering how, adequately furnished though it was, it retained its unfurnished air.

Pearlie, perched on the chair, said, "Yo trunk dere in de closet," and pointed through the open door—"de bafroom over dere. Well"—she hopped to the floor and, arms akimbo, took a final look about the room—"I gotta git down and set table for supper. Hit's at seben. Just come on down to de basement."

I sat on the bed and leaned my head against the footboard. "Thank you, Pearlie."

She glanced at me sharply. "Yu pore leetle thing. Yu's down in de mouf fur sho. Why don' yu stretch out on de bed and rest yoself? Yu is too beat down."

When she clattered her way out I closed the door and, not waiting to take off hat or coat, unfolded the somewhat grimy slip of paper I had held all this time.

So vividly I see again my twelve-year-old self seated on the side of the bed in hat and coat, reading what Mr. Dolph had scrawled on the back of a used envelope.

> *Little one, if I ain't gooned somebody thinks as she is cock of the walk, but don't let her whup you down and if you don't see me as per custom remember there are reasons and know I ain't eating hay but skivvying for you best possible.*
>
> *Your true friend,*
>
> DOLPHUS QUEEN

Good Mr. Dolph. Kind Mr. Dolph! Did he know what his brief, hastily scrawled note written from the goodness of his heart would mean to me? How in the friendless, formless life which confronted me it was my only link with the past I mourned? The only hope I held against the unknown future.

In my first weeks at the Seminary for Young Ladies I had the extraordinary sensation of existing in two dimensions of time. One moving at a bewildering pace in which I was so harried and hurried I might have been a leaf borne on a torrent, hurled from bed to breakfast, from breakfast to Assembly Hall, from Assembly Hall to one class after another. In this dimension time itself, like a deflated balloon, shrank to nothing. There was no time in which to grieve or wonder or even think.

In that harried, hurried, timeless time I make, however, a few observations. I mingle with the other young ladies (all of enviable family backgrounds) and discover that they are girls like myself, some older, some younger, some near my age. They accept me without undue interest or curiosity; they are casually friendly. But opportunity for the intimacy foreseen and forbidden by Mrs. Plummer fails to present itself. There is no time. The other young ladies are also hurried and harried. After morning assembly they too are hurled from one class to another, with only a brief recess, until two o'clock. Then, being day pupils, they dash off for home.

At two o'clock the school day ends. The seminary, swept bare by the departure of pupils and teachers, looms empty and silent, except for Miss Mabie and me. And I move into the second dimension of time which, lacking anything to fill it, looms, like the seminary, empty and silent. Companioned by loneliness and homesickness, I drift about the seminary grounds (how somber they were in winter). After supper I study next day's lessons in the deserted schoolroom, and with lessons done continue to sit at the desk, my head on my hand, postponing return to my third-floor room. Knowing that when I return Miss Mabie, who rooms next to me, and hoards her strength as a miser hoards gold, will be in bed. That my slightest noise, placing my books on the table, my steps across the floor, will bring a rap on the wall and her fretful voice, "Jessica, please. I must have my rest."

The Seminary for Young Ladies was, I believe, typical of the private schools that in 1902 flourished in the South. Some perhaps were better, though education in general was inept and inadequate. Judged by what was taught and what was learned at Mrs. Plummer's, none could have been worse. The teachers, broken-down gentlewomen with impressive degrees (from schools like Mrs. Plummer's), knew little of the subjects they taught; which wasn't important, for they were thoroughly informed on the subject that took precedence over knowledge: the South's enviable family backgrounds. They knew also that in Mrs. Plummer's seminary there must be no lazy pupils, no careless pupils, no pupils who were merely stupid. That the report cards issued monthly for the edification of enviable family backgrounds must bear only excellent grades. A necessity which so affected the eyesight of Mme. Mornay, the French teacher, she failed to see what she could not avoid seeing: that the majority of her pupils took examinations with "ponies" on their laps. The power of observation of Miss Truitt, the math teacher, was equally affected. Or the startling similarity of test papers attained by correct answers passed surreptitiously from one to another could not have escaped her.

Instruction in English and history, taught by the ailing Miss Mabie, was equally lax. She sat behind her desk, tall and thin, her brown eyes sick in her sallow face, her thin hand trembling as she downed raw egg and sherry taken, she was careful to explain, to give her strength and by doctor's orders. Often as we left her classroom, the day pupils, callous as youth is often callous, would ridicule her. In pantomime imitate the manner in which she gulped her egg and sherry, making their hands tremble, their teeth clatter on the glass as hers invariably did.

I never laughed at their play-acting. Not because I was wiser or nobler, but because at night I heard Miss Mabie's tortured cough, sometimes heard her crying. Hearing, I was reminded of an old horse I'd once seen as Mitty and I went to Mr. Bratton's store. A gaunt old thing with mournful eyes staggering before the loaded dray it pulled as if each step might be its last. No, I did not laugh at Miss Mabie.

But I had lived too long with Mitty, had been taught too conscientiously by Miss Key, not to perceive the lack of discipline, the slipshod methods employed by the broken-down gentlewomen; their total disinterest in the young minds entrusted to their care. Fearfully I waited the day when Mrs. Plummer, discovering it, would loose the bolts of her wrath upon their heads. I waited in vain. The day of Mrs. Plummer's discovery failed to arrive, and for the simple reason that discovery of what you already know is impossible. Instead I made a discovery. I discovered Mrs. Plummer; realized, and in a short time, that the formidable exterior, the manner of stern authority suggesting capabilities equal to ruling a nation, were a cloak worn to impress the world in general and enviable family backgrounds in particular; that whatever capabilities the real Mrs. Plummer possessed, she made no use of them. But being a snob herself and recognizing snobbery in others, she devoted her time and mind to the exploitation of snobbery; and made a very good thing of it.

How vividly I recall her talks at morning assembly, the only activity of our day in which she participated. What an impressive figure she was as she faced us from the rostrum, her billows of flesh cuirassed into the fashionably cut skirt and high-collared shirtwaist. How stern her face, how grave her voice as she delivered her talks on such vital subjects as: How a young lady should enter a room; how a young lady should leave a room. How she should greet her elders or pass cream at table. How she should walk, talk, eat, sit (with knees together lest she appear vulgar); how she should go to the bathroom. Listening, I gathered that Mrs. Plummer considered "good manners" more valuable than good sense or character. And the Fall of Rome insignificant compared to using the correct fork.

Her service in the cause of snobbery was not restricted to talk. There were "contacts" to be maintained with those families whose offspring either attended the seminary or might in the future be inveigled to attend. These were achieved by an institution known as "calling day," when with carriage and Negro coachman hired for the occasion, her best dress topped with a seal jacket, her cardcase clutched in kid-glove hands, she made her round of calls. There were also her "Evenings." Then, in dainty notes delivered by hired messenger, the parents of the young ladies were invited to partake of an insipid concoction called "punch" and nibble small cakes from the bakery. While her gawky overgrown daughter, who constantly cracked her knuckles, fiercely lashed the piano and Luther, her ten-year-old son, tortured the violin,

Mrs. Plummer as imperially as a dowager duchess circled among the bored parents, saying, I'm sure, the things they most wanted to hear.

Now and then, Pearlie being unable to stay and help with refreshments, I was pressed into service. At such times it struck me that Mrs. Plummer's evenings inflicted a great deal of undeserved punishment on everyone except Mrs. Plummer.

Watching her benign and queenly progress as she passed from one set of parents to another, I wondered if they suspected that the Mrs. Plummer presented to impress them did not exist. That the real Mrs. Plummer was the most indolent, most futile of women. Who left the running of the seminary to broken-down gentlewomen; her husband and children to an orderless, planless existence, to food prepared by a slovenly cook that was either underdone or overdone, but never done as it should be, which concerned her not a whit. Her own meals were eaten not with her children, Miss Mabie and me, and occasionally Mr. Plummer, but from a tray carried to the cottage by Pearlie. She enjoyed, I learned from Pearlie, far more appetizing menus than those served to the rest of us.

I was at the stage when hunger is constant, with mealtime its only opportunity for satisfaction. Miss Mabie, I came to know, fortified hers from tins kept in her room and numerous cups of tea managed with a spirit lamp. I had no such recourse. Now and then at night I found a few grapes or a slice of cake left for me by Pearlie; swiped, she admitted, from Mrs. Plummer's supplies. I doubt if any food will ever equal those stolen delicacies eaten in the dark.

When Mr. Plummer joined us in the basement dining room, I noticed that he too disdained the food and resorted to tall glasses of milk instead. Seeing him as he sipped it, his pale eyes gazing abstractedly into space, I would be reminded that Miss Mabie said he was a "brilliant" man, that he taught not only mathematics at Boys High School but astronomy as well. And I wondered if his thoughts roamed not in the basement dining room but on some distant star.

Beyond "Good morning" or "Good evening," Mr. Plummer had spoken no more than a dozen words to me. But I liked him. He came and went quietly, aloof but always courteous, managing somehow to transcend the confusion of his life. Often as I studied at night in the schoolroom, he in another graded papers or made out report cards, fleeing, I thought, though this was speculation, Claribelle's noisy knuckles and Luther's violin. Once, my lessons done, I passed the schoolroom where he sat and saw him through the open door, his papers pushed aside, his head leaning on his hand. And I knew that Mr. Plummer was lonely too.

In all these weeks I had no news of Mitty. No answers to my numerous letters, though each morning I looked hopefully through the mail on the hall table. Now I began to worry. Had my letters failed to reach her? Had Mrs. Plummer, who apparently took no interest in what I did, taken more than I believed? Enough to intercept the letters I wrote or those that came for me?

Whatever the reason, I determined to search it out, for the idea of Mitty's not hearing from me, thinking perhaps I was forgetting her, distressed me. So I went to find Pearlie. And after she had extricated herself from the tangle of brooms and mops in which in the process of preparing for Mrs. Plummer's "evening" she had snared herself, I questioned her about mail. Had she noticed any addressed to me?

She shook her head regretfully. "Honey, I wouldn't know. Don' you know, I kain't read writing?"

No wiser or happier than before, I turned away disconsolately, to worry all day about Mitty. I worried in classes, worried as I wandered in the grounds after school, worried as I ate the tasteless supper, working myself into that state where disastrous possibilities are the only likely ones. In imagination, I saw Mitty lying sick and helpless in the little house, saw Mitty dead. But this I could not contemplate. To picture Mitty other than cheerful and quick-moving defied even my morbid imagination.

Because of Mrs. Plummer's "evening" I had to study in my room that night, a change which proved not wholly satisfactory. The necessity of absolute quiet lest I deprive Miss Mabie of her rest, the poor light provided by the single gas jet were more conducive to sleep than industry. Time after time I found myself nodding, and once so nearly asleep I went to the window and, raising it, let the cold air sweep my face.

My window overlooked not Peachtree but the street on the side, a narrow block, connecting Peachtree with West Peachtree. Usually it presented little of interest. The back garden of the house on the corner was across from us, and at its rear was the brick building which housed Segadlos. From the chatter of the young ladies, I knew that Segadlos was a school of dancing concerned with nothing but dancing and, like the seminary, catering to enviable family backgrounds. Leaning in my window, I knew by the brilliant lights that beamed from Segadlos, the carriages which lined the curb, the music that drifted on the night air, that Segadlos was having a dance. Through its tall windows I could glimpse the glasslike floor of the ballroom, the figures that glided and swirled and dipped, and, leaning in my window, I watched as entranced as if I glimpsed fairyland. A sound in the room pulled me from the window, and turning I found Pearlie at my shoulder, a warning finger on her lips. "Yu is to come downstairs," she whispered.

Believing she came from Mrs. Plummer, I sighed, "Oh Pearlie, do I have to?"

She hissed, "Down on de side porch. De big plat eye." Suddenly I knew whom she meant. "Pearlie-is-it—?"

Grinning, she nodded. But already I was speeding down the third-floor stairs and the flight below and through the side door to the little porch. And there was Mr. Dolph. As big as ever and as brown, the same erratic eye, the same whip over his arm; but in my eyes so beautiful I could only throw my arms about his waist (which was as high as I could reach) and lay my head against his stomach. Which caused him to exclaim in amazed awe, "Well sir, I'm whupped! Really whupped for fair."

When I had wept my foolish tears and left his stomach somewhat damp in consequence, I straightened and, with the big red handkerchief he offered, wiped my eyes.

He squatted Indian-fashion before me. "Now, little one, tell me how do you make out?"

When I told him I made out very well, he looked at me suspiciously. "That fat cock of the walk now? She don't bear down too hard on ye?"

I explained that Mrs. Plummer, for all her air of bearing down on everything, bore down on nothing. That she bestowed no more attention on me than on the seminary or her family, which meant no attention at all. And after gazing at me dumfounded he, for the first time in my knowledge, laughed. And laughed so hard and so long he must ask me to pass the handkerchief and, panting and puffing, wiped his eyes. "Well sir," he gasped, "that whups me. It really whups me for fair."

We talked of important things then. He assured me that Mitty was "fine as silk" and sent word "she missed me dreadful" and my letters were the light of her life. But with certain parties ordering no letters, she didn't dast write, not wanting to make trouble for me.

I, of course, was crying again, so again Mr. Dolph passed the handkerchief and I dried my eyes once more and asked about Petey. Petey, Mr. Dolph said, and without pulling down his mouth the least bit, was alive and kicking and had lungs like a mule. He went on to say that orders being orders, and certain parties ordering otherwise, he hadn't dast try get past the fat cock of the walk. But trying to skivvy something, he'd driven by the seminary time and again hoping to see me, and seeing nothing except the little colored wench skittering about the place. Tonight, he said, he waylaid her. And here he was and here I was. And here, he groped in the dark, here was a box sent, Mitty bid him say, from Mitty and that fool bird.

He left soon, promising to take Mitty my very dearest love and (here his mouth pulled down just a little) to kiss Petey for me. I, in turn, promised to be of good heart and remember *there were reasons* and that he was ever skivvying for me as best he could.

I watched his huge figure, the whip swinging, lunge toward the street until it was dissolved by the night. Then, carrying Mitty's box, I went to my room and opened it. And what a box it was! Mitty's biscuits enfolding slivers of country ham, Mitty's teacakes, to me not teacakes but the flavor of all the happy years with Mitty. A loaf of Mitty's nut bread. Little pots of Mitty's jam and jelly and piccalilli. A bag of the small sweet apples she called "pippins." At the bottom, one of Mitty's chocolate layer cakes, rich with such icing as only Mitty could make, and tucked in a corner a small crocheted purse containing a silver dollar.

Tenderly, I returned each article to the box. Later I would share with Pearlie and Miss Mabie. But tonight, torn between the happiness of Mitty's love and the misery of being away from her, I could not have borne to taste them. I knew the sacrifice Mitty's box had cost. Yet to see her, which would cost nothing, was not allowed. And though, true to my promise to Mr. Dolph, I told myself *"there are reasons,"* it did not help. I was not reconciled.

The years that followed, as I passed from childhood to adolescence, were like a river coiling through a countryside, so monotonous, so unchanging there is no sense of progress; when the passage can be endured only because of a belief that rivers inevitably lead somewhere.

Looking back I perceive, nevertheless, signs of progress. I have passed from the age of twelve to that of thirteen. I have discarded my childish plaits for a soft pompadour in front and a curl down my back, like the other young ladies. I have also shed the repulsive middy blouses ordained by Mrs. Plummer for dresses made by Mrs. Plummer's dressmaker. As a consequence, despite their plainness, they have a not unfashionable air.

I am aware of other changes, but these are not visible and are known only to me. My breasts, to my great embarrassment, are beginning to swell and round, though why I am embarrassed I do not know. I have also begun to experience what the young ladies in whispered lavatory sessions call "the monthlies." Due to a Doctor Book slipped from home by one young lady and read in the lavatory by all the young ladies, this affords me the feeling of being very mature indeed. Though, again, I do not know why.

Signs of physical growth outweigh, I confess, any signs of mental; though even here, despite the broken-down gentlewomen, I detect progress. Not in the excellent grades I receive nor the fact that I advance from one grade to another, that I pass from the confusing world of arithmetic to the equally confusing one of geometry, that I absorb a hodgepodge of literature and history from Miss Mabie. But because I have come to view education as a means by which I may eventually escape dependence and aloneness, and attain for Mitty and me a life together and safe. If I was young to take such a practical view, and I think I was, it was because the circumstance of my life required it. For I had only myself to lean on.

Christmas and summer vacations I spend with Miss Mabie at the seminary, the two of us rattling around in the vast deserted place like dried peas in a pod. Mrs. Plummer and her family, at these seasons, retire to "the farm"—a destination so lacking for me in direction or tangibility I would not have known surprise to learn that the Plummers, even ponderous Mrs. Plummer, simply floated in space at these times; as cherubims float in religious pictures.

Christmases at the seminary were strange and terrible things and without resemblance to any I had ever imagined. Certainly they bore no resemblance to the simple, happy ones I'd known with Mitty. Neither did they resemble those enjoyed by the other young ladies. Listening to their chatter, I heard of eggnog parties and open house, of the Christmas dance at Segadlos, of towering Christmas trees with decorations from Germany and Paris, of gifts unbelievably numerous and less believably costly, of Christmas dinner with thirty at table and three huge turkeys and champagne cup. Yet as I listened—and, I admit, marveled—I would have exchanged a dozen such for one of Mitty's.

One Christmas spent at the seminary, I think the second, remains with me vividly. How gray and lowering Christmas morning dawned. How devoid of any spark of Christmas cheer. That Christmas breakfast of tea and crackers in Miss Mabie's room because neither the cook nor Pearlie would appear 'til later. The somber little ceremony Miss Mabie made of presenting me with a handkerchief and of accepting the flannel penwiper I had for her. Afterward, leaving her to "take her rest" and wandering about the empty house disconsolately. The Christmas dinner, cooked the day before, and consisting of underdone turkey and scorched pudding. Sitting after dinner in Mrs. Plummer's parlor before the open fire, while on the street outside carriages filled with merry people swept up and down, their horses' hooves beating a tattoo, the tinkling bells hung on their harness mingling with the silver blasts of Christmas horns. A lovely sound against the still gray day that brought the joy of the outside world close and alive. And emphasized its lack within.

To make dull minutes seem less dull, I traced pictures in the coals of the fire—lovely pictures. Castles rising in a glowing wood, ships full sail on a crimson sea. Yet seeing more clearly the picture limned across my heart—Mitty's Christmas alone in the little house. Then, as I traced, Miss Mabie, silent across the hearth, began suddenly to cry. Not crying as I thought of it, quiet, almost secret. But wracked and tortured, as if against her will the jagged sound was torn from her. While she cried (and I thought she would never stop), not knowing what to do or say, I did and said nothing. And finally the dreadful sound diminished, after a little stopped. The quavering voice asked me to fetch a raw egg and a glass of sherry from her room. When I brought them, she broke the egg in the glass I held and gulped it down, her teeth clattering against the glass.

I went back to my chair and was tracing pictures again when, as if the tears had dissolved a barrier, she began to talk. Talking in a light, hurrying voice, almost gay, as I hadn't dreamed she could. She talked of her papa and mama, of the white-columned home in Washington County, of the wonderful Christmases she'd known there. There was the year her papa gave her the pony and riding habit. Another—she was sixteen then and her mama had died—when Papa had taken her to Paris for Christmas. And, oh the gifts she received that Christmas morning! Underwear sewn by the nuns. Worthy of a princess, which Papa had declared her to be. And the jewels! She laughed raggedly. One needed to have seen them to realize—

"Poor dear Papa," she mourned. "I'm glad he doesn't know—so glad. . . ."

The day darkened and the fire died and the hurrying voice stumbled and fell into silence. Then, no longer swift or gay, quavered in the dusk, "I must rest, I am tired. Very tired."

Together we went along the dusk-dim halls, each step seeming to require more strength than she could summon. But I did not offer to help her. Something in the lift of her head and trembling erectness warned she would disdain help. Once in her room, she was past caring when I helped her undress and brought her nightgown and turned down her bed. Like a sick animal she crept into it and closed her eyes. Then opened them and looked up at me.

"It hasn't been a happy Christmas for you, Jessica."

Awkwardly I protested it didn't matter, but the head on the pillow moved restlessly. "I should have tried . . ." She closed her eyes again. "But I hadn't the strength—I hadn't."

I protested again. I was old enough to look after myself, I said. She was not to worry.

She looked at me, startled, as if for the first time seeing me clearly. "Why, you're just a child. A lonely little child. Life isn't kind, is it, little Jessica? Maybe better for you, though, than for me. For me, everything in the beginning. Mama and Papa to love me, give me all that my heart desired." She put her hand over her face as if to shut out a vision she could not bear to see. "Now, at the end, nothing. Maybe for you, the other way. Begin with nothing. Everything at the end. Better that way. Better."

When at last she slept, I left her and went to my room. And for a long, long time sat at my window and watched the Christmas dance at Segadlos. Watched the figures whirl and dip and sway while the music throbbed against the night and the voices called, "Merry Christmas, a merry merry Christmas to all." It was very gay. Even when I found myself almost asleep, I could hardly bear to turn back to the sterile emptiness of my room.

Barren as that Christmas was, it bore strange fruit. A sort of bond between Miss Mabie and me, not of friendship—difference in age and upbringing prohibited that—but of something that served our lonely state almost as well. It led to my being served quantities of tea that I did not want, and greater quantities of talk about the past, which I wanted less. It led also to my having numerous tasks thrust upon me.

Filling her hot-water bottle, fetching her shawl, preparing her sherry and egg on holidays, which she viewed merely as another opportunity for hoarding strength, bringing her breakfast tray from the basement kitchen. Even walking down Peachtree to Kampers—if Mrs. Plummer was at the farm—to replenish her supply of tea and crackers. Tasks neither heavy nor arduous, yet sometimes, running up or down the two flights of stairs for the third time in an hour, I felt I carried the exhausted Miss Mabie on my thirteen-year-old shoulders. But then I would think of Mitty, and her belief that only by helping others you could "justify," and feel ashamed.

It did not strike me then that there was a strangeness in our association—a thirteen-year-old girl and a haggard old maid—or in the picture we made. With my teacup balanced on my knee, I sat and listened while, propped against pillows, she talked. Always of a glorious time, a lost time, its loss festering through the years like a malignant growth obscuring both present and future with its pain; her obsessed clinging to a past that no longer existed was only another way of dying. An idea that so depressed me that at her first hint of needing "to rest" I fled, eager for fresh air. And, to avoid further repetition of a past already unbearably dull, lingered later and later at night in the empty schoolroom.

On one of those nights—a night of gusty wind and rain and muttering thunder—I sat over my books, but not concerned with lessons. Possessed by restlessness because of the storm, perhaps, my mind refused to settle, but drifted aimlessly and without purpose. From the equinoctial storm bombarding the seminary, to Miss Mabie waiting to demand her hot-water bottle or an extra blanket, to the approach of summer vacation—only a few weeks away—a subject which with Mrs. Plummer's young ladies had superseded all others in lavatory sessions, even the Doctor Book. Their chattering voices uncaging a flock of names—Isle of Palms, Tybe, Cumberland—to flutter about like birds and conveying, somehow, the same sense of enchanted flight.

Other vacation plans, though not discussed in the lavatory, were in the air. The Plummers would go to the farm. The teachers—except for Miss Mabie—to summer with relatives or take "lodgings" at seashore or mountains. Even Pearlie, Mrs. Plummer dispensing with her services until the reopening of school, would go to her granny's in the country. Only Miss Mabie and I—and the slovenly cook—would remain at the seminary, an aspect it depressed me to contemplate. One long lifeless day after another. Days in which as in a painful dream I would hang suspended, unresolved with nothing to look forward to, with no promise of change.

Absorbed in this gloomy contemplation and no doubt deriving a sort of morbid pleasure from it, I was startled when a voice spoke my name. More startled when, looking up, I saw that Mr. Plummer leaned in the doorway and surveyed me with frosty, unsmiling eyes.

"Child, child! What a drab life you lead. Night after night"—his gesturing hand encompassed the schoolroom—"in this place. Or up in that barracks on the third floor with that half-dead woman, Maud Mabie. No friends, no fun, none of the foolishness that belongs to youth; that those gabbing idiots, the day pupils, are cursed with." His eyes probed mine. "Tell me. Is it because you scorn fun and frivolity? Or do you belong to a different species?"

His eyes were not smiling, but neither were they curious or prying as on that long-ago day Miss Pack's had been. They were kind—almost the eyes of a friend. And I found myself telling him as easily as I would a friend that the difference in the day pupils and me was not of species, but other ways.

I half expected him to laugh, to ask "what way," to point out that I had a head, two hands, two feet, and differed in no particular from the others. But he didn't. He continued to survey me attentively.

"Does it surprise you," he asked abruptly, "to learn that you've been the subject of speculation on my part since you first came to this place?" Without pausing for an answer he went on. "From my wife I heard something of your story. That you were more or less alone in the world, and at the age of twelve." His hand raked his hair abstractedly. "I unpacked my pity—seldom used, I assure you—and had it dusted and ready to invest you. Young and alone, I thought, thrust into the cage with the jibbering flock of snobbish geese." His eyes looking down at my upturned face were warmed by his sudden smile. "I came to know, and soon, that you had no need of pity. Mine or anyone's. You walked into this mare's nest of a life so trustingly. Young and yet so—only one word comes to mind—so womanly. Quiet but cheerful. Helping when and where you could. Allowing that hag-ridden Maud Mabie—oh don't think I didn't see—to use you as a servant. As earnest over lessons as if anyone in this mockery of learning knew or cared. Child, no need to tell me you are different. But tell me, if you can—Why?"

Though I was baffled by much, I told him, clumsily I'm sure, the difference between the young ladies and me. They had their families, I said. Fathers and mothers, sisters, brothers, uncles, aunts, cousins. They had a place in the world—their own place. This gave them, I said, the feeling of being valuable and important; of being wanted.

When I finished he asked quietly, "And you have none of these? No relatives at all, even distant ones?"

I shook my head. "Not that I know of, sir."

"Do you mean you've lived twelve, thirteen years—"

I interrupted to point out, "Nearly fourteen."

He smiled briefly. "I accept that important correction. Nearly fourteen years. Without kith or kin. Or anyone to give you affection?"

"No, sir, I don't mean that. You see, I had—Mitty."

His hand raked his hair again. "Mitty, Mitty. And who is Mitty?"

I told him of Mitty. Still clumsily, I know. For how take all the Mittys I knew and loved—the loving Mitty, the competent Mitty, the tart, the cold avenging Mitty, and with words mould them into one? Yet when, having tried, I met his eyes, I knew words had not wholly failed. For a sort of glow had grown in his as if, behind their frost, candles had been lighted.

He left the door where he leaned and came to sit on the desk across from mine, his lean hands clasping his sheaf of papers. "Tell me, child, how long have you known you were orphaned and alone?"

As long as I could remember, I said, or since I was five or so. But, I added quickly, I had Mitty then and didn't mind too greatly.

"And do you ever wonder if your aloneness is one of the accidents nature perpetrates? Or if in some gigantic design it was predestined—planned?"

I admitted that I had wondered. But I couldn't believe the part about the plan. There was no plan in such a life. Belonging to nobody—and nowhere. With no home, no place, not even a past to remember.

His eyes left me to gaze over my head at distance.

"You may not believe your life was planned. But I think it quite possible. Have you ever heard the phrase 'the child of destiny'?"

He did not see my puzzled glance. He continued to gaze into space.

"In every civilization we find a legend that springs—all of them, from a basic image of mythology. The story of the foundling. Cast away in infancy, found and reared by a foster mother and tempered and ennobled by hardships, achieving greatness." His gaze, deserting space, came back to me, his lean hand reached to pat my cheek. "Moses in the bulrushes, Romulus and Remus, Siegfried. All children of destiny. With lives not unlike yours." His eyes, still brooding, gazed into space again. "I wonder."

For a little he sat motionless, not speaking. Then, with a long sigh, pulled himself up from the desk and looked down at me, his eyes brooding. "Destiny is faithful to her pattern, child. What *has* happened can happen again."

When he said good night, I went to my room and while the wind shook at the windows and the rain beat against their panes, I lay and stared into the dark, my whole being strained toward something I could neither see nor touch, something that hovered above and beyond, yet so near I felt by reaching I might almost touch and grasp it. How reach it? Would I be shown the way? Was there, somewhere out in the universe, a powerful all-knowing destiny keeping watch, even over me? Lying in the dark, I could almost believe it.

The young century is five years old. I am fifteen and feel older and wiser than I will ever feel again. Logical reason for this sense of mature wisdom is not apparent unless it can be ascribed to my new acquisition, a whaleboned corset, and that I am now old enough to "go into" shirtwaists and skirts. The last, however, bear no resemblance to those worn by the young ladies. Their shirtwaists are the sheer, lacy, new "peek-aboos"; mine dark and plain, built for washing and wear. Their skirts of voile reveal taffeta underskirts that give an enchanting rustle. Mine of brilliantine reveals nothing except the greenish tinge effected by time.

Time, I find, has a way of effecting a great many things, among them Mrs. Plummer's list of young ladies. For, as time goes by, various pupils, for obscure reasons, drop from the lists; others, for reasons also obscure, are added. Yet, despite this constant state of change, the young ladies manage to seem unchanged. The faces may be different, and are. But enviable family backgrounds, thanks to Mrs. Plummer's contacts, adhere to identical traditions and the chatter in the lavatory revolves in identical circles. Boys—and Segadlos dances! Boys—and fraternity pins! Boys—and football games or parties! And since this was the South, long and repetitious harangues on "family," as tiresome and futile as those I still hear from Miss Mabie.

It was from these discussions that I learned that Southerners, in the opinion of the young ladies, consisted of two kinds of people only: the *Somebodies* and the *Nobodies*. The Somebodies either had money, or background enough to make up for its lack. Somebodies invariably lived on the North Side, preferably Peachtree, and belonged to the Driving Club. They sent their children to private schools similar to Mrs. Plummer's. They moved in an inner orbit as unattainable as the moon's. The rest of the population, which could neither attain nor afford this orbit, constituted the Nobodies. If they greatly outnumbered the Somebodies and consisted of valuable human beings, it failed to concern the young ladies. When they tossed their heads and exclaimed, "But she's nobody," it was with confidence that "she" existed in a fathomless limbo beneath their consideration.

After a time I was able to recognize and evaluate this for what it was and defend myself against it. But not at first. Then I not only lacked any defense, I was not conscious I needed it. It was Renette Collquitt, who looked like Queen Victoria, pudgy and proud and smug, who made me aware. Passing me in the hall one day, the center of the group of young ladies who served as her satellites, she called my name. And when I turned back she approached me, her manner so friendly that I was deceived. She bet my ears had been burning, she said, for they'd been talking about me. Or arguing, rather. They—she meant her satellites who stood listening—claimed my family didn't live in Atlanta but she claimed they did. Wouldn't I tell them where my family lived and settle the argument?

Reluctant to admit I had no family, yet equally loath to deceive, I answered evasively that my people lived out West End way.

"West End?" Her eyes widened before they slid away from mine to the other young ladies'. "Then of course you know Grace Stribling and Bess Follensbee! And Kate Madison—"

Trying to forestall further questions, I broke in to explain to her that I lived not in West End exactly, but further out Gordon Road at the cemetery, and once more the pale eyes circled the satellites. One of them, small, curly-haired Pet Pittinger, the seminary's acclaimed beauty, regarded me with open mouth. "But nobody lives away out there!" she protested vehemently, then finished, "That is, nobody that is anybody, I mean."

No one spoke for a moment and, seeing their eyes slip one to another and the half-smiles they half concealed, something sick and hateful twisted within me as once it had at Miss Pack's prying. A mouse ringed with hungry cats could have felt no more at bay than I, which was silly. For they were neither cats, nor were they cruel. Later, I would realize that they were products of the world of somebodies which believed itself to be the only world, a belief they accepted, being too young to question. I, also being young, did not tell myself this nor even perceive it. So my sense of separateness, my agonies of embarrassment each time Renette and her satellites giggled in corners, the conviction that they whispered of me, persisted. But time taught me that keeping myself more to myself would protect me.

It was Mr. Plummer who gave me a clearer understanding of the young ladies' attitude and who inspired me to begin to think for myself. He paused one night in the door of the schoolroom where I studied and from the door surveyed me from the frosty eyes.

"Do you know," he asked abruptly, "that you are growing up?"

Conscious of my rigid corset and high pompadour, I replied that I did.

"And do you realize that you give promise of being a beautiful young woman?" Then, as I moved my head deprecatingly, "Oh, I don't mean wax-doll beauty, thank God. We have enough of that. I am speaking of the beauty of intelligence and sensitivity. Let me assure you, you need not be embarrassed nor vain. It means nothing if you propose to use it to inveigle the first man with a substantial bank account that comes your way. Which, I'll take my oath, is the sole intention of the silly magpies that curse my existence." His bony hand raked his hair. "What manner of idiocy do they chirp? Dancing! Clothes! Beaux?"

Smiling, I nodded and added gravely, "And family, sir."

"Ah!" The hand dropped to rub the sharp jaw. "I should have known. The Southern balderdash of ancestors. Soothing syrup, Henry James called it. If his involved ladylike spasms can claim to call anything."

I looked at him, puzzled. "Soothing syrup, sir? For what?"

"For the humiliation of defeat and a sense of inferiority that defeat engendered. A soothing syrup compounded by the Redeemers. They took the romanticism of a Lost Cause, added their concocted legend of an 'Old South' that never existed, and with the mixture enticed the Old Order to their conniving scheme of looting, with the help of Northern interests, our forests and railroads and land. And selling the refurbished dubious Old South aristocracy, not just to the South but, by God! to the Yankees." The thin mouth smiled wryly. "Did a good job, too. Good enough to make genealogy the permanent avocation of the South and racial discrimination the curse. For mark this, child. The Yankee Reconstruction government gave us the idea of white supremacy. And the Redeemers found it a good flag to wave while they kicked in with the Yankee looters." Now his smile turned bitter. "Child, child. The South will in time recover from the war. But those two legends will retard her a hundred years."

He stared at me a moment as if suddenly aware that he had an audience. "There are books you should read, Jessica. If I get a card for you to Carnegie Library, will you read them?"

"I would like to read the books, sir."

"You shall, then. I would like to put them into the hands of every young Southerner so they could know what has happened to their world, what is happening." Then, with an abrupt "Good night, child," he turned and padded down the hall toward the side door. I wondered if he would remember about the books.

He did remember and a few nights later brought them to the schoolroom as I studied. As he laid them on the desk, he told me that he, with Mrs. Plummer's consent, had obtained a membership card at Carnegie Library for me; that on Saturdays, when tasks were done, I might go for books and return them. Surprised and pleased, I asked him to advise me on books to read. But he shook his head. "Find your way among them, child. That's half the pleasure. Read anything—everything—that comes to hand. How else can you learn to discriminate?"

From that night on I was never again without books. Walking back to the seminary on Saturdays, the single book the library allowed under my arm, I might have borne priceless treasure, so rich did I feel. And treasure books proved to be. For through them not only was my imagination nourished, but my hope of something beyond that time and place was kept alive. Avidly, because I wished to please Mr. Plummer, I read everything I found about the South. At least one young Southerner would know what had happened, what was happening to her land. And, in a small way, make his wish that all could know come true.

In all the time I had spent at the seminary I had not achieved, with a single pupil, the intimacy foreseen and forbidden by Mrs. Plummer. This is not meant to imply that I met with unfriendliness from the young ladies. I did not. But by the intuitive perception granted the young, they sensed that I—no more than Pearlie—belonged in what they considered their "circle." In the ordinary routine of classes and lessons and whispered discussions in the lavatory of the Thaw case—the sensation of the daily papers—the line of separation was not apparent. Only when they discussed their social activities was I conscious of the line, and as definitely as if they reared a tangible barrier.

Because of Mr. Plummer, this failed to disturb me as once it might have. Yet I do not deny that often I envied them their parties and pretty clothes, even their beaux; which I think was no more than human. Most of all I was envious of the friendship that bound them one to the other. So much I would have liked a friend of my own. But my few overtures toward friendship, while not actually repelled, went unrecognized. And I realized that for the young ladies, friendship was possible only for those within the circle. From necessity I resigned myself to the tiresome companionship of Miss Mabie.

One morning, I think the Monday after Thanksgiving holidays, Mrs. Plummer, having delivered her usual morning assembly talk on *How a Young Lady Should Walk, Talk, Eat, Sleep, Breathe and Go to the Bathroom,* did not, as was customary, immediately dismiss us. Instead, she halted the surge of movement that foretold departure and raised a restraining hand.

"Young ladies! If you please!" the stern voice warned. "I have an announcement to make."

We sank back in our seats.

Standing on the platform, she contemplated us with the calm gravity with which she managed to bestow significance on the slightest utterance. "This morning we enjoy the high privilege of welcoming a new member to our seminary family. One who, with her family, returns to Atlanta after sojourning in the capitals of the world. However, she is not to be regarded as a stranger, for stranger she is not. She descends from a family of native Georgians. And, I might add, illustrious Georgians. Distinguished since pioneer days for their services to Atlanta, the South and the nation. We are happy to welcome her back to Atlanta, honored to add her illustrious name to our rolls. Young ladies, I present Miss Laura Lee Carr. Miss Carr, please rise."

A girl rose from her seat in the front row. As all eyes, including mine, turned toward her, a gasp that might have issued from one throat instead of sixty breathed over the room. Not alone because she was such an exquisite creature; with black curls cascading to her waist, and eyes dark and large in the small pointed face. But because her dress of stiff black taffeta, unrelieved by a single flash of color, its bodice tapering to slim waist, its brief skirt flaring like a dancer's, was such a dress as we had never imagined. Moreover, it revealed not merely an inordinate length of slim leg, but legs sheathed, our unbelieving eyes perceived, in black silk stockings.

Standing before us, the center of all eyes, no duchess could have been more unaffectedly nonchalant than she. Not because she was vain or proud—it seemed to me—but because the adulation of strangers meant little. Proof, I thought, that she had never lacked admiration and love.

Mrs. Plummer said, "Young ladies, you will say good morning to Miss Carr."

We chanted in unison, according to rote, "Good morning, Miss Carr."

Whirling lightly she turned to face us. And with the slightest of bows, careless but as graceful as a dancer, responded.

"Bonjour, mes amies."

You could have heard a pin drop as, poised before us, she sent a buoyant but unconcerned smile over the hall. Then whirling, faced Mrs. Plummer again. *"C'est tout?"* she asked carelessly.

Mrs. Plummer's answering "That is all" signified dismissal, but instead of the usual noisy scampering up the aisle the dispersal was accomplished sedately and without the customary hubbub. Faces were almost blank. Eyes shone with something not unlike hostility. As if, confronted by that which deflated their smug assumption of superiority, they realized, for the first time, that there might exist standards which transcended theirs.

In the days that followed, their efforts to win the newcomer, who darted among them like a hummingbird in a flock of bluejays, amounted to siege. Observing, I wondered at their fawning overtures, wondered more at their insensitivity which her prettily worded withdrawals failed to pierce. For, like the hummingbird, she winged her way alone. When Renette, social arbiter of "the circle" for reasons unknown to me, called and beckoned, she flashed her buoyant smile and, waving airily, went on.

Yet she was neither disagreeable nor supercilious. She was gay. Her laugh rippled constantly. She was like a fresh wind wafted through the musty odor of snobbery. Through information brought from without in whispers and in whispered conclave redispersed, I learned that her father was "stinking rich," that they'd opened their old home on Peachtree, that Laura Lee arrived at the seminary each morning in a shining automobile—one of the few to appear on Atlanta streets—and with a young chauffeur. We learned, too, that her mama was an invalid and it was for benefit of her health that they'd traveled all over the world. Why this last bit of information engendered still deeper awe, I do not know, unless it bestowed still another touch of something beyond experience.

In the ensuing weeks, as I went to classes, studied in empty classrooms (and ran errands for Miss Mabie), I knew that the siege staged by Renette and her satellites to win Laura Lee Carr to their circle continued. But I was no longer interested. For, with the approach of Christmas, I was sinking into the unhappy state in which the season invariably thrust me. To contemplate with dread the holidays at the seminary alone with Miss Mabie, and my thoughts turning back to Mitty, as always. Startled, I realized how long since I had heard from her; since Mr. Dolph had stolen to the little side porch to remind me *there were reasons*. The sudden fear that they had slipped away from my life altogether became almost obsession.

As if thought had the power to wing through space—and who can prove it hasn't?—a few nights later as I prepared Miss Mabie's supper tray in the kitchen, Pearlie stopped beside me. And with an eye on the sullen cook said guardedly, "Somebody's on de side porch to see yu."

I dropped the lettuce and, wheeling, faced her. "Pearlie—you mean—?"

Grinning, she batted one eye to suggest Mr. Dolph's wayward one. "De big plat eye. Dat's who, honey."

Hurriedly I asked her to finish the tray and take it up to Miss Mabie. "Don't tell her," I warned.

She nodded. "I tell Miz Sack of Bones nuttin. Go on! Git up dose stairs fore plat eye put conjur on yu."

Needing no further prodding, I ran up the basement stairs and out to the little porch and Mr. Dolph. But oh, such a different Mr. Dolph from the one I'd always known. True, the whip was the same, and the wen and the uncontrollable eye. But the huge body no longer swaggered straight and tall but was stooped and shrunken. As if the vitality formerly housed within it had vacated and left it empty.

He told me why when I had hugged him, and hugged him again, and, unable to say anything except "Oh, Mr. Dolph," hugged him again. He, with one thing and another, he said, had been run through hell with a soot bag. First that blasted horse throwed him and broke his leg. Second the damfool doctor set it crooked. Still, in a manner of speaking, it healed, but like a crooked stick. And ever since he'd been plagued with rheumatism. Not just in the leg but all his body. Sometimes, he thought, the head too. He added, spinning his hat on his finger, that 'long with the rest, Poteat & Whidby, him being no good to anybody any more, had let him go.

Telling, he worked so hard to appear his old self, to hold defeat and humiliation from his voice, that I wanted to cry, but I wouldn't. Too clearly it would have revealed my pity. And pity, his attempt at the old cocksureness warned, was the last thing he wanted. So, as if to me he was unchanged—and the kindness and loyalty of his great heart were unchanged—I changed the subject and asked about Mitty.

Mitty, he said, was fine as silk and sent her unbounding love. And Petey—how desolate the smile he gave me—was spry as a cricket. And now, grunting, he leaned laboriously and looked into my face, now how would I like to go see Mitty and Petey?

Thrilled to a state of speechlessness by the very thought, I stared at him, again unable to manage anything beyond an ecstatic "Oh, Mr. Dolph!" But the indomitable figure of Mrs. Plummer flashing before me darkened my fleeting hope. "But would I be allowed to go, sir?"

Straightening, he propped his huge hand against the side of the house for support and looked down at me.

"Little one," he spoke slowly, solemnly. "When I was flat o' my back with this cursed rheumatism, you were heavy on my mind. Knowing you was worrying about Mitty—and that fool bird—was worrying to me. When a man is laid low, little one—and I don' know why it's so, but so it is—his mind clarifies like hog fat over fire. So mine did. And I see what a sharp thing were done to you. And was ashamed of my part in it."

For him to blame himself was unthinkable. "You had your orders, Mr. Dolph," I reminded.

"Orders I had, but I got no orders now—I'm a free agent. If it lets me do you a good turn I thank God for it."

As I repeated my foolish "Oh, Mr. Dolph!" I did not look at him. I could not. I knew quite well that kind as his intentions were—and they were kind—I would not be permitted to see Mitty. And trying to talk and swallow the lump in my throat, I managed to tell him so.

He asked gently, "Do you want to go, little one?"

I gasped. "Oh, Mr. Dolph. If you knew—how much—"

His hand reached to pat my cheek. "Then go you will. They could break Dolph Queen into a million pieces but there'd be enough of him left to skivvy it. Now"—grunting, he leaned close again—"I recollecks as how you said you and a teacher-lady are here alone—from time to time. And that you and this lady are in a way of being friends. Right?"

I told him dubiously, "Right," and he went on.

"It comes to me that along of being friendly with this lady and having done her favors, which knowing you I know for a fact, that mebbe she'd be willing to favor you. Right?"

Still more dubiously, I said, "Right."

"Now next time the cock of the walk goes wherever she goes, if you ask the teacher-lady a favor and to keep that favor under her shirt, I calkerlate she'd be willing to oblige. Right?"

That, I could not answer. I could only stand before him, torn between wishing and doubting. When I reminded myself that I had talked to Miss Mabie of Mitty and had found her not unsympathetic, I dared hope. But I recalled also that to oblige me might jeopardize her situation, and hope dwindled. But when I remembered that Mrs. Plummer planned to spend the next week end at the farm—that this very week end I might see Mitty—I knew I must try. And, asking Mr. Dolph to wait, I re-entered the house and skimmed up the two flights of stairs to the third floor.

Miss Mabie, propped on pillows, had just finished supper when I entered. And going to her side, I took the empty tray from her knees. After her customary weary "Thank you, Jessica," she requested her flannel bed saque and, when I'd drawn it about her shoulders, sank against the pillows and glanced at the tray I'd placed on the nearby table distastefully.

"You know soiled dishes disgust me." She was almost peevish. "Remove the tray, Jessica."

I said placatingly that I would. But first, I added respectfully, I had a favor to ask of her. Then, hurrying lest she postpone hearing to rest, I told her of Mr. Dolph. How he waited on the side porch. Of his plans for me to see Mitty. I asked, almost I pled, that she allow me to go. I would go at the time she named, stay as short a time, I said, as she wished, obey any orders she might give me. If she would just let me go; only let me see Mitty again.

She waited so long to answer that hope began to die. But before it wholly expired she said thoughtfully, "You couldn't stay overnight. I would be here, alone."

With hope reviving, I assured her fervently that I wouldn't stay overnight; then waited again, hardly breathing.

"You couldn't spend the day. The cook or Pearlie might miss you. Might mention it—"

Quickly I protested I wouldn't stay all day.

While I waited again she considered. "It couldn't be on a Sunday. Mrs. Plummer returns from the farm too early in the day. Perhaps Saturday—right after dinner—"

I asked breathlessly, "Miss Mabie, you mean you will let me go?"

She sighed. "I know I shouldn't. I know if Mrs. Plummer found out—" She contemplated her hand. "Tell this—er—Mr. Dolph person he's not to come to the seminary. You'll meet him, say at Kampers. At two o'clock. He must get you back by six."

She hardly heard my thanks. Sinking deeper into her pillows, she closed her eyes. "Go tell your Mr. Dolph, child, what I told you to say," she said wearily. And I left her lying there with closed eyes.

When Mr. Dolph and I had arranged where and when to meet, I watched his labored passage across the grounds and then went back to my room. And, lying on my bed, I cried for the first time in a long time. Cried for happiness because I would see Mitty again; for unhappiness because of what time had done to Mr. Dolph; and the goodness of his humbled heart. A mixed-up sad and happy sort of crying it was. And, as finally I dried my eyes, I wondered if life ever allowed total happiness or woe; or if always it tempered one with the other.

I have never ceased to marvel at the contrariness of time. Its way of dawdling before anticipated pleasure and hastening pell-mell to foretold disaster. Certainly between that night and Saturday, time exerted this dubious propensity. Yet while to me it seemed to stand still, like a rebellious child pushed along by elders, it did move forward hour after hour. And finally Friday came. Mrs. Plummer, whose decision fluctuated all day with the weather's on rain or no rain, finally departed for the farm. Time at last, laggard though it was, brought Saturday. And Mr. Dolph and I in his buggy, which like Mr. Dolph appeared somewhat dilapidated by time, were on our way to Battle Hill.

As we went along Atlanta's streets he, pointing with his whip, directed my eyes to this or that sign of Atlanta's growth, his manner at once disparaging that growth, yet admitting a grudging pride. There, he said, whip pointing, was the new Candler Building, Atlanta's big skyscraper. Seventeen stories! Built of Georgia marble! Sculptors brought over by Candler from Italy, France and England to do the fancy carving. A seventeen-story building! And all because of a soft drink—the receipt bought, 'twas said, for twenty-five dollars.

Later, with the same mixture of pride and disgust, he pointed out the new Terminal Station that, with its turrets and spires, stood like an overdressed lady in its shabby surroundings. Why, he grumbled, Atlanta would spend a million dollars on something that looked like one of the old Exposition buildings was beyond him. Still, it could take care of the six big railroads that used it. So it warn't all waste.

Though he talked, I know, so the way to Battle Hill might seem less long, how long it did seem. In my state of expectancy, the time Mr. Dolph's horse took to amble along Peters Street toward West End and on to Battle Hill was endless. But at last we turned into the shadowy pineland that led to Mitty's house; where every tree, every rock was well-remembered, its sighing pines, its air of summer days or winter rain so familiar that my heart, passing among them, was full. Then Mitty's house came into view. Smaller and humbler than my memory of it, but no less dear, for it was home, the only home I had ever known. Only the sight of Mitty waiting on the little porch stopped the tears that rose to my eyes. And when Mr. Dolph, perceiving it, reined in the horse and said, "Jump out, little one. I know you wants to run," I was out of the seat and on the ground, and running as I'd never run before, straight to Mitty's arms. And what a wonderful thing her "My ever ever blessed!" was. How wonderful to see Petey cock his tiny head as wisely as ever; to see again the fire on Mitty's hearth, the flowers in Mitty's windows, the shining spick-and-spanness of the little house; to find my little room waiting unchanged, with May Queen propped against the pillow of my bed; to stand at my window again and look out over the tombstones. To think back to the time when they were my only playmates; more faithful, I thought, than any I'd known since.

Then Mitty tiptoeing in and leading me from the room and taking off my hat and stepping back to survey me. Her amazement on discovering that I was taller than she—how small she was and how dear. And insisting that I stand, my back to the door, while she marked off my height. And Mr. Dolph limping in as she marked and exclaiming, "Things in general are springing up, eh, Mrs. McDaniel?" And all of us laughing too heartily to hide from one another that we felt more like crying.

When we stopped laughing, Mr. Dolph said while I visited with Mitty he'd ride down the road a piece for a visit with Zed McNair who he hadn't seen in a whet of a time; and come back for me around five. Then he was gone. And Mitty and I sat before the fire and talked. I told her of the seminary and Mrs. Plummer. Of the young ladies and Mr. Plummer. Then she had her turn. Janey moved "down country" to her sister's, she said; other Negroes lived in her cabin. And Janet Stopper—Janet of the dark eyes and dark flying pigtails—had run away and got married, and her not turned sixteen; and was going to have a baby. She'd married that no-count Wills boy. Folks said he was half-witted and you'd reckon it woulda took the starch out of that stuck-up mother's sails, but it hadn't. And now, she said, rising, I must have some of the fresh batch of tea-cakes.

She brought the teacakes and milk and I ate them, feeding Petey crumbs through the bars of his cage as in old days. Then I sat on the floor at Mitty's knee and put my head in her lap. And for a long time we sat not speaking, her hand smoothing my hair. After a little I began to talk; to tell her what I planned to do. How, when I left the seminary, I could find a situation and be, I said, independent.

Her small, work-worn hand patted my head. "And you will be, my blessed."

"And I'll come back to you. And we'll live here in the little house, won't we?"

"That we will, God willing."

"And I will buy Petey his new cage. And you a silk dress and a gold watch. Just as I planned when I was ever so small."

She didn't speak for such a long time that, raising my head, I looked up into her face and saw the tears that trickled down her cheeks.

She dashed them away with her hand. "Fire makes my eyes water," she defended hastily.

I smiled up at her. "Just as the sun made you cry the day you told me I couldn't go to Battle Hill school?"

But she would admit nothing. "Brightness always makes my eyes water."

I sat gazing up at the tiny wrinkled face.

"Mitty," I said softly, why wouldn't they let me go to school?"

"Why you know why. The county line—"

"Mitty—" I interrupted, "tell me the truth. I need to know. It isn't good—not knowing, Mitty. Not knowing who I am or why I am so alone."

Her eyes returned my gaze untroubled. "I know it ain't good, my blessed. And I'd tell you if I could." Fiercely she added, "I'd tell you everything you wanted to know. But I don't know myself. All I know is that Mr. Dolph came and told me he'd been ordered to place—a child. And knowing Charlie was dead and me living here alone, he'd thought of me."

"But Mr. Dolph knows, doesn't he?"

"No more than me. 'Place the child,' they told him and not another word. So he brought you to me. A forlorn little mite you was as ever I see. I told myself if it took my last breath you'd be happy with Mitty."

"I was," I told her. "Oh Mitty, I was."

We were engulfed by another silence. But after a little she said, "I know it's hard being alone and not knowing, Jess. Nothing can change that. But let Mitty tell you this. You are good and you have a loving heart. And a fine mind, Miss Key said. And you're wonderful pretty. That's *what* you are. If they call you Jess Kildare or Queen Victoria, it don't change *what* you are. Wear it like a rose in your hair, and be proud. As I am of you. And that's prouder than a queen."

Leaning, she gathered me to her arms and put her soft, wrinkled cheek against mine. And so we remained until we heard Mr. Dolph's buggy wheels as they came through the woods. Then I clutched her tighter. "In two years, Mitty, I'll be eighteen and can come back to stay."

"Of course you can, dearie."

"Perhaps two years won't seem so very long."

"They'll go like greased lightning."

"And when I come back I'll never leave you again."

"Never again," she echoed. "Now go wash your face and make your hair neat. We mustn't give Mr. Dolph cause to worry."

While I did her bidding she packed the remaining teacakes with jars of her jelly and jam into a box. Then brought a soft, lacy shawl crocheted, she said, in spare time, and wrapping it in tissue put it in the box. "For that teacher, Miss Mabie," she told me, "for letting me have my Jess."

With Petey's cage in one hand and her other arm around me, she walked to the porch with me, and holding Petey's cage high, stood there as I got into the buggy and Mr. Dolph clucked to the horse. Looking at her with suddenly cleared vision, I saw how tiny she was, how old, how helpless, for all the undaunted courage in the face turned toward mine. As we moved away I leaned over the side of the buggy. "I'll be back, Mitty, in two years," I called. And she called back, "Two years, my blessed"—as cheerfully as if she believed it to be true.

Christmas marched toward us, heralded by the young ladies' chatter of dinners and open house, of the Christmas dance at Segadlos, this year superseded by Renette's private dance, occasion for much whispering and giggling in corners. Naturally, in this I had no part. But I didn't care. Not now. Seeing Mitty had acted upon me like a tonic. With my plans uppermost in my mind, I determined to learn everything there was to be learned in order to assure their fruition, and labored over lessons more than ever. So it was without volition on my part that I was involved with Renette's Christmas dance.

One day after school as I straightened classrooms, a task recently relegated to me by Mrs. Plummer, I entered Miss Hine's room, to find it, not deserted as I had expected, but occupied by "the circle" of young ladies including Renette, all ranged closely about Laura Lee Carr. At my entrance they looked at me resentfully as if I intruded. All except Laura Lee Carr. She, seeing that I hesitated, called to me over the circle of heads.

"Come in, Jessica. This isn't a private room."

"I can come back later to straighten—"

"No no. I insist. We're talking of nothing important, they only want to know if I will attend Renette's dance. Or rather"—her face was suddenly impish—"if my beautiful brother will attend. *Là, là.* A beautiful brother makes one very popular, *n'est-ce pas?"*

All the young ladies except Renette giggled appreciatively. She continued to regard me sullenly.

Laura Lee, observing this in turn, regarded Renette. And breaking through the circle they made, she danced toward me. "Jessica, what will *you* wear to Renette's dance?"

A hush fell over the young ladies and with eyes slipping slyly one to the other they waited to hear what I answered. When I only said, "I am not going, Laura Lee," I could almost see their relief. Relief that was dispelled when Laura Lee exclaimed, "No? But why do you not go? You are one of us." Wheeling, she faced the circle of blank faces. "Tell her she must," she ordered imperiously.

It was Renette who answered, who said sullenly, "She can't very well if she isn't invited."

Laura Lee whirled toward her, the dark eyes sweeping Renette's dumpy figure slowly, insolently. "Ah!" she exclaimed softly. "I see. But this is bad. Very bad." Mockingly she surveyed Renette through bright eyes for a second, then exclaimed carelessly, "I almost forget—my brother and I can't attend your party."

Wailing protests rose and broke around her like a wave. "Oh Laura Lee! But it's really given for you. You can't mean that. Why, what on earth—?" And eyes surveying them gleefully, curls tossing, she murmured brief regrets, "So sorry, simply impossible," yielding to their pleas not an inch, not once telling them why she refused.

But Renette knew why; and as she left the room with the others she sent a venomous glance my way. It did not escape Laura Lee. When the door closed behind them she whirled toward me on her toes, her face alight with mischief. "Did you see, Jessica? Their faces? And that fat peeg Renette—" She clapped her hands childishly. "Ah, it was exquisite!"

"You shouldn't have," I told her. "It was unkind."

"Are they kind to you?" she asked sharply. And, as I started to speak, "No no—don't answer. I see with these eyes. Hear with these ears." She tossed the long curls. "They are jealous of you. The cats."

When I pointed out that they had no reason for jealousy, she danced to stand before me. And, cupping my face in her slim hands, bestowed a birdlike peck on my cheek. "You goose. It is because you are prettier."

Doubtfully I repeated, "Prettier?"

Her laughter trilled over the empty room. "But of course. My brother —who they oh so much want to meet—swears you are the only girl in the place he'd give"—she snapped her fingers—"*that* for."

Skeptically I pointed out, "But he's never even seen me."

"You think not? Oh! But he did. One afternoon when we drove by the seminary you were out in front. When I tell him that peeg Renette didn't invite you to her silly dance—"

"I couldn't go if I was invited," I pointed out. "Mrs. Plummer wouldn't let me."

She tossed her curls. "Mrs. Plummer! Bah! As for the stupid dance, Papa will make Oakes and me go. But at least I can worry Renette. It will teach the dunce a lesson. Perhaps now you will be my friend?"

"Your friend?" I asked dubiously.

"Of course. Do you think I like not having a good friend? I do not, I can tell you. But these others? They're so dull." The light voice mimicked: "My grandfather Governor Poopepoop—my uncle Judge Folderol—all dead, mind you. They are like turnips, the best part growing under the ground." Grasping my arm, she whirled me to face her. "You are not a turnip. You don't talk talk talk and say nothing. I like you." Grasping my other arm, she shook me lightly. "Now are we friends?"

"Oh yes. I'd like to be."

"Well then. Now we are. Tomorrow at little recess we'll walk in the grounds together and we'll—" She broke off to turn her head toward the street and the honk of an automobile horn. "There's Bucky and the motor. Now I must go."

She smiled, she waved her hand, she curtsied with mock respect. She said, "Until tomorrow," and danced toward the door; at the door, hand on knob, turned back. *"Au revoir, mon amie!"*

I could not believe she meant it. I never believed she meant it deeply. From the first I realized the impermanence of her friendship; nor did I blame her for it. As foolish to censure the hummingbird for its inconstant flight, I thought; and at least for the time, we were friends. We walked about the grounds at recess, arms entwined, on rainy days sat together in Assembly Hall, I, with uneasy eyes watching for Mrs. Plummer, unable to forget that this was the intimacy she had forbidden. Recalling her reason, "intimacy leads to revelation," I thought she need not have worried. To Laura Lee I revealed nothing except that I was an orphan, a state which she instantly invested with romance. Prophesying with sparkling eyes the appearance of my dead papa's friend who, having cheated my papa out of a fortune, would make me—like Sarah Crewe—heiress to a "magnificent" fortune, she clapped her hands, her dark eyes mischievous. And that fat pig Renette, who said I was nobody, would, *là là,* expire with envy.

Smiling, I pretended to accept her pretense, though I took it no more seriously than a child's belief in fairies. To me, she often seemed like a child. So artlessly she discussed whatever flashed through her mind: her mama's illness, the breakfast quarrel between Papa and Oakes, Miss Belle who ran the house for Papa and who, she confided gleefully, was madly in love with Papa. As if Papa would look at such a dried-up old stick, even if Mama died. Such an old silly, Miss Belle! Such a softie! Why, she let them—she meant Oakes and herself—wind her around their fingers. She knew they slipped off in the car with Bucky, the chauffeur, sometimes even at night, and didn't tell Papa. Oakes said if Papa ever found out, it was twenty-three skiddoo for her.

Listening and watching the slim gesturing hands, hearing her thoughtless laughter, I was sometimes seized by the conviction that, like the little boy in Mr. Barrie's book, she would never grow up. Yet this was only one Laura Lee; there was another who made me feel that I, not she, was the child.

It was this other Laura Lee who found me on a rainy winter day, spending recess at my desk checking report cards for Miss Hines. Perching on a nearby desk, she talked as I inked in records. Last night, after Papa left for the club, she said, she and Oakes had slipped off in the motor with Bucky and gone to a horrid little place on the viaduct off Peachtree to see that moving picture of the Thaw case. Stupid and cheap and not a bit like the real Thaw case, and horribly dull. Just the same, she finished impishly, Papa would have a duck fit if he knew.

I stopped checking papers to look at her, puzzled. "You enjoy doing things more if you think they displease your father, don't you?"

Her fingers twining one of the dark glistening curls, she retorted coolly, "Yes. Shall I tell you why?"

"I think I know. Your papa loves you and gives you everything you want. So you are spoiled."

She shook her curls at me. "Papa never gives what you want. Only what he wants you to have."

"He gives you what he believes to be good for you."

"Is it good for me when he is unkind to Mama?"

"Your mother is sick. What you call unkindness is no doubt for her good."

It was then that I met for the first time that other, older Laura Lee; saw her looking at me from the dark eyes as an adult looks at a child who babbles of something it does not understand. But she only said, shrugging, "There! You see. You don't know what Papa's like."

"I do know that he gives you a fine home and trips to Paris and motor cars and pretty clothes."

She looked down at her brief-skirted frock. "Pretty? You think I like these horrible black dresses? Always black? I hate them. But I have to wear them because the daughter of Madame de Chalfont, a friend of Papa's in Paris, wears them. He thinks them chic. It's the same with everything. Even Mama. Oakes and me too, if we let him; but we won't. He shan't do to us what he's done to poor Mama." She stared at me with mutinous eyes. Then in a breath the strange Laura Lee yielded to the imperious child again. "Jessica, I'm forgetting what I came to tell you. Mama says you're to come home with me some afternoon. And stay for tea so she can meet my friend."

Regretfully I told her I couldn't, that Mrs. Plummer, I was sure, would not permit, and she tossed her curls. "Mama will write her a note. She won't refuse Mama."

The bell warning the end of recess prevented further discussion; and gathering up Miss Hines' papers I delivered them to her classroom. But as I returned along the hall it came back to my mind. Greatly I hoped Laura Lee's mama would write the note, that I be allowed to go to their home. So often I pictured to myself the way a home would be, and a family in a home, happy and contented as I believed they must be. But if my picture was true I was not yet to know. A day or so later Laura Lee said her mama had been taken suddenly worse. Papa, she added, was taking her to White Sulphur; for the springs.

The last half of that term, except for Laura Lee, made little impression upon me. Inspired by books from Carnegie Library and my resolve to win independence for Mitty and me, I plunged into lessons, determined to learn everything and anything I could.

Final examinations over, I emerged from my absorption to find the seminary already whirling in the activity that precedes commencement.

Then commencement, held in the Assembly Hall at night, was over. Mrs. Plummer, regal in black satin and jet, had delivered prizes for the prettiest, the most popular, the best-mannered, with scholarship kept in the background like a poor relation that might embarrass. The graduates in foamy white and clasping roses to young bosoms had received their beribboned diplomas to the applause of fond parents and friends. "Auld Lang Syne" had been sung by the entire school—and the school year was over. Vacation had begun.

This summer, I told myself, I would not yield to the hopeless, shapeless resignation of other summers. I would continue to study; I would read books with something more than pleasure to give; I would employ the long hours usefully. To this end I spent a great deal of time on a schedule in which each hour was allotted its special duty. So much time for lessons, so much for reading, so much for tending my clothes, so much for my daily tasks. So much to work in the small garden I planted in a corner of the grounds. Bravely I started in to adhere to it. But as the withering heat of June advanced, with one arid breathless day after another, the nights that bridged them hardly less breathless, my courage, like my garden, wilted. Working in the garden on hot afternoons, the smell of city dust mingling with the heat, the vision of Mitty's burgeoning flowers would be before me, and my spirit would pant for Mitty's world of green growing things; of little brook and dim cool woods. Why, I wondered, must I be shut away in this gloomy place? Digging and weeding, I dreamed back to the carefree hours beside the little brook when I watched it dance its way over sticks and stones. Or, lying on my stomach, peered at the tadpoles that skimmed its surface. Yet knowing even as I dreamed I could never escape to that world again; nor ever be free of the conviction that my life would be not dreaming, but striving.

Often as I worked in my garden or, reading, closed my book and sat thinking, I would think of Laura Lee's fervent promises not to forget me, to contrive some way to get me away from this "horrible" place and "horrible" old Miss Mabie; promises in which I had scant faith even when she made them. I knew that she and Miss Belle and Oakes, immediately after school closed, had departed for Cumberland Island. A poky place with a poky hotel, she declared, with no dancing, no beaux, no fun. But this I had discounted. And the time that seemed to stand still for me, I thought of as whirling with excitement for her. That she should forget her promise not to forget struck me as no more than natural.

As if to prove my lack of faith, she fulfilled her promise and came. In the late afternoon of a hot July day she—her brother Oakes too—circled the seminary to the side steps where, while Miss Mabie took a "little rest," I sat and read. Dashing up the steps, she hugged and kissed me, said "Jessica, this is Oakes" all in one breath, then dropped to the step beside me. Oakes stopped on the bottom step and leaned against its rail.

"Oh Jessica!" This was Laura Lee. "That horrible Cumberland. Imagine! Not a man under thirty. And the girls—*Mon Dieu!* Oakes and I nearly died."

I said I didn't believe her and I didn't. For she and Oakes actually glowed, and not, I felt, from sun and sea alone. Now, laughing, she tossed her curls, then was suddenly serious. Truly she didn't enjoy it, she said. She kept thinking of me stuck in this horrible place—

"Jessica." Her voice dropped portentously. "Oakes has a peachy plan. To get you away from here." Then, as I started to speak, "Now wait. It can't get you into trouble. You see, Miss Mabie is in it too. Jessica, listen—"

With an air of conspiracy that suggested nothing less than a gunpowder plot, she unfolded the plan. They would persuade Miss Belle to invite Miss Mabie for tea and suggest she bring the "pupil" along. Miss Belle and Miss Mabie would take to each other like duck soup, and we'd be asked back because with Papa away Miss Belle was horribly bored. And while they drank tea and gossiped, we would slip off and have oodles of fun. Didn't I agree?

Listening, I looked from one to the other and thought how could I *not* agree? Seeing their faces alight with mischief, their eyes that sparkled with plotting, I knew the delight their gay companionship could be. Yet, to deceive Miss Mabie and involve her—

As if he suspected what I thought, Oakes for the first time spoke, to ask coolly, "You aren't afraid to do it, are you?"

"Not afraid exactly," I said. "But I don't think I should."

Laura Lee wailed, "Oh Jessica!" and he told her to shut up, and came back to me. "Why do you think you shouldn't?"

I explained about Miss Mabie. How disregard for Mrs. Plummer's rules might mean her situation. They pooh-poohed this, called it silly. People didn't fire people for going to tea with friends. If old lady Plummer tried it, they'd tell Papa. Papa would tell her twenty-three skiddoo.

They finished, they looked to see if they had convinced me. And when I said nothing, Oakes lifted his dark brows. "I don't believe you want to come."

"Oh yes," I told him quickly, too quickly. "It's just—you can't always do what you like."

"Why not, if you want to? We do."

"Not if it's wrong," I reminded.

He laughed impishly. "If we want to do it, we tell ourselves it isn't wrong."

"Then you are spoiled," I accused.

He laughed again in a way that made me feel very young. "Of course we are."

I looked down at his upturned face that was warm and alive with laughter. No easier not to spoil him, I thought, than Laura Lee. For they were so alike. His eyes deep and dark in the pointed face which, like hers, revealed every mood and thought that flashed across it.

A sound somewhere within the seminary startled us from silence and Laura Lee sprang to her feet. "That's probably old Miss Mabie. We'd better run." Skimming down the steps, she looked back over her shoulder. "Don't be a lemon, Jessica," she pleaded. But Oakes, trailing her toward the street, said nothing. Nor did he look back.

When they were gone I stood a moment thinking and absently twisting my single curl. For some reason feeling guilty and a fool. As if I had been invited to a delightful party, one I wished to attend, yet perversely wouldn't. I wondered why earlier my reasoning seemed so unquestionably right, yet now lacked reason as well as sense. I had not learned that the traitorous heart, to gain its desire, betrays both mind and conscience.

In the days that followed, the conviction of being a fool persisted. For how endless those days! How arid the silent seminary grounds, gray with the summer's dust! How dull the dreary kitchen where, cook being on vacation, I prepared the food Miss Mabie decreed. My room at night after another session with Miss Mabie's dead papa, when my heart, too, would feel dead. The city below my window that panted beneath its winding sheet of heat as if it too lay dying and deserted. And down the street, Segadlos, dark and silent—deserted. Segadlos, too, was on vacation.

Each morning when I went to the mailbox at the gate I hoped to find the note from Miss Belle, but, the days passing without its appearance, I concluded that Oakes and Laura Lee had abandoned the plan. I reminded myself that it was no one's fault but my own; I had been silly, and I couldn't have gone in any case, so I was being sillier now. Yet each day as the note failed to arrive, I sank deeper into depression, finally reaching the state where I viewed life as a veritable Death's Valley where I was doomed to languish without hope, testimony of how silly I really could be.

However, both Death Valley and self-pity were instantly vanquished when the mauve envelope addressed to Miss Mabie finally appeared in the mailbox. With lifting spirits I took it up to her. And after inspecting its exterior and wondering aloud, as she turned it over and back again, who on earth it was from, she opened and read it; then reread it, this time aloud, pleased and excited, as those who lead lonely lives are excited by the smallest attentions. The discussion of what she should wear and the addition of a great deal of white frill to a dress became her sole occupation from then on. Listening as propped against pillows she talked, I gathered that she regarded the invitation as due to Miss Belle's recognition of "blood," thereby proving that Miss Belle herself possessed blood. For, as dear Papa phrased it (and on blood Papa had no peer), "It took blood to know blood."

Her excitement by Friday had progressed to a state of palpitation that required in consequence so many eggs in sherry, I began to doubt her ability to descend the stairs. However, she managed, and with only a slight weaving, to climb into the auto which Miss Belle had sent. Then Bucky, the Carrs' chauffeur, was cranking the engine and hopping in. We were careening with a series of sharp explosions up Peachtree, going, Miss Mabie gasped clutching her hat, at least fifteen miles an hour. She only hoped we reached the Carrs' alive.

For me this, my first ride in an auto, seemed much too brief, and too soon we turned into a drive that led to the huge ugly house of gray stone. A house so turreted and balconied in the manner of British castles, I half expected to see a moat. But as we chugged up the driveway and stopped under the portico, I saw only the iron deer poised on the lawn, one foot forever lifted.

Bucky, as if pulled by strings, was springing out to open the door, and Laura Lee was flashing from the house with Oakes behind her. Chattering and gesturing, she conducted us along a narrow corridor, from which we caught glimpses of vast handsome rooms, to the library. Here Miss Belle, a very thin lady with very vague eyes, advanced to greet us, her floating ends of chiffon wavering in movement like octopus tentacles. Enjoying to the hilt, I knew, her role as lady of the house.

Tea was served by a Negro butler. As straight and stiff as if carved from wood—and as unbending—he impressed Miss Mabie no little; and me as well. But then I was impressed with everything. With the heavy handsome furniture, the damask draperies sweeping the floor, the tea tray handsome with silver and china. Yet I was not so impressed that I failed to be aware of Oakes on the sofa beside me; of his shoulder touching mine, of the dark eyes that each time I turned were upon me. Sipping my tea (which I still didn't like) and nibbling the tiny sandwiches, I sat wrapped in content, listening to Miss Mabie and Miss Belle exchange first pleasantries that became, as they took on more tea, confidential and contained considerable "blood." I gathered that Miss Belle, like Miss Mabie, regarded her present position in life as a comedown; and I wondered if Laura Lee's claim that this pale fluttering lady had romantic designs on her papa was valid.

As if my speculations had penetrated the fog of talk that swirled about her, she broke off suddenly and peered across at us to exclaim, "You young ones don't want to listen to our nonsense." Fluttering, she waved us from the room. "Go somewhere and amuse yourselves."

"Somewhere" turned out to be a large glassed-in porch overlooking the back garden (a room less elegant than the rest of the house, but more comfortable with its wicker furniture). Its table held one of the new gramophones and its sofa, the young chauffeur Bucky. Smoking, he lay stretched upon it, his boots disdainful of cushions, his eyes, when we entered, just as disdainful of us.

When Laura Lee said carelessly, "Jessica, this is Bucky," he swung his boots to the floor with a curt "Hello," and I saw that his face, which under the chauffeur's cap had seemed handsome, was less pleasing without it. His blond good looks were marred by eyes as round and hard as marbles. Laura Lee, whirling in the center of the room, demanded, "What shall we do? Dance?"

Oakes said, "Let's," and crossing to the gramophone wound it and, when the music started, came back to me. "Will you dance with me, Jessica?"

He showed no surprise when I said I had never learned, but accepted it matter-of-factly. I wouldn't learn any younger, he said, and offered to teach me. He taught me the one-step and the waltz, holding my hands and counting as I tried them; not laughing when my feet were clumsy, but saying patiently, "Try again." Gradually I caught on. At the end of the room Laura Lee danced with Bucky, gliding round and round without so much as speaking. Somehow I felt guilty; that in this time of summer's dusk, a magic time for me, she should have no one but Bucky.

It was, that afternoon, only the first of the many Miss Mabie and I spent at the Carrs'. Between Miss Mabie and Miss Belle a mutual admiration developed. The admiration that discovers in another the identical virtues it claims for itself. Over their tea, Miss Belle fluttering her appendages, Miss Mabie touching her frills, they would be almost girlishly gay. Tea over, they settled down for a "little visit" after laughingly, as if we were children, telling us to run along.

We were content at first to withdraw to the glassed porch to dance or play the new game "Carrams." But later we grew bolder and slipped off for a spin in the auto, with Laura Lee in front beside Bucky, Oakes and me in back. As July turned toward August, we became even bolder. Our little spins lengthened to long rides. Out to Peachtree Creek or Stone Mountain, sometimes to Grant Park, where we paddled about the lake in a rented canoe. Oftenest of all we went to Ponce de Leon Springs. There, standing on the slippery rock, we drank from the rusty tin dipper the sweet spring water that welled from its rocky bed.

It was a wonderful place—Ponce de Leon Springs. Lying many feet below the street, reached by wide wooden steps, it was a secret place, as lovely with its encircling hills and trickling water as a glade; and so still that as we sat or strolled beneath the trees, our voices were unconsciously hushed lest we disturb the cathedral quiet. Yet at other times Laura Lee, as if she must overcome it, would spring up unexpectedly to run madly, her voice daring us to catch her, enticing us to join her game. Then we would run like wild things; the hills returning our shrieking laughter in ghostly echoes. A delicious game—and exciting. Yet I sensed danger in it; though where the danger lay I did not understand.

I understood better on the afternoon that Oakes, pursuing me as we ran, caught me. And holding my arms, forced me to turn and face him and gradually, as laughing breathlessly I struggled, forced my face to his. Seeing his eyes, I broke off laughing. For they gleamed with something more than the challenge of the chase, something strange and not displeasing; yet sent a quiver of uncertainty through me, made me stand motionless waiting, for what I did not know. Not until his face bent to mine and his lips, soft and seeking, found mine did I know. Knew too by the sharp dizzying sweetness that engulfed me, that this was the danger.

With a little cry I broke away and stepped back, stepped back again when he pled, "Jessica," and moved toward me. Then Laura Lee and Bucky, emerging from distant shadowing trees, came toward us. And in unspoken agreement we traversed the darkling place together, Oakes and I side by side, yet not touching. And it was as if I was borne on the swirling veils of dusk. For I had glimpsed a strange and enchanted land. One I had never dreamed might be.

It was almost dark when we turned into the driveway where the iron deer stood unmoving, but not so dark that we failed to see the carriage waiting under the portico while its driver lifted traveling bags to the little stoop. And at Oakes' "The devil! The old man's got home," I sensed the apprehension that like an ominous little wind passed between the others.

Laura Lee gasped, "The letter said next week," and Oakes, leaning close to Bucky's shoulder, said swiftly, "Back out, Bucky, scoot around the block. Maybe the old man won't see us."

The suggestion came too late. For, as Bucky moved to obey, a tall figure stepped through the door, and gesturing that we come on, waited until the auto stopped. Laura Lee, Oakes and I, feeling sheepish, got out.

He answered their subdued "Hello, Papa" gravely and, in a voice equally grave, told Bucky not to put the auto up, he was to drive the visitors home; then he turned back to Laura Lee and Oakes. "Go inside, children. Mama is anxious to see you." With the same grave courtesy he said, "I am sure this young lady will excuse you."

They went in, Laura Lee sending an uneasy glance over her shoulder, and, expecting Mr. Carr to follow, I braced myself against the portico column to wait. He said, "Perhaps you would like some light," and touching a switch, flooded the stoop to brilliance. Then he would have gone in but stopped, his eyes upon me so intently that I looked up, startled.

After a little he asked, "You are a pupil at Mrs. Plummer's?"

"Yes, sir."

Another little silence—then, "I don't believe I know your name."

I told him my name.

He repeated, "Kildare? There are Kildares in Augusta whom I happen to know."

My head disclaimed the Augusta Kildares. And folding his arms he gazed down at me. "There are also the Kildares in Athens. Perhaps you—"

I moved my head again.

His dark eyes regarded me, amused, though gravely amused, and his thin lips were touched by a smile.

"You are a clever young lady," he said, not as if he intended a compliment but as if, aware of the plan that brought me here, he considered it mine. An impression due no doubt to my sense of guilt, which now induced such discomfort that when Laura Lee unceremoniously flashed through the door and, seizing my hand, pulled me toward it, I was relieved.

"Jessica, I told Mama you were here and she wants to meet you." Then, as I hung back, "Come on, Jessica!"

I glanced at Mr. Carr doubtfully. "But your father—"

She tossed her curls with the old imperiousness. "Don't be a lemon. I said Mama wants to meet you."

Darting ahead, she led me across a vast and vaulted reception hall with massive fireplace and paneled walls to a small room that opened from it. Here her mama waited, still wearing her hat. Her pale face gleamed pearllike above the dark handsome gown, her eyes almost concealed by weary lids. At our approach they lifted to bestow upon us the gaze of one too ill to care. But when Laura Lee said, "Mama, this is Jessica," she smiled as if she tried to be kind.

"So this is Laura Lee's wonderful Jessica?" Her voice, weary and toneless, was a fragile thread of sound. When I said, "Yes, ma'am," I tried to speak as quietly. For so frail she seemed, so detached from the tangibility of earthly things, I thought it possible for her to wholly vanish.

"Laura Lee has told me so much about you." As the muted voice spoke, the wide sick eyes looked into mine. "She tells me that you—you have been orphaned?"

"Yes, ma'am."

Again the lids drooped over the eyes but after a little lifted. "I'm sorry." The thread of voice had thinned. "Your mother—your parents would have been proud. You are—so lovely."

I said, "Thank you, Mrs. Carr," and stood there for a moment, my eyes held by hers. Then Mr. Carr came through the door and, crossing, leaned over her as if concerned. "You are tiring yourself, my dear." He spoke in the grave voice that seemed to belong to him. "Come, I will help you to your room."

The listless eyes left me and drifted about the room. "Yes, I am tired." The thread of voice trailed into nothing; and Laura Lee and I left quietly and returned down the narrow corridor to the stoop where Miss Mabie waited. She and Miss Belle fluttered their last good-bys as we racketed down the drive, Miss Mabie chattering on the way home of Mr. Carr; so distinguished, so charming, and with such polish—but then he had spent so much time abroad. It was really quite tragic, she added thoughtfully, that he should be burdened with an invalid wife. She wondered if it wouldn't be better for everyone concerned if—She failed to complete her thought or her sentence. Just the same I knew what it was; and it struck me as strange that Miss Mabie who had so much pity for herself had none in her heart for others.

September had come again. Mrs. Plummer returned from the farm, teachers from relatives or rented lodgings. Pearlie, back on the job, scrubbed and cleaned the seminary. Vacation was over. School had begun. The halls resounded with chattering voices and hurrying feet; the young ladies, some the same, others new, poured in and out of classrooms, whispering and giggling. Conversations circled again in the lavatory. The much-worn Doctor Book was produced for the education of the uninitiated, and Mrs. Plummer at morning assembly began once more to inform us how a young lady—a well-bred young lady—should walk, talk, eat, sleep and breathe.

This year, however, though life in the seminary went forward in its usual hurrying, scurrying manner, apprehension ran like a poisonous wind beneath its customary slipshod routine. It swept the young ladies to huddle like sheep in whispering groups, drew teachers together in halls to murmur one to another. The subject, of course, was the continuing attacks on white women by Negroes.

Each day as I brought the newspapers in from the porch, the headlines, tall and black and somehow ominous, met my eyes. But even as I read "Schoolgirl in Copenhill . . ." "West-End Matron . . ." "Housewife on Northside . . ." I had no realization of their inherent tragedy or the effect they might have on a city already tensed to violence. Even when many young ladies were kept from school and those who came were guarded by fathers or brothers, no cognizance of the dark potentiality pierced me. For the strange and enchanting world I'd discovered with Oakes had triumphed over reality. It was the real world that had become fantasy.

In the third week of September, the fickle Atlanta climate banished with lashing rain and blustering wind the golden Indian summer and settled down to a spell of bleak, bone-seeking rain, and colds and grippe, its camp followers, flourished. Even more day pupils, prey to grippe, were kept at home; among them Laura Lee. Lacking her company I was thrown back upon my own, but this I did not mind. For the first time I was happier when alone. Not that solitude was easily come by.

In my room, subject to Miss Mabie's demands, privacy was almost impossible. Empty classrooms after school hours offered even less. For no sooner would I withdraw to one than Pearlie, with brooms and mops and pails of water, invaded it. Only on the steps of the little side porch could I be alone. And though it rained still and blew, I would slip out to huddle on the top step in my coat, to know again in remembrance Oakes' teasing laughter, his dark eyes, his kiss beneath the trees at Ponce de Leon. Memories that colored and warmed the succession of bleak rainy days.

Then that Saturday in September.

Waking that morning, I found that the rain had stopped; dripping trees and rain-black roofs were drenched by sun, and delight rushed through me. It was Saturday, the sun was shining, Mrs. Plummer would take off for the farm, and the sum of all of these—Miss Mabie and I could go to the Carrs'. Dressing swiftly, joyously, I thought, not without wonder, "This must be what happiness feels like. So light, so buoyant as if you floated high—high."

I was pulled back to earth by the prosaic fact that Miss Mabie's breakfast tray, Saturday being her morning for "a little rest," must be brought up to her room, and I stopped at her door to ask what she wished on her tray. I found both bed and room empty. This, so early, surprised me; and as I made my way downstairs, I wondered what could have got her up and out at such an hour.

On the first floor I paused to ask Pearlie, who mopped yesterday's mud from the entryway, if she'd seen Miss Mabie. She stopped work to lean on the mop handle and gave me a solemn nod. "She over to de cottage. De cat sen' fur her. A while back."

This was even more surprising, and I repeated, "Why at the cottage, for goodness sake?"

Pearlie's solemnity deepened to mournfulness. "Honey, hell's done broke loose fur sho!"

I looked at her skeptically. "Hell? Pearlie, what are you talking about?"

"De onliest thing I knows is Miss Laura Lee's pa come stomping in here lak a bull—an' it not eight o'clock—saying he gotta see Miz Plummer."

I turned apprehensive. "Mr. Carr—was here?"

"He wuz here. Sitting lak a iceberg while he wait fur Miz Plummer to come. And when he walk out stiff as a poker she sen' me up to tell Miz Mabie she wanna see her, at de cottage. An' dat pore ole sack o' bones. Hardly could she dress herself fur shaking lak a leaf; her eyes jumping lak a skittish mule's. Honey—yu shoulda see her."

I did see her. The eyes sick in the sallow face, the gaunt trembling figure, the head she tried to hold high. And I was wrenched with guilt and remorse. This—I told myself miserably—because of Laura Lee's plan, the plan I had abetted willingly, even eagerly. Not dreaming when we involved unsuspecting Miss Mabie that she, ill and defenseless, would have to face Mrs. Plummer's icy arrogance—perhaps loss of the situation she so desperately needed. Because of me, she must face this; was, it flashed over me, facing it now.

Almost without volition I found myself darting past Pearlie and out the side door and racing across the grounds toward the cottage, my feet sinking in the soggy earth. As I ran, my mind shaped words with which to declare Miss Mabie's innocence. "We pulled her into it. . . . She knew nothing. . . . She must not be blamed. . . . It was Laura Lee and I. . . ." For a miserable second I shrank from the betrayal of Laura Lee; but knowing as I shrank that Miss Mabie, with nothing, must not be sacrificed to Laura Lee.

I crossed the porch of the cottage and went toward the door, to have it, as I reached for the bell, jerked open by Claribelle Plummer. In her usual distraught manner she hurried out, hardly pausing when I asked to see her mother, but motioned vaguely toward the hall and plunged down the steps.

In the long narrow hall, I sank into the small chair against the wall, in my apprehension so oblivious to the dusty disordered place it surprises me to find that I can recall it. The hatrack piled not only with hats and coats, but other sundry articles, including—of all things—a rusty teakettle. The straggly dusty palm in the hideous jardiniere, the crusted mud along the hall runner. For then I was not conscious of them; or anything except the voice that came through the half-open door down the hall.

It was Miss Mabie's voice, desperate, pleading as I had known it would be. "I did not see it so," she quavered. "Foolish? Yes. Thoughtless, I admit. But oh! Not dishonorable. Not that! Not that!"

"In my experience"—this was Mrs. Plummer's relentless authority—"my not inconsiderable experience, I have found betrayal of confidence generally regarded as dishonorable. You have betrayed the confidence, Miss Mabie, reposed in you when I accepted you into my establishment. Moreover, you have betrayed the reputation, I might add, the spotless reputation, of the seminary. That, as you must have known, I will not tolerate. I must be guided accordingly."

Guilt, like a wave of heat, possessed me, and I started up from the chair to go to that room, to cry out Miss Mabie's innocence. But before I reached the door Miss Mabie spoke again; her voice no longer pleading but light and cool, and so ugly with contempt it stopped me in my tracks.

"Perhaps you forget, Mrs. Plummer"—how sharp, how vindictive her small laugh—"that it was you, not I, who accepted Jessica into your establishment, who allowed her to associate with your precious young ladies. I consider *that* a far greater betrayal than what I did. And far more dishonorable."

"Circumstances sometimes force us to accept situations, Miss Mabie, which are, shall I say—unpleasant." Mrs. Plummer's voice had also undergone a change. Weighted it still was, and officious. But its authority lacked its usual invincibility. "That, I trusted you to understand."

"I did understand, Mrs. Plummer. Very well indeed. Why else would I allow you to thrust Jessica upon me? She was your responsibility, not mine. One you were paid to assume. As for accepting me in your establishment"—again the ugly little laugh—"I am not deceived by your professions of 'confidence'—I was never deceived. You knew my straitened circumstances, knew I was forced to accept the niggardly salary you offered; just as you knew when you burdened me with the girl I dared not resent it. You were indifferent to the humiliation of my position. I, Maud Mabie, as sheltered and protected by dear Papa as any of your young ladies, forced—and by you, Mrs. Plummer—into constant association with a—a bastard child!"

"Take care! You have no proof of that."

"No proof, Mrs. Plummer? What better proof do I need? A child, homeless without kith or kin or friends. No letters, no visitors, no one to care if she lives or dies. I'm not quite a fool, Mrs. Plummer. Only *one* sort of child is shunted off like that."

"You forget yourself, Miss Mabie."

"Forget myself? Oh no, Mrs. Plummer. For the first time since I came to—to this place I remember myself. And other things too, Mrs. Plummer. I remember that parents of your young ladies are careful to shield their daughters from, shall we say, undesirable contacts. They might be interested to learn that you have been less careful. I remember that, Mrs. Plummer."

For a moment Mrs. Plummer remained silent. When finally she spoke, the unction, the suavity in her voice was proof, to one who knew her, that the threat beneath Miss Mabie's words had not escaped her. That her wily brain was seeking means to avert it.

"I think we're overwrought, Miss Mabie." With what grave consideration she intoned it. "Perhaps unnecessarily. No doubt with prudence and co-operation this can be less serious than I feared." Her pause gave significance to the question that followed. "Can I count on your cooperation, Miss Mabie?"

Miss Mabie's faltered "Why—I suppose—if in any way—" revealed her bewilderment.

"Then all is not lost." Mrs. Plummer was again her assured managerial self. "Though the loss of Laura Lee is, I fear, irretrievable. However, if Mr. Carr sends her and the boy off to school, and he seems quite adamant, it cannot in the slightest iota reflect on the seminary. That leaves only this Miss Belle in whom you unwisely confided, who may conceivably talk. Since, due to this—er—unpleasantness she finds herself without situation, I might make a place on my staff for her. She too could live in. Occupy Jessica's room, be a pleasant companion for you—"

"Jessica's room?" Miss Mabie quavered. "But what about Jessica?"

Leaning against the wall, I waited for Mrs. Plummer to answer the question which I echoed soundlessly.

"Jessica must go." How cold the three words, how final. They rang against my homeless, anchorless mind like a knell.

"But go where?" Miss Mabie's cry was near hysteria. "Where can she go? She has nobody—no place—"

"That is not our problem, Miss Mabie."

Miss Mabie's "I didn't know—I didn't foresee—" broke hopelessly. "God knows I wouldn't hurt her, whatever she is. She's a good girl, good to me, willing—" Her voice crumpled and dissolved in weeping, the desperate, helpless weeping I'd heard so many times.

With the sound of it in my ears, I turned and went along the hall and out of the door; on the porch stopped to stare in amazement. I found it unbelievable that I could have become a formless disintegrated nothing, of value to no one, even myself; and the seminary stand unchanged, the sun shine on undimmed.

Standing lost and dazed, I hardly knew when Mr. Plummer came hurrying out the door, pulling on his coat. Passing, he reached to pat my shoulder and smile. "How rare," he said, "to find a child of destiny on my doorstep." Then, before my dazed mind could absorb his meaning or shape words for answer, he was gone, hastening toward the street. Blankly, I went down the steps and crossed the grounds and made my way to my room. For what seemed a long long time I sat on my bed, my head against its footrail. But when I looked at Mr. Dolph's forget-me-not watch, it was only nine o'clock. There was time to do what I knew I must do.

It was easily done and so quickly I felt a sort of cold wonder, if anything as numb as I could feel, that I hadn't done it long ago; that I had ever allowed the voice of duty to drown out the call of the heart. For I was going back to Mitty. Not proudly as I had dreamed of returning. Not independent and sure, a strong staff on which Mitty could lean. But fleeing to Mitty as a lost child instinctively turns towards home.

Packing my few clothes in the little trunk, I listened, dreading Miss Mabie's step on the stairs, the fretful demanding voice. That I could not have borne. The anger or hurt roused by her contempt still burned. I never wanted to see her again.

Locking the trunk, I put its key in my little crocheted purse, making sure that my hoarded seventy-five cents was safe. Then, hatless and coatless, I left the room and without looking back went down the stairs and quietly walked out the front door.

I turned up Peachtree, following the route that led to Carnegie Library. I could have boarded a streetcar, one passed every few minutes, but so strongly was I bound by habit it did not occur to me. Walking, I was aware of the life flowing along the street. The wagons and drays, the gleaming carriages, their wheels flashing in the sun. An occasional auto followed by cries of "Get a horse." Once a tallyho, allowing a glimpse of beautifully dressed women, their tiny parasols shading hour-glass figures and huge plumed hats; and gentlemen elegant in gray bowlers and yellow gloves. How gay, how safe they seemed. Looking, I thought of the seminary as it was at this hour. The vast, empty classrooms, the solitary grounds where I wandered. Hard to believe that this abundant life flowed continually past its door and the two remain as separate as the poles, just as I walked in this teeming, joyous life yet had no part in it, did not belong, but moved within it as isolated as an invisible shade. A terrible, almost poisonous despair pierced the numbness that enclosed me. Was I always to be separate? Always isolated and lonely and held out?

I was asking this question when the auto passed and, slowed by the press of other vehicles, allowed me to see its occupants. Mr. Carr at the wheel, elegant and cold and grave. Beside him a veiled and begoggled lady I did not know. And in the tonneau Laura Lee, no less merry or buoyant, laughing and tossing the curls, the gaiety in her face echoed in Oakes'. And between them, beaming, Renette.

The snarl of vehicles eased and the auto chortled on its way—they were lost to me. Remembering what we had been to each other, our afternoons at Ponce de Leon, Oakes' kiss beneath the trees, was remembering a dead self, the young, happy self that had lived so briefly its passing failed to dent my numbness; that made it possible for me to accept without pain the truth. I had only myself—and Mitty.

When I left the Walker-Westview streetcar it was as if, miraculously, I had become another person. The numbness and despair were dissolved. I felt lighthearted, almost happy as I turned into the little path; and running along it, under the pines, I pictured how it would be. I would go in the door (never closed in fair weather) and make my way quietly to wherever Mitty worked. She would look up and stare as if she couldn't believe . . . then, believing and crying "My ever-blessed," she would come toward me. I would tell her I'd come to stay. I would never leave again.

I rounded a curve and came within sight of the house. It stood in the cleared spot unchanged, the tall pines sighing above it. But something, what I could not have said, was like a lifted hand, warning me. Nearer, I saw the dust and leaves that drifted on the porch, the curtainless windows that stared out blankly, like the eyes of the blind. I was running again and at the front door, not open but closed, its knob yielding beneath my hand. Opening it, I was confronted by emptiness and deathly stillness. Calling Mitty, I was going from room to room, all of them empty, as if a giant wind had swept through leaving nothing, except for one thing. Petey's battered, rusted cage that, empty, still hung on its hook in the kitchen, its door sagging open.

The conviction that Mitty was dead was darkness flowing through me, drowning my heart, leaving my limbs dissolved, my mind possessed by darkness. To keep from falling I groped for the window and clung to its sill while the darkness ebbed. Seeing again this kitchen as I had loved it.

Its bright and shining spick-and-spanness, Mitty mixing a batch of tea-cakes, popping them into the oven while I licked the pan, with Petey chirping in his cage. And suddenly, unable to bear it, I was fleeing from the house, all that had happened rushing back upon my consciousness: my lonely childhood warmed only by Mitty's love, and torn away from it; the separateness that had been mine at the seminary; Laura Lee and Oakes; they, in turn, lost; the bright illusions I had cherished of a future enriched by all the past had denied me now only darkened the aspect of my life.

In that darkness I had no awareness of where I ran or why until, pushing through the cemetery hedge, I sank upon a marble footstone and became aware that I had sought my old playmates, the cemetery angels. With marble robes trailing, they stood, unchanged, in a world where all else had changed. I sat among them a long, long time. Some Negro workmen passed bearing spades, and one, the whites of his eyes slanting in his black face, looked at me wonderingly and hesitated as if, concerned, he would speak to me, but didn't.

A little distance beyond they stopped and, marking off a space of ground, began to dig, the thup-thup of their spades sounding in rhythm as they opened a grave. Such a grave, I thought, had been opened for Mitty, held all that remained of those busy tapping feet, the hands that were never idle, the twinkling eyes, the cheerful voice.

Like a cold wave breaking over me, shocking me awake, I found it inconceivable that Mitty should be dead, should lie unmoving in a narrow space. But if not, then where? How find out where? I thought of asking the Negro workmen, but dismissed it. They worked from a piece of paper with a numbered space. Who then would know?

As if in answer, remembrance flashed a name before my mind, the name of Miss Pack. I saw her again at the sewing machine, heard the sharp tongue that raveled reputations as the needle stitched up seams. Miss Pack would know, if only I could find her. I would stop at Mr. Bratton's store and learn where to find her. Find her I would if I had to knock on every door in Battle Hill.

Rising from the stone, I pushed through the hedge and returned along the little path, not running now; there was no need to run. But walking swiftly, stubbornly. As I walked, thinking, no longer in dazed unrelated fragments, but clearly; as if my mind, gathering up those fragments, shaped them into resolution. That willed Mitty should be alive, willed that I would find her; yet with each step something deep within me, hard and tough and stubborn, knowing that whatever I must face I would face.

If Mr. Bratton's little store appeared smaller than my memory of it, if the candy behind the fly-specked showcase failed to tempt as once it had, I did not scorn it because of this change. It held the ghosts of my childish self and a time I had loved. Here Mitty had met me after school. Here I had waited beside Mitty as she shopped. Corn meal and streak of lean! Channel cat fresh from the Chattahoochee! In winter wild rabbits supplied to Mr. Bratton by the Battle Hill boys. Coffee ground in the coffee mill, its wonderful aroma arising to float around us as he turned.

Mr. Bratton, leaning on his pine counter exactly as my childish eyes had seen him many a time, had not changed. Whether previously he had been an old-looking young man or now was a young-looking old man, I do not know. But there he was, no older and no younger, wearing the same alpaca coat or its twin, the pale eyes no paler in the long, seamed face, a straw that might have been the identical straw plucked from the identical broom in his mouth.

When I told him who I was it brought a dawning remembrance that was neither excited nor in any way roused by the recollection.

"Remember? I used to come with Mitty—Mrs. McDaniel," I reminded.

Without shifting the straw, he said, "Yep."

I explained how, coming to see her and finding her moved, it had occurred to me that he knew where she lived now.

He said, and not without a sort of complacency, "Sent away."

Glad he could not know the horror the two words sent through me, I echoed, "Sent away, sir? Sent away—where?"

As if sending women away was a natural and everyday occurrence, he remarked that he didn't call the "pertic'lers" to mind. And his offhand manner convincing me that either he would help me if he could, or could and wouldn't, I decided to seek out Miss Pack. To that end I asked Mr. Bratton where I might find Miss Pack who sewed by the day.

He admitted nothing at first, but finally answered as shortly as before. "Moved away."

I asked if he knew where she had moved.

He couldn't say right off, he said. Mebbe South Georgia. Mebbe again North Georgia, according to where her sister lived. For that was where she had moved to.

At this, my heart sank, and with such a thud I did not doubt that he heard it; and perhaps he did. For now, unexpectedly and unasked, he offered advice.

"If you're hunting Mrs. McDaniel, reckon Mrs. Stopper's the party you ought to see."

Blankly I repeated, "Mrs. Stopper? You mean Janet Stopper's mother?"

"That's right. She can tell you 'bout Mrs. McDaniel being sent away. She runs the Ladies' Circle."

I hope I thanked him, though I have no memory of doing it. Nor do I remember any more clearly the next half hour. Vaguely, I recall going up the path to the Stoppers' home, which once had impressed me as handsome, now shrunken and shoddy for all its tawdry pretention. I remember too, but also vaguely, that on my ringing the doorbell it was opened by a stout young woman, a fat baby cupped to her hip; that the young woman, sloven and heavy-faced, surveyed me, head on one side. And when I asked for Mrs. Stopper, motioned me inside. That when she asked, "Ain't you Jessica?" I at first failed to recognize Janet of the soft brown eyes and dark flying pigtails. How when I said, yes, I was Jessica, I thought that her face lightened, that the warmth I remembered grew in the sullen eyes. But she only said shyly, "I thought so," and, the stout baby's cold blue eyes (like Mr. Stopper's) gawping, led me to the parlor, and said she'd tell Ma.

In the parlor I sat on a hard chair of oak—the room contained enough of this wood to deplete a forest—and waited. Overhead, drawers were pulled out and shut, footsteps clacked back and forth and at last clacked down the stairs and, approaching, brought Mrs. Stopper into the room. And with eyes suspicious behind gold noseglasses, she demanded, without greeting of any sort, what I wanted.

As courteously as I could I explained. How I wished to locate Mitty. Mr. Bratton suggested—with flattery I tried to propitiate the beady eyes—that only Mrs. Stopper could help me. Clasped hands on stomach and beady eyes unpropitiated, she asked why I wanted to know.

I looked at her, genuinely surprised. "Why, I have to know. Mitty is like—like my mother. You see, I have to find her—"

The sharp eyes glinted like bits of glass. "If she's like your mother, do her a kindness and stay away from her."

I looked up at her vacantly. "Stay away?"

She rapped out, "That's what I said. As a good Christian I say it."

We looked full at one another, and I knew by her rigid body and the eyes that glinted like bits of glass that for some reason she was resentful, that she would never help me; that I would have to begin afresh.

"I don't think you quite understand." I was careful to speak with respect. "You see, Mitty would want me to come."

Her shrill laugh was a hen's cackle. "I got no doubt of that. She's a addlebrain if ever there was one. If you knew the trouble we had with her; though Lord only knows what woulda become of her—"

Through stiff, taut lips I asked what had happened to Mitty.

"Happened?" She lifted her thin brows. "Nothing. It's what coulda happened. Old as she was, living alone in those woods. And niggers close by. And her weak in the head—"

Startled, indignant, it was I who laughed now; not sharply as she had laughed, but quietly and sure. I spoke quietly, too. "Weak in the head? Mitty? Oh no. You've made a dreadful mistake."

"Mistake, is it?" She was angry. "Why, she's crazy as a bedbug. Spending the five dollars the Ladies' Circle donated to stand her awhile and—of all ridiculous things—for a bird cage for that dratted bird. But me"—the cackling laugh again—"I made a mistake."

I didn't hear her rasping voice, I was hearing Mitty's. Mitty's saying, as so often I had heard her say, "Just you wait 'til my ship comes in,

Petey dear, and you shall have your new cage." And Mrs. Stopper talking on, I stared up at her—in my wretchedness losing the sense that this was happening to me; that I was anything more than an audience for her ranting. The good ladies of the Ladies' Circle, she said, her pointing finger emphasizing, had placed Mrs. McDaniel where she would be looked after. It hadn't been easy either to get her taken in. On account of keeping me all those years, me being what I was. But what with her age and liable to become a charge on the church, and Pastor Cantrell bringing influence to bear, exception had been made. But one thing was sure and I might as well know it. Regulations had to be conformed to. And if I went snooping around Mrs. McDaniel, they'd put her out. As a good Christian, she warned me.

I did not ask in what way I might jeopardize Mitty. There was no need to ask. The reason was contained in a single word, the word that only this morning I had heard for the first time. It struck me suddenly how that word had shaped my whole life, could affect my life, and Mitty's too even now; lose for Mitty whatever dubious haven she had gained.

I rose from the rocker and faced Mrs. Stopper, not boldly but humbly. If she would just tell where Mitty was, I said, I promised not to see her or write or disturb her in any way. If I could just know where she was—

Hands on hips, the ferrety eyes hostile, she heard my plea, then laughed, her laughter sharp and knowing. "Don't think you'll take me in with that mealy-mouth talk. I know your kind. Easy promise—easy broken. You don't fool me." Stalking to the front door, she jerked it open, held it so I could pass. "I warn you. Don't go bothering Mrs. McDaniel. She'll not thank you to get her thrown out on the streets. And another thing. Don't come here again. My home is a Christian home, dedicated to the service of our Lord. 'Tain't proper for the likes of you to be coming here—"

I walked past her and out of the door and down the steps without speaking or turning my head. At the sidewalk, turned up the street. But when Janet's voice called, "Good-by, Jessica," I looked back and saw her mother's hand flash out to slap her cheek. And I was sorry. Pretending more courage than I felt, I waved and called "Good-by"; then I walked on up the street.

On the Walker-Westview car I rode back towards town in the waning afternoon, my resolution to find Mitty lying strewn and broken in the path of this day. Now I was too weary to revive it. Tomorrow when I was rested I must think of a way, a plan—but not now. I knew vaguely that I had no faith, no trust, nothing in the wide world to lean on, but I was too weary to face it. Now I craved nothing so much as sleep.

In the center of town where I transferred it seemed a long time before the Peachtree streetcar came. Leaning against a building, I saw the throng of people that milled around Five Points, where five streets converged, and wondered if some celebration had brought them out. But I dismissed this idea, for they moved, not with the air of a crowd bent on pleasure, but quietly, as if intent on serious business. Then, my streetcar coming, I forgot them. I was too concerned as we clanged along Peachtree with my own affairs.

Reaching the seminary, I found the reception hall and parlor brightly lighted—evidence that on Saturday nights foretold visitors. So, hopeful that my arrival might escape notice, I crossed the grounds to the little side porch and quietly, warily opened the door and stepped inside, to find Mr. Plummer seated on the bottom stair, his frosty eyes regarding me humorously.

"Child, child! A whole hour I've played the part of Sister Anne in the fairy tale. To watch for you."

Closing the door, I leaned against it, unable to speak. So he asked—and how kind his voice—"Where have you been? Or would you rather not tell?"

At his kindness, the tears, withheld all this long day, fought for release.

"I ran away," I said, "to Mitty."

The look he gave me was troubled. "So I thought," he said quietly, "and learned with considerable difficulty, I admit, of certain events that explain why. What I fail to understand is why you've come back. Why?"

The tears that would no longer be denied rolled down my face. "Mitty—she wasn't there—"

"You mean she was away?"

I shook my head. "The house was empty. She's gone. I don't know where. I couldn't find out—"

He let me cry awhile before he rose and with his handkerchief dried my eyes and face, made me blow my nose. "So you considered me a fatuous old fool when I called you a child of destiny. You must run out to seek it; as if it would fail to find you."

I looked at him dumbly, not knowing if, to lighten my spirits, he spoke in jest or in earnest. He gave me a little shake. "Try to look less doleful, child. You have a visitor. And since he has already waited an hour, you must not keep him waiting longer." His hand on my arm, he turned me, guided me up the hall toward the parlor. "And don't look so startled. In no single particular is your visitor extraordinary. Even his name—Poteat—is common in the South. Try, child, to be a little less funereal."

I tried to assume a less funereal expression, which was not easy. For I had no illusions as to the purpose of Mr. Poteat's visit. I had heard—as he had not—the cold finality of Mrs. Plummer's "Jessica must go." I suspected, as he did not, that Mr. Poteat was here not of his own volition. He had been summoned in order that I, like surplus baggage, might be removed from the seminary to a place where I would be out of the way.

As we approached the parlor, a trio of voices came floating from it to meet us. Mrs. Plummer's, like the French horn, sounding the motif, with occasional pips from Miss Mabie's and, but only rarely, Mr. Poteat's beautiful organ tones. As vivid, I realized, in recollection as if heard only yesterday.

Mr. Plummer's hand on my arm detained me. "Listen," he ordered.

I listened and, hearing, could hardly believe my own ears. For this Mrs. Plummer was not the inflexible, invincible Mrs. Plummer but the benign and regal grand duchess reserved for enviable backgrounds. "I will not," the duchess was saying, "bore you, Mr. Poteat, with the subject of Jessica. But I am, and I think I may claim to some degree, an observer of character. And I will not conceal from you, indeed to conceal it would be to fail in my obligation to you and to Mr. Whidby, for whom I have the highest regard, that of the hundreds of young ladies I've taken under my wing—I speak literally, of course—not one has possessed in toto the qualifications of Jessica."

Aware of her opinion of my qualifications, I could not still the nervous trembling that shook me. Mr. Plummer patted my shoulder. "Wait," he cautioned. "Wait." When my eyes questioned he said, as gleeful as a mischievous boy, "Don't judge them too harshly. It isn't the first time that Southern ladies have trimmed their sails to the winds of cold cash; nor, I promise you, the last."

"But I don't understand." I shook my head as if to clear it of its confusion.

Almost at the parlor door he paused. "It's really quite simple," he explained gravely. "Mr. Poteat informs us that destiny is about to catch up with you. Now, let's delay no longer."

When we appeared in the doorway, Mrs. Plummer, halting her French horn solo, swept toward me, hands outstretched, her manner playful, almost affectionate. "My dear Jessica! At last!" She clasped my arm and turned me toward Mr. Poteat, who waited beside the mantel; saying as we advanced, but still playfully, "Our little bird who will flit here and there returns to the nest. Jessica, my dear," she prodded, "you haven't forgot Mr. Poteat?"

He came to me with the agile swiftness I remembered, his eyes still young behind the crisscrossing lines that cobwebbed his face. Taking my hand he looked at me intently. "Do you remember me, Jessica?" the beautiful voice inquired.

"Yes, sir."

He looked at me sharply, as if he would read my mind. "You are exquisite," he stated as if it was fact; not said merely in kindness. Then he asked gently, "Tell me, Jessica, are you happy?"

My heart was so filled with unhappiness and so affected by his gentle inquiry I could only stand motionless and silent; and what was in my thoughts I cannot say.

He whirled, his eyes flying to Mrs. Plummer. "She is pale and, for one so young, much too tired. I hope it isn't a case of all work and no play—"

"That, Mr. Poteat, I assure you is not the case." For a moment the duchess yielded to the grave, judicial Mrs. Plummer. "However, I take the liberty of reminding that on that point, and indeed in toto, Mr. Whidby and I concurred."

"Mr. Whidby is a sanctimonious old fool," Mr. Poteat retorted caustically, "and in his second childhood. He forgets that pleasure is as essential to youth as bread."

"I wish to point out, Mr. Poteat"—this was Mrs. Plummer again—"that Mr. Whidby's instructions have been followed, in toto. Jessica, however, *has* enjoyed pleasures. Simple ones, I admit. But such as she, being neither frivolous nor giddy, would choose. Jessica loves books. She has enjoyed a magnificent library. Jessica likes gardening. She's had her own. Moreover, she's known young ladies of enviable family background, has had the privilege of being a guest in the home of Mr. Algernon Carr, whom perhaps you know . . . and"—she took on a roguish air—"ask Miss Mabie about the little frolics she and Jessica have had, the delicious little feasts—"

Mr. Poteat cast a cynical eye at Miss Mabie, but he directed no inquiry toward her. Instead, he pulled out his gold watch, consulted it and announced firmly that we'd delayed long enough. He turned to me. I would need a light wrap and a hat.

I said, "Yes sir," and left the room, but at the door turned back. "About my trunk, sir. It is packed and ready—"

Mrs. Plummer's precipitate "Never mind that, Jessica dear," was obviously flustered. But if Mr. Poteat noticed, he ignored it. We'd attend to the trunk later, he said. But his eyes meeting mine across the space between us were mocking.

As I leaned against the cushions of his carriage, the effusive good-bys of Mrs. Plummer and Miss Mabie—even Mr. Plummer's "Bless you, child"—were shadowy and unreal. For the combination of bewilderment, weariness and hunger (I had eaten nothing all day) had reduced me to that state of apathy when the mind, confronted by too many speculations, closes itself against the contemplation of any. Clutching Mitty's crocheted purse, I watched Peachtree roll by; the homes safe behind their gold and russet screens of September trees, the misty veils, forerunners of dusk, beginning to sift among them. But the strange place I went to, the strange life I was bound for, I did not contemplate. The present, rolling in Mr. Poteat's carriage along Peachtree, sufficed, and my mind refused both past and future. Not for long could I hold future and past at bay. For Mr. Poteat, silent before, touched my arm lightly. "Jessica—"

"Yes, sir." I turned my face to his.

"Will you explain something that puzzles me?"

"If I can, sir."

"You spoke of your trunk's being packed and ready. I wonder. Ready for what?"

"Why to go, sir."

He looked at me, his eyes narrow. "But you didn't know you would go. Unless," he smiled, "you claim clairvoyance as one of your—er—numerous talents."

My head denied the talent. "I knew I was to leave the seminary, sir."

"Then you are clairvoyant. How did you know?"

I was puzzled. "Why, I knew Mrs. Plummer meant for me to go—I heard her say—"

"Ah—" He drew that "ah" out lingeringly. "And what did Mrs. Plummer say?"

I didn't answer right away; I shrank from answering. Since the day in his office I had believed he could never be unkind. Now I knew how kindness could turn unkind. And I was reluctant to reveal Mrs. Plummer's opinion of me lest it lower me in his.

I still sat stiff and unspeaking when he touched my arm again. "Forget the question, child," he ordered gently, "and don't torment yourself. While you fetched your hat and wrap, Mr. Plummer contrived to have a few words with me on the porch." He added significantly, "Without the ladies. I know why your trunk was packed and what happened today."

Quickly turning, I saw his ravaged face and its attentive concern and I believed anew in his kindness and understanding. They would, I thought, encompass anything. So, reassured, I found myself relating all that had transpired: Oakes and Laura Lee and the plan; going to the Carrs' with Miss Mabie; Mr. Carr descending upon Mrs. Plummer; what in her dusty hall I had heard this morning. Running away to Mitty—not finding her.

When I finished, he reached and took my hand. "Jessica, do you feel that you can trust me? Rely upon me to do what I consider right?"

"Oh yes, sir!" And I did with my whole heart.

"Then believe that I am your firm friend. You only need to ask and I will serve you in any way I can." His penetrating eyes looked out from the crisscrossed face. "Remember it, Jessica. There will be times when you'll find it difficult to know your real friends—" He put my hand back on my lap. "This—this Mitty that you couldn't find. You love her very much?"

I told him more than anyone in the whole world.

The horses had clopped on their way towards town, as we talked, and darkness had fallen to shroud the streets. In the silence that followed I looked about. Surprised, I found we were nearing the Candler Building. More surprised, I saw that the crowds of men and half-grown boys which earlier had caused me to wonder had increased. And when Mr. Poteat suddenly sat erect, his eyes turning alertly from side to side, I knew that he too sensed that something unusual was happening. Something sensed, rather than seen, that passed along the street like an evil wind, touching the knots of men into motion, drawing shadows from deeper shadow to acquire form. To resolve into other knots of men that spilled along the sidewalk and street, merging as they moved towards Five Points with the others. Soundless except for their shuffling feet, all moving in unison, as if they—and there were hundreds—pursued a single quarry.

Mr. Poteat spoke to the Negro coachman. "Cut over to Pryor, Joe, and drop us at the Kimball House. Then stable the horses, and get back to the Kimball House—with us."

Joe spoke from the box without turning his head. "Can't, sir. Gotta get home. Wife home by herself with the chillen."

At Houston Street he swung the horses around the Candler Building and turned them down Pryor, their hooves ringing out sharply. Once, halting to let the milling crowd cross, he said, not turning his head, "Looks like trouble, sir?"

Mr. Poteat's quick eyes sweeping the crowd were scornful. "Depend on poor white trash to make trouble."

"Reckon those cards tacked up round town had got anything to do with it, sir?"

"Cards? What cards?"

In answer Joe thrust a hand backward to give Mr. Poteat a card. "Just little cards like this, sir. Tacked up on buildings round town."

In the dusk I leaned to look at it. Only a small white card, blank except for the K K K crudely lettered on its center. But Mr. Poteat drew a sharp breath. "Don't stable the horses, Joe. Use them to get you home. Keep to the side streets."

"Thank you, sir. I'll do best I can about the team."

"Of course, if you can. But look after yourself—"

We moved down Pryor Street still leisurely and reached the Kimball House entrance, where policemen held a cleared lane to the door against the crowd that, overflowing from Five Points, moiled about it. We had to wait while a party of ladies in evening gowns and gentlemen in high hats entered their waiting carriage; the ladies surveying the ill-dressed crowd as disdainfully as royalty would regard the rabble. Their disdain, however, seemed to stir no resentment in the coatless staring men who pressed close around them; and I wondered if human beings dared show resentment only to those beneath them; never to those above.

The other carriage pulled out, and Joe maneuvered ours to the curb. Mr. Poteat, rising, murmured as if giving a casual order, "Twenty dollars under the seat cushion. Just in case."

"Yessuh. Thank you, sir."

We stepped out then, and Joe, erect and impassive, slapped the reins on the horses' backs. As they moved off, Mr. Poteat and I entered the lobby of the Kimball House.

The lobby, high and spacious and impressively columned, was strangely empty when we entered, except for a gentleman behind the desk. He advanced to meet us and informed Mr. Poteat, whom he seemed to know, that the management had withdrawn the Negro help —just in case things thickened up. He hoped we wouldn't mind having to use the stairs. Talking, he ushered us toward the rear of the lobby and, opening a door, revealed the service stairs. With Mr. Poteat holding my arm as he would hold a lady's, we started up them.

Wide and carpeted, though considerably frayed, the stairs at each floor were broken by a landing, closed off from the hotel corridor. On the third floor this landing was occupied by two young men so meticulously and soberly dressed that to find them seated on the stairs absorbed in a game involving pennies and toothpicks struck me as peculiar—and even more peculiar when I noticed the basket that waited nearby. For of all baskets I had ever seen, this was the longest. Surveying it with a measuring eye, I wondered what so large a basket would be used for.

As we pushed through the door to the corridor, I asked about it. Mr. Poteat explained that it was used to collect sundry large articles which in a hotel must be disposed of. And pausing at one of the doors that lined the corridor, he put his hand on the knob and at the same time met my eyes steadily.

"Trust me, Jessica, to guard your interests."

Beyond a vague idea that the words offered reassurance, for me they had no meaning. I was too puzzled as to why I was here—or where, from here, I would go. That it would not be to Mitty or to Mitty's house, I was certain. Beyond that I had not inquired, or even speculated. I was not eager to have confirmed the alternative that loomed before me, that undoubtedly would be confirmed in the room we now entered.

It was occupied by three gentlemen: a young one who sprawled in a chair; another, less young and a minister; the third, Mr. Whidby, his ruler-edge mouth clamped tighter than ever. All, as we entered, looked around at us, and Mr. Whidby rose from his chair to meet us.

"Thank God you've come!" he exclaimed sourly through the thin, tight mouth. "You delayed too long."

Mr. Poteat asked swiftly, "He isn't—?"

Mr. Whidby admitted ungraciously that he—whoever he meant—wasn't what Mr. Poteat suggested. "At least," he added grudgingly, "not quite."

Mr. Poteat put his hand on my arm. "Then we'll delay no longer."

But when he would have led me toward a door at the end of the room, Mr. Whidby deterred us. Having delayed so long, he said, it might be best to delay a bit longer, at least until Dr. Etheridge came out.

Mr. Poteat's shrug implied that Mr. Whidby's opinion was of no great concern. Nevertheless, he acted upon it and, leading me to a sofa against the wall, told me to try and rest, informing the room in general when I obeyed, "She's had an exhausting day."

The minister brought me a glass of ice water and the young man deserted his chair to give me a palm-leaf fan. Each, I noticed, regarded me with something not unlike wonder. It caused me to wonder if they knew the alternative I would presently face, and knew it to be so uncomfortable, they tried to make me more comfortable now.

Somebody turned on the ceiling fan and, resting my head against a cushion, I watched it, soothed gradually by its rhythmic gyrations into a state that was, yet was not, sleep, as if one half of me slept leadenly as the very weary sleep, while the other half remained alert and attentive and on guard. It was this half that was conscious of Mr. Poteat, that heard his recriminations against Mrs. Plummer, who, he said, had treated the child as a servant, allowed her no more freedom than a prisoner. Surely something better than that could have been arranged.

Mr. Whidby retorted drily that the matter had boiled down to taking what he could get or nothing, which would have meant no school at all for the girl.

Their voices, sharpened by anger, roused me from my half-doze and, sitting erect, I smoothed my rumpled hair and skirts. The minister, who sat near me quietly, observed this and asked in a voice purposely loud if I had had a "nice nap." This put a stop to the argument, which would have stopped in any case, for at that moment the door at the end of the room was opened and an impressive man with a leonine head plumed with gray hair came from the adjoining room and closed the door behind him.

Mr. Poteat went toward him swiftly.

"Ah, Doctor! How is he?"

In answer, the doctor lifted his hand and turning its palm to the floor pressed it slowly downward, conveying—at least to my mind—the impression of something that slowly, surely was ebbing away.

Mr. Poteat asked, "But the mind? Is he conscious?"

The doctor seemed to have no power of expression except in his hands. He now spread them so that their upturned palms asked "Who knows?" as unmistakably as a voice. Mr. Poteat, moving decisively, called, "Come, Jessica," and waited for me before the closed door. Then, his hand on my arm, he opened it and we passed through to the next room.

It was such a large room and so dimly lighted, I received scant impression of anything it contained except the huge bed between the windows and the figure upon it. Dimly I was conscious of a white-clad nurse hovering, of a table crowded with bottles and glasses, of the mingled odor of sickness and drugs. But I had little thought for trivial things as, directed by Mr. Poteat's guiding hand, I moved to the bed and looked down at the motionless figure. The figure, I thought at first, was strange to me; then, shocked, knew it was not wholly strange. For this was the old man of Poteat & Whidby's office. The gnarled hands that had curled on his cane like tree roots now stretched motionless on the counterpane. The bright foxlike eyes that had watched me then, watched again, not with the old sharp knowing, but with something in their avid gaze I could not fathom.

We stood there a few minutes, and they might have been as many hours. I did not know what I was expected to do and so only stood returning the gaze of the eyes that looked up at me from the pillow. I saw the carved emaciation of the face, the straggly mustache that drooped lifelessly. It came over me that this was death. Before my eyes, the old man's life was being wrenched from his body as Man's had been wrenched from his. I felt myself being whirled into a void, sinking deeper and deeper into darkness. Then Mr. Poteat's steadying arm supported me. His voice said, "Steady, Jessica," and my faintness passed. My thoughts cleared. I wondered *why* had I been brought to watch this old man die? What did I mean to him—or he to me? Seeking an answer, my eyes searched his now as his had searched mine. Bending over him, I laid my hand gently on his gnarled one.

As if my touch somehow penetrated to the minute spark of self that persisted within him somewhere, a faint stir, no more than a shadow, moved across the old face. The sunken mouth, as if struggling to shape into words the unintelligible gurgling in his throat, was suddenly contorted.

The nurse came swiftly to the bed, her fingers poised for the pulse, but she stopped when a voice cautioned her to wait. A man emerged from the shadows, the young Andrew of brick-red hair and cheerful freckled face, and came to stand beside me. "Perhaps he is trying to speak," he murmured to the nurse. Leaning, he watched the writhing mouth intently. Whether he read its message or only tried to ease the dreadful urgency of those eyes, I could not know. Straightening, but still looking steadily into the dying eyes, he put his hand on my shoulder and drew me nearer. Clearly he said, "This is the child, sir. This is the child."

The other sturdy hand dropped to clasp the gnarled ones on the counterpane. "I understand, sir." He still spoke clearly. "Everything."

Almost before he finished speaking, the face had fallen back into its sunken immobility, the mouth hung lax and motionless again. Only the avid urgency of the eyes remained, and as Mr. Poteat led me toward the door, I felt as if they followed me. Stopping, I looked back. They still stared at the space where I had stood and I wondered if they had actually looked at me or only at the space I occupied.

In the next room, the others no longer sat stiffly on chairs or paced restlessly as before. They clustered at the windows that overlooked the railroad tracks beneath the viaduct, and through the raised windows I heard a sound, not recognized at first, but which I recognized after a few minutes. Years ago, lying in my room at Mitty's, I had heard that sound. But it was multiplied now a hundredfold into an angry roar, broken by shouts and screams, by the clattering hooves of horses, the crash of splintering glass, and the flat, staccato bursts of gun shots.

Mr. Poteat, exclaiming softly, "By God! It's happened," moved swiftly to the windows. He asked, "Where the devil are the police?"

The doctor, looking down into the street, spoke in a voice of impersonal calm: "There's a mob of five thousand down there." He shook his head, turning away from the window. "I'll take a look at the patient."

Mr. Poteat moved into his place at the window, and I went to stand at his shoulder. I could see but little. The viaduct stretched above the dark void of railroad yard. As I watched, a crouched figure of a Negro boy slipped swiftly along the viaduct toward Alabama Street, his head twisted frenziedly to watch the men who, brandishing guns and sticks, pursued him.

Seeing that they gained, he paused, his head jerking from side to side, as if seeking help. Finding none, he clambered up onto the viaduct wall and stood poised, arms outstretched, a slim dark figure against the glow of street lamps, and, his pursuers closing in and reaching to grasp his feet, he dived down onto the steel tracks eighty feet below, his scream rising against the darkness. And that darkness overflowed all the world and me.

I came back from the darkness slowly, aware of cool water on my face, of the sharp pungency of ammonia. I heard the matter-of-fact voice of the doctor.

". . . perfectly understandable at her age. Pulse strong. No cause for alarm."

The pungent smell of the ammonia stung and I turned away from the bottle. A waiter was placing sandwiches and coffee on the table next to me. The rising and falling roar still came through the windows. I heard the waiter say, "The niggers are fighting back. Shooting into streetcars. Turning carriages over. Holed up in their shanties down Butler Street shooting—"

He was interrupted by the abrupt opening of the door to the room where the old man lay. The nurse called urgently, "Doctor!" and promptly but with deliberation, as if knowing what he would find, the doctor walked into the next room, closing the door. His going was followed by a solemn quiet. Then the door opened again and the doctor came out briskly, his bag in his hand. He gave a short nod.

"Yes," he said matter-of-factly, "it's over. Now we can go."

His words released the others from inaction. Rising almost as one man, they gathered about the table of food, laughing and talking, almost gay in their sense of release. But I did not share their relief. Too much had happened in the last few hours. I could not forget the slim, dark figure that had dived through the darkness or the gaunt old man who lay dead in the next room. It was monstrous, I felt, that the Negro boy and the old man should be swept out of the world of living with no one to grieve or care or hardly notice. Hiding my face in the cushions, I cried for those who had no one to cry for them. The others, engrossed with food and talk, did not notice me, and finally I cried myself to sleep. On the edge of sleep I heard a tolling bell and Mr. Poteat's sharp "Ah! They're calling out the militia"; and Mr. Whidby's "And high time!" Then I slept again and it was not Mr. Whidby's voice at all but Mitty's saying, "And high time," followed by Mr. Dolph's, "The dander is up . . . the dander is up . . . the dander is up . . ."

Waking, I looked with startled eyes at the room where everything was strange; the girl on the bed in the nightgown of fine nainsook and lace stranger still, though the girl was myself. I had no memory of coming here, of undressing, or of anything since I cried myself to sleep in that other room while the old man lay dead in the next. I did not know where I was, or how I had arrived. I did not know why last night —or some night—I stood above an old man who lay dying; an old man I did not know. And, weighing heaviest on my mind and heart, I did not know where Mitty was; even how I might find her.

The sum of all I did not know regarding my life gave that life an aspect I did not like to contemplate. So, to avoid it, I turned my thoughts and my eyes again to the room. It was then I discovered that the sweeping velvet drapery at the windows, as well as the wall paper, were—except for color—identical with those in the room where I had cried myself to sleep. From this I concluded that I was still in the Kimball House, only in a different room; and that undoubtedly this morning had followed last night in logical sequence. I had no knowledge of how I had come here or where from here I would go. But for the present, at least, I knew where I was. And as I slipped off to sleep again, for that I was thankful.

I waked again to the pealing of church bells and a day hardly less gray than dawn. It came through my open window, not as it came last night, with screams and shouts and the roar of the mob, but so still and hushed that certain small sounds nearby, unnoticed before—one a sibilant undefined whisper—now caught my attention. Following the direction from which they came, I turned in the bed and faced—not the wall I expected, but an archway that afforded a view of a small parlor. And before a mirror on its wall, with her back to me, stood a lady I never before had seen.

Reluctant to be confronted with a stranger, I closed my eyes and pretended to sleep; but from under my lids I watched her. And oh what a wonderful lady she was! Not that she was so very beautiful or because of her elegant clothes. But her face looking out from the mirror, at itself not at me, was so frank and friendly, and at the same time brimming with such lively good humor, it flashed in the shining blue eyes and curved her mouth in a smile. Leaning, she tucked a lock of chestnut hair into place; then, dissatisfied with what she saw, pulling the pins from the luxuriant coils and tossing her head, she tumbled the gleaming mass down on her shoulders and began to redo it.

Watching, I wondered who she could be, why she should be here with me. And it was then that fancy, no doubt made irrational by the strange events of the past hours, retraced them. With my own vague conjectures regarding my past I wove a chain of reason—or so it seemed to me—that led inevitably to this gay lovely lady. She was the reason. The reason I was here, why, as I stood by the old man, young Andrew had said, "This is the child."

Now as she arranged her hair, humming a small happy tune, the logical part of my mind noted that the stupendous idea hovering on its edge was not beyond possibility. Her charm was not of youth but maturity. It was conceivable that she might have a sixteen-year-old daughter.

At the tap on the door of the other room I held my breath, hardly daring to breathe lest this bright illusion be shattered. Thrusting the last pin into newly done hair, she moved with a whisper of silk to open it. But when she admitted only Mr. Poteat, I dared to breathe again. He put his hat on a table and after a sharp glance toward me took the lady's hands and, holding her at arm's length, surveyed her, his head moving in wonder.

"Clever, clever Miss Camilla! How did you manage to get here?"

Her quiet little laugh was nevertheless gay. (Once I dreamed I heard my mother laugh.) "Even governors," she said, "can be useful."

"The governor?" He shook his head again. "I would think he had enough on his mind this morning."

She freed her hands and turned to the mirror to touch her hair, then turned back, shrugging. "The riot? Oh! that! The militia's in control." She demanded, "Did you have breakfast? You look tired, worn—"

"I thought we'd have it up here when she wakes." His eyes turned toward the bed. "Is she all right? She seems to lie very still."

She laughed at him. "Yes, yes, yes! She's all right."

As if not fully convinced, he came toward the bed and, though I closed my eyes fast, I knew by the silken whisper that she followed. For a moment I lay there, feeling their eyes upon me. Then he asked guardedly, "Well . . . what do you think of her?"

Believing the very tone of her voice would confirm or deny the wondrous thought that filled my whole being, the blood in my veins seemed to stop and listen. But at her "Why—she's almost a beauty," it started to flow again; and the dream I dared dream for a little shattered. Her voice was not the voice of my mother. I, who had never heard my mother's voice, knew it.

She spoke again, said thoughtfully, "I see what you meant . . . sensitive, intelligent . . . Yes, it's all there. Of course I can't see the eyes. Do they go with the face?"

"Yes. Wide, very gray, steady. Asking, 'Are you for or against me?' "

"No wonder. Still there's strength in the face, young as it is."

"Oh yes. She has a mind of her own." He paused. "We must go carefully."

"Yes. We must. We will."

Another instant and the silken rustle moved to the other room, her voice receding with it. "Go down and order the breakfast," she commanded. "I'll wake her, have her get dressed."

He asked, "You don't think waking and finding a stranger, she'll be upset?"

Laughing, she ushered him out. "Go on! Of course not. My dear man, you forget that I have a daughter older than she. And do hurry that breakfast. I'm starving."

She touched my shoulder, she cried gaily, "Jessica, my dear, time to get up!" and when I sat up and tried to look surprised the friendly voice went on, "I am Camilla Carrebee, a friend of Mr. Poteat's, but call me Miss Camilla, everyone does. Mr. Poteat is sending up breakfast, I've run a lovely hot bath for you. While you dress I'll take a look at the *Journal*."

I bathed and dressed, aware that in the other room she leafed through the Sunday papers until the waiter appeared with breakfast. When Mr. Poteat arrived at the door she cried, "Oh, there you are!" And, as if she'd known me for years, called, "Jessica—breakfast, my dear."

In every life there are times which, viewed back through time, thrust themselves up like signposts to mark a place where the face of life, affected by events, was altered. Because that breakfast marks such a time for me, it rises in remembrance so clearly that the very air of the gray day, the blended aroma of hot coffee and country ham, rise about me again, especially the last. For, having eaten nothing whatever the day before, I now was almost ravenous; and the country ham and eggs and griddle cakes, after Miss Mabie's pallid menu, were so delicious and I in consequence ate so much, I feared Miss Camilla and Mr. Poteat might think me greedy.

But, absorbed in talk, they failed to notice me. Mr. Poteat had heard down in the lobby that the militia had the "trouble in hand," though there was still sporadic fighting out in residence sections. A meeting of Atlanta citizens had been called to pass on rules for law and order; which—his smile was mocking—in his opinion was locking the barn after the horse had got out.

As if he were a small boy Miss Camilla said he should be ashamed. What, she demanded, were people to do?

He lighted a cigar, he drew on it leisurely and, head tilted, expelled smoke toward the ceiling. "Ah! . . . I see. You agree with Ben Tillman, 'To hell with the Constitution if it interferes with lynching. . . .'"

"Oh . . . you," she scoffed. Then her eyes noticed my plate. "Jessica, do have the rest of the ham and eggs."

I glanced at her quickly, suspecting that she might be amused by my hunger. But already, with gesturing hands and flashing eyes, she had plunged back into discussion. So I helped myself to the rest of the ham and eggs.

Breakfast over, the waiter cleared away the dishes and I withdrew to the windows to look down upon Decatur Street where the brown-clad militiamen stood at attention, guns over shoulders, guarding—for all I could see—nothing. The streets except for police and an occasional vehicle stretched bare and silent, with only shattered shop windows to testify to the violence of last night. Nevertheless it revived in my mind pictures I would rather not have seen. And deliberately I turned back to the room.

Miss Camilla, who leafed through the papers again, looked up to ask, "Is it time?" and Mr. Poteat, roaming restlessly, consulted his watch. "I'm waiting for Andrew. He shouldn't be long."

I turned back to the window and stared out, but unseeing now. Time for what, I wondered, or where? I recalled reading how an English queen who waited to be beheaded asked each time footsteps approached, "Is it time?" I told myself it was futile to think unpleasant thoughts and, seeking one that was pleasant, thought of Mitty; and though no other thought could hurt half so much, was unable to think of anything else until the young man Andrew arrived.

He came in quietly and, after a "Good morning" equally quiet, waited within the door, his manner cheerful yet so unassuming and his freckled face so good-humored that I found myself returning his smile.

Miss Camilla put on her hat. "I'll wait in the Ladies' Parlor." She moved to the door and went out and Mr. Poteat, closing it after her gallantly, turned and looked over at me. "Come sit here, Jessica. I must have a talk with you."

Obediently, I crossed to the chair he designated, thinking *now I will know,* and sat down and waited. Mr. Poteat said smoothly, "Sit down please, Andrew," and waited until Andrew was settled. Then, disdaining a chair for himself, he began to pace back and forth, his fingers rolling his watch chain, his eyes thoughtful.

"For so young a girl, Jessica," the melodious voice began, "you have exerted extraordinary patience, and I commend you for it. You have passed through a confused time, have undoubtedly been bewildered and disturbed. I saw it, I deplored it, and I would have dispelled your distress had it been permissible. Unfortunately, it was necessary that er—shall we say—a certain event transpire before it was. When that time arrived you were asleep and tired, and I considered it unwise to distress you further." He halted his pacing abruptly and his hand flashed toward me as if to thrust me away. "Don't look at me like that, child," he exclaimed.

Unaware of how I looked or how he wished me to look, nevertheless I tried to look differently and looked, I felt, nothing but blank. When

Andrew said with quiet cheerfulness, "Perhaps if Miss Jessica knows she will hear nothing too unpleasant—" I thought Mr. Poteat's glance toward him was impatient. But I was too torn between confusion and wonder to be sure.

Now Mr. Poteat swung a straight chair to face me and, taking possession of it, leaned toward me. "Jessica," he asked gravely, "did it strike you as strange that last night I should have brought you here?"

"Yes sir."

"And did it perhaps strike you as strange that you should be conducted to the room of Mathias Purefoy, the old gentleman who later died?"

"Yes sir."

"And did you figure that in some way this old gentleman might be connected with you?"

I did not tell him I had thought nothing clearly, that my mind had been a whirling confusion of shadowy speculation in which nothing was resolved. Instead I shook my head. "I didn't understand, sir—"

As if he found it impossible to remain seated, he sprang from the chair and began to pace again, his eyes on the ceiling; mine and Andrew's following the pacing figure as if attached to it by wires.

"Being a bright girl, however, you realize that nothing happens or exists without cause. And without knowing the cause, you knew the cause was there. And of course you were right."

He paced up, he paced down, then continued. "To trace this, Jessica, we must go back a number of years. To a time when Mathias Purefoy owned a farm near the small Georgia community of Flowery Branch and had on his farm a tenant farmer by the name of Angus Kildare."

At the sound of the name that was mine I clenched my hands in my lap to hide their trembling. And pacing and talking, he went on.

"Now Mathias Purefoy was a strange old man and a hard one, some said. So when this tenant farmer Angus Kildare and his wife were carried off by typhoid I daresay he was little concerned. And I doubt if he was more concerned for the child their death left homeless and unprotected."

I raised my head. "Their child, sir?"

As if aware of the hope kindled by his words, his voice was compassionate.

"No, Jessica, not their child. An abandoned child. Left in the little depot at Flowery Branch, taken by Angus Kildare and his wife, who were childless, to raise."

I gazed at him dumbly, hearing again Mr. Plummer's voice: "In every civilization there is the legend of the foundling, cast away in infancy—" But Mr. Poteat was speaking.

"However, Mathias Purefoy, strange and hard though he was, did not leave the child to the dubious protection of charity. Instead he instructed Poteat & Whidby—we had served him in a legal capacity for some time—to place it. And assumed responsibility for the expense."

My eyes transfixed by his, I waited, feeling that my breath having run away altogether, my rapidly beating heart tried to follow. At last he asked quietly, "Jessica, do you know who that child was?"

I found enough breath to stammer, "I think— Was I the child, sir?"

"You were the child and Mathias Purefoy your benefactor all these years. Still your benefactor. For in his will he provides for your care until you are of age, with Poteat & Whidby as executors and your guardians. His instructions regarding you are specific. You will be placed in a comfortable and congenial place—not too expensive. You will receive an education that will prepare you for a useful, self-reliant life. At the age of twenty-one you will receive a sum sufficient to maintain you on a modest scale until you can maintain yourself."

Even as the beautiful cadenced voice went on, realization of what it had revealed was a black abyss yawning before me; and sinking into it one by one the dreams, the hungers of the years: the father of the lost and radiant eyes, the mother whose laughter had echoed in my room; my little morsel of faith that I had once been loved and wanted. Now, confronted by reality, my heart almost died within me. I had never been loved or wanted. I had been cast away. And the thought was a black wind sifting across my life. The shape of that life rose before me—anomalous, desolate, loveless, poorer in this moment than ever before; yet even in this moment of ultimate despair my inner self moved by some strange impulse to refuse reality. To believe that I had been loved and wanted. Those to whom I belonged had been too poor or troubled perhaps to keep me; perhaps by keeping me would cause suffering or shame. They had not left me in a thicket or on the side of a hill but in a warm and sheltered place where people came and went; where I would be warm and would be found. With that thought I tried to warm myself against the bitter cold which crept upon me now; though the others could not feel it nor know how deep its chill.

I came back to Mr. Poteat, who leaned toward me, his eyes intent upon my face. "Jessica, did you hear what I said?"

I stammered, "What did you say, sir?" and patiently he repeated what I had failed to hear. Poteat & Whidby, he said, realized that Mrs. Plummer's seminary was not an atmosphere Mr. Purefoy would approve. Last night, prevented from making other arrangements by the—er—trouble and faced with a dilemma, he had telephoned his dear friend Mrs. Carrebee. She, being a charming and tenderhearted woman and knowing something of my story, had come to his rescue. She not only offered me refuge in her home but was here to take me to it. Mrs. Carrebee was a charming lady, moreover she was a distinguished member of Atlanta society. And, having a son and daughter of her own, she understood young people. No doubt, I could be most helpful to Mrs. Carrebee. She was not only a busy lady, but, with her daughter off at school and her son out a great deal, a lonely one. He believed it would be a mutually happy arrangement—unless there was another place I would be happier.

When I said I would be happier with Mitty, he regarded me worriedly. "But didn't you tell me this—er—Mitty had moved? That you have no idea where?"

"Yes—yes sir."

"And except for this—er—Mitty there is no other place you would prefer?"

It dawning upon me that there was no other possible place, I answered in the only possible way, "No sir."

He brought his palms down to his knees with finality. "Then that's settled. And all we can settle for the time. In short, Jessica, you enter upon a new and I hope happy existence. Now—" As if he had remained seated beyond his allotted time, he sprang up and the hand diving into his pocket jingled the coins it found. "Now have you any plans? Anything you wish to do?"

Bewildered, I asked, "Plans, sir? Do?"

Andrew said quietly, "Did you tell her that Mr. Purefoy left her a home of her own?"

Turning to him blank and unbelieving, I echoed, "My own home? And he leaned across the table, his cheerful eyes smiling into mine. "Hickory Hill it's called. Out in DeKalb County. Not fancy like the new ones. Sturdy and foursquare, built to last."

Mr. Poteat broke in, "We'll take that up another day, Andrew. Right now"—laughter crinkled the lines around his eyes—"I want this young lady to chirk up. For one about to enter on a new life and, I hope, a pleasanter one, she looks deuced unhappy. Eh, Andrew?"

But Andrew did not laugh. Instead his eyes questioned mine. "I'm wondering what it would take to make her happy."

I didn't answer or even speak until Mr. Poteat said gently, "Yes, tell us, Jessica. What would make you happy?"

I told them then what would make me happier than anything in the world. I wanted to find Mitty. His hand reached to touch my shoulder lightly. "Did you think I would forget, Jessica?" he asked, then added gravely, "Trust me—not to forget."

"We are nearly home," Miss Camilla said.

In the humid gloom of her carriage I had hardly noticed as the horses clopped their way through the Atlanta streets, which, devoid of the life that usually swarmed along them, appeared ominously empty and strange. But now I straightened and looked out of the window.

She asked, "Are you wondering where you are? Or do you know the Boulevard?" And when I shook my head she went on in her casual, friendly way, "Well, this is it, at least part of it; it runs for miles you know. The group of visionaries that planned it—my husband was one of them—had a dream of a boulevard like those in Paris. A magnificent sweep of avenue, sold profitably of course, that would be Atlanta's exclusive residence avenue." Her laugh was deprecating. "It didn't come off. Atlanta moved north on out Peachtree, and the Boulevard was never more than a middle-class neighborhood with a handsome home here and there that the visionaries built for themselves. Now the refined boardinghouses are moving in and it's going downhill fast. Not that I would trade my home for a dozen of the new ones further out Peachtree." Then, as the horses swung into a drive that curved through a vast stretch of tree-shadowed lawn, "Anyway, here we are."

The driveway brought us to stop before a house in no particular different from many in Atlanta, built in the Gingerbread Era of the 'seventies and 'eighties. But its snuffbox turrets and broken roof lines, its scroll-saw trim and leaded windows were blended by clambering Virginia creeper and wisteria into a house of handsome and comfortable appearance. Looking about as I stepped from the carriage, I saw that it stood in spacious grounds which on one side shelved away to a sunken park. A shadowy, withdrawn place of high trees, somewhat gloomy now. But the invariable summerhouse rose in the distance looking with its circular tower like a miniature Swiss chalet.

Miss Camilla led me up the front steps to the door. "Thank Heaven, Jessica, we won't be bothered with people today. Nobody home except Ad and the servants. Ad is Mr. Carrebee's unmarried sister. She lives with me, and I promise she won't talk you to death. She's a mute and has been since some illness she had as a child."

As we entered the house she pulled the pins from her hat and, thrusting it toward the colored maid who came up the hall to meet us, began firmly but pleasantly to issue orders.

"Drusilla, this is Miss Jessica Kildare who will make her home with us. Tell Miss Ad we're here, then bring tea to the morning room. And —oh yes! You'd better light the fire in Miss Jessica's room, to take off the damp."

Then, as she led the way down a passage running from front to rear, "I don't suppose Mr. Wes called," and at Drusilla's "No ma'am" she went on, "I hope he stays where he is, though he won't if he hears about the riot. That one! He thrives on excitement."

She preceded me into a room which made no pretensions except toward comfort. But what a comfortable room it was! With its wide windows overlooking the sunken garden, with its open fire and ruddy light and warmth, its distant clatter of pans that suggested preparations for supper, what a comfortable, welcoming room it struck me as being! In a few minutes we were sitting on the sofa with the light of the fire upon us, Drusilla was bringing the tea tray and Miss Camilla, still talking in her frank, lively manner, filled and gave me a cup.

"You know, Jessica, it seems very natural to have a young lady in the house. Cissa—she's my daughter—is off at Sweetbriar in Virginia.

Wes, that gadabout, is never at home. He's in Savannah now on some house party or other, and I only hope—" She broke off suddenly at something she saw in my face. "How stupid of me," she exclaimed, "babbling on like a brook when we're all strange to you and you're probably wondering about us, and perfectly natural too. Well—let me see. I'll start with myself. I am Camilla Carrebee, born and raised in Atlanta and Southern to the bone, and I'm one of those terrible Southern girls who back in the 'eighties married a loathsome Yankee. Mr. Carrebee was from Philadelphia. He came down to the Cotton Exposition in 'eighty-one and his old friend Mr. Hannibal Kimball—he built the Kimball House, you know—not only persuaded him to remain in Atlanta and go into textiles but introduced him to me. He lived only four years after we married, left me with two children and Carrebee Mills to raise. The last more trouble than the children. And still is." The lively voice halted as she glanced toward the door. "Come in, Ad."

The small woman in the doorway came toward us, and, halting before Miss Camilla, she held up the suit on her arm for inspection.

When Miss Camilla said, "Ad, this is Jessica," her head bobbed my way and while Miss Camilla inspected the suit, continued to bob; as if to convey the welcome she could not voice. And the chinquapin eyes were as bright as a child's and as friendly.

Miss Camilla said the suit would do and she hoped that I wouldn't mind. Cissa had never worn it, so I might as well until we could get to town. The suit of fine broadcloth in glowing wine color I thought just about perfect. For a fleeting moment I wished that Laura Lee and Oakes could have seen it; and sensed anew the perverseness of time that ignored what the heart desired.

As Miss Ad took the suit and bobbing her head departed, Miss Camilla went to answer the phone that rang in the hall outside. Nevertheless, the gay spirited voice floated back from the hall as she talked over the phone, and her image was clearly before me. The poised reliant figure, its youthful manner of moving, the friendly good humor that made her so charming. Yet beneath the charm and apparent frankness I sensed strength of will and wondered if anyone dared to oppose it.

Now, preceded by her voice, she re-entered the room. "Yes—that was Callie, just as I expected. Callie Peacock, I mean. Such a lovely girl, you must certainly meet her. Phoning to report that Wes called her last night from Savannah. For the moment they seem to be terribly in love—she and Wes I'm speaking of now—though how long it will last who can say—I certainly can't. . . . Anyway Wes told her he would leave for home this morning. That means he'll get in tonight."

She moved to the hearth, stirred the fire briskly, adding a log, said, "That one! He's so afraid he'll miss something." She moved to the windows and, reaching, drew the curtains and shut out the gloom of the darkening day, making the closed-in, firelit room as withdrawn and quiet as a small cove beyond the reach of the turbulent sea; and I was immersed in stillness. The small sounds that had no shape, the murmur of Miss Camilla's voice were all mingled now; a casual wave ebbing and flowing gently against my mind.

". . . but they seem to be really in love"—this was the casual wave flowing in—"so I hope . . ." It subsided to nothing, after a little flowed back again. ". . . women spoil him. Of course he's the darling of my heart but I don't have to be an utter fool. . . ." And still later, the impatient "That Wes!"

Consciousness, as if asserting itself before the tide of sleep that rose in soft undulations, echoed the words "Darling of my heart, darling of my heart" over and over again. Then the tide rising softer and softer engulfed them. And consciousness half-drowning thrust up with terrible clarity Mitty's house, empty and desolate. Pain was a cold hand closing about my heart—but not for long, for the tide flowing up and over the pain engulfed that too. And sinking, I sank to nothing.

Later I woke to eat, like one in a trance, the supper she brought me. Then followed her up the stairs to a wide dim room all pale-green and white. Mr. Poteat had phoned, she said. He would come by for me at nine in the morning. I said, "Yes, ma'am," too sleepy to wonder. Conscious of nothing except the slumbering fire on the hearth and the wide bed as enticing as a heavenly cloud. She patted my arm, she said, "Good night," and closed the door behind her. And still in a trance I undressed and put on the nightgown I found on the bed; and as if the bed were indeed the cloud it resembled, I floated off on it almost before my head touched the pillow.

I was a child again, standing lost and desolate in the center of the glowing ruby carpet that stretched endlessly before me. There was no reason for terror. In my gingham dress I stood alone and unmolested. But my sense of desolation, mounting, pervaded the vastness and climbed toward terror; on the edge of terror was dissolved by an unknown voice that called my name. I started up and, waking, found myself sitting tense and stiff in a wide bed staring at Miss Ad. She stood above me in a sun-bright bedroom, her chinquapin eyes smiling at my bewilderment. And I knew no voice had called my name, for Miss Ad had no voice. It too had been part of the dream.

Dutifully I said, "Yes ma'am," and smiling and bobbing, she turned to leave, pausing on her way to point to a chair on which clothes had been laid out. "For you," the gesturing hands explained, designating the various garments: the wine suit, a shirtwaist to wear with it, a hat with darling baby plumes cupped on its brim, a pocketbook and gloves. When I said, "Yes ma'am, for me," to let her know I understood, she smiled, she bobbed her head, and continued on her way.

Dressing, I wondered where with Mr. Poteat I was to go, but not for long; for I was young. I doubt if youth can too long be concerned when the sun shines bright on a new day and new surroundings that please.

And mine did please. My room, wide and quiet, was a lovely room. White furniture gleamed against sea-green walls; the dressing table was ruffled like the bed in white. There was a chest of drawers, a desk, and at the windows the tops of trees flaunted autumn. Accustomed to that stark unlovely room at Mrs. Plummer's, I found the knowledge that this was mine, past believing.

The figure I saw in the mirror when I had dressed was even less to be believed. The elegant young lady in fashionably brief jacket and velvet-trimmed skirt was a stranger; but I admit one I found quite irresistible. And if it was silly of me and vain—and it was—I told myself it was only human.

Quietly I made my way downstairs, where the wide rooms stretched, sunlit and ordered. In the hall I paused at the huge mirrored hatrack, my eyes attracted by the man's hat that hung there, that had not hung there before. So Wes came home, I thought, and touching it lightly tried to invoke a picture of Wes. "—Darling of my heart," his mother had said, and I visioned someone golden and godlike, the heroic figure that walks forever through girlish dreams. It was dispelled, and quickly. For the aroma of coffee and frying bacon drifted up the hall and, forgetting Wes, I went to find Miss Ad and breakfast.

A little later in Mr. Poteat's carriage we turned out of the drive and rode down the Boulevard in the most glorious sunshine, Mr. Poteat in fine humor, though his face looked in the revealing light as if additional spiders had spun additional webs across it in the night. With admiring eyes he surveyed me—and my clothes. He felt like a prince, he said gallantly, whose kitchen maid overnight turned princess.

I was pleased, of course, but for fear of sounding young did not admit it. Instead, finding his eyes upon me, I tried to thank him for his kindness; and sounded, no doubt, just as young.

When I finished he said quietly, "At least I hope to deserve such gratitude this morning," and at my questioning glance, explained. Yesterday, he said, after I left the Kimball House with Miss Camilla, he had ridden out to Battle Hill to make certain inquiries. They led him to a Mrs. Stopper, a cantankerous shrew! But he had forced the information he wanted from her regarding Mitty. Mitty being old and weak in the head, she'd said, and likely to be a charge on the community, the Ladies' Circle had sent her away where she'd be cared for.

With what voice I could find I asked, "Sent where, sir?"

He said quietly, "The county almshouse," and ignoring my "No—no—" went on. I must not be too distressed, he said. For Mrs. Stopper's daughter had told another story. What they claimed about Mrs. McDaniel, she'd said, was a lie. Mrs. McDaniel wasn't weak in the head. She'd looked after herself, washing and ironing and cleaning by the day. It was just that the "nosy old Ladies' Circle wanted to run folks' lives." She had laughed in her mother's face. At that, it took them a year to outsmart Mrs. McDaniel.

Listening, I sat beside him not crying; no more able to cry than if I had turned to stone. But I felt that my heart was broken. The past year of Mitty's life passed before me. Washing and ironing as Janey had, cleaning out by the day. Coming home at dusk to the empty house with only the specter of the poorhouse to greet her. A specter more fearful to Mitty, I knew, than death. I saw her again on the step that last day when Mr. Dolph and I drove off, so little, so fragile, so old; and remembered how when I called, ". . . in two years, Mitty," she answered, holding Petey's cage high, ". . . in two years, my blessed." As cheerfully as if she believed it.

I turned to Mr. Poteat and he put his hand on my arm. "Don't try to say it, Jessica. Your face says everything. And don't grieve. We are on our way to get your Mitty."

The road we followed after that or how many miles we traveled as the sun slipped higher in the sky, I did not know. Paved road was left behind. The carriage lurched over red clay, slashed and rutted, that ran between stretches of pine or fields of sere brown cornstalks. Here and there a small house stood alone and lonely, its dog rousing to bark as we passed and dropping to sleep again. On the quiet day distant sound fell clearly; bird calls from the russet woods, the creaking wheels of a wagon, the mournful singing of Negroes at work. Such a wonderful land, the South! I thought. Such a gentle land with its tapering pines, its deep quiet forests carpeted with wild violets, jeweled with dogwood and honeysuckle. The nights of long sweet summers made wondrous by the mockingbird. The winters, gentle too; except for sharp brief flashes, spared the bitter cold and snow that other sections knew. As if far, far back in time it had been created, a gentle land, where people might live in gentleness and friendship. From its fertile earth reap abundance for a million lives. But its heritage betrayed, and often by those whose land it was.

As if he read my mind, Mr. Poteat began to talk. The almshouse must not upset me, he warned, though God knew it could stand improvement. But, as always, the poor outnumbered the provision made for the poor. And had since the 'seventies, when Atlanta through a number of court rulings compelled the county to assume the extra burden of Atlanta's poor, as well as its own. Added care had been provided for young folks, the Home of the Friendless, and the Florence Crittenden Home for Girls (and how the Mrs. Stoppers fought against that!). But for the aged and decrepit there was only the almshouse. Even the King's Daughters Home for Old Women, built a year or so ago, was not enough. No doubt the county farm did the best it could on what it had. So I must not be too upset, he repeated, for we were almost there.

We were riding along beside a stretch of split-rail fence, its whitewash peeling in grayed scales. What it fenced in, or out, I could not determine, for it enclosed nothing except a bleak sweep of earth as flat as the palm of my hand and almost as bare. But a minute later we came in sight of the rows of shanties that stalked across the land where no tree or shrub or plant lifted a leaf or spot of shade. Here and there between the rows a rusty pump stood forlornly and in the rear water-closets leaned drunkenly. A moment later we pulled up before the sagging gate, and as we stepped from the carriage and made our way toward a sign that said *Superintendent's Office* I, regardless of Mr. Poteat's warning, thought of Mitty's little house. Of her flowers rioting in garden and on window sills, the cheerful spick-and-spanness of its comfort; and of Mitty forced from it to this. And I felt a rush of gratitude toward Mathias Purefoy. If he had done nothing more than let me take Mitty out of this, my debt to him could never be repaid. As we went toward the superintendent's office, like a child with an unexpected gift I soundlessly said my thanks to him; and promised to be good.

The superintendent's office occupied the first cabin on one of the rows, and was either better kept than the others or seemed better kept because of their general unkeptness. Inside we found a placard stating the superintendent's hours, but we found no superintendent. A tall, rawboned young woman who surveyed us from the door asked if we "wanted" something.

Mr. Poteat with his customary courteous deference stated that we wished to speak with the superintendent. She stated in return, with neither courtesy nor deference, that we couldn't speak with him; for the good and simple reason that he hadn't showed up this morning. He might, she concluded, walk in the door the next minute—or the next year.

Mr. Poteat said in that case there was nothing to do but wait. We seated ourselves in the straight chairs against the wall, the cantankerous young woman disappearing into the adjoining room. We waited, I unhappily. The idea that I was so near Mitty, who might be sick and neglected and certainly lonely, was almost too much to bear. And though I scolded my rebellious heart for impatience when Mitty had endured with patience far more, it was rebellious still; storming against the door of time like a frantic child.

Trying to divert my mind, I listened to the conversation that went on in the next room.

"More complaints about Nine." This I recognized as the voice of the cantankerous young woman. "Listen to this." Miss Cantankerous was gloomy. "Goings-on again in Number Nine. Laughing, feet stomping like dancing. Figgers called . . . 'Dosey do . . . Chicken in the straw' . . . What do you think of that!"

Another voice, edged with laughter, said, "I think it's grand if they have a little fun."

Mr. Poteat leaned toward me and murmured, "I'm sure if you go out quietly and ask someone, you will find Mitty. I'll wait here just in case."

With a whispered "Thank you, sir," I acted on his suggestion and, careful to move quietly, rose and stepped outside; and almost guiltily went down the "street" between the rows of cabins. These, I perceived, contained two small rooms, each room with its front door opening on the street; an arid place as devoid of movement or life as a desert; and under the September sun almost as hot. Passing the doors invariably open, I glanced into each, seeking for someone to direct me—without success. In the first I saw an extremely old woman who nodded in her chair. In the second a still older old woman napping across her bed; and in the third no one at all, for it stood empty.

At the fourth door, however, I met with better luck. For a young woman, who perhaps seemed young only because the others had seemed so old, sat at a rickety sewing machine stitching away so busily and—the machine being old, too—so noisily that she neither saw nor heard me. But when she stopped stitching to push dank hair from her eyes, the eyes, roving idly, roved to the door and found me.

"Yes?" She intoned the word in a delicate ladylike voice, the hand at her hair quirking a ladylike finger. When I explained that I sought a friend "in residence" and wondered if she could direct me, she sat with head dropped demurely, a thoughtful, not overclean finger against her cheek. Then she shook her head.

" 'Tain't likely I can"—she was gently patronizing—"seeing as how I don't consort with the others, their being the sort I ain't accustomed to."

Beneath her efforts to transcend her bleak surroundings, her faded wrapper, the torn and ragged shoes, I discerned a courage that refused to yield to ignoble circumstance; and was touched by it. Sensing that pity would be the final indignity, I spoke with the courteous deference I had learned from Mr. Poteat and told her Mitty's name; and asked if she knew where I might find her.

It turned out that she did. If I went straight down this row, she said, at the fifth door down I'd find Mrs. Mac. Thanking her and almost running, I slipped down the street and came to Mitty's door and looked in and saw her. Not sick or neglected, not even lonely, but as cheerful and unchanged as if she were still in her little house, where she might well have been. For flowers rioted on these window sills as they had on those. Her clock ticked as faithfully on this mantel shelf as on the other. And in his new cage by the window Petey chirped no less blithely as Mitty, scolding, removed his bath water.

". . . a rascal you are"—this was Mitty scolding—"sploshing water all over your nice cage. As if cages just grew on trees. If you ain't careful you'll end up at the poorhouse and that's a fact." How tartly she said it, how cheerful her laugh as she said it. "And what will poor Petey do then, I'd like to know."

She pattered to a shelf, placed Petey's bowl upon it and turned, and—as I had known she would—stood motionless and stared unbelieving. Then believing, cried out, "My ever ever blessed!" and ran toward me, arms reaching. Then they were around me, holding me tight so tight. And I, happier than ever before in my life, was crying as if unhappier. And crying and trying to talk and the words tumbling out this way and that and like Mr. Dolph's eye every way except right, I managed to tell her that I had come to take her away. Then Mr. Poteat was suddenly in the room, was holding her hands and saying gently, "So this is Jessica's Mitty?" And Mitty was dashing the tears from her cheek with her tiny fist and explaining that light always made her eyes water. And I was hugging her again and crying again and laughing because I cried. And it was a confused time and a foolish time and a time altogether wonderful.

We dried our eyes and packed Mitty's things in preparation for leaving, which we were not able to do with the dispatch we intended. For when we stepped from the door the "street," devoid before of movement or life, was alive with people. Old people and young; straight people and twisted; the quick and the lame, the sick and the well. All down at heel and branded with poverty but all Mitty's friends; and as glad for her luck as if it had been their own. One old man with merry eyes in a shrunken face bowed as she stepped outside, as he would to a queen—a difficult feat because of his wooden leg. And when Mitty exclaimed, "Go 'long with you, Mr. Dent," all of them laughed delightedly. Mitty and Mr. Dent most of all.

While she circled among her friends saying good-by, Mr. Poteat and I stood at the door and waited. And I saw the number on Mitty's door. Then it was I who laughed. For Number Nine with its dancing feet and "Dosey Do" was none other than Mitty's. Now watching as she came toward us, so little, so old, so dauntless, I knew that Mitty could never be vanquished; that her love of living and giving would transcend any time, any place.

We left, and her friends trailing us to the carriage watched with quiet eyes as Mr. Poteat gallantly handed her in. The horses moved off, Mitty, her head out of the window, was waving, and followed by their "Good-by, Mrs. Mac—Good-by," we finally rode out of sight.

Mitty sank back on the cushions, her twinkling eyes childlike with wonder, her small hand smoothing the cushions.

"Now anybody that tells me this ain't nice," she remarked without rhyme or reason, "can go roll their hoop." Then, Mr. Poteat collapsing with laughter, she and I had to laugh too. But when our laughing was done she looked up at me with loving eyes.

"I knew you'd come, my blessed," she said softly. "I knew that some day you'd come."

When we turned into Miss Camilla's driveway again, dusk drifted beneath the trees and the grounds stretched dark and forbidding; but the windows were lighted and friendly and Miss Camilla, waiting on the porch to greet us, was all warm smiles. Her "Here you are!" spoken in a clear, ringing, pleasant voice conveyed far more welcome than the words implied. Her manner as she took Mitty's tiny hand in hers was as cordial and natural as if they'd known each other for years. "I thought you all would never get here."

She led us into the reception hall and, pausing, informed Mr. Poteat with bantering imperiousness that he was to stay for supper. While Mitty and I went to our rooms to freshen up, he might have a drink; to Drusilla, hovering in the background, she relegated the placing of Mitty's possessions, including Petey, in the room next to mine. Then she ushered Mitty and me to the stairs, saying, "Dinner at seven, more or less; anyway you'll hear the gong." And as we started up, the picture she made all bright and glowing went with me.

In our rooms—Mitty's, wide and comfortable, adjoined mine—we postponed freshening up. Instead I dropped to the floor to sit at Mitty's knee as in the old days, and we talked; and said all the things held in our hearts this long time. When she told of her losing battle against the Ladies' Circle and the poorhouse—and what a valiant battle she fought! —I cried. When I, in turn, told of fleeing to the little house and finding her gone—she cried. And the realization sweeping over us that we were together and need never be parted again—we both cried. And had a thoroughly enjoyable time.

A gong sounded downstairs, warning us to hurry with our "freshening up," and with much scampering about and muffled laughing we gave ourselves, Mitty said, a "lick and a promise," and went down to dinner. Miss Camilla's warm, husky voice called for us to join her and Mr. Poteat.

In a high, wide room that glowed in mellow lamplight and stretched to wide, tall windows, we found Miss Camilla on one side of the hearth and Mr. Poteat on the other, a tall glass beside him. Miss Camilla interrupted what she was saying to smile at us and, her dimpled white hand briskly patting the sofa, ordered me to sit beside her.

"I told Eula to hold supper a bit," she said. "I asked Wes to get here on time for once, but no telling about that one. He can get tangled up in more . . ." Her throaty chuckle hinted of such delightful knowledge that I wished I might share it too. She added dryly, "He's a plain scandal."

Mr. Poteat observed that Wes was not as black as she painted him. "The wild oats of young men, Camilla, are seldom remarkable. They've come up with no really unique devilment since Nero."

"You don't know Wes," she retorted.

"My dear Camilla, you are victim of the doting mother's prejudice that believes her black sheep is the blackest," Mr. Poteat advised. "Wes's activities, if you knew them, would no doubt disappoint you by their innocence."

While they continued to banter the subject of Wes's behavior, I looked about the room and wondered if it was that fabulous room met in books —a drawing room. Since I had never seen a drawing room, even known anybody who had one, I could not be sure. For the Carrs', Laura Lee had said, was unlocked only for "grand occasions."

Certainly it was unlike any room I had ever seen. It had neither the cold elegance I had seen at the Carrs' nor the sterile correctness of Mrs. Plummer's. It was even a little shabby. The silk on chairs and sofa was faded, the marble mantel discolored by fires that had blazed on its hearth. But it was a friendly room and serene—and immensely comfortable.

A clock chimed the hour and Miss Camilla announced that we could wait on Wes no longer.

"That one!" she exclaimed humorously. "We might starve to death waiting for him."

She led the way to the dining room and, waving us to our places, took hers at the head of the table. Its immaculate expanse of damask sparkled with old silver and glass, and the bowl of roses in its center was flanked on one side by a great platter of fried chicken, on the other by a brown-crusted ham.

As I slipped into my chair, my eyes took it in. The blackberry jam, amber watermelon pickle, the spicy scarlet and green of piccalilli—I received, as never before in my life, the sense of abundance where nothing was stinted or cost even considered. When Drusilla passed dishes of string beans, yellow squash and okra, as well as two kinds of hot bread, biscuits and corn pone, my sense of abundance increased. And Lem, his dark face deferential above the spotless white coat, was not Lem transformed from coachman to butler. To my naïve, wondering eyes he was a figure from Arabian Nights, who filled Mr. Poteat's glass—not with wine, but enchanted elixir.

As we ate, Mitty and I listened to the talk that went back and forth between Miss Camilla and Mr. Poteat. Casual and wandering, it drifted from mutual friends to business, and on to cotton prices and "brokers" and inevitably to Carrebee Mills. Listening, I marveled at Miss Camilla. All womanly and generous charm, yet directing the affairs of a cotton mill. But nothing, I decided, would be too difficult for Miss Camilla.

Now her voice drew me back to the conversation by mentioning Mr. Algernon Carr.

"You know perfectly well he's one of the most important men in Atlanta. In the Southeast, for that matter. Why, think of all he's accomplished, heads up every worth-while movement, responsible for the Cleanup Campaign that closed all those dreadful places."

"Oh! They left town for a while," Mr. Poteat admitted, "though I hear the highly esteemed Pet Belleau only moved her prosperous business to a more desirable neighborhood. But then, she was less vulnerable, since her establishment is undoubtedly as well known as Mr. Carr's bank."

With her brusque laugh she called him incorrigible, but not in the least disconcerted, he smiled at Lem who was refilling his glass and told him just to leave the decanter. Then he looked down the table at her. "To get back to Algernon Carr's varied talents. You forgot to include his most intriguing activities. President of one of our leading banks and"—his brows lifted—"at the same time, head of the powerful cotton mill combine."

"That's just talk! He's only on the combine's board of directors," Miss Camilla answered.

"Ostensibly," Mr. Poteat said. "For the president of the bank to admit control of the combine might make his strategic position too obvious. The public might realize the extent of his inside information regarding mills in distress and . . . in need of a timely loan. For Mr. Carr's combine to eventually take over those mills from Mr. Carr's bank might suggest that there is more to 'high finance' than meets the eye."

Beneath his rich voice there was an undertone of delicate irony and Miss Camilla, amused in spite of herself, laughed again. Yet she still defended.

"Well! And why shouldn't he?"

Mr. Poteat shook his head reprovingly, "I'm afraid, Camilla, you are a zealous disciple of the New South."

She tossed her head. "What's wrong with the New South?"

"I refer, of course, to the New South," he said, "that out of defeat and Reconstruction managed to push its way to the top. But it isn't hard to forgive so charming a lady for that particular sin."

"Gracious!" she exclaimed, with her husky bark of laughter. "You sound as if you don't approve of the New South."

He spoke quietly. "I find the new rulers offensive. They hire out to Mr. Morgan, like a certain Confederate officer we know, as head of his Southern interests. Or as directors of Alabama coal mines and iron mills. This naturally is the result of Georgia's Mr. Henry Grady, who in a speech to the New England Society declared that the South could be saved by becoming like the North. An industrial heaven—and at lower wages."

"Heavens, how you do go on, Poteat. Mr. Grady was a fine man. And a wonderful orator."

"I only say that his oratory auctioned off the South to Yankee bidders. I also find offensive, dear Miss Camilla, the New South's bought politicians who, by waving the bloody shirt and appealing to racial intolerance, which every intelligent Southerner hates, win the cracker vote. And most offensive of all are the gangs of yokels—with two Biblical quotations and one mule whip—who ride out in bed sheets to impose their will on men who call themselves free."

But Miss Camilla had enough. She said tartly, "Poteat, you're mad and making a bore of yourself. I'll have Lem bring the brandy. The wine doesn't seem to set well."

We were having our dessert when I happened to lift my eyes and saw the young man standing in the doorway. With something like disappointment I realized this must be the long-expected Wes. While he made a pleasant enough appearance in his gray suit, it was no more than that. I found nothing at all extraordinary about him. He was tall, but hundreds of men were taller. His deep tan was the rule among Southern men and in no way exceptional. Neither was his dark hair. I felt that I had been taken in, led to expect too much. For certainly there was no evidence of the irresistible charm his mother had claimed. He was only a young man who made his way with careless ease to the empty chair. Miss Camilla's introductions produced polite nods for Mitty and me and an equally polite "Good Evening." Taking his seat, he told his mother he'd had dinner in town but he'd join Mr. Poteat in a drink.

Miss Camilla signaled to Lem, then turned back to Wes. Where had he been? she asked.

"Oh, out with a bunch I ran into."

"There!" she exclaimed to the rest of us. "You see! He tells me nothing. And I'll wager he's been up to no good." Her tone was proudly doting and she reached out and placed her plump white hand over his that looked so brown on the gleaming white cloth. "I never know what he's up to. The plain truth is he's a useless scamp."

I knew his eyes had passed over me and decided that I was a schoolgirl who rated no serious interest. But now, as with an oddly quirked smile he deliberately freed his hand from his mother's, he looked into my face. And suddenly I was lost in the endless, shapeless gray world of his pupils, caught and wrapped in their warmth, knowing the eternal inquiry and expectancy with which they met the world and the aching hurt of their disappointment.

His turning to me, I sensed, had been no more than the result of his drawing his hand free from his mother's dimpled hand, and he only spoke to cover his avoidance of her caress. Moreover, he did not speak to me alone but also to Mitty, and I was even jealous of Mitty for sharing in the sound of his words. Yet they were unexceptional enough.

"My mother often forgets that I am not one of her lintheads," he explained with mock gravity.

At the mention of lintheads, Miss Camilla plunged into talk of the mill and its reaction to the "little trouble" of Saturday night. But I heard her no more than if she and all others at the table had been swept by a wind into the distance. Only Wes and I remained.

When I recalled that only a few minutes past I had considered him unextraordinary, I was incredulous. Could I have been so blind? Somehow failed to see his gold and brown coloring, his dark, ruffled hair? That his slightest movement was made with hard, careless grace? That his face might have belonged to a young huntsman who from a high place views distance upon distance with eyes innocent yet wise, knowing and humorous and kind and heartbreakingly alive?

Watching him surreptitiously, I forced myself to finish my dessert. That it took will power to eat maple mousse, my favorite, reveals more clearly than words the state of my feelings. Yet common sense did not wholly desert me. What little remained carefully pointed out that I was nothing to him. I was merely a girl who needed a home and had been given one because of his mother's kindness—kindness which made her pretend I could, by trivial service, justify my keep. For me to even think of Wes Carrebee, warned common sense, was as ridiculous as the passion once conceived by Mrs. Plummer's young ladies for a clerk who passed the seminary on his way to work.

At the time I had thought them absurd. But no more so than I was now. But my absurdity filled me with an aching splendor I would not have exchanged for all the reasonableness in the world. Which proved how absurd I really could be.

Now Miss Camilla addressed him. He promised to be at the mill, she said; she had waited for him all morning. Why, she demanded briskly, hadn't he done as he promised?

He straightened and echoed vaguely, "The mill?" then recollected. "Oh! I went to East Lake for some golf. Rode out with Charlie and Breck." He laughed and his eyes were mocking. "I'm sure the mill will survive."

She retorted, "It won't if they put teeth in that child labor law. Heavens! The way newspapers take on when they want to build circulation. Saying conditions are worse in the mills than they are with the Russian serfs!" Her laugh was light and scornful. "And—they certainly don't overpay reporters. And certainly they don't provide houses and doctors and stores for them, which the mills do."

Wes inquired blandly, but the mocking gleam in his eyes, "They don't employ children either? Or get longer hours at lower pay?"

But she only exclaimed, "Oh, *you!*" and plunged straightway into discourse. Oh! she knew, she said, that noble hearts bled over child labor without knowing a thing about it. Not that she agreed with Asa Candler. Certainly she didn't think a child at work was the most beautiful sight in the world. But she knew what a child labor law would do to linthead economy. And who would they blame and hate? The do-gooders who had pushed the law through? Oh no! The millowners would be the villains. Look how they rioted when Loring put in modern machinery. Just because it would mean fewer hands.

She threw out her hands, she exclaimed, "Don't talk to me about lintheads!" Glancing around the table, she said to the hovering Drusilla, "Coffee in the living room," and with resolute steps led us toward it.

We sat in the other room as a family would sit, each doing as he wished with no effort toward conversation. Lem placed the decanter beside Mr. Poteat. Miss Camilla with Mitty vanished to meet Miss Ad, too shy because of her muteness to come to table.

Wes strolled to the hall, picked up the mail that he found there and coming back to the room, went to one end to read it. Still separate, I thought, holding himself to himself.

Mr. Poteat said, "Jessica," and beckoned me nearer, and I crossed to the hearth and stood by him. "Yes, sir," I said. Over his glass of wine, his eyes, quick again, smiled. "I want to know, child, if you'll be happy here, at least 'til you go off to school after Christmas? If you would be content—to stay on?"

I said, "Oh yes, sir," but I hardly knew what I answered. My eyes had gone back to Wes who read his mail by the lamplight. Watching him as he stood there, I thought: How describe him? How separate him from what I felt, what I would feel in the future? How see him again as he looked when my eyes first fell upon him? Just a young man, rather tall and certainly not handsome. A face that missed the ideal, the nose even slightly beaked. That was the way I had seen him. I saw him like that no longer! Now I saw—or thought I saw—a sort of dark potency in the brown, alive face; the eyes, merely clear and gray before, now gleamed with a lambent flicker. No longer just a young man, in no way extraordinary. But the only reality in the room—in the world. Beside him all others were shadows.

Miss Camilla came back through the door, said to me, "Mitty is visiting with Ad." Then, seeing Wes at the end of the room, she exclaimed, "Wes darling! It's—nice you're staying at home tonight. Perhaps we can get up a whist game. Mr. Poteat and I will take you and Jessica on. . . ."

I wished he would stay and I turned so I might hear his answer. He pulled himself up from his chair, said courteously he was sorry but not tonight. He had a date with Callie. With a brief "Good night" he went quietly from the room.

Miss Camilla watched until he vanished from view, then the white hands flashed out impatiently. "That one!" she exclaimed.

Part 2

So I began a new life in strange surroundings, lived among those who were strangers. A circumstance referred to in fiction as "a new life"; but the phrase is deceptive. For I learned as everyone learns that there is no such thing as a "new" life; but only the turnings and windings, narrowings and broadenings of the old that is one, and forever one only.

A great many things were changed but I was not changed. Nor was there change in the special aloneness which from the first had been mine; except that I felt even lonelier. For Mr. Poteat had told me I was one of those not wanted; and if other things were changed that unchangeable fact was unaltered. I spent many hours—some that were bitter, rebellious—considering this fact.

I still felt that I was the pawn of forces outside myself. A piece of cumbersome luggage to be checked this place or that until time to move me again. I admitted that Miss Camilla's was a pleasant place to be checked. That those with whom I was checked for the time showed me friendship and kindness. I do not deny that being young—and sufficiently vain—I derived pleasure from new clothes chosen by Miss Camilla. For while they were plain, as that strange old man Mathias Purefoy had decreed, theirs was the plainness of taste, not poverty. And because they were becoming, they freed me from that torture reserved for the young of being different. Certainly I enjoyed deep rugs and soft restful chairs and food attractively served. The girl who occupied my cheerful room, where the two courtly elms at my window woke me with autumn bouquets, was a happier girl than the dreary one of Mrs. Plummer's.

But had my new life lacked all of these I still would have been content. For I was with Mitty again. And oh! such days as those first days together were. I, running to Mitty time and again to hug her, she pattering over as often to me. And oh how we talked. As if words were glue that could mend the broken pieces of time and make it whole again. And what with talking and laughing and hugging—with considerable crying thrown in—we, as dear Mr. Dolph would say, were "whupped down for fair" and, being whupped down, we would start all over again.

As one day became another, I began to feel less like a guest in the house, became more familiar with the Carrebee traits and habits. I found them unlike any picture of family life that I had ever imagined: the family close-knit and fond, each for the good of all. The Carrebees were not like that. They were a law unto themselves, and while they belonged to the outside world, they held themselves separate from it. Miss Camilla, charming and cordial with friends who called or telephoned, when they left or hung up would forget them, laughing and shrugging. As if they were only a silly game that interfered with business. For I came to know that it was she who held the reins of Carrebee Mills in her dimpled and rather blunt hands. Wes held a position of sorts, learning to grade and buy cotton, but he took his duties lightly and refused to let them interfere with the more amusing side of his life.

As I came to know Miss Camilla better—or as well as I would ever know her—I understood, or thought I did, the reason for his attitude toward work. Gradually I realized how relentless was her control. How even her throaty, infectious laughter was used for gaining her way, her sudden melting warmth employed to win obedience. Yet awareness did not lessen her power or free us from it. I sensed that it was impossible for her to share control or domination. Compelled by something within herself, she must decide and direct and manage. Even for Wes, whom she worshiped, she could not be otherwise. Like Caesar, Miss Camilla was absolute as a sovereign; governing her affairs as if they too were a kingdom.

Several mornings each week she rode out to De Kalb County to work at Carrebee Mills, not in the carriage but in her buggy, handling the reins of the chestnut mare herself. On her days at home she kept equally busy working in her sitting-room office on the second floor, from breakfast straight through the midday meal, hers carried up on a tray by Miss Ad. Later, often as not, she dressed and went out in the carriage to attend a reception or tea, perhaps return a few calls. She came home in time for dinner to talk, glowing, unweary, of where she had gone and whom she had seen. Listening, I would wonder if she ever grew tired and weary. Or if the boundless vitality heard in her resolute step, in her husky, delicious laughter, sprang from an inexhaustible well that supplied her with tireless energy as a motor supplies a machine.

Now and then when she worked at home, as I went up or down stairs, I would pass her. Absorbed and abstracted, she would send me a glance, almost I thought of annoyance. As if I were a stranger who carelessly stepped in her way. The first time this happened I worried. No doubt, I thought, she's tired of me. Regrets that she took me in. When the dinner gong sounded I descended almost with dread. I thought, I'll try not to get in her way. But her husky voice, warm again, cried, "Darling, what have you done all day?" She gave me a comradely squeeze. "I'm afraid you've been dreadfully bored. Now—if you were only a year or so older. You could go places with Wes. Meet his crowd." Her hand patted my cheek. "But your day will come." Head on one side, she regarded me. "You do have the loveliest hair. Those gold streaks in the brown . . . they're intriguing."

She slid her hand through my arm. "I'm starving. Let's go in to dinner." We went and she came back to my hair. "If you'd just touch the gold streaks with peroxide. Not enough to be detected. Just enough to point up the gold a bit. It would make you a downright beauty." From the head of the table she flashed me a smile. "I must teach you the tricks of the trade, Jessica. You know there are tricks, my dear, whether it's cotton or charm you're selling."

Next morning—a morning of misty, gusty rain that sifted from a lowering sky—I lay on my stomach on the window seat in Mitty's room and, propped on elbows, pretended to read. But this morning my book was neglected. I was too occupied on one hand with watching for the arrival of Mr. Poteat and on the other with cogitating the question of going away to school, which we were to discuss. I could not contemplate with pleasure the prospect of having to meet more strangers, or the even unhappier fact that I would be without Mitty again.

My eyes surveyed her as in the low rocker she hemmed dish towels for Miss Ad. It struck me that in my changeable existence only she was changeless; that this Mitty who hemmed dish towels so cheerfully was the identical Mitty of the little house; of the one small room at the poorhouse; that change of place failed to alter her; instead she altered the place. That even this room of Miss Camilla's, with Mitty's clock on the mantel, Mitty's Star and Moon quilt on the bed, her pots of flowers on the window sill and Petey chirping away in his cage, had become Mitty's room.

I asked abruptly, "Mitty, what do they do to a person who runs away?"

Without missing a stitch she answered cheerfully, "Why they bring 'em back most likely, once they find 'em."

"But what if they don't find them?"

She finished a hem and turning the towel began on the other end.

"Most likely they do find 'em, dearie. It's a funny thing about Runners Awayers. They start out to run, not knowing to what or to where but wanting to be somewhere else, wherever it is. Like a bluebottle fly at the windowpane. Buttin' his head without using his head so to speak. Or stopping to think if he'll be better off outside or worse."

I said, "Oh Mitty! Flies don't think."

She stopped hemming and, head to one side, looked at me thoughtfully. "Well now, my blessed, I'm not so sure. I've met some mighty smart flies in my time. There was one fly in particular . . ."

She told me at length of "a fly in particular." Met up with, she said, back in her little house, and him making as free in her kitchen as if he paid board. And smart? When she went at him with a fly swatter he lit on its edge. A tight-twisted paper, and he lit on her very best china. And the broom was no good at all. For when she smacked the place on the wall where he was, he outguessed her and wasn't; but had zoomed away out of her reach.

Though I knew she only tried to turn my thoughts from the subject of running away, I was interested in spite of myself. I asked if she ever outsmarted him.

Holding her needle mid-air, she shook her head slowly. "No, that I didn't, dearie. He outsmarted me 'til the last."

Her words suggested an unhappy end and I asked what had happened.

In trying to outsmart her, she said, he plumb outsmarted himself. From zooming so much and zipping so much she reckoned he frazzled himself plumb out. And unexpected-like just dropped down dead from the ceiling. And dead he was as Dick's hatband.

We considered the miserable end of a particular fly for a moment, then I returned to the subject in hand.

"Mitty," I said, "what would happen if you and I ran away?"

She thrust the needle in the towel and put it aside; and, leaving her chair, crossed to me on the window seat.

Putting her arm about my shoulders, she drew me to her. "Now tell me. What's this all about?"

So I told her. About Mr. Poteat's coming to discuss sending me off to school. In itself, I said, unsettling; and the fact that I would wait until after Christmas to go, also unsettling. Because I felt that I wasted time, I said. In fact, I felt about as unsettled as a girl could feel, and I was sick and tired of it!

Though she patted my shoulder lovingly, her voice was matter-of-fact. It was natural for me to feel like that, she said, me being so young. But she believed that in a body's life there was a time for "full steam ahead," and also a time "to tread water"; so why didn't I just "tread water"? And try to be happy. Pulling me close, she held me tight. "Be happy while you can, my blessed. Let happiness in when it comes to your door. The other pushes in of its own self. Of that you can be sure."

She held me at arm's length and gave me a little shake. "Now I used to speak a piece—something 'bout gather the rosebuds while it's May."

Careful not to reveal that she misquoted, I teased, "But it's almost November, Mitty, and there are no roses to gather."

"That's what I mean," she said gravely. "For November, when there ain't any roses, comes every year."

Her gentle gravity shamed me and, putting my arms about her, I laid my cheek against hers.

"Then I'll gather my roses, Mitty. And do my best to be happy."

Her small hand smoothed my hair. "And now I hear Mr. Poteat's voice downstairs. Make your hair nice and go down."

Later I listened as Mr. Poteat and Miss Camilla discussed the question of school, though when only Miss Camilla's opinion seemed to count, it could hardly be called a discussion. It was her opinion, she stated, that I should go to Vestal Hall. Not too far from Atlanta, it attracted girls of family from all over the South.

Mr. Poteat, refilling his glass, remarked that unless he had been misinformed Vestal Hall was generally referred to as Half-Wit Haven. Certainly it did not seem to offer the practical education which Jessica would need.

Miss Camilla brushed this off with her favorite word "Poof."

"The kind of education that Jess needs can't be found in books. Surely you don't want a lovely girl like Jess to turn into one of those dreadful females who have a purpose in life. They wear such terrible clothes."

Mr. Poteat turned caustic. To expect any young lady, he said, any *Southern* young lady, to have any purpose whatever would be to beggar practicality. However—he made one last, though rather futile effort—why wouldn't it be practical for Jessica to return to Sweetbriar with Cissa? After the Christmas holidays?

"That would never do in the world."

"But I don't see," he began. Almost crossly she interrupted him. "Of course you see." Her dimpled hand emphasized. "She's headstrong, she's vain, she's jealous—and her temper . . . When she's home . . ." She threw out her hands. "Spoiled. Spoiled rotten."

Mr. Poteat said quietly, "You're too hard on Cissa. In view of the fact that it was probably you who spoiled her."

She shook her head, her face for the first time in my knowledge stern and masked. "No," she said flatly. "I wasn't the one who spoiled Cissa. But I won't let Jess go to Sweetbriar." Her smile returned as her eyes met mine. "Jess is going to Vestal Hall."

True to my promise to Mitty, I did my best to be happy. And as if the effort crumbled away a barrier, I found myself laughing at small things; kicking through the piled-up leaves dropped by the oaks and hickories and blackgums. Sampling persimmons I found, which, having been touched by no frost, were bitter and puckered my mouth. Often I crossed the Boulevard and plunged into the fields that stretched on the other side.

Rainy days I spent in the house, followed Miss Ad and Mitty, helped with household tasks, sometimes wandered alone exploring, coming across rooms and corners I had not seen before. It was on such a day that I discovered what to me was treasure: a small dim storeroom on the third floor containing hundreds of books. They had belonged, Miss Ad explained in sign language, to Mr. Carrebee her brother, stored here after his death by Miss Camilla, who called them "dust catchers." Sitting on the floor, I dived into them as one who is hungry for food. Though none had been published since the 'eighties, they opened up wondrous vistas. Dickens, Thackeray, George Eliot, and a complete set of Shakespeare. Numerous volumes of fiction. Numberless technical volumes on cotton; its growing and manufacture. In the dim dusty place I leafed them, engrossed, and pausing, studied the *John Wesley Carrebee* written in each in fine Spencerian hand, invoking from it a picture of the man himself. A quiet man and cultured, I thought, kindly and earnest. A man with a delicate chest, according to Miss Ad. Who had come to a gentle land and, finding it gentle and promising health, had remained to establish his kingdom. Who met Miss Camilla and married her and began to build toward his dream. And built his home and Carrebee Mills and fathered a son and daughter; then came down with typhoid and died—not from the delicate chest but from the secret adversary that lurked in the gentle land, the land he had loved and trusted. His dream had survived in the mill and Cissa and Wes; but nothing was left of the dreamer except these books stored away and forgotten; inscribed in fine Spencerian hand.

The small room and its contents filled a lack in my days and many hours at night, but often I was lonely for someone nearer my age. Sometimes I thought: If only Cissa were here. As for Wes, I saw him only as he departed or, returning, changed and departed again. Now and then I would catch a glimpse of him as he descended the stairs, bound for a formal affair. Tall and—I thought—beautiful in the gleaming white against black. I would imagine him dancing with Miss Callie Peacock to music tender, beguiling. And dramatically I would declare to myself that this was not to be borne—that I would surely die. But after I'd eaten an apple and a slice of Eula's gingerbread I would feel in such excellent health, I wondered if perhaps my suffering had been caused—not by love, but by hunger.

I asked nothing except to see and be near Wes, to be met with the casual friendliness grownups bestow on children, which was precisely what he had bestowed. I did not hope even for friendship—or even that he might select me as someone to talk to now and then.

I did not really hope for such favor as this, but I sometimes pretended I hoped. Being young, a female, and worshiping Wes, I even dared dream a little. I imagined he might call upon me to sew on a button, or fetch a book or mend a snag in his coat. Sometimes I imagined him ill; and, a convenient epidemic removing all competition, I was privileged to nurse him and hold his hand through the crisis. It occurred to me that wishing Wes ill might really bring sickness upon him, that imagination might mysteriously be infectious and I by my thoughts expose him. But my fear was useless. He was not struck down by a fatal disease. Neither did he call upon me to sew on a button or fetch a book or darn a snag in his sleeve.

He called upon me for nothing at all.

Little by little, like the shoots of a plant that appear one by one, the traits of those whom I lived among emerged from behind first impressions, and I began to feel that I knew them. Not completely. For who knows any single person completely? But at least I learned that each contained not just two people, but many. I learned that Mr. Poteat, the courtly and gallant, disappeared now and then (to lie drunk for days, they said). He reappeared, courtly and gallant and meticulously clad, with only the ruined face to betray him. "Nobody blames him." This was Miss Camilla's matter-of-fact voice. "He married Myrtle Luttrell. She was as beautiful, I'll vow, as you would never believe, but like all the Luttrells she had a weak streak. Now she's as mad as a hatter. He's faithful to her in his fashion. But after a few weeks of her tantrums—unfortunately she isn't the dangerous type that can be exciting; she's just dull—he goes off on a toot to forget. And"—this was to me—"don't look so scandalized, my dear. Atlanta has its quota of family skeletons and always has had. It's most interesting why certain homes and buildings were 'missed' when Sherman burned everything else in Atlanta."

The unsuspected side of Mr. Poteat's character was not the only one I came to see. I found that Miss Camilla when she played solitaire, which she played a great deal at night, cheated herself. The first time I observed this, she knew and laughed up at me impishly. "Don't forget," she reminded, "that there are tricks in all trades." When I cried, "But you're cheating yourself," she told me calmly, "My dear, everybody cheats themselves one way or another. If they didn't they'd blow their brains out."

Of course there was more than one Wes. I had intuitively sensed, before, a Wes who held himself aloof and distant. But now still another appeared. Brooding and almost sullen, sticking to home for a change; keeping close to his room for the most part and at meals abstracted and silent; ignoring his mother's overtures, quiet and moody, not speaking. As I talked with Miss Camilla I was aware of him silent nearby. I wondered if the auto he wanted was the reason for his moody behavior. If, like a small boy denied something he wished, he was testing his will against a stronger. At the thought, careful that he not see, I smiled to myself. And suddenly felt older than he.

Then, as suddenly as it had fallen, his moodiness lifted. He was himself again: seldom at home, constantly departing, returning; talking of going this place or that, the dance at the club, somebody's dinner party. The name Callie Peacock dropped from his lips over and over, to me as annoying as water that drips on a rock. But when Miss Camilla artlessly inquired if he and Callie "were making plans" yet, his sudden smile would flash down the table at her, derisive and taunting, and he told her nothing at all. And each time—so silly I was—I drew a deep breath of relief; like a condemned person hearing that execution, though inevitable, has been postponed.

On a soft gray day in early November, the first without rain, in old skirt and jacket and shoes, I plunged into the fields that loomed beyond the other side of the Boulevard and went for one of my walks. I came after considerable distance to a range of thickly wooded hills and a narrow circling footpath which, leading around them, joined them one to another; drawing me on toward where I did not know, nor did I pause to wonder.

The path landed me in a hollow cupped among hills, somehow

strangely familiar. Then I saw the toboggan slide, stark and bleached as a skeleton, and knew I had stumbled on Ponce de Leon Springs. It was deserted now and silent, except for the trickling water and murmuring pines. I shivered a little, for in the dim, shadowed place I saw again Laura Lee, dark and mischievous, and Oakes, so sublimely sure of getting his way. And there was another ghost, I suddenly realized. Ghost of the only youth I had known. For how gay and silly we'd been. Chasing each other madly, our shrieks echoed by the hills; and the time Oakes caught me and kissed me. . . .

I stood in the quiet place, smiling in memory a little. Oakes was so terribly young.

It was when I returned from my walk, wind-blown, draggled and muddy, that I saw, my eyes round with awe, the automobile that stood in the drive. More magnificent than I knew an auto could be, a thing of cream trimmed with royal blue, its seats, back and front, crimson leather; polished and gleaming with wire wheels that glittered, it stood in magnificent disdain. So alluring that I, sure that no one observed, was drawn to approach it. Yielding to impulse, I ran my hand over the satiny surface. I thought, So Wes got his auto; and pictured him, gallant behind the wheel, the dark head lifted—and Callie Peacock beside him.

Absorbed in the car and my picture, I saw or heard nothing else, and when Wes spoke behind me, startled I whirled to face him. He stood with his slouching grace, pulling on leather gloves. His eyes were not upon me, but the auto.

"Like it?" he asked and I said, "Oh yes!" as I tried to bring order to my hair and brush the twigs from my skirt; but finding that he watched, amused, I gave up trying; pretending again that I did not care if he saw me wind-blown and disheveled.

He strolled to the car, opened the door; then, foot on the running board, turned back to say, "I've got to run out to the mill. Like to come along?"

"Come along?" I repeated blankly and, nodding, he waited, his hand on the door. This was what I had longed for. He was eager to show off his prize and with no one else to impress, I would do. Whatever his reason, inconceivable that I should refuse.

I said, "I would love to go but I'll . . . I'll have to change. It won't take but a minute. . . ."

His eyes appraised my brier-hung skirt, my muddy shoes, my blown and untidy hair. "Oh! you're all right." He was casual. "Who'll see you except the lintheads? Anyway, there's a duster right in the auto."

I did not argue for fear he would regret he had bothered, and he brought the duster and held it for me, pulled from its pocket a veil—reserved for Callie Peacock, no doubt—and wrapping it about my head, tied it with matter-of-fact briskness beneath my chain. His brown hands, neatly but strongly shaped, deftly knotted the veil scant inches from my lips. My heart turned over when his fingers brushed my throat.

"Now," he said humorously, "you look like a dyed-in-the-wool motorist."

He guided the car down the Boulevard past polite lawns behind the line of huge trees along the sidewalk that still clung to their leaves. From yards and porches housewives and children and Negro servants looked up startled as we passed. I felt an absurd pride at the idea that some among them might take me for Wes's wife or sweetheart. And though I knew they stared not at me but the car, I do not deny that I felt a vicarious glow at the homage the public paid.

We roared with regal disdain past streetcars, buggies and wagons, left the city behind and followed a road with railroad tracks on one side, stretches of field on the other.

As if lured by the long empty stretch that loomed before him, Wes shot the auto ahead with a throaty roar of its engine, going faster and faster. So fast that the railway lines and dun-colored fields and red clay gullies swam together and merged. Holding onto my seat, I looked at Wes and saw the lifted head and on his face a strange blind intentness—somehow frightening. But before I had time to wonder why it was frightening he slowed the auto down to a speed that was less exciting and, as if just remembering me, said, "Scared?"

When I told him I had not been scared he glanced around at me reflectively. "Most girls would have squawked like all hell. You're all right, Jess."

I was warmed by glowing pride. "I expect I would have squawked too if I'd been scared," I admitted, "but I wasn't."

"No"—he shook his head—"I don't think you're the squawking kind of youngster."

I felt the flush creep over my throat to my face. "I'll be seventeen before very long." I tried to make seventeen sound older than seventeen.

His sudden laugh filled with private amusement stopped with equal suddenness. "I'm sorry," he said gravely. "I didn't mean . . . Dammit, Jess, don't start making me feel in the wrong."

I said quickly, "But I don't want to. For then you won't like me. . . ."

He glanced at me and started to speak, then decided against it and, turning his eyes back to the road, drove faster and we rode on in silence. It was hopelessly clear that I, to him, was no more than an agreeable child to pat on the head with tolerant kindness; though it was what I had expected, now unreasonably I resented it. Why couldn't he see how easy to span the difference in years? I was sorry now I had come, wished only to be back in my room. . . .

His car suddenly gasped, coughed and slowly spluttered to silence, then stopped. He got down, swearing under his breath, and looked under the hood. I followed and standing beside him held wrenches and pliers while he tinkered, watching over his shoulder as he performed mysterious rites, impatient because I did not know one tool from the other. But when at last he cranked the car, it burst into life with sharp explosions.

He tossed the crank and wrenches into the toolbox, wiped his grease-smeared hands on a rag, and it was then that I saw the cut across the back of his hand. It was bleeding slightly, I noticed, and smeared with oil and grease.

When I called his attention to it, he shrugged, said it was nothing. Nevertheless, I produced my handkerchief and, cleaning away the blood and grime, managed a small neat bandage. He thanked me with amused gravity.

"Maybe I should hire you to take care of me," he said. "I think you like to take care of people."

Without answering, I made the bandage secure.

"Better yet, I could take you on as my doctor. How about it?"

"Why not?" I tried to match his lightness. "You can be my favorite patient."

"It's a bargain," he said cheerfully. "Do I have to call you Doctor or will plain Doc be all right?"

"Doc," I answered, "is much less formal."

He gave his quick, bright flash of laughter. "Good. I'm glad you're not a stickler for formalities. I'm not good at following rules." Then, "Hop in, Doc, let's be on our way."

So Doc I was to Wes from that day on. Half joke, half game at first, but later settling into habit. "Doc" I was and "Doc" to me was precious because he had bestowed it, and if the gift was carelessly given and held little significance for him, it was more than I had ever hoped for.

We drove on silently. Wes listening to the sound of the engine anxiously, but it churned placidly, throatily, and his anxiety was gradually soothed. A few minutes later with a flick of his hand he indicated that this was our destination. This was Carrebee Mills.

I thought as we approached the mill that never had I seen so bleak a place. A large wooden building high and gaunt, the windows that marched across it curiously cold and blank, the name CARREBEE COTTON MILLS. EST: 1882 painted in giant letters of weathered black. Stark and unlovely it rose above its expanse of bare cindered earth. At its feet smaller buildings clustered and beyond, on a slope, I saw the straggling mill village. Rows of loosely built frame houses, all of the same barrack-like pattern. Before them the bald hard-packed earth that served as a street was rutted and behind them shambling water-closets tottered on stiltlike legs. The very air of the place was heavy with sordid and hopeless defeat.

I remembered Miss Camilla's saying that the lintheads came from the farms, and I wondered how they endured this desolation.

I wondered, too, as Wes turned the automobile through the gate what the lintheads thought when he dashed up in his shining car, a handsome young man of leisure.

In a voice flicked with scorn, Wes said, "The source of the Carrebee fortune, Doc, such as it is. Not the prettiest goose in the world to lay our golden eggs."

He brought his car to a stop near a small building with a sign OFFICE and we went up a short flight of steps and without knocking entered a large room containing two desks, and before each a man, one very large and one very small.

At our entrance they glanced up, and the large man bounced to his feet, his greeting almost too hearty. He clapped Wes on the shoulder. "How are you, boy? Ain't seen you in a coon's age."

He was a big, soft man with paunchy cheeks and a huge paunch of a stomach. His protuberant eyes, paunchy too, had the cold glint of silver quarters. When Wes said, "Ed Wangle, who runs the mill for us," their cold glint turned upon me.

"Howdy do, ma'am. Glad you dropped in." His eyes roved over my figure.

Wes suggested abruptly that they get on with the business, and Wangle agreed, flapping a large hand toward me.

"Maybe Miss Kildare 'ud like to go through the mill, while you and me dicker." Turning his head, he called, "Hey, Darty, how 'bout showing Miss Kildare aroun'?"

The small man hunched over a desk left his chair and came over with a sidling, crablike gait. He was a stooped, nondescript figure with a scowling face and a thatch of gray-sprinkled hair—but I liked him. His eyes peering through spectacles were as ingenuous as a child's. When Mr. Wangle said, "Darty Land, ma'am," and smiling I offered my hand, he gave me a quick shy smile, then was scowling again, even the scowl oddly endearing. For all his gray hair, he was like a small boy compelled by his mother to come forward and greet politely her visitors.

As he jerked his coat from a nail and, scowling fiercely, slipped into it, I thought I liked Darty Land as much as I disliked Mr. Wangle. He led me across the yard with his crablike, sidling gait and, scowling even more fiercely, muttered, "Know anything about mills?" When I told him I didn't, he informed me that Carrebee did both spinning and weaving, something you didn't see often in the South.

He conducted me through the great wooden shell of a building which enclosed vast stretches of space crowded with machines. They sprawled, row after row, ponderous and ungainly, their rising and falling thunder numbing my mind.

From the machines, I saw, raced hundreds of shining strands sweeping, swerving and darting. Swooping under and over rollers and twisting and gliding and shifting, they wound on giant spools, then instantly raced on again, and racing and thinning and tightening, spun quivering webs of light that, merging with other webs, made glossy, intricate patterns; emerging finally, unbelievably, in giant bolts of plain cotton too ordinary, I thought, to have been wrought by the miracle I witnessed. Yet, greater than my wonder at these, was my wonder at those who worked them. Moving swiftly and surely, adjusting and aiding and guiding, they seemed unimpressed by the pounding rollers or flailing arms.

But my greatest wonder was roused not by machines nor people but by the world in which they must work. A world of pale, luminous haze, stifling the air. For the first time the term "linthead," heard at the Carrebee table, held meaning for me. Only now did I know the meaning of lint itself.

Lint! Lint filled every inch of the air; a white, diabolical blizzard that blinded and confused me. Lint got up my nose, clustered on my lashes, burned my eyes, tickled my face, sifted in my ears, got under my clothing, and worked down to the roots of my hair. Each time I inhaled I drew in countless motes of lint that parched my throat, rasped my lungs, made each breath a half breath, plunged a knife of pain beneath my ribs.

Lint! I was utterly defeated by lint. I only wanted to run, run away from it, to leave it forever behind me. When Darty Land led me from the building and we stepped outside, I stood gulping the damp autumn air. Even when I was with Wes again in the car, the clean wind could not sweep away the memory of lint.

I had no illusions as to why he asked me to go on that ride. I had none when we returned. He would have no reason to ask me again. So I need not expect it.

Nothing was changed by the ride except that he called me "Doc," a nickname so unromantic it could not be counted as gain. His attitude was plainly that of a grownup tolerating one terribly young, which with my mooning and moping I obviously proved that I was.

Sensibly, I told myself that my whole future stretched before me. No doubt at some future time I would fall really in love. A sensible, reasonable love, not schoolgirl infatuation. He would be a practical man, I was sure, who had his feet on the ground. And when we were married we would have a good laugh at the silly young thing that was me. I would be wise and sedate with all foolish fancies discarded. I would scoff at the idea that I ever fancied I loved Wes Carrebee.

I could not, I did not love Wes, I assured myself. Still, I found myself writing "Jess and Wes" over and over again; and wondering if the fact that our first names rhymed did not have some deep significance. I found myself searching through the musty books in the storeroom for technical volumes dealing with cotton-mill operation. I found myself reading until my eyes burned; about carding and roving and combing; about warping and slashing and spooling; about spindle-winders and drum-winders, and twister rolls, rings and travelers.

To myself I gave explanation for my sudden interest in cotton. Did I not live among people who owned a mill; had I not visited that cotton mill in person? My interest had nothing to do with Wes Carrebee or any connection he might have with cotton. Of course, if Wes should happen to wish to discuss cotton weaving and should happen to ask my opinion, it would be no more than politeness to answer; and as sensibly as I could.

If, for instance, he should happen to ask a question on card construction, I would tell him a card required close and accurate adjustment and must therefore have firm and rigid framing. However, Wes either knew all he should about cards or did not care to know, for never once in my presence did he mention the subject of cards.

But it was nonsense to imagine myself in love with Wes. I was too sensible to allow myself a silly crush. Nevertheless, when Miss Callie Peacock and her parents came for dinner, I did not take to Miss Callie Peacock at all. I felt an antagonism to Mr. and Mrs. Rayburn Peacock, her parents, who, while to blame for *her* existence, had never harmed me. Yet dislike them I did.

I had no reasonable complaint against Mr. and Mrs. Peacock. They were well thought of in Atlanta society. Furthermore, Mr. Peacock, tall, sporty, with a white mustache and red face, was prominent in mule-trading circles; since Atlanta was mule center of the world, a man not to be treated lightly. Nevertheless, I disliked him and found his voice, a booming, rumbling sort of voice, extremely offensive. But at the same time, illogically, I disliked thin retiring Mrs. Peacock because she had almost no voice at all. I found her quietness as distasteful as her husband's booming.

Most of all, I disliked Miss Callie Peacock herself. I admitted she was dashing and perhaps rather pretty—almost twenty I'm sure. In consequence I felt horribly young, a feeling not helped by Miss Peacock. True, Miss Peacock was terribly "sweet" to me. When introduced she exclaimed she'd heard "oodles" about me from Wes (which I did not believe). But she hadn't dreamed I was so *young* . . . and crying out musically, it was wonderful to be so young, she made me feel I had only just been born.

I could hardly be jealous of Callie Peacock since I was not in love with Wes. Yet I was annoyed, though I did not show it I trust, when Mr. Peacock at dinner talked so loudly to Miss Camilla I could not hear a word anyone else said. I saw Callie Peacock's head bending to Wes, knew by their lips that they murmured to each other, but her father's voice, like a cannon's big boom, boomed out whatever they said.

Mr. Peacock boomed from the subject of mules to the subject of family, which naturally led to ancestors. He and Miss Camilla discussed not only their ancestors but the ancestors of their mutual friends. Then Mr. Peacock reverted to mules; discussed *their* ancestry and breeding; came back to ancestry of friends; returned once more to mules. Finally he discussed ancestors of both mules and friends at the same time so that I was hopelessly confused as to which was which, and who was descended from whom; and unable to hear one word that Miss Peacock and Wes had to say.

It struck me however that Wes was not particularly attentive, and this

—though I did not know why—gave me satisfaction. But as dinner came to an end, he leaned toward Callie to murmur, smiling his faint mocking smile, which she—silly thing—no doubt thought utterly charming. In response she threw back her head and laughed extravagantly. When her father glared at her fiercely, she became prettily confused, hiding her face in her napkin.

I heard her whispered "Wes, you old crazy! You're perfectly awful!"

In the living room later when Miss Camilla said I might be excused, I accepted dismissal gladly, but in my room threw myself on my bed and wept the furious tears of hate and despair.

How ridiculous, I stormed to myself, to imagine I might love Wes Carrebee!

A week or two later I went for another ride, not however with Wes. He had gone a few days before to South Georgia to hunt; and occupied with rugged shirts, clumsy boots, and running a greasy rag through the barrel of his gun, he had no time for me. The only tangible proof that the ride had really happened was that he continued to call me Doc.

My second ride was with young Andrew Hardee, and it was taken more for business than pleasure, for we drove out to Hickory Hill, the house left to me by Mathias Purefoy. Heretofore, I had given little thought to Hickory Hill, but when Andrew called and I knew I would actually see a house that belonged to me, I was transformed in the wink of an eye into a "woman of property."

When Andrew appeared, driving a brown, discouraged-looking horse and a rusty buggy hired, I learned, from a livery stable, I greeted him in my woman-of-property manner, but to my disappointment he failed to be impressed. With his usual calm cheerfulness and twinkling blue eyes, he helped me into the buggy and taking the reins, clucked at the horse, which, as if disapproving of the outing on principle, reluctantly pulled out of the driveway.

Delude myself as I might that I was a changed person, I could manage no such delusion in regards to Andrew. He was exactly the same, except for a somewhat thin overcoat. His dark, neatly brushed suit was the suit he invariably wore, his tie was the tie with the identical speck of egg. However, both tie and egg fading with time, they had reached a state that was not unharmonious.

As we turned out the driveway I, assuming a pleasant businesslike air, asked if it was a long drive to the property.

He raked his fingers through his rustyish hair, a habitual gesture, I was to learn, and gave cheerful consideration to my question. "It can be far," he explained, "from the point of view of a horse."

"Because this horse is slow, you mean?"

He made the admission so good-humoredly that I too was amused. Listening to Andrew's comments on the character of the horse and offering a few of my own, I quite forgot my determination to behave like a property owner.

We had traveled several miles when I realized our route was the same Wes had followed to Carrebee Mills. I asked Andrew if it was near Hickory Hill. He told me that, as a matter of fact, it was. That both were beyond the city limits out toward Decatur. However, Hickory Hill was a mile or so further out than the mill.

It was well past noon when we turned off the road to Carrebee Mills into another that carried us over rolling, sparsely settled country. I caught glimpses of a Negro cabin or small farmhouse squatting among fields of orange broom sedge or patches of winter corn; heard the cawing of crows in the serene distance. Later, we turned off again, this time along a narrow red dirt road that curved toward a rise. Suddenly Andrew pulled the horse to a stop and pointed with the buggy whip, and looking up the slope between dark trunks of leafless trees, I saw Hickory Hill.

It was a plain house and, even from a distance, I knew that for a long time it had been lonely. Though two-storied and strong, it was not a large house and it claimed no particular grace or charm; a house built by a man, I felt, who had learned that life, even when good, is hard. A long porch, set high, stretched across the face of the house, and at one end a blunt wing jutted. At the other, a warm brick chimney lunged tall against the vast sky of November. The house was coated with yellow plaster, rain-washed and sun-faded by the years to the grayed delicacy of sunlight mingled in mist.

The emotions the first sight of Hickory Hill aroused I cannot define. But I know that they were nothing like the earlier shallow pride in myself as a property owner. Yet there was pride, deep and solid as the house. I was proud and expanded; it is the best word I can find for my sense of being increased by every foot of space contained by wall and roof; by every yard of hill on which they stood. This, I told myself, was mine. Hickory Hill belonged to me and I belonged—for seeing it had silently forged an indissoluble bond between us—I belonged to Hickory Hill.

Absorbed in my house, I had forgotten Andrew beside me. Even when he spoke, my gaze did not waver.

"It's like Mathias Purefoy in a way."

"Yes." I realized that this I too had felt, and I wondered if Andrew knew Mathias Purefoy and his history better than I had supposed, if their relationship was more than one of business as I had assumed. Later, I told myself, I must ask him.

He slapped the reins against the horse's back and we began to climb the red dirt road that swung along the ridge toward the house.

At the top of the hill, Andrew guided the horse into a small swale stretching between the chimney and a chinaberry tree, and, leaving it with its nose in a canvas feed bag, we circled to the front of the house.

Black tortured trunks of wisteria writhed up the posts of the porch roof. From the porch itself, reached by a flight of long steep steps, I could see stretches of yellow and brown fields, scarlet gullies, smoky woods and dark gleaming streams. I told myself that it was here a family would take its ease; settling in rocking chairs in the long glowing dusks at the end of July or August days, catching the first breeze, watching the lightning bugs flicker in patches of blue night thickening under the trees. But the steps, I thought, would be dangerous if there was a child.

I heard a small clink of metal and turning saw that Andrew had taken from a pocket four old-fashioned heavy keys, rusty but new-oiled and hung on a twist of wire to which a tag was attached. He fitted one of the keys to the lock of the front door set deep in its solid frame, and swinging it open, stood aside for me to enter. His freckled, friendly face was cheerful beneath its habitual Scotch reserve.

"Do you want to look over your house, Miss Jessica?" he asked gently.

I nodded and entered a breezeway hall that ran through the center of the house from front to back. A wide sturdy staircase rose from the front of the hall, and doors opened from either side. I noted as I went from room to room that they were high-ceilinged, airy and generous, with massive hearths and solid mantels. But I did not gain detailed knowledge of the house in that first exploration. I did observe that a few pieces of old pine furniture, a tall, massive secretary, a table, a chest, satiny and glowing with age, had been left behind. These, Andrew told me, belonged to the house, as did sundry odds and ends stored in a carriage shed in the rear.

However, I was not disturbed by the scarcity of furnishings—I had expected none—nor the need of repairs, which I had been told to expect. Much more important to me was its basic strength and firmness. As if rooted in earth, it had been formed from clay and stone and wood into something as enduring and elemental as the hill on which it stood. The big kitchen, reached by a narrow strip of covered porch, had its open hearth; the great upstairs bedrooms with windows so high one would look out upon a brambled treetop world of squirrels and birds.

Inexplicably, I was aware of the richness of living the house had known in the past; the happiness and gaiety, the grief and hurt. And my awareness enveloped not only the past, but the joy and pain, the human, breathing, feeling life this roof would shelter, these walls protect in the future. For a moment—a moment set aside from time and by time unmeasured—I almost heard laughter not yet sounded, saw faces not yet born, felt warmth from fires not yet laid with wood from trees not yet cut down. And in this moment of time outside of time, there was upon me the feeling that I penetrated both past and future. What lay ahead I knew no more than any other mortal, what lay behind I knew a great deal less than most. But in the moment of time, outside of time, I felt I held both in my hand.

The air was filled with the dust Andrew and I had stirred, and suddenly I sneezed. Then it was Andrew who sneezed, and, overcome by a simultaneous spasm of sneezing, we retreated, our eyes red and teary, to the porch. And the house and my conviction that I knew both its past and future dissolved.

As we sat on the long steep steps of the porch to eat the basket lunch put up for us by Folsom's, which Andrew brought from the buggy, my thoughts were engrossed with the future when Mitty and I could live at Hickory Hill. I had started on my second sandwich before I recalled the difficulties I must overcome before this could be. As a consequence my enthusiasm for both future and food disappeared and, holding my unfinished sandwich, I sat silent a long while.

Andrew, observing my change of mood, suggested I try another kind of sandwich. Since the lunch was furnished at Poteat & Whidby's expense, he had ordered a large variety, he said. It would be a shame, he added, to waste them.

I told him I just wasn't hungry, and the blue eyes regarded me steadily. He was always suspicious, he remarked matter-of-factly, of a young lady's loss of appetite. It meant she was either in love or was worrying about something or other.

I said quickly, "It isn't love."

He persisted, "Then you are worried?"

I admitted the worry but added quickly it was nothing serious. It was serious he said, if it prevented my taking nourishment at Poteat & Whidby's expense. Moreover, foolish. As my legal advisor he should be informed of whatever it was, because if people should stop informing their lawyers, it would be the end of lawyers and he would be out of a job.

He said this in his dry, half-humorous fashion but his freckled face expressed genuine concern, so I told him in a businesslike way my concern about Hickory Hill. That wonderful as it was, I could neither furnish nor repair it, either now or at any time in the foreseeable future; that even if I managed somehow to furnish and repair, I could not keep it up nor buy a horse, though one would be essential so far out. Which meant, I concluded, that I didn't see how I could live at Hickory Hill.

He listened attentively, gravely eating sandwiches at Poteat & Whidby's expense, until I had put the case before him. Then he nodded, finished the last bite of the sandwich in hand, and wiped his fingers on a Folsom napkin. It was plain to see, he announced, that I was suffering from an attack of "contingencies."

"Of what?" I asked, and he repeated "Contingencies" gravely. And on my asking if it was serious, he said it was and it wasn't.

"If it's handled the right way it's not," he explained. "But it's not always handled right, not even by lawyers. Not even, what's more, when a lawyer himself is laid low by contingencies."

I asked if lawyers were "laid low" often and he said quite often; that it was something of an occupational disease. He happened to know a young lawyer who from eagerness to obtain a client had suffered a disastrous case of contingencies. Yet, he continued, placidly munching his sandwich, curiously enough, it was finding not a client on his doorstep but finding himself on the client's that brought on the case of contingencies.

Interested in the young lawyer's contingencies and forgetting my own, I asked how it happened.

"It was like this," he said. "He was trying to get a start and clients being scarce he was considerably behind with his board. To put it bluntly, he was about to be thrown out of his room and lose his trunk, when, luckily, his landlady met with an accident. With a trolley car."

"A serious accident?" I asked.

He shook his head dejectedly. "Unfortunately not serious. The landlady—I met her—was a good-sized landlady—a very good size. And the trolley was only an ordinary-sized trolley. The trolley got the worst of the accident, to tell the truth. Still, the landlady had a suit, and this young attorney saw his chance to handle the suit in return for keeping his room and trunk. Naturally he hoped he'd win her case and get her money for damages and that others who had accidents with trolleys would employ him."

"It seems reasonable," I admitted and Andrew agreed.

"It was reasonable on paper. Reasonable except for contingencies. You see, this young attorney was green, and knew he was green. But he figured on making up for that by being well prepared. He read all the law on accidents and read as many court decisions as he could dig up. Also, he got advice from everybody—lawyers or non-lawyers, interviewed all the witnesses, tried to think of everything the lawyer for the trolley company might possibly bring up, tried to have an answer ready for him. And, what's more, he *did* think of all the possibilities. If ever a man thought of every possible argument, courtroom maneuver or legal device, that man was this young lawyer."

"And did he win the suit?" I asked, feeling I was nearing the secret of contingencies.

He swallowed the last of another sandwich and brushed crumbs from his coat.

"No. He lost the case by contingencies." He was solemn. "Contingencies being the arguments he thought up for the defense. He worried about everything they could say and everything they might say, and about every possible contingency." He shook his head again. "Contingencies."

"What happened?" I asked. "Was there a contingency he hadn't thought of?"

"Oh no." He was mournful. "He'd thought of all of 'em. That was his trouble. When he stood up to address the court, he was struck dumb.

Choked by all those contingencies. His mind went blank from weeks of foreseeing contingencies; so he lost the case."

"And did his landlady throw him out because he lost?"

"Threw him out the same day," Andrew said, "and kept the trunk."

He returned the napkin to the lunch basket and closed it. "That's why I say you've got an attack of contingencies," he explained with a small smile. "And the cure is to trust in the future, let them take care of themselves."

The sun was far down in the west when we got in the buggy and the horse, settling into his shambling, unhurried gait, started toward home. The excitement and wonder of discovering Hickory Hill, which had buoyed me all afternoon, was lulled by the unbroken quietness to calm. Hickory Hill had been a discovery. No less momentous to me than those that the history books taught of Columbus, Hudson or Drake. And I was puzzled again, as so often before, that Hickory Hill should have come to me who could not possibly use it.

At this I emerged from my thoughts and pulled Andrew from his to ask about Mathias Purefoy. Was I right, I inquired, in believing that his acquaintance with Mr. Purefoy had been more than one of mere business?

He raked his hand through his hair. In a way, he said, I was right, but in another way I wasn't. He knew Mr. Purefoy, he reckoned, as well as anyone knew him. Which wasn't to know him well. For nobody could claim they had known him well in business or otherwise. A strange old man, Mr. Purefoy. Strange and hard, some had said, for 'twas rumored he'd done hard things. But he could do kind things too. When young he'd been a dirt farmer and he never forgot how it felt to be dirt-farmer poor. Which was the poorest poor that was.

I asked Andrew how he first came to know him and, talking quietly, the reins hanging loose in his hands, he told me.

Andrew had been born down Darien way, he said, the town that the Scotch had settled, and orphaned when young had lived round with kinfolks. This one, then that one, and wanted by none of them much. So at sixteen he struck out for himself. Worked his way upstate to Athens and got a job in a box factory and came to know Mr. Purefoy. The factory belonged to him, and he dropped in ever so often to mosey around and check up on things. One day he stopped and talked and—well, that was the beginning. Mr. Purefoy had been a good friend. But for him, the university and law would not have been possible. When he graduated it was Mr. Purefoy who got him placed with Poteat & Whidby. . . .

He concluded, eyes twinkling, "All leading to my meeting one of Poteat & Whidby's most highly valued clients. To wit: Miss Jessica Kildare."

After this we rode along in silence, I deep in my thoughts of Hickory

Hill, and Andrew quiet beside me. The dusk, sifting down, slowly veiled the face of the road that led back to Miss Camilla's.

That day I had gained a house and a friend; enough, I thought, for any one day to bring. But there was another gain no less valuable. I was pulled back to earth, though I had not been aware I had left it. If Mitty and I were ever to live at Hickory Hill I must give more thought to the future. I must not allow myself to be smothered by the soft, luxuriant ease that made life at the Carrebees' pleasant. As Mitty often remarked—and, I knew, with a purpose—this rich kind of life weakened the stomach for living close to the bone. For me such a life was as unattainable as my dreams of Wes. Well, I would dream no more. When I felt an attack of Wes coming on, I would firmly refuse to give in.

These resolutions were not easy to keep, but when I was downcast I would remember Mitty's cure for "feeling low" and give my room a thorough cleaning, or help Mitty and Miss Ad about the house. Keeping hands and mind so busy, I had no time to watch for Wes.

I told myself I was recovering from Wes, that after Christmas, when I went away to school, recovery would be complete. I did not look forward to leaving. After all, I would leave Mitty too. Though she would remain at Miss Camilla's, where she had made herself a valuable cog in the household, and with Miss Ad for company would not be too lonely, still I dreaded to leave her.

There were others I would miss too: Miss Ad, that shy, silent and kindly little creature of whom I had become so fond, the cook Eula, Drusilla and Lem. And because the dread of new surroundings and strange people again almost overwhelmed me, it caused me to view the approach of Christmas with some apprehension. Yet there was one reason to look forward to Christmas. For then Cissa would be home. And moreover, Miss Camilla informed us, she was bringing three school friends with her to spend the holidays.

From the constant talk of Cissa I had developed considerable curiosity about her and, as you do with someone as yet unseen, tried to evolve an idea of how she might look. The photographs I had been shown told me nothing except that she was slim. Nevertheless, I sensed that Cissa was beautiful, not merely because her family admitted this to be true but because other witnesses, silent but nonetheless eloquent, testified to her beauty and proved it to me beyond doubt.

For instance, there were her dresses to bear witness to her beauty. Rows and rows of dresses in one closet after another, dresses impossible to be worn by someone who was not beautiful. There were other witnesses too. Rows of small slender slippers in which only beauty could walk or go dancing. And final intangible witness, Cissa's delicate fragrance drifting over her room, voicelessly proclaiming, "I am Cissa."

I needed no pictures to tell me of Cissa's beauty. Yet I knew nothing of Cissa beyond the effect she had upon people, the impressions she left on possessions. Almost I seemed to see her at times as we see light; by reflection from surfaces that cannot of themselves give light. Or as we see wind, by fluttering of leaves and grass that bow as wind passes. Then I happened to come upon something with the power to bring her alive.

The cold day had kept me inside reading by Mitty's fire, so wrapped in warmth and content that I found myself feeling drowsy. I got up and put on my coat and went out into the garden and in the still, hard chill of the late afternoon strolled about for a while. I kicked through heaps of rattling leaves, stooped to examine a pebble which had the look of an emerald but was only a lovely green stone. It was then, aimlessly wandering, that I finally came to the summerhouse and, pausing, stood and regarded its deserted and desolate air. Then, lured by some strange attraction, I peered in its door that hung open, and the dusty shadows beyond somehow seemed a little forbidding. Then almost without volition I stepped through the door.

My eyes gradually adjusting to the dim leaf-broken light, I glanced about idly, for there was nothing to see. It was the summerhouse invariably found in Southern gardens, but dusty now and deserted, its scabrous iron furniture peeling in flakes, its floor rotting and littered, the smell of mouldering decay hanging in its still air.

It was not until I turned to go that I saw for the first time the little stairway and, curious, crossed to inspect it. Narrow and steep, the steps mounted to an opening in the ceiling, and when I had warily tested their strength—they might have been built for a company of elves—I began to ascend them. What a wondrous play place this must have been for Wes and Cissa! Ascending, I had a picture of them slipping up the stairs, their excited delight as they planned the game they would play. Wes being older and male would have been a bandit, no doubt—or a pirate; Cissa his worshiping slave. Almost I could imagine his scornful intolerance because she was weaker, less daring.

At the top of the stairs I had to stoop to enter the low octagonal niche. It could hardly be called a room, for it was no more than a pocket designed to pull and hold the rising heat from below. A raw, unfinished place with its unsealed walls and rough plank floor and two small high-placed windows, cold I knew in winter, hot in summer. With nothing to offer children except freedom from adults and the feeling of privacy; yet that Wes and Cissa had played here was evidenced after all the years. By mouldering litters of paper and bits of old crayon, a doll that lurched in a corner staring from empty eye sockets. By an unpainted wooden box that stood beneath the high window, its top stamped with the words MACCABOY SNUFF.

Without stopping to wonder at my desire to know what it held, I raised the dusty lid and looked inside. Its contents were, I thought, exactly what might be expected. A scrapbook half filled with the pictures children would choose: animals, flowers and ships. Others intended to fill it but never pasted in place. A crude childish drawing in crayon, obviously of a small girl, who looked more like a goblin, with yellow corkscrew curls and monstrous blue eyes. Above her head the artist had added storm clouds, blue, black and purple with zigzagging streaks shooting from them to indicate—I presume—streaks of lightning. And under the figure in the unsteady scrawl of childhood I read:

This is me
Cissa Carrebee
Me in the rain.

My dust-smudged fingers returned it to the box and pried among a tattered pile of old ball gowns salvaged, no doubt, by small Cissa many long years ago. Now their colors were faded and dim, the materials fragile and rotten. Folds of once beautiful silk crumbled at my touch to nothing. Kneeling there, I looked at the shreds and visioned a small girl who played lady, saw her as regally she trailed her silken robes. The small head imperiously lifted, her airily poised hand lifted too and crooking its tiniest finger. I thought of how Wes must have hooted in masculine scorn of her pretense. And robbed her game of its magic; shattered her lovely illusion.

Convinced by my own childish fancy, I illogically felt sorry for Cissa. And as I lowered the box lid I thought, Poor little Cissa.

Rising, I moved toward the stairs but paused at their top for a moment, my eyes attracted by something they had failed to observe on ascending. Something carved on the wall such as boys carve on trees with a penknife to enclose their name or initials. This, however, was more intricately done, had taken time and effort. Wes had carved it perhaps to relieve boredom as Cissa sat drawing. For here was imperishable proof that for that day at least they were friends.

Brushing the layers of dust away, I looked at the words he had cut and, though clumsy, uneven, some even misspelled, they were easy enough to read. And for an instant I felt a swift sense of shock as if they were meant for me.

WES & CISSA CARREBEE
THERE PLACE
KEEP OUT . . . THIS MEANS YOU

The summerhouse and its turret room where Wes and Cissa had played soon passed from my mind but were brought back one night by Mitty. A night when Miss Camilla gave a dinner party for some "stuffy New York brokers" and Mitty and I dined from a tray in our room with Miss Ad. I, engrossed with my thoughts, while they—never handicapped by Miss Ad's inability to talk—carried on a mysterious but satisfying conversation.

My head whirled with the party in progress downstairs. With the great bowls of flowers from the florist which I had helped to arrange. With the table rich with its point de Venice cloth, its flowers and tall candelabra. With the gold-necked bottles arrayed in the butler's pantry, the extra butler "brought in" to pour them. The kitchen a strange and wondrous place when its high priestess Eula had showed me the big ice-filled tub with its unshelled oysters. "Blue points, honey," she said, "fur them whut kin swaller the nasty things. And dese"—she opened the oven door—"is de quail. No more dan a mouful apiece but one yu don't disremember. Now gits yu upstairs 'fore I sends up yo'alls trays by Drusilla. . . ."

Ascending the stairs, I had met Miss Camilla descending, not the everyday Miss Camilla but in her rich, silvery gown queenly and ever so beautiful. When I gasped, "Oh Miss Camilla, you're lovely!" she said absently, "Thank you, Jess. Will you knock on Wes's door and tell him it's seven o'clock? And to hurry . . ."

Before I could say, "Yes, ma'am," he answered her from above. "She won't have to bother," he called, as he turned down the stairs impeccably dressed, but his face was bored, almost sullen. "I'd rather be hung to a hickory limb"—he was grim—"than eat with that damned Holy Carr."

From the foot of the stairs she watched him descend, her eyes not doting but cold and appraising. "If you want your bread buttered you'll hide what you think."

Reaching her side, he shrugged. "He puts no butter on my bread—much as he'd like to. And he never will, by God, if I can help it."

Together they turned toward the living room and unnoticed I went up the stairs as Miss Camilla's voice, floating back, lifted lightly: "You may eat those words some day."

Later, when Drusilla brought up our trays, I had asked if the party was terribly dull. "Dull? No, ma'am, it sho ain't. Deys is havin' dereself er time. And dat Mr. Wes! Keepin' 'em all in stitches wid his goin' on. Dose gennamun 'bout to bust wid laughin'. 'Cept one. He jes sits dere. An' Miss Callie. . . ."

Casually I asked, "Miss Callie . . . she's at the party?"

"Yas, ma'am. An' lookin' at 'im lak she ready to eat 'im up. . . ."

After we had finished our meal and Miss Ad had said good night and gone down, I washed my hair, soaped and rinsed it and, sitting on the bed, rubbed it dry, listening as Mitty related the conversation she and Miss Ad had managed somehow. And it was then that the summer-house and its turret room came back to mind. Miss Ad had talked, said Mitty, meaning that Miss Ad's flashing fingers and expressive eyes had conveyed how Wes and Cissa, left to the care of servants—Miss Camilla being busy with the mill—had been spoiled on one hand and neglected by the help on the other until they were like two wild young goats; practically living in that dratted summerhouse except for nighttime, of course. And no one to notice or care. Only Heaven, Miss Ad had commented, that takes care of drunks and children, had protected them. From fire or a bad fall or maybe a terrible scare. At that, she believed it was the cause of the way Cissa was. High-strung and skittish, quick-tempered. And even when a little thing, raging and storming; saying nobody loved her.

Because I too had wished to be loved I foresaw that this might be the foundation from which friendship with Cissa might grow. For I still believed that to have a best friend and to be one was one of the greater glories provided by life. And so I do still. I did not view it as illogical to hope that Cissa would be such a friend.

With this hope, I was even more eager for the arrival of Christmas and Cissa. And I counted the days, ticking them off one by one. Tried to spend them with work as room by room the house was refurbished and polished. Aware as the four of us worked—Miss Ad, Mitty and me along with Drusilla—of the fragrance of Eula's fruitcake about us.

Lem dragged in the Christmas tree, tall and tapered, and set it up in the living room, where it scented the house with cedar. That night while Miss Camilla and Wes were away at some party or other, I trimmed it. Mitty and Miss Ad looking on, sipping the eggnog Miss Ad concocted and feeling chipper enough, Mitty said, to cut the pigeon wing. When I finished the tree she surveyed it, small hands on hips, with the eye of a seasoned woodsman. "Well sir," she announced, "it's a tree as what is a tree. And more than that I can't give it." Tired and sleepy, I laughed, but I thought, Cissa arrives tomorrow.

It was tomorrow, and Lem, also refurbished and polished, drove off in the carriage to meet Cissa's train, leaving me to drift from window to window and watch for his return. After a seemingly endless time I saw the grays turn into the drive and dash to a stop by the steps. Cissa had arrived. Only a cyclone could have produced a hubbub comparable to the arrival of Cissa and her guests. And Lem who had departed to meet them proudly, erect and correct on his box, was returning a man caught in the path of that cyclone, crushed under an avalanche of baggage, hat boxes, wilted bouquets and fluttering handkerchiefs. His passengers, a confusion of hats and coats and whirling skirts, springing from the carriage almost before it stopped, swooping on Miss Camilla like a flock of chattering sparrows.

While they clustered about her, rapturously proclaiming that she was a love to have them—and what a love of a place Atlanta was, what a love of a house, and what a love of a gown she wore—I stood and watched from the veranda. To my dazzled eyes they were wonderful, the most wonderful girls in the world; and when Miss Camilla ushered them up the steps and drew me forward to meet them, I knew that I was the homeliest. Conscious, as I stammered "How do you do" to each, that their bright birdlike eyes appraised and dismissed me. Then Miss Camilla was saying, "It's time you two met. Cissa . . . this is Jessica. And this, Jessica . . . is my prodigal daughter, Cissa."

On the verge of speaking to one of her companions, she turned at her mother's voice to give me a quick glance and automatic smile. "Oh of course! I'd forgotten that you were here—though Mama wrote me."

I hoped to put into my smile my wish to be friends but my greeting—I had heard so much about her, I had wanted to know her—was halting and schoolgirlish. I was not surprised when she murmured, "How sweet of you," and whirled gracefully but firmly away. Not to join her friends who gathered around Miss Camilla, but standing apart, watching their fawning homage to her mother with a faintly scornful smile as if she found them amusing. She was, I perceived, the most stylish, the most perfectly poised of the four; yet she had at the same time a wistful childlike quality that was somehow heartbreaking. The word "pretty," which fitted the flesh-and-blood attractiveness of her friends, did not apply to her; nor did the word "beautiful" occur to me. With her slim silverness, her reckless changeling eyes and scornful mouth, she might have belonged to a less earth-bound race; a snow queen out of an old folk tale magically created from frostgleam and snow sparkle, moonglow and fern shadow into the semblance of mortal; giving allegiance to some Prince of Darkness who reigned in darkness beneath an enchanted hill. But the snow queen was replaced a moment later by a shameless imp.—At a remark made by one of the others, she suddenly yelled, "Spearmint kid, you know me!" throwing them into gales of hysterical laughter, though why I did not know. Nor did I ever learn why, though throughout the holidays the meaningless phrase, repeated on every and all occasions, invariably caused an explosion of shrieking laughter.

A house occupied by an army could not be thrown into turmoil comparable to that of a house occupied by four young ladies. An army would observe routine. The young ladies observed none. An army would rise and retire and have meals, but not so young ladies. They slept half the day and stayed up all night. And they were constantly on the move. Moving out the front door to go to this or that party. Moving in the front door to change and go to another. They moved upstairs and down to the telephone and from it. To the bathroom and back, unable to move so much as a foot without calling back to each other messages of such vital importance they could not wait. When not on the move or absent from home, they lounged on their beds in frilly wrappers, devouring the boxes of chocolates sent from Nunnally's by various beaux, their low-voiced confidences punctuated by screams of laughter.

However, in one particular they were not unlike the army. They demanded unceasing service and accepted as natural that they receive it. The dresses that had to be pressed, the trays that must be prepared. The telephones that had to be answered, the sashes that had to be tied. The candy papers and handkerchiefs, the scarves, fans and flowers which must be retrieved from wherever they dropped them, the beds that had to be made after each session of lounging. The sandwiches made when they went out each night, and left on their bedside table. The devastation they left in the house as they swept through it. So politely they prated their thanks to Drusilla and Miss Ad and Mitty. Not to me. For eagerly the first day or two I also had served, pressed dresses as they unpacked; later when they got into ruffled wrappers and lounged on the bed took them a bounteous tea tray. Thought as I worked: Now we will get to be friends. And seeing the tray as I entered the bedroom, they did call me a pet and a love and exclaimed they were "simply starving" and how did I ever guess? . . . then promptly forgot me. After a little I went out of the door and closed it, but not quick enough; for I heard the voice and the question. "But, Cissa, who is she? She's really terribly pretty . . ."

Swiftly I walked down the hall to avoid Cissa's answer, but again not swiftly enough. "Oh, she's nobody—" How lightly and clearly she said it. "Mama's forever taking in some stray or other. . . ."

The careless words and the careless voice followed me down the hall and I knew as never before I had known the terrible strength of shame. Once those who had scorned me mattered but little; though I often had been lonely and hurt, I had not deeply cared. But now I cared. I had dreamed—foolishly, God knows—of friendship with Cissa, and of course Cissa's friends; of being one of them—belonging. I could not delude myself that they did not matter or that I did not care. I cared and, caring, knew fully the power and horrible authority shame holds over his victims.

For a long time I sat in my room, bitter and filled with self-pity. Then, happening to think of Andrew, I was suddenly contrite. Was this being like Andrew, steadfast and uncomplaining? Andrew who would call my failure to make friends just another "contingency" and trust it to work itself out? Smiling and no longer bitter, I left my room, and went down the back stairs to the service telephone in the pantry and, first making sure that no one observed, I found Poteat & Whidby's number and called it; and asked for Mr. Andrew Hardee, wondering as I waited what on earth I could say when he came; and able to think of nothing.

His voice, cheerful and twinkly somehow like his eyes, said "Hello" and waited and said it again, and like a silly I stood there as silent as if I were struck dumb. He called to somebody nearby, "Phil, did you say the call was for me?" And after another unanswered hello, "There seems to be nobody on. Well—they'll call back if they really want me," and I heard the receiver go click. And smiling I went back to my room, thinking how cheerful he sounded and how much like himself.

It was in an Andrew-like frame of mind that I went downstairs to wait in the living room for announcement of dinner. But my change of attitude toward the other girls who had preceded me was, I fear, strictly female. For the warmth of my admiration, I found, had dropped several degrees. Not for Cissa; my conviction that Cissa was the loveliest, wittiest and most charming of girls was unchanged. But toward her three guests, who clustered about the piano and looked over some sheet music, I had definitely chilled. The titian-haired empress Lucinda from Alabama, called Cindy for short, was not, I discovered, the devastating creature I had believed her to be. Her use of the broad A even in such words as the name of her native state and banana, which earlier I had considered distinguished, now was only absurd. The small girl Flo made me think less of a dancing kitten—to which I before had compared her—than a cat. And the dark quiet girl Clare with the tragic eyes was not, I realized, the victim of a sad love affair but probably bilious.

Only Cissa remained as first I had seen her. Snow queen and magic. Even now as she stood by the fire, the small scornful smile on her lips, I saw her not perhaps as she was; but as a small lonely child trailing her ball gowns in the turret room of the summerhouse.

It was then that Wes entered the hall and, handing his suitcase to smiling, white-coated Lem, careless, with hands in his pockets, sauntered into the room. The three girls at the piano plunged like three wild horses to meet him, the titian-haired Cindy actually throwing her arms about him with "Wes, you old crazy! And handsomer than ever, you scamp!"

Shocked, I glanced quickly at Wes, certain he too would be shocked, and perceived with surprise that he rather seemed to enjoy it. Laughing, he stood among them, said the usual things, while small kittenish Flo clung to his arm and fluttered her lashes, in baby talk asked if "bad Wes" had missed her. He assured her with face perfectly solemn that he spent the third Wednesday of each month crying in his licker, he missed her so much, and the others simply shrieked in laughter. Not that he was at all witty, at least in my estimation. Had he merely recited the alphabet they would have laughed just as hard, silly things. Then Flo, clinging once more to his arm, recalled a house party that had been "too simply divine" and really such loads of fun—though he had been a "bad boy." She shook her finger under his nose as she scolded, "Wes Carrebee, it's just an old miracle I've got any reputation at all."

He drawled, "Oh, I hear you've got more than ever, that it reaches even to Memphis. . . ."

With feigned fury she began to berate him, her small fist pounding his arm. "You're just a low-down old . . ." She halted to grope for a word but before she could find it, Cissa, who had watched with the small scornful smile, moved forward and interrupted.

"If you're angling to get Wes back on your line, Flo"—the clear, lilting voice was lazy and edged with a secret laughter—"it's another lost cause. He's Callie Peacock's private property now; with her 'No Trespassing' sign hung on him."

There was challenge in her voice, or at least so I thought, and I wondered whom she challenged or why. Neither Flo nor Wes seemed to catch it, or at least failed to betray doing so. For Flo wheeled to face Wes, her fluttering eyes stilled and incredulous. "You're not really serious, are you? About Callie Peacock I mean. Why, Wes, you've known her for ages! Everyone has . . ."

He smiled but his eyes were cool under his dark quirking brows. "Perhaps that's why I'm serious, Flo. I've known her for ages. It has its points, you know. Especially when what I know is all good."

Cissa, gracefully swirling, cried lightly, "Don't let him fool you, Flo. I don't know the bait Callie used on her line to get him but I'll never believe it was goodness. Not that I blame her. He's a taking rascal, I have to admit, even if I'm his sister. . . ."

Wes leaned on the piano and watched her as he would watch a star on the stage. "You don't mention that I have a kind heart," he offered lazily.

"I don't need to, darling. It speaks for itself—through Callie. It must have been ghastly for her, poor dear. Out such a long time and all the girls she came out with married and raising families. I'm so glad that at last . . . even if it had to be you . . ." Head tilted and eyes bright with malice, she added, "I'll probably end up by marrying Syl Crowley for the very same reason. . . ."

The name she called was strange to me but obviously not to the Three Graces, for the shriek they sent up testified that they not only knew him but the knowledge was somewhat unsavory. But Wes remained undisturbed. His "Why not?" was amiable. "He's rich as all get-out. And pretty damned shrewd. Collects his nigger rents with one hand, sells 'em Kink Out with the other. . . ."

"What difference, my pet, if niggers or mules or lintheads? As long as it makes enough money. You can't have the world and a whitewashed fence around it to boot. Or can you?"

He said sharply, "Are you hinting that I give a damn about Callie's money . . . ?"

"But I'm not, Wes." She faced him, eyes wide and childishly sweet. "I know Callie will take just wonderful care of you."

"She will at that," he said briefly. Then his eyes, roving idly, happened on me in my corner. "Come to think of it"—he spoke carelessly still—"better than anyone would . . . except maybe Doc. . . ."

Apparently no one heard my furiously beating heart though it would not have surprised me; for Cissa, starting to move away, turned back to regard him, puzzled. "Doc?" she repeated. "Who do you mean by Doc?"

Straight-faced, he said, "My doctor, of course."

Slowly she said, "You've never been sick in your life. You don't need a doctor." Her eyes narrowed. "You're a case all right, but no doctor will be able to cure you."

Lem sounded the dinner gong and Miss Camilla came down the stairs and led us in to the table. While the chattering voices spun their mingled yarns of this or that or the other, I sat quietly and, deep in thought, hardly heard it. I could not figure why Wes did not tell Cissa who "Doc" was. She would have known that for me to be Doc was not to be taken seriously. If my obdurate heart had leaped when he called the name that he alone had for me, I knew it was said only in fun.

Yet as I braided my hair that night and got into bed, we agreed—my heart and my head—that what to Wes had seemed fun, we did not think funny at all.

Confusion reigned in the house and all in the house must serve it lest it overwhelm and submerge us. A constant stream of what Mitty called "Comers" and "Goers" entered or left through the front door calling "Hi" or " 'By" like gay birds of passage. Flocks of strange young men descended upon us and like locusts devoured the mountains of food and rivers of punch that constantly appeared from the kitchen, where Eula, weary and sullen, threatened to quit and Drusilla wept into the dishpan. Miss Camilla continued to go to the mill and work in her second-floor office, appearing only for dinner, when she would turn on her charm like a faucet. Dinner over, she told them fondly they didn't wish to be bothered with an old woman and over their protests fled to her "office," getting her own desire by pretending to yield to theirs. Entranced, they called her "a brick" and "a peach," and "a wonderful mother" in a mounting chorus of praise, until Cissa stopped it with "Spearmint kid, you know me," and the invariable spasms of laughter.

I too retreated when I could and slipped up to my room to read, perhaps just to putter; take a bath, wash my hair, thread fresh ribbons in my corset covers. And though the music and voices floating up from below perhaps stirred the wish to be dancing and gay, reason warned it was not to be had by wishing. Then Mitty would come in and start to talk, and first thing I knew I was laughing.

It was on one of the nights when I sat alone that Miss Camilla tapped on the door and came in, a dress box under her arm. "Ah, just as I thought! Sitting up here by yourself." Before I could speak she rushed on. "Well maybe you're smart at that. It's Bedlam downstairs. I thought if I had to hear Flo Henry giggle just one more time . . ." As she talked she cut the string on the box and took off its top. "This just came . . . I wanted to see . . ." She broke off to lift something pale-green and silky from the box and, shaking it out, held it before me. "I had Mrs. Bonner make it. She sews for the very best people and makes the loveliest things. Well . . . do you like it?"

I liked it, I said. It was lovely. "But, Miss Camilla . . . you shouldn't."

"Now don't think you have to feel grateful. To me anyway. Mr. Poteat told me to get it. There'll be occasions at Vestal Hall when you'll want to dress up a little. Here . . . hang it up in your closet."

I hung the green dress in the closet and turned back to the room. She sat on the side of my bed, a lighted match to a cigarette. She glanced at my incredulous face and threw back her head, her laugh husky and infectious. "I'll vow, Jess, if you'd found me with a gun at my head you couldn't look more horrified."

I said, "But I didn't know—"

"Well, I do and have moreover for years. On the sly of course."

I asked doubtfully, "But—do you like them?"

"I certainly do. But then," she added mischievously, "I come from a family of tobacco fiends. My mother used snuff along with almost every other Southern woman of that day. Picked it up from the colored help. They never admitted it, of course. Papa and Mama were married for thirty years and he died without finding it out. She ordered it by the case in our cook's name from some place in Virginia."

"But how all that time and your father not know? Didn't they dip it with a sort of brush?"

"The crackers and niggers did. Not the nice people. They put a pinch in their bottom lip. Mama was never without one until time for Papa to get home. Then she'd scrub her teeth and chew cloves. I used to wish Papa would catch her. She was thoroughbred stock. Big South Carolina plantation and all that—lost in the war of course. Papa was middle-class from across the tracks. But with more get up and get in his little finger than you'd find in the Ravenals, whole kit and boodle." She leaned and thrust the stump of her cigarette into one of Mitty's small pots of flowers placed in my room to "brighten it up."

"Don't give me away to Mitty," she warned. "I'm sure she'd have me arrested." When she settled back on the bed and said, "Jessica," the tone of her voice had changed.

"Yes, ma'am . . ."

"I want you to tell me why you stick up here by yourself when there's fun going on downstairs." Then, as I started to speak, "Now don't tell me you like it better, for I won't believe it. I expect those insufferable brats—and I'm including Cissa and Wes—haven't made things too pleasant for you."

Earnestly I denied this. It was myself, I said, that made it—well, uncomfortable for myself. That I still had to learn not to be shy. It made me awkward and clumsy and unable to join in the fun. So I decided I would rather be uncomfortable in my room in a comfortable sort of way than be so thoroughly uncomfortable as I knew I would be downstairs.

While she listened she drew another cigarette from inside her shirtwaist, lit it and smoked until I was finished. Then she said flatly she didn't believe me but she also knew that I would be drawn and quartered before I told tales, and she liked that. She liked it very much. Just the same, she knew how selfish and self-centered young people could be. Cissa for instance. She had written Cissa frankly that the mill wasn't doing so well . . . that it took more of her time than ever. "And Cissa brings three lazy wenches home and spoils everybody's Christmas. Moreover, all of 'em looking down their noses at you. Don't think it doesn't make my blood boil."

"Not Wes," I said quickly. "Wes . . . he couldn't have been nicer."

She gave me a long, deep look. "He has?" she asked. She continued to stare at me thoughtfully, then nodded gravely. "Wes is a very discerning young man." After a little she added, "Now I want you to plan to come down to the New Year's party. And wear the new dress. And let me tell you something, young lady." Her square dimpled hand reached and lifted my chin. "Don't let those silly girls intimidate you. You are quite a girl. Intelligent, pretty and, best of all, a good head on your shoulders." She tilted her head to survey me with narrowed eyes. "We must be sure that it isn't wasted."

Dressed for the party, I stood before my mirror and was suddenly glad that I had decided to go. And if I wished the new dress might have been less schoolgirlish, still I had to admit it was lovely, its pale-green tint becoming. I was confident that the girl who returned my gaze from the glass could hold her own anywhere; and I felt a glow of excitement as I went toward the stairs. It heightened when I looked down at the scene below me. I caught the gleam of shining floors cleared for dancing, the punch bowl in a corner with Lem, white-coated and proud, presiding; the clatter of gay voices; and I seemed to float down the stairs against the rising thrum of the famous Mr. Frederick Wurm's orchestra.

At the foot of the stairs, the cluster of early guests in the hall dissolved, revealing Cissa who stood in their midst. Cissa laughing and gleaming in a gown all white and silver that stripped my pale green of all charm, made it prim, unexciting and dull. How different Cissa's dress! Not made of earthly material like the dresses of mortals but of sparkling frost spun by unearthly hands to Cissa's quicksilver figure.

She was more snow queen than ever, I thought. More startlingly breathtaking and lovely. Beside her, all others were dimmed to no more than colorless shades. The Three Graces were safe, ordinary and human, though in the grandest of party gowns they were far more imposing than I. Moreover they had donned with their gowns a fashionably world-weary manner. Their tolerant smiles, their languor, their gently cynical laughter suggested that they had been everywhere and seen everything and nothing was left worth experiencing. Life henceforth could offer only a procession of dull anticlimaxes. It struck me as inconceivable that creatures so experienced and so worldly-wise and so bored with that world could in any conceivable circumstance ever have cried, "Spearmint kid, you know me!"

Only those who endure it know the effort it takes to be at a party but not of it; to stand idle and partnerless this place or that, yet look like the belle of the ball. The punch consumed in order to appear less idle; afterward, awash with punch, floating about the table with its platters and platters of food.

As I sipped and nibbled and tried to look very festive, I pondered over the young men who constantly strolled, despite the cold night, out to the porch and back again, returning a little more flushed, a little more gay, at each sally. As if on the porch they partook of a magic potion. Taken perhaps, like my punch, to give time that seemed so empty the illusion of fullness.

There was a limit however to time spent at punch bowl and table. I withdrew to a strategic wall, out of the path of the dancers yet not so close to one of the clustering groups that I might appear to intrude. Standing against this wall with—I hoped—graceful, nonchalant ease, I held my vivacious smile and looked brightly over the room. Over heads and between them, but careful not to look at them lest they think it a plea for attention.

Shifting from wall to wall, always gay and poised and expectant, I kept up my pretense of waiting for a mythical beau-retriever. But after a number of moves I found my pose more and more wearing. My bright expectant expression felt as stiff as a plaster mask. The effort required not to glance at young men who passed without girls on their arms took more and more self-control. More difficult still was control of my eyes—and persistent heart—when Wes and Callie danced by, her face possessive and triumphant, seeming so at home on his shoulder!

The penalties a party extracted were, I decided, too heavy to willingly pay. I would retreat to my room and be miserable in comfort.

Touching my hair, my skirt, I braced my courage for my ignominious retreat to the stairs. But I was granted reprieve. Someone touched my arm, someone said, "Will you dance this with me?" and it was Wes. Wes standing before me, Wes wearing his formal clothes with less formality than any man present, Wes who asked me to dance; and I could only look at him blankly, unable to utter a word.

And then, as the orchestra swung into "Are You Sincere?" he led me out on the floor and . . . I was dancing with Wes. I was spinning faster and faster, my body a feather that whirled in obedience to his. My tedious wallflower waiting, my too-bright smile of defeat, my legs that had ached—and my heart—all of them gone and forgotten; for . . . I was dancing with Wes.

"Why, you're as light as a leaf, Doc," he said. "Where did you learn to dance like this?"

I explained that Oakes Carr had taught me, and he looked down at me, surprised. "So you know Oakes Carr," he said. "Doc, I'm surprised."

When I asked him why, he laughed as he shook his head. "Damned if I know. It just never occurred to me . . . that you had a past."

I began, "Everyone has—" then remembered that on the subject of pasts I had little to offer. I told him, instead, of Laura Lee and a little of Mrs. Plummer's. He knew of the school, he said. It stood across from Segadlos, where he'd gone to many a dance. How strange, I thought, if on one of the nights that I watched, Wes had been one of those dancing. Strange and somehow mysterious. Then—as far apart as our two separate worlds. Now—I was dancing with Wes. He was talking and,

I realized, talking of Mr. Carr: Everyone called him Holy Carr, he spouted so much about virtue. He found it hard to believe that his son even knew how to dance, much less teach it.

"He didn't teach you to dance like this," he accused.

I said, "You make me dance well," and wished the words back as I said them. But taking them at face value, he asserted that he could neither make a silk purse from a sow's ear or a dancing leaf from a millstone.

Holding me off as we whirled, he surveyed and appraised me. "In that dress you look like a leaf. A young one that comes out in the spring. You're not old enough for a summer one."

"Nor gay enough for fall," I suggested.

He replied, teasing, "You don't strike me as the gay sort or a serious do-or-die, either."

That he had thought of me in any possible way, once would have made me dizzy with joy. But I was not dizzy now. For I was aware that dancing, he held me close but no closer than he would hold any girl, not as close as he had held Callie. But, for the moment, I cared nothing for Callie. I cared for nothing. For—I was dancing with Wes.

We danced and somehow it didn't matter when his next words revealed that he had seen through my stiff, smiling pretense and in pity asked me to dance.

"First parties are pretty dull," he remarked. "You'll go to better ones before long."

"Will I?" I asked, and he nodded.

"Wait 'til some of these young whippersnappers wake up and take a good look at you," he advised. "You'll get such a rush you'll give old man Wes the go-by."

"Do you think they'll ever wake up and take a look?" I asked.

He glanced down at me, his eyes smiling, amused. "Don't worry, Doc," he reassured. "They'll look. They're a little young yet to get their eyes open. Like puppies, you know. But they'll grow up pretty fast."

"Like you?" I taunted, then was afraid he'd be angry, but he threw his head back and laughed.

"God forbid! I'm the most backward case of all. Some say pretty damned hopeless."

I was dancing with Wes and then, suddenly, I was dancing with Wes no longer. He no longer held me, we no longer swayed to the music. The music had stilled, the dance was done; the orchestra leader shuffled his scores, the bald violinist mopped the pink dome of his head. With Wes sauntering beside me we left the floor, and it was then I saw how Callie, laughing and chatting with others, followed Wes with eyes that were watchful.

Wes did not see her, however. Halting, he looked with frowning surprise at a late guest just arriving. As he was welcomed by Cissa the stranger bowed over her hand, and continued to hold it, smiling down at the taunting face that turned confidingly up to his. He was rather distinguished in a strange sort of way, almost handsome, yet with something about him not pleasing, though what I could not have said.

I asked Wes, "Who is he?" and, abstracted, he answered, "Crowley. Syl Crowley."

Though the name was familiar it was a moment before I remembered that I had heard it from Cissa as the name of the man she had teasingly threatened to marry. I had not believed her to be serious then, and now that belief was confirmed. For Mr. Crowley was an old man; he must have been at least forty. Though he had a certain distinction in a lean, hard sort of way, his pale waxen face with its thin blade of a nose and thin tight mouth was wrong somehow and displeasing, even a little frightening. To imagine that Cissa would marry his kind was too much for the wildest fancy. And seeing the confiding, almost intimate, way she slipped her slim arm under his black-sleeved one, I wondered what game she played at now.

Wes, still beside me, drawled, "I guess I'd better see that Mr. Crowley is taken care of," and I watched him stroll carelessly across the room to shake hands with the gentleman. Then the orchestra started again, the couples moved out to dance, and in the whirling and swirling they were shut from my view.

I returned to a wall and a vacant chair and for a little I watched the dancers. With time it grew rather confusing. Or perhaps it was I, weary and sleepy, who was confused. The dancers blurred, the music clashed in a tuneless crash, and my head began to ache. Midnight arrived and the brand-new year of 1907 was noisily greeted with a blare of horns and ruffle of drums, the usual shouts and hurrahs. And of course with "Auld Lang Syne."

It was the repetition of the song perhaps (though as a song I had nothing against it) that made me decide finally and irrevocably that I would go to bed. I went, not through the maze of shouting and singing guests who blocked the path to the stairway, but escaped through the small side room that would land me in the pantry.

I did not dream as I entered the room that it might be occupied. Seldom used, it was dark except for the faint glow that came from a door left ajar, and only vaguely I saw the large, deep chair and not the figure that huddled within it; or heard through the distant singing, Callie's racking, heartbroken sobbing. The strangled, hopeless weeping of grief and despair and defeat.

My foot struck a small footstool and she lifted her face, a pale shape of grief in the dimness, her eyes wide and unseeing like the unseeing eyes of the blind. "Get out," she ordered harshly; and then, aware of her rudeness—as if it mattered—she said, her voice contrite, "Please get out. Please leave me alone. . . ."

I wished I might stay and give her whatever comfort I could, but misery gave her power impossible not to obey. So, closing the door behind me, I left and went on my way to the pantry stairs and to my room and to bed. I did not know the reason why Callie had cried. But I did know the hurt had been deep, and I wondered if Wes, who could make her flame with triumph, inflicted the hurt. Surely if she cried for some other cause, he would have been beside her.

But Wes, I thought, wasn't there. She had wept in the dark alone and I felt no gladness at this as once I had thought that I would. I could not be glad for so much hurt or grief even if by it I gained. For I would never forget how she cried, I thought as I got into bed and turned out the light. It even seemed to sound in the room, that strangled, desperate weeping. And its unhappy ghost sobbed on and haunted my dreams.

Vestal Hall! What a grave, studious, scholarly front its ivy-clad buildings, tall and white-columned, turned to the world. How convincingly it conveyed to the world the impression of earnest young faces bent over books, of young minds drinking in knowledge. How hushed its very air. And how inconceivable to suppose that a voice might be raised, a door slammed, or a strident young laugh ring out to desecrate the quiet where young minds quested for learning.

How extensive the preparations made for learning at Vestal Hall. The classrooms and teachers and pupils; the books and blackboards and chalk, the pencils and paper and erasers; the pianos for music, the laboratory for science, the maps and the charts and the graphs. What stupendous equipment for learning where nothing was ever learned.

How reverent my feet that first morning as they traversed (quietly, of course) the spaces of hall! How awed my eyes as they surveyed Professor Murphy across his desk as he suggested the courses I take. How ungrateful I felt when I refused a course in Geology (which he taught) and selected a course in Modern Design instead, though I had no idea what was to be gained from Modern Design except escape from Geology. How desperately I retraced the spaces of hall to my room where, sitting on my bed, I looked at my curriculum and wondered how English and History and Math and Elocution would fit me to make my way.

Yet some things I did learn at Vestal Hall. From morning chapel conducted by Miss Ebbett, a well-bred woman with a voice like a raven, I learned how the Vestal Hall young ladies should conduct themselves. From her I learned too the dangers that lay in wait for young ladies from monsters who, lurking under the guise of MALES, waited to ravish females in general and Vestal Hall young ladies in particular. This perhaps accounted for their absorption in the subject of males, which surpassed by far their interest in all other subjects—in fact, was the only subject in which they evinced any interest whatever.

What else did I learn? —I learned from Doctor Posey, the president, frock-coated and mousy, a draketail of hair over his collar, that Vestal

Hall young ladies must have "cha'c'ter." And that the way to have it—was to have it. The way *not* to have it was to think about boys or look at boys or turn your head when boys whistled; especially the boys who worked in the cotton mills on the edge of the town.

Where were the studious young minds of my fancy, questing for knowledge? Certainly not among the two hundred talking, screeching pupils I moved among who devoted hours to the discussion of males and hair styles; of males and fashions; of males and food—but never, never of books. Who were constantly quarreling and making up, who whispered and giggled and had "midnight feasts," who made fun of the teachers and disparaged the food and regarded the students who attempted to be studious with the contempt bestowed on a traitor. Yet from this giggling horde I did learn. How to choose clothes that were beau-catchers, how to wear my hair, how to send a man a "come-hither" look. Even as I wrote Andrew that I feared I had learned nothing of value at Vestal Hall, I knew I had learned. But I did not tell Andrew that.

What a scrambling, confusing, noisy half term it was, with my class in Modern Design the only oasis. Here—being the only pupil to have chosen Modern Design (taught by Professor Kerlich)—I at least knew quiet again. Listening to Professor Kerlich, I began to realize the magic of color. His pale eyes gazing out the window, he talked of the eye for color that sees beyond color—of Pissarro, Seurat, Gauguin—of the science of color, how when each color assumes its place in the whole, the artist reaches the control of a musician who has mastered the character of each instrument in the orchestra.

Much that he said was confusing, or so I thought. But later his words would return and render me useful service; so those two things at least I learned at Vestal Hall. The magic of color and how to choose beau-catcher clothes.

When I stepped off the train at Atlanta's Terminal Station, feeling fine as the June day in my new tan suit and sailor hat with the darling green feather, I found Andrew waiting to meet me. He too looked downright distinguished in a new suit, and his good-humored face was as friendly as always, as he answered my questions all the way home.

Mitty and Miss Ad waited on the veranda when we turned in Miss Camilla's drive, and while Andrew carried my bag to the porch I dashed ahead to hug them, aware with a pang of dismay what little armfuls they made. Then, laughing and watery-eyed, I introduced them to Andrew and they, speaking, as it were, through Mitty, insisted that he must stop for a glass of iced tea. Lem, who had to drive into town on an errand, would take Andrew along, Mitty said. So he could dismiss the cab and "set" awhile.

Miss Camilla, they said, was at the mill. But in the house I received warm welcome from Lem and Drusilla and Eula; the last exclaiming in a spontaneous burst of amazement that I had "gloried out like a sizzling bum"—which meant, Mitty explained, a skyrocket.

On the side porch, where the wisteria was in bud and where bees were having a preliminary look at the silvery-yellow frills that would eventually be white and lavender torches, Eula brought our iced tea and an "oven-fresh" cake. When Mitty and Miss Ad had settled us into chairs, we had our tea and cloud-light cake and chattered away, Miss Ad and Andrew content to drift on the current of talk that flowed between Mitty and me, listening with smiles and nods to prove they remained afloat.

Mitty had never met Andrew so she did not know of his quietness, and when she realized that he had little to say, she gave him a glance of concern. Mitty firmly believed in the benefits of good talk and encouraged others to share it by what she called "warming them up." As if they were kettles and must be "at boil" to be happy.

The glint in her eye told me that Andrew was in for a warming-up on the spot—and he was. Being Andrew, the result fell short of a furious boil but attained an agreeable simmer. For with the profession of law as a starter, Mitty plunged into talk of writs and injunctions, mandamuses and habeas corpus with the familiarity of one whose entire life has been entangled with law. And when Andrew left to ride into town with Lem, they were like friends of long standing. When he told me good-by he spoke of her. "All wool and a yard wide," he said.

"To tell the truth," he added, "it eases my mind to know she's on hand to look after things at this end."

"At this end?" I was doubtful.

"I mean," he explained, "in case of a contingency. Just as I keep an eye on things at the other end," he added, "along with Poteat & Whidby. It means that somebody," he finished, "is keeping an eye on both ends."

I went to my room and found Mitty unpacking for me, and I kissed and hugged her all over again, then asked how she liked my friend Andrew. With her hands on her hips and head on one side, she told me. "With that smile—" she informed me in the invincible manner she adopted when stating what she firmly believed, "with that smile, mark my words, that young man will go far!"

I agreed. Then as I changed from the tan suit to a cool summer frock, she brought me up to date on the Carrebee household.

Cissa, she said, had graduated at Sweetbriar but wasn't home yet, still visiting school friends up in Virginia. Miss Camilla meant to go up for the exercises but at the last minute couldn't because of the mill, where things warn't too smooth so kept her busier than ever. Wes had taken a cottage at Tybee Beach with some of the Bell House boys and was spending the summer there, more or less.

Without comment I heard that Wes was away and denied that the slight twinge I felt could possibly be regret. I was cured of my crush on Wes. The girl who had imagined a crush on Wes no longer existed.

And if the excitement of return had calmed, I ascribed it to being with Mitty again and content; and naturally settling down.

When I went downstairs before dinner Miss Camilla, just getting home, gave a gruff cry of delight when she saw me, and left me almost breathless with the warmth of her hug. It was a joy to have me back, she exclaimed.

"You'll never believe how I missed you. The house has been like a grave."

I said I was glad to be back and she ordered, "But let's have a look at you." Plump hands on my shoulders, she held me off and with critical eyes surveyed me. "Goodness! You've really grown up. Haven't you?"

"I must have," I smiled, "since everyone seems to think so."

"You have. You've shot up like a weed." Her eyes suddenly widened with that strange habit they had of seeming to look deep inside you and seeing what no other eyes saw. She said, and her voice seemed to weigh the words, "You've turned into a beauty, you know. I don't know just where the change is. Who on earth fixed your hair in that way?"

I was solely responsible, I said, because I refused to wear "rats."

Head tilted, she said that she liked it. "Plain but rather distinguished. And at least not with a million puffs like every other head of hair."

"Mr. Poteat," she called over her shoulder, "come see what Vestal Hall did for this young lady. We've a beauty on our hands."

From the hall he called back, "Coming," as he handed his coat and hat to Lem. Then Mr. Poteat came into the room and crossing, bowed gallantly over my hand. His beautiful voice said, as I knew it would say, "Miss Camilla was right. Vestal Hall has done well"—and I thinking that he had aged, that he looked neither happy nor well.

Miss Camilla at dinner talked of the mill, of the shiftless and lazy "lintheads." At her comments, caustically gay, the contempt in her voice, I felt a stir of resentment. Why were the millworkers so despised—not just by Miss Camilla, but by everyone? Still, she was kind to me, and I could not doubt her kindness to others—even her "shiftless lintheads."

When the conversation lagged and Mr. Poteat turned to his wine, Miss Camilla sat silent, her eyes narrow and thoughtful. Lifting my eyes from my plate, I caught hers fixed on my face. As if in it she found some answer she was seeking. Meeting my eyes, she did not shift hers as if I had caught her staring. She accepted my glance with one warm and completely disarming. And though the idea persisted that her thoughts had been upon me, I was wholly convinced that they had been kind—and no doubt concerned my own good.

How different the days of this summer from the summer days I had known. How astonishing that the hours that once seemed to drag on heavy and leaden feet should dance blithely by and so lightly I am hardly aware of their passing.

Who would dream, I muse, that the attractive young lady in the sheer summer frock who dines at a candlelit table is the same nondescript girl who this time last year cooked in Mrs. Plummer's silent kitchen? Who would dream that the girl declared by Miss Camilla to be "lovely and clever and with such excellent taste" is the same who last year was deemed less than nothing? And the fashionably clad young lady who with Miss Camilla goes to call on Atlanta's best people, the same girl who last year was called "bastard"?

We called on the Old Guard, who, it was said, "stood for something," though I never heard what; unless for the lost and irrecoverable past. Now they carried no more weight in Atlanta's affairs than they gained at their genteel, frugal tables.

Because of family connections, the Old Guard forgave Miss Camilla for marrying a carpetbagger and joining the commercial New South—liabilities which to the owners of coal yards, the manufacturers of iron stoves or hair-kink remover were assets. They had taken a leaf from the book of the enemy as well as possessing the Yankee talent for trade and knowingness with a dollar. Their parlors bore no resemblance to those of the Old Guard. They were sumptuous and overfurnished and gleaming with gold leaf and crystal, and they smelled not of moth-eaten tradition but of money.

There was still another circle where Miss Camilla was greeted with awe because she was Southern, her family had once owned slaves, and her family name was as familiar as a page from history. This was the Yankee circle. Its membership included families of men stationed in Atlanta by Northern interests to manage enterprises owned by Yankee stockholders and to insure that profits winged steadily northward so those who received dividends might winter in Florida. They were from Boston, Philadelphia and New York. They were, I discovered, the most Southern of all Southerners. They used colloquial expressions constantly, they defended Southern prejudices and attitudes, they spoke harshly of Negroes. They were amusing—and often irritating. There was the recital by one of this circle on the subject of grits. "Can you all imagine—Henry just won't come to the table unless there's a little old dish of grits. And as for black-eyed peas—"

My mind became a storehouse of names without faces to fit them and faces with no names attached. However, as time passed I began to put faces and names together and brought order out of confusion; then with Cissa's arrival was plunged into further confusion. By the dozens of young men who each Sunday afternoon came to call. Descending upon us in droves like vagrant and restless blackbirds that lighted to eat and drink and winged their way to their next stopping place.

The first time or two this happened, I believed it was Cissa who drew them and I marveled that beaux drawn by her charm came in droves like bees drawn to honey. Cissa herself pointed out that I was mistaken. Sunday afternoon calls, she said, were an old Southern custom that had less to do with charm than with food. The beaux, she said dryly, like sparrows, went where crumbs were the most plentiful, and the charm that drew them to "us" was Miss Ad's chicken salad and Lem's freezer of ice cream.

Whatever the charm, each Sunday afternoon the place was thronged with young people, the young men lured by the food, the girls, Cissa said dryly, by the young men. We played the gramophone, and feeling incredibly wicked—it being Sunday—we danced. We gossiped, we flirted, we quarreled and made up. We were often absurd, as young people too old to be children and too young to be adult have always been and will always be.

There was a great deal of love dished up with the chicken salad the young men consumed, and as with chicken salad they were ready for a new dish each Sunday. To one like myself who had regarded love as a rare and priceless commodity this at first proved disturbing. But I realized that they were only playing at love, like young birds teetering on the edge of the nest with a great flapping of wings in preparation for actual flight.

How amazing the intangible thing popularity! How difficult to acquire before you have it; once acquired, how simple its acquisition seems to have been. How astonishing to learn that popularity begins as almost everything does, in a small way, but handled rightly grows rapidly. Popularity with males follows this universal law. One young man is attracted to you for a reason entirely devoid of logic. It may be because your hair waves nicely or because it is straight as a stick. Because you toe in or toe out, because you are a "nice dancer" or can't dance a step. Whatever the reason, if the first young man remarks to other young men, "Some peacherino," your popularity is assured. The first young man may be a silly young man whose opinion carries little weight on other subjects, but on the subject of peacherinos he is not to be scorned.

The beaux came, pomade on hair and with shoes newly shined, in twos, then fours, then eights; for popularity multiplies not by simple progression but by squares. I was second to none in my conquests—not even to Cissa. For while she was exquisite, they had known Cissa for years. They sensed no doubt as I did that Cissa, if you drew too near, would cry "Don't touch" as she fled.

However, she came to accept me, and if not as "Best Friend" at least as a convenient companion. We did our nails together or shampooed our hair, planned elaborate wardrobes that never went further than planning and, being female, discussed as a matter of course the subject of men. We spent a great deal of time and breath on this subject. I do not deny my interest in men, not only as a topic of conversation but also as—well, as men. I did not object to a "date" with a young man. Nor did I object in the least to numerous dates with numerous young men of various shapes, dispositions and sizes.

I had for instance a date with a shy young man, a gulping young man with large ears who, it was said, wrote poetry in secret.

I also had a date with The Cynical Young Man, a young man who knew everything about everybody and none of it good. The Young Man With An Eye To The Future appeared, with three newly sharpened pencils in his breast pocket and notebook always at hand. He was replaced in time by The Sporty Young Man, The Young Man Who Was Kind To His Mother, The Brilliant Young Man, The Young Man With Ancestors. Finally and momentously, I was asked for a date by the most desirable of all the young men, The Dangerous Young Man, and braced for dangers too "awful" to mention, waited with icy hands and pounding heart the night of our date.

Though The Dangerous Young Man did not appear dangerous, I was not misled, for I had been warned by girls who *knew* that his pretense of not seeming dangerous was what made him so dangerous. When the dangerous young man was hardly civil but sat morose and glowering and even refused lemonade, though the night was warm, the signs foretold danger as plainly as the heat lightning on the horizon foretold gathering storm. And impatiently I waited for him to be dangerous.

At last the moment of danger came. The dangerous young man turned slowly and with brooding eyes looked into mine and commanded in a steely voice, "Kiss me." It was a royal command and as arrogant as if an eternal law decreed that it be obeyed. Too awed to resist eternal law (and also being curious), I kissed the dangerous young man. But as I lifted my face I made the fatal mistake of laughing.

The dangerous young man bounced to his feet and pacing the floor delivered an impassioned and bitter speech on the subject of shallow and frivolous women. Who played with hearts as if they were toys, who trampled great love in the dust, who, like mermaids, lured young men with dulcet song to destruction. He, said the dangerous young man, would not stand for it. He was warning me he would not stand for it. His temper . . . ungovernable, his will . . . like iron. The love which seemed to amuse me was a cruel love, a dangerous love when crossed or denied. A love that must master. A terrible love perhaps, but there we were. He could not change.

He finished his speech, which had consumed considerable time and shoe leather, and sat beside me again in the swing. He was, the ruthless voice said, going to kiss me. I need not struggle—and I need not think laughing would stop him. Kiss me, he would. I denied it. He insisted. I insisted he wouldn't. He accused me of leading a fellow on. I rejected the accusation. With a lunge he grabbed me and tried to hold my face in a kissing position. I turned my head. I continued to turn my head, his continued to follow. It became ridiculous and comical. And I laughed again.

The dangerous young man went home, and I went to bed. I felt that he had betrayed me. I could not forgive the dangerous young man for not being dangerous.

It was on one of the Sunday afternoons that I saw Oakes Carr again. The usual crowd of young people drifted about the grounds and porch, sang around the piano in the living room, danced to the gramophone, or clustered at the buffet.

Standing in a circle of young men all very gallant and sweet with me and stiff and sour with each other, I looked up as Oakes, just arriving, entered the room. For a second, surprised, I stood still, then called his name sharply and, murmuring excuses to the young men, went to meet him. He was no less surprised than I and for a little we could only exclaim at the changes we found in each other, then insist illogically that neither had changed, and meaning both statements sincerely. For oddly enough while Oakes was changed—he was taller and somehow seemed older—he was also exactly the same. The dark eyes—like Laura Lee's somehow—still promised when they laughed into yours the most delightful of secrets.

Now they were puzzled, not laughing. "So the peacherino I've been hearing about from the fellas . . . was you all the time? When did you come to the Carrebees'?"

I told him and his eyes were thoughtful. "You mean right after . . . ?" he began—and did not finish the question. But I knew what he meant.

I answered, "Yes. Right after—"

He said regretfully, "I wish Laura Lee could have known. She . . . we worried a lot about you. Laura Lee called old lady Plummer to ask where she could reach you. Talked through a handkerchief to disguise her voice—but didn't find out a thing. She tried to pry it out of Miss Belle . . . did you know she taught now at Mrs. Plummer's?"

I said I knew.

"Then the old man shipped us away to school. Me to Dahlonaga, Laura Lee to Normal at Milledgeville. To learn to sew and cook and keep house. And is that a scream?"

I said it was.

"She hated it like all forty. Came home for Christmas and told the old man she wouldn't go back. And by golly she didn't."

The old gleam of excitement started to light up his eyes. "She ran off and married you'll never guess who . . . Bucky."

I gasped, "Bucky? Oh, Oakes! Why did you let her?"

"Hell, Jess, how could I stop her? She wanted to spite the old man. Knew that would make him see red."

"And did it?"

"He came up with the usual. Don't darken my door—you know, right out of *Way Down East.*"

"Where is Laura Lee . . . now?"

The light died in his eyes, his face sobered. They didn't know where exactly, he said. The old man had forbidden her to write. Just the same, Laura Lee got a card to her mother now and then. Sent it to the Negro washwoman's house. She delivered it along with the wash. The cards were all from different places. The last was from Buffalo. He reckoned they were having a pretty rocky time of it.

I saw Laura Lee having a "pretty rocky" time of it and I wanted to cry. Laura Lee like a hummingbird, shackled to Bucky of the hard-fleshed face and eyes like blue marbles. Drifting from this town to that, living in one squalid room, eating—when they ate—in cheap cafés.

I said, "Oakes—your mother. How is she?"

He shrugged. "You know, I expect."

I knew, and I knew great pity. But to Oakes I said nothing of pity. Instead, as I turned to go back to the waiting young men whose eyes were sharp knives at my shoulders, I paused and told him please to remember me to his mother.

Nodding, he said that he would. He added, "She'll be glad to hear that I found you. She's asked lots of times if I had."

This, I thought, was my growing-up summer that was not in the least concerned with corsets or clothes or hairdos but was concerned with a new awareness of people, of the invisible life flowing beneath the surface of the thoughts.

This growing up was painful. Because of it I realized that Mr. Poteat's quick eyes could be bleak and unhappy, Miss Ad's lonely and unfulfilled. Even in Miss Camilla I would fleetingly catch its presence as she talked of her worries regarding the mill or brokers or worn-out machinery. She would talk of such matters to me, I knew, not because I could help them. But simply for someone to talk to and by talking perhaps ease her burdens.

Gladly I tried in small ways to give her what help I could, for it dawned upon me that there was no one on whom she could call for small but important errands which, engrossed with the mill, she was unable to do herself. Cissa never offered to help nor did Miss Camilla ask her. Cissa, like Wes, went the way that she pleased and nobody dared to obstruct it.

On a blistering July day I went downtown on one of these errands. It took me to Chamberlain Johnson's new store. In its dim and cool shadowed comfort I selected material for new curtains which would go in the morning room. Something "smart" Miss Camilla had said, "and please God no cabbage roses."

The sun had gone down behind the big old oak on the lawn when I reached Miss Camilla's, and as I turned in the driveway the air was perfumed with the sweetness of Dorothy Perkins roses. I was content with myself and a world that seemed content to swing serene in its orbit. But it was a deceptive world which, as I neared the house, lurched and whirled giddily in space. For Wes had come back; and I knew by my plunging heart that my cure had not been complete, that I was not over Wes. I had just had a relapse.

He came round the house from the side yard, wearing rumpled and grass-stained old trousers and his white shirt open at collar and with rolled-up sleeves, his face and arms deep brown from his stay at Tybee and—I thought—incredibly beautiful.

He saw me and called, "Hi, Doc!" giving me a friendly, careless wave, and I called back a greeting, hardly aware of my words. His brows lifted as he came toward me.

"Everything around the Carrebee place has blossomed out since I left," he said.

"The Dorothy Perkins are wonderful," I agreed.

His eyes looked me over. "I wasn't thinking of the Dorothy Perkins." His voice was dry.

I said, "We didn't expect you home . . . so soon. Wasn't Tybee fun?"

"It was time I got back," he said briefly, ignoring my question. "It must have been hot in town. Wouldn't you like a cool drink?"

"I would love a cool drink," I said.

We went in to find it, I trying to act as if the world were a safe ordinary world even as it swung wildly in space. I insisted, when he asked, that I wanted a tall glass of ice water, and he said he would have ice water too, but added a good deal of whiskey, explaining it was to "lay the dust."

We went out to the side porch, where the wisteria vines seemed to cut off the air, and I sank into a chair and pretended to be quietly at ease though I was filled with a tumult of excitement combined of happiness, anguish and misery, all at one and the same time.

"I hear you're the belle of Atlanta," Wes said, smiling. "That you've broken the hearts of half the young fellows in town."

"I haven't broken any hearts," I answered. "Who told you?"

Lazily he said, "Oh, I have my lines out, you know."

"Obviously they are unreliable," I accused. "You shouldn't believe them."

"I believe my own eyes," Wes said.

I recognized the old teasing note in his voice and knew that my surge of elation was absurd.

"There must be one you like best," his voice still teased.

"One of—what?"

"Of the young men who Eula swears descend on the house like the plague of locusts swooping down on old King Pharaoh's Egypt."

"They come for Miss Ad's chicken salad; and Cissa," I replied.

His eyes slanted at me. "Yeah? Eula claims they cluster around you like flies around a watermelon cutting." He shook the ice in his glass and surveyed it thoughtfully. "Besides, I hear that Cissa's been giving her time to Syl Crowley."

"Oh, he's here now and then," I discounted Syl Crowley. "He doesn't really matter to Cissa."

He gave his head a brief, noncommittal shake, his eyes scornful, and dismissed the subject. "Never mind Cissa," he said. "We were talking about your beaux. Who's on the heartline?"

"No one," I answered.

Already he was bored with the subject of my heartline for he asked about Vestal Hall. Had I liked it? I said well enough, and talked a little about Professor Kerlich's course in design. I tried to make it amusing, and he obligingly laughed at the right place but I was not convinced that I had succeeded.

He drank the last of the ice water in which he had "laid the dust" and said he'd better clean up for dinner and went up to his room; and I went to mine and leaned close to my mirror.

I was shocked to find it reflected the same face that had been there this morning, unchanged. For whatever the face betrayed or concealed, I was no longer able to pretend. I loved Wes and my pretense of not loving him was shattered and swept away.

I loved Wes and, despite the unaltered face in the mirror, I was convinced everyone would know it. As I changed for dinner to a dress of pale yellow, I knew everyone would know I wore pale yellow for Wes. I felt as if a powerful lamp had been lighted within me, that its glow must reveal my innermost secrets as the shape of a letter in an envelope is revealed when held against light.

I had read somewhere that criminals feel that their guilt must show, that this is the cause of their furtiveness, their flinching, evasive eyes. It suddenly struck me as strange that love and guilt should brand humankind with identical marks, and to love without being loved in return is like guilt that, try though you may to conceal, you always betray.

When I went downstairs I was braced to face the music and there was no music to face, though I thought that Miss Camilla glanced at me down the table curiously now and then. However, this was later. At first I found only Wes and Cissa.

As I went toward the sitting room I heard his voice and her swift, mocking drawl of laughter. She cried out when I entered.

"Jess, you should really hear Wes." Her laughter spilled over again. "He's warning me against Syl Crowley."

Wes, apparently not annoyed by her ridicule, shrugged and smiled good-humoredly. "I just tried to tell you what people think when a nice girl runs around with him. Not that nice girls do. His friendship with the other kind is too well known."

Cissa turned wide ingenuous eyes toward me. "Jess, don't you think he's being terribly moral for a young man who is so popular with so many odd—people?"

I had no intention of being drawn into their argument by Cissa and

I let her know it by shaking my head. At the same time, with a slight pang, I wondered if what she implied about Wes could be true.

In the next moment he, by his own words, seemed to admit it. "At least I don't ride around town in Pet Belleau's victoria," he retorted, "and I'm not a 'business associate' of hers."

"Maybe you should be, Wes." She pretended thoughtful concern. "Think! You could make piles of money like Syl. We could use more money, couldn't we, sweet? And you really should take an interest in some sort of business. Why not Pet Belleau's?"

Her gibe at his failure to "buckle down" was one she used often, but I was puzzled about the woman named Pet Belleau. For I knew, as everyone knew (though nice young ladies were assumed not to know), that Pet Belleau was one of "those women." That Wes might know her came, I admit, as a shock, and I was relieved when he said, "I don't know Pet Belleau." He grinned. "We've never been introduced."

Like a saucy child, Cissa surveyed him, her eyes bright with mischief. "I had no idea Pet's kind had to be introduced. But why not ask Syl to arrange it? I'm sure she's more attractive than the women we know . . . all the way down the line."

Wes straightened up and his face was hard and unsmiling. "That's enough," he said evenly, quietly. "You forget about Jess."

Cissa's laughter rocketed skyward. "Wes," she went on serenely, speaking to me and turning back to him, "is just plain old-fashioned about women. Especially me. It's really quite touching but a terrible waste of time. He knows I'll go to hell in my own way . . . just as he'll go in his."

Wes looked at her closely, coolly, and his gray eyes were glacial. "You're well on your way when you run around with Syl Crowley."

For a moment I thought he was angry. But I was wrong. For he laughed, and the sound was genuine and tolerant and amused.

"You forget, Cissa, I know you. I know how you say things to shock yet never *do* anything shocking."

Lazily Cissa asked, her voice as amused as his, "Do you really know me that well?"

His remark had flicked home, however, as I knew by the lifted head, and she instantly dropped the subject—at least, I thought, 'til the next time. For they habitually teased and bantered in a half-joking, half-serious way and, though I attached no importance to it, often I found it boring and dull. I was concerned, tonight, only with Wes.

Nevertheless, there was more dissension at dinner, though not between Cissa and Wes. This was between Cissa and Miss Camilla about Cissa's going to Europe. Listening, I gathered that Cindy, with a number of Sweetbriar girls, was making a tour of Europe under the wing of an impoverished gentlewoman, well known for *Mrs. Cooley's Cultural Old-World Tours for Distinguished Young Ladies.* It would be a wonderful trip, Cissa said, and would get her out of Atlanta, which bored her to death, and she'd see new places and people, all the marvelous old ruins in Europe. She'd have to rush like crazy, of course, for the party sailed in two weeks and, with loads of new clothes to buy—

Miss Camilla, who had listened abstractedly to Cissa's talk of the trip, broke in at this point to declare brusquely that Cissa could put going to Europe or anywhere else this summer out of her head.

"You've cost me enough at Sweetbriar this year and," Miss Camilla continued briskly, "I can't afford right now for you to go traipsing off to Europe with a lot of giggling girls. You can just stay home for a while."

"But I wrote Cindy I would . . ." Cissa began.

"Then write her again that you won't," Miss Camilla ordered.

Cissa flushed and her lovely face hardened. Coolly, she said, "I'm going, I'm going, and you can't stop me."

"Maybe not"—Miss Camilla was matter-of-fact—"but I can stop the money. So if you go to Europe or anywhere else you'd better find someone to provide it. For I won't."

She did not so much as glance at Cissa, but sat at the head of the table, her frank, friendly self, her composure calm and unruffled. If she was aware of Cissa's steady regard, she did not betray it. But I was aware—and shocked—at Cissa's eyes. They were the eyes of a snow queen still, but careless, deliberately mocking, a snow queen balked by cloddish and clumsy mortals unable to comprehend her enchanted world. When after a little she spoke, her voice was not a child's treble but tinkled like ice in a glass.

"If I don't go," the chilled voice said, "you'll be sorry."

Miss Camilla, unperturbed, turned her frank, friendly eyes down the table. "That's enough, Cissa. You can't go and that's all there is to it."

I was surprised at how swiftly Cissa recovered from both disappointment and anger. Like a changeling she swiftly veered to teasing and impish laughter, and dinner ended in a lighthearted mood.

My mood, however, was neither gay nor lighthearted. For I had just recalled that tonight I had a date—a very dull date with a dull young Mr. Carter. If fate deemed it fitting to lay Mr. Carter low with a trivial accident—a broken ankle for instance—I would not, I admitted, quibble with fate about it.

But Mr. Carter appeared on the dot, bearing a box of chocolates which, as we sat in the swing, he ate. Over the creak of the swing and Mr. Carter's crunching I was aware of Wes and Cissa inside, of their gay spontaneous laughter. The gramophone playing Cissa's favorite record, and I knew they were dancing.

When finally Mr. Carter departed I went in to join them. I found them turning out lights preparing to go up to bed. Cissa's " 'Night, Jess" was vaguely kind, the smile Wes threw me with "Pleasant dreams, Doc" kindly careless.

So I went to my room, though I knew I would not close my eyes once in the night, and, heavy of heart, got into bed—and instantly fell asleep. My dreams were not pleasant, however. For all night I fled from young Mr. Carter who, crunching chocolates, pursued me across a desert. I waked out of breath and loathing young Mr. Carter, but alas —still loving Wes.

Summer heat descended upon us. Long hot days when day after day the thermometer reached the high nineties. Long hot nights when the motionless air hung unstirred and unbreathing. This in the South was the season for "taking it easy"; for midday siestas, long lazy days when bodies yielded with grace and instinctive wisdom to the merciless sun with no thought of complaining. For even as they exclaimed, "Too hot to live," they added, "But fine for cotton," unconscious admission that cotton was the weft and the warp of their and the South's existence.

They altered the pattern of days—of life—in respect for heat's hovering presence. Kept the house cool and shadowed and immeasurably quiet; and withdrawing to porches and yards or bedrooms, left the house to heat's domination. With freezers of lemon sherbet and high cool glasses heavy with ice shaved from the block in the icebox, they cooled off with icy sweetness. "Too hot to eat," they declared, mopping perspiring faces; or "Too hot to live . . . but fine cotton weather."

Even Wes stayed at home. Slept late in the mornings, came down to exclaim over coffee, "Gee! What a scorcher!" Later he sat on the side porch, a cool glass in hand; but not long at a time. Bored and restless, he roamed into the house and out again, strolled to the carriage house to polish his auto and, mopping his face, would return. "Phew . . . too hot for work!" he exclaimed as with another iced glass he sank into his porch chair again and, still bored, ordered, half-teasing, "Come talk to me, Jess." And I, like a well-trained child, would obey.

On the side porch, shadowed by wisteria and Virginia Creeper, we would talk. It was rambling talk and idle and of nothing important, yet for me touched with a sort of magic. Not because of what we said or might say, but because of the moments when his face unconsciously was suddenly gay and boyish. Or, catching his swift careless smile, my heart would thunder so fiercely that I could hear nothing he said. Yet at one of those times he said something I have never forgotten nor will ever forget to the longest day that I live.

The dress I wore that hot afternoon had been chosen for coolness alone, since I considered it somewhat too young in its style for the mature young lady I believed myself to be; which was really too bad. For the material, though only voile, was lovely. Fine and soft with a print of petals in delicate pink, not patterned in prim pink precision but scattered and drifting and wind-blown.

Wes, having a drink of something to "lay the dust," had been for the most part silent, but his eyes from time to time over the rim of his glass surveyed me.

I did not know why until, rather abruptly, he said, "I like that dress." I looked at him in surprise.

"This old thing?" My little laugh deprecated my dress. "Well . . . at least it is cool. . . ."

"What is it?" he asked. "Silk mull, linen, chiffon?"

"Wes . . . of course not. It's cotton . . . just cotton voile."

He said slowly, more to himself than to me, "With new machines we could turn out goods like that at the mill . . . goods that would go in the market like hot cakes. If my mother would only see . . ."

I waited for him to continue but he sat silent again, his eyes on the glass in his hand, almost scowling in his concentration. It occurred to me that this was the logical time for me to reveal my knowledge of manufacture; of cards and looms and rovers. But I did not, moreover I could not. For I believed I had glimpsed—for an instant—something. Something in Wes, long preparing, perhaps formless still, but forming. . . .

Tentatively, quietly, I said, "You are the one who should make it happen, aren't you?" Then, as he raised his brows in a gesture of inquiry, hastily I explained, "I mean, make the mill produce the kind of goods you would like."

He twisted his glass slowly, making the unmelted ice tinkle. "You forget," he said flatly, "it's my mother who runs the mill."

I said, still quietly, "I haven't forgotten. And I know how much it would please her if you wanted . . . to try."

His eyes flickered up at me, but before he could speak I went on. "Why don't you talk to her, Wes? Tell her what you want to do. I think you will be surprised how glad . . . I think she wants . . . well . . . not so much on her shoulders . . . that she's tired . . . though she would never admit it. . . ."

The late afternoon sunlight that sifted in through the vines outlined the dark head and browned face into chiseled beauty. My heart, catching, seemed almost to stop when I found his eyes steady upon me, and I thought, He is angry. Because I said what I said. . . .

He suddenly shook his head as if he tried to clear it. "I can't get it," he said flatly.

I asked blankly, "Get what?"

"A saying I heard years ago back at school, but I can't remember . . ." He added, with a quick grin, "Not that I do remember a hell of a lot from school."

Puzzled, I repeated, "A saying?" and he nodded.

"Hadn't thought of it for years. Until I saw you as you are now. With the light falling on you like that. . . ."

"What is the saying?" I asked. "Perhaps I would know . . ."

His eyes did not waver from mine. "The good and the beautiful," he said gravely. "I reckon I thought of it, Doc, because that's how I see you."

Joy wrenched my heart, but not unalloyed, for it was mingled with guilt. For Wes to see me like that made me feel somehow dishonest, and I managed to say it though my voice tried to stop in my throat.

But he overrode my protest. "Oh yes, you are, Doc," he asserted. "And a damned rare combination. Beautiful women are usually spoiled and arrogant and self-centered. But it hasn't spoiled you. You're still just Doc. Doc the good and the beautiful."

"You're wrong." How steady I kept my voice. "It doesn't make everyone self-centered or arrogant."

I thought, You are beautiful, and he was, but of course I could not say it. Because of the silly convention, conceived by no woman who ever had loved, which did not permit it for men. So I said, instead, "Cissa is beautiful."

His brow quirked. "Oh yes, Cissa's a beauty. God save her."

"She's good too," I insisted. "Spoiled perhaps sometimes, but not in the way you meant, a way that's really important. Cissa is good."

"Cissa behaves if you watch her," he said dryly. "And watch her damned close."

"You're not fair to Cissa," I protested, and remembered that Mr. Poteat had once said the same words to Miss Camilla.

He did not argue but shook his head, his smile wry, "Doc, none of the Carrebees were cut out to be saints. Goodness isn't our strong suit."

"You've been good to me," I said. "All of you. Miss Camilla and Miss Ad and Cissa too . . . and you. You've been kind and generous and good."

He looked down into his glass and, finding his drink finished, sat jiggling the lumps of melting ice again as if keeping time with his thoughts. Then he stood to go and refill his glass, but paused to give me my reply.

"I hope you're right, Doc," he said. "I hope we've been good to you. It would be one star at least in our crown." He added, as he went toward the door, "The Carrebee crown could use a star, Lord knows."

Now instead of writing "Jess and Wes" on vagrant scraps of paper, I wrote "the good and the beautiful," for they had become the most wonderful words in the world. Now no dream seemed impossible. I did not doubt that Wes, if he wished, could be whatever he wished once—as Mitty would say—he put his hand to it. I was in that delightful state which we speak of as "being in love," butt of old jaundiced jokesters and, I admit, often amusing. I was as absurd and silly in the throes of first love as any woman. But to me it was not absurd, nor can I laugh at the absurdities I find in others. I cannot scorn or scoff at those who love. For we scorn and scoff only because we forget. And the wonder and meaning of that wondrous time is lost . . . lost forever.

If it is a foolish time—and it is—it is also a glorious time, an unselfish, ungrudging, an unstinting time. A time of willingness to sacrifice, of happiness when we can serve: a time when, if we genuinely love, we are pure of heart and generous as kings would be if they were always kingly; so for all of the foolish moments I cannot laugh.

Then suddenly . . . it was all over. The silly dreams and long tranquil talks on the porch, the comfortable feeling of friendship . . . the half-awakened hope that some day . . . all of it ended. Wes was no more as he had been, Wes had changed. Amiable still and still calling me "Doc," gay and teasing at times, flashing his swift sudden smile, yet changed. The change a wall that closed me out, holding me at a distance; and if I dared draw near, he withdrawing, retreating and—on some pretext—strolling out of the room.

At first I said to myself I only imagined it, that it was only one of Wes's bad humors and not directed at me. Tomorrow, I thought, he will be himself and we will be as we were. But tomorrow came and it wasn't true, nor the day after, nor days that followed.

I wondered if I could have said something or done something to destroy the friendship that to me was so . . . precious. If what I had said regarding the mill had, when he thought it over, displeased him. I wondered if his talks with his mother could in any way have caused the change toward me. They had talked, I knew, in her office and I, believing I had brought it about, had felt so pleased—and so wise. But now I wasn't so sure.

Now I thought it not improbable that, observing the friendship between us, she had warned him that our friendship must not develop to more. Jess was a fine lovely girl, she would say, and kindly—but there was her dubious background. And Wes was not to encourage Jess. Jess was too fine to be hurt.

So there it was, the old shadow full-bodied beside me again with its somber reminder of the dominion it held over my life. Reminding me I had forgotten that its shade was ever beside me, a jailor that kept me imprisoned in my aloneness.

Unhappily but firmly, I picked up the threads of my days, resolved to fight free of all that bound me. Shocked, I reviewed the time—it was almost a year—since I came to the Carrebees', and saw how aimlessly I had drifted.

I would drift no more, I determined. I would not be lulled, as I had been, into the feeling that I was wanted. For nothing could change the unchanging fact that I had no place of my own. And however fond of me people might be, their fondness could never transcend it.

I forced myself to have dates, to go to parties and outings, pretended that I enjoyed them and deceived everyone but myself. Now and then I went into town to lunch with Andrew who, I realized, in his quiet way still "kept an eye on me." At one of these times, as we left the restaurant and moved slowly along the sidewalk, he glanced at me sharply and asked if I felt well. I looked a little pale.

"Just the heat," I said.

As we crossed the street I remembered his saying he had something to tell me—something important. Now I spoke of it.

"I said important to me," he corrected good-humoredly. "But it will wait. Right now you must get home. You still look peaked."

I was grateful when he immediately put me on my streetcar and I was on my way home. The heat, oppressive all morning, had increased. Sullen, lowering, torpid, it was as still as if all forces of weather, down to the last parched breath of air, had been withdrawn in preparation for furious assault, and as I went up the driveway, it was obvious that we were in for a storm. The sky seemed to hang heavy over Miss Camilla's roof, ominous, tarnished, brassy. And a low vanguard of clouds, crouching in the distance, muttered and grumbled on the horizon and sent up battle flares of heat lightning. The leaves seemed to tremble on the trees, and as I passed turned pallid faces toward me; the flowers flaunted their richest and most brilliant hues, as if making a show of defiant splendor on the eve of disaster.

Still, I told myself, the storm might pass over. It might be only a heat storm that would vanish as the sun dropped down, and I recalled other days when, after a similar display, the sky had suddenly cleared, becoming as serene and content as if on a pension. All thoughts of the storm were banished, however, when I entered the house. For in the hall I was confronted by the small, childlike figures of Mitty and Miss Ad. They sat on chairs primly, like good children, and I started to laugh—then saw their faces and halted.

"We're keeping an eye out for Miss Camilla or Wes," Mitty said, without other greeting. "Wes would be best. He has to know, and the sooner the better."

"Know—what?" I asked quickly.

"About Cissa," Mitty said in her calm, sensible manner.

"What about Cissa?" I looked at her, puzzled. "Has something happened to Cissa?"

Mitty was brisk. "Whether something's wrong or not depends on how you look at it. Anyhow, an hour or so ago Ad sees Cissa talking on the telephone and what she sees she don't like."

"What did she see?"

"She was talking to somebody named Syl!" Mitty exclaimed. "Though I don't call it much of a name. Anyhow, Cissa told this Syl she'd meet him at the Terminal Station by the information desk."

"Perhaps she's going on a week end with a crowd. It doesn't mean anything."

"Ad thinks Cissa is eloping." Mitty was definite.

"You mean Cissa and Syl Crowley?" I asked incredulously.

"That's what I've been trying to tell you."

I felt a sagging relaxation of tenseness and a sudden desire to laugh.

"But that is ridiculous," I gasped. "Miss Ad misunderstood. Cissa wouldn't!"

"Wouldn't what?" Wes's voice asked.

We whirled and found him in the doorway.

"Wouldn't what?" he repeated. "What is it Cissa wouldn't do?"

I told him what Miss Ad and Mitty suspected. He listened, not smiling. He glanced at Miss Ad.

"Information desk at the Terminal, Aunt Ad?" he asked, and I saw how set his face suddenly was, his eyes bleak.

Miss Ad's frantic bobbing head gave him his answer.

He nodded, said "Thanks" and went out. We heard the front door slam, then the sound of his car as it went down the drive.

I was less sure now that Cissa and Syl Crowley were beyond possibility, for I saw Wes's face as it had been when I told him. So set, the eyes so bleak. Restlessly I paced, waiting though not knowing for what. I saw that Miss Ad was herself again, she and Mitty in and out of the kitchen, checking on dinner. Life was no different, I thought. Perhaps it was really no different. Cissa would come back—

The first fat, lazy drops of rain splattered and from the veranda I saw the tiny funnels they made when they struck and were sucked up by reddish dust. Then they were beating swiftly, and I saw Wes turn his car into the driveway with Cissa beside him. And at the same moment the storm broke upon us with its pent-up fury.

Lightning unraveled across the sky, a peal of thunder shook the house, and the heavy clouds abruptly released a crashing torrent as Wes and Cissa scrambled from the car and ran for the veranda, Wes carrying Cissa's suitcase. They leaped up the steps to the porch, like sea creatures gaining land, already sopping and soaked to the skin. Wes's suit hung limp and shapeless as he stood in squelching shoes, his face glistening with rain. Cissa's dress was plastered to every curve and line of her exquisite figure and her hair had become a dank mop.

She gave a delighted laugh, jerking off her ruined hat and tossing her head to swing the sodden hair back from her face. Even as she was, wet as a drowned rat, she was ravishing, and not the least disturbed by the collapse of her plans.

She called to me, gleefully, "Jess, I've been saved again! By dat ole debbil Wes. And practically at the altar."

"Cissa, you didn't intend . . ." I began and stopped.

She knew what I did not say, and her eyes widened in mock amazement. "Of course I did!" she exclaimed. "I'd marry General Sherman, if he had plenty of money and would promise to burn up Atlanta again. I was never so sick and tired of any place in my life."

She looked like nothing so much as an adorable child glorying in the magnificence of her wetness. She had lifted her head defiantly when I said she would not have gone through with it. But now she giggled.

"I would have married Syl all right." She was impish. "Though I'll confess he bore up when Wes showed up and took me off his hands. I reckon I did kind of force myself on him by my take-me-or-leave-me basis." She wheeled to Wes lazily. "You do have to admit, Wes, he was a perfect gentleman."

"Imperfect gentlemen generally are," Wes said briefly. "And after they reach Syl's age they hanker after respectability."

Cissa gave a cry of delighted admiration. "Wes, you're just the smartest thing. Syl's just dying to settle down and lead a respectable life. He's always talking about the 'right people.' "

Wes nodded. "That's why he wants to marry you. You're a respectable girl, more or less."

Before she could fling back a retort Mitty spoke up. If she didn't get out of those wet clothes, she told Cissa flatly, she wouldn't live to marry anybody at all. And Cissa, laughing down at her, said, childlike, "Mitty, you're so mean to me," but went toward the door, swinging her sodden hat. At the door she paused and, a hand propped on its frame, looked back at Wes pensively.

"Don't forget, Wes. You promised to talk to Mama . . . about Europe. She'll give in to the *darling of her heart* . . . even for me. And I'm not jealous, my sweet, because she loves you better than anything—except, of course, the mill."

Wes said shortly, "I told you I'd talk to her."

She turned languidly to go, then she faced us again, not pensively but alive with malicious mischief as she gave a delicious chuckle.

"You know, Wes, if Syl wants to marry someone respectable, I really should take him up on it. It would be such a wonderful joke on him."

The next day I heard that Cissa would get her trip to Europe. She was to leave right away for New York to join Mrs. Cooley's Cultural Tour for Distinguished Young Ladies at the Astor and have a few days to shop for new clothes before the ship sailed. When I heard it—it was Cissa herself who told me over coffee—I stared at her dumfounded, then laughed.

Over her cup her eyes, meeting mine, narrowed shrewdly. "Why do you laugh like that, Jess?"

"Because I was right. You didn't intend to go through with it. It was only your way of getting . . . your way."

"Of course," she said lightly, then her voice hardened. "But don't be fooled, Jess. If I hadn't got my way, I would have gone through with it."

"That would be silly. You'd only cut off your nose to spite your face."

Biting her lip, she shook her head. "Not to spite my face. But for spite."

"But spite who, Cissa? Except yourself?"

"Whoever interferes with what I happen to want." Trailing from the table, she said over her shoulder, "It's a trait I inherit from Mama."

Finishing my coffee alone, I admitted the truth of her parting words. It was the cause of the conflict between them: Cissa, with tantrums and threats and childish acts of revenge, fighting to get her way; Miss Camilla, with charm and friendly directness that told nothing, fighting for hers. I did not question which was the stronger; and while Cissa had triumphed this time, even by the threat of Syl Crowley, it was not easy to believe that Miss Camilla could be intimidated. Yet, I conceded, perhaps I was wrong. For Cissa was going to Europe.

Her departure was preceded by a vortex of work and confusion in which Miss Ad, Mitty, and I spun like leaves in a whirlwind. Even with the luggage closed and locked, Cissa, suited and hatted, threatened to unpack everything to make sure a favorite fascinator had been packed. Searching the rooms swiftly, I wondered who ever thought up that silly name for a scarf.

When at last she left in Wes's auto for the Terminal Station, I sank into a living-room chair, feeling as if I had been struck by a cyclone, too tired, I told myself, to lift a finger. But my tired eyes fell upon the lost fascinator, lying on the floor by the table from which it had slipped. I picked it up and replaced it on the table. Not for Cissa who, I thought crossly, managed to get service even when away. But I recalled that Miss Ad had made the fascinator for Cissa from treasured heirloom lace and had sewn the flashing rhinestones onto its fragile beauty painstakingly by hand.

Cissa was gone and the house, like a meadow when the bright and ruthless wind has passed, seemed strangely calm. It was not unwelcome, yet I had the flat, let-down sensation that follows excitement, and the bursts of temper and mocking laughter of Cissa.

It was increased that night. Miss Ad and Mitty, tired after the busy day, went early to bed. Miss Camilla was at some social affair or other and Wes, after driving Cissa to the Terminal, had not returned. So I had the house to myself, and it was suddenly a vast house and lonely, with a surprising number of mysterious sounds.

I was tired but not at all sleepy, I discovered when I went to my room, so deciding to read myself sleepy, I went downstairs to get the book I had left in the sitting room.

Only a few lamps burned, and the room had become vast and shadowed, and cloaked in mystery. I was not aware that Wes had returned until I reached the archway between the reception hall and sitting room.

Surprised, I paused, half inclined to retreat, recalling how he had seemed to avoid me, but wishing to stay, and held by the division of impulses in the archway. He was, I knew, unaware of my presence, for he did not move from the empty hearth where he stood, his head bent and his attention fixed on something he turned in his hands.

In the glow of the single lamp I could see only that the thing he held hardly had substance, but was tenuous and fragile. Then I caught the tiny glint of icy fire in the folds and knew it was Cissa's fascinator, which I had left on the table. He had noticed it and picked it up to put away for her.

But then I concluded that I was mistaken, that Wes had no plan for keeping it safe but seemed bent instead on its destruction. For his hands wrenched at the tenuous folds, straining and twisting and jerking with all his force in the effort to rend it.

I cried in protest, "Wes, don't!" and his head jerked up, his eyes startled, as if he were confronted with some shape of terror. Then he laughed, and the laugh was careless, and he spoke, his voice careless too, yet undertraced with emotion.

"I didn't know you were still up, Doc," he said. "Don't worry." He held up the fascinator. "This lace is damned good and strong. Won't give an inch."

He flung it carelessly at the table and, landing on the edge, it skittered again to the floor.

Entering the room, I picked it up. "It's so lovely," I offered, both in reproof and in explanation of my protest. "The lace was your great-grandmother's," I told him. "Left to Miss Ad. She spent hours making this for Cissa."

"I didn't hurt it," he answered curtly. "I didn't know about Aunt Ad . . . or the lace. I just knew it was Cissa's."

I looked at him, puzzled. "But why should you want to tear it?"

He shrugged. "Just a damnfool impulse. And . . . well, I'm fed up with Cissa right now. Tried to take it out on that watchamacallit."

He dropped into a deep chair beside the hearth and, with his head against its back, closed his eyes. His face, I thought, looked desperately weary. I felt a stir of compassion, and thrust it away. He did not seek my compassion, nor, I thought, my company. That, he had proved beyond doubt in the last few days. I murmured good night and started to leave the room, and was stopped by his voice.

"Sit down, Doc," he said without moving or opening his eyes. "It's early yet."

It was not late, nor was I sleepy, but the voice suggesting I stay was not his voice. It was a sleepwalker's, or how I would imagine a sleepwalker's to be. I hesitated, and he spoke again, his eyes still closed.

"Sit down and talk awhile, Doc," he said. "Unless you're sleepy."

"No," I said. "I'm not sleepy."

He opened his eyes and smiled at me gently. "Don't read tonight, Doc," he said. "There'll be plenty of nights to read. I'm damned poor company tonight even for myself."

That his voice was weary and lonely did not escape me. But I closed my heart. He could not veer like wind and when he chanced to veer in my direction, expect to find me eager and waiting.

Perhaps he believed from my silence that I wished him to beg—though I did not—and he gave me a small, apologetic smile.

"Stick by me, Doc. Please."

The "please" naturally touched me, and it struck me that it was unkind not to relent, with talk keep him from the unwelcome companionship of his thoughts.

I sat in the chair across from his. "All right," I said, "I will." The words were merely polite, without significance for him. But they meant more than I dared admit.

He did not talk, however. With his head back against the chair, he gazed ahead abstractedly, kneading his forehead with his finger tips. He worried about the affair of Cissa and Syl beyond reason, I decided. Especially with it settled and over.

In a voice that I kept practical, I told him so. Cissa would forget Syl Crowley in Europe, I said. It wasn't as if she cared for him or had meant to marry him. Like a child, she had acted thoughtlessly.

When I finished he said quietly, "Cissa is never thoughtless when she's trying to get her way."

"You're too hard on her," I said gravely. "She's young."

"Not as young as you, Doc," he returned.

"But I had to grow up faster than Cissa," I pointed out. "I had to face situations that sometimes weren't . . . fun. Not that I'm as grown-up as I should be."

"Sometimes, Doc," he said, "you seem older than Methuselah. And wiser. But you're wrong about Cissa and me."

"About you?" I questioned.

"About my being hard on her," he answered. "I'm not. I get mad as the devil at her. I'd like to slap her face when she deliberately shocks people or play-acts and insists on being the star of the show."

He straightened, then leaned forward, elbows on knees, and as if remembering, he said slowly, thoughtfully.

"But I'm not hard on her. I know too damned well why she grew up to be what she is."

"Cissa isn't as bad as you make her sound," I told him. "She's spoiled . . ."

He picked up my word. "Spoiled," he repeated. "That's the polite word, Doc. There's another for spoiled food. We say it's rotten."

"Cissa isn't," I defended.

"She is, or so damn near it you have to look close to tell the difference. But you see, Doc, I know why. We didn't get much attention when we were kids. Our mother was so wrapped up in that goddamned cotton mill she couldn't take time to be a mother."

"She didn't have any choice," I said.

He shrugged. "I won't argue that. I'm only telling you what it was like."

He went on. "When we were older, and Cissa wanted something, she could get it only by forcing Mother's attention. She used to run away. Once they found her ten miles away, eating supper with a colored family and keeping them all rolling with laughter. And another time she managed to get to the depot. Told the ticket agent she was Cissa Carrebee and her mother owned cotton mills and to please lend her a hundred dollars to take a trip. She was nine then."

With astonishing vividness, I pictured the nine-year-old Cissa telling her elaborate lie, her eyes wide and solemn and innocent. And I laughed.

He laughed, too, though without mirth. "They sent her home in a carriage, and everybody thought she was so cute. It isn't so cute when she grows up and the running away means Syl Crowley."

"You care about Cissa a great deal, don't you?" I asked.

He shook head and shoulders as if shaking off water. "Not always. She can be a devil. Not a cute little devil, a real one. The kind that is respected in hell as being particularly efficient at his job. It's just that . . . when we were kids, I had to be with . . . sort of responsible for her and whether I like it or not, I still feel responsible. I can't break away from it. I wish to God I could."

"You shouldn't wish it. She is your sister, Wes. You grew up close to each other."

His mouth twisted. "We had to be. There wasn't anybody else."

"I used to get so bored with Cissa," he said. "I was older, of course, and when she cried I'd tell her stories, sing"—he shook his head—"play silly games, just to keep her quiet. There was one game"—he grimaced—"I reckon I played it a million times. *Chicka-ma, chicka-ma, craney crow.*"

I tried to repeat the jumble of sound, and failed. He laughed at my efforts, then told me about it. It was a crazy game, he said, that one of the Negro nurses taught him, and it really needed three to play it. A mother, the child, and the old witch, so he had to play two parts—the child and the witch. It went like this: The mother returned home and found her child gone. She went to the old witch singing:

"Chicka-ma, chicka-ma, craney crow
I went to the well to wash my toe
And when I got there my child was gone.
What time, old witch?"

Then the old witch tried to catch the mother, naturally—and he usually did though he pretended she could outrun him.

The brown hand raked the dark hair. "God—I used to get so sick of that game."

"Cissa must have adored you," I said, with a little pang of envy. "She still does, in spite of her teasing."

But he shook his head. "She knows I'm no great shakes, Doc." He said matter-of-factly, "I've worried about it. I've wondered if I've poisoned her in a way. If I'd amounted to something, been some damned good, she might have been . . . different . . . trying to imitate me . . ."

"But you will amount to something," I protested.

He gave me a rueful grin. "Doc, I'd like to do something worth-while for a change."

"But you will," I said. "I know you will!"

He shrugged. "Maybe. But I'll be honest with you, Doc. I don't believe anybody ever amounts to a tinker's curse without somebody who wants it for them . . . to give them incentive. You see, I've never had anybody that cared enough to . . . even believe I could if I would. Maybe if somebody really believed I could, I might after all. It might help if somebody came along who believed in me. God knows I don't believe much in myself, and most men who get somewhere do. So maybe you need a sort of partner who can supply the believing part."

He had spoken lightly, half-jokingly, and I was not sure that he was serious. But whether he was or not, I answered seriously, my voice as grave as his had been light.

"I believe you can be whatever you want to be," I told him firmly. "So if you want somebody that believes, there's always me."

It was simple truth. I had never meant words more sincerely. With his charm and quickness of mind, I did not doubt that he could win any heights to which he might aspire. It crossed my mind that there might be many who'd think I had spoken too boldly, too frankly, but I did not care. I had only said what I truly believed, and truth, Mitty said, shamed the devil. I came back to Wes to find him watching me steadily with a faint smile.

"You know, Doc, you surprise me. I've believed all the time that you were gentle and—well, retiring. But, by God, I believe you'd fight if you believed in your cause."

"I would," I said defiantly.

He still looked at me steadily, the little half-smile playing over his face. "You know, Doc," he said softly, "it might be that everyone, including me, is wrong and you are right. It just might be."

After that we chatted of other things, and for me it was an hour of quiet happiness, enclosed with him by night and the dim-lighted room; to watch his face as he talked, gaily now and not depressed, to listen to his laughter that had a quality of its own, subdued and mellow, yet—it is not easy to put into words—as different from other laughter as he was from other men.

Happily, I went to my room when we said good night, and before I got into bed, stood at my window and asked the stars if this was happiness I must never have again, and gave myself the answer that it was . . . unless the stars themselves decreed otherwise.

And they did. For there was that happiness again . . . and yet again.

That happiness was waiting again next morning when I went down to breakfast and found him there, not gay and teasing but all grave loving-kindness. And when I stirred under his gaze and looked up at him quickly, he said simply that my face always asked a question and he wondered what that question was. And I caught my breath to stem the love that swept me, for I had determined to be sensible above all things. Yet I did not feel sensible but only joyful when he informed me that Eula was packing a basket lunch, that we would ride out in the country for a picnic. And so we did. In his auto we set out and spun along the road, which, in the early morning, seemed dew-washed; that happiness keeping pace with us all the way no matter how fast Wes drove.

There was that happiness on that day and the next, and on the days that followed, as the Georgia summer, enriched and brightened by the heat, approached its final ripening. As August, wheeling toward September, turned more golden and more scarlet, swelled and rounded, and beneath the velvet skin of sunlight attained the piercing sweetness of the peaches ripening on the trees.

Almost every day there was that happiness. It was there as we drove along green-tunneled side roads and let them lead us where they would, or in the glowing purple dusk, slipped between lofty walls of emerald corn, past fields of luminous, fleecy cotton; the wind that buffeted our faces with its warmth, gentler now that the sun was down, heavy with the smells of clayey soil, of sun-soaked grasses, and with the dank, dark, oozy smell of river bottoms and the Chattahoochee.

We stopped to eat at places where Wes invariably was a familiar and welcome guest. From a plank table we ate barbecue prepared by an old Negro who had pride and a fiery conviction about the mixing of sauces to which Wes deferred, as did I, once I had tasted them. The meat was hot as the distilled essence of red peppers could make it, but sour, sweet underneath; an experience mixed equally of torture and delight.

We stopped for watermelon, sugar-sweet and icy, brought from the springhouse or from a brook. Other times we dined in more formal surroundings, in hushed and ordered stretches of snow-white tables and gleaming glass and silver, where long-bladed fans stirred the air and muted music throbbed not too nearby. We were served by Negro waiters in white jackets, elderly and with the grave and stately dignity of prime ministers, and as solicitous of our comfort as if they were indeed prime ministers of a kingdom where Wes was king and I shared his throne.

But these formal outings were rare. They called for planning and arranging which Wes avoided. His idea for each day produced on the moment was bright, newly minted. We lived in the present, or, more exactly, as if there were nothing but the present; no past behind us, no future to arrive.

There was that happiness on the Sunday we drove out to the river. It ran low between its banks, for rain had been scarce, but when Wes turned off the road and stopped on a flat stretch of bank, under a heavy covering of live oak and willow, we caught the coolness and the wet, muddy smell of the saffron water, heard the ripple and slap of its current against roots and rocks and drifting limbs of trees.

"It's nice here," I said, but Wes did not reply.

"Did you notice, Doc," he asked abruptly, "how, when we spent a lot of time together a while back, I changed . . . toward you? And kept out of your way?"

"I noticed," I said.

"And did you figure," he went on, "that there was a reason? Why I changed."

"Was there?" I asked, my voice, against my will, small in my throat, as if to make itself inconspicuous lest it attract and bring back those days of bewildered hurt.

"I changed"—he apparently did not notice my voice—"because of a talk my mother had with me. About you. A serious talk."

I carefully held my face still and waited. He said, "You know she thinks the sun rises and sets in you. She would, everything considered. That was the idea, you see. When she'd spent a couple of hours telling me what a fine girl you are, how sensible and down to earth, how pretty —which I knew for myself—God knows I got the idea. And it stuck in my craw."

"What," I asked, still unable to produce a normal voice, "what stuck in your craw?"

He shrugged. "You've been around her enough to know she likes to run things," he answered. "The mill, the house, everybody. Everything. I've got in the habit, I guess, of balking on principle when she tries to run me or use me to get her way—about something."

"But I don't see"—I was puzzled—"how saying nice things about me would help her get her way."

His short laugh interrupted. "Don't you, Doc? Neither did I, at first. But when she began to point out the sort of wife you'd make some lucky chap, how you'd help a man settle down, get his feet on the ground"—his mouth twisted wryly—"I knew she had it all figured out. You were the wife for Wes Carrebee."

"And that was why you avoided me?" I asked, my voice even smaller.

He stared ahead at the slow, turgid river, his face hard and his mouth thin. "I wasn't going to have her meddling in your life. And you feeling you had to go along with it because she's been kind to you. It would be damned unfair," he said shortly. "For both of us."

"That would depend," I offered tentatively.

He shook his head. "No. It was no good. I wouldn't let her play God with you, cajole you into marriage."

He would not, I thought, understand, no matter what I said, that I who had sworn to control my own destiny should now gladly, eagerly, accept control as wise and generous as Miss Camilla's. Nothing less than the truth could make him understand that I loved him. I felt hopeless, then desperate, then was swept by recklessness. I groped and fumbled for words with which to shape the sentence that would say "I love you."

Before I could, his voice interfered. "And that, Doc, is why I kept out of your way. For a few days I even made a go of it. But I'm not a strong character, Doc, and I'm afraid my foot slipped. So here I am . . . back again."

Still trying to shape the statement of my love, I said nothing.

"I'm back, Doc," he said. "And without my principles. If I've been pushed into your arms against your will and mine, I don't care. Or to be exact I care too much. Too much to care how I get you just so I get you."

"Get me?" I said it warily, not daring to assume too much.

"If you don't think marrying me is a good idea, forget the whole thing and no hard feelings," he told me. "There're reasons, God knows, why you wouldn't. You'd be better off with somebody else."

He had turned to look at me now, and I stared up at the brown face and, blinded, I shook my head, feeling dazed. I saw my hand lift of its own volition, I saw my fingers touch his cheek. I had forgotten my carefully prepared speech, entirely and utterly.

"There couldn't be anybody but you . . . ever," I said.

He sat gazing steadily at me, his eyes deep and grave. Then he lifted the hand with which I had touched his face and kissed my palm gently. He raised his head, which had bent down to my hand, and his eyes were gentle.

"When you look at me like that I know I could never harm you. My good and my beautiful."

He kissed me then, so I answered, not with words, but in a way that transcended words. His lips were not hard or hungry against mine but tender and gentle. He held me close for a while, my head against his heart, and its strong steady throb was in my breast as well as his and it was my heart, our heart. We were silent, each thinking our own thoughts, but mine were of him, his no doubt of me, and so they did not travel separate paths. But mine led me to something I must make clear to him. And I sat up and drew away a little.

There was something, I said, that I must tell him. Perhaps he knew already but I must be sure. I told him then. That I knew nothing of my parents or who I was really, nor would I ever know, it seemed. But from the little that was known it seemed only logical that I was a . . .

He laid his hand gently on my mouth, and when I raised my eyes I saw that his face was wrenched with pain and anger.

"Goddamn it, Doc," he said, "don't apologize to me or anybody for being you; or for anything about you. I'll hear that from no living human being, not even you!"

"But it's only fair . . . " I began.

He would not let me finish. "I know what you would say, so there's no point in saying it. It's not important enough to repeat. Besides, it's you who'll get the worst of this bargain, God knows."

"It's the only bargain I want."

He gave his head a quick little shake. "I'm no prize, Doc."

"You are to me," I assured him. "And you have to be happy, Wes. Please be happy. I want you to be happy."

He was, I thought as we drove home, completely happy and content. My own happiness welled up in my heart and spilled over. Yet under all my laughing, poignant recklessness was the quiver of tears. I thought, I am to marry Wes Carrebee, though I did not really believe or comprehend it yet—and when we passed a tall, stooped Negro driving a sad-looking cow I would have liked to stop and tell him, and the cow too, that I was to marry Wes and that Wes loved me.

This reminded me of others I must tell. Mitty first, of course. And Miss Camilla. Then the rest of the house. Then suddenly I remembered that Andrew was coming out this afternoon. We would have to tell Andrew, I thought—not happily. Then Wes was turning in the drive and in my excitement at telling Mitty, Andrew was forgotten. She would, I thought, be thunderstruck with surprise at the news.

We went upstairs and, after knocking, entered her room. She was seated in her rocker, her basket of quilt scraps on her lap, and she gave us a quick, shrewd glance as we crossed and stood before her.

"Mitty," I began gently, and was suddenly aware that it wasn't "fun" to tell Mitty. Mitty so loyal, so loving. Who had no one but me. I dropped to my knees and put my arms around her. "Mitty," I said, "I have something to tell you. But first I want to tell you this. No one can ever take your place. And you must never leave me. Never. Promise."

She said matter-of-factly, "Why, I do promise, my blessed. And if you're trying to tell me that you and Wes Carrebee—"

"Mitty!" I exclaimed. "You mean, you knew?"

She laughed her loving little laugh. "Why shoot, dearie, of course I knew." And getting up, she hugged and kissed me and stroked my hair. Then shook hands with Wes in a sort of man-to-man fashion in spite of being a woman.

I had recovered my surprise a little. "But Mitty, how did you know?" She smiled serenely and patted my hand which she held.

"Well, dearie. Don't nothing happen 'less it gives warning. I mean in the growing-up line. Eye teeth, twelve-year-old molars, not to mention other developments. I always knew when to look out for 'em. This warn't different. And I saw this coming too."

"But you didn't say a word, Mitty."

She still smiled gently and wisely, and as if, I thought, she knew some secret I could not know and would not understand if she revealed it.

"No, dearie," she agreed, "I didn't say a word about expecting those molars either. One word or a million wouldn't a stopped 'em."

The only surprise I encountered as Wes and I went to tell the others was the lack of surprise. Miss Ad expressed her lack of surprise silently, Eula with a wise, knowing laugh. Miss Camilla was the least surprised of all. She kissed me calmly, giving me a brusque hug and telling me it was without a doubt the best thing that could have happened to Wes.

It left only one person who would be surprised, I thought, and that was Andrew, who would arrive before long. Then it dawned upon me that I wished to surprise him no more than Mitty.

When he came, we sat on the side porch and without delay I said I had something I wanted to tell him.

The twinkle of his blue eyes brightened in response to my own excitement.

"It must be good news, judging by your cheeks."

"It is," I said gently. "It's wonderful news!"

"Why, then," he said with his quiet smile, "I guess I'd better hear it right away."

"I hope it won't be as big a surprise to you as it was to me," I said.

"Well, I won't know that until I hear what it is," he said with quizzical patience.

"Andrew, I am going to be married," I said. "To marry Wes Carrebee!"

If I expected it to shake his steady quiet, I was mistaken. For he grew even quieter and his calmness, I felt, became even deeper. The only sign he gave of surprise was the disappearance of the twinkle of his blue eyes. It was gone, and the eyes regarded me gravely and thoughtfully, as if he pondered on what I had told him.

Nevertheless, when he finally spoke, his voice was not quite steady, though as quiet and unhurried as ever.

"Well," he said at last, speaking slowly, "that's a contingency I hadn't expected."

"Nor I, Andrew," I assured him. "I've told Wes all about you, of course. How patient and kind you've been with me."

He gave his head a little shake of denial. "I've just taken care of contingencies," he answered.

"You've done much much more than that," I protested. "You've been my friend. You are my friend. That's why I was so anxious to tell you about me and Wes. I knew you'd be glad too. Andrew, it's such a perfect contingency."

He continued to look steadily into my eyes for a moment; then the twinkle returned and his face was its calm, cheerful, freckled self again.

"Since you are happy," he agreed, "why then it's a very agreeable contingency. I couldn't, I guess, ask for a better."

Mitty came out with a pitcher of ice tea and, to my surprise, kissed Andrew on his cheek as if he were a very old, very dear friend. But I reminded myself that she had liked him immediately, and made him her fast friend, which amounted to an old friend in Mitty's estimation. Wes joined us and shook hands with Andrew and received Andrew's congratulations. I was positive that Andrew must admire Wes for his looks, his easy poise and his charm. Andrew, however, gave no evidence of such ardent admiration. He was with Wes just Andrew, which means friendly and cheerful and agreeable. Wes was the charming one. He suggested that since Andrew had showed up at an opportune moment, it would be an ideal occasion to drink to his undeserved luck and to my future in something more fitting than ice tea.

Andrew agreed, and Wes insisted Mitty and I have a drink too, since it was a very special occasion. I had never tasted whiskey, except once when Mitty gave it to me during a weak period after a siege of grippe, and assured Wes I was in sufficient daze as it was. He would not accept a refusal, however, and Mitty, instead of backing me up, said she would not only have a dram but told Wes to make it a double one. She felt, she explained, the need of a good dram to steady her down. I wondered if Mitty had been more affected than she admitted.

Wes brought out the drinks and passed them around, and then all three of them drank to me. They stood, the three people dearest to me in all the world, and lifted their glasses "To Jess." The sight of their smiling faces and my awareness of all they meant to me, of their goodness and love and beauty—for they were beautiful to me, every one—so overwhelmed me that I choked up at my happiness that seemed suddenly too great to bear. My eyes brimmed with tears, so that I saw them through a salty flood that made them float in a watery mist, that made their smiles blur and the glowing faces dim. I heard their voices wish me happy, golden years, many and long and rich with content, and knew if their command would have made my years all they wished for me, I would have lived, as the girls in fairy stories Mitty had read to me as a child, happy ever after.

I saw them dimly as they stood and drank to me on the day Wes asked me to be his wife. And so I have seen them since, more often than I can count, through a swimming, watery blue of tears. And many times as on that afternoon, my eyes are too full to see clearly and the shapes and faces melt and fade. And those three most loved and most loving are lost and drowned in my weeping.

It came at last, my wedding day, and having come, was unbelievable. So unbelievable that when Mitty's voice called my name and penetrated sleep, and waking I found her by my bed, the day for a moment was as any other day.

She twinkled down at me. "And don't you be dawdling on your wedding day. The hairdresser comes at nine, Miss Camilla says."

Her words lifted me from sleep on a wave and I gazed at her solemnly. "Oh Mitty!" I said and reaching, put my arms about her waist and hid my face against her breast. "Oh Mitty!" I said again. "I—I think I am a little—scared."

I felt her hand upon my hair. "Scared, dearie? You needn't be. I told you everything—"

I stopped her. "Oh Mitty! I don't mean—*that.*"

Matter-of-factly she asked, "Then whatever do you mean?"

Still hiding my face in her bosom, her hand still smoothing my hair, I told her how last night, deliriously happy, dread had swooped down—and dark wonder: What if Wes didn't love me? What if it all happened too quickly for him to know? What if he came to know afterward? Realized that he did not, could not love me?

Having told, I raised my face to Mitty's. "Why would I think such things, Mitty?"

Her eyes lost none of their cheerfulness. "Well now, blessed, it's funny about women. Always hunting happiness, worrying and fretting to get it. And when they do, mistrusting it because it don't carry a twenty-year guarantee against tarnish. Like silver."

"But love and marriage—do they tarnish, Mitty? Do they?"

"Why, dearie, some of the shine wears off with the new. It does with anything; and anybody that says different can just go roll their hoop. But the Good Book don't say love, honor and obey 'til the new wears off. But as long as ye both shall live."

I smiled up at her earnest little face. "And cleave unto—" I reminded.

Remembering, her smile was loving. Then she exclaimed, "Now get up! Eat your breakfast. And don't dawdle. This is your wedding day."

This is my wedding day. Over and over I said the words to myself in the hours that followed, but still not believing. The evidence that it is somebody's wedding day is undeniable. The doorbell rings as persistently as if a finger had been hired for that purpose alone. Delivery wagons from florists and caterers circle in and out the drive as if engaged in a silly parade. From downstairs comes the sound of furniture shoved about, ladders pulled around, always to the accompaniment of voices calling and suggesting; with Miss Camilla's voice rising to dominate like a general's in the thick of battle. And still I do not believe.

Miss Theresa arrives to do my hair and I sit imprisoned in a nebulous haze so golden it might have been spun by the sun. It separates me from the world of reality—even the sphere of thought. When the baggageman comes to take my trunk to the station and, puffing and panting, bumps it from my room and down the stairs, I wonder who is going away; when it dawns upon me that it is I and the trip is my honeymoon, still I refuse to believe.

Somebody comes to tell me Wes is calling and I stare astonished until they mention the telephone. I slip down the back stairs to the pantry telephone lest somebody see the bride, and I can't believe that I am the bride. When Wes's voice, slurred and a little thick yet laughing, says, "This is your black sheep, Doc," I manage a lifeless, "How are you?" Still laughing, he talks of a bachelor's dinner and how many quarts of champagne; and Jim who went to bed in white tie and tails; and it is like hearing strange irrelevant things about someone I know only slightly.

Back in my room I eat the lunch Mitty brings, unconscious of flavor. Mitty's voice that comes from a vast distance talks of the handsome presents, of the house being decked with smilax and lilies; a wedding cake three tiers high; and still it has nothing to do with Jess Kildare. I simply cannot believe it.

Miss Ad comes in with Drusilla, who carries a box which Miss Ad opens. It is my wedding dress and Miss Ad gently, as if it were made of glass, hangs it from the gas jet for us to see, and all white and misty it twirls there, this way and that. I see Mitty's tear-bright eyes and Drusilla's O of wondering mouth and Miss Ad's reverent face, and I want to cry. For their eyes shine as if they believed the dress might be theirs. Not mine, who does not believe.

Miss Ad hangs the dress in the closet and she and Drusilla depart, and Mitty declares I must rest and makes me lie on the bed, and leaves. In the shining haze I lie there like a thing suspended in space, neither happy nor unhappy but thinking of many things: of the pines around Mitty's house that never ceased their sighing; of the cemetery angels trailing forever their marble robes; of Mrs. Plummer, huge and grotesque, moving lightly with grace. I think of how Mr. Plummer had called me a child of destiny and I had not really believed. But knowing now that since a faraway day when Mr. Dolph said "The dander is up," destiny had watched and waited. And at the time ordained had led me to this day and Wes.

Yet, it struck me to wonder was this—the present—final destiny? Or only a turn in the road that would lead on somewhere from here? I could not believe that destiny was wholly achieved by love, important though love might be. Destiny, I sensed, would transcend self and the loneliness of the heart. Destiny was of God. And who except God could know what final destiny was?

It was Mitty who waked me a second time, who stood smiling above me. "Hop up, dearie! Mr. Andrew's sent you a wedding present. It'll be right up."

Obeying, I looked at her, puzzled. "Andrew? A wedding present? But he sent me a present already. What on earth can this be?"

"The sooner you see it the sooner you'll know. Now smooth your hair a bit, while I go let it come up."

I smoothed my hair, retied the sash of my dressing gown and, turning to face the door, waited. And when someone knocked I crossed to the door and opened it and saw with incredulous eyes—Mr. Dolph. As big as ever and as brown. With the whip swinging over his arm, the bad eye dancing and prancing, and a smile all over his face.

I cried, "Oh Mr. Dolph!" and hugged him and stepped back to look at him, he laughing delightedly all the while and I finally laughing as delightedly. For delighted I was. Not only because I had found him at last. But because he was straight and hale and his swaggering self again. And never was the great heart more evident than when, leading him to a chair, I sat beside him and told him all that had happened. For while he could only ejaculate, “Well I'm whupped! Whupped for fair,” what he felt shone in his beaming face.

My story finished, I asked for his. Where had he been? I questioned. And how had he been? I had wondered, I said, and worried. He had been so good to me, so kind. He listened, the good eye regarding me with thoughtful fondness, the bad one out of bounds. When I finished he laid his big brown hand upon mine. “Little one”—how steady his voice—“Dolph Queen looking at you sees a little gel, one with a true and loving heart. That's growed up to a fine lady. That lady also with true and loving heart. But, little one, Dolph Queen's right as Dick's hatband. At present I've got the bull—meaning life in general—by the tail.”

I rejoiced to hear it and when I had told him so, I asked what had brought about this wonderful change.

He slapped his broad thigh a resounding blow. “Well now, I'll tell you. I've joined up with the gypsies.”

I stared at him incredulously. “The gypsies?”

He gave his thigh another resounding blow. “Gypsies I said and gypsies I mean, though spoken of by some as Irish horse traders.”

A glimmer of light dawned on my mind. “You mean, that come to Atlanta every spring? In their painted wagons? To bury their dead?”

“Them I mean. Gypsies.”

“But, Mr. Dolph”—I leaned toward him—“tell me how?”

It had all come about, he said, 'long of that blasted rheumatism; which showed that bad sometimes had a way of working for good. For it was 'long of that rheumatism he'd gone over in Cobb County to stay with Zed McNair a spell. And the gypsies coming south as per schedule and making camp on the land next to Zed's, also per schedule, he got acquainted with 'em. And took to 'em in a manner of speaking.

Wide-eyed I echoed, “Took to 'em?”

“Took to 'em. Took to their way of jousting about in them dazzly little waggins. Staying no place long. Pitching camp sleeping in waggins and tents, trading in horseflesh or prope'ty or whatever notioned 'em. Yet reg'lar and set in their habits in their irreg'lar way. So I took to 'em. And havin' took to gypsies in general, I took to one in pertic'lar.”

I echoed again, “One, in particular?”

He confirmed it with a solemn nod. “A widow lady handsome as ever you see and smart as a trivet.”

“Mr. Dolph, what are you trying to tell me?”

He slapped his thigh a resounding whack. “Lor' love ye, little one, I up and got married.”

“Married, Mr. Dolph? You—married?”

“Married I say and married I mean. A year come spring. To a widow lady with cumbers.”

“Cumbers?” My echo was doubtful. “Cumbers, Mr. Dolph?”

He nodded gravely and held up four fingers. “Four little gels.”

I gasped. “Daughters you mean, Mr. Dolph?”

"For a fact. Four of 'em! Two years apart. Two to eight."

Too astonished for words, I could only stare speechless. But finally I again found my voice. This was a surprise, I said. My head moved in wonder. Such a thing had never entered my head. Had it entered, my head would have refused it. He nodded slowly as if his surprise equaled mine. "It whups me," he said, his voice that of a man struck by a cyclone. "It really whups me for fair."

But I hastened to add wholeheartedly, I thought it wonderful, too. No one knew better than I the great kindness the four little "cumbers" would have from him. Rubbing his nose he listened, thoughtful and solemn.

In a way, he replied, I war right. They war a joy. In another way they warn't. Those little gels smart as whips and so lovin', put him in mind of one little gel and in that way they war a joy. But if I was acquainted with little gels, and being one it was likely, I had er idea what jousting about in the waggin meant in the way of four little gels—and water. How stopping to take on water and stopping to let out water, that waggin in a day's travel made more stops than a switch engine.

He laughed, and so violently the tears ran down his face, and I laughed too almost as violently. When we could laugh no more we looked at each other in exhausted silence, his good eye steadfast, the bad one anything else. It was like this Mitty found us when, opening the door, she herded the gypsy wife and four young "cumbers" into the room. And then such a time as we had. I telling Mr. Dolph how lovely they were and meaning it; and telling Lorna his wife how wonderful he was, and meaning that too; and all the time the four little girls hanging on Mr. Dolph like kittens and pulling his hair and kissing his nose and peeping around at me. As if they found me as wonderful as I found them, and their mother as well. For she was a beautiful woman. Straight, deep-breasted and brown as a berry, she moved like a queen, vivid skirts swinging, the tiny bells on her high red shoes tinkling.

Then Mitty said Miss Camilla waited downstairs to serve them wedding cake and ice cream, and after dozens of hugs and kisses ushered them out of the door. But not Mr. Dolph. Hat in hand, he stood before me steadfast and grave again, as I pled again that they stay for my wedding.

"Little one, 'long of pitching camp tonight over in Cobb County we best be taking off. But afore I go one thing I got to know. If ye don't mind my askin'."

"Dear Mr. Dolph ask me anything—anything—"

He turned his hat in his hands. "When Mr. Andrew's letter finally reaches me by way of being forwarded by Zed from Cobb County, it bein' my standing address, it tells of you anxious to know my whereabouts. But nothing more. And thinkin' p'haps you're needin' a friend I come lickety-split. Aiming if things pull on you too sharp-like, to take you 'long in the waggin with me and Lorny and the cumbers." The smile he gave me was so humble I had to wink back the tears.

I took his big hand and held it. I loved him for the thought, I said, but it did not surprise me. Too well I knew his generous heart. Too often it had lightened mine. I would have said more but words failed me. And after a little he spoke.

"I comes lickety-split." The good eye twinkled humorously. "And what do I find? That things in general has sprung up. Into as fine a lady as ever I see. And pretty beyond any way to say it."

In spite of the tears I was laughing again. "Now, Mr. Dolph!"

"Pretty I says and pretty I mean. But here's whut I'm wantin' to ask. If things in general—is happy?"

I told him how happy I was. Of the kindness of everyone. I told him of Wes whom I loved, who loved me. Wes whom tonight I would marry.

He heard me gravely but when I finished the twinkle had returned to his eye.

"Tell him whut is to be your husband," he said, "how Dolph Queen says this. That you are loving and willing and eager to please and not needin' a touch of the whip. That you handles best to er easy hand. And if he'll be rememberin' it Dolph Queen will be thankin' him."

Later, I watched from my window as he and Lorny and the four little "cumbers" clambered into the painted wagon that waited in the rear drive and with a pop of his whip and unbelievable clatter drove off. And as, leaning, I waved at the numerous hands that waved back, I thought what a wonderful wedding present they were. I must not forget to thank Andrew for making my wedding day perfect.

"Dearly beloved, we are gathered together here . . ."

Now I believed. And knew I had believed nothing before this moment because I had been afraid it would never come. Afraid, as dressed at last I stood, all misty veil and trailing white, before them; Mitty smiling as her small fist dashed at her eyes; Miss Camilla calmly surveying me, and with competent dimpled hands arranging my veil again; Miss Ad smiling and nodding like a wind-up toy that must go until it runs down. But I was afraid to believe.

Mr. Poteat came in the door and with him, distant, muted music that, closing the door, he closed out. For a moment he stood against it, slim and distinguished in his evening clothes, the hair like tarnished silver, the quick eyes in the ruined face taking me in. "And this beautiful bride I must give away?" he asked gallantly and, crossing, kissed my cheek gently, and said, "I am proud of you, Jessica." Smiling I thanked him and we chatted, though of what I do not know; but I was afraid to believe.

Miss Camilla moved toward the door, said, "It's almost time. I'll get the bridesmaids—Ad, don't forget. Be at the top of the stairs and watch for my signal." Through the door she left open I saw the bridesmaids slip down the hall to cluster at the head of the stairs like a huge bouquet, heard from the rooms below the discreet buzz of talk and the rustle of skirts that rose from the wedding guests gathered there. Who waited, I told myself, to see a wedding, and that wedding mine. Still I was afraid to believe it.

Someone put my shower bouquet on my arm, showed me the right way to hold it, then someone else hissed suddenly, "Now," and I heard the hush that pervaded the rooms below and after a little the music that swelled and soared. "Here Comes The Bride," it said; and the bridesmaids poised behind Miss Ad like quivering butterflies waited for the signal. Mr. Poteat, bowing, offered his arm and on it I moved toward the door; then on sudden thought looked back and saw Mitty's eyes. And breaking away from Mr. Poteat's arm, I ran back and put my arms around her again, not caring for my flowers. She patted my shoulder cheerfully, matter-of-factly. "Now run on, dearie, you don't want to be worrying your bridegroom."

So I went and on Mr. Poteat's arm followed the bridesmaids down the stairs, pacing my steps to theirs as I had been told, seeing as in a dream the faces, most of them strange, that lifted to watch me; their eyes as still and rapt as if they watched their youth march by. As in a dream, I followed the aisle between the white ribbons to the improvised altar of flowers and palms; saw the surpliced and solemn minister and the young man Breck. Then I saw Wes. Tall and grave and beautiful, his eyes meeting mine, not gay and teasing but serious and intent; almost, I thought, troubled. Mr. Poteat placed my hand in his and as together we faced the minister awareness flashed through me. Wes too had been afraid to believe; the last few weeks had been for him—as for me—a time in which utmost bliss in the new and unknown life was mingled with utmost dread. And at this thought love filled my breast and grew stronger and stronger. And uncertainty and fear dropped away. Now I believed. Now I was not afraid.

"With this ring I thee wed . . ."

His warm brown fingers holding my cold ones, he repeated the wondrous words quietly, steadily, but I felt the brown fingers quiver as he slid the wide gleaming circle on mine. I thought, surprised, He feels this as much as I. Then it was my voice I heard. "I, Jessica, take thee, Wesley," it repeated, my mind absorbed in the words but going along two paths at once as it does in moments of deep feeling; one leading back to my childhood and Pastor Cantrell's sermon and Mitty's voice saying, "For better or for worse and let no man put asunder . . . and cleave unto . . ." And knowing that I would cleave unto my love until death and even beyond it.

"I pronounce you man and wife. . . ."

I looked at him with lifted head as the words married us, thinking swiftly and with a rush of wonder, "Now I belong. Now I am wanted." All the old life was ended, the new life beginning. Miss Mabie had said, "Better for you perhaps. Beginning with nothing, everything in the end." And for an instant my radiant flowing happiness dimmed. For this, I realized, was not end but beginning—and what would the ending be?

Then, as swiftly as it had dimmed, happiness flared again; for Wes was taking me in his arms and his lips, leaning to mine, murmured, "Hello Doc." And I knew. We were one now. Now and forever. At the end as in the beginning, I belonged to him. I belonged.

Against a palm-banked wall Wes and I stood with Miss Camilla beside us while the guests filed by two at a time, as—Wes whispered—the animals entered the ark. They took our hands, they voiced their congratulations. "Hope you'll be happy" . . . "Our sincere good wishes" . . . and the jokesters having their jokes. Wes and I said "Thank you" and "Thank you" and "Thank you" over and over until the words had no meaning, nor did time; and the faces that floated before me like unattached balloons, separate and single but passing, were merged with the others, the soft beating music, and the fragrance of flowers and perfume.

The ladies, handsomely dressed, their arms encased in their long white wrinkled kid gloves, murmured, "Lovely wedding . . . lovely bride . . . lovely table . . ." their eyes slipping over my figure with the same avid gleam I had seen on a long-ago day in Miss Pack's, and reviving her wheedling voice: "Who was your fokes, sweetie?" Now my heart swelled in my breast with joy almost too great to contain. I looked up at Wes, brown and vivid beside me, and thought, "He is my folks. Now and forever. 'Til death do us part."

They passed on, the beautiful ladies and the men they pulled in their train; drawn, as by a lodestar, to the dining room and the bride's table, where the cake rising high and in splendor was flanked by platters of food; and where butlers poured from gold-necked bottles the dancing, golden champagne. And finally Wes and I stood deserted against the banked palms.

Wes breathed, "Thank God, that's over!" and Miss Camilla said briskly, "Now's your chance to slip up to change for the train, Jess. I'll go find Mitty. I know she will want to help you." She moved off a step but stopped, her voice breaking out pleased and surprised. "Why, Mr. Carr, how delightful! I didn't know you were here. I was afraid that Miriam's health . . . and Miriam, you too! Wes"—she turned back to us—"Mr. and Mrs. Carr could come after all. . . ." She put her hand on my arm. "This is our Jessica. Jess, you must know Mr. Algernon Carr. . . ."

He took my hand, the tall grave man with the cold black eyes, and the quiet voice said, "How do you do, Mrs. Carrebee," but the eyes probing mine were saying, "You are a very clever young lady." Even his tall straight back, as he moved away, repeated "very clever young lady." Then Mrs. Carr was before me, the delicate cameo face under the nut-brown hair looking miserably ill. I said, "Oh Mrs. Carr!" as she took my hand, not shaking it like the others but holding it tight within hers.

"I'm so glad you came to my wedding," I said. "I didn't know you were . . ." Almost I said "invited" but caught myself just in time, and said "coming," instead.

She smiled such a sad little smile. "Nor did I. But I wished to come. Very much. I hadn't forgot you, you see. Or that my Laura Lee loved you."

I asked about Laura Lee but she could tell me no more than Oakes had told me before. "We hear from her now and then"—her eyes were wide with their pain—"but always from a different place so we never know . . . just where she is." A quiver barely perceptible swept over her face. "It's a terrible thing not to know where your children are, or if they are safe . . . or well treated. . . ."

Fervently, I wished for words that would offer some sort of comfort but, without pretending, I had none. I was too convinced that Bucky would never treat anyone kindly; that, callous, indifferent himself, he would be blind to the need of another. So for a moment we stood, each thinking of Laura Lee; then, as if just recollecting her husband, she glanced uneasily over her shoulder to where his tall figure waited, his eyes watching, I thought, as a jailor watches his captive. The thin face quivered again and her hand dropped away from mine, nerveless, and as if irresistibly drawn she forgot me and all else and moved obediently toward him. But before turning to go on beside her, his dark eyes met mine again as if impelled to say for one last time, "A very clever young lady."

Miss Camilla hissed, "Now! Go while you can!" and Wes and I slipped up the stairs, Wes scooping my train up in his arm as we ran. In the upper hall he drew me out of view and, taking me in his arms, held me close, and whispering "Hello Doc," kissed me a long, long time. And a little later, floating on clouds, I went to my room to change and found Mitty waiting, as always, to help however she could.

What an extraordinary thing it was to be married! To believe as I did in the first days of honeymoon that one added to one equaled not two, but one. A stupendous discovery which mathematics, reputed to be an exacting science, ignored, and language, with no pretension of exactness, recognized. *My* luggage and *his, my* room and *yours* became *ours,* and the narrow, cramped pronoun *I* was banished—not forever as I believed but at least for the time—and replaced by the all-encompassing *our* and *we*. Such miraculous, breathtaking words that each time Wes used them my heart felt as if it stopped in its tracks. A fancy which, had it been fact, would have led to my early demise, for Wes used them often. In the morning he said, "Shall *we* breakfast in *our* room, Mrs. Carrebee?" and later, "*We* must get tickets for Maxine Elliot," or "*We* must hear Patti" or "*We* must go to the opera. Caruso is singing."

We go to the theatre and the hero compared with Wes to me is insipid. *We* go to the opera and Caruso is equally so, except for the wonderful voice (though I'm convinced if Wes wished he could sing better). And

I wonder if, watching and hearing, he hates me because marriage deprives him of fame he might easily have.

Such thoughts I kept locked in my breast lest Wes think me lovesick and foolish, not the sedate, settled wife which after a week I knew that I was. Though the truth was I loved him each day more and more—and logically; for each day revealed a new Wes to love. One never seen before. There was the Wes who dealt with head waiters, those starched and pontifical purveyors of privilege, and by his courteous assumption that he would receive only the best, always received it. There was the Wes, no matter where we happened to be—walking along the crowded street, having supper in some little place he would find—who would suddenly break into what he or I said and send me a long deep look and say quietly, "Hello, Doc."

There rises another Wes. We stroll back to the Astor in the silver dusk unbroken as yet by the lights of the night. Wes, with his easy slouching grace, pausing to wait, hands in pockets, while I peer into the windows of shops. Before one—it was a florist—I stop and look and linger and ask, "Wes, what are those lovely bluish flowers?"

His eyes follow mine and he tells me, "Those are Parma violets, Doc."

"Violets?" I gasped. "Why, I never saw violets like those."

He took my arm gently, led me into the shop, and a small prissy man tripped to meet us. Bowing, he said, "Madame," then, "can I help you, sir?"

"Please. I want all of the Parma violets you have."

The little man's eyebrows shot up, his voice was gently reproving. "But we have quite a quantity, sir. At least fifty dozen, sir, more or less."

Wes took out his wallet. "I'll take them," he said, and the salesman, his face smoothly polite once more, tripped to the rear of the shop.

I asked helplessly, "But Wes—why so many?"

He did not answer or glance at me. Hands in pockets, whistling softly and bemused, he sauntered to the rear of the store where the salesman counted and boxed.

"This must be a very special occasion, sir," the salesman said.

"Yes . . . it is," Wes answered briefly.

He came after a little, carrying the box with the violets, and we left the shop and continued down Broadway. A street of silvery dusk no more but jeweled now; brilliant and dazzling.

I scolded, "Darling, you shouldn't have spent—"

His voice flashed over mine and he sent me a glance so wary that for an instant I thought, Why this isn't Wes— Then the stranger went out of his face. He said to me gently, "Don't ever say that again, Doc."

Dismayed because he misunderstood, I said, my lips trembling, "I just wanted—I wondered." Struck by a sudden thought, I looked up at him. "Did you buy them for me?"

"Of course."

"You see, I meant I would have been happy . . . with only a few. So I wondered why . . . so many. . . ."

He asked, "Don't you know?" and I shook my head.

"Ah Doc!" He thrust his hand through my arm as we walked and drew me nearer, smiling at me. "Don't you see? I've got to make up for the violets you've never had."

Reaching, he touched the tears on my cheek. "Doc," he accused, "not crying?"

I moved my head to deny. "Bright lights make my eyes water." But Mitty's excuse served me no better than Mitty. He didn't believe me. Laughing, he said, "Forget it, sweetheart. We'll go to our room, put on our best bib and tucker and have a hot time in the old town tonight." Then with our lifting tension a fit of merriment came over us both; and our eyes laughing and devilish, we took longer and longer steps, rose higher and higher on tiptoe; and prancing like two happy children, like this went to the Astor and through the revolving door; and inside stopped and looked at each other—and burst into laughter.

"Forget it!" he had said. But, remembering, I knew as long as I lived I would not forget. That when I was old and my honeymoon blurred by time, this little fragment of time would shine, radiant and undimmed. Wes wanting to give me the flowers he thought I had missed; Wes like a devilish schoolboy as we tiptoed our way down the street.

"Forget it," he said. . . .

For the first week of our honeymoon we might have been two invisible shades slipping through the throngs of the city. Unknown and knowing no one, our privacy remained uninvaded. Unnoticed we strolled down Fifth Avenue, drawn by windows into the shops, in them beguiled into buying. In one, silk for Mitty's "handsome" dress, in another her watch of gold. In still another Petey's new cage, a magnificent Chinese pagoda, painted green and trimmed with gold just as once I had dreamed it. For Miss Ad silk too for a dress, for Miss Camilla from Tiffany's one of the new fountain pens, solid gold with her monogram. Presents for Drusilla and Eula the cook and the coachman Lem. Telling the salesgirl, "Mrs. Wes Carrebee, Hotel Astor," and feeling very much married, yet with a heart that sang.

"Cissa!" I said as we left the last shop. "We must buy Cissa a present."

It was easier said than accomplished, for Wes, as if bored with shopping, would give me no help. When I asked, "Do you think . . . ?" and held up whatever I pondered—a lace fan—an inlaid dressing case—and at last a bracelet of moonstones—he would shrug, lift his brows, say each time I asked, "Whatever you think, Doc."

I touched the moonstone bracelet as it lay on the black velvet pad. "I think this. It's like her somehow. Cool and misty . . . and lovely. . . ." He looked at it with expressionless eyes, then turned away. So I had to make the decision and buy it without his approval, thinking, He has been sweet and so patient but he's bored with shopping. Yet next day, in a small darkling shop, he bought Cissa a present himself. One he found on a shelf of hand-carved toys imported from foreign lands. It was a tiny hut, a gingerbread hut right out of a fairy tale, and happening upon it, he stood above it, his gray eyes intent. The old man wrapping my parcels noticed. "In a minute I show you," he called.

Wes turned and repeated, "Show me?"

"Ya ya." The old man came from behind the counter and crossed to the fairy-tale hut; and reaching, wound it. The music, light and tinkling and incredibly sweet, started to play, and two tiny figures, a boy and a girl, swung through the door of the hut to the stoop; and stood there, tiny hands clasped, tiny heads turning stiffly.

The old man asked in delight, "You recognize—yes? Hansel and Gretel?" One veined hand tapping the other, kept time with the tinkling music. "Humperdinck's score," he said. "Now—comes the children's prayer." Softly he sang the words, his head keeping time too.

"When at night I go to sleep
Fourteen angels watch do keep."

After a little he warned, "Now, the grand chorus—

"When misery is at its lowest ebb
God the Lord stretches forth His hand."

The music clicked and stopped, the children with another click swung back into the gingerbread house, and the old man, head on one side, smiled up at us. "From Switzerland. Nice, *ya?"*

We agreed and Wes said, "I think I'll get it for Cissa." The old man put the hut in its box and when he had wrapped and tied it, we said good night and left. As we strolled up the street, I asked Wes if he would tell me the story of Hansel and Gretel.

"Of course," he replied. "Don't you know it?"

I said I couldn't seem to remember. Mitty had read me so many stories. . . .

But when he told it to me I knew that Mitty would have cut out her tongue before she would have read me that story. Yet now oddly enough I needed very much to know it. For standing before the gingerbread hut as the sweet tinkly music wound on, I had glimpsed on Wes's face a sadness that in turn made me sad. How darling of Wes, I thought—to suffer for Hansel and Gretel. Which, he explained, was the story of two lost children.

It was nearing October when Wes and I came home to Hickory Hill, and as we chugged up the rise in his auto my happiness was as high as the hilltop. Such a wonderful house it seemed as we wended our way toward it. Plain and strong and friendly, like the earth in which it was rooted, its delicate faded yellow overlaid with the color of autumn, as if autumn herself had, through the years, laid her patina upon it.

Wes gave a low whistle. "Say, Andrew's done a good job! The old place doesn't look bad."

My laugh was contented and proud. "Bad? It's a wonderful house!"

Reaching, he tousled my hair. "Sweetheart, that's what I said. To tell you the truth, I'm surprised. It didn't look much before, though you'll admit I was pretty damned noble about it. I still think we could have lots more fun in one of the new apartments, where they practically breathe for the tenant."

I smiled at him lest he perceive the small pang stirred by his words, which reason banished by leaping to his defense. Why, reason demanded, should he feel as I felt about Hickory Hill? He had never been homeless, nor faced homeless tomorrows, nor felt, wherever he was, like a stray, unneeded, unwanted. He had been sheltered, protected, had known but one home in his lifetime. Perhaps that home would always be home, regardless of where he might live. But I also banished that thought. Win Wes, Hickory Hill would. Manlike he would admire its good unpretentious strength, respect its simple solidity.

The wheels of the auto lurching over the seldom traveled road laboriously reached the top of the hill and I saw Andrew and Mitty waiting on the veranda. At their welcoming wave, Wes said, "Oh-o, the welcome committee," and we gaily waved back. He parked the auto and together we walked over the land toward the house. I thought *Mr. and Mrs. Wes Carrebee coming home,* and though the walk was a brief walk, consuming no more than two minutes, in that time I lived a lifetime—brought forth children who grew up, went to college and married, Wes had advanced to control of the mill—all by the time we reached the front steps.

At the steps Wes stopped to measure their steep ascent with his eye and called up to Andrew, "What's a fella to do if he arrives slightly drunk? Break his neck on these steps?"

Andrew, as he shook our hands, admitted that not being a drinking man, he had overlooked that contingency. But with the new prohibition law he did not anticipate any trouble from licker if we'd just keep an eye on Miss Mitty.

He looked at her with a fond chuckle but Mitty remained unperturbed. "Now go 'long with you. You talk like I'm a reg'lar toper."

We moved to enter the house but when Wes ordered "Stop" we turned back to face him. Hands in pockets, he faced us gravely and I was nonplused. So serious he seemed, so solemn, yet I fancied I caught in his eyes the familiar glint of his teasing.

"My friends," he said, slowly, funereally, "I am confronted by a serious problem. One on which I request your honest opinion."

We waited, not sure whether or not he was joking.

"It is an old Southern custom," he proceeded judicially, "for the bridegroom to carry his bride over the threshold. Now I want you good people to tell me if you agree that since Jess, contrary to rule, owns the threshold, she should uphold tradition and carry the bridegroom over."

Of course we all laughed, and so heartily that I knew Mitty and Andrew, like me, had half believed he was serious. His own swift laughter flashing, Wes grabbed me up in his arms and carried me over the doorsill. I called him crazy and mad, and kissed the tip of his nose, and he put me down and spanked me on the place where I sit and I thought no more of it. I had not learned, as I was to learn, that joking and lighthearted teasing are often a flag that a valiant pride waves to conceal that it has been humbled. I did not know, so as we went through the house no shadow dimmed my elation. If it struck me that Andrew as he led us about to show what had been done here and there talked more to Wes than to me, and constantly asked his opinion, I thought it only the nature of men to be absorbed by gasoline pumps and cesspools and the best kind of gutters. Soon Mitty and I left them and slipped off to look at the kitchen, to a woman ever the heart of the house.

And oh, what a kichen it was! Not gleaming white, like Miss Camilla's with white gas stove and icebox coldly efficient and sterile. But its wide oak floorboards and old-fashioned pine cabinets glowing and warm and friendly. On the open hearth, which Andrew had left as it was, snapped one of Mitty's incomparable fires, and the big coal range in the corner murmured in homely comfort. It was no trouble a-tall, Mitty said of the range, viewing it with an affectionate eye. You banked it at night and pulled this or that in the morning, and a widow with a beau didn't perk up any quicker. Did I know that Andrew had arranged for the Carrebee mill to supply us with coal when 'twas needed? And now why didn't I take off my coat and make myself right at home? I could start out feeling at home by helping her dish up the dinner.

We dished dinner up, set the table before the fire, I thinking as we worked how already the kitchen was Mitty's. Her flowers at window sills, with Petey chirping above them. Her gay curtains crisp, framing the view that they gave of the long slope of the hill with its tangle of flaming treetops slipping down to the hollow where a Negro cabin nestled. Occupied, Mitty said, by Adeline, a mighty good woman who'd let us have all the fresh eggs we needed. Now, if I would call the men folks, dinner was ready to eat.

A gay and lightsome dinner that was. Andrew proudly produced a quart of champagne brought along, he said, for the "christening," and, he confided, hidden out until now on account of Miss Mitty's failing. One of the reasons, he added, he'd brought only one quart, the other—his eyes twinkled—being financial. And now—he filled our glasses and held his own high—he'd like to propose a toast. To the master of Hickory Hill. So we drank to Wes, then I proposed a toast to Andrew and Andrew toasted "the noblest of her sex—when not in her cups—Mrs. McDaniel." And we were all tremendously gay.

When we had eaten of Mitty's dinner heartily enough to please even Mitty, we sat contentedly over coffee, and talked. Then Wes, with an exaggerated Southern drawl, said it was an old Southern custom, ma'am, for the old marster of de ole plantation to hep hisself to a leetle snooze every day after dinner. He leaned and kissed the top of my head. Ole mistiss, he advised, could stay with the field hands and do up the dishes.

After I helped Mitty clear table, she, claiming she had a few special things she wanted to do, shooed Andrew and me from the kitchen. Together we went through the house. Our progress was slow, so I might more fully absorb the quiet simple charm Andrew had achieved for me. For it was Andrew who had arranged for all that was done while Wes and I honeymooned. The house made sound, the floors scraped and polished, the walls not papered but painted in the new fashion, a soft luminous yellow that increased the feeling of space and restfulness. It was Andrew who had found the old pine and oak pieces and had them rubbed to the mellow glow of the old secretary left in the house.

When I had admired and exclaimed over all he had achieved at so little cost, he told me, "There are a few odds and ends in the carriage house you haven't seen."

Swinging the keys on his finger, he walked with me across the yard to the carriage house. "I was thinking it might be a good idea for you to get rid of the stuff inside so Wes, come bad weather, will have a place for his car."

"What is inside?" I asked as he put the key in the lock.

"I expect the sort of thing most people chuck out. I didn't look at it."

He tugged at the double doors and when they creaked open, we stepped inside. Except for the dust, it was ordered and neat, the stacks of storage swathed in old blankets or huge squares of coarse cloth. It was under such a dusty cloth that I discovered the portrait in the carved, massive frame and, curious, dragged it out to the light and with Andrew's help stripped its wrappings away.

I saw a dark square of painting, held in an ancient frame, ornate and curlicued and with its gilt rubbed off in spots. Out of the dark background, shadowy and deep and mysterious, appeared the head of a child. A boy, his face slender and sensitive, with luminous, dark eyes that gazed at me from the canvas as if, in a moment, he would ask to break free of the world of paint, and join the world of the living.

I gazed at it, startled by an unaccountable sense of familiarity, though certain I had never laid eyes on it.

I asked Andrew, "Do you know who it is?"

"Well, I can't say for sure. It might be a real boy. Again it might be just a picture some artist dreamed up."

I looked at the portrait again, puzzled but fascinated by the feeling of familiarity—and suddenly it was explained. There was something of Wes in it. It could easily be Wes as a child. It wasn't, of course. But if

I had tried to imagine Wes before time had banished the infantile expression it would be of a child such as this. I asked Andrew, "Do you think it has a look of Wes?"

He cleared his throat—I thought, rather uncomfortably. "Well . . . they both have dark hair. But Wes's eyes . . . they're lighter, aren't they?"

Wisely, I remarked that you couldn't judge by eyes. For one thing, the artist might have made them darker and larger to get a certain effect. Or Wes's eyes might have changed.

He nodded so agreeably that I concluded the discussion held little interest for him. "Shall I wrap it and put it back?" he asked.

I almost said yes but with a quick change of mind said, "No. I want to take it into the house and hang it over my sitting-room mantel. I can at least pretend it is of Wes."

He said teasingly, "Yes, ma'am, boss lady. Whatever you say," and picked it up. "We'll clean it a bit and I'll hang it for you."

In the kitchen, he asked Mitty for soft clean rags. She brought them and watched without comment as he dusted the painting carefully. When I asked if she didn't agree that it had a look of Wes, she pursed her lips.

"Blessed, if you see it thataway, I reckon it does. I figger folks see in pictures what they want to see."

I said, "Oh, Mitty! Andrew wouldn't agree with me, but I thought you would."

She laughed her soft little laugh. "Why, I do agree, dearie . . . that you likely see some favor to Wes. For I see favor to a little brother of mine who died of the summer complaint." She reached into a drawer and handed Andrew a picture hook. "Reckon you'll need this," she said.

He smiled at her admiringly. "Mitty, if you had run the Civil War for us, we'd have licked those Yankees."

She tossed her head. "I don't know about that. But I do know that President Abe could have kept us from fighting that war, easy as pie, if he'd understood folks down South. All he needed to do was tell the South they *couldn't* free the slaves and they'd a freed 'em or killed theirselves trying. Just like this business of closin' saloons. Folks what never put foot in one will start drinkin' at home. More than ever, most likely."

Andrew said, slyly, "I know of a case . . . a mighty fine lady . . ."

She exclaimed, "Go 'long with you! And put up that picture if you're intending to. Time is wasting."

Laughing, Andrew and I went to the sitting room, and when he had hung the picture over the mantel, we stepped back and surveyed it. The fire on the hearth was reflected in the depths of the child's dark eyes and made them glow even more with life, and impulsively I turned to Andrew. "Don't you see now that Wes *might* have been like that?"

He smiled at me. "Well, now . . . I kinda agree with Mitty that we see what we want to see."

I asked, "Then what do you see?"

Smiling, he shook his head. "I won't spoil yours by telling. But, like you, I see a trace of somebody. . . ."

My eyes went back to the picture, speculatively. "I expect," I ventured, "you see Mathias Purefoy?"

"Maybe," he admitted. "I was mighty fond of the old gentleman."

Though I could not find in the glowing child's face even a trace of the old man with the sharp fox-eyes, I held my silence. He refused to spoil it for me, so I would not spoil it for him.

"Wait and see," I told him. "I'll prove that I am right."

His hand raked his hair. "And have you figured out how you can prove it?"

"Why," I said airily, "when you see my first son."

Andrew drove off in his rented buggy and I spent the time until Wes woke from his snooze settling in, which, thanks to Mitty's thoroughness, was more of a state of mind than of actual work. However, like a child with a new dollhouse, I made a great pretense of being housewifely and busy: looked over the wedding presents stored away by Mitty, wondering as I surveyed the array of glasses and vases, the six carving sets, the eight clocks, how in a lifetime I would ever manage to use them, unless, like Mr. Dolph, I joined up with the gypsies.

This, I thought, as I peeped into closets and opened mysterious doors on I knew not what unexpected treasure, this was the real beginning of marriage. The deep tranquil joy, impossible in the beautiful, fascinating, fearful time of the honeymoon; equally impossible in the deluge of parties and dinners given in our honor on our return by, Miss Camilla said, the "very best" people, none of whom we must offend. So we went to the Old Guard's dinners, where over the frugal table the Civil War was refought, with Fort Sumter fired on as the soup came in; with dessert, General Lee "outnumbered." We dined with the People of Substance in sumptuous extravagant splendor, where the talk was of stock in railroads, cotton, and timber, their voices hushing with awe as they intoned the name Coca-Cola; as if it was an all-powerful God that held their fate in its hands.

We dined with the gay and untroubled Young Marrieds; the women so pretty, or, if not, with soft eyes and hands and beautiful clothes attaining the semblance of beauty. The men not all handsome, but friendly and, with their slow Southern way, often gallant. They asked me to dance, they paid me extravagant compliments, asked Wes, their eyes accusing, "Where did you find her?" or whistled the popular song "Where did you get that girl?" And no one asked, even to make polite conversation, where was I from? Was I kin to the Augusta Kildares? Or Rome's? Or Savannah's? And though I had learned of the mazed and crisscrossing threads of kinship that knitted the South together, it did not strike me as strange that I was asked for no credentials. To be Mrs. Wes Carrebee, I assumed, was sufficient.

When they, who accepted bounty as kings accept divine right, were friendly and, in their way, made "homefolks" of me, a stranger, I was pleased and I was grateful. If some of them said in casual conversation that "Any nigger would steal, even a good one" or "Keep Jews out of our clubs" or spoke contemptuously of "poor white trash" or "lintheads," unsure and uncertain, I would sit silent. But I would remind myself that they were Wes's friends who, for Wes's sake, had been kind, had given wonderful parties for us, had taken me to their hearts. So, for Wes I would sit in silence. It was Wes who made possible these exciting friends, who laughed and danced and played with no thought of tomorrow. Wes who made it possible that I laugh and dance in gleaming gowns, low-necked and sleeveless, seeing in other eyes that at least to those eyes, for the moment, I was beautiful, too. Aware at that moment that Wes strolled across the floor, aware of the women's eyes trailing the tall easy figure and fluttering at his approach as leaves flutter in sudden wind. And, as they fluttered and preened, thinking, He's mine . . . he belongs to me.

Often, watching, I pondered on the secret of his fascination, which was—or so it seemed—impossible to resist. That made him his mother's darling and favorite, and made adoring slaves of servants. That made even his creditors (and of these I found he had many) love him, and the sternest dowagers melt.

I did not learn it, of course, though there was much I did learn about him. I learned that his voice could at one moment be as gentle as a woman's, in the next cut like a whip. He could be a devilish boy laughing and teasing, and as relentlessly cold as a blade. He could be the tenderest of lovers or a mocking young satyr, jibing at something I said. At times, everything was a game. Passing me, he would suddenly seize my hands and spin me wildly in "Stiff Starch" and when, weak with laughing, I cried, "Wes, stop!" he would pull me to him and hold me close for a moment. "Ah, Doc," he said at one of these times, "life's been too, too damned serious. You don't even know how to play."

He was right, I thought. I did not know how to play. I—and this shocked me—I was older than he. Not in years nor superior wisdom but in awareness that life is challenge that you, of yourself, must meet. Yet when, with brooding eyes, he sat withdrawn and silent, I would be . . . not so sure. What did I know of *this* Wes? I would ask. His thoughts, his dreams, his awareness? What did I know of Wes at all, except I knew nothing about him?

In the seclusion of Hickory Hill, days and weeks slipped by almost unnoticed, and autumn, sadly dropping her leaves, withdrew at winter's approach. I did not grieve at her leaving; for if marriage was not as I dreamed it, the different happiness reality brought was not in any way lessened, and we, for the time, were happy and oblivious to all of the world.

On bright mornings, I would stand on my hilltop with Wes, or alone perhaps, when Wes slept late, and it was delight to be young and in love, and contented with love's fulfillment: to feel myself borne up above the landscape that stretched below me; to breathe in the sharp winter air with its flavor of sedge fields and earth and pine trees. I would think, My world is this hilltop, the new world I many years dreamed of; lifting me high above that lowland of being unloved and lonely. Now I was never alone, and even alone, was not lonely. When Wes drove to town as he would now and then, separation, too, brought delight; for returning, he strode, his eyes eager, to the steps where I waited. Taking me close in his arms, he would kiss the tip of my nose or tousle my hair and murmur his wonderful foolishness that was never foolish to me.

In those first happy days, he never came empty-handed, but produced from this pocket or that, small presents for Mitty and me. Inconsequential gifts without value, except for the thought that prompted their giving.

There was the winter dusk when, returning, he opened the kitchen door and announced, "Ladies, I want you to meet a gentleman," and wheeling, we found the pointer dog regarding us from the doorway with enormous and noble dignity. When he had taken us in, as one who is royal he walked and stretched himself out at the hearth, as much at home as if he had known no other fire, no other home but this, which 'til the day he died would be his.

Such events as these made up those first days of life at Hickory Hill. These and a thousand others, so little considered then, we were not conscious that they would be remembered. The first time Wes ate Mitty's own special battercakes and her spoon bread; the night Wes having forgot to stop by the store and fetch home the kerosene oil for the lamps, we ate supper by fire glow and sat in the dark by the fire; the night the bat slipped into the house, and with broom and mops we all chased him, laughing hysterically.

I would have said, had I been asked, that these were of no significance, for so it seemed at the time. Of these, I thought, I would remember only the love which absorbed us, that made our days constantly gay, the nights passionate, warm and tender. The enchanted world that love created, where the binding seams that had held me ripped apart and allowed the seed of self to expand, where I learned what all lovers learn, that only when you love are you truly alive. And it was Wes who showed me this world of enchantment those first days at Hickory Hill.

Each morning the drowsy cheeping of the birds that lived in the treetops outside my windows woke me at daybreak, and lying beside Wes I watched as the day advanced, each groping finger of light lifting from darkness the furnishings of the room. First Wes's tall chest of drawers, then my toilet table, the low chair beside it, the sofa against the far wall where Wes often napped in daytime.

Marriage, I thought, was like that. Not knowing swiftly, completely, the one you have married, as before marriage you expected. But a gradual dawning which unveils one by one the various faces of love and of loving and living. And if the happiness marriage brings is quite different from that once imagined, you know, and before long, that the lost dream of two hearts beating and dreaming as one had no more to do with marriage than the heroic dreams a young warrior dreams have to do with the actual battle.

I cannot say when the first small shade of doubt moved across consciousness like a surreptitious tenant that takes possession without giving notice, its existence unknown until timidly it makes itself known. At first I was hardly concerned. It was a small weak thing and transient, banished, I believed, when I called myself silly and demanded (of myself) if I was a drivin' woman determined to change my young husband into what he was not? Had I imagined, I asked of myself scornfully, that marriage would take all the variable strands that made up Wes—his lighthearted gaiety, his teasing and jibing, his love of play, his abstracted moods, his swift and sudden angers—and, like the vast looms at the mill, weave them into the dull ordinary stuff of the marriage-tamed husband?

I had imagined no such thing nor did I now want it. There was nothing I would change about Wes, I protested, even if I could. For change, however slight, brings loss as well as gain, and what could I bear to lose of Wes? He had not shown interest in the mill before marriage. Why should I expect it now? His amusements away from home then—golf at East Lake, his hunting, poker games with the Bell House Boys—had been a vital part of his life. Only a fool would expect him to lop it off. Thus, I argued the case for Wes against that first small doubt, sent it humbled back into the limbo from which it had sprung—or so I thought. But a day or two later, I knew it had not really been banished. It had only withdrawn deeper into consciousness and now, as if strengthened and rested, it emerged larger and stronger, and would not be thrust away. Like many another before me, I was forced to accept it as a permanent tenant; and learn to live with it.

I tried to forget it in work. With Mitty's help I gradually transformed Hickory Hill from a house to a home, conquered the cold stiff unfriendliness which a house shows to presumptuous intruders. With satisfaction I saw it become a pleasant place and comfortable, its fires, as winter came on, as bright and glowing as those which long ago burned on Mitty's hearth. Sometimes as she and I worked and Petey warbled in his cage, I had the strange feeling that time had turned back; that we were still in the little house and all that had happened between that time and now—the seminary, the Carrebees, even Wes—was only a dream. Would I ever feel as content and as safe in any house—even Hickory Hill—as I had in the little house? I wondered. Yet . . . it was borne upon me I had been companioned there, too, by doubt as well as loneliness.

As least my misgivings about my feeling for Hickory Hill were resolved as day by day it tightened its hold upon me. It was, I thought, with its simple goodness, its toil, its peaceful rest after toil, the shape of what life should be; but like life it had its problems. Standing beyond the city's limits, it afforded neither gas nor electricity. We burned oil lamps which had to be cleaned and refilled each day. The kitchen range devoured kindling and coal; the oil pump that brought water into the house demanded as much attention as a spoiled child, and was so contrary that Wes, in perfect good humor, announced himself defeated in the struggle for a decent bath; henceforth he would bathe at the club or the Bell House.

He made this announcement to Mitty as he ate his late breakfast in the kitchen. And I in the storeroom checking supplies overheard. Mitty, who stood at the stove cooking the battercakes which he loved, said we'd have to get Mr. Andrew to come out and have a go at that pump.

Wes laughed at her fondly. "You think Mr. Andrew can work miracles, don't you, Mitty?"

She said cheerfully, flipping the cakes on the griddle, "Well now, I don't know about that. I do know he'd have a go at that pump."

She brought the cakes, placed them beside his plate, added the butter. "Now better eat them while they're hot," she advised, and started to turn away, but he reached and caught her hand. "Mitty, I'm not worth my salt as a husband, am I?"

He said it gravely, not laughing, and something caught at my heart; at Mitty's too as I knew when I heard her answer. "Why of course you are." Her voice was gentle and loving. "The best kind of husband there is—at least for some women. Now"—her voice was its cheerful sensible self again—"there are women, I don't doubt, what wouldn't have you on a stick. The kind that don't want a husband but one of those performing dogs they can make jump through hoops on their say-so. But for a loving heart whose name I won't call you're just the right ticket."

He asked slowly, "Do you think that, Mitty?"

She said cheerfully, "And that I do. And I don't think things like that pump mean a hill of beans to 'somebody.' But the way you come in laughing and teasin' and the way you've got of ever letting her know you love her . . . Well sir! that's a reg'lar Stone Mountain of beans, I expect."

His laugh was not quite steady. "Bless you for that, Mitty."

In a moment she exclaimed, "Now you've set there and let those battercakes cold up. I'll cook a fresh batch." Then, as she went toward the stove, "Of course it wouldn't hurt you to have a go at that pump."

He let out a delighted whoop of laughter. "All right, all right! Bring on the cakes and I'll have a go at the damned pump."

He ate his battercakes, got into old clothes and, calling Mitty Simon Legree, fixed the oil pump. As he tinkered Mitty peered over his shoulder, suggesting he try this or that as she handed him pliers and wrenches, and both talking and laughing as they worked. They came into the lunch

I had ready, grease-smeared but triumphant, Wes frankly admiring of Mitty. As he cleaned up at the pine washstand in our room he said quietly, "You know, I've wondered what made you such a damned wonderful person. I guess I know now. It was Mitty."

"I'm not that wonderful," I smiled, "but whatever I am . . . it was Mitty."

He nodded, his eyes abstracted. "I think with a mother like Mitty even Cissa and I . . ." His voice trailed into nothing.

"But, darling, Mitty wasn't my mother," I reminded.

He looked at me, his dark brows quirking. "You mean you weren't born from her body? That doesn't make a woman a mother. Or Mitty less a mother."

Rather surprised at his having opinions on motherhood I asked what *did* make a mother.

"Not taking what you want at the expense of the child."

Prompted by something I saw in his face or intuitively sensed in his mind, I said, "You have a wonderful mother too."

His sharp sudden laugh was a bark.

I said firmly, "Yes she is, Wes. If she wasn't the sort . . . well, like Mitty, you must remember her life was different, her responsibilities . . . It must be terrible for a woman . . . "

His shrug and "Yeah, I guess so" were careless. "Let's go eat that lunch," he said gaily. "You know, I think I'll stay at home with you and Mitty today. It's so quiet out here . . . and peaceful. . . . That is, I'll stay if Mitty will make spoon bread for supper."

We went down to lunch, I gay and lighthearted and telling myself, "See . . . he is beginning to settle down . . ." Entering the kitchen, I cried to Mitty, "Wes says if you'll give him spoon bread for supper he won't go into town today."

Lunch over, we put on coats, hardly needed for the November day was almost like spring, and strolled with Mitty over the grounds of Hickory Hill. She pointed out the different plants she had discovered. These were lilac bushes, she said, and those, over there, oleander; and here two fine cape jessamine bushes though she couldn't abide 'em, they put her in mind of a funeral. They all needed "soil-loosening" though, if they was to thrive in the spring. If she only knew a good strong young man, here she cast a mischievous eye at Wes, one willing to give her a hand.

He told her she need not make sheep's eyes at him. What did she think? That he was a performing dog . . . ?

She laughed when he threw her own words back at her. "Go 'long with you."

"I'm going," he retorted. "This minute." He threw out his arms, stretched and yawned. "I think I'll go catch a little snooze. You see," he told her accusingly, "you've tuckered me out with that pump." Reaching, he took my hand. "Come tuck me in, Doc."

We left Mitty puttering about the yard and hand in hand went to our room. He dropped to the sofa against the wall, hunched the pillow under his head, and I knelt on the floor beside the sofa to unlace and take off his shoes.

He said, "Why are you so good to me, Doc?"

"I love you."

He reached and, pulling me close, his dear dark head against my breast: "I love you too. You don't ever doubt it . . . do you, Doc?"

"I never doubt it," I said, and I didn't.

"Don't you ever doubt it, Doc. Promise me . . . you won't ever . . ."

"I promise, my darling, I promise . . ."

"That's why I need you, Doc . . . somebody who never doubts me. Who won't doubt—come hell or high water. You see, Doc, people are always wondering what's wrong with me. My mother wonders why I don't take hold at the mill . . . my friends wonder why I don't settle down . . . and, Doc, do you know who else wonders what's wrong with me—why I don't settle down? Me, Doc. And *I* don't know why."

With my arms round him to hold, to protect, now it was I who wondered: if there could be worse hurt than this? Someone you loved needing comfort and not knowing just how to give it. Able to do nothing at all except just kneel there in silence cradling his head. Thinking, This is my love, not heroic and unconquerable as once I had dreamed my true love would be. But beset and bedeviled by—I did not know what—but something. With everyone wondering—his mother, his friends, even himself—why he didn't do this or the other; trying to make him over into what they thought he should be. Their doubt and mistrust a seeping poison undermining his faith and his pride in himself.

When I was sure he slept I went downstairs and brought in an armful of logs and built up the sitting-room fire, pulled his chair close before it, placed a small table at hand. He must find home so pleasant, I thought as I worked, he won't want to leave.

In the kitchen I found Mitty mixing a cake. "Thought I'd have a go at the kind Wes likes best," she explained, "devil's food with thick chocolate icing. And where do you think you're going?" she asked as I pulled on a jacket.

"Take the wash down to Adeline and get some of those sweet gum leaves down in the bottom . . . I'll be right back."

I went outside and made my way down the hill that sloped to the bottom, not using the dirt road but slipping and sliding on the carpet of needles put down by the pines that stood straight and tall, sighing just as they had about Mitty's little house. Between their disordered ranks I caught glimpses of the open, almost flat country that surrounded the hill and tried to imagine again what Old Mathias Purefoy had in his mind when he chose this spot as the place to build his house. Had it been because in its isolation it nevertheless afforded a view of the country that stretched flat and unbroken around it? Even now, ahead in the distance I could see across the lowland the vague smudge of smoke that rose from Carrebee Mills.

Reaching the hollow, I peered in Adeline's open door and said, "Hi." She looked up from her ironing, her doleful face breaking into a grin. "I seed you racin' down de hill lak a kangleroo, Miz Carrebee. You better come in an' res' yosef'."

I said, "I can't. I've got to gather some leaves and hurry back." I placed my bundle on the floor. "Here's the wash, Adeline."

"Yassum." She looked toward the dusky recess of the room. "Sparrow," she said severely, "kain't you trouble yosef to pass time of day wid Miz Carrebee?"

Her emaciated little husband—more skeleton than man—oozed from the shadows, a half-empty bottle of Coca-Cola in his hand. "I'se aimin' to pass time o' day iffen I git a word in edgeways," he whined. "Howdy, Miz Carrebee, ma'am."

I said, "Hello, Sparrow. Still drinking Coca-Cola?" I smiled.

Adeline answered for him, "He drinks 'em. Eight, ten a day."

Sparrow, his duty done, oozed back to his rocking chair in the depths of the room. "I'se goin' right on drinkin' 'em," he said in his unvarying whine. "Someday I'se gonna hab me a roomful ob dopes."

Adeline picked a hot iron from the fire. "Someday you gonna kill er baar," she intoned ominously, then leaning, replaced the iron on the fire. "I'se goin' to help Miz Jess gadder her leaves," she announced in Sparrow's direction, "and git me a breaf ob outdoors. You stir dose collard greens once and awhile so as dey don' stick to de pot. . . ."

As we went outside, Sparrow's whine threaded after us. "Don' you be gone long. Hits gittin' time for my rest."

Adeline, walking straight and proud as an Indian, snorted. "Res' he say. He don' do nuthin' else but."

I looked at her wonderingly. "Why do you put up with him? He's like a child."

She stalked beside me. "Yassum. Dats de reason, I reckon. If he war a proper man I'd run 'im off wid de broom. I speck de oneriest trick ter play on a woman is hitch her up wid a man dat needs 'er. Nuthin' to hol' onto an' gotta hol' on jes de same." Without effort she reached and pulled down a tree limb. "Dese sweet gum leaves is righ' colorsome. . . ."

We gathered leaves red and bronze and gold, and when we had enough she put hers in my arm, then stood, arms akimbo and head back, to look up the slope at Hickory Hill. Her chuckle held genuine mirth. "I neber see dat place but whut I thinks whut I thunk w'en I was itsy bitsy. Dat it sho is a fine place to trow rocks at. . . ."

I held my voice careless. "Was it empty when you were—itsy bitsy?"

"Oh no, ma'am. He lib dere den—de gennamun dat own it—an' her long wid 'im."

"Her? His wife, you mean?"

"Dat I cain't say fur true 'cause I don' know. I was no more dan knee high to er duck an' wedder she wife er daughter er whuteber I neber hear or mebbe don' recollecks." She chuckled again. "All I recollecks is dat she put me in min' of er hant."

"Hant?" I repeated incredulously.

"Yes ma'am. Every evening 'long 'bout dusktime she walk, summer an' winter, round and round de top ob dat hill. And w'en her die he walk de same way come dusktime. Roun' en roun'."

"She—she died, you say?"

"Yes ma'am. En dat was er sad ting. W'en she fall sick he come fotch Ma to hep out wid de cookin'. I hear Ma say not a soul come near 'em. I watch de day de burial waggin bring 'er down de hill, him ridin' behin' it in de buggy. An' nobody else. Dat was a lonesome ride fur bof ob 'em."

My imagination, fired by the desolate picture her soft mournful voice painted, flashed a conjecture across my mind. Suppose the man had been Mathias Purefoy—the woman who walked round the top of the hill, his daughter. The two driven to live in isolation at Hickory Hill. . . .

"Adeline," I asked, "was his name Purefoy?"

Her bony hand rubbed her jaw thoughtfully and her face puckered in the effort to recall. "Wall now, I kain't just say. It mought a been and agin it moughtn't. A youngun's remember is lak a flour sifter. Things jes slip fru."

"But you know how long ago that was, don't you?"

"Miz Jess, I don' fur a fac'. Neber did I learn how to tell time, needer clock or passing."

Perhaps Andrew could tell me, I thought. And turned to go back up the hill. But stopped as Adeline spoke again. "The mostest ting I recollecks is she die de year ob de Exposition. Pa was aiming to hitch up and drive Ma and me in to Atlanta fur to see it and Ma coulden go 'count ob helping out up dere. Just afore she die dat was. Me and Pa go by ourself and I ain't neber fergit dat Exposition. No ma'am. Piedmont Exposition . . . 1887 it war an' I see a man riz up in er balloon an' fly in de air lak a bird." Then, as Sparrow whined from the door, "Hit's done past my restin' time." She gave me a wry grin. "Now dere's a man whut is a bird. A real sad bird."

The sun was low in the west and late autumn's smoky haze was sifting among the trees when I made my way toward the top of the hill where our house rose sturdy and plain from Georgia soil, the scent and feel of Georgia rising around it. The plaintive call of the bobwhite, the hot smell of supper cooking, the loneliness of a dog's distant howl. This, I thought, was the real Georgia. A quiet land, but not soft. Strength in its pine-shadowed woods slashed with roads of red clay, in its flatlands and careless yields of peaches and corn and cotton. A land of small humble people and small humble houses, both worn with living. The yards and porches where in shabby rocking chairs people talked in the vast brooding night, their voices lost in the darkness. Like that since the beginning, when in the Indian town, The Standing Peachtree, the Cherokees planted their patches of corn and fished in the Chattahoochee. When Hardy Ivy, first settler of Marthasville, later renamed Atlanta, put up his hewn log cabin. When Mathias Purefoy built his house on top of Hickory Hill and built it plain and strong and friendly like the earth in which it was rooted. As Mathias Purefoy himself had been. With hands gnarled like the roots of trees, he had carved his life from its soil.

Toil and rest and peace among the humble and unpretentious. How wonderful if I might persuade Wes to that simple enduring pattern. He and I at Hickory Hill, his work at the mill; and on the hill where the woman, Adeline said, walked round and round, our rosy-cheeked children would run. With the years Wes, his devils banished, would turn gray—I lose my figure and that wouldn't matter. We would be bound to that other invisible house of our life, reared on the homely, familiar things.

Perhaps tonight after supper, I thought, when we sat at the sitting-room fire, closed in and content, I would speak to Wes of our future, the future which I had visioned; but suddenly I knew I dare not. He would laugh, he would tousle my hair and say I was crazy. This was a modern world not pioneer days, we couldn't turn back the clock. No—I must win him to my way slowly like Miss Camilla. Let him believe that it was his own idea.

At the back door I suddenly halted, struck by awareness. *Like Miss Camilla,* I had said. Like Miss Camilla and others trying to mould Wes and shape him into something he wasn't, something I thought he should be. Forgetting how he had said, "That's why I need you, Doc, somebody who won't ever doubt me. . . ."

I would not doubt, I said fiercely. Nor nag him to be otherwise than he was. Why should I? This was the Wes I had loved from the first, loved and adored beyond telling. What right had I to want him to change . . . to fit a groove of my digging? What would it profit to win him to my way if the winning destroyed the man?

I entered the kitchen door and Mitty, taking her cake from the oven, said, "You're back just in time. I hear Wes upstairs."

I said, "Good!" and fetching a wide-mouthed earthen jar for the leaves, placed them on the sitting-room table, where the log fire leaping and snapping lighted them with new glory. How pleasant they made the room, I thought, how pleasant for living and loving.

Wes's footsteps above warned he was coming down and I went to the stairs and, clasping the newel post, waited. As he came into view my clasp on the post tightened. I knew by the evening clothes he wore that he was not staying at home as he had promised.

Descending the stairs, he asked, almost cross, "Where on earth have you been?"

I smiled a carefully careless smile. "To take the wash down to Adeline. It's more to the point"—I kept my voice light—"to ask where on earth you are going?"

"I forgot the frat smoker tonight. They have one every year, you know."

"No . . . I didn't know. . . ."

He stopped on the bottom step to look down at me quickly. "You don't mind, do you, Doc?"

"Of course not, my darling. It's just that I'm sorry . . . you'll miss your go at Mitty's spoon bread."

"I know. And I hate it. But I sort of feel obligated. It's a mighty poor sport that won't give one night a year to the bunch. . . . You see how I feel, don't you, Doc?"

"Yes, darling, I see."

"And don't wait up for me, sweet. These smokers can go on all night." He suddenly leaned to peer into my face. "You do understand? That going is sort of a duty?"

"Of course I do, Wes."

He ran down the steps and in the deepening dusk I watched while he got in his auto. Wheeling slowly, he turned it toward the road, lifting his hand in good-by.

I waved back and held my hand high, glad that the dark prevented his seeing my face clearly and my smile that felt stiff and frozen. I did not feel noble at all, I thought, I wanted to kick and scream and ask when he talked of "duty" to a silly old frat, what of his duty to me?

I sat on the back steps a long time while the resentment that burned slowly cooled. When I went in to eat supper with Mitty I tried to appear unruffled, but I knew that my pretense would not deceive her for a moment.

We ate at the kitchen table before the fire on the hearth. As we ate she told me how after Wes and I had come in, she'd found out back of the carriage house—I'd never guess what—a passel of sweetshrub bushes! She'd wanted 'em all her life. And now to have a peck of growed-up ones dropped in her lap so to speak . . .

She brought the coffeepot from the stove and refilled our cups and took her seat again.

Stirring mine, I asked slowly, "Mitty . . . how long after marriage does a man need to settle down?"

Lips pursed, she considered the question. "Well, blessed . . . that depends on the man. You see, dearie, it's like this. Some men are fast settlers, some are slow, some, being of a nonsettling mind, never settle at all. Which kind you get you don't know, at least not 'til you're married. And as far as I can figger there's no way to provide against it. Why, even if folks could draw up a list of habits they'd rather not marry, how could they put down a habit they never happened to hear of?"

"But, Mitty," I said impatiently, "isn't it time that Wes— We've been married more than three months. I think he should—"

She interrupted me firmly. "Jess, if I've learned anything, it's not to be saying what others should do; or shouldn't. A woman can make herself miserable about an unsettling man or if a man don't settle as she'd like; or accept, which is all she can do. For the Scripture says nothing of settling but only for better or worse."

"And cleave unto," I reminded, smiling across at her.

She nodded, not smiling. "And one thing more. Don't traitor your love to another . . ."

I cried, "Mitty, I didn't mean—"

She put the worn little hand over mine. "I know that, Jess. But traitoring you are when you talk it—even with me. You see, dearie, love is a flimsical thing, hard to come by. Easy tore by doubting and carping and nagging. I've seen some mighty fine love tore to shreds by a woman's sharp tongue. Tearing what can't ever be mended on account of some little thing or other."

Earnestly I leaned toward her. "Mitty . . ." I said, "listen . . ." Then I told her or tried to tell why I was troubled . . . and sort of scared. I loved him, I wanted Wes to settle and be a successful man. Not for myself, I added quickly, but because I sensed that's what he wanted. But it seemed as if—I didn't know why—he had walled off his wanting, and I wanted to break through that wall somehow so he could find himself. . . .

She reached and patted my hand. "And he will, my precious. And you're a good wife . . . good as ever I see. But remember this. Folks can act mighty quare without knowing what makes 'em act so. Witch-rid, we used to call 'em. All a wife can do 'bout a witch-rid husband is cleave unto 'til the witches get tired of riding."

As she talked I listened and pondered. From where did she glean the wisdom that led her unerringly to the heart of my worry? What was it that drove Wes at times to silence and dark abstraction? That reared a high wall between us and closed in the gay Wes, the Wes warm and tender, the Wes I so desperately needed? That made him like a stranger indifferent to me and my needing? And returned as from a far journey, and holding me close, sometimes murmured, "Oh, Doc . . . if I lost you I'd die."

I looked over at Mitty and smiled. "Don't worry, Mitty. I won't traitor my love. . . ."

Cheerful again, she replied, "I know it, my blessed," and, rising, she began to gather up dishes. Then her quick hands were stilled for a moment and her eyes gazed out of the window. "It feels like a change of weather. 'Twon't surprise me if we're in for some real winter."

Oh, such an exciting night in the house of the young Wesley Carrebees! Such running about, such calling, one to another! So many "Do you know where I can find this—or that—or the other?" Mitty, wearing her best silk, was thrusting sundry articles into what she called her "go-way bag." Wes was getting his bath, complaining about the oil pump; and I, feeling very important and, I admit, very fetching, had just finished my hair and was getting into an evening gown.

Mitty was going to spend the night with Miss Ad, which failed to merit—in my opinion, at least—her excitement. But perhaps that rose from my own excitement at the evening Wes and I would spend. For Wes and I were going to a *Formal Affair,* which I write in italics because it's written that way on my mind.

Now, formal affairs were not at all rare in Atlanta. In the course of the social season there were many formal affairs, but without italics. Beginning with debutante balls in the fall, going on to the Thanksgiving Dance and the Christmas Ball, and the ball on George Washington's birthday; exclusive of private dances and dinners, and receptions and teas, and numerous banquets.

Our *Formal Affair* was a different affair altogether. It was given by Mr. and Mrs. J. Cuthbert Scoggins, and Mr. and Mrs. J. Cuthbert Scoggins were *very* important people. I did not know why and no one I asked could tell me why, but Mr. and Mrs. Scoggins were very important people. Mr. and Mrs. Scoggins were also very exclusive. They saw *very few* people. Naturally that did not mean that they did not see their friends in the social set, and their friends' daughters and sons who were the Young Married set. It would be absurd to assume that Mr. Scoggins did not see the various persons in his employ—at least a few hundred—or that Mrs. Scoggins did not attend a church with an extremely large membership. But Mr. and Mrs. J. Cuthbert Scoggins saw *very few* people.

Mr. and Mrs. J. Cuthbert Scoggins lived in a house (naturally, way out on Peachtree) that looked outside like a Spanish grandee's palace and inside like anything you might mention, from walls hung in amber silk in the drawing room to General Lee surrendering his sword in the library. Its marble reception hall was surpassed in size only by the State Capitol's foyer, and the magnificent swinging staircase had nothing to fear from the Hanging Gardens of Babylon.

Since Mr. and Mrs. Scoggins saw *very few* people, everyone wanted to see them and so they were wined and dined and entertained, and no event that was an event was considered really exclusive unless Mr. and Mrs. Scoggins were present. They entertained little themselves. But once every two or three years, they gave a *Formal Affair* and with one fell sweep repaid all the dinners and balls and suppers they had enjoyed. It was Mr. and Mrs. Scoggins' *Formal Affair* that we would attend tonight . . . and oh, what an exciting night it was in the home of the young Wesley Carrebees!

Wes came in from his bath, tall and handsome, and as he sauntered about the room and got dressed, we carried on unimportant husband-

and-wife conversation. I said it was rather nice to be going to a party again, that we'd stuck awfully close to home, it did us good to get out now and then. Wes said "Yeah" and "Yeah" and "Where do you hide my dress socks?" and "Where's that new dress shirt I bought?" Dressed, I sat and buffed my nails, surveying myself in the mirror from time to time and thinking I looked rather lovely.

Wes put on his dinner suit, which was as formal as Atlanta men ever got except for a wedding, and folding his handkerchief, thrust it in his pocket, the lean brown fingers deftly bringing it to point, his eyes on the Wes in the mirror.

He said abstractedly, "Did I tell you that Cissa got home today?"

I extended my hand, inspected my nails. "No." I, too, was abstracted. "But I knew she was expected. Did you see her?"

"Nope. I called the house but Mother was at the mill and Cissa was resting." His voice lifted sarcastically. "What else does she ever do but rest?"

"It will be nice to see her again. I haven't since we married, you know."

"Why shouldn't I know? I was in the wedding, remember?"

"I wonder if she'll be the same," I mused, unable to imagine staying in Europe all these months and coming back unchanged.

"That's what I'm afraid of." Wes sounded rather grumpy.

"That she'll be the same. Wes . . ." I was reproving.

"Don't be the dear little scolding wife, now."

I laughed. "I did sound like it rather, didn't I?"

"And don't say rather. It's affected."

I snapped back, "All right, I won't say rather."

Sighing, I went to the closet and got out my coat. We had started out sort of gay. How had we slipped into this?

The *Formal Affair* was in full swing when Wes and I entered the marble foyer of Mr. and Mrs. J. Cuthbert Scoggins. From the vast high-ceilinged rooms that led one to another through great archways the steady hum of many voices rose and fell like the hum of the mill machinery. The swinging staircase was lined with pretty women, ascending and descending, their delicately toned gowns billowing softly, their necks and shoulders gleaming like marble in the brilliant light of the chandelier.

At the foot of the stairs, Wes and I separated, he to go to the gentlemen's coat room, I to the dressing room, agreeing to meet at the foot of the stairs again. The dressing room was crowded and noisy, offering, as I waited by the door, a view that consisted mainly of bare arms and shoulders twisting and writhing as their owners struggled to reach the dressing table at the end of the room.

Standing just within the door, I was conscious of the slightly sickish feeling induced by too many pairs of lungs and too little air. The chattering, laughing voices sank for an instant to a drone, and a single voice shrilled strident across the room.

"I just heard about Callie Peacock. It's really the most dreadful thing . . ." Then as the drone crescendoed again, her words and voice were wholly engulfed.

What would her completed words have revealed of Callie Peacock, I wondered, who had, months ago, sunk below my horizon? What so dreadful could have happend to Callie, wrapped as she was in her parents' adoring protection? I must remember to ask Wes.

I finally got to the mirror and, reassured about my appearance, made my way to the foot of the stairs, feeling lighthearted and rather gay when I heard the strains of the music. I had the triumphant lift that all women know when they feel they are looking their best. My dress, *à la princesse* in a sort of soft mauvish blue with the bodice embroidered in pansies and creamy lace outlining my shoulders, was becoming, I thought.

At the foot of the stairs I found no Wes and, leaning against the wall, I waited, watching the crowd sweeping back to the ballroom and thinning out. I said "Good evening" to this pair of oldsters, and "Hey" to the Younger Marrieds, as, with excited voices and eyes, they passed. Finally, except for an occasional hurrying butler or maid, I stood marooned in vast splendor in the ornate reception hall of Mr. and Mrs. J. Cuthbert Scoggins.

But not for long, for someone unseen, approaching from behind me, touched my arm lightly and said, "Hello there," and I turned to find Oakes Carr, handsome and smiling, beside me; Oakes, whom I had not seen since that Sunday at Miss Camilla's.

Before I could even say hello, he said, "So you married Wes Carrebee?"

Smiling, I asked, "Surprised?"

His eyes looked me up and down. "Not at Wes."

"Surely not at me?" I accused.

Gravely he said, "At you . . . just a little."

I felt a small flare of displeasure at the implication contained in his words, then remembered that Oakes was terribly young and not to be taken seriously. I changed to another subject.

"Oakes, what do you hear from Laura Lee?"

He frowned as if to call her name called also troublous thoughts. "Mighty little, Jess. A card now and then. One short note, from a hotel in New Orleans. I wrote and sent it there quick on the chance that it would reach her." He shook his head. "I don't know. I told her about finding you, you being at Carrebees'. I knew she would want to know that you were all right. I hope you don't mind."

"Oakes, of course I don't mind."

He shook himself as if to shed his unpleasant thoughts. "Aren't you ready to go where the fun is?"

I picked up my train. "I think I will. Wes seems to have been detained."

On the arm of Oakes Carr I entered the ballroom just as a dance ended, and we paused within the door while couples surged from the floor toward friends or the small gold-painted chairs standing against the wall. The great room with its tall windows festooned in rich gold damask, the stretch of floor gleaming like satin, made an impressive picture, yet I did not call it a fairyland, as once I might have called it. It occurred to me that we invest only that which is unknown or new with magic. Such a scene as this was no longer unknown to me. To some degree, I knew most of the dancers who, over the long room, were collected in groups—the dowager groups, the people of substance, the Young Marrieds. There was Mrs. J. Cuthbert Scoggins resplendent in turquoise velvet, the paradise feathers in her flagrant red hair emphasizing with their ethereal delicacy her broad red face and gross figure; there shone the gleaming bald head of Mr. J. Cuthbert Scoggins; and there, too, I spied Cissa, her exquisite figure and head reducing all women present to dull dowdiness. She wore a startling narrow black sheath, unadorned and utterly sleeveless and slashed to her knees in the front, which was Atlanta's first view of the much-discussed hobble skirt. And there was Wes beside her.

Oakes asked, as the music started again, "Shall we dance?" and not waiting for my consent, circled my waist with his arm. I laid my finger tips on his shoulder and we began to move lightly over the floor.

I said to Oakes, "It was you who taught me to dance. Do you remember?"

"Of course. We had fun, didn't we? You and me, Laura Lee and Bucky. By God, if it had entered my mind that Bucky . . . I'd have killed him." He leaned back to look into my face. "Did you know?"

I shook my head. "I felt so sorry because Laura Lee had only Bucky . . . and I had you. You were a very special person to me in those days."

"But not now?"

"Well, yes, even now. But in a different way. I have a warm place in my heart for you and Laura Lee. You were my very first friends."

"Now that you have plenty of friends, no doubt we are less special."

I shook my head. "No. There will always be a special feeling about you, and your mother. She was kind to me and I did not get much kindness. How is she, Oakes?"

"Hell, Jess, I don't know. Better one day, not so well the next. Sometimes I get the fool idea that the old man decides which . . ."

The music crashed to a stop and his arm dropped from my waist. "Where would you like to go? Or would you try the next with me?"

"No, thanks. I must go to Wes and say hello to Cissa. She just got back from Europe today."

As we made our way through the milling crush, he laughed, his eyes impishly smiling. "I hope Cissa didn't add to the ruins over there." Then, contritely, "Sorry, I forgot. She now belongs to your family."

"Cissa is very lovely." Levelly I said it, and would have said more, but there was no time to say it for now we drew near Cissa and Wes. He stood tall and grave behind her and she, speaking to him, tilted her head back to his, her slim body arched, her little feet in black slippers with golden heels, her beautiful legs and ankles revealed by the new hobble skirt.

Turning her head, she saw me, for a breath stood unmoving, then moved toward me, her eyes flying over me cool and appraising as she came.

"Jess!" Her hands dropped to my shoulders holding me at a distance, and she raised on one toe and dropped a light kiss on my cheek. "Or should I say 'Mrs. Carrebee'?" Her eyes slanted demurely. "I reckon Mama was right. It's the quiet ones you'd better watch." She held a disinterested hand out to Oakes. "Hello, Oakes. You're getting to be quite a big boy. Would you ask me to dance?"

He grinned at her. "Grandma, will you dance with me, sharp claws and all?"

They swirled out to the shining floor. With every swirl Cissa's slim ankles and legs were revealed by the skirt, and Wes, observing it, glowered. I said, "Darling, don't look so cross. Aren't you going to ask me to dance?"

He said, "Of course, Doc," and we danced, but his mood did not lighten. "You wondered if she'd be the same." His laugh was dry. "Well, she's the same, all right." He was grim. "She looks like a two-bit whore."

"Wes!" My voice was shocked and I tried to lessen its shock when I went on, "She's your sister."

His laugh was a bark. "Do you think I'd give a damn if she wasn't?"

"And probably everybody in Paris is wearing the hobble skirt," I consoled.

His eyes slanted down at me. "Oh, for God's sake!" He was exasperated but, after a turn, he was penitent. "Pay me no mind, Doc. Cissa riles me, that's all. Anyway, I love you. It's just that Cissa . . . well, forget it."

We danced on, I bowing and waving over Wes's shoulder at people I knew, at Miss Camilla, resplendent in silver, arriving with Mr. Poteat. I told Wes where they were, but he gave them not even a glance, and I sighed. He was still cross.

The orchestra struck up a waltz, a dance that had been pushed almost to oblivion by the one-step, and Mr. Poteat, with his correct little bow, swept me out to the floor.

Wes and Cissa danced by, not seeing us, and I expelled a tiny sigh of relief, for Wes's bad humor had vanished. He was smiling now at something Cissa had said, and as delightedly as if he hadn't a care in the world, which he hadn't. They were a beautiful pair, I thought; Wes's tall handsomeness, the brown sensitive face; Cissa's exquisite figure etched by the narrow black sheath, her slim white arms by Wes's black coat, the shining hair like an aureole, the lovely face with its terrible eagerness. Yet still with the spirit of the childish Cissa hovering, Cissa who, in the summerhouse turret room, had trailed her silken finery, where she and Wes had lived in a world of their own, bound by dependence, one on the other. Later, of course, it had changed. Wes, sent to the University, had found other friends, other loves, and nothing was ever the same. But I did not doubt that he still was the pivot on which Cissa's universe turned.

The band was playing one of the new popular songs, but its rhythm did not prevent the words of another from drifting across my mind; and dancing with Mr. Poteat, I murmured them under my breath.

"Chicka-ma, chicka-ma, craney crow
I went to the well to wash my toe
And when I got back my child was gone.
What time, old witch?"

Smiling, I remembered the game; how Wes had been both old witch and child, and how he would run and run but always in the end, because she was smaller, he let her win.

The evening progressed to supper served in the new buffet fashion, serving oneself from platters arranged on table and sideboard, the butlers and maids moving noiselessly, presenting additional platters and gold-necked bottles from which they refilled the glasses with champagne. The hum of conversation rose to a gigantic roar, more than ever like the mill, but, I thought, producing nothing. After supper, there was dancing again, but the dowager set, weary husbands docilely trailing, began to take their leave, and Miss Camilla, catching me between dances, said she and Mr. Poteat were leaving. She'd had a long day at the mill. Would Wes and I ride Cissa home.

I danced with various young men, and heard various small talk—football, the price of "licker," the burlesque shows at the Bijou, the "big time" vaudeville at the Forsyth, of an act named The Four Keatons with a kid . . . funny? You just had to see him to know . . .

I listened, I smiled, I tried to appear entertained, but privately concluded that I was not one of those who could "die happy" dancing. When Wes, cutting in, announced he was ready to go, I was more glad than regretful. "But Cissa? Is she ready to go? She seems to be having a wonderful time."

"She'll go now if she wants a ride," he said. "I'll cut in and tell her so. You wait here for us."

Weaving in and out of the dancers, he reached her and a little later they joined me, Cissa rebellious and storming. "I hoped with a wife to boss you'd stop trying to run my life."

Wes said, without expression, "Get your wraps. I'll wait at the front door," and stalked off.

Cissa and I got our wraps from the yawning dressing-room maid, Cissa's face mutinous still, with angry eyes. She did not speak nor did I as we made our way to the front door, she always a pace ahead, as if fleeing both time and place.

Pausing, we said good night to Mr. and Mrs. J. Cuthbert Scoggins, uttered the usual trite thanks. "Such a beautiful party. Such a wonderful time!" Mrs. Scoggins, her paradise plume at a rakish angle, responding vaguely, "So happy . . . so nice" to see us . . . she and Mr. Scoggins saw *"very few* people," Mr. Scoggins even more vaguely echoing "very few people." Then we were walking around the corner to the machine and, with Cissa in the tonneau, were speeding up Peachtree.

Cissa leaned forward and rested her folded arms on the back of the front seat. "Wes," she said brightly, with no trace of her former anger, "I almost forgot. I ran into friends of yours in New York."

Wes, lighting a cigarette behind his cupped hand, waited until it was lit to ask without interest, "Who?"

"That silly old mother of an old flame of yours, Callie Peacock. She was in a horrible state. Insisted I go up to see Callie. They were at the Astor, too. And, Wes, she looks dreadful. Really, more dead than alive. Her mother is taking her to that doctor in Switzerland who makes them sleep naked out in the snow—or some such weird idea. Did you know about her, Wes?"

"Of course. Everyone does."

Cissa's laugh was brittle. "Aren't you rather cool, considering . . . ?"

After a pause, Wes said evenly, "That's a lie and you know it."

"I only know what her silly old mother said, with the tears digging ditches through her face powder. Callie started going downhill, she said, right after you all broke up."

Wes said flatly, "If it's true, you know better than anyone who's to blame."

For a moment, she sat silent, then suddenly spit her words like an angry kitten. "Yes, I do know. And a lot of good it was."

"That's right," Wes said smoothly.

I thought wearily, It's begun all over again, their quarreling and stabbing and jabbing; and in an effort not to hear, I said over and over the words of that silly song, *"Chicka-ma, Chicka-ma, craney crow . . ."*

I came back to Cissa's voice, light, gay, telling of the young Englishman who had, she claimed, wanted to marry her. He would inherit the title when an older brother passed on, but the brother was so disgustingly healthy. Poor Reggie! Not a dime to his name. If she only had piles of money, real money, he would marry her in a minute, for he adored her.

But poor dear! He simply must marry money. So—no husband, no title, damn it!

"When I got back my child was gone . . ."

Now—she turned suddenly wistful—now no one left except Syl. Tomorrow she'd give him a ring. She hated to deprive Pet Belleau, but Pet Belleau had a whole city of men, while she had nobody now. . . .

Wes swept up Miss Camilla's drive and stopped at the steps and, reaching back, opened the tonneau door and stonily faced ahead. Cissa got out, and standing beside the car, asked softly, "Won't you come in for a nightcap?"

"No."

I said, "Thanks, Cissa, but it's terribly late."

Without moving, she asked, "When shall I see you again?"

Wes's cold, hateful voice said slowly, "I wish to God I never had to see you again."

She took a quick step forward, and on tiptoe looked up at him, throat arched as her laughter rippled. "I know," she cried. "But you can't get away from it, pet. There's many a fight left in us yet." Then suddenly, swiftly she turned and without a good night went up the steps toward the door; and Wes and I drove out to Hickory Hill, a dark drive and silent, for he was still cross and I knew it. The *Formal Affair* had not, after all, been exciting.

There are periods of our lives when we stand by helplessly and watch life being moulded by forces beyond our control, into a shape from which we recoil. It is not a period of great suffering, for usually we are only vaguely aware that the change is permanent. Not until the transformation is accomplished do we realize the period in which it was achieved as critical . . . and then, of course, it is too late.

The next weeks and months were such a period for me though I did not know it. There were many happy days when my cup filled to the brim and ran over with content. If there were those that were less happy and troubled, it did not strike me that they were in any way extraordinary. When Wes spent more and more time away from home I smiled with fond tolerance and declared it was but natural, that the novelty of marriage wearing off, he now returned to normal ways again. I knew he rarely went to the mill, that Miss Camilla had actually alienated him by her constant nagging . . . and that I would not do. For I still held to my resolve that, like others, I would not try to twist and shape him into something he was not. Even when I realized that he was drinking more than he ever had before, I was not disturbed. The first time he came home exhilarated and singing, and, seizing Mitty, made her waltz about the kitchen, she and I laughed in delight. This was a new Wes and one we thought enchanting.

But what at first had been an innovation settled into accepted routine. He brought his liquors home now, appropriating a small closet for his "cellar," arranging it as carefully as a housewife, singing happily and off key as he worked, pausing to force me to a game of "Stiff Starch," spinning me to dizziness and when I pled to stop, spinning me more furiously, his eyes gleaming.

At first I was not perturbed. My experience with drunkenness was too slight to be familiar with the pattern of its insidious progress. Moreover, there were intervals when for days Wes, declaring he was on the wagon, would disdain a drink; when he spoke contemptuously of "Jim, who can't handle his licker" or Pete—a "no-good sot." On those days he was gay and, I thought, marvelously content. He rode me down the hill road to the little general store near the mill where I laid in food supplies, he waiting in the auto while inside the small dark store that smelled of kerosene, I shopped. I preferred that he should wait; for the few times he had gone inside had played havoc with my spending. Each order I gave he doubled, maybe tripled, and he bought enough sardines, which he liked, to supply the mill.

I did not censure him for considering cost so little. To me it was a constant worry. But accustomed all of his life to the lavishness of Miss Camilla's table, he did not suspect the hours that I spent with Mitty over lists of food and prices. Had he for once known of our concern with these matters, I do not doubt that he would have arranged a regular sum with which to meet them, realized that the five and ten dollar bills he dropped irregularly on the kitchen table as he finished breakfast were insufficient. He did not dream—he would have been indignant had he dreamed—that most of my modest allowance from Mathias Purefoy was used to augment what he gave. And I did not tell him that many a night I lay long awake and troubled. Every day I drew nearer to my majority when I would receive the last small sum Mathias Purefoy had left me. After that we would have no income except Wes's monthly check from the mill. He would have to get down to cases then, I told myself grimly. Tomorrow I simply must have a talk with him.

But when tomorrow came he would be gay and untroubled. At breakfast he would say, "You look extra beautiful this morning, Mrs. Carrebee." He would warn Mitty with the devilish glint in his eye to keep away from his cellar. His breakfast eaten, he would rise to go, pausing to drop a ten-dollar bill at my plate. "Come walk to the car with me, Doc," he would say, tousling my hair. And I would get my coat, Colonel rising from his place at the hearth automatically when he observed it, and the three of us would walk to the car. He'd give me a kiss and Colonel a pat and we'd stand and watch him turn and head down the hill, then go back to the kitchen and Mitty, I with my heart singing; and there was no cloud in my sky.

Then the weather and Wes would change. He would "fall off" the wagon, the drinking would start again. He would be at home less, sometimes not returning even at night. The first night this happened I was frantic with fear. All night, after Mitty persuaded me to bed, I stared into the dark, picturing him lying on the road somewhere, dying and calling my name . . . or dead. I was up and dressed at dawn and, wrapped in my coat, paced round and round the hill like the woman Adeline told me about, Colonel pacing every step with me, stopping when I halted to peer down the road as day lightened; but seeing no overturned car, no sprawling, lifeless body. Mitty came out and forced me back to the warm kitchen for coffee. "Why, dearie, nothing's happened to Wes. Likely that gas buggy fell to pieces on him and no way to let you know he couldn't get home. He oughter get him a horse."

Unconvinced, I drank my coffee, pacing from table to window, watching the hill road. Saying to myself, "Dear God, just let him come . . . bring him back safe . . . don't let anything happen to Wes. . . ."

At ten o'clock I could bear the suspense no longer, and I put on my coat and wrapped a scarf around my head. "I'm going to walk down to the mill," I told Mitty, "to a telephone. I've got to know . . . something."

I started out, and finding Colonel's eyes watching me longingly, I said, "Come on, boy," and we made our way down the rutted road of the hill. It was a bright cold day and the sharp air cleared my thinking. I was probably acting very foolishly and new-wifish, I thought. Nothing had happened to Wes. Wes was unpredictable. If he decided to stay in town overnight, he would stay. Reaching the hollow and Adeline's cabin, I almost turned back home, but the idea of facing the whole day without reassurance decided me. I turned down De Kalb Road toward the mill. On a day like this it was a pleasant walk and the two miles between home and the mill not too far. I had walked it several times when we needed supplies, and when Wes had not come home, there had been no other solution. It was a lonely stretch of unpaved road without house or building of any sort between Adeline's cabin and the little store, in rainy weather a sea of mud.

When I turned in the mill gate the hum of machines beat against my ears like the droning of giant bees, and I remembered the dazzling, shifting world of lint which had seemed so horrible; strangely, less horrible now because I had learned that without lint, the world could be a confused and dizzying place. Colonel and I crossed the bare, hard-packed earth of the millyard, and went toward the office. I left him at the bottom of the wooden steps, feeling, as I went up them, embarrassed and awkward. I hoped I would find, not the hearty, moist Mr. Wangle, but the little man I had liked, Darty Land. The office was empty except for Miss Camilla, who sat at Ed Wangle's desk, a sheaf of papers before her. She looked up and saw me and her eyes widened. "Why Jess! Come in, my dear." She peered beyond my shoulders. "Wes with you?"

I shook my head. "I came to use the phone . . ." I began, and stopped because, foolishly, I wanted to cry, was afraid I would cry if I said more.

She rose briskly, crossed to where I stood at the open door, and reaching behind me, closed it. Then she put her arm about me, led me to the chair beside hers, put me in it and went to sit at the desk again. "Now, what is this all about?" she demanded.

I told her, not crying but quietly, and listening she rolled the pencil she held between her palms.

When I finished she said flatly, "That one!" And getting up, went to the telephone on the wall and called a number. Waiting for an answer, she looked over at me. "Stop worrying, Jess. Nothing's happened to that one." Then into the phone she said, "Hello . . . Mr. Maddox, please . . ."

With my eyes on her face I waited too, wondering if she was really unworried or if, for my sake, she pretended.

She said into the phone, crisply, "Jim? This is Camilla Carrebee. Sorry to bother you but I want to get in touch with Wes, the scamp. Have you any idea how I could?"

She listened again, then, her voice rising, she cried, "Oh no! How dreadful!"

I held my quick indrawn breath . . . until she laughed her infectious throaty laughter. "Serves you right," she said to the invisible Jim. "You will play with those sharks . . . well . . . thanks for the information. Good-by."

Turning, she said, "Wes stayed at Jim's last night. Jim said they got mixed up in a poker game that went on all night and cost Jim a hundred dollars . . . the fool."

She came back to her chair. "Jess, what are we going to do about Wes?"

In my concern the desire to confide in her was almost too great to resist. But I remembered that Mitty had said, "Don't traitor your love," and I only looked at her gravely.

She said, "All right! Forget that I asked it. I'll do the talking. I've never really worried about Wes before. Oh I knew he hadn't settled down, that he refused to take interest in the mill, but that's no different from most young men in Atlanta whose families have means. They sow their wild oats, then settle down into solid citizens, at least most of them. Some, of course, don't. But I didn't believe that Wes belonged to that species." Her fist hit the desk. "Still don't, I'll vow. But somehow I can't get *at* him. He evades, he laughs, he gets mad as a wet hen . . . but I never get *at* him. This"—her hand gestured—"this is a going business—and it's his. And he hasn't the gumption to run it."

She stared across at me. "And that's not the worst. He's taken up with a bunch he used to despise . . . the Souse Club, he used to call them. The hard drinkers. Why, Deke Keddy hasn't drawn a sober breath in five years! Not that he needs to. His father made a pile out of patent medicine. Hap Langel's off the same bolt of cloth. So is Shep Patton. I could name you a dozen. Spend their lives gambling in hotel rooms. Soaking up rotgut licker!"

She reached in her pocketbook that lay on the desk, pulled a cigarette from it, and lit it. "I sound like a mother-in-law. As if I blame you for Wes's bad habits. I don't."

She regarded the tip of her cigarette. "But you know, Jess, a clever wife can do lots with a man—and I don't mean by bossing him. Certainly not Wes. But she can influence, direct, without his knowing it, turn his thoughts and attention as she wills. If you knew something of textiles and their tremendous future—enough to stimulate Wes's interest—"

I broke in. "I do know a little. I read those books of Mr. Carrebee's up on the third floor."

She looked at me thoughtfully. "You did? I didn't know it." She was brisk again. "Tell you what I'll do. I'll send them . . . the whole kit and boodle out to Hickory Hill."

She ground her cigarette out in a nearby tray. "You know, Jess, Wes should buckle down. After all, it's really his mill. I've just been carrying on until he was ready to step in. Someday he'll have to— There's nobody else. And it's the Carrebee bread and butter. Yours too."

I said, "Yes, ma'am, I know. And I am . . ."

I was shocked to silence by a shrill and piercing scream that flayed the silence, a kind of prolonged shriek that rent and tore at the air. . . . I started up, for an instant alarmed.

She laughed. "Just the whistle blowing for dinner. They have twenty minutes for it. Sit down and relax. Now . . . what were you saying?"

Laughing, I dissembled. "I . . . the whistle blew it right out of my mind. And I really must go. I told Mitty I'd come right back, I'm afraid she'll worry."

Halfway down the steps I paused and looked across to the slope of the mill village where the workers scurried in their doors as if driven by whips. Small wonder, I thought, recalling Miss Camilla's "twenty minutes for dinner," that they looked thin and pale, if always they must eat in such hurry.

I continued my way down the steps, at the bottom found Colonel had vanished, and my eyes roaming the deserted grounds suddenly spied him. He stood at the wall of one of the smaller buildings, his eyes fastened on a boy who, sitting on the ground against the wall, ate his dinner and read at the same time.

I walked toward the pair quietly and halted near them, noticed by neither. The boy's eyes glued to his book saw nothing else and Colonel's, glued to the food, moved in unison with the boy's grubby hand that pinched off small portions and carried them to his mouth. And I remembered how I, as a child, had eaten by pinches, to make it last a long time.

I thought that Colonel should be ashamed: that he, with his generous three squares a day, should beseech with his mournful eyes the boy's dinner of cold corn pone and fatback. It was little enough for a growing boy working from sunup to sundown. I moved toward Colonel, intending to take him away and let the boy finish his dinner, but after a step I halted again; for the boy, turning a page, saw Colonel for the first time and a slow shy smile of surprise slipped over his sallow face.

His hand deserted the book and lifted to pat Colonel's head. "Hey, ole feller," he said, in a voice that seemed very quiet for a boy.

Colonel's eyes did not waver but his tongue quickly licked his chops and his whine fairly pled for pity.

"Air you hongry, ole feller?" The boy looked down at his corn pone and breaking off a sizable hunk, held it toward Colonel. He ate it with one swift snap and stood as beseeching as before.

"Now you looky here, ole feller," the boy began, but the sad eyes riveted on his face were too much for him. "Wal, being as how you air hongry . . ."

Then I moved toward them. "Don't give him all of your corn pone. He's making you think he is hungry when he isn't."

The soft dark eyes looked at me shyly. "I reckon er dog like er boy air allus hongry."

I assured him that Colonel was not. "He gets three big meals every day."

He ran a measuring eye over Colonel. "This here air a purty big dog."

"You're a pretty big boy," I answered. "Do you work in the mill?"

"Yes ma'am."

"Do you like it?"

"I ussen ter live on er farm." He said gravely and added nothing more as if he considered this sufficient answer, which it was.

I would have liked to talk with him further but his manner did not invite it. Perhaps it was shyness, but there was pride too. And his reserve abashed the curiosity of a stranger.

I told him we must go and leave him in peace with his book and his dinner. He said—I knew it was the pride speaking—"I air eatin' out here today 'count of my ma bein' porely."

"I'm sorry she's porely," I said. "Is it very bad?"

"Jest porely 'count of another youngun."

"A baby!" I said. "That's wonderful!"

His slow, direct glance caused me a twinge of discomfort.

"Have you other brothers and sisters?" I asked.

"I only got Mady."

"Mady . . . is your sister?"

"Yes ma'am. Mady an' Ma an' me. We'uns air all."

"And your father . . . ?"

"Our paw he died. Afore we come 'way from the farm. There air jest Mister Luckett, Ma's husband."

"Oh," I said, "your stepfather."

Again he sent me his slow, direct glance.

"No ma'am. Ma's husband."

The twinge of discomfort tugged at me again.

I repeated, "We must go, but first won't you tell me your name?"

"Yes ma'am. Hit's Cade Pilgrim. Hit were give me after my pa."

"I like that name," I said. "Do you remember your pa?"

A simple statement once more encompassed all to be said. "When he die I were goin' on twelve."

I still did not go. I was held by the thin young figure in its patched and faded overalls, its battered shoes that were far too large, by his scraggly lint-dusted hair that emphasized the look of age.

"You like to read?" I asked.

"Yes ma'am."

"What is the name of your book?"

"Black Beauty," he said. "It air 'bout a horse."

"Does Mady like to read too?"

"Mady ain't a good reader, 'count of so leetle schoolin'. She'd ruther to play with her doll." With a tolerant smile he explained, "Hit ain't er real doll. Hit's jest a stick doll."

As if suddenly aware that treasured time was wasting, he returned to his book and his corn pone, and my "Good-by, Cade" fell on unhearing ears. When I reached the gate and looked back he still sat with his eyes glued to the book and the grubby hand pinching off corn pone. He had made it last, I thought, a long time.

Walking back along the hill road I was a different woman from the panic-torn wife who an hour ago had come down it. I had found two interests to help fill the days that often stretched long and empty. I had dreamed of a life together, a life of fullness, achievement, and that was the life I still wanted and I believed somewhere existed; but I was no patient Griselda to sit placidly waiting for Wes, his coming the end and beginning of living. Moreover, I was going to have a talk with Wes. Miss Camilla had said the mill was his job—and she was right. Our futures, his, mine, our children's, would depend upon it, and that I must make him see. For only in doing that job, I knew, would Wes find any true fulfillment.

At the top of the hill I saw Mitty on the back steps waiting, I knew, as I had waited for Wes, her face anxious.

"Everything's fine," I told her as I drew near. "Wes just stayed in town."

As we ate lunch I told Mitty about Cade, the small linthead, of Mady who had only a stick doll, and of Mr. Luckett, Ma's husband. Afterward I went to the upstairs closet where my childhood books were stored and thoughtfully went through them, laying out those that would appeal to a boy's taste. *Swiss Family Robinson, Robinson Crusoe, Treasure Island,* my school editions of *Ivanhoe* and Cooper's *Leatherstocking Tales.* Perhaps they would give Cade, too, a magic and secret life to brighten the days.

With my arms full of books, I went back to the kitchen. It was empty except for Colonel, who slept at the hearth, and I wondered where Mitty had gone. But soon she came in and I saw that she held my doll, May Queen, in her arms.

"Now I just got to thinking. It would be bad to carry a present for Cade and not one for sister Mady." She sat down and propped May Queen on her lap. "I remember the day Mr. Dolph brought her to you. How she perked you up more than a passel of pills. She ought to do it for Cade's sister, too."

Such a lovely afternoon that was. While she washed and ironed May Queen's clothes, I read *Swiss Family Robinson,* but stopped to watch as she pattered about as perky as the first robin. What was the secret that made her the person she was? I mused. That filled the great well of love in her heart, so it never ran dry of loving? The little I knew of her life, which had been mostly working and serving, had held nothing of radiance or joy, except that she brought to others.

I came back to the room where, ironing doll clothes, she was having a talk with Petey. "Now I'm tellin' you man to man," she was saying, "you're laying down on your singing. An' don't be excusin' yourself by puttin' on that you're gettin' old or that you're moultin'. Remember you this: A bird that can sing and just won't up and sing is mighty apt to be pushed to it."

I laughed to myself and went back to my book, and the slow winter afternoon waned; and it dawned that Mitty's lecture to Petey might contain some wisdom for me. A bird that can sing and won't, I thought . . . is mighty apt to be pushed to it. And a woman who can be happy and won't . . . might well receive the same treatment. And I must be happy, I thought, try very hard just to be happy.

The dusk came down and the supper cooked, and we lit the lamps and waited; and as if life would repay for the waiting, we heard Wes's car on the hill. Taking a lamp, I went out to the steps, and holding the lamp high, I waited until his tall figure strode towards me, was by me, was gently lifting the lamp from my hand and placing it on the top step; was taking me in his arms and was murmuring, "Hello there, Doc."

We went into the kitchen as glowing and warm as our hearts. And though we heard the wind rise outside, a restless wind and tormenting, inside there was peace and content. Wes had come home.

An afternoon or two later I waited again for Wes to come home. He had promised he would ride me down to the mill to take Cade his books and my darling May Queen to Mady. But when four o'clock came and he had not appeared, I gave up hope. I told Mitty I would walk down instead.

She examined the sky dubiously and said the weather looked doubtful. She didn't want me to get caught in a rain and maybe catch my death of cold. I laughed, reminded her I was neither sugar nor salt to be hurt by a little wetting, and kissed her good-by. And with the books under one arm and May Queen and her go-way bag under the other,

I made my way down the hill road, left muddy and slippery by yesterday's rain.

Reaching the bottom of the hill, I found Adeline regarding the sky from her yard. She came to the road when she saw me. "Miz Jess, you best git back home. Hit's gonna rain cats en dogs."

She was probably right, I admitted, but I hoped to outwalk it. She cast a calculating eye at the clouds. I mought, she said, and I moughtn't. But it was bad for a bride to git bone-wet. "Dey say de fust chile comes wid water on its brain."

I promised her to avoid getting bone-wet and went on, aware that Sparrow had oozed to the door to peer over Adeline's shoulder. I remembered what she had said on the day we had gathered the leaves; that the oneriest trick was to hitch up a woman with a man who needed her. Nothing to hold onto and gotta hold on just the same. It had worried me only briefly. Now, recollecting, I felt a qualm of uneasiness. Deeply as I loved Wes, I was beginning to have the disquieting sensation that I didn't have much to "hold on to."

I reached the mill before the rain fell, though the billowing clouds, scudding swiftly and merging, had increased in their threat as well as their size. The wind had died. Now there was only a still breathlessness that foretold—sooner or later—a furious downpour. But I no longer cared. If the rain was too heavy, no doubt Darty Land or Ed Wangle could find a way to get me home. However, I did not now go to the office; I picked my way across to the slope where the mill houses crouched in the somber light of the day. Here and there on the meager little stoops small children played and one, when I asked, pointed out Cade Pilgrim's house. And walking gingerly, lest I tumble—with books and May Queen—in the slimy mud, I came to the house which the child had designated. Identical with the others, it was no better or worse, no cleaner or less clean, but merged into the general shoddy pattern.

Its front door was closed and, both hands being occupied, I kicked gently at the base of the door with the toe of my shoe. While I waited I looked around, not from curiosity but because of things I had heard and read about mill houses. I recalled reading that mills employed not individuals, but families; and a man to get employment must have two, three, even four in family who could work in the mills. The number of rooms your house had was influenced by the number of workers the house contained. Cade's house, I found, had four rooms, two to a side, each side with its front door, but the small stoop serving both doors. Perhaps his family used only half of the house, which accounted for no one's answering the door.

I stepped over and kicked against the second door and immediately it was opened by a girl of nine or ten years of age, her eyes so grave, so sedate that I had a startled sense that I looked at myself at that age. She stood holding the door, not wide, but only half open, the lovely eyes in her intent face turned up to mine, questioning.

I smiled at her. "Are you Cade's sister Mady?"

"Yes ma'am."

"Then I've come to see you and your mama and the baby."

With the smile that quivered at the corner of her mouth, two dimples flashed in her cheeks . . . and vanished. Quietly, she stepped back, the door widening. "You kin come in, ma'am."

I stepped into a room that was almost bare. There was a double bed in the corner, a broken-down chair or two, a rickety table holding a cracked bowl and pitcher. A potbellied stove jutted out from one wall. Beside it, in an old Morris chair, a woman drooped, a ragged quilt about her shoulders. I knew this was Cade's mother who was "porely."

She drew herself straight at my entrance and regarded me with courteous inquiry. " 'Evening," she said, and waited.

When I told her I was a friend of Cade's, her eyes widened. "I warn't knowing as how Cade hed any friend." Her voice was puzzled. Then understanding dawned in her thin face with its spattering of freckles. "Why I reckons you air the lady whut belongs to the dawg."

I admitted Colonel's ownership and said that, hearing from Cade she was porely, I wondered if there was anything I could do.

Her head lifted. "We're makin' out, thank you kindly," she replied quietly.

I was perplexed. Here was the same sort of pride I had met in the woman at the poorhouse, a pride which refused to yield before circumstance. Holding my bundles, I smiled at her. "May I sit down a moment?" I asked. "I've walked a long way."

Now that it was I who asked help, she was no longer standoffish. "Why yes, ma'am. Mady, push up the cheer for the lady." Then as I took it she said regretfully, "It's a crying shame you muddied yore pretty shoes. Mady, hep the lady ter rid herself of her bundles."

I said, "Thank you, Mady. And this"—I laid the box holding May Queen in her arms—"is for you."

Her eyes, a deep radiant blue, their irises black-rimmed, brightened. But when her mother said, stiff-lipped, "Thank you kindly, ma'am, but we ain't needin' no hand-me-downs," their glow dulled.

I put my arm lightly about her shoulders and spoke as if I hadn't caught the resentment in her voice. "It isn't hand-me-downs, Mrs. Luckett. It's something that meant a great deal to me when I was"—I smiled into the upturned eyes—"a big girl . . . like Mady. I hope it will to her too."

Mrs. Luckett's mouth remained stiff. "I ain't doubtin' hit's kindly meant, ma'am, but Mr. Luckett, my husband, is er proudful man. I don' aim ter displease 'im."

I took the box from Mady and untied the string. "I don't think he'll mind this, Mrs. Luckett. Anyhow, you decide. . . ."

As I lifted May Queen with her glory of golden hair and pink silk dress, I heard their quick indrawn breath, and I saw Mady turn rigid, her small fists clenched at her side.

The mother saw, too, and her thin face was suddenly guarded. For a moment she sat silent. Then she spoke dully. "I jest kain't tell her she kain't. I don't keer how much ruckus he . . ." Her voice faltered and her sick eyes stared over my shoulder.

I would have put May Queen into Mady's arms but she did not notice; her wide eyes were too intent on something behind me. Turning I saw the man in the doorway, with hands thrust deep into pockets, and hat pushed back on the foppish hair. His flat eyes, incurious and indifferent, regarded me.

The silence and his unwavering regard held until Mady broke it, her clear child's voice propitiating, "Ma done said I kain't hev hit, Mr. Luckett. Fer true, she say I kain't hev hit."

The cold eyes moving slowly to the small taut figure caught the light from the window and glinted.

"What say, Mady?"

The valiant treble repeated, "Fer true she say hit . . ." Her voice trailed off and merged with the silence. But when, without speaking, he held her with the flat expression in his eyes she tried again. "Ma says I kain't."

Impulsively I put my hand on her shoulder. "Never mind, Mady, he heard you. . . ."

He said with insidious softness, "That's right, Mady . . . you kain't keep hit."

She nodded and I hope that never again shall I see in another child's eyes what I saw in hers. Swaggering, he crossed to stand before me, his eyes sweeping my figure.

I asked, "You are Mr. Luckett?"

He drawled, "That's right. And I reckon you're the lady that stuck-up Cade talks about."

His wife's voice warned, "Dude . . . Dude." Then, covering her warning with a small laugh, she said genteelly, "Dude, be acquainted with Miz Carrebee."

The meaty figure, half turning at his wife's voice, pivoted back, no longer swaggering but with a pretense of gallantry. "Why you must be Miz *Wes* Carrebee." He was as unperturbed as if we had casually met.

"Yes, I am Mrs. Wes Carrebee."

"Well now! I'm mighty proud to welcome you. Likely it didn't seem so when I come in. Reckon a man forgets his manners when he's carrying too heavy a load."

Hands in pockets, he moved to the stove. His voice was aggrieved. "Hit's enough to drive a man out of his mind, Miz Carrebee, ma'am. Kate there ailing, not able to do. But we're making out all right." His eyes slid to small Mady, who watched him intently. The insidious softness was back in his voice. "Ain't we, Mady?"

Mady nodded agreement as if her head was worked by a string.

I said evenly, "So I see," and picked up May Queen. "This was my doll when I was small, Mr. Luckett. I brought her to Mady. I hope you will not object."

The meaty hand rubbed the pale jaw. "Why no, ma'am. It's mighty kind of you."

I placed May Queen in Mady's arms and she lifted her eyes, her breath catching. Leaning, I kissed her cheek, then crossed to Mrs. Luckett and took her thin hand. "I'll come again, Mrs. Luckett, if I may." Then, at the dry burning heat of her hand, I inquired, "Mrs. Luckett, have you had a doctor?"

Proudly, she answered, "Yes ma'am, Dude had Doctor Myley drop by." Her eyes sought his. "Didn't you, Dude?"

"That's right," he drawled.

"I just run down from birthin' he say," she explained. "He tole me ter ease up a mite."

My eyes searched the room. "Why, where is the new baby?"

"Mady settled 'im out in the kitchen, 'count of my cold and coughin' right smart. She'll be proud ter show 'im." Her laugh was gentle. " 'Pears like he's more hers than mine, with me so puny."

In the small cheerless kitchen the baby slept in the splint basket that served as crib, his tiny fists doubled on the worn, spotless blanket. Whatever strength he had taken from his mother he had failed to use for himself. He was scrawny and pale, the blue-tinged white of skimmed milk.

But Mady's eyes were adoring. "Ain't he pritty, Miz Carr'bee?" she asked, her small hand smoothing the blanket.

"He's a beautiful baby. And you keep him so clean."

"Yes, ma'am." Her laughter brimmed over. "He do purely keep me ahumpin'."

At the warning rat-a-tat of rain on the roof I went to the window and looking out, saw the first big spattering drops of rain. I turned back to Mady. "I must hurry or I'll be caught in the rain," I said as I kissed her.

In the next room I hurriedly told Mrs. Luckett good-by and left; Dude Luckett, swaggering, saw me to the door, and I felt his eyes following me down the hill.

Crossing the millyard I looked at the sky. Thickened and darkened, the mountainous masses of smoke-black cloud hung heavy with rain. Even as I looked, they seemed to split wide and release a wall of swift pelting water. Running, I sped past the mill with its rumble of machinery and windows brilliantly lighted, and reaching the office, dashed up its steps and entered, and stood shaking the rain from my coat.

Darty Land, scowling, looked up from his desk and, rising, came toward me with his sidling crablike gait, his child's eyes peering over his glasses. "What you doing out in this rain?" he growled.

Laughing, I put out my hand. "Hello, Darty Land. How are you?"

"Terrible." Then, not to be diverted, he repeated, "What you doing out in this rain?"

"I'm more concerned with how I'm going to get home."

He peered over his glasses at me. "Got a few things to clean up. Soon as the whistle blows we'll hit the road to your place." He turned to his work and forgot me.

Waiting, I wondered if Wes had got home, if he was worried about me, and decided he wasn't, for Mitty would tell him where I had gone. I could hardly wait to tell him of Mady and Cade—how grown-up both of them were—and of Mr. Luckett, "Ma's husband."

How foolish women could be when it came to the man they loved, as if they were compelled to follow love to the end. I wondered why. Could it be because custom gave them so little else? And were men less foolish in love because they had so much besides?

The mill whistle's shriek jerked me from my thoughts. Darty, shrugging into his coat, went to the window and I crossed and stood beside him. Together we watched the millworkers pour from the buildings like ants.

Jostling and twisting and pushing, their hurrying shapes dissolved in the rain as they went toward the slope and home. Lights began to splutter in windows as women, weary from work, went about the supper.

When the mill lights had winked out one after one, Darty said, "Let's go," and we left the office and went down the steps, feeling the rain on our faces. He led me across the grounds to a building still brightly lighted, and I saw CARREBEE MILL STORE painted across it. Darty said, "Over there's our carriage," but it was only a grocery wagon, used, Darty said, by the store to fetch supplies from the markets.

While he untied the horse's reins that were looped to a post, I stood before the store window and watched the people inside. Swarming, they bought their supper, picking and testing and choosing, the women in faded gingham with a pinch of snuff in their lips, the men in overalls which, like Cade's, were faded and patched, not overclean. All, both men and women, had the sharp bitter look of struggle. Their eyes were quick and knowing, though weary now at day's end, wanting only a bite of supper, and then bed; shrieked out again at daybreak by the whistle.

Darty called, "You want to go home?" and I turned and went to the wagon. He helped me up to the high wooden seat and got in and picked up the reins. As we drove along the dark soggy road he told me what he knew of Dude Luckett. Raised right here in the village, and not worth the powder and lead, he said, it would take to blow out his brains, but quite a man with the ladies and hell on wheels when mad. On a trip upstate met a widow with a little farm—that was as good as he wanted. Reckon he didn't rest 'til she sold the farm and he got his hands on the money . . . and now those kids working in the mill.

"But isn't there a law against that?" I protested.

"Yessum, we've got a law. It don't mean a thing. Wish it did."

I could not see his face but by the tone of his voice I knew he was scowling. I asked, wonderingly, "Darty, don't you like the mill?"

"Oh—it's all right."

"What is it you don't like about it?"

He chuckled. "There's only one thing wrong with mills. It's the way they're run. Take the mill store for example. Most mills have their own store. They charge higher prices than anywhere else but the hands better trade there if they want to do well. Yet the millowner claims he's doing it to help 'em."

"Is that true of Carrebee Mills?"

"Don't get all het up about Carrebee. All of 'em do it."

"Is there anything else?"

"Plenty. Now take Dude Luckett. I'm holding no brief for Dude, but he's got his side. He had four pay envelopes in his family, now just two. And Ed Wangle don't want a two-worker house."

"But Darty . . . couldn't things be different?"

"Millowners like it the way it is. And the hands dassn't show any gumption."

"I didn't know about all this. . . . Maybe someday things will be different."

"Might—if they don't get worse."

We reached the top of the rise where Hickory Hill glowed warm and cheerful with lights. "Looks like you're home." He pulled up the horse near the house and I asked him to have supper with us. But he shook his head. He had to get the wagon back to the store.

I put out my hand. "Thank you, Darty . . ." I began, but stopped, for I heard the back door slam and footsteps that strode down the steps and came toward us. I called, "That you, Wes?"

He called back, "Hello, Doc," and strode on, straight and so imperiously tall, I wondered if he had worried and was displeased because I was late.

Darty said, "Good evening, Wes."

Wes's greeting was friendly, "Hey, Darty! Looked like the dam burst, didn't it? I'm glad Jess thought of the mill. I was afraid she wouldn't."

Laughing, I retorted, "Of course I thought of the mill. You talk like I'm half-witted."

He reached in the dark and tousled my hair. "I do or you'd have known it was going to rain."

"I did know it. But I wanted to go." Without volition, I remembered that he had promised to come home, ride me down in the car.

Wes said to Darty, "How about a drink for the road."

Darty said he'd better not. He'd better get back. Ed would have a convulsion. He climbed in the wagon and took up the reins and Wes moved close to the wagon and looked up at him.

"Thanks for bringing my wife home, Darty."

Darty, embarrassed, said 'twas nothing at all. Glad to oblige any time.

Laughing, Wes warned not to tell me that, or I'd probably take him up on it. Then his voice changed, was somewhat less gay, "And oh, while I think of it, Darty, next time don't bring her home in a grocery wagon. . . ."

There was a moment of silence. Then Darty, clearing his throat, broke it. "It was all I had handy . . ."

I said quickly, "Darty, I can't thank you enough."

He repeated, "Nothing at all," and with a good night started down the hill. Wes and I, slowly and walking apart, went to the house. I was angry. Darty had been embarrassed. And Wes had been arrogant. And I was going to tell him so.

As we ascended the back step I stopped and said, "Wes . . . that was—I can't tell you how—"

I was not allowed to go on. I was in his arms, his mouth was on mine. And when he raised his head, I said again, "Wes". . . and his kiss stopped me again.

At last he said, "Doc, I was so damned worried." He gave me a little shake. "Don't ever do that to me again."

He went on talking, his voice muffled and tender; but I looked over his head and out into the night; and saw that it was still raining.

This was fulfillment at last, the child I carried within me. All my unrest was calmed, as were my troubles and worries. I seemed to exist in a nebulous space where nothing of earth could reach me, my whole being curved to protect the life that I carried.

This was fulfillment at last, the fulfillment not found in marriage, which I now knew was impossible to attain. For marriage was union of two separate souls, each alien one to the other, each impelled by its hidden self to impulses beyond understanding. Not so with the child of your womb, small spirit that springs from your love, that is sheltered and nourished within you: existing only because you exist, breathing because you breathe, loving because you love, two bound one to another by an indissoluble bond. For you an extension of self, its joy and pain inseparably yours until you can feel pain no more.

This was fulfillment at last, double fulfillment for me. For now at last I would have my own. I would hold my own in my arms. I would be to my child what no one on earth could be, would spare it the pain of rejection, the hurt that a mother, caring too little for what she has borne, without mercy robs the child of what no other on earth or in heaven can ever replace.

I told Wes I was going to have a baby, not as timid young wives would reveal it in books, showing a tiny garment bashfully, which I always thought silly and prudish. My "Wes, I'm going to have a baby" was happy and proud, as if I alone had accomplished this, this miracle so astounding. Nor did Wes take me in his arms and in reverent voice whisper, "Dear little mother." He salted his eggs and grinned at me over the table. "Well, that's what you wanted, isn't it?"

"Of course it is. Wes . . . aren't you glad?"

He pursed his mouth as if he gravely considered. "Well, now, Doc, I think I'll wait and see. If it comes here redheaded and freckled . . ."

"Wes," I scolded. "It will be a beautiful baby. It will look like its father."

Quickly he shook his head. "No, Doc. It must look like you—and be like you. Straight and clear-eyed and good." He pushed back his chair and rose. "Listen, Doc, I'll be late tonight. Going with Breck and Jim and a bunch to the auto races at Hapeville."

Later, as Mitty washed dishes and I dried, I asked her how most men reacted when they heard about the first baby. She chuckled. "Well, blessed, it depends on the man. The average man, which to my way of thinking is consider'ble below any average I know, looks on a baby as something to be expected, which a woman don't do. Every woman thinks she is the first to pull off this smart a trick. She never stops to think that everybody already on the earth or ever was on the earth or ever will be, gets here the same way. And that she ain't killed no bear."

I teased, "And what has all that to do with how a husband reacts to the news?"

"I was acoming to that, given time. Husbands don't do what you call react. Fact is, when the baby comes, they're likely to look sorta sour and think it a mighty pore package. Then somebody ups and says, 'Just like his father,' and he's caught, hog-tied, and slaughtered. He throws out his chest and goes struttin' around as proud as a bantam rooster. And all because it looks like him."

I laughed. "But suppose it doesn't?"

She chuckled again. "It generally don't, 'cause new babies look like nothing I ever see in this world. But only you say it, and he'll believe it." She hung the dish towel over the stove and turned to face me. "Don't be fretting yourself. You're a good healthy girl with plenty of sense. Your baby will be the same. Next time you're to town lay in some goods. We can start sewing."

So as summer came in with its long warm days and in leisurely fashion began to turn toward fall, I tranquilly went about living my life, but with an added awareness. I arranged the books Miss Camilla sent out on the shelves I, myself, built of pine two-by-fours, inveigled from Darty Land. Painted and filled with the books, they looked well, ranged against the sitting-room wall.

As I arranged them, I wondered if, now that our baby was coming, Wes would settle down. For now it was not our future alone but that of our child. Occupied with my thoughts as I sat on the floor, I idly examined the small hand loom Miss Camilla had sent with the books. Sometime, I thought, it might be fun to try my hand at weaving.

In the cool of the evenings I helped Mitty weed in her flower beds that flashed their color and fragrance, and thought how human beings, even as plants, responded to care, that it was Mitty's love that brought hers to their final splendor. So it would be with children; how they developed, dependent on the love and care they received, from the time the small seed was planted.

Often, I walked to the mill to visit with the Lucketts, and each time I came away worried about Mrs. Luckett. There were days when she would be up, stirring around, saying she did believe she was over the hump. But when, on my next visit, I found her on the bed—"Jest restin' awhile," she would apologize, " 'count o' not feelin' so peart," and I would worry again. But gaining a day and slipping a day, she was finally able to go back to work in the mill.

Mady stayed home and kept house and cared for the frail little brother who, for reasons I never learned, had earned the nickname of Poky. Always when I went with books for Cade or clothes sewn by Mitty for Mady and Poky, I would find her busy at her cleaning or washing or ironing. I would feel guilty because of the little I did, for small Mady's tasks were too heavy. Yet so great was her courage and wish to serve, she never once thought them a burden.

Yet I conceded that Miss Camilla might be right, that it was easy to overdo giving. Meeting me in the millyard and stopping to chat, she had brought up the subject.

She was friendly, casual, forthright. "Jess, what's this I hear about you taking a mill family under your wing?"

Briefly I told her of ailing Kate Luckett and the children, of Mr. Luckett, "Ma's husband."

When I finished she patted my arm.

"It's nice of you to take an interest, my dear, but don't overdo it. You mustn't make them dissatisfied with their kind of life."

I rebelled at the thought of Mady and Cade, bound to this life.

"Do you mean they can't have another kind?"

Patiently she explained. "Jess, this *is* their life. Their families work in the mill from one generation to another. They wouldn't be happy away from it. And they'd be just as unhappy here if they had a taste of the other."

Reluctantly I admitted the logic of this and she patted my arm again. "I knew with your sensible head you would." Her hand moved up to pat my cheek. "Have your little game of Lady Bountiful, my dear, but don't upset their lives."

It did not prevent my going to see Kate Luckett and Cade and Mady; but I was careful not to overdo giving, not because of any conviction that Miss Camilla was right, but because I was loath to cause trouble for her or the Lucketts. I did not admit that Cade and Mady were bound to the mill and Dude Luckett. Often as I crossed the mill grounds, I caught sight of him walking with a dark-eyed, flaunting girl whom I knew only as Cora. No bonds whatever seemed to irk him.

The dry arid days of August went by and autumn, rainy and drear, dragged like a whining woman damply, morosely toward winter. Held in the house by the weather, burdened with my clumsy and thickening body, I was forever fidgeting at some task, seeking release for the energy which nature had stored. And on these unlightened days, I was not brave or gallant—I was a woman. Without knowing why, I would find myself weeping slow tears as I dusted or sewed. There were days when, convinced I would die, I spent hours preparing for death, arranging my few possessions, marked them with cards that read "for Wes" or "for Mitty"; and folding my hands when I went to bed, in saintly and pure resignation, I would think, *Like this Wes will discover my body in the morning,* and drop off to sleep with the pensive but pleasant conclusion, *So young to die . . . so young and so fair.* But next morning, waking to find myself in excellent health, energy would flow through me like a stream, and all day I would work like a beaver, singing happily and laughing at trifles. And Mitty would say, "The baby moved last night. And took off the pressure."

Sometimes I thought I bored Wes, and no wonder. For my world had shrunk to a small arc that held nothing but myself and my baby. With the candor natural with me, I talked to Wes of them, like the whippoorwill repeating, over and over, one tiresome tune. The date the baby would come (counting on my fingers), the tiny clothes finished and waiting, the doctor who must be called when Mitty said. Then beginning all over again. The date (counting on fingers again)...

He was considerate, thoughtful. Yet I would feel him edging away as I talked, and if I happened to pause for breath, which, breath at this stage being short, I had to do often, too quickly he changed the subject. Had I heard, he would ask, or did I know . . . ? And, smiling, I pretended to listen, but waited like a cat at a rathole to pounce on *his* pausing for breath so I might return to *my* subject.

I did not walk down the hill often now, for the climb back was too steep for a body as heavy as mine. On fair days, Mitty plodded down to take things I wanted the Lucketts to have, and bring back word that they were "gettin' along." Later she brought back the news that Kate Luckett was down again with the grippe and she reckoned must be right sick. The mill doctor told her she ought to lay off the job.

This weighed on my mind, and I determined that I would ask Wes to come home early one day and drive me down to see her. Sighing, I thought if there was any one thing I would change about Wes—though there wasn't—it would be his uncertain absences, his still more uncertain returns. Then when I asked him that night, I felt a small twinge of remorse. "Why, of course, Doc," he said gently. "Tomorrow, at that. Will two-thirty be early enough?"

"Plenty," I said, "and I won't stay long and keep you waiting. Maybe" —I looked at him eagerly—"you would go in and meet the Lucketts."

He shook his head. "Not me, Doc. And for a very good reason. I feel guilty and I can't do a damned thing about it."

I insisted softly, "Oh, but you could! You could do so much about it. If you took over the mill. Wes, don't you realize . . . it is *your* mill. Your father left *you* in control."

Stretched in his chair on the other side of the fire, with Colonel at his feet, he looked at me with shrouded eyes.

"Listen, Doc," he said quietly, "I'm telling you once and for all. I won't work in the damned mill. Oh, I dived in a couple of years back. I had ideas about running it, but didn't get very far. My mother saw to that. To her, the mill is a cow. She feeds it just enough to keep it alive so she'll get that last little drop of milk. And for fear she won't get that last drop, she's got to be boss, and she will be boss, come hell or high water!"

Slowly, I asked, "Is that why you won't . . . ?"

"That's why. And because I couldn't wring my dirty profit out of . . . say, your Lucketts."

"But why, Wes? Why should Miss Camilla . . ."

"Ask your young friend Cade how many hours he works a day, how much he earns. Ask Mrs. Luckett what the mill store charges her for a sack of flour. Check it against what you pay. And I'll tell you why. She's money-mad. She always has been. It's why she married my father, why she let Cissa and me grow up like we did. And I'll tell you something else. She had the idea that you had real money coming to you or she'd never have spent a minute's time on you."

Shocked, I asked, "How could she think such a thing?"

He laughed. "She did. She'd sell you or Cissa or me down the river to get it, and don't forget it."

"But why is she like that? Why so much emphasis on money?"

"Because her mother was a Ravenal, planter aristocracy . . . they thought. Plantations, slaves, rice floating down the river, yassa, boss, suh . . . and after the war, bone-poor. My grandmother married the first man that came along and lived low and talked high the rest of her life. My mother was raised poor and proud, and to have pride and not have money to support it makes money the most important thing in the world. Because without it you can't be proud. A Southerner that can't be proud is a dead Southerner. And then she gives Cissa hell for being what she is . . . and me. She forgets that

"Degenerate squires make degenerate seed,
Soon we will have a degenerate breed."

I changed the subject. "What's Cissa done now?"

"What hasn't she done? She's running around with Syl Crowley, making herself the talk of the town."

"Wes . . ."

"Uh-huh . . ."

"What's wrong with Syl Crowley?"

"He's a big-time pimp and partner to Pet Belleau, prominent whorehouse madam, among other things. He can buy you a woman or a state legislator, if you've got the price."

"Then it's ridiculous to worry about him and Cissa. Cissa is proud."

He stared across at me somberly. "That," he said briefly, "is what worries me."

Next day I gathered the articles I would take to the Lucketts into a basket and waited for Wes to come drive me down as he promised, but even as I waited, chatting with Mitty, I knew that he would not come. For he had left in the morning angry, his temper suddenly flaring, had flashed out of the door without saying good-by, leaving Mitty and me with shocked faces.

"What did I say, Mitty?" I asked in wonder.

Shaking her head, she said she didn't exactly recall, but she believed it was something about the mill.

Helplessly, I cried out, "But I was only going to ask him to stop and tell Darty Land to send us a load of coal. Why, he didn't even let me finish."

All morning as I went about my tasks, a small hard core of resentment lay in my breast at his temper which, I felt, had no justification. Not waiting to hear what I would say of the mill, but at the word mill itself, flying up like a peevish schoolboy indulging himself in a tantrum. Not knowing or caring that the coal pile was getting low, that the weather, suddenly colder, promised to be colder still.

At two o'clock, I put on my coat and sat in the kitchen waiting. Mitty, seeing, remarked, "Now, blessed, being it's bad weather, Wes likely'll think you won't be going."

Calmly, lest she suspect my resentment, I told her whether Wes came or not, I would go. With tight-pressed lips, she surveyed me, hands on her hips.

"Now, you wouldn't. And you goin' into eight months?"

I only laughed at her. "Mitty, it won't hurt me to walk. It's good for me."

"It ain't walking that worrits me, dearie. But the weather. Not that it's terrible cold, but I'm thinking it's mighty dampish. And I needn't tell you it's pneumonia weather."

"Mitty," I said, "I've got to get out of the house. I've been cooped up so long. And I want to see how Kate Luckett is, see Mady and Cade. They'll think I've forgot them."

"Well, if you've got all of those reasons I reckon you might as well go. Don't forget to tell Darty Land about the coal. And don't leave Colonel behind unless you want him to throw a conniption fit."

She followed me to the back porch and, peering out, doubtfully shook her head. "It's fogging up. Now you go careful, my blessed."

I called back, "I will," and with Colonel pacing beside me I crossed the yard and started down the hill road, and almost turned back; for the fog blotted out what lay below with swaths of thick white mist, engulfed in a swirling white sea what had once been the world.

As Colonel and I descended, its coldness clung to my face, and my hand, touching Colonel for guidance, felt the dampness upon his coat. Groping our way blindly through it, I thought he and I might be the only living creatures on some hellish nightmare island, where one false step would send us spinning into fathomless space. Carefully, all the while touching Colonel's head, I put each foot warily down, each time feeling the tricky wet clay, uncertain and slick. I wondered how far down the hill I had come, and peering ahead tried to discern a familiar landmark; the fork in the road, the roof of Adeline's house, the branch that ran through the hollow. I saw, or imagined I saw, the ghostly shape of Adeline's roof, and knew an easing of tension and laughed to think I had been tense. . . . Then, my foot slipping, I fell and was suddenly hurtling down through the fog. Down . . . down, with Colonel frantically barking, and I going down . . . down . . . was there no end to this hill? And smashing against I did not know what, I lay still, feeling something within me rip like a seam. Then I was falling again, swirling faster and faster and faster, not into fog but a soft, enveloping darkness, while far up, and receding, Colonel was frantically barking. . . .

The deepening murmur of rain spread across all the vast darkness, reached me and roused me from it to waking. For a moment I lay with closed eyes, too tired for the effort of waking, then opening them, saw with clearing vision the shimmering light at the rain-streaked windows; and knew I lay in my room and, although she made no sound, that Mitty was somewhere near.

"Mitty," I said, and heard the small metal tap of the crochet needle as she placed it upon the table and the gentle stir of her skirts as she moved to the bed. Then her face, dear and familiar, and softened now with concern, was hovering over me, and though I could manage to speak no word, she said, as if I had spoken, "What is it, my blessed?"

"Mitty," I finally managed, surprised at the strange thready voice I forced from my lips, "my baby . . . it didn't . . . ?"

There was no need to complete the question. She knew and had known what it would be. She gave me my answer gently.

"No, my blessed, your baby . . . never lived."

It was the answer I had expected, the answer I somehow had known. Yet hope must have feebly persisted and now, fleeing, dragged in its wake pain that, tearing and searing, ripped through me, closing out all else but pain; and one part of me thought as, shrinking, I cringed before it, that the pains of birth and death were identical, all-devouring, all-encompassing, leaving the emptied body and heart gutless and ravished shells.

I had not meant to cry, I did not want to cry, for what use was crying? But I felt the tears well up and break over and slowly crawl down my cheeks, and tasted their bitter salt on my lips. Then I could not hold back my weeping, and Mitty, kneeling, took me in her arms and held me as she had when I was a child, and, crooning, dried my eyes with a corner of her apron.

"I'm sorry, Mitty," I said through my crying. "I didn't mean . . ."

She shushed me, lovingly. A good cry would do me good, she said. "Tears wash away sorrowing like spring rain washes winter out of the ground. Just have yourself a good cry."

"Mitty," I whispered—for I could make no more sound than a whisper, "Mitty, my baby was . . . ?"

"A boy, my blessed." Then as I cried afresh for the son I had carried and lost, my son with the dark, glowing eyes, she said, "I know, I know." She offered no shallow and useless comfort, but held me gently, yet fiercely, protectively, her work-roughened hand stroking my hair and cheek. And after a little, I grew quieter. The pain was there undiminished, for the crying had not eased the sorrow, but like rain that, dissolving, softens the earth, so my sorrow was softened.

In the leaden exhaustion that followed, I hung suspended in a vast vacancy that stood me in comfort's stead. I hardly knew when I took the broth which Mitty brought and fed to me from a spoon. This, I thought vaguely between spoonfuls, was as we had been when I was a child and ill; held against Mitty's breast, fed with a spoon from a cup, Mitty's voice saying, as so often it said in the long ago past, "Just one more spoonful, my blessed." And, as in those lost days, I obediently took the last sip and fell back, asleep.

I slept and dreamed, and in my dream I was a small child again and, with Mitty, walked again in the cemetery, strolling among the pale tombstones. Mitty and I were laughing at a big, snowy pouter pigeon that flopped down and strutted before us as pompous as Mrs. Plummer, his pink eyes glaring indignantly as we stood there laughing and laughing. He saying not what pigeons usually say, but "in toto, in toto, in toto." Yet as I laughed at him harder still, I knew all the while I must hurry and find what I had come to find. A green mound belonging only to me and infinitely precious. I must find it, and knew somehow that once it was found I could never leave it again, for it would be helpless and lonely, and too small to be left to itself.

It was night when next I woke in the dim, quiet room and took the broth and cream junket Mitty fed me. "Try to eat it," she pled. "It will give you strength, my blessed." And I ate it, vaguely recalling how a long time ago a voice sweet as syrup had chanted, "Whut use I got fur strength now?"

I waked again, though if an hour later or a day or a week, I did not know. A man in a rumpled black suit whose round cheeks were rosy as plums sat at the bed beside me, blunt fingers on my wrist, eyes on a big gold watch. Gently he put my wrist on the bed, shoved the big gold watch in his pocket. "Progressin' nicely, ma'am," he said, turning to Mitty, and, finding my eyes upon him, repeated, this time to me, "Progressin' nicely, ma'am."

I asked, "I have been . . . very sick?"

He looked down at me through sharp little eyes that were kind. "I won't try and mislead you. You've been a mighty sick lady. But then," he smiled, "I couldn't call childbed fever a piddling sickness in any case."

I stared up at him as my mind dredged up vague things heard and forgotten, that now, moving beneath the surface of thought like sluggish fish in a pool, stirred and brought to the surface widening eddies of doubt.

He saw it, perhaps, in my face, for he asked, "Something troubling you, ma'am?"

I said there was a question or two I would like to ask and I wanted a frank, honest answer. I told him then the things I had heard and asked him if they were true.

He answered me quietly. Yes, ma'am, he said, it was true "in some cases." It depended, of course, on a number of things . . .

I broke in to ask, "Is it true in my case?"

Even before he answered, his sharp eyes, veering from mine, gave me my answer. But he came up to taw. "Yes, ma'am. In your case it's true. I'm sorry."

"I can't have other children—ever have other children?"

He laid his big freckled hand over mine. "Ma'am, I want to be honest. So I won't say *ever,* for I've known cases that fooled us. But I do say, in your case—not wanting to raise false hopes—in your case, it ain't at all likely."

I felt Mitty's hand on my shoulder, as if she would help me to bear it; but this time I did not cry, and that, it struck me, was strange, for now I had lost not one son, I had lost all of my children. All of my rosy-cheeked sons, all of my small, lovely daughters. They would never play on Hickory Hill, never clamber over me like Mr. Dolph's little "cumbers."

The doctor rose heavily, picked up his shabby bag. "I'm sorry, ma'am," he repeated. "A bad streak of luck. You could have mothered a dozen." He shook his head, said abruptly, "Good morning, ma'am," and padded his way from the room.

I lay, not speaking, while Mitty brought warm water and gave me what she called a "spit bath," her voice brisk as she sponged. She was proud as a queen, she said, that I was on the improve, and for more reasons than one. Maybe Wes and Andrew wouldn't be underfoot every minute, looking as sad and hangdog as Colonel. When it came to sickness, she declared, men was worse than a dog with fleas. Amoping and pacing, apacing and moping, and twisting and scratching . . .

Gropingly, my mind went back through the dark lost time, seeking its last awareness. How did they know I was sick, I asked, that I had fallen?

She dried me gently with a soft towel. Didn't I remember? she asked matter-of-factly. I'd been "taken" in Adeline's cabin and Adeline, who was a smart woman, sent Sparrow to the mill to tell Darty Land. Darty couldn't get in touch with Wes nor Miss Camilla either. So he called Andrew, Andrew found Wes. And both of 'em came lickety-split; Wes mad as a hornet because I had walked to the mill.

I asked, "Who told him, Mitty?"

"Why, he didn't have to be told. He knew where you was when it happened. But that's water under the bridge. And I reckon it's true about that ill wind blowing some good. It's blowed you a horse and buggy."

"A horse and buggy?"

"That's what I said, and all your own, Wes says, to cart you about. Moreover, Sparrow to tend it and tend it good, Wes ordered, or he'd dynamite the Coca-Cola plant. You'll be as upcoming as Miss Camilla when you drive out, for a prettier filly you'd go far to see. High steppin' as a girl at a dance."

A sharp little flick of anger pierced me, and my small laugh was bitter. "What difference now, if I walk or ride?"

She brushed my hair in silence awhile, then with utmost cheerfulness said, "I remember the day of your wedding and you asking me if the shine wore off of marriage. And I told you it did and anybody that claimed different could go roll their hoop. Do you remember, my blessed?"

"Of course, Mitty."

"Now me getting old, I gotta admit that my recollector . . . well, some of *its* shine has worn off. But I don't recollect you wanted to back out because Wes would lose some of his shine." She peered into my face. "Or did you?"

"No, Mitty."

She gave my hair an extra-firm stroke. "And had you backed out, I tell you right now, I'd been plumb put out with you. 'Cause it's a mighty poor sport that will take all the good, then goes running out on the bad."

Slowly I asked, "You don't blame Wes, do you, Mitty?"

She began to brush my hair again, and her voice was thoughtful. "Why, yes," she said, "I reckon I do, but I feel downright silly to do so. For it's just blaming Wes for being Wes. Same as you're to blame for being you and me for being me. Wes acted like Wes. Like Wes and like nobody else, like you acted like Jess by peltin' off in that weather."

"But then nobody would ever be to blame for anything," I protested, impatiently.

She shook her head. "No, I don't see it that way. I see it the other way round. We're all to blame for the thing we'll be judged by, according to preachers, when Gabriel hauls off and blows that horn of his. We'll be judged, I reckon, for what we are."

She brought me more broth, and, to please her, I took it; then, pausing before returning the tray to the kitchen, she said Wes had been hanging around my door, like Grant hung around Richmond, and Dr. Tilly had said he could see me for a few minutes.

She went out with the tray. Then Wes stood tall in the doorway, beautiful as ever, I saw, almost with surprise, as if I expected to find his face corroded by the acid of my bitterness. But it was unchanged except for the eyes that looked as if they had never known sleep.

"Doc," he said quietly, and knelt by the bed and gathered me into his arms; and crushed me against him and buried his face on my breast. "I'm sorry, Doc!" he said. "I'm so damned sorry."

It did not ease the pain of the son I had lost, the sons I could never have, and I could not truthfully say "It doesn't matter." And though he was contrite and miserable, and I felt the desire to comfort—I would not. He would not twist me, as he did his mother, into whatever he wanted, with his beautiful careless hands, or think that what had happened could be obliterated with "I'm sorry."

When I failed to speak, he raised his head and looked down into my eyes, and I met them squarely and without flinching. He said, and his voice was gentle, almost humble, but, I thought wryly, its arrogance and pride unchanged and unlessened, "I know I can't make up for . . . what's happened, for your not being able to have . . . children, but Doc, I'll try damned hard. And I'm not trying to make you believe that I've turned lily-white overnight. But I will take better care of you. I will be a better husband."

As I listened, my eyes upon him, I knew he meant it sincerely, as a careless boy is sincere when unwittingly he makes trouble for others. "But he isn't a boy," I told myself, "he is a man, a husband, almost a father, with responsibilities. If he doesn't take them, it's because—as Mitty said—he's Wes. Perhaps he will never take them, but will go on being just Wes. . . the Wes I loved at first, that I love now."

I stared at him as he sat on the side of the bed, his brown fingers playing with mine, his eyes watching me, the questioning half-smile on his face. And suddenly I was weeping again, not outwardly, but that dreadful feeling of weeping inside, that slow and desperate wasting . . . weeping not for the child and the children lost, but for Wes. Wes whom I loved, who had come to me seeking comfort, who had been refused.

I raised my hand—it seemed so heavy—to his hair, and stroked it, wound a lock of it on my finger, smiling into his eyes. "Be happy, darling," I said, annoyed with my voice that came thin, not strong as I wished it to be. "Let's just be happy."

He said, "Oh, Doc!" and buried his face in the pillow beside me. And I stroked the dark head again. I was tired, I thought, and sleepy.

He went out then, pausing at the door to give me a quick grin, and Mitty came in to dim the lamp even more and tell me quietly that now I must rest. As I tried to obey, I thought of Wes. He would continue to be beautiful and gay, moody and aloof, considerate and thoughtless, selfish and generous, all the virtues and faults that were merged into one man and one pride. And yet I would not have him changed in any important way. He was still Wes, and Mitty, as usual, was right. Wes could be blamed for only one sin. The sin of being Wes Carrebee . . . himself.

While I was sick, Wes seldom stirred off Hickory Hill and each day came to sit on the foot of my bed and talk, a more efficient cure than Dr. Tilly's iron tonic and, unlike tonic, easy to take in large doses, the taste of his kisses sweet upon my lips.

Those hours brought us closer than ever. He was tender, thoughtful, and eager to serve me, proud when Mitty, busy, left to him the task of soft-boiling eggs, or making a cup of tea and taking a milk pudding from the icebox to serve to me for lunch.

Overdone or underdone, hot or cold, the toast and eggs were more delicious because he prepared them. His bad cooking and small failings somehow became endearing virtues. I thought it was rather sweet that he should not know how to soft-boil an egg.

I could not resist his charm nor help adoring him. I could not resist his gaiety, restrain my laughter at his jokes, or control my response to his love-making. And if the bitterness was still there—and it was—it was no longer directed toward Wes, but life itself. I felt I had been cheated and betrayed by life. A discontent possessed me, like an actual physical presence in my body. I knew it was neither brave nor admirable to be possessed by the sullen humor. When I snapped at Mitty, always patient and cheerful, I was ashamed. Yet the knowledge that I behaved badly did not dissolve the bitterness.

But this did not prevent my mending and swiftly regaining my strength; and when Dr. Tilly allowed visitors, Andrew came to see me. His visit gave Mitty so much satisfaction that I guessed she expected that he'd set me right.

He was his cheerful, matter-of-fact self when he came in, but I was suddenly aware of how he had changed since I first saw him at Poteat & Whidby. Now, in his sober, well-cut suit, he had an air of authority and importance—though not self-importance—that the young Andrew had lacked.

Yet he was as good-humored in his quiet way, as kind and modest as always. Raking his fingers through the rusty hair in the same thoughtful manner, he said he was glad to find me better. Though according to Mitty, he added, I still wasn't too chipper.

"You can't expect to bounce right back," he went on calmly, "but you'll pick up fast. And now that you keep your own stable"—his eyes twinkled—"you'll be sashaying around in no time."

When I said I supposed so, he gave me a thoughtful glance.

"You don't sound very enthusiastic."

"I don't suppose I do," I admitted. I was aware of the steady gaze of his blue eyes.

He said quietly, "You will when you're stronger."

"No." I avoided his glance. "It isn't that. I guess . . ." I hesitated, then I told him, still avoiding his eyes, "Andrew, I can't ever . . . have children."

His voice was matter-of-fact and for that I was grateful. "That's a contingency you didn't expect, isn't it?" he asked.

I said it was.

"That's what hurts, isn't it, Jess? That's your trouble."

"Yes," I said, "to know I can't ever . . . I feel so . . ." I searched for a word to express how I felt and found it. ". . . so useless."

"I'm sorry." His voice was still matter-of-fact. "It's a very foolish way to feel."

"Foolish?"

"Yes." His fingers raked his hair. "Because you're not useless. You can still have children, you know."

I frowned, puzzled, and told him I did not understand.

"To my way of thinking," he said, "to have children, you don't have to give birth to them. You do have to give love and understanding. And the world being what it is, children who need them are not hard to find."

"Do you mean I should adopt a child, Andrew?" I asked.

"It isn't important how you arrange it. It's caring that matters."

I said, "But it wouldn't be the same as your own child."

He bent toward me and asked, in a voice completely unlike his, and with iron in it, "Has Mitty cared less for you because you aren't her own child? Do you need her less? Do you belong to her less?"

The change in his voice, as well as his words, was strangely shocking, though he had spoken quietly as ever. I shook my head. "No."

"It's not being of the same flesh and blood that makes people belong to one another. It's giving love and care and faith. And it doesn't matter if it's children or men and women."

He straightened in his chair. "So don't talk to me about being useless. There's one sure-fire cure for anybody who feels useless. To go out and be useful, by God, and in God's name put an end to it."

I tried to tell him how right I knew him to be, feeling a surge of shame and at the same time a sense of relief. Within me the cold hardness dissolved and allowed warmth and feeling to re-enter.

"Im afraid I'm not very useful where you are concerned, Andrew," I said. "I don't know why you are so good to me."

"I feel responsible," he said. "After all, Poteat & Whidby are still your guardians even if you are married and keep your own stable."

The Georgia spring came in early, its air balmy and still, as if it had hurried on my account and arrived warm and breathless. It blurred the dark limbs of the hickories in a fuzz of yellow light and scattered mild blue wood violets across winter's dark decay of fallen leaves.

Wes took me out in the buggy and gave me lengthy and detailed instructions regarding the handling of Moppet, the name that I gave the filly. I made so many mistakes that Wes and the filly were both disgusted, Wes and I snapping at each other and things in general. Yet it was a pleasant kind of unpleasantness, a husbandly, wifely tift that ended by Wes's laughing, delighted, when I landed a wheel in a ditch.

However, I finally got the knack of it, and the freedom I gained helped me mind less when Wes, slipping back into old habits, kept odd, unpredictable hours. Now instead of moping in the house, waiting for his footsteps, I hitched up Moppet and drove along country roads, keeping at first to those seldom traveled. But then, gaining confidence, I drove to the mill to see Cade and Mady for the first time since my illness.

My newly won confidence was close to being shattered again as we entered the mill gate. The mill whistle broke on the quiet spring morning, and Moppet, frightened, reared frantically, almost wrenching my arms from their sockets. By the time I had calmed her, the millworkers were jostling and shouldering from doorways into the cindered yard and racing toward their dinners, unwilling to waste a precious minute of their freedom.

As I secured Moppet to the hitching bar near the gate, I searched the hurrying crowd for Cade and Mady, but they were nowhere in sight. Instead I saw Duke Luckett. With his measured swagger, he moved beside his companion, a sharp-faced girl of a thin, defiant prettiness, who at something he said threw back her head and laughed raucously.

As I crossed the cinder yard and went toward the mill houses, the unpleasant sensation his manner always induced sharpened, as if the sight of his mealy strength in which he took pride stirred in me some deep, automatic fear, as the mill whistle had in the filly.

On the Lucketts' stoop, though the door hung open, I received no response to my knock. Nor to my voice when I called "Cade" and then "Mady." And concluding that no one was at home, I turned to go back to the buggy.

As I stepped off the stoop a voice behind me said politely, "We heard you knocking but we couldn't come right off. We war takin' keer of Ma."

I wheeled, startled, and saw Cade in the shadow cast by the door.

"Cade," I said, "I decided no one was home."

"We war lookin' after Ma," he repeated. He added courteously, "We ain't aiming to be unsociable."

"I know that, Cade," I assured him. "Is your mother—sick again?"

"She's took worse'n here lately," he answered. "That's how come Mady and me ain't on the job. They's got to be somebody to do fer Ma. She ain't able to git about."

"I'm sorry," I said, wanting to help but afraid of intruding.

He said, "It'd purely pleasure Ma if you'd step in and set er spell. She air askin' most ever' day if we see you."

When I told him I'd like to sit a spell, he led me to the rear room. It contained a large old brass bed with sagging springs, a straight chair, and by the bed an upturned box that served as a table to hold the oil lamp and a worn Bible. Beside the Bible someone had placed a bunch of the pale-blue wood violets that grow in the Georgia woods.

Though the day was mild, a spring chill hung in the air. And in the fireless, sunless room it was intensified into a clammy bone-seeking cold. I wondered how Mady, standing beside the bed in her thin skimpy dress, managed to keep from shivering.

She said quietly, "Howdy, Miz Car'bee," and I saw that the blue eyes were troubled, and I knew why when I turned to Kate Luckett on the sagging bed and saw the emaciated body under the worn quilt and the sunken eyes, the ominous leaden face that seemed to have caved in upon its bones.

Concealing my dismay, I took her hand, and it seemed impossible that the furious furnace of heat I felt in it could be generated in the meager body.

As I told her I was sorry that she wasn't well, conscious of the inadequacy of words, the sunken eyes gazed up at me, the bright dark pain of desperation in their depths.

"It were real nice of you to come." Her voice was a husky rasp. "I bin wishing you'd be droppin' in." Her eyes left mine and moved toward Cade and Mady. "Though Mady there and Cade kin be as good as a show, when they see I'm low in my spirits. But hit's tejous fer 'em."

When I told her I would have come before but I too had been sick, she was concerned.

"I ain't hear you war ailin'," she said, her voice hardly more than a whisper. "I hope it warn't nothin' too bad."

"No," I answered, "it wasn't bad. I'm fine. It's you who must get well now."

She did not answer, but looked up at me with deep and passionless comprehension that already said what she would not say before Cade and Mady: That just as I saw death on her face, she felt his shadow within, and had no fear of him—except for her children.

I bent over and said quietly, "Mrs. Luckett, I'm going to get some things I think you should have. But I won't be gone long."

"I'm purely sorry to trouble you."

"It's no trouble," I told her and turned to Cade. "Cade, I'll need your help."

As he and I went down the slope I questioned him and learned that the situation was as I suspected. There was no coal, he said, and except for sorghum and flour—no food. "Mr. Luckett ain't to home much lately," he said quietly.

On a used envelope I found in my pocketbook I wrote a hasty note to Mitty listing things that she should send and, giving it to Cade, I told him to take the buggy and go to Hickory Hill. He nodded in understanding and straightway got into the buggy. And I turned toward the mill office to ask Darty Land's help. But Darty wasn't there. At my entrance, Ed Wangle heaved his large, soft body from his swivel chair. With blatant heartiness he boomed that it was "a shore nuff treat" to see me up; I'd been mighty sick, he'd heard. I thanked him and said I was quite well now. But I needed help for someone else who was ill. It was Mrs. Luckett.

His heavy delight was replaced by a sententious compassion. He placed a chair for me, and tilting ponderously in his, pulled at his lower lip with a forefinger that needed its nail cleaned.

"Now that you bring it up," he said more quietly, but still loud enough, "I reckon I did hear something about you looking in on one of the women. Dude's woman, you say?"

I nodded. "I'm afraid," I said, "she is seriously ill. I've just come from there."

His finger circled slowly from the lower lip toward his fleshy nose, his eyes giving me shrewd, flickering glances from behind his mask of massive commiseration.

"You say Dude's woman is right bad off?"

"Mrs. Luckett is desperately ill," I corrected.

His eyes widened in aggrieved innocence. "Sho, that's what I said," he agreed.

"I'm afraid, in fact, Mr. Wangle, she hasn't long to live."

He was mournful and he was astonished. "You don't say! Why, look here, that's bad." He wagged his head slowly, his lower lip conveying his sympathy by thrusting itself further out. "I didn't have no notion she was that sick."

"She is, Mr. Wangle. And no coal to heat the house. And there are two children and a baby."

His profound sigh indicated his wonder that such tragedy should strike. "I tell you, Miss Jess, a man has to keep a strong holt on hisself or he'd plain break down."

I was glad to find him sympathetic, I told him, because I needed his help. I wanted the Lucketts to have a load of coal. I also wanted the mill doctor to see Mrs. Luckett—and at once. The coal would be charged to Wes, I added.

He would send the doctor, he agreed. That was what the mill hired him for, and he might just as well earn his money. But—he was mournful again—he was plumb sorry but he couldn't oblige with the coal.

I was incredulous. "But, Mr. Wangle, Mrs. Luckett is dying in that house, and it's cold. You must, Mr. Wangle."

He leaned toward me in confidential disbelief. "Why, Miss Jess, if it got out that the Lucketts got a load of free coal, I wouldn't git another minute's peace. Every linthead on the place would want a load."

"Nonsense, Mr. Wangle."

"Now, Miss Jess," he said, his great face reproachful, "that ain't no way to talk. I got to think of mill policy. Sholy you can see that."

"I don't think policy matters when a woman is dying."

"Miss Jess, you don't know what you're saying." He was genuinely shocked. "You oughten to be more careful. Suppose that kind of talk got started? Where'd we all end up?"

This was no time to argue on the subject of policy, and I returned to that of the coal. He again insisted that my request was impossible. He continued to evade, shift ground, protest his helplessness. It struck me that for all his contempt for "lintheads," he was strangely apprehensive of the enormities they might be encouraged to commit. The most trivial of bad examples . . . the least consideration accorded . . . the slightest kindness or generosity directed toward lintheads, would inevitably lead to the direst of consequences.

"I jest can't, Miss Jess," he said again. "Why, we do everything now for 'em 'cept wipe their noses, and most of 'em don't get wiped, come to think of it. Not in wintertime anyway. But that's aside from the point, as the feller says. The point is, I just can't do what you're asking. It would be against policy," he said solemnly, as if this would lift the question above discussion. "And you wouldn't want that, would you?"

As he talked, my annoyance had mounted. Not only because he refused the coal, but at his pious protests of sympathy even as he shifted and evaded. I was outraged because to him a suffering human being was less important than mill policy or routine.

I rose impatiently. "Mr. Wangle," I said levelly, "there's no point in discussing it any further. My husband is the head of this mill, and if you don't send that coal immediately I will call Wes and ask him to buy a load of coal and deliver it to your office—in person."

He stared at me in blank surprise for a moment, then tonelessly, as if unaware that he spoke aloud, said, "And Wes'ud do it, by God!"

I had spoken impulsively and in anger and I was surprised to discover that I was prepared to carry out my threat.

Evidently Ed Wangle was also convinced, for abruptly he gave in, and so suddenly that I concluded it might be against policy to anger the wife of the head of the mill.

He said ruefully, "Why sho now, here I'm gettin' you all upset and you ain't hardly up from being flat on your back. Sometimes, I think I'm the biggest jackass in Georgia, and all over a little coal. I don't know what I was thinkin', making so much over nothing. If you say you want it, I expect we can send it."

I told him I did want it, and immediately.

He was his bombastic self again. "Now don't you worry, Miss Jess, I'll have that coal at Luckett's in ten minutes." Then, as he escorted me to the door, "And I'd appreciate your not mentioning our little business confab to Wes. He might get the idea we'd had a sure-nuff blowup and I sholy don't want Wes gittin' any bee in his bonnet 'bout me."

His wide grin implied that he spoke humorously. But as I went down the steps I carried the impression that the idea of Wes with a bee in his bonnet about him did not strike Ed Wangle as comical.

The coal arrived at Luckett's almost as soon as I did. And by the time Cade returned from Hickory Hill with the things I'd sent for—and Mitty as well—Mady and I had fires roaring in both stoves.

While I put the food supplies they'd brought in the kitchen safe, Mitty redded up the house. Then she cooked supper, and while the children ate I sponged Kate Luckett's body and changed the sheets and slipped one of my nightgowns on her. Lightheaded from the fever, she was hardly conscious of it, yet she did not neglect to give me a courteous "Thank ye kindly, ma'am."

It wasn't long after that the doctor came and reaffirmed what I already knew. That Kate was beyond any help that any doctor could give. If she'd done what he said—he shook his head—stayed off the job and rested and et good nourishing food—he shook his head again.

He left, a sad little man who was, I sensed, no stranger to defeat. As he went out the door Darty Land came in it. He'd heard from Ed Wangle how bad off Mrs. Luckett was—was there something he could do to help out?

He could find Dude Luckett, I answered grimly, and send him home. Kate Luckett was much too ill to be left only with Mady and Cade.

Scowling, he discounted any good the no-count Dude would be—even if he could be found. He had a better idea. Ed was just waiting to move a widow and her daughter who'd been boardin' with the Higgins family in with the Lucketts as soon as— He did not complete the thought nor did he need to. Meantime Widow Handy and her daughter was boarding with the Higginses just up the street. He'd just step up and have a word with her.

When he returned he brought the Widow Handy with him, a rawboned woman whose granitelike exterior suggested that before the onslaughts of existence she had hardened. Yet she had not been in the house ten minutes before I perceived the good intent beneath that unyielding exterior. Her big capable hands took the reins from Mitty's small ones without fuss or bother. And when Mitty and I turned toward home in the buggy, knowing that she remained afforded me almost as much comfort as she would be to Kate Luckett.

As Moppet climbed the rise I was eager to reach home, to tell Wes of my afternoon. I knew why I was eager. It was because I believed that if Wes knew the Lucketts—could know Cade and Mady—he would realize the important work to be done at the mill. See that their lives were too vital to be controlled by the crazy quilt of myth and prejudiced blindness which Ed Wangle called "mill policy."

But when we reached home, the auto was not in its place, and we found the note left for Wes undisturbed. And though I was disappointed, I was not surprised; for his valiant but sporadic efforts toward more dependable habits had not persisted. He had gradually slipped back to the old patternless existence.

As Mitty and I ate our snack supper, I listened for the sound of the auto. If he would just come home, I thought, so I could talk to him of the subject of which I was so full. For regardless of other faults, Wes was openhearted, kind and generous, and would give his coat or last dollar to someone in need.

Later, when Mitty, declaring that she was plumb tuckered out, announced she'd go to bed, I told her I would read a while, that I wasn't sleepy, and knew she was not deceived, by the wise glance she gave me.

"Now, you got no more use asitting up waiting for Wes than a pig has for a sidesaddle," she said. "And you know it as well as me."

I smiled and said no doubt she was right, but I would wait up just the same.

She said, "Well, dearie, if you'll be all right, I'll go tuck myself in," and when I said good night, she pattered up to her room.

Then with every intention of following her in a few minutes, I fell asleep in my chair. I was awakened sometime near dawn to find Wes coming in the door. When he gave me his careless grin, hugged me and asked why I wasn't in bed, I knew he had been drinking, though I did not realize how much until later. He did not stagger or slur his words or act in the least like my idea of a man gone in drink. Neither was he gay as sometimes he was when he'd had a little too much. He appeared to be completely himself, and it was only when I had closely observed him that I realized that his eyes were oddly unfocused. And there was another sign. Speaking of something he had done, his voice suddenly, for no reason, stopped. He stared at me in puzzled good humor, then, after a little, switched to another incident and again broke off, as if—it occurred to me—a connection had snapped. Though he was not aware of what happened, I could almost see in his eyes the unconscious effort his mind made to re-establish the lines. Then without warning he was asleep, sleeping, as they say, like the dead; and I had to tug and struggle and coax to get him upstairs and to bed. But this I knew I must do, so Mitty, next morning, would neither see Wes nor be witness to his shame.

It was late when I woke and went quietly down to the kitchen. I found Mitty collecting supplies for the Lucketts while Sparrow hitched up Moppet. Sparrow would have to drive her, I said. I must stay with Wes who wasn't well. Later if he felt better he could ride me down. If she suspected Wes's ailment, she did not betray it, but, blithe as a cricket, went out to see that Sparrow "hitched up" right. A brain, she remarked, floating in Coca-Cola warn't to be trusted.

I sat at the kitchen table and drank two cups of hot coffee. Yesterday's strain and actual work, the long waiting for Wes and lack of sleep, had left me on edge. However, the coffee helped, and when I heard Wes stirring upstairs, I took him a cup, black and hot, in hopes it would help him as much.

I found him a very sick man, his face deathly white, his hands tremulous, shaky, paying a heavy price for last night's dubious pleasure. However, he managed a wry, rueful smile and, rubbing his knuckles against his temple, informed me, almost with pride, that he didn't remember a single damned thing about getting home, or in bed. He did sorta remember starting for home and of considerable argument about driving. After that he blacked out. He must have laid enough dust, he ruefully laughed, to soak up the Chattahoochee.

I was unable to share his amusement, and I did not pretend to. I was not only shocked, but to see Wes, with his strength, reduced—and so quickly—to this, stirred a vague, nameless fear. It was followed by a strong tug of anger that he should inflict this on himself.

No doubt he read what I thought in my face. As he got out of bed and unsteadily pulled on his robe, he sent me a mocking grimace.

"Ouch, Doc! Do you have to look like a tight-faced Carrie Nation?"

His laughter annoyed me.

"I do not find it amusing," I said, "to see you like this."

"It's only a hangover, Doc," he explained with good humor. "Not fatal, though this head almost makes me wish it would be. Your frozen face doesn't help."

Not trying to conceal my resentment, I retorted, "There's more black coffee in the kitchen, if you need help."

He still smiled but his eyes were wary. "Black coffee is easy to take, Doc. It's your black looks I can't stand."

I remarked that cheerfulness was too much to expect when he refused to take care of himself.

He buttoned his shirt, and crossing to stand before me, lifted my chin in his hand and held it. "Hell's bells, Doc! When did you ever hear me put in a claim of being sensible or taking care of myself?"

But as I led the way to the kitchen, where he tried to manage more coffee, my resentment still burned, and my plans to talk of the mill, and the important work to be done, were abandoned. In this frame of mind, he would only flare up, perhaps make any future talk even more difficult.

So I was careful to speak casually of Kate Luckett's illness, of Mady and Cade caring for her and the baby with no heat in the house and so little food.

As I talked, I saw the frown that clouded his eyes and thought perhaps I had touched him. But it was only his fear that I might catch Kate Luckett's disease. So many young women had it—Callie Peacock, for instance. He didn't disapprove, he protested, of what Mitty and I had done—"but for God's sake don't take a chance." However, if I wanted to go down and give Mitty a hand, he'd drop me when he went into town. And he silenced my protests that he wasn't well enough for town, with a grin.

With a man of principle, he asserted, it was a point of honor not to give in to a hangover.

He came down, shaved and dressed and spruce; he was his tall handsome self though still pale. Dropping a brief kiss on the top of my head, he casually mentioned he'd probably be late tonight—and not to wait supper. Then, seeing my face, he frowned. Maybe he'd get home early after all. Anyway . . . he'd try.

"It doesn't matter," I lied.

"It does," he contradicted gently. "I'll try to make it for supper, Doc. Honor bright! I'll get out of—what I had planned with the fellers. I'll come home and we'll sit by the fire, you and I, and gossip like old married people."

The promise, sincerely made, was inspired by his wish to please me. And it did, because it proved that pleasing me still mattered. Yet, returning his kiss, I knew he would not come home early. And I wondered why his code of honor should be invincible in regard to a hangover and worthless in regard to his wife, even when he swore *"Honor bright."*

Later, as he drove me down to the mill, I watched the road ahead without speaking. I was puzzled. How could I know Wes so well, and yet so little? How could we be so intimate, yet he remain a stranger? Were other wives puzzled by this contradiction in their husbands? Were their husbands familiar yet strange, the least known man of all men? Did they know them as I knew Wes—his mannerisms, tastes and gestures? His step and the tone of his voice? His gaiety and depression, his humors both good and bad? How he looked in the morning before he had shaved or brushed his hair? How he slept at night, the face young, guileless, serene on the curved arm?

All this I knew yet knew nothing. I had no clue to the compulsion that made him refuse to conform, to avoid all responsibility; to accept no task that required more than brief, casual effort. I did not know why, fleeing what he called boredom, he pursued only more dullness. None of these answers I knew as to why Wes was Wes. He was unsolved and beyond explanation; a mystery that stirred in me, now and then, a sort of dim apprehension, like that in a dream when, faced with impending evil, we stand frozen and helpless and powerless to avert it.

This dim, undefined apprehension hung like a shadowy haze on my mind's horizon, as Wes let me out at the mill. But when a few minutes later I looked down on Kate Luckett, and saw the shocking change the night had wrought, it retreated. And made way for a greater apprehension.

On a day when the fruit trees—peach, apple and plum—trailed color across the Georgia fields, Kate Luckett was buried in the stark little cemetery not far from the mill. And afterwards I walked back to the house with Cade and Mady. None of us spoke—or wept; though I felt enough like weeping. Not for Kate but for them. Yet I dared not cry or take them in my arms to give the comfort arms should give to children who sorrow. They might consider tears a weakness; one they had long since outgrown.

At the house I found that Mrs. Handy, who had stayed at home with Poky, had moved her few possessions while we were gone. And with her daughter Clytie—a slim and flaxen-haired girl with eyes of clearest cornflower blue—had settled in.

As we drank the tea she had ready I was aware of Dude Luckett's measured footsteps elsewhere in the house and, Mady and Cade leaving the room on some errand or other, I spoke to her of them, and of Dude's treatment of them and Kate.

Her gray head lifted belligerently. "No man whut trods shoe leather air goin' to pick on younguns I'm around." She was scornful. "So don't you worry, ma'am. They air good younguns. An' iffin he lift his hand agin 'em I'll—"

I did not doubt that she would manage. Nevertheless when I said good-by to Cade and Mady on the stoop, I felt great tenderness for them. Except for each other, they could look to no other human being for love, given generously, gladly. They had no one, except Poky to whom Mady was mother, though a child still and without a mother now of her own.

"I know you'll make out," I told them. "You can take care of yourselves. But I hope you won't mind if I help a little. I want to help."

They were silent a moment and briefly their glances met as if consulting each other. Then Cade gave me their answer.

"Whut you done for Ma war a comfort to her. And we air beholdin' to you fer it. We don' want you troublin' for us. But if you air of a mind," he consented courteously, "we'd be proud."

When I saw other mill children—so old, so sedate, so weary!—I felt guilty. I did so little and the need was so great. Still I knew satisfaction as I saw Mady's thinness fill out, Cade's body strengthen. And that spring I needed to feel useful and important to somebody. For regardless of the explanations and reassurances I offered myself, I felt more and more that as a wife I had little meaning, that my importance to Wes was of a casual nature. He bothered to come home for dinner even less often, and usually came so late he might as well have stayed out all night, as sometimes he would. The old feeling returned, that there was a special part of his life —and his mind—into which he was unwilling to admit me.

This infected me with the disease to which many wives before have fallen victim and, convinced that there must be another woman, I turned suspicious and jealous. But my suspicion forcing attention by sharp hints directed at Wes, failed, to my surprise, to make him look guilty. He looked only bewildered; then, the truth dawning on him, he was overcome with hilarity.

Crossing, he put his arms around me and lifted me off the floor, laughing until the tears came to his eyes.

"I'm damned, Doc! If anyone had told me you'd go green-eyed I'd have thought he was clean off his head!"

"Put me down!" I ordered as icily as my precarious and undignified position permitted. "Put me down! And this minute!"

He did not put me down nor did he stop laughing, and my annoyance increased.

"No, Doc," he assured me happily. "You're on the wrong track. I'm not traipsing after women. Not because I'm noble, mind you, or have principles. But because you're all the woman I want."

Convinced of his truthfulness, I gained dubious solace from it. Almost I wished there might be another woman. I would, at least, have a definite cause for his indifference to me and the reasoning by which he could love me—and I still did not doubt it—and explain to himself his cavalier treatment of love.

I went through the process also endured by all wives of wondering if I, somewhere, had failed. On nights when he stayed out, I lay in my bed that stretched lonely and wide—and retraced the time since our marriage, seeking the point at which I had made my mistake. And though common sense knew this for what it was, I still dared hope by changing myself to make the miracle come to pass.

Perhaps, I reasoned, I needed to be gay for Wes and exciting. So the very next night he came home, an evening slow to arrive, I was determinedly gay and exciting. I exclaimed a great deal, I recall, dashed about and sang snatches of songs—tried to appear vivid, vibrant, alive. The result was not that expected. He asked if I felt all right, and when I cried out gaily, "Of course, I feel wonderful," he asked dryly if I'd been hitting the bottle? I wondered, since gaiety failed, if I had been sufficiently loving. This led to my lavishing love and succeeding, I fear, only in boring Wes. When I put my arms about him he gave me a casual pat—and continued to read a newspaper. It looked like my friend Holy Carr was going to clean up the town, he remarked. He had finally pushed through the City Council decision to abolish Collins Street, which would play hell with Pet Belleau and Syl Crowley's business. He broke off to exclaim, "Doc, for God's sake, are you trying to choke me to death?"

It wasn't, I told myself, that I was unhappily married. I was unhappy because my marriage was given slight opportunity to be a marriage at all. I was not unhappy with my husband. I was unhappy because I was so often without him. Yet on the rare times that he came home early and spent the evening with me, he was good-humored and fond and we could be quietly cheerful together. Often as we went up to bed he would say, tousling my hair, that I did him more good than medicine, and wistfully I would wonder why he took me in such small, occasional doses.

When he put his hands on my shoulders and pulled me toward him, I was weak with the old fatal sweetness; and his smile, steady and mocking, his quirking brow, had the power to make my heart totter. When he returned after an absence of days and, kissing me, said, "Hello Doc," the cold knot of anger would crumble and I was grateful for his return and his kiss. To me nothing else mattered. To me he was Wes. Too long had I had no one to belong to me, to relinquish easily that one. Over and over I fiercely reminded myself, "He is mine—he belongs to me."

There were times, and not a few, when I, in the way of a woman, would, working myself into a fine state of indignation, rehearse scenes in which, wielding a broom or preparing a chicken for the oven, I made grandiloquent speeches. But, often as not, my indignation had worn thin before he came in its range. And I was indulging myself in a spell of such bitter tirades one hot afternoon in mid-June when I heard, with my usual mixture of joy, resentment and anger, the signal gun of the backfiring auto—and I promised myself that for once I would have a few things to say on the subject of husbandly obligations, and this time I would not let myself be diverted. Wes would not make me laugh, try as I knew he would, and destroy the dignity essential to indignation.

The front door slammed—never to my knowledge had he quietly closed a door in his life; then he called "Doc" as always and entered the kitchen, where, braced by my anger, I sat stringing beans. But my wrath was quickly dissolved when I saw the shock and emotion stamped on his face. His drawn, tight mouth was flashed by white lines, his jaw rigidly set, and he spoke in a tone of hateful amusement.

"The Carrebees have done themselves proud again, Doc, and added new blood to the line," he informed me, his short laugh utterly lacking in humor.

"New blood?"

He nodded, and going to a cupboard, brought out a bottle of whiskey and a glass. "I've been presented with a new brother-in-law. A well-known—I might say notorious—fellow. Highly connected with all high-class houses of ill repute and the high-class ladies therein. Prominent in the most exclusive circles of shady society."

"Wes—what are you saying?" I asked, though I was beginning to realize only too well.

He filled the small glass from the bottle. "Our little Cissa has become a bride," he said. "You'll never guess whose."

I exclaimed, "Not . . . not Syl Crowley!" my voice small with shocked disbelief.

He nodded again. "The same."

"But," I burst out, "I can't—Wes, Cissa wouldn't."

"Cissa did," he answered. The paleness of his face was slowly replaced by a dark, slow flush, due perhaps to the drink, and his grin was forced and tight and contemptuous. "She said she would and by God she did!" he said. "And I hope her spiteful little soul fries in hell!" He tossed down the glass of whiskey, grimacing, and added, his voice rasping, "And with Syl tending the fire, it probably will."

Unable to comprehend swift, bright Cissa's belonging to Syl, I saw again her soft, white arm held in the bony crook of his impeccable black sleeve. But then I remembered something else. The faded child's drawing I had found in the box in the turret room of the summerhouse; the drawing of a pathetically misshapen figure with yellow corkscrew curls, standing beneath a sky of darting black lines. I remembered the childish scrawl:

This is me
Cissa Carrebee
Me in the rain,

and I was sorry that I had remembered. It only revived the small lonely Cissa of the turret room and made more unbelievably tragic her marriage to one like Syl Crowley.

Wes, in jerky, caustic sentences, related what he knew of the marriage. Cissa and Syl had been married by a country preacher and had left last night for New Orleans. It must have been on the spur of the moment because she'd carried no clothes but left Miss Ad a note with explicit instructions regarding them. Syl, she said, would buy what she needed. The newspapers, Wes added, would blow the story high as a kite, since Cissa was what society editors considered "society" and Syl the guttersnipe type. Sort of a reverse on the usual "Tycoon Weds Chorus Girl." Well, let 'em splash it all over the front page and see if he gave a damn.

He tilted the bottle, pouring another drink, but sipped it, leaning against a low shelf, his fingers turning the glass between sips. He laughed briefly, sarcastically, when I asked how Miss Camilla felt about it.

"Don't worry! She's not tearing her hair and wailing for her lost chick. Syl, whatever he is, has the one great virtue, in her opinion."

"Virtue?" I asked dubiously.

"Money," he answered dryly. "He's supposed to be rich, though you can bet nobody gets a look at his books. My mother won't find it too hard to accept him."

"You exaggerate, Wes," I said, and he surveyed me, his brows mockingly lifted.

"Do I? Well, she certainly wasn't hysterical about her daughter throwing herself to the wolves. Not that I blame her, I'm not crying either. I wash my hands of Cissa. How she chooses to go to hell is her own business."

"Maybe," I offered cheerfully, "maybe it won't be so bad. If they love each other—"

His laugh was scornful.

"Do you think she gives a damn about Syl Crowley? Well—she doesn't. She'll make his life a hell, and he'll make hers hell right back. He'll do it a damned sight more efficiently than Cissa. He's an expert. I know what he's like—in private. Cissa doesn't. But she didn't think about there being a private Syl. She only thought of two things, that Syl was rolling in money and the joy of spiting somebody she wanted to spite like all hell."

"People don't marry for those reasons," I pointed out.

"Cissa would and did," he returned flatly. "Those were her reasons." He nodded slowly, "Yes," he said, "those were her reasons, all right." He added, "She wanted to get even with Mother."

"But why? Even for what?"

He shrugged. "To punish her. Why do people want revenge?"

"Wes, that is simply nonsense."

"It's true. You see, Doc, you don't know how it was when we were kids. Left by ourselves, rattling around in that damned house like a couple of peas in a boxcar. Our mother—we hardly laid eyes on her. Always busy. With her rich Yankee friends or milking every cent she could from the mill." He said carelessly, "She didn't give a damn what happened to us."

"But nothing did happen to you." I was impatient of his desire to blame Miss Camilla.

His eyes lifted and met mine quizzically. "No?" he asked lightly. "But Cissa marries Syl Crowley," he added meaningly.

"Your mother adores you," I said, still impatient.

He agreed, "Oh yes! I was her favorite. Cissa always came off second-best. She'll let me squander money, God knows. Cissa too. Her weakness is for getting money, not holding it. But money won't make up for many things," he said more slowly. "You know that. Maybe that's why I loved you. My mother has never known it and never will."

"But to blame her for Cissa's marrying Syl," I told him quietly, sensibly, "isn't reasonable."

"I blame her," he stated. "I blame her for everything Cissa is. For bringing her up—or *not* bringing her up—without giving her a way to evaluate the difference between what is, and what isn't, worth a tinker's dam. For ignoring Cissa until she learned that only in one way could she get attention: by making trouble and doing crazy things that forced attention upon her."

"But Cissa doesn't need to force attention now," I pointed out. "People turn around on the street to look at her. Cissa is beautiful."

He finished the second glass of whiskey and said, frowning, his voice coming slowly, "She grew up without anybody except whatever niggers were around the house—and me. She grew up with no father, no mother—which was worse, because there was a mother, yet not one. Nobody gave a damn about her, as far as she knew. Christ, Doc, do you think she *felt* beautiful?"

"But Cissa's not a child any longer, Wes. She's a grown woman."

As we talked Colonel appeared at the back screen door of the kitchen and, discovering Wes, pushed the door open unaided, and gave his master a sedate but cordial greeting. Wes let his hand drop carelessly to the dog's head, and his fingers massaged behind the soft ears. Now, he removed his hand from the dog and without a glance toward him spoke in a moderate, unemphasized tone.

"Steady, boy."

At the words, Colonel dropped to a flash crouch, haunches strained and the tendons straining against the hide, his body frozen except for the tense rippling of bunched muscles at the shoulder.

Wes, speaking again, released him from the relentless vise that had held him motionless and he rubbed his head against Wes's leg, his tail flailing happily. Wes dropped to one knee, and pulling the dog's head into the curve of his arm, mauled it with rough affection.

"He was broken to hold like that when a pup," he explained. "A good man had the breaking of him. A long time ago, the way a dog's lifetime is gauged. He's grown-up now too."

I knew what he tried to prove but I was not convinced. "Human beings aren't animals," I said. "People can learn and change."

"Can they, Doc?" he asked quietly. "I haven't noticed they're so different from other animals. Maybe they can learn to work algebra or memorize a poem or pick up the knack of sewing on buttons. They can change cotton into cloth. A tree into a mast for a ship or a wagon tongue. But I haven't noticed that we've learned how to change ourselves any more than Colonel."

I would not agree with him, but I was faintly astonished that he had thought deeply enough on this to come to his own conclusion. So seldom he gave any indication of being concerned enough to analyze in an effort to understand.

He picked up the bottle again, said he might as well have one more, and I realized that these drinks were not the first of the day. I had learned by now to recognize the subtle change that liquor induced. The flushed face, the narrowed bright eyes, his voice deeper, warmer, with a velvety texture.

He filled the glass to the brim, offering, as if in reply to my unvoiced disapproval, "After all, Doc, I ought to drink to Cissa. Once, anyway, for taking herself off my neck. Now she's Syl's responsibility."

"She's yours too," I said. "You won't stop caring just because she is married."

"Maybe not, Doc," he answered and swallowed the whiskey, this time without a grimace, and, corking the bottle, put it back in the cupboard. "Maybe I won't stop caring," he said, almost as if he spoke to himself. "But I can sure as hell try."

He might try, I thought, but he would always care what happened to Cissa. They were still bound one to another, not by the usual, casual tie of sister and brother but by the intangible web of the past, of aloneness, neglect and dependence.

By such ties a family was held together; by them were made into a family. So it was, I thought, with Wes and his family. In spite of his animosity and criticism, often unfair, he was bound to his mother and Cissa, and his reaction to Cissa's marriage revealed how firmly bound. For he had been shocked and was deeply disturbed, I knew, in spite of his caustic pretense that he washed his hands of the whole business.

His pride had been affected by Cissa's marriage, as if Syl's connection with "houses of shame" somehow, through Cissa, touched Wes. Though I told myself that this was absurd, I felt that Wes's conception of himself had been shaken; his idea of what he believed himself to be, disturbed. For the first time in my knowledge, his pride had been penetrated; he felt that the honor of the always impervious, imperious Wes had been tarnished. This, frankly, struck me as nonsense. Moreover it occurred to me that a little humility would do him no harm. Remembering his treatment of Darty because he had driven me home in a grocery wagon, I decided it was likely to help him.

Certainly something seemed to have helped Wes. His attitude toward Cissa's marriage did not change. I knew Syl and Cissa had returned to Atlanta and were living at the new Ansley Hotel, but Wes had not seen them and seldom mentioned Cissa's name. I believed that with Cissa, as with everything else, time was the healer. His habit of worrying about her, of being concerned, like everything else would pass.

This, however, was not the change that I noticed in Wes which gave me the greatest relief. That there was any change at all, I was not at the first even conscious. I attached no special significance, though pleased, on the morning that he announced he would stay home all day—not go in to Atlanta, and as I went about my household work, he strolled around the grounds, came into the kitchen to nibble at a cold chicken in the icebox and to tease me and Mitty. In the afternoon we sat on the front porch while he drank a few glasses of something to lay the dust, and it brought before me again the wonderful days before marriage when we sat on the side porch at Miss Camilla's, in the shadow of the wisteria. Such wonderful days they seemed, and my heart ached now with love as then, so this day was wonderful too.

It was followed by other days of staying at home, but in such gradual progression that at first I was not aware of a difference in Wes's pattern. I was delighted. As we sat on the porch and talked as he had his drinks, I had a deep sense of relief. This too, I thought, time had resolved. Wes was settling down.

When the extent of the change in Wes finally dawned upon me, my satisfaction at his changed pattern was shattered. Summer had dawdled lazily halfway through its chore of months and the heat lay arid and breathless on the Georgia country, on the day that, coming downstairs, I went to the front door and saw him. He sat in a rocking chair, a drink in his hand, but not rocking, not moving at all. His eyes were turned out over the sweltering miles of field and wood and valley spread before him; his eyes, those clear gray eyes, as blank, as devoid of life as that aspect, from which even dogs and birds had fled to escape the fierce flailing of sun.

"Wes," instinctively I spoke his name, and he turned and, seeing me at the door, smiled crookedly.

"Oh, it's you, Doc. What is it?"

"I just wondered if it isn't too hot out on the porch." I didn't know what to say or do or why I should feel this yearning desire to comfort.

He shook his head. "It's not too hot. There's a breeze, now and then."

I was moved by the impulse to seize him and shake him, to jolt him back into life and action. But, of course, I could not, I did not dare to kiss him, even touch him, for fear he would resent it; and this also shocked me. What had come over us? I wondered.

Puzzled, I went on to the kitchen and, standing at the window, drank a glass of cold water, slowly, my mind recalling and weighing—and as it weighed—frightened. I did not tell myself now that I was being notionable; I knew better. For three weeks, going on four, Wes had stayed close to home, and in all that time had done nothing but sleep and eat and sit placidly drinking. I was conscious of shock. That was not like Wes, I thought, but in the next second was forced to admit that it was Wes; the Wes he had become.

Was it the drinking? I asked. Could it slip up that quietly? Yet had it been so stealthy? Had I not been aware that he had drunk more and more heavily? Hadn't I noticed the nights when he was slightly fuzzy, when his mind became fumbling and slow with its responses? And there was something else. I had observed when I spoke to him on the porch that he was unshaven, that he needed a haircut, that his shirt was not only soiled but damp with perspiration. It struck me like a blow that I would have noticed a sudden departure from fastidiousness; that I had not, proved that his descent into slovenliness had been so gradual, I had failed to perceive it.

Sometimes I was persuaded that this was only a mood, that he would come out of it. And there were times when he was almost the old Wes, gay and laughing, or teasing Mitty and me, and almost, I believed; and it was as if darkness moved out of my heart and out of my house. There were days too when, with a resurgence of energy, he would busy himself with a job; paint porch furniture, dig a new flower bed, start to put down a walk of flagstones to the carriage house. But his interest waning, the project was deserted, unfinished, and he lapsed back into his lethargy and the porch chair and the glass.

One morning in early fall, when he came downstairs, carefully dressed and groomed, I was pleased. He looked like the old Wes again, handsome and with his easy grace—and though the difference was there, perhaps I alone would have seen it. There was a certain slackness of his expression, some spark was gone from his eyes, though the pink flush on his face gave a false semblance of health. No doubt it would do him good to get out, I thought, and asked where he was going. He had noticed, he answered, that the coal was low, so he thought he'd drive down to the mill and tell Darty Land to send up a load.

"I thought I'd better put on some decent clothes," he explained, indicating his suit. "Wouldn't do for the heir of the founder of Carrebee Mills to show up looking like poor white trash."

I laughed. "You couldn't look like poor white trash," I told him, gratified by the little display of pride. "Why don't you drive on into town after you see Darty?" I suggested.

"What for?"

I said I couldn't offer any ideas but what about Breck and the gang? Or he might go see his mother, I added. "Though you may find her at the mill."

His shrug implied he had no desire to see his mother, and I went out to the porch to watch him drive off. I knew he had been drinking, though it was early, but he seemed completely in control of himself, so I did not worry until he turned down the hill road between the hickories, and I saw that he went too fast for so steep a hill. I felt a quick tug of fright, and, annoyed, told myself not to be absurd. Wes was an excellent driver. And even as the thought hung in my mind, I saw his car skid sickeningly and swerve from the road, to rear frenziedly over the rutted ground and crash with a shivering, rending reverberation into a tree.

Then I was running down the hill, panic choking my throat, aware that Mitty was calling from the porch and following. Stumbling to my knees, I scrambled up, stumbled again, got to my feet again, unaware of a bleeding elbow, and was running again, my breath knifing my chest. It seemed that I ran for hours on a treadmill that allowed me to gain on the tree and the wrenched and twisted car only by a fraction of inches.

Yet I finally arrived at the place where the smashed car lay shattered, horrified at finding how broken and mangled the shining thing had become, and knowing a numb astonishment that in so short a moment it could become nothing. One wheel, clear of the ground, was still indolently spinning and a thread of vapor curled up from the engine. But where, I asked frantically and with mounting horror and panic, where was Wes?

I heard him laughing and, wheeling, found him lying but propped on his elbows, where he had been flung clear, several yards from the car. He was laughing, not hysterically nor as in shock, but in pure delight, as if he found the accident and the smashed car the most delightful joke in the world. Startled, I stared at him, unable to believe he was safe and capable of such laughter, with no more damage than the dirt on his face where it had been shoved when flung clear, and the fresh, neat suit stained and torn.

Gasping from fear and my run downhill, I managed to ask if he was hurt. Still laughing, he shook his head.

"Don't you know that God takes care of drunks and idiots, Doc?" he answered. And then, with a wave toward his auto, "But it looks like I won't be going to the mill today, after all."

I felt a sudden flood of anger in reaction to the fright he had given me and to my conviction that the accident had been caused by his drinking.

I cried out furiously, "You might have been killed!"

"Not me," he replied cheerfully, getting slowly to his feet. "No such luck, Doc. I was bored with that automobile anyway."

And now it was easy to stay at home, content with his chair and his bottle. Unhappy and bitter, I worried, my anger and pity so intermingled, I hardly knew one from the other. There were desperate nights when he would not go to bed but remained sitting downstairs before the fire until the night came pale toward the dawn. And I lay awake staring into the darkness, unable to sleep for listening to his clumsy, stumbling steps lurching against furniture, as he crossed the room to pour again from the bottle.

Those nights were evil, those hours of waking, horror. But there were worse; when, his brain sodden, his nerves jangling, he lost all reserve, and his emotions, released and debased by alcohol, swept out beyond his control. He would cry, his face in my lap, in great gulping sobs that seemed as if they must tear his throat wide. Through trembling lips, he would insist, "I'm no damned good, Doc. No good. Ought to be horsewhipped for marrying you. Too good for me, Doc. You, I mean. Too good. Any decent woman too good."

There was no comfort I could give him; but I held him tightly, held him as you hold a frightened child, and stroked his head, murmuring the meaningless sounds a woman makes over a child.

With his face still hidden in my lap, the slackened voice stumbled on as if it repeated a half-forgotten lesson. "Don't know, Doc—what's matter—with me. Can't help myself—weak—too damned weak. Can't get—hold of myself."

Sometimes I could not keep the tears that filled my own eyes from running over, though I wept not for what he said, but for the awfulness of his saying it, for the terror of his having become . . . this. Sometimes, happening to glance up, he would catch sight of my tears, and his unsteady fingers would reach up to brush them away.

"Don't cry, Doc," he would plead. "Nothing for you to cry 'bout. I'm not worth crying 'bout, Doc."

"You are, you are," I cried out.

But he shook his head owlishly. "Lotsa people worth crying over . . . not me." Then, with a strange flash of unendurable insight, he pled, "What in God's name is wrong with me, Doc? What makes me like this?"

But I was as helpless to help him as he was to help himself, and he dropped his face to my lap again and hid it from the world.

Oh, my Wes, whom I love. Wes, with your easy beauty and reckless grace. Wes, with your shining arrogance. How many times I have recalled our standing together as we were married, and how I thought that now you belonged to me, that at last I had somebody. Somebody who was mine so long as we both should live. And so you were, and so you will always be, while we live. You were mine at that moment of marriage and, God help us both, you are mine with your head in my lap and your man's throat choked with child's weeping; and I would not have it otherwise.

That winter was a hard one. There was no snow to smother walks and drift over roads, but the cold was bitter, and Mitty and I were kept busy feeding the fires that, for all their roaring, could hold only a small field of warmth against the chill of the rooms at Hickory Hill. The frost prying deep into the ground reached the hearts of the hickories and, lying awake in the still nights, I heard them snap and pop with rending explosions, like giants cracking marrowbones.

Wes was the same. At intervals he made desperate efforts to pull himself together, swearing never to touch another drop. He would hold to his resolution, and with gray face and quivering hands tried to conceal his shame with humor directed at himself; singing in what he called his "whiskey baritone," *"Father, dear father, come home with me now."* But I sensed the shame within him and the desperate battle he fought to regain his control and self-respect.

Mitty, of course, was my rock. With love and tenderness she helped me care for him when he was past caring for himself, and with never a word of blame or reproach. When, shaking and fumbling, he spilled and dribbled his food, with loving regard she helped him, and cheerfully cleaned it up.

Miss Camilla's attitude was less generous when she rode out to Hickory Hill to "have a talk about Wes." But for this I could not blame her, for I knew that her anger sprang from the anxiety a mother feels for her son.

Somehow I lived through the days and somehow clung to the hope that Wes would be better. And to help him, as well as myself, I held to my regular life, in an effort to keep my outlook on life as normal as I could.

I continued to go to the mill to watch over Cade and Mady, and the courage I had found in them helped me keep my own—and so often mine was a poor faltering thing, near to panic. But I hoped that Wes too might be helped, that by knowing of their hungers and longings, the valiant courage with which they and many like them daily endured, his own might be strengthened.

My hope never came to fruition. When I talked of Mady and Cade and Mrs. Handy's daughter Clytie who had worked in a mill since the age of ten, he would—on his better days—apparently listen with interest. But I finally came to know this as only the pretense of courtesy. On days that were not good, he drank and slept and woke to drink again. White and weak from lack of food, which he refused to take, he crept about, his face and brain as blank as a sleepwalker's. Then his body, rebelling at its punishment, would be seized with severe cramps and nausea that called a halt to the drinking. I would put him to bed and with Mitty's nourishing broths gradually bring him back to food and sobriety. Then, for a brief season, I would have the old Wes again, laughing and joking, and raising his hand to swear, "Never again."

It was during a lucid period that I asked him to go to a doctor. Perhaps, I said, there was a physical reason that corrected might solve—everything. Gravely, he promised to go to Doctor Townsend, who was the best doc in town. And go he did the first day he was able to get up and dress. I shall never forget the tall handsomeness of him as he walked across the yard—not to the buggy, which he scornfully refused, but to the automobile Miss Camilla sent for him. When three nights had passed and he had not returned, I hitched up Moppet and drove into town. With Andrew's help I traced him to the small sordid hotel on the back street, and there, in a tawdry room, not even clean, we found him stretched across the bed in his soiled and rumpled clothes, so stupefied by drink and sleep he hardly woke as Andrew and I, pulling and pushing, dragged him downstairs and into the buggy.

As I took the reins, Andrew, standing beside the buggy, asked quietly, "Perhaps I should ride out with you—"

I said it wasn't necessary. I could manage. Wes was asleep—

He said, "Can you manage if he wakes?"

"Oh yes." I spoke proudly. "Wes would never be ugly to me." Then, under his steady, unsmiling regard, I realized the mockery of a love which must be proud of so small a fact. And sitting there above Andrew I thought, Death must be like this . . . this slow draining away of your hope. . . . Yet, as I thanked Andrew and turned Moppet up the street, I knew that I still hoped. Hope, it seemed, did not easily die.

Once more time for me assumed two dimensions controlled by Wes. The quiet, placid days when he was himself and life flowed like a leisurely shining stream, when once more hope would strengthen. The other of dark tormented days when fear ran like a swift and perilous current beneath their surface, when the past year seemed longer than all the years of my life and I had the sensation of having aged far beyond the twenty-one years which before long I would reach.

Absorbed with other matters, I gave no thought to the subject of birthdays until, a week before the date which was mine, I received a note from Andrew. In it he congratulated me on "a certain contingency" which had occurred twenty-one years ago, and reminded me that the provision made for me by Mr. Mathias Purefoy would become effective upon my reaching my majority. In that connection, it was necessary that I be present at the offices of Poteat & Whidby on the day in question in order that this provision might be carried out. A postscript suggested that Wes should accompany me.

Andrew's note stirred conflicting emotions. Mitty and I for some time had been forced to many small economies in order to cover expenses, for Wes had contributed little to the support of Hickory Hill. If Mathias Purefoy's bequest should be a sum of money—however small—I could certainly use it.

But there was another consideration. This provision intended by Mr. Purefoy to aid me in establishing myself was the last. There would be no others. The small monthly income which had been our chief support would cease. And when the sum that was to help "establish" me had been exhausted, we would have to depend entirely on Wes. For a brief moment I was shaken by irritation at his undependability that placed all of our futures—Mitty's and mine—and his, in jeopardy; but in the next, I reminded myself fiercely that even had I foreseen this day, I would have loved him no less, nor been less eager to wed him.

I told myself that I would deal with that problem when the time came. Now my task was to keep Wes in condition to go on the appointed day to the offices of Poteat & Whidby. Luckily, it was one of his better periods when he held his drinking to steady but moderate amounts, and when we set out for Poteat & Whidby's in the buggy, he looked almost himself again. Only the slight puffiness of his face and its bright, abnormal pinkness betrayed the change in him. He was still handsome; still wore his clothes with casual perfection. When we reached town, I saw the eyes of women flicker toward him, even as they passed, and the secret measuring desire with which they responded to his imperious maleness.

He had drunk just enough before leaving home to put him in fine humor and, for the first time in weeks, we were close and good companions, at least for today. I was proud to be with Wes, proud to be walking beside Wes, proud to be the wife of Wes. Walking beside him when we were first married, I felt this pride, and I felt it now in spite of his puffy face with its bright pink color.

But as I moved with Wes toward the doors of the offices of Poteat & Whidby, another fragment of the past was revived. For a swift, trembling fraction of time, time seemed to slide backward with unbelievable swiftness and I came to those impressive oak doors as a twelve-year-old girl, walking beside Mr. Dolph with his wildly rolling eye and coiled whip. I saw the strange faces of two older men. I saw another, the freckled face of a young man with rusty red hair. And I saw still another, the face of an old man, seamed and hard-bitten as hewn timber. With those faces rising about me out of the past, for an instant I saw and felt as a child again. Then the past fled back to its shadows and it was the present once more. I was a grown woman, I had known love and marriage and happiness and grief. There had been many changes, but one thing remained unchanged: the riddle of my existence.

Nevertheless, there had been changes, and one, I realized, startled, stared at me from the door of Poteat & Whidby. For it no longer merely read Poteat & Whidby but Poteat, Whidby—and to my extraordinary delight—a third name, which made Poteat, Whidby & Hardee. Andrew had become a partner.

When he came to the outer office to greet Wes and me, I told him how glad I was—and how proud. And smiling humorously, he said he had been made a partner several months back and had intended to mention it. Not, he added, that it was a world-shaking event. When I retorted that I had been deprived of knowing that he was on his way to the fame I had predicted, he looked uncomfortable but in a comfortable way, and said that Mr. Whidby and Mr. Poteat were waiting.

We found them in the large impressive office—which no longer appeared so impressive—with Mr. Whidby on one side of the enormous carved desk and Mr. Poteat on the other. When we entered, Mr. Poteat rose and came to meet us, with his usual gallantry. Otherwise he had changed shockingly in the months since I had last laid eyes on him. The crest of hair was lusterless and the gray cobweb of lines on his face had deepened, and I thought he moved, not with his old swiftness, but with a vague, fumbling indefiniteness, which later I found also affected his thinking.

He was not, I reminded myself, a young man. It was natural that he too should age. But I did not deceive myself. I had learned in bitter hours the meaning of the vague fumbling hands, the stumbling brain, and knew too well the cause of the rapid decline. Mr. Whidby had also suffered the inroad of years, but he only appeared drier and wispier, not "broken" like Mr. Poteat. He remained seated behind the desk, explaining that his doctor had ordered only essential exertion. And I wondered if his and Mr. Poteat's condition was their reason for taking young blood—in the guise of Andrew—into the firm.

That my surmise was correct was proved when, after the amenities had been observed and Wes and I had been seated in the chairs before the desk, it was Andrew who took the chair behind the desk and opened the folder that waited upon it. As I watched him, admiring his calm, quiet, unruffled manner, it occurred to me what a fine appearance he made. His dark suit, of excellent material and cut, gave him dignity and the air of what Miss Camilla called "a man of stature." Yet the cheerful, unassuming manner and the twinkle were as unchanged as if he wore the old threadbare suit.

The blue eyes twinkling across at me, he said that Mr. Mathias Purefoy having, in his last will and testament, left specific instructions in regards to the care of one Jessica Kildare—now Mrs. Wes Carrebee, he added with a good-humored smile—Poteat, Whidby & Hardee, as executors of that will, had followed those instructions to the letter and were of the opinion that those instructions had been satisfactorily executed.

"However," he went on, "one instruction has not yet been carried out. This is in regards to a provision which Mathias Purefoy instructed that you receive on reaching your majority. Which as we know is—today."

He paused to allow Mr. Poteat and Mr. Whidby to congratulate me on achieving the age of twenty-one (as if I had the least thing to do with it), and I found myself smiling at Andrew's manner. He observed with perfect propriety a legal tone and look, yet managed at the same time to laugh at the perfect propriety of the law. I was puzzled as to whether he was behaving in a splendidly lawyerlike fashion or caricaturing, by a shade of overemphasis here and there, the whole tribe of lawyers, with their portentous language which concealed facts rather than revealed them.

When Mr. Whidby and Mr. Poteat sank back into their chairs, Andrew again took the center of the stage. But I suddenly perceived that his humorous manner and the amused twinkle had disappeared. His face, though not solemn, was thoughtful as if he pondered serious matters.

"And that brings us," he said calmly, "to the fact."

"The fact?" I echoed blankly, and he nodded.

"You, Jess, are the fact," he said, but as if he had a fondness for facts.

"You are the fact," he repeated, leaning back and settling himself, "on which Mathias Purefoy's intentions and instructions were founded."

I looked at him doubtfully. "Do you mean," I asked, "his instructions about—this last provision?"

"Exactly," Andrew replied. "The last provision is also a fact. As a matter of fact, there are a good many facts."

Because I was in a state of complete bewilderment, I waited in silence.

"But the main fact," Andrew continued, "is one that had to be dealt with a good many years ago, and of which I will tell you, as fully as I can, which isn't very full," he added, "because I only know what Mathias Purefoy told me. And he was a man of few words."

I waited, still silent, my eyes on his face, while he seemed to consider what he would say. He leaned forward, his elbows on the desk.

"First," he said, "it is necessary for me to tell you of Mathias Purefoy, whom you saw and spoke with in this office. The impression people had of him was correct, I would say, but with qualifications. He was a hard man and stern, but he was also a just man within his understanding of justice. Perhaps he leaned a little heavy toward the Old Testament when it came to justice, but he was a God-fearing man and a good man. He was also a money-making man."

I made no comment and he looked thoughtfully at the space above my head.

"I do not disparage that knack," he went on, "but it did not make Mathias Purefoy a happy man. He made his first money almost by accident. He was a farmer upstate, outside of Flowery Branch. After the war of sacred memory, many of his neighbor farmers were short on cash, and it just happened Mathias Purefoy had some on hand, and he loaned them money," Andrew went on, "and either got it back with interest or got a farm, worth considerable more than he loaned on it. This led to various investments that, due to the foresaid knack, usually paid good returns. And he being not a spender but the opposite, a man who liked to wear resoled shoes more than new ones, why—he made more money than he spent. A good deal more. At one time he was for the South a wealthy man, a comfortably wealthy man. That was Mathias Purefoy. Mathias Purefoy had the knack of making money but not enjoying it. He was frugal with himself, some said tightfisted. But he was not frugal with his wife and their child."

"A child?" I repeated with quickening interest, remembering of hearing from Adeline of the woman who walked on Hickory Hill at dusk; remembering too the child's picture which Andrew and I had discovered in the carriage house, which hung over my mantel and looked, I thought, as Wes must have looked as a child.

"Mathias Purefoy had a son," Andrew said. "An only child. I knew little about him, for Mathias Purefoy told me little. I gathered that he was a bright boy. Intelligent . . . handsome! He not only lacked his father's knack for getting money, his talent ran in the other direction. Young Purefoy had his horses and lived like a rich man's son. His father doted on him, and gave him more than was good for him, proud that the son of a dirt farmer could show the bigwigs and nabobs how to live like a gentleman. Well, he showed them. He broke his mother's heart and died before he was thirty, after a disastrous and tragic business that ruined him and caused considerable suffering. He left his father an embittered, cantankerous old man who blamed the bigwigs and society swells; but he blamed himself more for spoiling the boy and failing to teach him responsibility and self-reliance."

He paused, then after a stillness in which a dropped pin might have been heard, continued, "That explains, Jess, why his instructions for your upbringing were as they were. He did not want you ruined by money, as his son was ruined."

I was aware of a tenseness that had come over the room, as Andrew's story of Mathias Purefoy and his wastrel son led to me, though I did not know how or with what significance.

I gazed into his eyes and steadily his gazed back from across the desk, and though I knew the answer before I asked the question, still I must ask. "Why do you tell me all this about Mr. Purefoy's son? It isn't just to explain why Mr. Purefoy insisted that I be brought up in a certain way, is it?"

He shook his head, soberly. "No, Jess. There's a reason that concerns you."

I had anticipated his answer and, after his detailed description of Mr. Purefoy and his son, it must have been plain to anyone what was coming. Yet, as I put the next question, I felt a choking lump of emotion rise in my throat; not because I was shocked or surprised but because, after so long a time, questions I had asked as a child, and as a woman too, would at last be answered by something more than silence.

"Was it . . ." I began. "Was he . . ." But I was forced by my trembling voice and the tears that welled in my eyes to pause. But Andrew knew what I would have asked.

"Yes, Jess," he said gently. "The son of Mathias Purefoy was your father; Mathias Purefoy, your grandfather. Not important people but good, plain stock. You need never feel ashamed of your blood."

"Ashamed," I said. "You know me better than that, Andrew."

"I do know," he returned quietly.

Another question, the natural consequence of what I had learned, rose to my lips almost without volition.

"Do you know anything of my mother, Andrew?"

His face seemed to tighten beneath its freckles, and lifting a small silver knife that lay on the desk, he balanced it as if to throw, then replaced it precisely where he had found it.

"I can't answer that, Jess," he told me gravely. "Mathias Purefoy left definite instructions on that point."

"What are those . . . instructions?"

He answered levelly, his voice devoid of emotion. "That you will make no effort to ascertain whether she is living or dead or to learn who she was or, on the assumption she might be alive, endeavor to seek her out. None of which is to be construed by you as implying that your mother is still among the living, and you are explicitly informed no such implication is contained in anything I say to you."

I was silent, looking down at my hands that lay in my lap, trying to absorb the implications behind what I had just heard. I felt as if the strange old man who was my grandfather had wished to wall up some passage and seal it forever, a passage which he decreed should not be explored.

I asked Andrew slowly, "Why am I to know nothing of my mother? Did Mr. Purefoy—my grandfather—give a reason?"

Andrew's mouth became firm. "Yes. The knowledge could neither benefit nor hurt you, but might be the cause of great suffering and tragedy to innocent persons. Even disgrace."

I thought this over, aware that Wes reached and, taking my hand, held it tightly. Then I looked at Andrew squarely.

"You use the word 'disgrace.' That means, doesn't it, that what I've heard—that I was illegitimate—is true?"

"Yes, Jess, that is true," he said gently.

Even as he spoke, I was remembering how, for as many years as I could remember, I had dreamed that someday I would find my mother, who would cherish and love and help me; find a place of the spirit which would be mine—my place. But I had never dreamed that I might be a threat to her. Yet now for that very reason I must yield to Mathias Purefoy's instructions.

I felt an eerie shock and swift, faint terror. The separation from the chain of flesh and blood and life, by which most people are linked into both past and future of humankind, had been irrevocably broken for me. I was not allowed a place in the procession of life and death and life again. I was not—to use the word that stands so clearly for all I could never experience—I was not "related," as, in a greater sense than mere kinship, others were related through kin to humanity, to human life itself. And I knew, I thought, how a lonely ghost must feel when it attends a gathering of happy, laughing celebrants and can only hover invisible and unknown and never share the gaiety.

I suddenly realized how long I had sat silent and that Andrew and the others waited patiently while I gave attention to the thronging thoughts that pressed against my mind. I saw that Wes's face was drawn, with tenderness for me and with anger for a situation that caused me hurt. Andrew waited, concerned for me, and with only kindliness and goodness in his eyes as they met mine. Then he took a document from the folder on the desk and gave me his smile again.

"Now we take up the final provision in Mathias Purefoy's last will and testament," he suggested.

In view of my recent concern about finances, the stir of interest I felt in what he would tell me was, I think, only natural. I halved the optimistic figure I had mentioned in a discussion with Mitty last night, which we figured we could stretch for a year's expenses. Now I knew I would settle for far less and be grateful.

Andrew, very erect and grave and holding the document opened on the desk before him, began to speak again with quiet directness.

"As I said, Jess, Mathias Purefoy had the knack of making money, and there was a time when he was holding on to a considerable sum as well as real estate and other various investments. Since he had named one Jessica Kildare as his sole heir, you, Jess, it appeared, would eventually be a well-to-do young woman."

Still not knowing if Mitty and I would be able to manage another six months' expense, I held my breath. But Andrew was speaking again.

"Unfortunately for you, the value of Mathias Purefoy's estate, due to his son's extravagance, the changing economy, had drastically shrunk at the time of his death. There was just enough to provide the small allowance you have received and a tidy little nest egg."

I asked, "Andrew, what is . . . a tidy little nest egg?"

He twinkled. "Well, to some folks—the Vanderbilts, for example—a pretty uncomfortable sum. Others—like me—would consider it—quite comfortable."

I repeated, "Comfortable?"

"Which means—not talking like a lawyer—that it can do what Mathias Purefoy wanted it to do. Establish you—not extravagantly—in life. You can own Hickory Hill clear. And you will receive approximately ten thousand dollars besides. It is not the fortune Mathias Purefoy hoped it would be. But it gives you a degree of the safety the old gentleman was anxious for you to have. Values of investments and property vary somewhat. You can't say what they are worth to the dollar until you turn them into cash. However, we've estimated approximately the total value; conservatively, I would say."

It struck me as a great deal of money, at least far more than I ever dreamed might be mine, though I had no understanding of its real value. It was inconceivable that the figure he quoted referred to actual money, belonging to me, which I might use as I wished. Even as, turning, I searched each face and found it smiling at me—Andrew's reassuring and pleased; Mr. Poteat and Mr. Whidby beaming benignly, Wes's half-smile gravely tender—I could hardly believe that Mitty and I need not worry, at least not soon, about expenses.

As Wes and I drove back to Hickory Hill, we were silent until we had left town behind and Wes egged Moppet to a canter on the dirt road. Then suddenly he broke into wild hilarious laughter and laughed so long that I turned to him wonderingly. "Wes . . . what on earth?"

He exploded again. "Ten thousand dollars!" he gasped. "What a whale of a joke on my mother."

"Darling, what are you talking about?"

He grinned at me. "Wake up, Doc. You're in a trance. My mother expected you to come into a pile of jack." The grin turned grim. "That's why I tried like hell *not* to marry you when she steered me your way. Remember, Doc?"

I said I remembered, though at the time I had not dreamed— Puzzled, I asked, "How could she expect such a thing? I didn't know. No one else did."

He grinned again. "She was guessing and willing to gamble on it. Maybe Poteat said something that started her thinking." He cut his eyes around at me. "Didn't you ever stop to wonder why she took you under her wing?"

"I thought it was because she was kind and was a friend of Mr. Poteat's," I said slowly. "Was there another reason?"

He laughed. "My mother is a great gambler when it comes to futures."

"Oh, Wes!" I sighed. "You are so unfair toward her. Miss Camilla is not like that . . . why, she's always doing generous things."

He drove unspeaking for a moment. Then he said quietly, "Have it your way, Doc. But don't try to tell me about my mother."

Deliberately, I changed the subject and, as Moppet joggled comfortably along the road, he drove with one hand and with the other reached for and held mine. "Did it hurt, Doc? All that stuff you heard?"

"Not as much as it would have once." I held his hand against my cheek. "You see, darling . . . now I have you."

"Oh, Doc," he said, so almost sorrowfully that I glanced at him quickly and saw again on his face that strange far-off rapt calm which now and then I surprised and which always—though I did not know why—made me shiver; as if a goose walked over my grave. But immediately he was cheerful again, and like old married people we talked quietly of this and that, and I felt peaceful . . . and almost happy again. He was so darling today, I thought. Perhaps if today he too was happy he might decide it would be worth while to keep all days happy . . . perhaps . . .

But he didn't keep all days happy. So teasing, so taunting he said, "I promise, Doc. Just one," and I do not doubt that he meant it. But one became two—and two, three—and then we counted no longer.

Always when I put him to bed there was a sense of relief as if, for the moment, the problem was solved; and as he slowly improved and began to take food again, always the new hope that perhaps now he would be better. And I would be aware of the world again as if I emerged from a bottomless pit into sunshine. But there were other days when I despaired, when my heart truly sickened within me. Somehow I must manage to go through the days of my life too proud to let anyone, even Wes, see. But bewildered and not knowing how on my sky so black a cloud could have been shaped.

Nights at home I began to delve in the cotton mill books which had belonged to Wes's father and, though they were confusing at first, I began before long to understand their terms. As a consequence, I sought the small hand loom Miss Camilla had sent along and the next time I went to the mill I asked Darty to get me some yarn. Mitty and I worked at the kitchen table for hours trying to figure it out; and when I had learned the difference in warp and woof, I dyed small batches of yarn, recalling as I mixed my small cans of dye what Professor Kerlich had told me at Vestal Hall of color, and managing to achieve what I considered spectacular results.

It was perhaps a childish way of passing time which moved on such heavy and leaden feet; but I was enthralled. On my next trip to Atlanta I stopped in Miller's Book Store and bought technical books on weaving and textile design. And childish though it might have been, for me it was a door that opened on a new and enchanting world, hardly glimpsed as yet; and not recognized as the world of my future.

The days I tried to fill with other things. With Mitty, I worked in the garden planting, transplanting, weeding; the sense of fulfillment the feel of rich loamy earth and plants gave me, not unlike my satisfaction at the improvement of Cade and Mady and Poky under Mrs. Handy's care.

Once on my way to see them I happened to enter the mill gate as Miss Camilla drove in, and I waited until, turning the horse over to a Negro helper, she came toward me, pulling off her driving gloves.

"What brings you to the mill?" Her manner as always was casual, disarming. "Didn't Wes come home again?"

Concealing the annoyance stirred by her bantering question, I told her Wes was at home. I had come to see some children whose mother had recently died.

Abruptly, she said, "Come to the office with me. I've been wanting to talk to you."

I followed the poised, efficient figure up the outside steps to the office and inside waited while she drew a slip of paper from her purse and gave it to Darty. "I want those figures," she ordered and after a quick questioning glance he went out. She sat at the desk and, taking a cigarette from her purse, lighted it from a kitchen match which she struck on the sole of her shoe. Then she settled back in her chair and looked over at me.

"I'm glad I ran into you, Jess. I've been wanting to speak to you about these mill children you've taken under your wing." She paused as if expecting me to speak, but when I said nothing, went on. "I hate to interfere with your role of Lady Bountiful. No doubt you enjoy it. But Ed Wangle tells me it's stirring up trouble. And I won't have that."

I was puzzled. Less by what she said than her manner of saying it. This was neither a suggestion nor a request. It was an order. And given so peremptorily that I glanced at her, astonished. She avoided my glance by regarding the tip of her cigarette. "What you fail to understand, Jess, is the fallacy of thinking of lintheads as individuals, instead of a community where each expects as much as the next. We've had pretty good employee relations at Carrebee because we treat 'em all alike. Now Ed tells me they're riled up about your attention to those children."

I was too familiar with Ed Wangle's attitude toward the hands to believe that this was any more than his petty tyranny. And I said so to Miss Camilla.

She straightened and her voice was almost arrogant. "Isn't it rather presumptuous of you to question Ed's opinion? He's an experienced and valuable man."

"I still can't see . . ." I began, but she did not allow me to finish.

"Since you can't, you must be guided by what I say." Her eyes holding mine actually seemed to dilate. "For right now I can't risk employee troubles. To tell the truth, if I don't lay my hands on money—and pretty quick—" She broke off, her outflung hands expressing what she didn't say. "I've borrowed everywhere I could, I've run the mill catch-as-catch-can, the bank's hounding me, the commission house is threatening suit. Even if I staved them off—and I suppose I could by hook or crook—it's hopeless unless I can modernize the plant. Sooner or later we'll be sold down the river and all our futures with it."

I tried to picture Wes without Carrebee Mills behind him. Surprised, I thought, But he would have nothing. None of them would. Cissa or poor little Miss Ad—or Miss Camilla. How did people who knew nothing but spending react to nothing to spend? Were they frightened? Was it fright that made Miss Camilla brusque, commanding—almost unkind?

I said uncomfortably, "I didn't know. I'll be careful about the children . . . help any way I can. I only wish I could in . . . other ways."

Her sudden, almost guttural laugh startled me. "I wish it too." She was grim. "And I don't mind telling you I was depending on your help. Otherwise I would never have let things pile up as they have. I knew when you came into your money you'd help . . . and should. After all, it's Wes's mill too."

I asked, bewildered, "My money? You mean the little I got from my grandfather?"

The square dimpled hand flashed impatiently. "Of course not. I mean the money I expected you to get."

"But how could you expect any such thing?"

She leaned toward me, her eyes holding me. "Because I'd heard from a long time back that old man Purefoy was a rich man. And I thought you were going to get it. All of it."

"But how could you? You didn't know—nobody did—that he was my grandfather . . ."

Her smile was cynical. "I wasn't fool enough to think old Skinflint Purefoy would support you all those years out of the goodness of his heart." Her smile was grim. "I'd like to know what happened to all of his money."

I sat dumfounded by what she had revealed. Wes had been right, I thought. She had believed I would come into money—had counted on it. Illogically, for an instant I felt I had failed her. In the next I had a qualm of nausea—as if I had looked upon something revolting.

I said again, "I'm sorry I can't help somehow. I wish I—"

Again the upflung imperious hand stopped me. "Wishing won't help." She was brisk again. "Nothing will, except money. Somehow I've got to get my hands on money."

Driving Moppet up the hill road, I realized that Miss Camilla had divulged two facts—both unpleasant. One, the precarious circumstances of the mill; the other, that the many kindnesses she had shown me had sprung from reasons other than sincere liking. If the second produced a twinge, not unlike hurt, it was quickly banished. Long ago, I told myself, I had realized that Miss Camilla was of the fast-growing New South which predicated worth on money alone.

The other fact gave me far greater concern, for it affected Wes, and so vitally that the mill in my imagination assumed the power to shape his life as the mystery of my birth had shaped mine. Hate it as he might, it was the force that made him the Wes Carrebee of fine clothes and spending and careless, arrogant pride.

Now, I told myself, hate it or not, he must concern himself with it. No longer with scornful laugh and bitter tirade could he shrug it off. Regardless of his resentment toward it—or his mother—he must face up to cold facts. He had no more right to sit by and let the source of livelihood for so many go to ruin than a ruler who watches his country crumble and lifts no finger to save it. The mill, in a way, was his kingdom, established by his father, left for Wes to guard and preserve. Without it he would no longer be the imperious Wes Carrebee with an unassailable place of his own. He would be nothing. What that would plunge him into, I dared not speculate. It must not happen. I must talk to Wes.

I must talk to Wes. It echoed against my mind monotonously as I watched for the opportunity—and humor. When today became tomorrow and tomorrow the day after, I determined no more time should be wasted. And when next morning he came down moody and irritable—familiar warnings—I knew we must have our talk before he in another bout of drinking further delayed it. So when he had halfheartedly eaten his breakfast and I held a match to the cigarette he pulled from his bathrobe pocket, I said, "Wes."

Brow quirked, he sent me a glance, "Yeah, Doc."

"Wes, I must talk to you. Seriously, I mean."

Brow quirking again, he said, "Well for Christ's sake, talk!"

He must promise, I said, not to fly off the handle until he heard what I had to say. For it concerned him more than anyone.

He broke in irritably, "All right. You don't have to knock your head on the floor, you know, to say a few words."

Privately I wasn't so sure, but I bypassed this and quietly, almost casually, repeated what Miss Camilla had said regarding the mill. Smoking, he listened with what appeared to be attention—and I drew a breath of relief. He wasn't going to be difficult, and fly off the handle. But when I finished and looked at him I was apprehensive again. For the attentiveness was gone from his eyes. They were bored, almost sullen.

"For Christ's sake, Doc, you're not letting that stuff worry you, are you?"

It did worry me, I said. If he would just stop and think what the mill's going under would mean . . . to all of us . . . his mother and Cissa . . . himself . . .

But I could not pierce his skeptical imperturbability. His mother had cried "Wolf" too often, he declared, to take him in with it now. If I let her fool me, he added, then I was weak in the head. By God! a wonder she hadn't tried to get her hands on that little dab of money from old Purefoy. His laugh was scornful, hateful. She couldn't stand to know there was money, however little, that she couldn't spend. As for the mill, I wasn't to give it another thought. He wouldn't.

He moved as if to leave the table, but I stopped him. "Wes," I said again and, troubled, leaned toward him. "She isn't fooling this time. She may have before . . . but not now. I'm . . . I'm convinced of it."

"Oh, she's always convincing," he retorted. "You're a fool to believe her."

He got up to go but, swept by a sickening sense of defeat, I stopped him again. Not quietly nor calmly but in frustrated anger that seemed to congeal my blood into ice.

"It is not I who am the fool." I could hardly believe the cold level voice was mine.

He had turned away but now he wheeled back, his eyes narrowed. Quietly he asked, "By that you mean I am the fool?"

I told him through set lips, "You have to hear it sometime. From somebody."

He stood motionless, the fingers of his hand resting lightly on the table; on his face the far-off rapt look he sometimes wore. And almost I cried out that I hadn't meant it—I had spoken in anger—he must forgive me—but I caught the words back. He should not put me in the wrong when I was right.

His eyes came back to me. "That is what you meant, isn't it? That . . . I am a fool?"

I raised my head and met his eyes. "You called me—fool—first," I pointed out coldly.

He looked at me with a flitting smile and something looked out behind the smile that sent a shadow of doubt across my mind.

"Yes," he spoke absentmindedly. "But it wasn't meant—as you meant it. I think you know it."

I did know it. He had spoken impatiently without real intent. I, with knowing and intention of hurting.

Suddenly I was weeping, my head down on my folded arms, weeping as Wes had never seen me weep. I could not clearly have said why. But I felt as if I had shattered something I valued, something that would never be whole again.

When finally I raised my head and dried my eyes, I found him standing just as he had, his eyes somber upon me. I began, "Wes . . . I didn't mean . . ."

He said gently, "Forget it, Doc. And . . . you mustn't ever cry like that again. For anything."

Yet only a few nights later when inadvertently I spoke of the mill again, he gave a short, harsh laugh, and getting up from the dinner table and flinging his napkin down angrily, he went out of the room. The show of temper disturbed me, and later, hearing the clink of bottle against glass, I was more disturbed—and frightened. Still not knowing the cause, I went to his side and asked why he was so annoyed?

He tossed off the whiskey, making the act somehow a gesture of defiance, and, his face still dark with anger, made no reply. I felt a hopeless ache of pity and fear and blind helplessness.

"Wes," I said. "Please tell me what is wrong."

He poured another drink before he spoke.

"I warned you, Doc, I get goddamned good and sick hearing about the mill."

I protested, "Isn't that rather silly of you, darling? It is your mill."

"Not mine," he said.

"Wes—it is. You are the head. Or could be if you wished. Wes . . . you could do so much, if you only would. There's so much to be done."

I spoke impulsively, almost before I knew it. But his eyes behind their puffs of sick flesh looked at me, level and hostile.

"You may as well get it through your head, Doc, once and for all. I hate the damned mill. I always have, and I always will. And I'll tell you something else. I don't want to be nagged about it every minute I'm with you."

I said despairingly, "I didn't nag . . . I only said that your mother—"

"Are you trying to say there's a difference, Doc?"

"Of course," I cried.

He shrugged. "Maybe to you. Not to me. My mother and the mill—they're the same. She's the mill, the mill is my mother—they're one. I never could figure it out. But the mill was all she gave a damn about."

To try to persuade him to any point of view but his own was silly and futile. Instead, I reminded him of his promises after his last bout that he was through with liquor forever, and pointed out the suffering and misery he must endure if he began again.

He heard me patiently, and then, his manner completely convincing, assured me he would not have another. His eyes steady and lips smiling now, he regarded me, tolerant and compassionate of my foolishness that feared he was capable of such behavior. He was gently amused, his eyes forgiving me for officiousness, yet a little hurt that I should have so little faith.

But I saw the sly glisten of wary cunning and delight that shone—so it actually appeared to me—through his eyes, as if another creature looked out from them. From Wes's eyes peeped the mocking eyes of the devil that haunted and drove him, and I knew his earnestness and lofty compassion, his wounded sensitivity, his forgiveness to me for my faithlessness, were lies. Not Wes's lies, but the lies of the devil fox I saw peer out through his eyes.

And I was right, for he drank again, and again I heard his stumbling in the night, and watched in despair the slow stages of destruction through which he was flailed by drink. It ended with another attack of violent pain and agonizing cramping of legs. The attack was more desperate than any he'd suffered before and I woke Mitty and ran down the hill to send Sparrow for Dr. Tilly. The sedative he left put Wes to sleep, and then it was to go through all over again. Nursing his wasted body, shrunken and white and helpless, soothing the tortured, guilt-ridden and shamed spirit that was, God knows, as sick or sicker than the flesh that housed it.

His strength returned, but more slowly than in the past and never fully. At his request, Mitty and I had made up a small room for him on the lower floor of Hickory Hill and placed a couch there so he could nap during the day without climbing the stairs to our bedroom. He spent long hours there alone, gazing at the pages of a book or newspaper, or looking out the window; at what I could not tell. He slept on his couch one night and, claiming he found it more comfortable, had us make it up every night and made it his bed. And with this increasing desire for aloneness, I marked another change. One day, entering the room with a bowl of hot soup, I saw that, though he was still young, the Wes who sat at his window and stared out at nothing was old, his hair slashed with gray, his eyes lusterless, his skin clayey and puffy. Only his smile remained young and flashing and holding such sweetness, when turning he gave it to me, that I felt my youth dying within me and, dying, take flight forever.

I would never forget that day. How I had come upon Wes and found him suddenly old. Even when both impression and shock lessened, when I even persuaded myself that Wes would be young again and made myself almost believe it, I did not forget the day when I saw Wes—suddenly old.

I did not go far from home now or stay long away when I went, for he wanted me always nearby. Like a child, if I only stepped from the room, he called, "Oh Doc!"

I would call back, "In the kitchen! Want anything?"

"Nothing," he would answer. "Just wondered where you are."

Then I would go and kneel by his chair, and putting my arms about him, would hold him tight for a moment; not as a wife would hold him but fiercely, as if to protect—as I would have held my son.

It was not until Wes was almost himself—or as much himself as he would ever be again—that I felt free to leave him with Mitty and drive down to see Cade and Mady. But at last came the Sunday afternoon when I drove through the mill gate. The mill idle, the houses bleak where the workers, drawn by the mild day, sunned themselves on their stoops, thin faces heavy with the sullen resentment that hung in the air as intangible as smoke, but as unmistakable.

Reaching the Luckett's stoop, I heard singing and the whanging of a guitar coming through the partly open door, the guitar strummed with skill and the man's singing voice hearty and vigorous with a nasal resonance that brought the words to me clearly.

> *"He stabbed her to the heart and the blood it did flow*
> *He stabbed her to the heart and the blood it did flow*
> *And into the grave Pretty Polly did go . . ."*

The lugubrious words raced with such zest, and the melody of the guitar leapt after them in such galloping excitement, that the death of

Polly seemed a gay and festive event, as I knocked at the door and Mrs. Handy called above the music, "Step right in." The voice had swung into the next verse, *"He threw some dirt o'er her and turned to go home . . ."* but it broke off as I entered the room and the guitar, with a final whanging chord, fell silent.

Mrs. Handy and Clytie, Cade and Mady ringed the room, while Poky, who had finally graduated from crawling, continued his bobbing, see-sawing dance as if the music still played.

The man with the guitar was tall, rawboned, with brick-red hair and a skin as fair as a young girl's except for the scattering of large freckles, but there was nothing girllike in his hard leanness and sinewy toughness. His eyes, a strange yellowish color, as alert and knowing as an animal's narrowed slightly at sight of me, and his long body rose from the chair, the guitar under his arm, his face wearing a proud reserve and defiance that his surface courtesy did not conceal.

He remained standing while Clytie introduced him as Yancy Jackson and then his wife. He gave me a nod and told Mrs. Handy he and Willie Mae had better be goin'. And I suspected that my arrival had hastened his departure.

I spoke to him pleasantly.

"Are you leaving because of me, Mr. Jackson?"

He was no whit disconcerted. "Since you ask me er outright question, Miz Carrebee, I give you er outright answer. Yes, ma'am. I'm leavin' because of you."

"Why, Mr. Jackson?" I inquired.

He was as direct with me as I had been with him. He said simply, "I reckon the reason is your name bein' Carrebee."

For the first time it dawned upon me that the name Carrebee might mean different things to different people; that to some it might mean what the tone of Yancy Jackson's voice implied it meant to him.

"I married a Carrebee, Mr. Jackson," I said, "but I don't come to this house as a Carrebee but as a friend, too good a friend to deprive them of your music. So please stay, Mr. Jackson. I will leave and come back another time."

Though the hostility in his face was diluted by a flicker of interest, he said nothing.

I went on, "However, I would much rather stay and hear some music too, if you wouldn't mind."

He rubbed his long, bony chin thoughtfully, then nodded imperturbably. "Since you put it thata way, ma'am, I reckon I can stay a while longer."

He turned back to his chair, his nod indicating to his wife that she might be seated also, and took his place with a dignity as impressive as that of a judge mounting the bench.

"Any particular tune you of a mind to hear, ma'am?" he asked, and I asked for the song he had sung as I came. It was named, he said, "Pretty

Polly." Knocking his heavy shoe three times against the floor, he struck a crashing chord on the guitar and swung into it again.

But after a few songs Yancy Jackson announced that he was sung out, and no amount of persuasion moved him a jot. He was a stubborn man and proud but, I decided, fair and generous. Having accepted my assurance of good will, he accepted me also, with reservations.

From the deference Mrs. Handy and Clytie accorded him, I decided he was a man of influence in the mill community, which was not difficult to understand. As he talked, I recognized a keen, tough mind that dug quickly and shrewdly to the root of a question, no less effective a tool because its shaping was not the result of formal schooling. Listening to the talk that wound back and forth between him and his wife and the Handys, I gained an insight not alone of the workers but of the mill itself, for he was bluntly outspoken. Where the others took cover in noncommittal evasiveness, Yancy with calm judiciousness condemned the juggling of prices in the mill store and damned Ed Wangle as the one to blame.

"Well, reckon it's his right to set prices up like he wants." This was his wife, worried perhaps lest the conversation reach Wangle's ears.

But Yancy, tilted in his kitchen chair, shook his head.

"If right means what I think, he's got no right takin' money out of folks' pockets 'cause he's got 'em over a barrel. Ain't a mite different from a thief that puts a gun to a man's head, 'cept a thief's got more gumption."

Upping prices at the store, he went on, was no more than an underhanded way of cutting wages, which already were cut to the bone. And, he continued, gettin' paid so unregular you couldn't figure your money. The rule said wages paid every two weeks, but the rule didn't hold with Ed Wangle lately. Made it easy to spread out a man's time and get more work for the same money.

"Not that we git our hands on much cash spendin' money," he said. "By time they hold out on your store account, there's mighty little left. And likely as not that ain't real money, but this here scrip."

I asked what he meant by scrip and he explained. It was exchange paper printed by the mill and given for wages in place of money. Good for face value at the mill store but discounted at other stores at twenty-five per cent, mebbe more.

"All this," he concluded, "is causin' talk. They're saying the mill's skimmin' on mighty thin ice. Reckon that's whut makes 'em so skittish. Thinkin' the mill's about to go bust."

He had addressed his remarks to the others but now he looked at me, and I gathered he had really intended the information for me.

There was no danger of that, I assured him. I would have heard if the situation was serious.

His nod admitted that possibility. "Ma'am, I ain't misdoubtin' you. But when you belong to a mill and eat and sleep and hear it day in and out, you get to where you kin smell how it's going. Like a hound dawg kin smell when the man he belongs to is readying to die afore anybody else. I reckon mill folks are kinda like that hound dawg."

Later, driving home, I told myself that in spite of Yancy Jackson's shrewd reasoning, his opinion regarding the mill was absurd; that to be disturbed by the devious gossip of mill hands, which no doubt constantly coiled among them, would be ridiculous. Even Yancy Jackson, though not an ordinary man, was not impervious to gossip. At least so it appeared.

Nevertheless, I worried, and though I said nothing of it at Hickory Hill, the nagging possibility that Yancy was not mistaken kept me awake most of the night. Turning and tossing, I thought, If I could only talk to Wes! And for a moment something like anger was added to anger. But in the next moment he turned in his sleep and I saw in the moonlight the thin quivering face, the closed eyes deep-shadowed under dark brows. And anger was dissolved.

It was nonsense to worry, I told myself again, then knew I would worry until I verified what I had heard or proved it false. Tomorrow, I resolved, staring into the moonlight, I would go to Darty Land. Darty would tell me what I had to know.

I found Darty in the office, fortunately alone, and without wasting time, told him my reason for coming and admitted I was concerned. And his face, like that of an old man who slips off uncomfortable shoes, was instantly relieved.

"Time somebody found out what's goin' on," he muttered. "Not that I know anything."

"Nonsense," I said, "you know more about the mill than anyone, Darty Land."

He scowled furiously but, obviously flattered, asked what I wanted to know.

"I want to know if it's true."

"What d'you mean, true?"

With a touch of asperity, I retorted that he knew what I meant. "Is the mill about to go bust?"

He looked at me steadily a moment. Then he said, "Yep, 'less somethin's done pretty damn quick, you can bank on it."

For a moment I was too dazed and shocked to speak. This was not the answer I had expected. The fears and worries of last night had failed to prepare me for the discovery that they were supported by facts.

I sank in the chair beside Darty's desk. I said, "But why has no one told me? Why didn't you warn me, Darty? I have a right to know."

"Didn't ask me," he growled.

"But I don't understand." I was bewildered. "After all these years! Why would it fail now?"

In answer, Darty swung to face his desk and began producing from various drawers documents, bills, statements, cost sheets, and piled them methodically on it, muttering he'd been wondering when Wes or I might come by to ask a few questions. He hadn't drawn an easy breath since that blasted loan went through.

Puzzled, I asked, "Loan? What loan?"

He answered harshly, "The loan for seventy-five thousand dollars Miss Camilla put through a while back."

Staring, I asked, "Put through how? Where?"

"The bank. The one Carr's head of."

"Do you mean Algernon Carr?"

"He's the one, all right. Besides being head of that bank, it's taken pretty much for granted around the cotton business that he's the bigwig in that there mill combine. Man name of Holly is chairman of the board. But it's what you could call a widely known secret that Carr cracks the whip. Holly, as they say, don't blow his nose less'n Carr says the word. I guess Carr figures Carrebee Mills would fit right nice into his string of other mills and near about fell over himself lettin' Miss Camilla have the money when she came to him for it."

"Because he expects to get Carrebee Mills for the combine that way?"

"That's the idea, all right. If Miss Camilla defaults on payin' back that loan, Carr's bank just moves in and takes over. Then all that's necessary is to shuffle the cards around a little between the bank and the combine, and the combine ends up with Carrebee Mills."

I had tried to be attentive while he explained, but I was distracted by my swiftly widening realization of what it would mean if, as he said, the mill went to bust sure as hell.

"Why did Miss Camilla borrow seventy-five thousand dollars from Mr. Carr if she knew he wanted the mill? Why should she play into his hands?"

"It ain't hard to figure out why," Darty answered. "Of course I didn't know a blamed thing about it 'til the loan was put through and it was too late to try and talk her out of it. Not that I can picture anybody talkin' Miss Camilla out of takin' seventy-five thousand dollars in real money when she has the chance."

"But if it means losing the mill, ruining her and Wes and Cissa, how could she be so—so irresponsible?"

"I expect seventy-five thousand cash was just more temptation than she could stand. Folks who want something bad enough figure they'll find a way to pay when the time comes to pay. She plays around on the futures market, might have counted on makin' a killin' and gettin' all in the clear. Nobody ever does, not that way. But she wouldn't be the first one to try."

"Why it's . . . it's like a bank clerk that takes money to gamble and means to put it back before he's caught!" I protested.

"Well, it ain't dishonest," Darty disagreed. "And in a way, the fact is, her makin' the loan ain't so unreasonable, except there ain't enough time to pay it off. She was squeezed tight about money. Pretty near desperate, to tell the truth. She was in debt pretty deep to the commission houses and they was puttin' the screws on her. The way she figured, or said she did, she could use the loan to consolidate her debts, ease the pressure, and at the same time put in modern equipment and improvements. With new equipment we could up production and cut the payroll. And better goods would bring more profits naturally. Maybe we could come out ahead, loan and all."

"If that's true, why do you think the mill will go bust?"

"Because Miss Camilla ain't done a blame thing she's supposed to do. Ain't ordered new equipment and as far as I can see, don't plan to. Said it'd make the lintheads rare back on their hind legs, if we tried to put in the new equipment. Sounded to me like she was givin' herself an out for not usin' the money per agreement. That's when I began to sweat hard. Of course she used some to pay off the debts to the commission houses. Had to. That was all right, too. But I don't know what she means to do with the rest. She's taken out some of it already and don't say what it's for. It ain't so much yet, but I'm practically certain she's playin' on the futures market with it, hopin' to make a killin' like I said. When I figured that, I got too scared even to sweat. She'll lose her shirt. There won't be a single piece of new equipment. Without it, the mill ain't got a prayer of makin' enough money to pay even the first note on the loan when it's due. She's only got a three-year loan—which is a mighty damn short one. She has to pay it off in three installments, one a year. It comes out at just under thirty thousand on the first payment, addin' on interest. And if she misses any one of 'em, that's when you can kiss the mill good-by."

I shook my head, frowning. "I can understand all but one thing. I can't understand how she borrowed seventy-five thousand dollars without Wes knowing about it. He owns more shares in the mill than anyone else in the family. More than Miss Camilla and Cissa own together. His father left him a clear majority. He's in control of the mill, legally. It seems to me that she couldn't arrange a loan without his agreeing to it, and he hasn't said a word to me about . . ."

My words trailed off. I saw Darty's head ducked and he was scowling at the floor, his eyes avoiding mine.

I felt a sick dismay. "Darty, did you know that Wes . . ."

He still avoided my eyes and the mottled red crept up into his face. "I know I ain't got the right spillin' something Wes ain't mentioned. But God Almighty, I couldn't sit here and see the mill go over the edge and say nothing!"

I said helplessly, "But Wes couldn't . . . he wouldn't let the mill go to smash . . ."

"Don't go layin' the blame on Wes, now," Darty told me. "Miss

Camilla probably outsmarted him too. Said she'd use the money for equipment and all those debts. If she'da lived up to it, the loan wasn't a bad idea." He shook his head, his face puckered in wretchedness. "Always wished Wes would take hold of things hisself. He could have, too. Got plenty of sense. And could do anything he wanted with the hands. Had his Pa's head . . . if he'd got the chance to use it."

"I wanted him to take hold too, Darty," I said, miserably and angrily. "I wanted him to take hold too!"

Riding home in the buggy, my misery and anger mounted higher, the more I thought of Miss Camilla's greedy, blind, and foolish risking of the mill, upon which depended the livelihood of all of us as well as of the mill hands. But even greater than my bitter resentment toward her, was my hard, heavy anger at Wes. Anger fed by my hurt pride because he had not mentioned the loan to me, because he had considered my advice of no value, my opinion unnecessary though this decision affected our lives. I was neither a child nor a fool! I had a right to know. At least I would have known that when a loan was made, somebody must see that the money was properly used and the mill put in a position to repay it. He had known I would insist on just that. He had known I would feel that it was he who should keep check. And that he did not want. He didn't want responsibility thrust upon him that he did not wish to take. But now he must take it. He must.

I found him, not seated at his window, but dressed and shaved and not too unlike the old Wes. He strolled about the yard, hands in pockets. When, topping the rise, I saw him as he had not been for so long, hope came again. Perhaps this was a good omen, a turning point. I cringed away from telling him what I had learned, yet knowing as I cringed that I must.

Tiptoeing, I kissed him. "Feeling better?"

He shrugged. "It gets damned dull when you're gone. Where've you been anyway?"

I told him. Told him what I had learned, all I had learned. Hands in pockets, he stood, his back to me, and I couldn't see his face. When I finished he neither by word nor gesture indicated that he had so much as heard.

I said, "Wes, you've got to act now. Do something."

He flashed to face me. "Do what?" he demanded.

"Why—" I stammered, flustered by the sudden attack. "Go in—take charge—do something to save the mill."

His eyes glinted from narrowed lids. "That's what you'd like, isn't it? That's what you've wanted? That's why you've nagged and bickered and left me not one minute's peace. So I would take over the mill. Go to the mill every morning, home from the mill at night. Back to the mill next morning—all cut down to a narrow little box you chose for me."

"No," I said heavily. "That isn't what I want."

He laughed scornfully, like a spoiled boy kicked a rock from his path. He was a spoiled boy, I thought swiftly. He should be treated as one.

"Wes," I said steadily, "it isn't enough to be handsome and attractive and—play in the sun. Not when you have the ability to accomplish. You do have that ability. And you waste it, though it means your whole life—and mine."

His body had braced defiantly as I began to talk. His mouth was a stubborn line. When I finished he said quietly, "Now get this. I'm not going to take over the mill. And, by God, if you don't leave me alone about it I'll hate you as I hate my mother."

I asked through tight lips, "So that's why you hate her? Because she wanted you to be a man—act like a man—be responsible for what was yours—" My laugh was bitter. "I've never known why before."

His face, white before, was suddenly suffused with red and his eyes were ugly.

"You don't know why I hate her. I hope to God you never will know. But it's also the reason I hate the mill."

Coolly, I asked, "Is it a reason? Or an excuse for running away?"

His eyes, somber, met mine. "Both," he said shortly.

"A coward runs away." I purposely edged my voice with contempt.

He admitted that too. "Yes. But there are times when unless you run away—you are lost. And"— he laughed bitterly—"if you run away—you are just as lost. You didn't know that, did you?"

Politely I said, "No, I didn't know that."

He passed his hand over his face as if to clear it. "You are like the rest. Measuring all humanity with your miserly rule of thumb." He added wearily, "It doesn't matter."

"Perhaps not," I prodded. "But the mill matters. What are you going to do about it? Let Carr's combine get it?"

He stared at the ground, his toe scuffing the dirt. Then his flung-up hand gestured as if to push it—and everything—away. "Maybe you'd better call Andrew," he said wearily. "Ask him what to do."

Perhaps that would be wiser, I agreed. Perhaps Andrew would put somebody in at the mill to guard Wes's interests.

His somber eyes lifted and something glinted in their unlighted dark. "Maybe he will," he agreed. "Anyway, tell him to handle it."

At the mill next day, I took advantage of a period when the office was empty and telephoned Andrew. Calmly he heard me out, and after a few questions agreed that we'd better meet with Miss Camilla and get down to cases. Meantime, I wasn't to worry. There was a moment of silence and as it persisted, I wondered if the connection had been broken, and spoke his name.

"I'm still here," he said. "I'm just wondering."

"Wondering about what?" I asked.

Matter-of-factly he told me, "Wondering how you would like to try running a cotton mill."

When I told Wes that Andrew would arrange the meeting with Miss Camilla, at his office, and wanted Wes present, he gave a small non-committal nod, and deliberately turned to gaze out of his window as if bored with the subject.

I did not press him further, so that I did not know if he intended to go. However, on the appointed day he was up early, and as if he'd acquired in the night an extra supply of strength, his appearance, shaved and dressed, was greatly improved. He complained good-humoredly that he couldn't find a single damn handkerchief for his coat pocket, and when Mitty produced one, freshly laundered, he patted her cheek and slipping the handkerchief into his pocket, twitched it into shape with the old careless air of elegance.

Relieved, I was, nevertheless, puzzled as to the source of this almost magic renewal. But as we drove toward town, it finally dawned upon me that his spirits came, not from health, but from the all-too-familiar bottle. And, reaching town, I was not surprised at the suggestion that I go on to Andrew's office, that he'd meet me there in ten minutes.

Conscious of passers-by, I concealed my dismay. But it didn't escape him and he promised, as if amused at my fear, that I could count on him.

"Please, Wes . . ." I began.

Laughing, he interrupted to promise. This time he wouldn't fail me. "Bright honor, Doc!" He smiled and with his careless wave went jauntily off. And I went my way, alone.

I had little faith in his promise, and when I reached Andrew's office I warned him not to count on Wes. But Andrew remained undisturbed. In that contingency, he said calmly, we'd do without Wes.

A clerk thrust his head in the door.

"Mrs. Carrebee," he announced, and Andrew, rising, moved from behind his desk. Then her throaty, husky voice was in the room, and turning, I faced Miss Camilla.

She smiled and said, "Jess!" in greeting, as unconcerned as if unaware of the reason that brought us together. But in her smile, and the warm husky voice, and most of all in her eyes, I perceived a difference in her. A set, hard ruthlessness moved now behind the mask of charm and good humor. And whether or not her position was defensible, she was prepared to defend it.

She maintained her pretense of ease as, accepting the chair Andrew offered, she slowly drew a glove from a plump white hand and opened the conversation. She understood, she said, that I had been upset because of circumstances at the mill. Because plans made for it had not been effected, at least as quickly as I thought they should be. Of course I had no least idea how difficult it was to get things done. Sometimes she felt as if she beat her head against a stone wall.

Andrew, from his chair behind the desk, interrupted with courteous firmness. It might be well, he suggested, to explain why this talk about the mill seemed necessary. Why the present situation was—to put it bluntly—precarious. Quickly, before she could answer, he outlined briefly but precisely the condition. The huge loan from the City Bank, the conditions of the loan, the limited time in which it must be met, the improvements on which that loan had been contingent. Item by item, he listed the changes and improvements which should have been made but had not been made. Moreover, he stated, the financial situation of the mill at present was even more hazardous than at the time of the loan. Payment of outstanding obligations insisted on by the bank had not been met. Considerable funds, however, had been disbursed.

Miss Camilla's short, brusque laugh was even harsher and blunter. "Are you suggesting I've stolen—from myself?" she inquired.

"I suggest nothing," Andrew returned calmly. "I merely state facts."

She shrugged. "It takes time to get things done, Mr. Hardee. Since you are unfamiliar with mill operation you don't realize that a layout of the plant must be drawn before machinery can be installed."

"The layout was drawn," I said, breaking in. "Some time ago."

Unaware that I knew this, her expression slipped for a moment before she adjusted it swiftly to my unexpected thrust.

"Of course it was," she said. "Which, as I say, took time. And I told Darty Land weeks ago to forward the orders for the machines. Most certainly he should have found out why delivery takes so long. But"—she spread her hands—"I'll have to see to that, too!"

"The orders have not been mailed," I told her, and her blue eyes widened in pretended surprise.

"You ordered them held until you gave the word," I continued. "You have not given the word."

"I did nothing so absurd," she returned, her voice sharper. "If Darty told you any such story, he's lying to protect his own slip."

I shook my head. "I'm sorry. But Darty isn't lying."

She gazed at me steadily before she asked, her voice cool, "Are you calling *me* a liar, then?"

But before I could answer Andrew interrupted again. Nothing would be gained, he suggested, by this line of discussion. He bowed slightly toward Miss Camilla, his voice matter-of-fact.

"Mrs. Carrebee, you have carried heavy responsibility in Carrebee Mills for a good many years. I am confident you will be glad to be relieved of it—let someone younger assume it."

She no longer smiled and her eyes had narrowed. "Who am I to let assume the responsibility for Carrebee Mills, Mr. Hardee?"

He raised his brows politely. "Why, Mrs. Wes Carrebee, of course. I assume that was understood. With Mr. Carrebee not well enough to take charge, his wife is the logical person."

She said drily, "I agree Wes is not able to take charge of anything, including himself."

He made no reply to this but continued, "Since he is unable to take charge himself, he has appointed his wife to act for him. I am sure you consider it only natural for him to trust her judgment and ability."

Her face stiffly set, she asked, "Am I to believe that Wes wants the mill run by a girl?"

"You may take it," Andrew said, "that he wants his wife to be in charge."

"In sole charge?" she inquired.

"She has asked me to act in an advisory capacity," Andrew answered. "Otherwise—in sole charge."

Her laugh was harsh now and angry. She turned toward me, her mouth scornful. "I don't believe it," she said flatly. "I don't believe Wes would be that big a fool even when drunk. If Wes wants her to take charge, as you claim, Mr. Hardee, then let him come here and say it. Until then, I'll continue to manage affairs as I see fit. As for the loan, that's the City Bank's concern, not yours."

If Andrew detected the vicious contempt in her voice, he ignored it. He replied, quietly, that no intention to bring legal action existed unless no other alternative could be agreed upon. She must know, he said, that unless Carrebee Mills was put on a sound basis and its equipment overhauled it must inevitably fail as a business enterprise.

"Then it will fail under me," she told him bluntly. "We may as well be clear about that. Wes certainly is not capable of making an intelligent decision about the mill, or anything. And certainly I don't intend to let Jess take it over. I'll run it as I see fit, as long as I see fit, and I don't believe, Mr. Hardee, that you or anyone can prevent me."

As she talked, the door behind her opened quietly, and raising my eyes, I saw Wes. Not aware of his arrival, she talked on, and, leaning in the doorway, he waited while she completed her speech. Then she picked up her gloves and rose.

"I wouldn't hurry," Wes said flatly, and came into the office, closing the door behind him, the shine of his eyes and flush of his skin revealing that he had been drinking. But he had himself in control, and his voice was clear and hard.

"I heard you say, I believe, that I am not capable of taking charge of anything, including myself?" he asked her.

Surprised by his sudden appearance, she was, for a moment, shaken. She regained her poise, was her invincible self again. "You know that," she retorted, "as well as I. You aren't well . . ."

He shook his head. "You mean I'm either drunk or pulling out of a drunk," he said. His raised hand stopped her denial. "Oh, don't apologize for telling the truth. I generally am what you say. But I can make an intelligent decision once in a while, if I try very hard. I've made one just now. I've decided that Jess has a stake in Carrebee too. My stock. And you shan't kick it out from under her with promises you don't keep and have no intention of keeping."

"You don't know the situation, Wes," she said. "You don't know the truth."

He laughed. "I haven't noticed that you're particularly familiar with it either," he taunted. "And we needn't argue whether I know what I'm doing or not. I'm doing it. I want to be damned sure if I'm not around to stop you that you won't ruin Jess the way you've ruined everything and everybody you've worked on. You shan't swindle her, then tell her to go to hell. I don't know if she'll do better with the mill or worse, but if she wants to try, by God, she'll get the chance."

"Don't be a fool!" she snapped. "She'll run it into the ground in six months. There won't be any Carrebee Mills."

"As I see it, there won't be one if you run it, either."

"I've run it for years," she retorted.

"You've milked it dry for years," he answered. "Now somebody else is going to get a chance."

"It'll be smashed, Wes!"

He smiled into her face. "You can't get it into your head, can you? I don't give a nickel-plated damn if it's smashed. I care about Jess and about her having a chance to make something decent out of the mill, and that's all."

She said hoarsely, "You don't know what you're doing, you fool. I said you couldn't take charge of yourself. But I see now that someone else is able to take charge for you."

"At least," he answered, "it isn't you. That's some gain."

For a moment her anger was livid, then she fought her way back to control, the set mask of a smile on her face.

"Very well, Wes. Have it your way—or Jess's," she said. "I don't think the experiment is likely to last very long. She'll find handling a cotton mill and a thousand-odd lintheads no easy job. If there's any mill left by the time she gives up, I'll come back."

As she spoke, she regained her composure and confidence, as if her own words reassured her. She strolled toward the door, her face arrogant and certain, pausing to turn back to Wes.

"I'll come back and run the mill for you, Wes, when Jess admits she's beaten!"

She went out, and Wes stood for a moment wearing the grin and the look of triumph. Then slowly he sank down in a chair and I saw that the clash with his mother had shaken him, after all. His forehead was wet with sweat and his hands trembled. But he managed a twisted smile as his eyes sought mine and held them.

"All right, Doc," he said. "There's your goddamned cotton mill."

There was no public announcement when the change-over at the mill was effected. And no evidence of it except that I—not Miss Camilla—drove through the gates in the mornings; often with a heavy heart. There were days when I felt I couldn't leave Wes. Not the "bad" days. Then he was past knowing if I was or was not there. But the days when, pulling back, he constantly called "Oh Doc!" only wanting to know I was near; or sat at the window staring out, rousing only when I slipped in with a cooling drink or Mitty's broth. Sometimes as I stood there, my eyes on the dearly loved face, a great dark bird of fear would swoop down and blot out the light. And something within me would cry out, "Oh God, what can I do? There must be something!" Yet even as I soundlessly cried out for help, I faced the bitter knowledge that there are times when you can do nothing—but accept.

Now, several days a week I worked in the office with Darty, and with the passing days I began to lose my first feeling of being an intruder. More and more as I passed among the mill hands they gave me a friendly "Good morning" or "Good evening." Often I stopped to chat with them. They had come to know, I realized, that I—not Miss Camilla—was head of the mill, for in their attitude I found the same watchful waiting I had met in the Lucketts at first. Yet each day I felt that my stock rose higher—as theirs did with me. Beneath their work-bitten faces and bodies I discovered kindness and a salty humor and shrewd common sense. Cast on a desert island, I thought, they would survive whoever else might perish. For the stoic acceptance which I had marked in Yancy Jackson and Mrs. Handy burned in each.

These two, if not actual allies, were at least friendly. Yancy Jackson treated me with a fine, grave politeness. And Mrs. Handy, granite-featured, austere and stern though she was, I had come to respect. Under her generalship Mady and Cade and Poky had not only cleanliness and nourishing food but protection from the sly cruelty which I sensed lurked in Dude Luckett. And this was to me a great help, for now I could devote little time to them. Every moment at the mill was devoted to learning what I could from Darty about the details of operation, and every moment away from Hickory Hill, thoughts of Wes pulled me back. At my first free minute I was in the buggy and heading for home again.

In his better periods I found him sitting at the window gazing out. Other times he would be stretched asleep on the bed, his swollen, puffy face with the horrible bright pink—not Wes. With work I tried to hold despair at a distance. At night I struggled with the hand loom or pored over the technical books and, overwhelmed by all I must learn, knew another kind of despair. But learn I did. Not swiftly or easily but slowly, laboriously. Yet, when the various operations demanded by spinning and weaving were no longer unfathomable mysteries but logical steps in a method, perversely I concluded it was really quite simple. And that running a cotton mill was not the difficult feat it was reported to be. At least not to me.

Had I been wiser, I would have questioned the unruffled surface which until now had prevailed—known that sooner or later the squall would break. The first was caused by Ed Wangle and was, Darty said, quite a big blow, and no more than he expected with that gasbag Ed Wangle on deck. Arriving at the office one morning, I found Darty and Ed going at it hammer and tongs, Ed bellowing and red-faced with anger, Darty ferociously scowling. The argument, it appeared, was over mill store prices, which Darty had ordered reduced to conform to prices elsewhere.

When I entered they calmed down somewhat, though Ed, I could see, was still angry; but he turned his hard blue eyes my way and his voice was almost fawning. "Mrs. Carrebee, ma'am," he said, "Darty here says you gave orders to price the foodstuffs we sell in the store the same as the outside grocers. Is that right, ma'am?"

I said that was right, and his bombastic voice rolled at length while he argued against it. The mill store had to charge more, he announced, because it carried the hands on credit. If it was to make any profit, that was.

When I informed him we didn't want to make profit he stared at me, his mouth hanging open. "Not want to make profit?" he asked blankly —then laughed his great bellowing laugh. "Then, ma'am, what use you got for the store?"

"The store is for the workers' convenience, Mr. Wangle, not to get rich on."

He scratched his head, then shook the same head as if to clear its confusion. "Twenty year I've worked at the mill and I ain't ever heard talk like this." He quoted, " 'For the workers' convenience.' " His voice mocking mine was mincing. "Well, God blow me down!" he exclaimed. "What use has a linthead got for convenience? Why, ma'am, you start treatin' 'em good and they'll be at your throat like a pack of wolves. They ain't used to good treatment."

"Then it's high time they began to get used to it, Mr. Wangle, for they will get good treatment from now on. And I hope, sir, that you won't forget it."

He gave me a long steady glance and picked up his hat from a desk and left the office.

"Perhaps we should have let him out after all," I told Darty.

But he wouldn't agree. "Plenty of time to do that if we have to. Truth is he'd like nothing better, for then he could go round shooting off his big mouth about the raw deal you gave him. Ed is a pretty bad talker. I figure if we can keep him cooled down 'til we got our foot in the door it's better for us. I sure want to keep him on our side 'til the new machinery gets in."

"What does he have to do with the new machinery?"

"Not a darned thing. But if he starts shootin' his mouth about it meaning fewer jobs for workers he can stir up considerable trouble."

In the cold of the winter morning I turned Moppet down the hill road, where each hollow left by the rain was skimmed with its layer of ice.

And the stark and bare trees, jeweled with prismed icicles, were like gaunt, unlovely old women flashing the family diamonds.

We turned in the mill gate, the droning voice of the mill all around us, and I guided the filly to the shed, where she could wait out of the cold. But as I turned to go back toward the counting house I stopped, my eyes drawn to one of the mill houses with an assortment of derelict furnishings piled in the street before it: an iron bedstead, some chairs, a torn mattress, dishes and pots and pans.

Beside them three small children shook and shivered, and even from where I stood I could feel the dismay that was theirs. I sighed as I started to go on my way. Another mill family moving, I thought, seeking in some other mill a life nearer the life that they wanted.

Then across the sharp winter air I heard a bellowing voice, and I stopped and turning, looked back and saw, as the voice had led me to expect, the burly figure of Ed Wangle. He stood at the door of the house, his big arm gesturing "hurry" to someone inside. In response, two women emerged, supporting between them a man with too little strength to walk alone. Huddled in their shabby clothes, they crossed the stoop.

Almost running, I went toward the house, reaching it just as Ed Wangle locked the door and thrust the key in his pocket.

I went to the edge of the stoop. "Who is moving?" I asked, my eyes turning from one to the other.

The man looked at me through sick eyes and the woman looked at Ed Wangle. His blustering voice answered. " 'Mornin', ma'am. Right snappy this mornin'."

I asked again, "Who is moving?"

His big arm swept the others. "This here is the Dodson family, ma'am."

I asked why they were moving, and his fat finger rubbed his red nose. "They ain't said, ma'am. Figger it's none of my business. They comes and they goes like blackbirds, not lightin' anyplace long."

One of the women—she was older, her eyes quiet in a worn face—said, "We'se bein' evicted, ma'am, an' no place to go."

I repeated, "Evicted?"

"Yes, ma'am." Her head moved toward Ed. "By him."

The man said quickly, "We ain't complainin'. He's got his side. Me down with pellagry. Ain't able to work. He's got to have workers in the house. 'Tain't his fault."

I sent Ed Wangle a meaning look. "Unlock the door," I ordered, and like a fat pouting boy he obeyed.

"Help them put their stuff back inside," I said next, then told the silent watchers, "You won't be evicted."

I turned to Ed Wangle. "I'll expect you at the office when you've moved them back in." And not waiting to hear his reply, I left, feeling the cold hateful eyes boring my back as I went.

In the office I waited for him alone. And he came, not blustering now but his big body seething with his anger. He closed the door behind him and faced me with bullet head forward and shoulders hunched.

I said levelly, "Ed, from this minute you are fired."

He stared at me from contemptuous eyes. "You can't fire me. I don't work for you. I work for Miss Camilla."

"You don't work for anyone here. You're fired."

His hand circled his jaw. "I don't b'lieve you've got the straight of this."

"Perhaps it's you who aren't straight about it."

He said, "I got it straight, and from the real boss. I knows why she's lettin' you play your little game to please her son whose driv hisself loony with licker."

"You aren't straight about it after all. The mill belongs to my husband. He's asked me to run it for him. I'm the boss, Ed, and you're fired. You've had orders about evictions. . . ."

He shook his head. "From you not from the boss. But"—he lifted his hand debonairly—"I'll make out I'm fired." He laughed, not his blustering, bellowing laugh but silent and evil laughing that, soundless, still filled the room. "But I'll be around. The boss pays me to be around. You'll probably be hearin' from me, on one count or another."

That was the beginning; and also the end. The end of the friendly " 'Mawnin' " and " 'Evenin'," the end of the neighborly smiles. The end of the unruffled peace of which I boasted too soon, of being accepted not as a Carrebee but as a human being.

The beginning I hardly noticed at first. When, passing, I said, "Good morning," and received no response I thought nothing of it. But each day the number of times it happened increased and, shocked, I realized that all of them passed me without response; and instead stared at me from cold, hostile eyes.

Darty said when I told him, "I knew it. That big mouth Ed Wangle." His scowl deepened. "Reckon you'd better stay at home for a while, let 'em cool down."

I said, "I won't stay at home. They shan't scare me."

He scratched his head. "You sure are a hardheaded lady to be so young."

I didn't stay home. I went to the mill just as often, but each day it was harder to go. It wasn't that I was frightened; I wasn't. But it takes courage to walk among those whose hate like a living thing walks beside them, leering and sneering when you wish to be friends, walking down the village street, stabbed by their hostile eyes, trailed by stealthy laughter, I felt numb and frozen inside.

Once Yancy Jackson stopped me. "Miz' Carrebee, I sholy don't think it's safe. It ain't that they're bad, they're scared fer the job. Did you stay home a while, they'd simmer down."

I didn't stay home. But now I turned, not frightened, but uneasy. A flung rock would come uncomfortably near, yet I would not see who had thrown it. Foolishly, I persisted, refusing to yield—not for myself but for Wes; and for Miss Camilla, who had said, "When she admits she's beaten, I'll come back."

There was the dusk when, hurrying to the buggy, I had the feeling that unfriendly eyes were watching; and turning, saw Dude Luckett's pale flat eyes shining with vicious glee. Then at last there was fear, not for myself: fear for Mady and Cade and the slight protection I had offered, threatened now by grim-faced defiant rancor. Driving up the hill road, I prayed, "Don't let me give up . . . don't let me be scared." Yet even as I prayed, the enmity engendered by Ed Wangle's malice walked beside me.

A thin rain falling through the afternoon had become sleet at dusk. Its fields of whispering hushed the world as I came home to Hickory Hill.

The damp and cold had seeped through my clothing and Mitty, seeing me shiver, made me sit by the fire and brought me a cup of steaming coffee. Wes seemed a little better, she said, though he was still powerful weak. She got him to take some soup a while back and he had dropped off to sleep; it would be best not to disturb him, she said, just let the poor feller sleep.

I told her dully, "He can't go on like this, Mitty. Each time it seems worse."

Her mouth crinkled in worried tenderness, but she refused to offer false hope or hollow encouragement.

When I went toward the kitchen where Mitty had laid our supper near the warmth of the hearth, I paused and, careful to make no sound, opened the door of his narrow room and looked in upon him a moment. When he was weak like this he would not have the room dark, and in the dim glow of his shaded lamp his face looked almost as pale as the pillow. But it was calm with sleep, and though wasted and bloodless, haunted still with the old beauty that I had seen my first night at the house of the Carrebees.

While we ate our supper, Mitty asked about the mill and I told her how the workers grew more and more sullen and angry until, I said, it was something that you could almost feel.

I heard Wes call out his name for me as Mitty and I washed and dried our dishes. His eyes were sunken and dark and sick when I went in to kiss him hello, but he did not feel like talking, he said. I sat by his bed until he slept again and then went to the sitting room, where Mitty dozed in her chair, her spectacles pushed up on her gray hair. I picked up a book and tried to read, but unable to see the words because Wes's wasted face thrust itself between me and the page. I read, vaguely aware of Colonel's barking in front of the house, but I paid it no attention.

Mitty, without opening her eyes, said, "I expect he's stirred up a 'possum."

But the barking continued, a steady, hoarse bay unlike the yelp of a dog excited by some creature, and I raised my head to listen. It was a deeper, throatier sound, now interspersed with growls, and I saw that Mitty sat up and, head to one side, listened too. I got up from my chair, and going to a closet in the hall, took out a coat and flung it around my shoulders.

"Wait, Jess," Mitty said, and the tone of her voice and her use of my name instead of the familiar one of my childhood made me pause.

"What is it, Mitty?" I asked.

"Hush," she said, and I listened, then I heard it too. Or rather, I felt a presence that was not a noise but a gathering of more intense silence, against which the bay of the dog was furiously hurled.

"Don't go out," Mitty said.

But this I rejected. "I must see what it is. Something might be wrong with Colonel."

But when I opened the door and went out on the porch the dog, braced at the foot of the steep steps, was unharmed, though the deep, throaty bark continued. Then came sound out of silence: a muffled sound on the hill road below the crest, a tramping of feet on frozen leaves.

I would not admit the fear that thickened in my throat. I said over my shoulder, "Mitty, go in," for I knew that she stood behind me. But she did not obey.

And then the dark, stumbling figures edged up over the crest of the hill and moved forward from the deeper darkness beneath the trees toward the house. I saw blurred featureless faces as they drew closer around the porch, though still keeping beyond the rim of faint light that came through the door.

I knew now who they were, where they were from. I even thought I recognized a figure here and there, among them Dude Luckett's, though I could not be sure. Some, I saw, had partially covered their faces with handkerchiefs. The air was tight, as so often it had been tight at the mill and I had felt it with anger.

"What do you want?" I called, forcing my voice to steadiness.

From the shadows a voice answered back. "Stay outen the mill. We come to warn you to stay off. We don't want you an' your new-fangled machines."

"The machines won't make less work," I began, but a chorus of shouts drowned me out, and a few of the dark, lumpish shapes edged closer. The same voice that had spoken before spoke again.

"We're givin' you warnin'. Stay outen the mill. If you don', what happens will be your own fault."

"I have a job to do at the mill," I replied.

Another, uglier voice from the back of the crowd cried out.

"Ain't no hedge-born bastard takin' bread outten our younguns' mouths!"

I was shaken by a burning fury of anger mingled with shame and fear.

"We come to warn you," I heard it again.

Before I could speak, the massed figures edged slowly backward in sudden withdrawal as if pulled toward the darkness by invisible wires. But I did not realize why until Colonel, leaving his place before the steps, flashed up them to stand with his head at Wes's knee. And then I saw Wes.

He stood with a hand propped against a supporting post of the porch roof, wearing trousers he had pulled on and a coat open and showing his bare chest beneath. His face was white still and his lips quivered with weakness. But he stood careless, arrogant, contemptuous, and smiled mockingly at the darkness.

"Who did you say you came to warn?" he taunted.

"To warn Miz Carrebee," a voice called out, "how we don' want no new machines to do folks outa work."

Wes turned his head toward the voice. "Then come talk to my wife like men," he called back. "Not like maulers crawling out of a manure pile!"

At their sullen surreptitious mutter he laughed suddenly, as if in delight. "You'll warn nobody in this house," he taunted. "You'll warn no one here. But I warn you, every louse-bitten lint-haired bastard. Keep away from my house and my wife. Because the first skulking, yellow one of you that raises a finger against my home or my wife will regret it to the last day of your life, by God!"

A hoarse, unintelligible shout came back and Wes wheeled toward it.

"What I said goes from now on," he told them. "I'll give you three minutes to get off of my land." His voice came stronger and snapped like the crack of a whip. "Now get going!"

He still held himself erect against the post, smiling defiance at their shadows, and I saw them slowly edge back and merge with the black lake of the trees, and expelled a great breath of relief.

But then a raw voice shouted again and there was a swift, speeding hum of wind and a stone hurtled out of the night.

It seemed as I watched in terror that Wes casually waited for it to come and accepted the blow as if too proud to avoid it. For a second after it struck—high against the side of his head—he leaned carelessly against the post. Then as Colonel, lunging, brushed him, with grave grace he bowed to the darkness before he was flung twisting and crashing down the long steps to the frozen ground.

Whether I cried out or not I did not know. I was beside him, holding him in my arms, raising his head with its black smear of blood and cleaning it of dirt with my dress. His eyes were open and his look amused. I asked if he was hurt badly and he shook his head.

"I'm all right, Doc," he said. He made an effort to raise himself and

I tried to help him to his feet. But then I saw his face, suddenly wrenched as if an invisible, massive force crashed his body. He sagged limply against me, his hand lifting in a groping gesture toward his head.

"Wes, what is it?" I asked.

He told me thickly, ". . . head . . . aches like hell, Doc."

With him inert in my arms, my eyes sought the circle of dark figures that had drawn further back into shadow. Straining, I tried to lift him alone, and Mitty, coming to my side, added her strength to mine. But thin though he was, his weight was too much for us, and despairingly I glanced over my shoulder. As I did, a figure came forward from the concealing blackness beneath the trees; a great hulk of a young man, his face vaguely familiar though I did not know his name. Kneeling at my side, he slipped his powerful, hard-muscled arms under Wes.

"I'll tote him, Miz Carr'bee," he said with rough gentleness, and as easily as he would lift a child, he raised Wes and carried him up the high steps and to the bed in the narrow room.

Driven by sickening fear, I paced from bed to window and back to the bed again, watching with frantic impatience for the young mill hand to bring Dr. Tilly. It seemed hours before buggy wheels grated on the frosty ground and Dr. Tilly's voice rumbled in the hall. Then he was in the room. His bulky body bent over Wes who lay, his face pinched and leaden-hued, his breathing rasping and hoarse.

Feeling helpless and useless, I waited until the doctor gently replaced the covers and straightened. Then I followed him out of the room. In the hall he turned to meet my unspoken question, his small, shrewd eyes giving me my answer even before he spoke.

When he did speak I listened impatiently to the gruff voice explaining that the rock only glanced; that the serious damage was caused by the fall and striking his head on the step. . . .

I stopped him. "Serious damage," I repeated blankly. "How much damage? How serious?"

The gruff voice sank to a mumble.

". . . no use building up false hope . . . in cases like this . . . extensive . . . cerebral pressure. May subside . . . not hopeful."

He was telling me that Wes would die but I heard it without comprehension. I was incapable of accepting his meaning. This could not be happening.

A voice asked, "Will he regain consciousness?" Astonished, I recognized my voice.

"No way to tell . . . possible . . . again maybe . . ."

I did not hear the rest. Turning, I sped back to the room. He might wake. Look for me. But he lay unchanged; his face leaden still and his breathing hoarse and labored, as if an engine, racing out of control, pounded toward self-destruction.

Then I knew. And with numbing comprehension came agony that

held my body in its frozen vise of pain. Nothing existed except the struggle for life raging hopelessly within the unconscious body of Wes. Everything else became distant and unreal. Time moved neither slowly nor quickly. There was no time. Once, aware of Mitty's arms about my shoulders, impatiently I shrugged her away. She was gone. I did not know if hours or minutes passed when I saw patches of pallid light at the window.

Andrew was there but I did not lift my eyes from Wes. Then Andrew was gone. Miss Camilla and Cissa were in the room. I hardly knew when they came or when they left. I was vaguely conscious of remote sounds: footsteps, voices, the opening and closing of doors. A steaming cup was held before me and without seeing who held it I shook my head and pushed it irritably away.

Rigid, I sat, my eyes fixed on Wes's face. Was his labored breathing weaker? Had the pinched look around mouth and nose deepened? But as if to reassure me his eyes opened suddenly. Strangely, they were clear and proud, carelessly amused, as they had been when I first saw them. He said, shaping the words with effort, "Bother you again, Doc . . . just let me know."

I knew that to him the hours had been minutes and that, as always, he refused to admit defeat.

"I will," I said, "I will!"

He was silent again and I was uncertain whether he had slipped away from reality again or not. But then he asked if I remembered the violets. I said I would always remember, and his lips twitched into a wry suggestion of a smile.

"Always overdid things, didn't I, Doc?"

I said, "Rest. Don't try to talk."

His eyes searched my face. "Don't go away, Doc. Promise."

I promised, and he appeared to think over my reply for a few moments.

He told me, frowning, "I stayed away too much."

"Don't worry about it now."

But he asked, "Why did I stay away, Doc?"

"You were never really away," I told him tenderly.

But his eyes in the expressionless, drawn face showed that he knew it was not so. "Was, Doc. Don't know why. You were all I had."

"And you're everything I have. Everything I want."

He closed his eyes wearily. "I won't go away ever again, Doc."

But though I held his body close, he slipped away, to return to a past in which I had no share. His lips shaped names I had never heard, spoke to boyhood comrades invisible to me and unknown. Once, with a faint breath of laughter, he said, "Cissa." Then, still faintly, but his voice lifting as if his mind called, he said, "Cis!"

Then in a remote timeless void he and I were alone with his harsh, hurried breathing and the patches of white that sharpened around his lips and nostrils. He muttered jumbled sounds which at first meant nothing to me. Then, as the slurred, indistinct jumble continued, I suddenly recognized some familiar rhythm and hint of words in the incoherence. It was the old song sung with the childhood game he and Cissa had learned from a Negro nurse, and so many times sung together during the long, empty days of their childhood.

He fell silent presently, and lay motionless and quiet, except for the hard rasp of breathing, for time that had no measure.

Then his eyes opened, gazing steadily with the strange rapt look at something infinitely far away. And, his voice rising in eager expectancy, he repeated the line from the game of his lost childhood.

"What time, old witch . . . ?"

Not long afterwards, and without speaking again, he left me once more and went away.

It was Andrew who led me from the bed, but in the hall I drew away from his arm and walked unaided toward the sitting room. At the doorway I paused, gazing with dull surprise at the circle of faces in the yellow lamplight—their presence had made no real impression on me until now.

The dark faces of Adeline and Sparrow peered through a half-open door; Darty Land scowled from a corner. The waxy face of Syl Crowley gleamed above the back of the chair where Cissa, white-lipped and ghastly, stared blindly from glazed eyes. And all alone on the sofa Miss Camilla, rigidly erect, turned the stone mask of her face toward me; and I was pierced by pity. The grief we shared made bitterness small and mean.

Stiff and motionless, the plump, dimpled hands clasped tightly in her lap, she spoke, "I hope you are happy now."

I looked at her with blank disbelief, thinking I misunderstood.

"I hope you are happy," she repeated in the same toneless voice.

Someone—I do not know who—made a sound of shocked protest.

She replied to it without shifting her eyes from my face. "Don't try to stop me. It's time someone told the truth. This is what she's wanted. What she's schemed for from the day I took her in and befriended her. Gave her a home when she wouldn't have been allowed to set foot in the back door of any other decent house!" Sarcasm edged her voice. "Oh, she fooled me, too, with her calf-eyed innocence. So shy! Such a little lady! Her heart running over with gratitude and love for the whole world!"

Bewildered, I thought, This is hysteria. And Dr. Tilly lumbered toward Miss Camilla, saying soothingly, "Ma'am, you're not yourself . . ."

Her raised hand stopped him. "I know what I'm saying," she flung at him arrogantly. "Nobody can stop my saying it. I owe it to my son who is dead, to tell the truth about her!" Her husky voice was raw and rasping, the chords of her white throat rigid and strained. "I'll tell it everywhere. To everyone who knew my son. How she tricked him too. Tricked him into marriage. So convenient, living in the same house!"

Stunned by the sudden fury of her attack, by her face suddenly distorted and ravaged, the others sat too shocked to offer interference. I heard Mitty's grim "I'll get Andrew," but Miss Camilla ignored her.

Her voice was a throaty gasp now as if near exhaustion. "She's got what she wanted. She turned my son against me. Against his mother! Dragged him down. Now he's dead. Dead so quickly, too quickly, and who knows what really happened? Who knows what really caused it? He's dead, and she's got what she was after from the first. Carrebee Mills. Everything. She's taken everything. And my son is dead!"

I heard Andrew speak with quiet authority.

"There'll be no more of this."

He seemed taller and more solid as he moved unhurriedly toward Miss Camilla. Her eyes turned to him, their blue chilled by contempt.

"Who are you to interfere with what I have to say?"

"I am your son's friend and his wife's. That is why I cannot allow you to speak to his wife in a manner he would not permit if he were here."

"I am his mother!"

"He would not permit even his mother to say what you have said."

Their eyes met for a moment. Then abruptly she shrugged in disdain and rising stiffly from the sofa, whipped out the folds of her heavy skirt. "I have no desire, God knows, to remain in this house."

Taking her coat from the arm of the sofa, she moved imperiously toward the door, pausing beside the chair where Cissa sagged, limp and crumpled. She commanded, "Coming, Cissa?"

But Cissa only looked slowly up at her with wide, grief-blind eyes, and it was Syl Crowley who answered.

"I'll see my wife home."

"Just as you like, Syl," Miss Camilla said. In the moment of crossing the room she had regained almost complete control, and she moved with neck arched and head lifted. There was something tragic and terrible in her proud aloneness as she went out into the night.

She was gone and I had seen her in a stark glare that left no pretense or deception. But the discovery of the full reality of what she was did not seem important. Her hatred and her fury did not matter. Her words could not hurt. Everything but Wes was insignificant. I felt nothing else, knew no meaning beyond the monstrous knowledge that Wes was dead. The black flood of numbing despair and agony that, widening and deepening, encompassed all else in the world.

Part 3

THIS, THEN, WAS WHAT I HAD BEEN traveling toward all these years. This future dark and unshapen as night, a future that without Wes stretched dreary and empty, with nothing to strive after, nothing to long for.

All the happy and unhappy past rushed back upon me. I was a child with Mitty, safe in the little house; with her walking among the green mounds and pale stones in the cemetery. I was a young girl lonely at Mrs. Plummer's; gawky and shy at Miss Camilla's, miserable with hopeless love. I was a bride, standing at Wes's side, my hand in his; a wife, proud, then hurt and bewildered, resentful but forgiving—and always loving. And all rushing toward this. A house that stretched wide and silent yet every room echoing his laughter, his swift-running feet.

To me it seemed unforgivable that the world should continue to turn and people continue to live—when Wes was gone. That the spring should rush toward green splendor of summer; that the clock on the mantel ticked toward the future when I counted—not forward, but backward. "This time last Tuesday"—then Wednesday and Thursday, then "This time two weeks ago"—three—four—

From time to time I was vaguely conscious that Mitty stood above me and with bowls of soup and tempting dishes urged me to keep up my strength. When with talk of her garden and mention of Cade and Mady she tried to rouse me from my brooding despair, I waved her away impatiently.

Andrew came and, sitting across from me in the shadowed room, talked of the mill and business, and I knew he too hoped to rouse me. Pretending to listen, I thought drearily, "If they'd only leave me alone."

I did not want to be roused, I did not want to feel. I only wanted to sit in Wes's chair, Colonel lying with his muzzle on my shoe as he had lain by Wes. Sitting there, I scourged myself because all those months I had sensed his dark will for self-destruction and failed to understand or help him. If I had tried harder, I thought in agonized self-reproach, been stronger and wiser, less tolerant! Or had I loved him less blindly, seen him with awareness, Wes might have been saved.

In unreasoning remorse I was scourged by a far greater guilt. It was I who had caused Wes's death, who had assumed charge at the mill, who fired Ed Wangle and earned the enmity that inflamed fear and anger. The anger that brought the sullen mob to Hickory Hill, to fling the stone that caused Wes's fall, had begun with me.

For the first time I understood Wes's hatred and resentment for the mill. Now I felt it too. Even as I blamed myself, illogically I blamed the mill too, and those who worked at its looms and spindles. Now the very thought of it was repugnant, whether it survived or fell, of no importance. I wished I need never see it again. Yet I knew that sooner or later I must go back. Whether I cared or not, responsibility for it burdened my shoulders, though reason for bearing the responsibility was gone. Hate and dread it as I might, I could not free myself from it. I was bound to it by Cade and Mady and Poky. By Darty Land and Yancy Jackson and all who depended on it for their living. Even Miss Camilla and Miss Ad.

I would have to go back to the mill, I told myself drearily, sitting in Wes's chair, Colonel's muzzle on my shoe. But not yet. Not for a little while. Not while the rooms of Hickory Hill were still haunted by Wes; not while my thoughts and dreams were crowded with Wes.

I would go back. Next week perhaps, or the next. But I still did not feel that the mill really mattered, and I continued to sit brooding in Wes's chair counting backward in time. "This time three weeks ago"—and when the mill intruded upon remembering, quickly I closed it out.

It was late one afternoon that Mr. Poteat came, impeccably dressed. With polished gravity he apologized for the unexpected call and, placing his hat on the table, took a nearby chair. He would have come before, he said, but he knew I preferred not to be bothered. And Andrew had kept him informed— As he talked the trembling hands and sick eyes betrayed his misery, and when Mitty brought coffee, I asked if he would like something stronger.

He admitted that he would. A little pickup would help. "Been a little under the weather lately. My dear, afraid I'm getting old."

Mitty brought a bottle from Wes's cellar and Mr. Poteat, pouring a generous drink, lifted his glass gallantly to me.

"Wanted to come out, my dear, since the night of . . . the night of your loss. Wanted you to know that I thoroughly disapproved of Miss Camilla's conduct—that night. Not easy to forgive her, though understood she was not herself. But I can't forgive her continuing to repeat . . ." He broke off, his face with its veil of gray lines crumpling with the effort of logical thought. "Continuing to repeat," he went on, "her vicious accusations. Told her so. Told her I can't condone her conduct. We—we—it was very ugly, my dear."

I told him I was sorry. He and Miss Camilla had been friends a long time.

His fingers moved across his face as if to brush something away. "No choice, my dear. No choice. I could not allow—even . . . an old friend . . ." He broke off to refill his empty glass.

I waited while he drank, holding the glass warily as if he felt unsure.

"Ordinarily I would not bring such information. But think it best for you to be prepared." He added, as if surprised, "Camilla is a vindictive woman, my dear."

Did he think her gossip would be believed? I asked.

He started to speak, then fell silent, and bending his head, let it rest on his hand. At last he spoke, but without directly answering my question.

"I did you no favor when I took you to her house."

"You must not be sorry for that. No matter what happens I can never be sorry."

He raised his face from his hand. "God knows if I was sure you meant that . . ."

"You forget," I told him. "I met Wes in that house . . . first loved him there."

He nodded then in understanding and after a little while said slowly, "The love of people in that house costs high."

Recalling what I knew of him, I felt a surge of pity. His tragic home with the half-mad wife, seeking the graciousness and charm he was denied, at Miss Camilla's. Yet—I realized suddenly there must have been something more to draw him to its leaping fires on the hearth and the bottle beside his chair. Then I realized. What I should have realized before—what others must have known and no doubt understood. He loved Miss Camilla.

"You love her," I said softly.

He nodded mechanically, as if admitting an old and familiar knowledge.

"I've loved her a long time," he said simply.

"And now you've quarreled. And because of me."

His head lifted and I heard the old fullness and richness. "No," he denied. "We quarreled about a principle of conduct."

"But you shouldn't have," I told him sadly. "I would have understood."

He drew himself erect with impressive dignity and his eyes momentarily lost their dullness. Such eyes might have looked along the barrel of a dueling pistol in an age when life counted for nothing when weighed against honor.

"You would have understood and forgiven. I could not have understood or forgiven myself."

His eyes dulled again. Fumbling for words, he said he must go, and rose. But Mitty and I persuaded him to stay, and when he had sent his carriage away we had supper. He ate but little, I saw, and afterwards returned to his chair in the sitting room and the bottle. His quarrel with Miss Camilla and the shattering of the friendship—or love—of so many years was a far more serious wound than his pride would admit. But I saw how he downed the whiskey quickly, hurriedly, as if impatient for surcease from thought, and I knew he too was seeking escape. And when he said good night and unsteadily climbed the steps to his room I pretended I did not notice.

I was sorry that he had been hurt. Sorrier still that so unimportant a matter had provoked it. That Miss Camilla deliberately attacked my reputation was too trivial to lose him what little happiness he had. Without Wes to approve or disapprove, I could feel no concern with what Miss Camilla said.

Going to my room, I heard a board creak as the house settled for the night, and its sound was somehow like Wes's step. His brief, aching image moving with swift, casual grace toward me was created among the shadows of the hall. Within me something writhed and cried out wildly, though I made no sound. For a breath it was as if Wes was there. But there was no one. The hall stretched empty and only the shadows kept me company. Little I cared for gossip or shame or lying slander now.

It was with heavy reluctance that I dressed one morning a week or so after Mr. Poteat's visit, to go to the mill. My distaste at shouldering the responsibility had not lessened, but I could not escape it. At home I found myself worrying about conditions at the mill, recalling problems I'd left unsolved or work I had left unfinished. Irritably I tried to push them away and shut out any concern for the mill, but inevitably they returned, persistent and nagging.

Nevertheless, I had little heart for what I knew I must face and I told Mitty in the kitchen I wanted no breakfast. She didn't insist. Maybe just coffee'd be best, she said as she filled my cup and, across the table, had hers.

She glanced at me sharply, her face puckered with concern. "Maybe you'd better put off going a day or so. For a fact, you don't seem to feel too spry."

"One day is as good as another, if I have to go."

"You might feel more like it tomorrow . . ."

"I don't think I'll ever feel like it."

She gazed at me thoughtfully. "You're wrong, dearie. You'll feel better."

I did not deny it but she read doubt in my face.

"You'll see," she promised me. "Right now, the part that feels, feels glad or feels down in the dumps, is like a finger you give a hard lick with a hammer. But it'll begin feelin' again and carin' again before long."

"I don't want to care again," I told her flatly.

"No," she said gently, "but you will. That's what's wonderful and awful, both at once. We ain't allowed to stop feelin' and carin'. In a way, nature is sort of policeman. He lets you loiter along with your not carin' and then he orders you to 'come out of it and get goin'.' "

"I suppose it's a law that we have to care, Mitty?" I asked bitterly, and she nodded solemnly.

"Yes, dearie, it's a law."

But driving down the hill road a few minutes later, I felt that I was outside of Mitty's law. Never again could I care desperately and terribly, again feel deeply and wildly—about anything. The frozen numbness permitted only a sluggish stir of emotion, like the dull anger I felt as I neared the mill gate, because from here the mob of men had come to Hickory Hill.

To blame all the mill people was neither just nor rational and I could not, with reason. Fear had sent them to Hickory Hill that night. Even the stone had been flung on an impulse; had been the defiant gesture of fear goaded to daring. Yet unjust though it was to blame them, I could not forgive them for Wes.

Turning Moppet in at the gate, the vast, familiar rising and falling moan of the mill machinery surrounded me and, hitching Moppet, I crossed the millyard, feeling the slight, steady trembling of ground beneath my feet. When I entered the office Darty Land looked over his spectacles and, leaving his desk, sidled forward to meet me, grumbling disapproval.

"What the dickens do you mean traipsing down here this soon," he demanded. "You ought to be at home taking care of yourself."

"I had to come back sometime, Darty. I'm all right. So don't worry."

He shrugged in resignation, pulling a chair up for me beside his desk.

"Well, seeing you're here, reckon we might as well go over a few things. There's enough trouble to keep us both busy worryin', I expect."

I accepted the chair, and asked what kind of trouble he meant.

"All kinds," he answered gloomily. "If anything can go wrong in a cotton mill that's missed this one, I never heard of it. Production down, costs up. Equipment going to hell and hands laying off!"

Controlling his disgust, he gave me a more factual report. Equipment failures had been neither unusual nor serious, but enough of 'em to slow production. Neither was there anything unusual about hands laying off the job. Coming from farms like most of 'em had, the habit of planting, tending and picking, then resting a spell, still hung on. But lately layoffs had increased so sharply that the spare hands reserve—the system by which mills manned the jobs of workers who took a day off—was running low.

That wasn't all, he said grumpily. We'd been turning out too many seconds. Moreover, the quality of yarn coming out of the spinning room was off; and that meant too much breakage. None of 'em serious, taken singly. But together they slowed production. We were turning out gray goods to fill back orders from convertors. If we failed to deliver by specified dates, the goods would rot on our shelves. For the convertors, unable to have it processed and in manufacturers' hands for fall selling, would cancel their orders.

"We got to deliver those orders as per contract. We need the money. Production will be at a standstill when they install the new machines, but wages and cost will go on. And don't forget. The first installment on that loan with Carr, plus interest, comes due before long."

"Darty," I asked, "are these things you mention, hands laying off, breakage, slowing up . . . is it just a run of bad luck?"

"Didn't say it was luck," he corrected me.

"Then why are they happening—all at once, Darty? Isn't there a reason?"

He shifted restlessly in his chair. "Sure. And it's always the reason when a mill starts falling apart. . . . The people. There's still bad feelin' among 'em. So they lay off the job, turn out sloppy work, neglect equipment. They plain don't give a damn if the mill goes to hell and that's all it takes to send it. Ed Wangle ain't helping. Keeps 'em riled up about the new machines. And there's something else. That bunch going up to Hickory Hill . . ." He broke off, confused and apologetic. "Sorry, Miss Jess . . ."

"It's all right, Darty," I told him. "But what does that night have to do with the difficulties at the mill?"

"Since that happened, they're uglier than ever."

When I demanded sharply, "Why should they be?" he rubbed his jaw thoughtfully.

"Here's the way I figure. Inside they ain't proud of that bunch trying to throw a scare into a woman. And it turning out . . . like it did . . . Lot of 'em knew Wes—seen him about for years, besides the time he hung around a spell meaning to learn the business. And nobody who knew Wes could help takin' to him."

Hiding a twist of pain at his words, I nodded. I said, "I know," and in an aching flash of memory saw Wes again as I first saw him across Miss Camilla's table.

I said bitterly, "I should think they would feel kinder—not uglier toward his mill."

He shook his head. "It don't work like that. The fellers mixed up in it belonged to the mill, so the others sorta feel they're guilty too. They figger you blame all of 'em and they're waiting to see how you'll take it out on 'em. So they turn ugly to get in the first lick."

"They're wrong," I said dully. "I won't take it out on anyone. It wouldn't bring Wes back. I've never believed they meant it to end . . . as it did."

Darty's nod was distressed. "They don't know that, you see. And there's been rumors. One—that the sheriff was coming to round up all who went up the hill . . . throw 'em in jail. There's been lot of talk. The mill was going to shut down. Their credit at the store would be cut off . . . dozens more just as crazy. That's why they're acting up and letting production go to hell."

Bleak discouragement settled upon me, and with it my earlier repugnance for the mill and the struggle.

I said despondently, "I don't know what we can do. If they are willing to let the mill go to hell, as you say, how can we stop it? We can't keep going unless they do their jobs."

Darty's small eyes peered concerned over his spectacles. "I'll admit it ain't easy," he consoled. "But when nothin' terrible happens to 'em, it'll blow over."

"But you said we must make delivery to the convertors—that we need the money—"

He waved a deprecating hand. "Now, Miss Jess, you know I always see the darkest side. It may not be so bad. If production picks up we'll get straightened out."

"I hope you're right," I said hopelessly as I rose to leave. I'd come back tomorrow, I told him—and every day. But now I wanted to stop by the Luckett house to see Mady and Poky, Cade too when he came in for dinner.

"Gosh! Almost forgot," Darty exclaimed, "to tell you. Mrs. Handy pulled out . . ."

On my way to the door I wheeled. "Pulled out?"

"Yep. Packed up and left two or three days ago. Daughter went off with some man, I hear. Her ma took out after her. Had it on my mind to tell you . . . didn't hear about it 'til yesterday. I know you—"

I didn't wait for him to finish, but turning, hurriedly left the office. I was anxious. With no one to defend them I was fearful of what Dude Luckett might have inflicted to satisfy the appetite of his swaggering, bullying arrogance. Impatiently I thought, Darty should have told me at once, then changed it to, I should have come before.

In my anxiety I was only vaguely aware of the occasional millworker I passed on my way to the Luckett house and paid little attention to the wooden defiance I glimpsed in their faces. Nor did the absence of even a single nod of recognition impress me as significant. Hastening up the hill, I crossed the narrow stoop of the house and knocked briskly on the half-open door and called Mady's name down the dogrun hall.

When there was no answer I called again sharply, "Mady! Are you in there, Mady?" Then I saw her. She came up the hall, Poky on her arm. And I had the odd sensation that the grave eyes did not see me.

Stooping, I pulled her close when she reached the doorway, giving a quick sigh of relief at finding her unharmed.

"I hear Mrs. Handy left," I explained. "I wondered if you all were . . . all right. I would have come sooner but . . ." I hesitated. "But . . . I couldn't. I'll wait to see Cade . . ."

She said tonelessly, "You don' have to wait. Cade air home now."

"Cade's home?" I was surprised. "He isn't at the mill?"

Only then was I struck by a difference in Mady; an intangible, disturbing difference. I asked swiftly, "Is Cade sick, Mady?"

Her eyes looked up at me and I found the explanation for my uneasiness lay in the unnatural brightness that glazed the brilliant blue of her eyes. In sudden fear, I demanded, "What's wrong, Mady? Is it Cade? Is he sick?"

"Hit ain't account a bein' sick," she told me. "Hit's somethin' else." Her voice like her eyes was a glossy and shallow tonelessness.

"Where is Cade?" I asked. "Is he inside?"

Before she could reply I sped past her down the hall and paused at Cade's open door and looked in. He was there, seated on the side of his bed, fully dressed. When he saw me he stood up slowly, warily as an old man would, holding his body stiffly erect.

Quietly I asked, "What's the trouble, Cade?"

He said deprecatingly, "Hit air nothin' much, Miz Carr'bee."

"But what is it?" Puzzled, I went toward him. "I don't understand."

I heard Mady's voice, still expressionless and somehow terrible, from the doorway.

"Show 'er, Cade."

Reluctantly he unbuttoned his shirt and with embarrassment bared his boyish back and chest.

"Hit war Mr. Luckett did it," the expressionless voice spoke from the doorway again.

I stood silent, choked by storming, wrenching fury at what I saw. Cade's back, welted and raw with purplish, sickening slashes where the strap in Dude Luckett's fist had lashed again and again.

When I cried, "But why?" again it was Mady who answered.

"Mr. Luckett say Cade spoke uppity," the blank voice said, "and he done it. Mr. Luckett war right bad lickered up."

Now I understood the blank eyes and the strange, placid terror of Mady's voice. They were the eyes and voice of hysteria. I thrust down my anger, with effort held my voice calm. Kneeling beside her and holding her, I reached out for Cade.

"It won't ever happen again," I promised. "Never again. I swear it to both of you."

"Mr. Luckett air gone," Mady offered. "He left right after he whupped Cade. The next day. He ain't say where to. Just up and went."

The blue eyes met mine, blank and depthless, like the painted, unseeing eyes of a doll. "Mady," I said. "Mady! It's all right now. It's all right, Mady!"

She continued to stand stiff and wide-eyed a moment, and then suddenly as if my voice broke through the wall shutting off and damming emotion, she raised her hands over her face and, her shoulders hunched like an old woman's, trembled with quiet weeping. Once, as she wept, she pinched up a corner of her dress between thumb and finger and wiped away one of her tears that had splashed on Poky's nose.

While her sobbing melted and washed away the pressure walled behind the blank eyes, I told her. She and Cade were coming with me to Hickory Hill.

"You can't stay here alone," I explained at Cade's dubious look. "And until we can make some arrangement, I'll know you're all right. We'll pack up your clothes. Just what you'll need for a few days."

Cade was still doubtful. "We wouldn't want to be puttin' you out none."

"You're not putting me out," I assured him. "I want you to come . . ."

We went down the hill, Mady holding Poky's hand; I carrying the scanty bundles of clothes, our progress slow because of Cade's sore, stiff back. As we went, the noon whistle sounded and the street of the mill village teemed with people on their way to their hasty dinners, and I was suddenly conscious as earlier I was not, of the hostility on the faces at sight of me. I told myself defiantly that I didn't care. I would not let myself be affected; that what they thought was of no concern one way or the other.

I was less impervious, however, than I pretended. The discouragement driven from my mind by outraged anger at Dude Luckett's brutality now returned to overwhelm me. Unreasoningly, I saw the mill only as a place where meanness and ignorance could inflict pain upon helpless children, as a place of suspicion and grudging distrust.

When Mady and Poky were in the buggy I helped Cade pull himself painfully up to the seat. Taking my place, I jerked impatiently at the reins, swinging Moppet around and making her prance in surprise at the unaccustomed treatment. I wanted only to get away from the mill, to escape from its ugliness.

I was not allowed to escape. For as I turned Moppet out the gate, with a raucous whoop a band of half-grown boys broke from the low growth that bordered the road and dashed toward the buggy. Yelling and catcalling, their grinning faces alight with glee, they ran alongside, flicking Moppet with switches, hanging on the sides and back of the buggy.

From the confusion of jeers I caught only a few phrases, but their coarseness was enough to prove the offensiveness of all. Cade's face flushed with anger, and I had to handle Moppet with one hand and with the other prevent him from jumping to the road to give combat. He shouted challenge to the boys in the road, calling their names, and they yelled back names I knew they would not have dared call if from their elders they had not picked up their attitude of contempt.

Holding my face expressionless, I concealed my indignant fury. These young hoodlums should not know that the names they hurled could hurt me. I did not have to pretend long. One of the boys, older than the others, ran at Moppet's heels, flicking her with a switch, making her dance and skitter; her eyes rolling, her muscles quivering in nervous apprehension.

I did not know where the switch cut her or if it cut her at all. But she gave a sudden snort of outraged fear, her ears went back and I felt a lunging jerk at the reins. Then, neck stretched and body low to the ground, she was bolting headlong, the buggy careening and skidding, leaving the mill boys behind.

The frantic beat of her hooves mingled with Poky's delighted screams of approval, while the buggy lurched and tilted and I yanked savagely at the reins. The brush and rocks along the side of the road were a rushing, sickening blur; my arms were wrenched and aching in their sockets, my body drenched with cold sweat. I braced my body, sawing fiercely on the reins, the leather cutting and burning the palms of my hands, and a choking lump of fear rising in my throat. And Moppet still plunged on, showing no sign of slackening.

My strength was giving out, I felt. The force of my pull on the reins weakened and my arms throbbed and pained. I could not hold on much longer. Then Moppet was tossing her head, fighting the bit but slackening, beginning to respond a little. She was slowing down. . . .

She came finally to a halt, quivering and sweat-soaked, her breathing a groan of weariness, her sides heaving. Getting down from the buggy, I stroked her neck and talked, soothing her until she grew calmer. Returning to my seat, I picked up the reins again, and Moppet wearily now and sedately ambled up the road.

Only then did reaction set in. My stomach felt hollow and trembling, I was icy cold, my teeth chattering. A state caused, no doubt, partly by fright but by something more. By sick fury and disgust and my hopeless knowledge. I could not go on with the struggle. I was beaten, and if I refused to recognize and accept it I was also a fool. There was even a sense of relief and release in defeat. Now I need not attempt what had become a sheer physical impossibility. To force myself to the mill was as unreasonable as egging myself to walk through a stone wall. I didn't care if I never saw the mill again as long as I lived.

That night after supper, while Mitty took the children up to inspect their rooms and prepared a hot bath for Cade's sore body, I paced from sitting room to kitchen and back to sitting room. Worn to weariness, yet unable to rest, I shuddered away—will-less and strengthless—from the problems that pressed in upon me. I did not even know how to run the mill without Darty's help, and the struggle to save it seemed hopeless. And without Wes to strive for—meaningless. Why should I worry? I thought irritably. I cared nothing for the fate of the mill—of anything. Even the clear child voices calling back and forth upstairs were reminders that they too were a problem; and one which promised no easy solution. Who would willingly take on the responsibility of three children?

Now they trooped downstairs, Poky's feet plopping awkwardly against the steps—and my rasped nerves. But I forced myself from the doldrums. It wasn't easy. Mitty had given each a big red apple "near 'bout too pritty to eat," Cade said, but all three were munching away noisily while Poky, with Colonel barking at his heels, dashed madly through the rooms, his small homely face ecstatic.

Mady's eyes sought mine in apology. "Hit's the fust time he ever be in a runnin' house," she explained. "At home iffen he run, ther folks next door knock on ther wall 'count o' the noise." She offered, "Iffen you're feared he'll break yore pritty things I kin stop him."

Ashamed, I said quickly, "No—no Mady. Let Poky run."

Poky ran. Round and round the circling path through sitting room, hall and dining room, his face radiant, his voice calling wildly, "Mady, Poky run. Mady, Poky run."

Mitty said, "That child'll be winded," and as the gnomelike figure hurtled past again, broke into laughing. Then everyone was laughing, even Cade—even me—Poky, lurching drunkenly, loudest of all. Between us, creating such a din, I did not hear the back door open and close or footsteps that crossed the kitchen—I heard nothing. But wiping my eyes, I glanced up and found Mr. Dolph in the doorway, the whip swinging over his arm, the bad eye stabbing in all directions. Then I was running toward him, calling, "Mr. Dolph! Mr. Dolph!" I found myself in his big arms, heard him saying, "Well sir, I'm whupped. Whupped down for fair!" I was calling the wide-eyed children over to meet him, he was shaking Cade's hand and saying, "Sir, your servant," and, "Ma'am, I'm honored," to Mady. Then he looked down at Poky, infinitesimal beside his great height, and at sight of the upturned wide-grinned face, he stooped and as gently as a woman picked him up.

"This," he announced portentously, "is a cumber as you would go a far piece to see." And everyone was laughing again—at what I'm sure no one had the slightest idea.

Later I sat at the kitchen table with him as he ate the bounteous supper Mitty had spread, and while she and the children chattered in the sitting room, he and I talked. It being near to April, he said, the bad eye dancing and darting, the gypsies had come to Atlanta as per custom and made camp over in Cobb County, also as per custom. And Zeb McNair had showed him the newspaper piece he'd saved about my sorrow. And when he read it he come lickety-split.

I told him how glad I was, and asked about Lorny and the little cumbers. They was right as a trivet, he said gravely, but still give him trouble 'bout water. Which being according to nature he didn't complain. Not but what with the waggin and six little cumbers it war wearin'.

"Six, Mr. Dolph?" I exclaimed. "But I thought there were only four."

His nod was portentous. "And you thought right, ma'am. Four there war. Two to eight. There ain't four now. Ma'am, Lorny blessed me with twins."

"Twins, Mr. Dolph?"

"Twins I said and twins I mean. Two leetle gels which added to four leetle gels adds up to a round half-dozen, and"—his glance was significant—"consider'ble water."

I saw that this was no laughing matter, so quickly I served him more coffee. And as solemnly as before he went on.

"There is a saying, ma'am, 'be keerful whut ye wish fur lest ye git it.' And truer word never war spoke. For along of being fond of one leetle gel—I'm speaking of Things in General, understand—I wish fur a leetle gel of my own. And whomsoever give me my wish has been whut I call over-freehanded."

Suddenly his gravity exploded and his laughter rang out through the house so contagiously that it brought Mitty to the doorway. "My," she said, "it's good to hear laughing in this house again." And I thought of Wes who had laughed in this house, the dark head thrown back.

When Mitty returned to the children, Mr. Dolph and I continued to sit at the kitchen table, and it was then that we spoke of Wes. And though I said little, I knew he sensed the despair that darkened for me the aspect of life—and of living.

Across the table the good eye regarded me with a simple honesty that imparted earnest goodness to every word he uttered. "When I know by the newspaper piece whut had been done to a heart whut I know is a lovin' heart, I comes lickety-split. To see whut help I can give."

He was so true—he was so good, and I told him so. But there was nothing that he—that anyone—could do. Nothing I wanted done. From the bottom of my heart I was grateful, I said. But there was—nothing.

His steady regard did not falter when he spoke slowly. "I am looking into a face whut I knows through the years, and never afore have I see it like this. I take it"—his voice was amazingly gentle—"that the dander is down."

I could not be otherwise than frank with him so I admitted that the dander was down. If I could only go away, I said. Perhaps sell Hickory Hill and with Mitty find such a little house as we'd had in Battle Hill. Get away—from everything.

For a while we sat silent. Then he asked, "Little one, recollecks you the time I war laid low by rheumatiz and laid off by Poteat & Whidby?"

I said that I recollected.

"It war then that Poteat & Whidby without so intendin' done me a favor. Fur being laid low and nothin' to do give me time to study out things. And it come to me clear that my life war"—he held up his empty cup—"empty like this here cup. And I had to fill it up or I war whupped. And for fair."

As he carefully replaced the cup, his good eye came back to me. "So fill it I did. With cumbers. And any man whut say a cupful o' cumbers ain't full and runnin' over will have me to whup."

He tilted his chair back on its rear legs, the good eye turned to the ceiling. "I comes here tonight," he spoke musingly, "expectin' to find a sorrowful heart and the dander sunk mighty low. And it do my heart good when I found them." His head jerked toward the sitting room and the children's voices. "Fur ain't nothin' can jack up the dander like a cupful of cumbers; or keep it up; or make you pull any hill whut you got to pull."

He had, I realized, misconstrued what he found, and quickly I undeceived him. What he meant, I explained, could not be. The responsibility was . . . too great. They—now my head moved toward the sitting room—needed and should have far, far more than I had to give.

The nod he gave me from time to time indicated—I thought—agreement. But when he said, "Yessir, the dander is low—mighty low," I knew the nods had affirmed not my words but his estimate of my dander. After that he was silent for another while, rocking slightly on the legs of his chair, his eye fixed upon the ceiling. Then he brought the chair back to earth and his eye back to me.

"It ever be a quare thing to me how the mind, like this here onery eye, go dartin' about willy-nilly. How it go back to a day when I war ordered to place a leetle gel whut had no home or no fokes. 'Genteel but cheap' they ordered, and my mind thinks on a number of ladies whut would likely take her. Most of 'em lived easier than Mrs. McDaniel and in some ways had more to give that leetle gel. But when I figger on no-count givin', she took the cake."

"No-count givin', Mr. Dolph?" I questioned doubtfully.

"No-count I said and no-count I mean, though not meaning how it sound. Fur 'long o' seein' differ'nt kinds of givin'—and lovin' too, I figger that no-count love whut don't stop to count whut it give, is the only kind to be trustin'. And one thing you can bank on. When its dander is up, which it generally is, it'll move Stone Mountain."

Before I could speak, he swept on. "So I taken up the question of that leetle gel with Mrs. McDaniel and clear I recollecks how her face—whut warn't ever whut you'd call a soft face—took on a set look that tells me the dander is up. She say sharp-like to me, "Whut you mean coming out here to ask me such a fool thing. Go on, fetch her to me. Whut leetle I got is hers too, so don't dawdle. . . ."

His eye meeting mine was almost stern, his voice firm. "She wan't young then and she war pore as a Methodist preacher. But she knew she'd give you the best she could, so there warn't no need to be countin'. I figger she never did."

I could see him but dimly through tear-blurred eyes. "She never did."

"And if I recollecks rightly, the dander stayed up right peart."

"The dander stayed up. It's still up."

He nodded and cocked his head toward the other room, smiling fondly at Mitty's voice as it spoke of the batch of teacakes she'd be baking tomorrow. Then he came back to me. "Still givin' in her no-countin' way, I figger."

"Still . . ." I could manage no more. But after a moment I tried again. "Mr. Dolph . . ."

He said quietly, "You don't need to say it. I see in your face whut warn't there afore. And it do my heart good. It tells me the dander is up."

With difficulty I corrected, "Not up. But rising."

Staunchly he told me, "Whut rises is bound to git up."

"It is getting up," I admitted, and then because it was, I was able to say what I wanted to say. How I could never repay him for saying what I needed to hear; for reminding me—not of Mitty's no-countin' love alone but all who had given such love to me—including himself; and last for getting my dander up—which I assured him was rising higher by the second.

In my gratitude, which perhaps the rising dander intensified, I no doubt overdid it. His face turned redder and redder, attaining after a little a violent red I had never seen on another face. His neck twisted so constantly and so vigorously that in alarm I concluded my thanks. And waited while he pulled the big handkerchief out and blew his nose so lustily that Petey, asleep under his cover, burst into ear-splitting song.

Mr. Dolph turned in his chair to circle the room with his eye, coming at last to the cage in the window. "Well sir!" His voice was awed. "If it ain't another fool bird." Then, overcome by sudden remembrance, he laughed so heartily that he must blow his nose again, which sent Petey into another gale of song. How long this would have gone on I can't say. But just then Poky's excited grin peeped around the door with Mady's and Cade's behind it, and Mr. Dolph, springing up with a great roar, scooped Poky up under his arm and headed back to the sitting room. With Poky enthroned on his knee—and the bad eye gamboling madly—he launched into tales of hair-raising adventures, all mythical, but drawing Cade and Mady to sit on the floor before him, their charmed eyes on his face. He had wrestled an alligator "twenty-four foot long if a inch," outwitted any number of "reptile snakes thick as my arm"—all along of travelin' about in them dazzly little waggins. Then, in answer to their plea, he must tell of the gypsies; of making camp, of singing at night round the big fires. He broke off to sing, and with as much dash as if he was young and handsome:

> "*'Oh gypsy . . . oh gypsy,'*
> *The fair young maid cried,*
> *'So handsome ye be*
> *I would fain be your bride.'*
> *'I be sorry, sweet maid,*
> *But a gypsy must roam.*
> *Moreover six wives be*
> *Awaitin' at home.'* "

Carried away by his own music, he put Poky down in order to dance what he called "The Fandango," the bad eye joining in madly. Then, laughing and gasping for breath, he collapsed helplessly in his chair, while the rest of us laughed as helplessly.

It was near to midnight when, explaining that Lorny expected him, he left; and we walked across the yard to watch him get in the gypsy wagon and, with a prodigious pop of the whip that as usual failed to touch the horse, plunge down the hill. As under the April night sky with its curved young moon we sauntered back to the house, I told Cade and Mady that they would remain with me, that Hickory Hill was to be their home. And though they said but little and that little was stiff and stilted in the way of children, their eyes, when they said good night and went up to bed, left no doubt as to what they thought.

Later, in my nightgown I stood in my window and again looked out at the night, and I felt that something of its soft serenity moved across my heart. And while it neither eased hurt nor lightened sorrow, the heart was no longer all-despairing; nor was it rebellious because life reached out and drew it back into tumult. Standing by the window, I leaned my head against the frame and wept as I had not wept since Wes died. But even as I wept, I knew from somewhere I had received strength with which to face the struggle ahead.

Next morning I woke in the darkness that precedes dawn and stared at it bleakly, the mill and what it encompassed flowing over me again. I recoiled with sickening distaste from its ugliness. But with night's almost imperceptible lifting, the strength Mr. Dolph had helped me find was revived.

Getting up, I went through the sleeping house to the kitchen and put on a pot of coffee, and back in my room dressed stiff-fingered in the chill silence. Passing their doors, I looked in on the children. On Cade, then Mady who slept, Poky's head on her stomach, her face soft and serene with sleep. I jotted a note for Mitty, then standing at the stove, drank a hasty cup of coffee, my mind considering and discarding the means by which I would do—what I had to do.

As, groping in the dark yard, I fed Moppet and led her to the traces I went over what was to be done. I must learn all I could, overcome the antagonism of the mill hands, get the mill back on sound operation and production back to normal. The new equipment must be installed when delivered and the hands trained to handle it. The quality of goods must be improved in order to increase greater demand and higher prices if the mill was ever to be free of the debt with which Miss Camilla's squandering inefficiency had burdened it. But looming nearer than these—and far more disturbing—was the note due Algernon Carr's bank. That, I must do something about—though I had no idea what the something would be. I had neither the money to meet it nor ideas as to where I could get it. Nevertheless, I must do something. This was of immediate and crucial concern. Others could wait at least for a while.

Though I knew that each of these problems must be dealt with, unhappily this knowledge supplied no solutions. Neither was I inspired by my cup of coffee nor the ride through the chill spring darkness with its first trembling hint of impending light.

When I drove the buggy through the gate and brought Moppet to a halt, I realized it was earlier than I had thought. The mill still slept. Its gaunt timber buildings were dense looming shadows against the fainter darkness of sky as I crossed toward the office through heavy cottony mist. On its slope the mill village was a black patch of sleep and silence, unrelieved by the faint, flittering yellow of even a single lamp. And the door of the office was locked. I would have to wait until Darty arrived, to get in. Wrapping my coat about me, I sat on the top step of the flight leading up to the office door, finding it extremely hard and amazingly cold.

My mind continued to revolve but now, as if clarified by the cold air, it marshaled circling thought into line. First, I wanted the mill to be a sound and profitable business enterprise, for I suddenly knew that was necessary before it could become more, have importance and meaning that transcended financial success. And that I wanted for the mill. I wanted it to have the respect of the community, not merely because it was prosperous but because it had imagination, generosity, taste; was trustworthy, fair and honorable. In other words, I wanted it to have a good character, to be held as a worthy man is held in respect by those who know him.

To achieve this would not be easy. It would be hard and wearing and tedious. It would often be ugly, frequently disheartening, sometimes almost hopeless. But it was a job that had to be done.

Sitting there in the half-night of dawn, I remembered how I had wanted to save the mill for Wes, had hoped he would find the incentive to take charge, be its head and have pride in his work. It was too late for that now. But when in desperation and despair after his death I felt that the mill no longer mattered, I had been wrong.

I realized now that this was his work. Work from which barriers, deeply and darkly buried, had barred him—but it was still his work; work to be done. To complete it as he would want it would be a far worthier monument than those of carved and unfeeling stone. It was the only service I could render him now. His work had become my fight.

Huddled there on the cold wooden step as the gray dawn spread in the east and washed down the walls of the buildings with pale, shadowless light, I acquired a certainty of purpose that had never been mine before. And a strengthened resolution that, recalling my earlier brooding apathy, now saw it as craven and abhorrent. It was as if, braced against the locked door of the office, I unconsciously had left girlhood behind me and become, completely and wholly, a woman.

The whistle that would startle the workers from sleep ripped the dawn just as Darty's figure, sidling through the gate, came toward the office. Seeing me, he stopped short and, peering over his glasses, demanded sternly what I meant by roosting on the step like a hen.

I told him, "I've been thinking. About the mill."

"Seems like you could find a better time and place than—"

"Darty, yesterday you said what the hands think is behind the trouble we're having at the mill. Didn't you?"

He had drawn a ring of keys from his pocket and now felt among them for the one to the office. And as he answered, "Yep," he didn't look up.

"You said," I went on, "that they expected me to be down on them and got in the first lick by being sullen and unfriendly. Didn't you?"

The right key found, his eyes lifted to peer at me. "Yep," he said again. Then, "What you got on your mind?"

I told him if he was right (and I believed he was), then all the trouble arose from misunderstanding. The hands, convinced of my animosity toward them; I equally convinced of theirs for me.

I looked at him inquiringly and he nodded.

"Then before we can clear up the trouble in the mill we must clear up the misunderstanding. Mustn't we?"

"Sure. The question is, how go about it?"

"Talk to them."

His laugh was grim. "How? One at a time? To hundreds of 'em?"

"Of course not. Call them together. You must have some place for meeting with them."

"Don't ever meet with 'em."

"Then how do you ever get orders or policy or praise to them?"

"Through department heads."

"Then use that way now. Have the overseers send all hands to the cotton shed. I can stand on the loading platform."

Standing before me, swinging the keys on his finger, he looked down at me worriedly. "I ain't sure it'd be smart."

"Well, it certainly couldn't do any harm." I protested.

He retorted dryly, "Any crowd that big can get out of hand. And a bunch of riled-up lintheads is like a keg of dynamite." He pursed his lips. "If I was fool enough to let you do it—what'd you say to 'em?"

"I—don't know—yet—exactly. I'll have to feel my way at first. I want to be frank with them—and honest—tell them what we plan to do—"

He stood without speaking a moment, his thumb and forefinger rubbing the key between them.

"I reckon I'm being a plain damn fool," he said grudgingly, "but it just might—I say might—work. But for God A'mighty's sake be careful what you say to the peppery fools."

I promised, and with a muttered "I'll see that they get there," he shrugged. "Preach, make a speech, talk at 'em, all the same thing. Feeling like they do, most likely won't believe a word you say. And touchy—? If they start, there ain't a prayer of stoppin' 'em."

He swung on his heel and sidled off to give instructions.

While I waited for his return I made a hasty effort to organize what I would say to the hands. I realized with horror that my mind was suddenly blank, incapable of shaping a single logical sentence; a state which no amount of jogging improved. I was still making frantic efforts when Darty returned to take me over to the cotton shed, and, helping me up to the loading platform, muttering he scurried off and left me alone.

I had never before realized that the loading platform was so high and so vast and so bare until I stood on it alone and faced the expanse of ground where the mill hands would gather. It stretched empty now, under the dawn swirled in the rising mist. And standing there, I was seized by the feeling that this had happened before, that a hundred times I had stood like this facing emptiness.

Then I knew from where the sense of familiarity came. Knew that in a hundred dreams I had stood alone facing, not colorless dawn, but the luminous glowing of the ruby carpet that stretched endlessly before me; feeling that all in the world that mattered had gone out of it. That nothing was left—or no one.

For a moment I was bewildered. Which, I wondered, was dream—which reality? Then I knew that it didn't matter. For in both dream and reality I was left desolate—and alone. In the dream, by what I did not know nor would I ever know. In life, left desolate and alone because Wes was gone from it.

The work whistle forced me back to actuality and, squaring my shoulders, I watched through the whitish mist as the hands trooped and jostled down the steep street of the village from their houses, and were directed by Darty's pickets in my direction. Gradually the space before the loading platform filled, the faces puzzled and curious as they approached; then, recognizing me, taking on the defensive animosity I had encountered yesterday as I left with Cade, Mady and Poky.

As I looked at the close-packed mass of bodies that spread across the bare stretch of mill ground, I knew suddenly that Darty had not exaggerated their explosive possibility.

But this sudden knowledge, I warned myself, I must not by a glance or word betray. I must conceal, too, that other fear which was not concerned with antagonism or violence, but with plain and simple stage fright. It glued my dry and swollen tongue to the roof of my mouth, locked my jaws and throat in an iron vise, and throttled my voice to dumbness.

Yet, I sensed that they waited, the sea of their faces turned up to mine, closed and cold and guarded. I had to speak. I had to say something . . . anything. . . .

Somehow I forced sound from my throat, sound so strange I covered it quickly with a cough and, stumbling and groping for words, began again. Then, like a friendly island in that sea of hostility, I caught sight of Yancy Jackson's lean, rawboned face and fastened on it. I could talk to Yancy, I thought. And I would.

I talked to him, my voice strengthening as I talked. Like one detached I heard it speaking clearly and to the point and, at least, making sense. Then, swept along by what I wanted to say, I forgot to listen. I talked of the misunderstanding that caused worry and anger, explaining that I talked to them now to try and clear up that misunderstanding. I'd heard the rumors that were going around, I added, and they were entitled to know that none of them were true or had any basis in truth. They undoubtedly had heard talk of the mill closing down. Then, at an almost imperceptible nod here and there, I went on. The mill would not be closed down by me. "But," I added, "it might be, by you."

The ranks stirred slightly as feet were shuffled. "Unless you want to keep it going, it might have to close down," I continued. "But I hoped that if I talked to you and told you about the mill as best I could, about our plans and what we hope to do, you would want to keep it running. I am going to tell you so you will not misunderstand what is being done and why."

I caught a quick, warning frown from Darty who stood below me, and knew he cautioned me against revealing too much lest their disapproval and anger be aroused. But I ignored his warning. I was going to put my cards on the table. I would not win them by deception or by concealing unpalatable facts. If I depended on their help to win—and I did—then it was no more than fair that they know the odds against them. I knew I risked their disapproval—perhaps enmity—but that chance I had to take. For this was the way Wes would have played it—all cards on the table, nothing held up the sleeve.

Even as I thought this, I heard my voice speaking of the new equipment which would be delivered soon. Of automatic looms, electric stops, self-winding bobbins. The increased yardage we would get per hour. The smaller number of hands required to operate it.

There was a sullen muttering, but this I had expected. I raised my hand.

"Let me finish." I spoke matter-of-factly, knowing a show of emotion would stir theirs to greater intensity. "The new equipment will require fewer hands, but we plan that only children under fourteen—who shouldn't be working in the mill anyway—will be let out. Husbands, wives, children over fourteen will stay on the job."

Nasal shouted words were flung from somewhere in the crowd, and turning, I faced the direction from which they came.

"Yes," I called, "I know it's hard on a man to lose the wages his children bring in. I know it's a hard squeeze even with their wages to make it do for food and clothes and heat. But with the new equipment and the mill producing as it will, you'll have as much, maybe more than you have now, even *with* the children's wages."

They were wary, but they were interested, too. And a square-built man near the loading platform spoke aloud.

"How?" he asked flatly.

"This is how," I answered. "First—stepping up production. Second—by switching from gray goods to fine-count cottons so we can compete in the market with quality goods. It won't be easy. But if we do it, we increase profits and you'll share in that increase by being paid better wages."

A number of voices called out at once. I answered what I understood as the general meaning.

"I can't tell you how long. That too will depend on you. But I can tell you this. Without new equipment and upped production and quality, the mill can't go on. It hasn't been operating on a sound basis for a long time. Cost is too high and there's too much waste. Of time and money and work. Too many mills are turning out gray goods. As a result, the market is glutted. That's why we have to do what we are going to do. To keep going."

In a swift circling glance I searched those faces which were close enough to read. And though they were intent still and wary, the hostility that had glazed them had given way to an almost imperceptible interest. As if they dared no more—lest it be shattered.

Suddenly any apprehension I might have felt was gone. For I saw them, not as hands or a mill community, but as a group of people made up of good and bad, weak and strong, kind and cruel, but each subject to worry and uncertainty, to grief and hurt. Like me, human and fallible and often afraid.

I forgot Yancy Jackson; I had no need of him now. Instead I talked to all of them, my eyes unconsciously moving from face to face, meeting their eyes. Still matter-of-factly, I told them, "You've heard promises before, some never kept, some not meant to be kept. I won't make promises I can't keep. I can't promise when we'll raise wages, for I don't know. But I say this. We will as soon as it's possible." Then, as a murmur swept among them, I added, "I know that means little, but I ask you to give me a chance. Since I came Darty Land, the new mill manager, has reduced store prices. Paid wages regularly—every week—and paid you in money, not scrip. They haven't been favors and we deserve no credit. We have only done what is fair and right. When the time comes that we raise wages . . . that won't be a favor either. No more than paying your wages on time and not cheating you in the store. You will be paid more because you earn more, and that is fair and right. And this promise I can make. To do my best to be fair. Whether you believe me or not or will give me a chance to prove it. . . . That's up to you to decide."

I paused, looking out at them, wondering what I should say next, and suddenly realized I was through. Yet the faces waited, I saw, still turned up to mine. I couldn't just let them stand there. I must end it somehow. Embarrassed, feeling awkward, I gestured futilely, then admitted the truth.

"I guess I wouldn't be a woman if I knew when I was through talking. Anyway . . . I'm through."

There were a few chuckles and the crowd began to shift with an uncertain restlessness as if unable to resolve itself into individuals again. Then it dispersed swiftly, moving in ragged lines and little groups toward the mill. And as Darty and I walked to the office, he admitted grudgingly that it could have been worse.

"Anyway," I pointed out, "the dynamite didn't blow up."

But he only returned dryly, "Don't brag. It could have."

I did not delude myself that my talk wholly dispelled ill feeling or solved all the difficulties confronting the mill. But production did step up and within a short time was almost normal again. It looked as if we would make delivery on the convertors' back orders on time, Darty admitted, coating his pill of praise in its usual gall.

"Reckon they figured they'd better pitch in or they'd have to listen to you make another speech," he said sourly.

When I replied airily that he had seemed to approve of my talk, he growled, "You ain't no female William Jennings Bryan. But meeting delivery on those orders is worth it."

Nevertheless, there was evidence that my talk had not been as ineffective as Darty pretended. The mill people, though still wary and stiff in their manner, were not openly hostile. They began again to nod and speak when we met, and I made it a point to seem unconscious of any strain of lingering hostility. For now I plunged into learning mill operation from top to bottom; learning not from books, this or that theory, but by actual doing; becoming familiar with each step required to change raw cotton into cloth. And though I failed to achieve the seemingly effortless proficiency of the mill hands who watched me tolerantly, I gradually learned the fundamentals of weaving.

I was always busy now, and though work did not cure grief, it helped me bear it. The aching sense of loss was always there beneath the surface of activity. But work carried me more quickly through the days and left me weary at their close. I did not lie awake so many nights, sleepless in the wide bed, searching the darkness for the ghosts of happiness and lost love. There were still nights when weariness failed to bring sleep—but not so many. I had learned to make tiredness anesthesia for pain.

The mill by day, nights at Hickory Hill with Mitty and the children, formed the pattern of my life. The voices and laughter of Cade and Mady and Poky filled not only the rooms of Hickory Hill but made less bleak the emptiness within me. They held long and extremely grave discussions with Mitty, whom they rightly considered the wisest of mortals. Or with Poky on Mady's lap and Colonel, who had adopted Cade, with his muzzle now on another toe, they listened to Mitty's stories of me when I was "knee-high to a grasshopper." And as anxiously as if I was not at the moment three feet away, waited to learn if I was found the time I got lost "over by Mr. Harbuck's."

Cade and Mady and Poky did not fill the void in my life. Nothing could. But they lightened it and gave me the strength Mr. Dolph had predicted. They warmed the evenings with Mitty at Hickory Hill, until I went wearily up to bed to sleep until time to get up and go off to the mill again. The mill, evenings with Mitty and the children, sleep, and back to the mill. It was not an unhappy or unrewarding pattern.

Now, wrestling at the mill with one crisis after another, barely avoiding one disaster before confronted by another, I often felt that the odds were too heavy for winning, that any one of an infinite number of possible ill winds could sweep the mill to destruction. Of these, the loan with Algernon Carr constituted an alarming and immediate threat. For the date when the first note plus interest must be met, approached; and with what seemed to me incredible speed. For I had no reason to believe that the money to meet it would be forthcoming.

My mind worrying at the problem, I senselessly repeated various *ifs*. If the new machines were installed . . . if we were turning out quality goods . . . But, I reminded myself, the new equipment was not in. The mill was not in full production. It was not making quality goods or selling at quality prices. We did not have the money for the payment or any idea as to where we could get it.

Darty glumly admitted he too was stumped. "I can't figger gettin' a quick thirty thousand dollars, and a slow one won't help. We might scrape up part of it. But not more than half, even if we use operation funds. Then we couldn't meet payrolls or operation costs. Either way we'd go bust."

Thoughtfully, I said what so many times I had said, "If only we had more time."

"But we ain't." Baffled, Darty scratched his gray thatch of hair. "Beats me how anybody figgered they'd get equipment installed and set up and switched over to a new line, to say nothin' of pullin' in the profits, in time to take care of this first payment."

"Didn't Miss Camilla realize how impossible it was, Darty?"

He snorted. "Miss Camilla was thinkin' 'bout gettin' hold of the money. Reckon she counted on talkin' Carr into givin' her an extension. She generally counted on talkin' folks aroun' if she needed to. Generally could, too," he concluded with grudging admiration.

Frowning thoughtfully, I said slowly, "Darty, if Miss Camilla could talk Mr. Carr into an extension, why couldn't I?"

He answered quickly and to the point. " 'Cause you ain't Camilla Carr'bee. You're a harder worker and fairer minded and I'll probably be sorry I said this—you're a sight better head of the mill. Leastways you're learning how to be. But you can't work her kind of spell."

Still preoccupied, I admitted the last. "But it might help if I talked to Mr. Carr," I insisted stubbornly. "Oh, I know you think he made the loan in order to get the mill. But that's only your opinion."

He gazed at me steadily above the rims of his spectacles. "Yep, just my opinion."

"I don't underrate your opinion, Darty," I explained. "You know that. But you might be mistaken. It might help if I asked for an extension."

"Might," he said.

"I know you called what he's trying to do unethical. But it isn't . . . well, illegal . . . is it?"

"Tain't nice but it's legal," he said dryly.

I went on earnestly, "After all, Mr. Carr is well thought of, highly respected. Known as a man of high principles and rigid standards. I'm always reading in the papers of his supporting some worthy movement or another. I mean, he surely wouldn't stoop to shoddy conniving and sharp practice."

"Maybe not," Darty agreed. "I don't claim I can't be as wrong as the next feller. If you think there's a chance of Carr easing up, go ahead."

"He might not, of course. But if there's the least chance he might, I have to take it. I can't just . . . not try?"

Darty shook his head. "Nope, guess not."

The earnestness with which I had spoken had been to convince myself more than Darty that an appeal to Mr. Carr was not hopeless. I had little enthusiasm for the prospect of asking Mr. Algernon Carr for consideration. But, I reminded myself, I too might be mistaken about him. My impression that he found my presence disturbing might be due to no more than the unpleasant incident at Mrs. Plummer's and the knowledge that he had disapproved of my friendship with Laura Lee. Since then, on our rare meetings, he had met me with his customary grave courtesy, and if it was something less than cordial, I told myself that was his way. At least, it was not as if he was a total stranger.

But I did not deceive myself. I knew I would far rather approach a stranger than Mr. Carr. I would go because I had to; because however slim the chance, I must avail myself of it. But I had no illusions regarding my own feelings on the matter. Only the mill could have forced me to it.

In the weeks of worry and struggle, my feeling for the mill had undergone a change. Now whether it survived or not mattered terribly. It mattered because of Mitty; of Cade and Mady and Poky. It mattered because I needed the income it provided for them as well as for myself, for Miss Camilla; it mattered for Darty Land, who without it would be adrift, and because it was the source of livelihood to the mill hands.

These reasons were important, but they were not the most important. The mill was Wes's work left undone, work that had come to me. It had become mine. It was my work. I knew that a woman in business, especially in the South, was a target for criticism. This gave me no concern. My concern was selfishly centered around my personal life and the work I had found.

It was mine. Mine to worry and scheme and plan for, mine to ponder and dream of. The thing I would create with my effort, the design I would achieve. It was a design that even in my thoughts had barely begun to take shape. But one I was certain no other could ever conceive exactly in the same way or find the same fulfillment. Another's dream would be different. Only I could realize mine.

I understood now what it was that men found precious and absorbing in their work—what, at least, a few men found. It was this, the exaltation of using their minds and strength to complete a work, to achieve a fulfillment that must be unique, because each living person was different from every other. This was my work. Nobody was going to take it from me. Not if I could prevent it. Even if I had to seek favors from Algernon Carr.

In the days since my talk with Darty it had become starkly clear that Mr. Algernon Carr offered my only solution. In two weeks the note fell due, and without additional time in which to raise the money I saw no possibility of staving off defeat. Even if granted an extension, I still had no idea where the money would come from. But time at least would give me a lease on hope, so time I must have. And it was this hope that carried me to Mr. Algernon Carr's bank.

Though the City Bank was one of the first established in Atlanta, this did not imply that it was an institution of venerable tradition, since the city had few buildings dated before the 'eighties. But it made up for its lack of age with impressiveness. Its lobby, of immaculately white Georgia marble, was sheathed with ornately carved paneling and an elaborate frieze that portrayed the rising of the New South from the ashes of the old.

However, I was much too absorbed by my errand to be impressed, either by the grandeur or the dignity of the venerable Negro in black alpaca jacket and spotless white gloves who opened the massive door for me, who directed me on my asking to the office of Mr. Carr.

"Straight back to the railin', ma'am. One of the gent'muns will be glad to help you."

Thanking him, I crossed the gleaming expanse of floor to the rail where I finally managed to attract the attention of a stiffly erect gentleman with hair of conservative gray, above a conservative face and wearing a conservative suit. Fixing me with a forbidding eye that warned whatever I wanted was out of the question, he inquired how he might be of service.

When I asked to see Mr. Carr, he literally braced himself for battle, but when I added, "Please say Mrs. Carrebee to see him," he withdrew from the field. Waspishly he summoned a messenger to escort me to a small anteroom. Here a correct young man who dangled a pince-nez —not on his nose but his finger—agreed to find out if Mr. Carr was "available."

He returned presently to inform me that Mr. Carr *was* and conducted me to another door which he opened, at the same time announcing my name.

I stepped into an office which, like the lobby, was lavishly supplied with marble and carved paneling and a great deal of ponderous furniture besides. And displayed on one wall, where it easily met the eye, was a veritable gallery of plaques, medals and framed citations, their Gothic lettering attesting to Mr. Carr's incomparable service for this or that worthy cause. And I wondered if they were offered as proof of his moral rectitude as a doctor's diploma attests his medical knowledge.

Before tall, richly draped windows, at a vast polished desk, Mr. Carr, dark and polished like the desk, studied a document, his head with its glossy black hair bowed as he read. Though he obviously knew of my presence, fully a moment passed before the opaque eyes lifted from the document to admit it. Even then he waited to replace the document in a drawer and jot a few words on a pad which methodically he put in another drawer. Only then did he rise and, in the cold, grave voice I remembered so well, move to greet me and gesture toward the leather chair facing his desk.

Thanking him, I took it, voicing a polite wish for his family's health.

He resumed his chair and I caught a fishlike movement beneath the surface of the still, dark eyes. But when they met mine it was gone.

"Thank you, my wife and son are well," he said quietly.

Neither emphasis nor intonation suggested that he purposely excluded Laura Lee. He spoke as one who did not have and had never had a daughter; as if by omission he would thrust her into the colorless nowhere of things never made and people never born.

I controlled my stir of resentment and the impulse to verify her existence by calling her name, then reminded myself that this was no place for recrimination. I was here on a matter of business and moreover had better get to it.

Trying for a businesslike calm, I explained the purpose of my call.

"Mr. Carr, you probably know that—recently, the controlling interest of Carrebee Mills came to me."

A grave nod and the grave voice admitted the knowledge. "I was sorry to hear of your loss," he said smoothly and, leaning back in his chair, waited, his hands relaxed on its arms.

With a slight bow I recognized his sterile expression of sympathy, then drawing a deep breath, I began to talk of the mill, of the plans for increased production and changing over to quality cottons.

"It means the mill enters an entirely new field," I acknowledged. "But one, we believe, that offers greater opportunity and profit—and in a reasonably short time will mean considerably increased earnings and enable us to put the mill on a sound financial basis."

Eager to inspire in him a share of my own conviction, I unconsciously moved forward to the edge of my chair.

"I know that change usually involves risk, even danger. But in my opinion the danger in this instance lies in refusing to change. For years the mill has tried with old methods to compete with mills equipped with modern, faster machinery and has found it—unprofitable. We are going to change all that. And I have every hope of succeeding. I am convinced that Carrebee can be one of the most prosperous and progressive mills in the state. Someday perhaps in the South."

In my enthusiasm I had escaped, at least for the time, the restraint his presence usually imposed. But now, noticing the tiny, dry twitch at the corner of his mouth, I was enveloped by it again. And feeling very young, I sat silent.

What I felt I would not betray, I told myself, and forced myself to speak again but levelly now and calmly. In view of these plans for the mill, I said, I wished to discuss the loan which had been negotiated with his bank prior to my husband's—to my loss. Obviously our plans could not be put into effect until the new equipment on which delivery was promised was installed and in operation. Even then we would not benefit until our quality goods were produced and sold. The period between now and then would be the most difficult. And to meet the bank's first note would impose an insupportable burden. It had occurred to me that the bank, to protect its heavy investment, might make some sort of adjustment that would give me the time I must have.

He had listened almost unmoving, his face showing neither attention nor abstraction, interest nor boredom. But now his finger tips, forming a steeple before him, beat softly like small noiseless hammers. "May I ask, Mrs. Carrebee," he asked smoothly, "the nature of the—er—adjustment you have in mind?"

"We would like to renegotiate the loan and extend it over a five-year period," I told him. "But if that can't be arranged, we would appreciate more time in which to meet the first note. Due—as you know—shortly. With six months' grace, I am confident we can manage it. Even three months would—we'd be grateful."

I finished and waited, and with a calmness I was far from feeling, watched his face for signs of favorable or unfavorable reaction. But unstirred and dispassionate, it told nothing and his eyes were concealed by his lids, as he gently, almost tenderly, stroked his smooth-shaven cheek as if finding pleasure in the feel of his skin.

Holding my impatience in check, I waited, deriving a measure of encouragement that he allowed me to wait while he unhurriedly considered my request. Perhaps he would give me more time. He must—I had to have it.

But when he finally spoke, his words neither indicated his decision nor concerned our discussion. Yet he spoke as if they followed logically, and with his usual dispassionate quiet.

"I understand, Mrs. Carrebee, that you recently made a most interesting speech to your mill hands."

I said I was surprised that he should have heard of it. I did not say that I was more surprised at the irrelevance of bringing it up now. Though I was.

"In the banking profession it is necessary to know what goes on," he explained sedately. "We have clients, and friends as well, who are connected with cotton. Naturally, they keep their ears to the ground. You will find it difficult to run a mill sub rosa, Mrs. Carrebee."

I replied with asperity that I entertained no such intention, and was tempted to add that he would know far better than I the problems of working sub rosa. But I let it pass. I was here to solve my problem, not to fence words with Algernon Carr.

He accepted my statement with another of his quiet nods. "Your speech has been the subject of considerable discussion among cotton mill interests. Also the changes you have made at Carrebee and those you contemplate making."

Thoroughly nonplused, even annoyed by the prolonged and boring discussion of my unexciting talk to the hands, I spoke impatiently. "Flattered as I am by your interest, Mr. Carr, I'm afraid the changes I've made are not that important."

"How you may regard my interest, Mrs. Carrebee, is not the point. But your innovations at Carrebee are—"

I said, "I don't understand . . ."

"I am sure of that. You are unable to comprehend the damage that can be done by a person who lacks both knowledge and experience. Or how thoughtless sentimentality and blind idealism can disrupt the cotton mill economy of the entire South."

Though he spoke quietly and without emphasis, I was none the less aware that something in the dark morose eyes caused me discomfort.

With as much will as I could summon, I spoke calmly, almost lightly.

"I fear you've had exaggerated reports of my talk, Mr. Carr. I doubt that I said anything momentous enough to threaten cotton mill economy."

The dark eyes, depthless and unwavering, stared across the desk.

"Unless I am mistaken, you told the hands that when mill earnings increased they would share by increase in wages. Am I mistaken, Mrs. Carrebee?"

"No . . . I told them that. It's only fair, if I want their cooperation . . ."

His eyes fixed on mine and for a slow moment we gazed at each other. Then, pushing back his chair, he rose and unhurriedly walked to the window, one pale hand holding the other behind his back. With his back to me, he looked out past the dark folds of drapery.

"It did not occur to you that such a statement endangered the fundamental concepts essential to proper relationship between mill management and hands? That you were attacking the rights and authority of management, which are necessary to preservation of our business system? Your thoughtless, gratuitous commitment to share increased earnings with your hands, which, I understand, seemed only fair to your mind, may well encourage hands in a dozen other mills to demand wages on the same basis."

When I failed to answer immediately, he turned toward the room and, over folded arms, the cold dark eyes waited.

"I find it hard to believe that my words could be so far-reaching or cause such drastic results, even if I were as foolish and mistaken as you believe."

"It is not a question of your words alone, Mrs. Carrebee. There are others—many—who through ignorance or sentimentality, or both, try to undermine and tear down what other men have built by intelligence and work. You aid in the destruction of something you could never build and cannot understand. And your weapons are words . . . speeches such as yours."

The bigotry of his words, the smug self-righteousness of his voice, the very elegance of his broadcloth, all asserting his invincibility, roused my resentment almost to actual anger. Anxious and with a sense of pressure, I had come to talk over the payment which was a heavy and constant burden. I had come in good faith, willing to be advised by superior knowledge and experience, to exert every effort of which I was capable to prove that faith. And I had been lectured like a schoolgirl whose interpretation of the lesson is not as the teacher's—a teacher who rejects all interpretations except that which is his.

I said briskly, "Mr. Carr."

He turned back to the room and regarding me over his folded arms, bowed his head slowly, not speaking.

"Mr. Carr, I came here to discuss the loan you granted Carrebee Mills and an arrangement regarding the first payment. Please—could we settle it? One way or another?"

With another bow, he leisurely returned to his chair, not relaxing within it now but sitting as stiffly erect as a dead man—and certainly as bloodless and cold. He waited for a little, then spoke with calm, judicious gravity, as he had before.

"Mrs. Carrebee, in considering any possible new arrangement regarding your loan, the bank must also consider how it might be affected by your mill policies. Funds extended are not, as you doubtless know, the money of the bank's officers. For that reason, the obligations imposed upon those who administer them are infinitely heavier than the obligation felt by an individual."

I felt a sinking, sickening disappointment as the dispassionate voice went steadily on and my hopes of being granted time in which I could make a desperate attempt to save the mill were crashing around me. Now I knew what his answer would be; Darty had been right about Algernon Carr. He wanted Carrebee Mills for the combine he had shrewdly and ruthlessly created. His desire for the mill, added to his hostility for me, unchanged since that long ago time at Mrs. Plummer's, had made the result inevitable from the first.

Yet even in the wretchedness of defeat which left no chance of saving the mill, the knowledge that as yet he had given me no answer moved across my awareness. The thin lips that so easily could mouth smug righteousness had found it less easy to manage a simple no. I felt there would be satisfaction if I could force it from him; a sort of bitter, miserable compensation to strip him of his pretense of lofty principles and impersonal ideals.

"The bank," he was saying as I drifted back to the meaning contained in his words, "must make decisions on the basis of certain factors which in the decisions of the individual figure less prominently. I hope that is clear."

Somehow I contrived to keep my voice steady.

"Mr. Carr, as yet I've had no answer to my request regarding adjustment of the loan or meeting the first note. I understand that the bank may wish to check—but when may I have an answer?"

The saturnine face with its somber eyes did not change. "You must know the answer, Mrs. Carrebee."

"Then I am to assume that your answer is no?"

The sleek, dark head was once more inclined.

"May I know the reason for the refusal?"

He said smoothly, "The policies you practice at Carrebee provide sufficient reason."

I sat thinking, my eyes on my hands on my lap. Without knowing how I knew, I knew nevertheless that mill policy was not his only reason.

I raised my eyes to meet his. "There are other reasons too—I think."

Again the dark head was inclined.

"I believe I am entitled to know them."

"Mrs. Carrebee, the bank avoids extending loans to mills that practice policies we believe unsound. Moreover, where there is a change of management and policies—as in this instance—the bank may decide the firm becomes a bad risk because of that change. The bank sits in judgment, is obliged to sit in judgment. And regardless of who the party is, when the bank's verdict is unfavorable they must go down."

"And that is the verdict on me, Mr. Carr?"

"Unless you are able to meet your note, plus interest, when it falls due. As you doubtless know, if the note is not met, the whole sum of the loan falls due immediately."

Rising, I stood drawing on my gloves, feeling my face stiff and unnatural, as if it were a wax face that might crack and shatter into thousands of fragments. On impulse I grasped the edge of his desk in my gloved hands and leaned toward him.

"Mr. Carr," I said slowly, gropingly, "you have said 'No' to my request and I accept it. But I am frank to admit that I find your reasons for that 'no' unsatisfactory. You agreed to a loan—an overgenerous loan—when the mill was a far poorer risk than now, far less likely to pull out of the red. It is generally known, Mr. Carr, that banks are not swayed by sentiment. And if this bank considered Carrebee a good risk under Miss Camilla—and a bad risk with me—I believe it must be because of me."

He lifted his eyes and stared at me while I talked, and I saw for the first time, not actual change but a tensing and tightening that drew the sallow skin taut and the mouth to a thin, compressed line. And under the surface of the somber eyes I caught again that brief fishlike glinting. But that face, forbidding as once it had seemed, could no longer intimidate me. And meeting the cold steady eyes that tried, I felt, to stare me down, I held my eyes as steadily upon him.

"It is because of me that you consider Carrebee Mills a bad risk . . . isn't it?"

The unctious voice slid in smoothly, "A bank must consider many factors. We must take into account the welfare of business enterprises of all kinds, in the area of the bank's influence. Naturally, activities or policies that will, in the bank's opinion, unsettle or disrupt . . ."

Deliberately I broke in. "I think you are evading me still, Mr. Carr."

For a moment he sat in the unmoving way that was part of him, his fingers tapping the polished desk. Then he looked at me, the acid smile barely touching his lips. "I wonder if you recall my telling you some years ago that you were a very clever young lady?" His cheeks were even paler, I saw, though his voice was still quiet and betrayed no emotion.

"I do," I said.

"I see no reason to change that opinion. You are a clever young lady."

"That means I am right. That it is because of me?"

"The reasons I gave are valid."

I persisted, "But there is another."

I wondered if at last he would come from behind his mask. His face was paler and so taut it seemed to gleam when light touched it.

"I would prefer not to tell you, Mrs. Carrebee. It is not pleasant."

"That's all the more reason to hear it. For I promise this, Mr. Carr. If your reason is based on truth, I cannot object. If otherwise, I must be vindicated," I said.

"Then you insist on knowing?"

"I do insist."

The slight bow was almost deferential.

"First, Mrs. Carrebee, please remember this is at your wish—not mine." He paused and went on, his grave, composed self again, and, I fancied, finding the telling not unpleasant. For a moment Laura Lee was before me. Laura Lee sitting on a desk at Mrs. Plummer's, swinging the slim silk-clad legs. Laura Lee saying, "I hate Papa. He loves to punish. Mama and Oakes—but he shan't punish me again—ever."

His voice thrust away by Laura Lee, now floated back.

"Loans, Mrs. Carrebee, are made on collateral. But since collateral is only physical property, its value can fluctuate sharply. Naturally, it is essential. But there is another more important collateral—one that is not physical. And in the opinion of the bank, both in making a loan and in the bank's attitude, of far more vital importance."

"Yes, Mr. Carr?"

"That collateral, Mrs. Carrebee, is character. What you are. Who you are. Your reputation. Your background." His slow eyes moved to touch darkly upon my face. "The first point we must consider in one who asks consideration, and our clients as well, is character, Mrs. Carrebee. Is he or she respectable, with nothing to hide? Or . . . is the person in question . . . shall we say—dubious?"

He went to the door and, opening it, stepped gravely aside for me to pass out.

"Good day, Mrs. Carrebee."

The insult had been delivered in his unemotional, measured tones, but its impact was intensified by his quiet, crushing force that seemed to smash across my face. The room and his dark shape melted into a swirling pallid glare in which my body floated oddly hollow and light, with no feeling at all. Pain, rage, humiliation would come later. But now I was incapable of feeling or thought except for a remote wonder that I should remain upright with no visible evidence of his attack. When I found I still tugged at the same glove finger I had been smoothing, I realized that what had seemed days encompassed only a second of time.

For a moment I was shaken by anger. At myself. Why hadn't I lashed out at his pretense of smug righteousness? Thrown Laura Lee in his face—or his wife who was slave to her master? But the anger loosening its hold, I knew had I been able to frame a retort, my throat could not have produced it. I should be grateful that I managed to walk past him, my chin high, my eyes not seeing his face.

Outside I crossed the anteroom, holding my body in a vise of rigid erectness, feeling if I relaxed a single muscle, I would slump in a shapeless, meaningless heap on the floor. Remotely I marveled, yet with grim humor, that I had forced him into the open. I had failed. Neither slipping nor faltering, he had led me into his trap. And I had insisted, as he knew I would, on hearing the reason that he gave with an assumed reluctance, to disguise his dark delight.

As I crossed the lobby with its ostentatious marble and paneling, feeling slowly returned. First there was anger, bitter, rankling, as much at myself for a fool as at Algernon Carr. Then actual sickness that sent me weakly to a marble bench against a ponderous column to sink down, jaws locked, my body cold, my stomach writhing. I heard my name called as from a great distance and, turning blankly, found Oakes Carr before me, a concerned smile on his face.

I managed to greet him, to make intelligible replies to his inquiries. What he said I heard in vague broken phrases, ". . . sorry as the devil to hear . . ." then he broke off, his face darkening. Was there anything he could do? he asked. Any way he could be of help? If there was, he insisted, I must call on him, and I think I promised I would.

"What are you doing here?" I asked, grasping at something to say, not caring what.

"I'm learning the banking business," he told me. "I've even an office.

All my own. Pretty stuffy, but I guess I'd better stop making a fool of myself and settle down. It was time I was growing up."

I made some reply, obvious and inconsequential, and he returned my question.

"Why are you here?"

I told him I had come on business, and he assumed naturally enough it was an unimportant, everyday business such as cashing a check or making a deposit.

"Were you taken care of all right?" he asked.

"Yes," I said, "I was taken care of."

He smiled, said he'd be seeing me and, standing there, the people eddying around us, we exchanged the small courtesies which precede departure. Then feminine voices cried out, "Oakes Carr!" in such obvious delight that we turned just as Callie Peacock bore down upon us, with none other than Renette Colquitt of the Mrs. Plummer days beside her.

Both, I saw, were fashionably, expensively dressed and wore triumphant smiles at meeting Oakes. As they approached I framed a smile—the sort reserved for friends seen only occasionally. But I need not have bothered. For when their eyes turned toward me, though I read recognition, their faces congealed to a stiff, relentless mask and their eyes were glazed and unseeing.

"Call me, Oakes," Renette murmured; her curious myopic eyes crept over me as she spoke. Then, wheeling in stiff-necked dignity, they swept away.

Uncomfortably I dissembled. "Callie seems to have recovered her health," I remarked lightly.

Oakes' face was tight with anger, ignored my dissembling. "Damn them!" he snapped, then red-faced went on, "Jess, you know I don't believe the talk that's being spread around."

I had spent little thought on Mr. Poteat's warning of Miss Camilla's gossip. But now Oakes' fervent protests, more than the slighting by Renette and Callie, told me that already I had been made an object of contempt, had become unacceptable among Atlanta's "nice" people.

Sorry for his embarrassment, I put my hand on Oakes' arm.

"It doesn't matter, Oakes. Don't be upset."

It was not quite true. No one is above minding public opinion or enjoys the role of outcast. But compared with what had already transpired today, this incident was no more than trivial.

Oakes and I said good-by and turned to go our separate ways. But hesitating, I looked back over my shoulder to ask, "Oakes, what do you hear from Laura Lee?"

He only shook his head. And so we parted.

I was on the street and moving through the busy, jostling traffic of Marietta Street, toward the statue of Henry Grady, before I became aware again that my attempt to gain time in which to save the mill had failed. The shattering stroke of Algernon Carr's calculated attack had blotted out for a brief while the sense of failure. But now it returned and reduced Algernon Carr's insult to insignificance, compared to the collapse of my plans and hopes.

Why had I been so shattered by a few words? They were only words, contemptible, shoddy and mean. Then suddenly I knew it had not been the words but the calculation and ruthless desire to hurt and shame. Yet that too was trivial now. Only the mill mattered. For in losing the mill I was robbed of my dream, of a conception of achievement with which to shape my striving and living. I lost the chance to fulfill a promise to myself and to Wes, to the hands, to Darty, Cade and Mady and Mitty. The failure of the mill meant not my failure alone. With it swept so many failures.

Standing on the sidewalk, feeling bodies brush past me, jostled by a heavy woman with bundles, I tried to decide where I would go. I shrank from the mill, from telling Darty I had failed. Face Hickory Hill, I could not. Or tell Mitty we must begin to worry and scrimp again. She would be cheerful and undaunted—more cheerful and undaunted than I. But I could not tell her . . . yet.

There was nowhere to go, I thought. But then I realized I was wrong. I could go to Poteat, Whidby and Hardee. I could talk to Andrew. He could not, I knew, save the mill or make losing it unimportant. But he could help me find the courage to lose without accepting a defeat.

Neither Andrew's name on the door nor the passage of time had been able to change the offices of Poteat, Whidby and Hardee, where, uncertain of the future and shaken with a sense of loss, I went after leaving the City Bank. And then as I turned the familiar doorknob I was overwhelmed by a rushing memory of another time long ago when I came to this door for the first time with Mr. Dolph. How erect I had held myself, I remembered, to help hold in the pain of having left Mitty and the little house in Battle Hill.

What changes the years between then and now had wrought! How restlessly life had rushed on. Yet nothing was changed. Life curled fat and lazy in a warm musty corner and would not stir.

Andrew, like life, had changed yet remained unchanged, I thought as he came forward to meet me. He had more certitude now and surety was as much a part of him as his clothes which, regardless of fine cloth and custom tailoring, never succeeded in looking like anyone but Andrew. To discover a spot of egg on his lapel would seem only natural.

But in other ways Andrew had changed. He had become what Miss Camilla would have called "a man of substance." He had Atlanta's and the state's respect and his opinion was listened to gravely by that small clique of Atlanta which, working silently and invisible between the "Big

Money Boys" and the Wool Hats, strove to free the real and more vital South which they loved from intolerance and hate and bigotry.

Sitting on the edge of his desk, I told him of my interview with Mr. Carr. And raking his fingers through his hair, he said that undoubtedly we had another contingency on our hands. But—he smiled up at me with utmost cheerfulness—we'd think of something.

"I've thought of everything, considered taking our operations funds, borrowing money on Hickory Hill. But"—I looked at him despondently—"it wouldn't be nearly enough. I've wondered if another bank might make me a loan, perhaps take over the loan from Carr. But I don't suppose there's time for that . . ."

"Time doesn't enter. But something does, almost as relentless. A matter of ethics. Bankers are a pretty clannish club. They don't interfere with the patients of other club members." He added dryly, "Ethics, you see."

Frowning, I asked, "Andrew, why would Algernon Carr dislike me? He does. And has, since I was at Mrs. Plummer's and was a friend of his daughter's."

"Well, I only know the gentleman in a casual business way and by reputation. But considering what you've told me, and what I've heard elsewhere, I know enough to make an informed guess as to why."

"Why—do you think?"

"I think to Algernon Carr, you're sin," Andrew said seriously. "You were a child without background, as he would see it, without family. He would say you were—a nobody."

"As the girls at Mrs. Plummer's saw me," I interrupted, "except Laura Lee."

Andrew nodded. "Like the girls at Mrs. Plummer's," he agreed. "Then you were presumptuous enough to marry a Carrebee, and as if that wasn't enough you maneuvered yourself into the kingdom where he thinks he is king—namely cotton—and right off, your attitude toward the mill people and the relationship between them and yourself threatens the system that put him at the top and keeps him there."

I shook my head miserably. "But I didn't know I was threatening him —or anybody. I just did what I thought was fair. I wasn't trying to disrupt what he calls cotton mill economy. I didn't even think of it. I wanted to get along with the hands. Not feel ashamed every time I saw those children standing there all day. And saw dirt and ugliness every time I went to the mill village. And it wasn't trying to play Lady Bountiful as Miss Camilla said. It was giving people their rights and expecting them to give me mine."

"It's a pretty good rule of thumb for cotton economy or any other economy," Andrew said. "It's even enlightened. But you didn't think of that. You did it because you thought it should be done. You saw a bunch of people getting a pretty poor deal and you wanted to give 'em a fair deal. That is a sin to Algernon Carr. He's money- and power-hungry with a streak of hell-fire-and-damnation religion—and no sense of humor. It adds up to Southern bigotry; the combination that convinces a man that God meant for his kind to prosper and rule the earth. It also converts him to the Republican 'trickle-down' philosophy: give those on top the mostest and some of it's bound to trickle down to the bottom."

Recalling Algernon Carr's gallery of citations, I told Andrew of them. "He probably does the good work just to get the citation."

Andrew shook his head. "I think you're wrong. He's as earnest about good as a Scotch Reform preacher, and as down on sin. That's why he's dangerous. He'd be burned in oil for what he believes right. And burn evildoers (and that's anyone who won't see it his way) as well. That's why he's agin you. You're sin and you've had the brass to stick your head up in his particular heaven—Cotton Heaven." His eyes twinkled. "Reckon we won't let him do it."

"He'll soon have the satisfaction of running sin out of the cotton mill business anyhow," I said wryly.

"Why let him run you out?"

"How can we help it? I don't know where to turn. You said no other bank . . ."

He sat thinking, his bright blue eyes intent, his fingers going through his hair now and then. After a few minutes, he brought out a piece of foolscap and a pencil, jotted down some figures. He shook his head, jotted down more figures. He looked up once to ask how many acres I owned at Hickory Hill. But before I could answer, he said, "Oh yes, of course," as he remembered, and put down another figure.

"What are you doing?" I demanded curiously and he gave me an abstracted glance.

"Figuring," he answered calmly, "how to get hold of nearly thirty thousand dollars."

Firmly I told him, "If you have any idea of lending me the money, it's out."

"Don't worry, my little dab isn't a drop in the bucket. I haven't been in the firm that long." He had an idea, however, and his face lighted. "Poteat might have something put away. Not much, probably. But every little bit helps."

I protested, "But I don't want you to do this. What if the mill did go under—and all of you lost—" Then, realizing he wasn't listening, "Andrew," I accused. "Andrew! You didn't hear a word I said."

He looked up, his face almost stern.

"Leave the high finance to me. You go run your cotton mill."

"I won't let you do it . . . whatever you're planning."

He looked up again, his face really stern. "Oh yes, you will! Holy Carr won't kick my client around and get away with it. I've got my pride too. If you're sin to Holy Carr, then I'll work like the devil to keep you in business! And you'd better go on and let me get to it."

Firmly he steered me toward the door.

On my way back to the mill I had a brief resurgence of hope. But it faded. Andrew would come up against the same walls that stopped me, except one. He did have the character Algernon Carr had mentioned, but his physical collateral was insufficient even if I would allow him to risk it.

Though I did not mention the impending crisis to anyone except Darty, it was seldom out of my mind. Often as I worked at one thing or another, I would stop to wonder why I even bothered when each day brought nearer the date the note fell due, when I would drive Moppet through the gate for the last time. Yet I continued to work, hardly knowing why, except that a core of stubbornness would not let me stop. It was the last thing I could do for my work. And Wes!

I did not accept defeat philosophically. I fretted and fumed, often railed in thought against the failure and the necessity of its arrival. At other times I reproached myself. If only I had interested myself in the mill sooner—had wasted less time—had—had—

When I listened to Cade and Mady at the supper table, heard them laugh in the old rooms, or, sitting on the front steps at dusk after their happy, busy day, in the deepening dusk sing softly, I would hardly hear it. Their faces still wore the soft light of wonder inspired by a home warmed by love and trust, with respect for all it sheltered. Not a house darkened by fear and ignorance. How would I keep it for them if the mill . . . ? And Mitty? At her age would she have to begin cutting corners again—have to scrimp and pinch?

And then ten days later the reprieve came. Not dramatically. With nothing to mark it as a special event unless it was the automobile Andrew hired to bring him out to the mill; almost as decrepit as the buggy which he drove when he first brought me to Hickory Hill.

Through the office window I saw him get out and motion the driver to wait. Then he came up the steps to the office. When I met him at the door his sturdy cheerfulness was undiminished.

Seated at my desk, the blue eyes met mine unperturbed. "Reckon I'll have to take your offer to mortgage Hickory Hill, at that. With that we may swing it."

Incredulously I said, "But Andrew, we couldn't possibly get thirty thousand on Hickory Hill."

"I don't want to if I could. We've got most of it. Mr. Poteat rounded up more than I dared hope. I think he must have touched a few of his old friends."

Darty, sidling over, watched and listened as Andrew explained the necessity of the mortgage on Hickory Hill.

"How much you count on getting on it?" he asked.

When Andrew told him he shook his head pessimistically.

"Won't get it. Not on property way out here. Figure on a couple or three thousand less."

"We'll have to try, Darty," I said. "It's our last chance."

Darty, with his most ferocious scowl, growled in his throat, "Well—ain't my money good? Got about three thousand laying up, not working. Been saving for ten years for a rainy day. Ain't likely I'll see worse weather than this."

I sank into a chair, looking from one to the other, helpless and incoherent. "How can I . . ." I began, "both of you . . ."

"Don't look at us as if we'd won the war," Andrew twinkled. "There'll be another note to meet next year. You've got a reprieve, that's all. And next time the mill will have to make the money to pay it. Everybody who owed me a favor—and some who didn't—has just had a chance to return it."

"But I didn't want you to . . ."

"I wanted to," he said grimly. "Remember, I have my pride. Also, while my attitude toward horses as toward money is not what you'd call reckless, I'll back a horse . . ." his eyes met mine steadily, ". . . or a person if I think they're a winner." He paused, then seriously, "You won't have it all your way. A mill is no Sunday school picnic. And there's Algernon Carr. And when the sanctimonious crusade against evil forces, they aren't always . . . nice."

Darty admitting, nodded. "Figure Carr don't run that combine with billet-do or love taps either. And that's damned near twelve mills under his thumb, come to think of it. It's pretty steep odds . . ."

We stared at each other a moment. It was Andrew who answered. "I'm backing a winner that's used to running against heavy odds," he said quietly.

Andrew handled the payment of the note, and I imagined Algernon Carr receiving it and in disappointment and chagrin gnashing his teeth like the villain in the melodramas, but I was perfectly aware of such fantasy. Algernon Carr would lift not so much as an eyelid. His bloodless, impassive face would remain exactly the same, though I did not doubt that his mind would dart to possibilities (all unpleasant for me) in regards to the next payment that might capture Carrebee Mills. For I intuitively sensed that Algernon Carr was a patient man, willing to wait for his prize plum to fall, of itself, in his hands.

But next year I would deal with when the time came. Now I was caught up in other concerns. The new equipment would arrive shortly, so the manufacturer wrote, and I knew despite the improved attitude of the hands there would be resentment at the actual appearance of the machines. I spoke of this to Yancy and a few others with whom I was friendly. The consensus of opinion was divided; some for, some against, some on the fence.

"Might be trouble," was Yancy's comment. "Then again, might not."

This information left me no wiser as to what I might expect, so I tried to close my mind against speculation and my ears against talk. In neither was I wholly successful. For, going about the mill, the snatches of discussion that reached my ears of "stretch-outs" and "work assignments" and "loom load" told me that they argued against the new machines.

Now, after supper at Hickory Hill while Mitty and the children held their discussions or had candy pulls or popped corn, I returned to the hand loom, so long neglected; determined to learn all that I could by the time the new machines were in. I turned the small room Wes had occupied at the last into a workroom. Here I dug into the books on cotton again. For the first time I began to get a slight idea of cotton's supreme importance. Not to the South alone—though we of the South thought of cotton as ours—but to the world and to time. I learned that cotton had been woven in the story of mankind almost since the beginning. In prehistoric days, the white bolls so ordinary to us of the South grew by the Nile and the Ganges, and, spun, woven and dyed, had formed the staple clothing of India, Egypt and China. 500 years B.C. Alexander the Great carried to Egypt cotton from India, where cotton textiles were woven with matchless skill.

Why the knowledge that a brown-skinned woman beside the Nile had more than 2,000 years ago sat, as I sat now, and weaved, as I now weaved, a design that was distinctive but practical from the standpoint of production, should give me such satisfaction, I did not know, but it did. Perhaps it bestowed an added sense of the dimension of time; or the suggestion of a fundamental law which—despite man's mechanical wizardry—controlled the basic needs of humanity: the making of bread, the building of fire, the weaving of cloth.

I saw—or thought I saw—other signs of this law. For the fundamental process of weaving, whether gray goods or the finest of fabrics, by hand or power machine, was identical. The fiber dried, pressed flat and twisted; the cleaning, ginning and carding. Then spun to yarn or thread strong enough for weaving. In weaving, the fabric formed by interlacing two or more sets of yarn or thread. The warp or lengthwise yarn stretched firmly on the loom, and the weft or cross threads slipping in and out the warp, then battened or pressed down to make the fabric compact. Exactly, I thought, as I worked thread over and under when I darned a stocking.

When I thought of the thousands and thousands of yards of cottons turned out by American mills each season, it was hard to believe that all fell into one of the three fundamental weave specifications: the plain, the twill and the satin. Yet they did. The plain, where the weft, crossed over alternate threads of the warp, became calico, homespun and tabby; or by variations with groups of yarns produced basket weaves, monk's cloth and such. Alternating fine and coarse yarns made the twills, like piqué, grosgrain and rep. Two weft threads interlacing four warp and moving a step to right or left on each pick formed close-woven fabrics of serge, gabardine, denim. In satin, the third weave, floating or overshot warp threads on the surface reflect light and give a satiny luster.

When the uncrossed threads are in the weft then it becomes sateen. The warp-pile fabrics were fabrics like terry cloth, plush; and the weft pile, velveteens and corduroys.

I began to try in a tentative way my hand at designing, calling upon the small nest egg of ideas Professor Kerlich at Vestal Hall had taught me. The feel for color and pattern, the excitement of design found by chance, returned to me like a long-deadened sense suddenly waking to life. I began to observe. Saw the gorgeous black splashes of deathly black where an oak twig with great, glisteny leaves hung between Georgia sun and a white fence. On the same fence I saw the exotic, oriental writing of a shadow cast by barbwire. I saw the damp, rubbery pattern of the undersides of toadstools, of pebbles and twigs in a sand patch. I saw the white and green niceness of Mitty's ribbon grass in the yard.

It was vague and formless at first and fleeting, but surprisingly I waked each morning to find it not quite so formless. And I found myself recalling Wes on Miss Camilla's porch, touching with knowing fingers the soft fine voile of my dress. "Once I had the idea of Carrebee turning out stuff like this," he had said.

There were other reasons why I wanted Carrebee to produce quality goods. I was beginning to weary of reading in *The Manufacturer's Record* that only New England mills could turn out fine fabrics; that the mills of the South, ill-managed and with incompetent labor, were capable of producing only low-price, low-grade goods. I determined that Carrebee . . . would show them.

As I worked with the loom and experimented with design, my impatience for the arrival of the new machinery increased; also my anxiety. I sensed among many of the hands a growing distrust and caution, a residue of the bitterness banked and hidden but capable of flaring up into open resentment again.

I warned myself not to expect too much. Their loyalty was of brief standing and tentative. A few weeks could not hope to cut through the jungle of distrust, tension and fear that were the result of long years of struggle between workers and owners. I was by no means confident that the actual, physical presence of the new equipment would not stir fear and more hostility. Some disgruntled hands—how many I could not guess—might break into open revolt. If these gave way to their feelings and affected the others, I dared not predict what might follow.

I braced myself to wait it out. But the exact delivery date was uncertain. Freight of this size and weight was slow to move and subject to delay. Confusion due to a mix-up along the line further delayed it and necessitated a voluminous correspondence on Darty's part. Neither manufacturer, railroad nor freight agent would assume responsibility for the delay and none of the three could inform us where the equipment had got to though they assured Darty that it was shuttling along railway lines somewhere. The manufacturer wrote politely, washing his hands of responsibility. The freight company washed its hands too. As for the railroad, it never admitted that there was responsibility to admit. So . . . we waited.

Summer arrived with a withering heat that climbed to the nineties and hung there, its air like the breath of a furnace. It was broken by little rain, though in the late afternoon thunderheads piled ominous and purplish above the dark stands of pine. Scorching noonday breezes swept up eddies of dust from clay roads and plowed fields, and twisted them into whirling funnels of hazy red that spun against the vacant blue sky.

In the office shades were drawn, and in the close, breathless gloom Darty, coatless and making no pretense of work, moved a palm-leaf fan. Even the breeze, he complained, was hot. He'd bet you could fry a egg on the millyard. As if the heat had failed to impress me he reminded me every few minutes and with growing disgust that it was hot. He'd bet you could fry a egg . . .

Stepping to the screen door, I looked out at the sun that still rode high and young. Shadows had narrowed to shrink into inky alleys or under ledges or buildings. There was only the sun, molten and brassy, beating down on the panting earth. And my eyes dazzled and blinded by its glare, I turned back to the dim office. Darty, mopping his face with an already sopping handkerchief, was thirstily discussing beer.

"If I had the sense of a mud turtle, I'd be settin' under a tree somewhere with a cold pitcher right by my side. Beer heats you up but it's worth it for my—"

He broke off suddenly at a faint sound which came from outside, and we sat silent and listened. Then we heard again, distant but unmistakable, the creak and clink of harness, the dull jangle of trace chains, the high-pitched screech of a wheel needing grease.

Outside on the top step, we gazed anxiously toward the rise of the dusty red clay of the road. Above the rise the ascending veils of red testified that something was mounting the crest, but now the road stretched, a narrow track with sparse, dust-dim grass along it, its bordering gullies flaunting May pops, briars and snakeweed.

As the clinking and screeching came nearer, the ears and noses of the two lead mules popped suddenly into view and moved forward with powerful, plodding hooves. They were followed by a second pair, and then another; great, black, vicious and sweat-soaked beasts, their hooves raising dull scarlet clouds of dust. The pistol cracks of teamsters' whips, their profane and lusty shouts at the mules shattered the quiet day in a manner that only Ireland and quantities of bad whiskey could have produced.

"It's them!"

Darty expelled the words in a sighed ejaculation of fulfillment.

The three pairs of mules descended the slope and now the great wagon: flat, splintery, silver timber and ponderous iron-shod wheels hove into view. From its bed rose ponderous masses covered and lashed to the wagon bed by hemp ropes, thick as a man's wrist, and heavy ring bolts. A second appeared at the top of the rise, then a third, and the red churning dust told that others followed.

Sounds of arrival must have reached the hands through the whirring and clashing noise of their machines, for now the heavy doors of the buildings slid back on screeching rollers and the hands deserted their looms and spindles and surged through, out to the yard. Jostling ranks of men and women and half-grown boys and girls swept as if by a common impulse through the mill gate and spread out in straggling lines along the road.

Customarily any break in the workday was invariably occasion for joking boisterousness, catcalling, whistling and shouting that expressed the relief of rare and unexpected escape from labor. This, however, was different. They moved with the loose-jointed, careless and relaxed walk of people whose work demands dexterity of their entire bodies, and they were not boisterous now. But, faces intent and eyes narrowed to alertness, they were curious.

They stretched along the road, now almost reaching the ridge, a hundred yards or so distant, their eyes on the lead team of mules which had progressed three quarters of that distance, their hooves, with those of the others, making a muffled, slow drumming that sent billows of red dust upward to spread and moil over the lines of mill people. The snorting of mules, the noises of harness and sharp, explosive pops of teamsters' whips, the discordant cry of the ungreased wheel, crowded the heat with sounds now. The last few teams and drays were not yet over the ridge, where banks of slick clay rose an additional four or five feet from the level of the roadbed, ending in tufts of brownish sedge through which the road had been cut.

Watching the ridge, my attention was attracted to the top of the cut on the left where a man's heavy body lurched into view. It looked like Ed Wangle, I thought, and the damp, rasping bellow of his voice in the next second verified my identification. Startled, I turned to Darty inquiringly.

"What's he doing here? Did you know he was still around?"

Darty shook his head, scowling. "Thought he'd cleared out—"

He broke off, and, looking back toward the ridge, I saw that three other figures had taken shape behind Wangle's mound of bulk. He stood, his hands on his hips and a straw hat pushed back from the big, meaty face with its ponderous jowls.

"Do you think he's here to make trouble?" I asked, but Darty shook his head again.

"He may count on her putting him back if he runs you out, but I figure this is Ed's own frolic . . . whatever it is."

My eyes on the big figure on the hill, I nodded. "So do I."

Wangle waved his hand in a brief signal, and at almost the same moment, I heard a commotion nearer the mill gate. And I saw that a half-dozen men, such as loaf before any country store, had formed a slovenly cordon across the road directly in front of the first team. The mules came to a halt, squatting back on their haunches and laying back their ears and snorting, their yellow, mean eyes malevolent. Behind them the line of others were jolting to a stop, some mules bracing their fore-legs, others bucking. One or two lashed out with their heels in surprised anger.

As I swung my gaze to the first dray, the Irishman was starting up from his seat, his arm rising, his long snake of whip flickering backward. I heard his indignant "What the divel you think you be up to . . ." But before he could lay the whip on those blocking his way, two of them clambered up the sides of the wagon to pinion his arms and jerk the whip from his grasp. His small, knotty body struggled and then, accepting the situation, he sat down again, crossing his legs and philosophically lighting his pipe.

Ed Wangle's vast wheezing voice drew my attention back to the rise of the road. He also had mounted a wagon that had come to stop on the crest, and stood high on its seat above the heads of the mill hands on the roadside. Hands on meaty hips and bent slightly forward, he began to speak, his voice rasping and powerful, carrying even to Darty and me. He repeated, I realized, arguments they had heard before. The new equipment would lose lot of 'em their jobs. They'd find out about the stretch-out. 'Bout losing their kids' wages. They were points that still had emotional potency and he extracted every ounce. A few yips of encouragement, a rippling mutter of response ran down the ragged ranks.

"Now you folks just listen here a minute, that's all I ask," he exhorted. "Just ask yourselves, who's goin' to be helped by this here fancy machinery on these waggins. Whose it gonna benefit? You?" He shook his head with gloomy conviction. "No sirree, bob. 'Tain't you. 'Tain't gonna benefit you po' folks. It's gonna benefit that widder lady living up in that fine house on Hickory Hill. That's who'll benefit, mark my words. To buy her fancy clothes and ribbands and fancy rigs to drive roun' in."

Darty growled and started down the steps, chin thrust out belligerently, his shoulders hunched, but when I called sharply, he swung back.

"Wait," I said, "don't interfere."

"What's got into you? You gonna stand here and let Ed's hoodlums mess up that machinery?"

Calmly I told him, "It will be all right. Stay here and watch."

"Watch while Ed . . ."

"Yes," I said. "Wait and see what happens."

He scowled in furious exasperation, muttering unflattering things about women, but mounted the steps reluctantly.

I hardly knew why I prevented his interference with Ed. Certainly Darty was capable of looking after himself. But I had the feeling that this was a test, a time when a decision would have to be made if ever. I felt that today, now, the hands would make that decision.

Wangle, encouraged by a few yells of encouragement, had gained confidence.

"I'll tell you good folks what these here machines will do for you, now. I'll tell you what kinda machines these are. They're pickpocket machines. Yes sir, they'll pick a pocket clean as a whistle. They're the slickest pickpocket machines ever made, so long as a linthead's got pockets in his britches."

His efforts at humor evoked laughter.

"They'll tell you," he cried in his big windy voice, "they'll tell you they wouldn't think of lettin' these machines pick yore pocket. But you see, they can't stop 'em. They was designed and built for pocket pickin'! If they didn't turn out more goods and take less hands to run 'em, why would anybody want 'em? Reckon millowners buy 'em because they's shiny and pretty?"

I felt Darty jerk impatiently and discovered I was holding his shirt tightly.

He snapped, "What the devil's got into you? You gonna let Ed ruin us while we just stand here?"

"Wait," I said again, hardly hearing his voice and shifting my gaze from the crest of the hill.

I knew now, sharply and clearly, the explanation of what had before been only a feeling, unformed into reason and not even fully understood when I acted on it. I had prevented Darty interfering because the decision had to be made by the mill hands. They must decide whether they would back me up, give me trust and stand by me. I must know sooner or later, for the mill and possibility of its success depended on them. This, I thought, was really between the hands and me. Ed Wangle, with his big blustering voice, was unimportant. This was between them and me.

He was mopping his steaming jowls as he talked, speaking slower but still in vast and fumbling tones.

"And that's what me and these here fellers is here for right now. To help you all. Every man, woman and child that makes his bread by the sweat of his brow. We're here to dump these here machines in the road and fix 'em so as they won't pick a mill hand's pockets. Or be good for anything else, fur as that goes. We're gonna do it 'cause we don't hold with puttin' machines made of iron and wood and stuff over folks with hearts and stomachs and souls what stands the same, ever one, before the throne of the Almighty!"

He wasn't important, I repeated. He was only necessary because through him I would find out.

Hands held outward, Ed spoke in doleful supplication.

"What about it, folks? We gonna dump these here machines off these waggins or ain't we?"

There was no answer and we waited, he and I, for whatever decision they would give. We waited. . . .

Then, I saw that Yancy Jackson had come to stand beside the wagon, near a front wheel. He stood, tall and lean, scuffing at the red dust with the toe of a clumsy shoe, his face bent as if he was far more interested in the puffs of red dust than what might occur. But his voice came sharp as the whack of a hickory stick.

"Talkin' now, about this here throne. How about it, Ed, when you was managin' the mill? Didn't stick to that kind of practice at the mill store, did it?"

"I tried to be good to you fokes. You know that," Wangle crowed hoarsely, arms outspread over Yancy's head. "Sho, now and then, a shiftless no-good had to be throwed out. 'Cause he wasn't pullin' his weight. I treated all of you that was ready to put in a full day—good. I tried to be good to you. Give you all I could plumb figger how to work it to give."

"Seems like that was the trouble, in a way," Yancy said. "You gave it. If it was ours and we had it comin', how the hell was that bein' good?"

Laughter this time was on Yancy's side. He drove it home, never smiling, yet his voice sharp with spiteful wit. He used the scrip, the irregular pay, the evictions, all an old story but new and fresh and as pointed as whittled darts of spiteful truth. They were laughing now. The men who had come to back up Ed Wangle were shuffling their feet. Those on the Irishman's wagon descended sheepishly, as if they hoped not to be noticed. Only Wangle remained on the seat of the wagon at the crest of the road.

Looking up at him, Yancy said, almost gently but clear enough for all to hear, "Come on down, Ed. Them there jackasses are all wore out and it looks like you're through hitchin' rides on other folks' wagons."

Wangle, looking around, scratched his head, leaned over and spat a great wad of brown tobacco into the clay road.

"Oh hell, Yancy! You know I was just foolin'," he said.

He climbed down from the wagon, using the wheel spokes for footholds, without hurry or embarrassment. Grinning, he looked about and then caught sight of me on the office steps. His big hands flopped high over his head in a careless greeting.

"Hi yu' been, Miz Jess? Better get in outen this here sun. You don't want to git sun prostration."

"I think I will, Mr. Wangle," I called back.

"You do that and take keer yourself. Sho nuff looks like you got yourself a cotton mill for keeps."

Again we exchanged waves and he lumbered off down the road. He was right, I thought. I had me a cotton mill for keeps. If I could keep it.

The Irish teamster's mule whip cracked on the air. The mules lifted their ears, lunged against the traces. The unoiled wheels began their screech. The wagons entered, separated by several yards with tailboard at one end, mule noses at the other. With the hands jostling alongside, it made a sort of triumphant march, I thought. A nice one.

Crossing the millyard on my way to the office in the crisp air of October, I was suddenly struck by wonder. Less than four months had passed since the big drays had delivered their load to the mill, yet the mill was back on production, even now winding yards upon yards of fine-count cottons onto the giant spools.

But, I thought wryly, the doing had not been so easy as the telling—or so simple. Our progress at first was unsteady and faltering, like a young child learning to walk. Taking one step, then another, pausing to balance, but with each step acquiring surety and able to quicken. The hands taught to operate the machines, at first disgruntled and critical of changed routine. But becoming proficient, and the astonishing, almost uncanny sensitivity and power of the modern machinery revealed, the remains of their hostility abolished. They could not withhold their admiring pride at the acquisition of swifter, surer tools; moving along the aisles between the massive and gleaming rows of steel, unable to hide their grins of possessive pride that these extraordinary creatures must obey their orders. The men with offhanded shrugs indicated it wasn't so much to put these contraptions through their paces if you were onto their little tricks. And the women with knowing nods and glances attested that they weren't fooled for a minute; that for all the talk about these modern machines they had their failings too.

But behind the pretended casualness, enthusiasm had quickened, and in the crisp fall of 1913, when the scarlet of oaks and gold of maples matched their colors against the pale sky, the mill rumbled into production and the first yards of fine-count cottons began to roll from the Carrebee looms in both woven and printed designs.

The woven designs were from yarns dyed before weaving; the printed, woven of yarn in natural shade, then put through the copper rollers of the printing machine which in one operation printed both pattern and color.

As the enthusiasm of the hands mounted, so did mine. Plans discussed for so many months at last attained tangibility. Words spoken or put down on paper resulted in machines and people working together, evolving from what had been only hope and a dream—actuality. This—the heady intoxication of achievement—lifted me above the ugly gossip which Miss Camilla continued to spread. When past acquaintances, passing me, carefully turned their heads, the realization that she had made of me a notorious figure outcast by the group which in Atlanta constituted "society," lost its power to hurt. Only work mattered, I told myself, as the mill gained momentum. Only work was real.

In the office I waited alone for the first of my own designs to come off the looms; eager, yet half-fearing to see the finished product. I had considered it worthy of production, the design distinctive, yet simple and easy to execute. But now I wondered if I had been overconfident.

Smiling, I remembered that it had been inspired by—of all people—Poky. How, discovering my small pots of dye in my makeshift workroom at Hickory Hill, he had indulged in a glorious orgy of wall-smearing, using every available color in patterns unknown to man. Arriving home I found him cheerfully nonplused at Mady's despair and not in the least concerned. Mady, apologetic for the damage, promised that Cade would repaint the wall tomorrow. "I'm purely sorry, Miss Jess," she repeated.

Kissing her cheek, I reassured her. "Darling, don't worry about it. It's nobody's fault but mine. It serves me right for leaving the workroom unlocked and the dye where Poky could reach it."

She lost her look of despondent misery when she found Poky was not less loved nor I, too shattered. But I viewed the results of Poky's labor with less patience. No inch of wall within his reach had been neglected, and my thoughts as I bleakly surveyed the chaos were not concerned with design. Yet it was then, irrationally and illogically, that inspiration came.

On one space of wall Poky, no doubt cleaning small finger tips to prepare for further dye-dipping, had left a vague, uneven tracery of slanting lines; delicate and illusive and suggesting summer rain seen through a window. It crossed my mind idly that it was interesting how a child could achieve by accident an effect of rain that was really a lovely pattern.

Thoughtfully, I said aloud, "Summer Rain," and knew I had the name and design for my first Carrebee Cotton. One part of my mind was testing color combinations. Rose with the illusive fall of lines in black; yellow with iris-blue; green with white; the other part figuring that the pattern was simple, easy to work out, yet delicate and lovely as childhood days of play in an attic while summer rain fell gently and quietly. Best of all, the idea had an almost native simplicity and directness. Why, even a child could have thought of summer rain!

It occurred to me that a child had brought it to reality and supplied me with the conception I needed. But I am sure Poky had no idea why he was snatched up by an excited woman who hugged him and planted kisses on his grubby cheeks. He was not grateful for this acclaim, but insisted on getting down to continue his voyage in the boat contrived from Mitty's sewing-machine top turned upside down.

Later, I turned my carefully charted design over to Matt, the master printer, and now in the office I waited to see what Matt called a "sampling." But when he laid it on the desk before me, I surveyed it with rueful eyes. It bore no resemblance to the thing my mind's eye had seen—the effect of fine summer rain. The lines were too definite, too boldly sharp.

I said quietly, "It isn't quite right, is it?"

He asked if I wanted his opinion. When I said that I did, he gave it.

"This here ain't no print job, Miz Carrebee. It's too sort of delicate-like, just a little ways off misty, yet sharp enough so you know it's there. It's real catch-on, as the feller says. But it should be wove in. Printin' gives you solid lines which you don't want. You want almost solid but now and then the background color running through for a thread or two."

He was right, I said, but how would we get that effect in the weave?

He shook his head. It was a right particular job. "Of course, if we could held hold of a real top-notch design man."

"Do you know such a man?"

He did not, but the man I wanted found me. He stumped into my office a few days later in a neat black suit, a derby that might have been cast in black iron and with bumps on his toes big as potatoes. His name was August Vogt, he said, his German accent heavy and thick as clabber. But he had a shy, kindly smile and the innocent, mild dreaming eyes of a child or an artist. He was a design man, he informed me, mentioning mills where he had been employed. He had heard Carrebee Mills was going into fine goods.

I said we were and asked why he had left his last position.

"Mizzes Carrebee, to earn a salary I do not need to sell my soul by humbling myself to vulgarity. They say of me, this squarehead is a hard man to work with. It is true. I spend my life learning to weave from the loom, not just the cloth but also beauty. I am hard to work with by those what think looms are made to make ugliness only."

I showed him the design for Summer Rain, watching his face as he held the squares of paper, the black iron derby under his arm. His round, pinkly plump face with its curled mustache remained inscrutable.

He returned the designs to me, and I put them on the desk.

"The man who those came from," he said bluntly, "will not have it hard working by August Vogt."

"Do you think you can put them in work without trouble?"

He shook his head. "Put them in work *with* trouble. If it was easy to put in work, it is not worth any trouble." He paused. "May I ask whose design it is, if you please?"

I said it was mine and explained that a child's smearing of paint on a wall had suggested it.

"I do not doubt it that something suggested Faust to Goethe," he replied. "You are not Goethe, ma'am, but still I will work in your mill."

Later, when August Vogt had proved his uncanny understanding of yarns and looms, I saw Summer Rain as a dream realized. Through his perceptive knowing, the delicacy and illusiveness of the pattern was even more fragile, more than ever like fine summer rain. Rain, I thought, that deserved to drift over the South, reach towns in the North and West, and refresh not only the market but the mill's low balance at the bank where we kept our running account. For Summer Rain with our other quality goods must stimulate the prosperity for Carrebee! And I did not doubt—I would not allow myself to doubt—that when enough people saw the quality of Carrebee Cottons, prosperity and reputation would come.

My optimism, however, was haunted by time. The time left in which to prove the soundness of our plans. In eight months the second note to Algernon Carr's bank must be met. As Andrew had pointed out, the first payment had earned the mill and me only a reprieve. Already I was holding onto every possible dollar toward the payment that as days passed loomed larger and larger. And always confronting me was the knowledge that now it was not only my own ruin, but others'. Andrew I knew had gone into debt for far more money than I liked to think. Mr. Poteat had put up money he could ill afford to lose. There were Darty's small savings.

Responsibility for them and the obligation to fulfill their trust weighed heavily on my shoulders, as did the obligation I had toward the mill hands. So many people and so much depended on success that often I felt that I was driven and goaded to use every ounce of energy and ability in the task before me. I often railed because it was not greater, my experience terribly limited, because I must learn so much by trial and error. Yet I gained a satisfaction from driving myself to work harder and yet harder. And though often physically tired, there was something glorious in honest fatigue, and my spirit in those first weeks soared to a higher level than it had ever known. If I failed for whatever reason, striving had its reward, one which did not depend on success.

There was an aspect of the cotton business with which I was unfamiliar. And I realized it when Darty asked me if we would continue to use the commission houses with which Miss Camilla had dealt, or switch to others.

The decision must be his, I answered, since I knew nothing about commission houses or their policies.

"If you want to change, by all means do," I said. "There might be advantage in dealing with houses that know nothing about the changes in Carrebee."

Snorting, he pointed out my mistake. Commission houses, all of 'em, were all on the grapevine circuit. What one knew all of 'em knew. They were like gentlemen's clubs, he explained, or fraternal organizations. Not that he expected resentment because of Miss Camilla. Another point had him stewin'.

"What is it, Darty?" I asked.

"Well, Carr's a pretty big stick in the gentlemen's club. He swings plenty of weight. Has lot of friends. Influence. He can help or hurt plenty of 'em. I just got to thinking . . ."

"Thinking what?"

But he made a sound of self-disgust and called himself a fool to cross a bridge 'fore he reached it. But I had an idea of the nature of his concern and I too was faintly disquieted.

But whatever possible trouble had worried Darty, it did not immediately appear. The work of the mill went on, and in addition crews were painting the mill houses and establishing more sanitary conditions. At least, I thought, the mill community would be neat and clean and reasonably healthy.

Meantime the rising sales of Carrebee Cottons brought a vast satisfaction. Now every bolt carried the slogan "Carrebee Cottons." The catch phrase caught on and helped to carry the name and reputation of the mill, and as Darty and I went over the financial reports I could assure myself that if business continued to increase and we met with no disastrous blows of chance, we could handle Algernon Carr's payment when the time came.

Often, in my anxiety that foresaw every dire possibility, I wondered if there was danger of blows directed against the mill from Algernon Carr himself. Or if he held my ability in such contempt that he would simply wait for the mill to go down to ruin without his assistance. What if he heard of the small but encouraging acceptance our new lines were meeting? Would he think, perhaps, that he had underestimated me because I lacked the character and background?

A few days later I regretted my gloating wish that he might learn of our success! For because he heard of our progress or for some other reason, he decided to wait no longer for time to bring the Carrebee mill to destruction. He would assist time, and with a directness almost as implacable.

Entering the office, I found Darty at his desk, reading a letter and wearing an expression that suggested he'd been summoned to attend his own hanging.

When I asked what was wrong, he faced me reluctantly. Just a little trouble with the commission houses, he admitted. He had used his own judgment and contacted Kirby and Marks, the commission house which had taken care of the bulk of Carrebee's business for many a year. But Kirby and Marks had written that they found themselves unable to handle Carrebee products right now. Perhaps in the future.

"If Kirby and Marks can't handle our goods," I advised briskly, "write to other houses. Kirby and Marks aren't the only commission house on Worth Street."

He stared at me owlishly for a space before he said, "I did."

He had written to every commission house with which he had the slightest contact. He had also written to the houses where he had no contacts, casual or otherwise. The results, in both cases, had been equally discouraging. The replies were courteous, stiffly correct, phrased in the formal style of the cotton business, which still retained something of the days when it was dominated by gentlemen planters. But from between the lines emerged one fact: The present situation made it impossible to accept, at this time, the honor . . . In brief, each letter said *no*.

My forehead furrowed with worry, I asked Darty what was behind the sudden disinclination of the commission house world to handle Carrebee Mills.

"I know blamed well what's behind it," he said glumly. "I've been expecting somethin' like this to happen. Tried to warn you once. But I decided it's no use crossin' bridges too soon."

"What is behind it?"

He gazed owlishly over his spectacles. "Told you once. Carr's a member of the club. Carries lot of weight there too. Mighty easy to drop a word here and there. Write a few letters. Get his friends to pass the word on. With a string of mills like the combine, Carr's good will is a pretty nice plum. Nothing open. Just a understandin' between gentlemen. You grind my ax, I'll grind yours . . ."

I surprisingly felt no surprise. I had realized, I told myself, that Algernon Carr would not long be content to sit back and watch Carrebee get back on its feet. He still wanted the mill, still wanted it in the combine. If we increased our earnings and built reputation, his chances of taking it were lessened—perhaps lost. He was not, I had known, a man who easily gives up. I should have known he would attack; that when he did he would strike at a vulnerable and vital spot to assure swift and complete victory.

The commission houses were that vital spot. Through them the mill's products reached country-wide markets. They were a vital link in the complicated chain that led from cotton field to store counters. I saw no possible way for the mill to survive if the channels which carried our merchandise to market were blocked. Nor did I know any alternative route by which we could reach customers and sell our goods.

But I was by no means prepared to admit that there was no way. Mr. Carr had moved with shrewdness and efficiency to cripple, if not destroy us, and the assault had hurt. But I was not ready to give up. There must be some way, I told myself, to get our cottons before people . . . before enough people . . . people who would buy. There had to be a way. But I did not know what that way was.

The answer still eluded me on Sunday when Andrew came to Hickory Hill for dinner. He had fallen into the habit of coming regularly almost every week. I was always glad to see him, always he gave me a sense of balance. But this Sunday I was worried and annoyed. That I could not devise or invent a solution to my problem made me irritable and anything but pleasant company.

I spoke almost crossly to Cade, pushed Colonel away when he placed his head in my lap to have his ears scratched, and when I saw the surprised glances of Cade, Mady and Mitty, my irritation increased. I did not care, I thought. I was tired. I was tired of worrying, tired of working myself to death. Without appetite I picked at my food, though Mitty's meal was delicious. Though she frequently insisted her hand was "out with biscuits" or "out with chicken pie," as if it went on unconventional jaunts with those dishes, today her hand was not "out." Everyone but me ate heartily, laughed unrestrainedly, chatted incessantly and made, I thought, a great deal of hectic confusion. As usual, Poky dropped a remarkable number of articles and banged on the table with everything in his reach capable of being banged. To climax his performance, he burst suddenly into song at the top of his lungs, to the general admiration of everybody but Colonel and me.

I remarked firmly that the table was not the place for singing and ordered Poky to be quiet. At this he looked at me in dumfounded astonishment and Mady, though adding her admonitions to mine, gave me a look of puzzled hurt. I admitted to myself that both Poky's reaction and Mady's look might have been caused by my unusual sharpness and by the taut, nervous strain I had heard in my own voice. But I did not admit that I was at fault. I told myself I had a right to demand reasonable quiet at my own table, without being subjected to wounded looks. Nor was it necessary for a dead silence.

I felt a tug of exasperation, pretending not to notice the general reaction to my show of annoyance. My humor was not improved, however, and after dinner as Andrew and I sat in the sitting room before the fire, I responded unenthusiastically to his attempts at conversation. Finally he gave up and sat looking at me steadily for a few minutes, and then asked what was the matter.

"Nothing in the world is the matter!"

But he disregarded my protest. "You may as well get it off your chest. And if you have to be cross with somebody, it had better be me than Cade or Mady or Poky. I think you're a pretty nice young woman, but I don't have any illusions about your being perfect, like they do. So I don't feel as if somebody's pulled the earth out from under me when you're thoughtless, ill-tempered and rude."

"Was I as bad as all that?" I asked wretchedly, and he nodded calmly.

"You were. If I had been Poky I'd have spanked you!"

Shamefaced, I said, "Maybe somebody should anyway. I'm sorry, Andrew."

"You're worried and worn out," he said, relenting and speaking more gently. "But snapping and being cross won't do any good. Why not tell me what's on your mind and see if I can't help out?"

"Of course I'll tell you about it, but I don't see how you can help. It's the commission house, and the whole business is pretty complicated. . . ."

He interrupted, sinking back in his chair, "Then you had better start explaining. There's no hurry. I've got all day."

The explanation did not require all day, of course, or even a half hour. Andrew grasped the essential facts connected with the marketing of cotton goods quickly and surely. I described the relationship of commission houses to mills, giving him quick thumbnail sketches of the parts played by cutters, convertors and so on. I explained that the merchandising of the goods produced by the whole industry centered on Worth Street, New York. Worth Street, I finished, was the heart of the weaving industry. If the connection between it and the mill was cut off, the mill had little chance of survival.

He heard me out patiently to the end and when I was finished sat thinking for a few minutes.

"Worth Street and the commission houses are the only instruments used by mills for selling their goods?" he asked. "Is that the way it is, Jess?"

I gave a shrug of discouraged assent. "The only one that matters. To all intent and purpose it is the only way to get your goods to manufacturers and from there to stores."

"And to people, I assume," he suggested.

"Of course to people eventually," I agreed. "But the mill first has to get its products to manufacturers so they can turn it into merchandise. We have to reach manufacturers who buy quantities of goods to make into thousands of different things. Worth Street is the only way to reach them."

"I understand the principle," he told me. "I'm not convinced your conclusion is sound, though. Did you know we have a wholesale market here in Atlanta?"

Faintly surprised, I asked, "Here?" and he nodded.

"They manufacture a good deal more merchandise every season than you would probably ever guess. Of course, it's not Worth Street. But there are men down there with brains and initiative. They know not many merchants in small towns down South can afford to send buyers up to New York every few weeks or months. Furthermore, the New York market doesn't cater to the taste or needs of small-town people or Southern farm families. Then merchandise made down here can be delivered faster, so it's just common sense for Southern merchants to buy in Atlanta. Besides, it builds Southern business and keeps money in the South, instead of following the usual practice of sending it all North."

I was interested, of course, and curious about his being so well informed about the manufacturing activity in Atlanta.

"How did you learn about all this?"

It was by now so ancient a joke between us that he looked a little sheepish as he answered. "Well, I've got a client down there in . . ."

Before he could finish we had both burst into laughter.

He had given me a glint of hope. A small one, but one that might grow larger and lead to a solution of my problem. Later, as I lay in bed, I told myself that Andrew's information meant there might be a market for Carrebee Cottons right here in my own yard. It might be even better than Worth Street in New York. I must not bank on it. I must not expect too much. Probably it would turn out to be impractical. But, drifting off to sleep, I thought, I can go see, talk to people, find out. It was a chance. I could not turn down any chance.

In the little space between sleep and waking, when the half dreams begin to drift in and obscure reality, I saw myself in one of those dreams, calling upon the businessmen in the wholesale section of Atlanta that Andrew had told me about. I saw myself enter the doors of offices, stand before desks, saw myself speaking to men who were always in the half dream—half-imagining little dramas—faceless and silent. I saw myself arguing, urging, pleading vehemently, attempting to remain business-like and matter-of-fact, yet unable to keep my anxiety from showing in my face. I was reaching across a desk, seizing a faceless man by the lapels of his coat, shaking him and tearfully insisting he must, he simply must buy thousands and thousands of dollars' worth of Carrebee cottons.

And then I was wide awake. Sleep was impossible. And I was scared.

I did not escape from that fear but neither did I give in to it. I was not strong. But I did not dare allow myself to be weak. There were checks for Miss Camilla and Cissa that the mill must supply money for every month. There was Mitty, Cade, Mady and Poky. There was the money loaned by Darty and Mr. Poteat; and Andrew, I knew, had obligated himself to a desperate extent to help me pay the first note on the loan. I could not fail them. I could not fail the people at the mill who had given me their trust and fastened their hope on my ability to pull the mill through. I was scared. But scared or not, neither hell, high water nor Worth Street was going to make me quit.

Darty prepared a sample book of my goods, a book about fourteen inches square, a sample of each design neatly fastened within. And on Monday morning, with it lying on the buggy seat beside me, I turned Moppet's head toward Atlanta, to call on the wholesale market. Seeing on every hand, Atlanta's growing and changing. Old landmarks torn down and huge buildings flung up, the smooth ribbon roads. A viaduct here, another one there; department stores growing and fattening. Another hotel, maybe two, and always the city rising up. Skyscrapers tall as New York's beginning to make Atlanta "the New York of the South." Where, I wondered, was the village of The Standing Peachtree, where the Cherokees jogged on their horses along the ridge or fished in the Chattahoochee? Or planted their corn that in spring grew tall and green and tasseled . . . ?

Wholesale Row, scattered along one of the dingy streets below Whitehall, was unprepossessing, and my hopes dropped as I stopped in one after another to show my samples. For these were not show places. These were workrooms with scant space devoted to front offices but all possible space used for turning out work. The people were Jewish and invariably kind and looked at my samples with what I felt was real interest. But always the shrug, and the hands expressing futility. "We got no call for this. No style in cottons. Yours nice . . . different . . . nice quality . . . but for what would we use them? Ladies' house dresses? Cotton? . . . No style value. Sorry."

Walking down the street to the next place, I thought over what they said. They were right. There was no style value to cottons. In the South women wore them during the warm weather, but simple little frocks they ran up at home. And that was not style.

The next place was a small one-story brick factory which, I discovered when I opened the door, consisted of one long room, the front occupied by a number of tables piled with wearing apparel, the rear containing two dozen or more sewing machines at which girls and women sewed without stopping to raise their heads. Seeing no one at hand, I drifted among the tables and briefly glanced at the clothes folded and piled upon them. They consisted of women's and girls' cotton house dresses and underwear, boys' shirts and pants. All of the flimsiest cotton in run-of-the-mill design. Yet, by the number of garments, all identical, piled high on each table, I deduced that the maker expected someone to buy them.

Behind me a gentle voice said, "Good morning," and turning, I saw a young Jewish man, almost as shabby and ill-kempt as the building; he had soft dark eyes that were friendly but also knowing. Not discomfited in the least by his soiled work pants and old shirt, he came to stand by the table of dresses I had inspected.

I gestured toward them now. "Are these made here?"

"Everything made under this roof." His shrewd eyes took me in. "You a buyer?"

"No." Then I asked, "But buyers do buy your merchandise, don't they?"

He shrugged. "So would I keep it for souvenirs, you think?" he inquired and laughed.

"Who buys it? Which firms, I mean?"

"Low-price. Walk down Decatur Street—out Peters Street. You'll see my goods hanging before the store." He gave it a glance of contempt. "Shoddy. Shoddy, cheap. For cheap trade."

"But is it profitable?"

"Profitable, she asks? Lady, what do you think? Resources I gotta pay for the goods. I gotta pay for trims. Buttons and braid. I gotta pay the sewing-machine girls. I gotta pay rent. The store on Decatur Street gotta make his profit. Lady, where is my profit?"

"I hope you don't mind me asking you so many questions. You see I never knew before that Atlanta had wholesale merchants."

"You in trade?" he asked.

"No. But I may have to be."

"How is that? *May* have to be?"

I told him I designed and manufactured cottons and his face was at once eager with interest. When I asked if he knew Carrebee Mills he answered indifferently, "Sure. Out in De Kalb. Gray goods. Sure I know them."

"Not gray goods any more. Now we turn out fine-count fabrics. Would you like to see samples of the new line?"

He shrugged, jerked his head as if to say "Why not?" and I put my sample book on the table before us. Turning the pages, I said, "This is an exclusive design. Summer Rain we call it."

The thin sensitive fingers slipped under the sample, their tips alert to texture and finish and count. He looked at me, a new respect in the wise eyes. "Fine," he said gently. "Soft. Beautiful."

We went through the sample book, his shrewd eyes missing nothing, in a sure instinct for texture, color and grade. When we completed the book, he asked, "You going in for fashion cottons?"

"Fashion?" I echoed, feeling poorly equipped for what I was trying to do.

"That's what the cotton industry needs. Put cottons back in the money," he said, "fashion cottons. You got the quality there." He shrugged. "Why not?" He slapped his breast. "Me? That's why I have this"—his arm encompassed the floor—"why I turn out drek. To get enough money together to go into high-prestige stuff. Where the real money is. Exclusive designs."

"But how would you merchandise it? Send it to the New York market?"

"The New York market? I spit on it." He actually spat on his floor. "Not to market. Exclusive, I said." He gave his chest another sound slap. "I put on my fine double-breasted suit that I ain't got—I call on all the fine houses, the big stores with the French saloons. Only six to you, modom, I say. Six only. But . . . those six exclusive to you. Lady, listen. Fashion ready-to-wear"—he threw kisses toward the ceiling—"is going to be . . . colossal. Now what do the ladies do at home? . . . They sew . . . make their own clothes. Soon—no more ladies sew at home. Everything ready-made. Children's wear too."

Doubtfully, I asked, "Would it be very difficult for you to switch from making"—I swept the table before me—"this . . . to style merchandise?"

"Difficult? Lady . . . easy like rolling off a log. A good designer, a good cutter." He waved toward the girls at the clattering sewing machines. "The sewing machines I got. But"—he held up a cautioning finger—"only one item . . . difficult. Money—money to get the start."

"How much money?"

As he spoke, he ticked off the items of expense on his fingers. "One, for a good designer. Two, for the high-class goods. Three, to travel to all the fine shops in the Southeast. Four, a fine double-breasted blue suit for me, and expense account." His soft eyes laughed into mine. "Nobody has that much money." Then his eyes fell once more on my sample book, and opening it, he slid his fingers under the sample of Summer Rain. "See," he said. "Here . . . you have the promotion. This, in a beautiful dress! Soft . . . light as the dandelion thistle—in assorted colors, of course." Now he began to act; in his soiled, shabby work clothes, advanced toward a mythical customer, pretending to lift with delicate, careful hands a delicate, mythical dress. "Modom . . . to you I present . . . Summer Rain . . . the jewel of our collection. Modom, just feel the texture. Carrebee Cottons . . . finer than silk. Exclusive, modom, with you in your city." He discarded his act. "Of course I would be wearing my double-breasted blue suit."

I asked, "How long have you been in this line of business, Mr. Saul?"

"How long I have been in the business, you ask? I was born in the business." Then, as I laughed, "No, but I'm serious. Mama had me in the busy season when she had to help Papa in the shop. I slipped in between shipments. I never got out. Not in Atlanta, that was, but . . . in Philly. I have to come south for my Marta's health. She is my wife. Her health is better where it is not so cold."

For a moment I stood there, not speaking. Thinking perhaps that so soon I should not speak. Perhaps first let Andrew investigate Homer Saul; his character, credit and background. But, I thought, my eyes upon him, why wait for investigation when the record was there before me? Young and shabby and yet with a young heart that was so easily gay. . . . Credit? He probably had little? Yet on little, managing to have his sewing machines, this small place to turn out his work . . . and a dream of someday making high-style goods.

Slowly I said, "Mr. Saul, why can't we go into business together? Makers of high-style cottons?"

He glanced at me, quickly. "Is this serious?"

"You see, Mr. Saul, I am Mrs. Carrebee . . . of Carrebee Mills. I'm starting to turn out fine-count goods of our own design. But I've run up against a problem . . ."

"Mrs. Carrebee!" he said in shocked tones. "Why didn't you say so? I would have brought you a chair. Or better still . . . come back to our place, mine and Marta's. Marta will give us coffee . . . this way, Mrs. Carrebee."

He led me to the rear of the store past the clattering sewing machines and through a door in the wall. We entered a small, spotless room where Mr. Saul's Marta sat, darning a sock that already appeared to be more darn than sock. Slim and pretty, her delicate face framed in dark curly hair and her large gentle eyes, like his, ready for laughter.

"Marta," he cried as we entered. "Coffee for everybody. We go into business!"

She put down her darning and rose, smiling at me as if she would say, "Isn't he a rascal?" But to him she calmly replied, "That will be nice," and went to the stove for the coffee.

Homer Saul pulled a comfortable chair to the table and, bowing gallantly, said, "Modom, do us the honor." Then, sighing, he pulled up a chair for himself. "For an occasion like this I really need that blue suit."

Now I came to know the real meaning of work. To know weariness beyond any weariness ever experienced before. Yet I could not rest but must go on, not knowing how or even certain in my numbed fatigue if there was logical reason for going on. I attained a thin, high place of nerves tightened to permanent tautness that made me forget, except for snatched, brief hours of sleep, that rest existed or mattered. I found that sleep was an enemy. It lulled you with the desire of more sleep and made you its victim again, until you only wished to give up—and you couldn't give up. You had to go on.

Now, with new hope and a new world to conquer, all else was subordinated to producing, and finding the channels through which our quality cottons could reach the consumer. Many hours I spent at the mill; and when not at the mill, I was at Homer's small brick plant where the same girls worked at the same sewing machines but where all else was changed.

In the front room, where the tables of what Homer had called "drek" had been displayed, he had installed his showroom. Nothing fancy, he protested, in case it should occur to me he was indulging in unnecessary extravagance. Nothing showy! But with a little partitioning, a few mirrors and secondhand furniture disguised with mauve paint, he had achieved an air of elegance and smartness. Here Homer, in a fine blue suit and a lofty air of assurance: "Modom, I present the jewel of our collection. Exclusive with you in your city. Carrebee High Fashion Cottons, Modom. Finer than silk. Naturally, Modom, you know Carrebee High Fashion Cottons and . . . Modom, an August Vogt design."

But that came afterwards. At first we went slowly, warily, like one who walks a tightrope. Each step carefully taken, the foot tentatively placed, and only when finding it firm, daring to take another, lest we plunge to disaster. And always working. Either at Homer's place or in the small unused room at the mill which I took over as a workroom; and where August and Homer and I crouched over its pine table for hours, engrossed with new designs or, brooding perhaps over small pots of dye, worked out color motifs.

In Homer's showroom a man of huge girth and long, heavy-lidded eyes looked at my Carrebee cottons and with languidly held pencil made a few lines on a paper. "Like this," Otto would say, or, "Here we have that . . ." or "perhaps" or "maybe . . ." and a few weeks later we'd inspect the Carrebee High Fashion Line for spring or summer or fall and I could hardly believe that the few languid lines upon paper had been his symbol for the frocks of cunningly simple lines he displayed. And Homer, in fine double-breasted blue suit, would throw unlimited kisses at the ceiling and swear he would sell five thousand of this number and seven of that, and we'd laugh at his overstatement. Then, in his fine double-breasted suit, he'd go on the road to call on the shops—and double his figures.

Even at first our quality fabrics and Otto's instinct for line found acceptance, and slowly but surely Carrebee High Fashion Cottons began to catch on. Orders, straggling in unsolicited at first, steadily mounted, and to fill them the tempo of work was stepped up to a faster and faster pace. Handwoven labels for every dress said *Carrebee Cottons . . . Finer than Silk* and a smaller hand-woven tag announced *An August Vogt Design.* For I was determined that each concerned must have full credit for effort and thought expended. And of credit—as of work—there was enough for all. For Homer, wise in the ways of merchandising, was constantly on his travels making what he called "a little arrangement": arranging with factories scattered throughout the South to use Carrebee stock for their products, their contracts calling for deliveries on a regular weekly or monthly basis. This steady production and sales was, Homer said, the bread and butter to keep us from starving while we established our high-fashion cottons and introduced them throughout the land.

Evidence that this was beginning to be accomplished (and more swiftly than I had dared hope) began to appear. Slowly at first, then like a snowball, gathering both speed and substance in its progress. Letters from fashion stores and exclusive Specialty Shops outside the South: "Will you have your representative call on his next trip?" Trade papers and magazines sent their reporters to "get" the story of the new fashion sensation . . . the *exclusive* Carrebee Cottons. And I feeling smug and patting Homer as well as myself on the back for being such clever operators.

Homer with his wise, all-seeing merchandising eyes placed a warning finger across my lips, said, "Sh-h-h. Lady, don't start with the big mouth."

"Homer, it's true! The line *is* catching on! Of course we've done a good job! A spectacular job! You have to admit it."

"So now geniuses we are, says the lady." Prayerfully his eyes sought the ceiling. "Jess, don't you see, don't you know yet what is happen?" His face was suddenly awed, his voice dropped to hushed wonder. "Jess, we hit a trend."

Puzzled, I echoed, "A trend? What does that have to do with our line going over?"

He wrung his hands at my ignorance, paced a few steps and came back. "Lady, I try to explain. For years the retail and wholesale trade everywhere saying 'Cotton is sick. Why don't they make cottons that we can sell?' The trade all over saying and thinking, 'Why don't they make good-looking cottons?' And that, my beautiful, ignorant Jessie-bug, is the miracle, a . . . growing demand, a trend. We happened to hit when the trend was toward high-class cottons, but tomorrow they say, 'I spit on high-class cottons,' and what makes with us, way up high on a trend? I tell you, Jessie-bug. We go boom. We go bust."

Such a wonderful person . . . Homer. So wise, so shrewd, so easy to laugh; bringing with laughter, the spirit of fun to hard work. Yet laughter was only one of the various Homers that I came to know. There was Homer the trader, who, discarding all laughter, was quiet, wary and knowing; who, without wasting a word or a gesture, gently but firmly pushed some dallying buyer (and the sale) to decision and the name on the dotted line. There was Homer the husband, who when frail Marta was ailing, gave her careful and devoted attention, preparing her meals, making her laughter ring out as he served; but later, coming to stand a long time at the windows, the dark eyes gazing into the street.

Once when I suggested that Marta should have the attention of a doctor, he led me into the little office off his display room and gently put me in a chair facing him.

"I thought, Jessie, you understood. Doctors! Marta has seen more doctors than I can count! They tell me this or that . . . maybe . . . perhaps. A bad heart. Something wrong. But all give me the same answer when I ask what can be done." His face was quiet and infinitely tender. "Just one word, Jessie: 'Nothing.' "

"Homer . . ." I said, trying to form words of sympathy, so trite and empty as they came to my mind I could not bring them to my lips. "Homer . . ."

"They are wrong, of course, Jessie. Something I can do. I can take care of her. She must not do practically anything. Rest often. Not become tired. Not worry. No children, of course. This way, maybe for many years . . ."

I understood now his gentle solicitude for her, evident every moment they were together; and understood too his depths of goodness and capacity for love and service.

Now that he had told me this much, he spoke more and more of the problems induced by her inability to stand worry or strain. The clumsy lies and inept excuses he must invent to keep the daily newspaper which she read regularly and thoroughly, from her. Knowing that recent headlines would hardly be conducive to calmness, particularly to one of Jewish faith.

"We are sensitive to such things, Jessie. Maybe too much so. But in so many centuries of persecution and ugliness we learned to recognize the bigots and the tyrants earlier. We can smell them. If Marta read the papers, with that news splashed all over, it would upset her." He shrugged. "I am upset myself."

"Yes," I said, "so am I, Homer."

I remembered a childhood friend, the Negro boy named Man. And I recalled the unknown young Negro who had leapt from the viaduct. I was upset too.

The violence which filled the newspapers arose from a number of causes. Tom Watson, one-time friend of the poor and less privileged, had adopted methods that appalled decent people and inflamed the thoughtless to lawlessness. His paper, *The Jeffersonian,* attacked bitterly the rich Jews who planned to usurp control of the South from its rightful masters and thereafter inflict God-only-knew-what iniquities on the poor white-Christian voters of the South. In the mounting atmosphere of tension which spread not only over Georgia but the South, the Klan, or its later-day imitator, rode again to inflict the usual outrages with riveted leather straps upon the backs of a few and the conscience of all.

I read of the ugly, brutal forays of the Klan. I also read the reports of speeches by Watson and other politically prominent, or would-be prominent, orators, and saw that the bloody shirt was still valiantly waved, states' rights defended indignantly, and the sanctity of the home, motherhood and the Confederacy employed in toto to defend a bill to erect an unnecessary bridge, to protect the speaker or defame his rival. It was familiar and threadbare, yet apparently still effective. And I was reminded of Mr. Poteat's talking at table my first night at Miss Camilla's. He had talked, I remembered, of the New South and those who employed the demagogues to blind the common people with passion and make them easier to lead to the fleecing.

In the struggle at the mill I often forgot the ugliness. Homer came to Hickory Hill with Marta, and he, who was not permitted the children he longed for, labored with such tireless and selfless energy to win the friendship of Poky, I could have wept for that talent for fatherhood, wasted. Meeting Marta's eyes, I knew she would have wept with me, had it not been essential for us to be women and smile so a man would not know of our pity.

Poky responded nobly and allowed Homer to serve and wait upon him, to carry him on his back, crawl on the floor like a horse, pursue a kite or a June bug. Poky was, in fact, so responsive that Homer invariably returned to Atlanta a wreck of blissful fulfillment. But I could not help thinking many such happy days would bring about his collapse if not his finish.

In a small room above the carding room, reached by a narrow stair, I had arranged a place where Homer and August Vogt and I could work in comparative quiet. Often now, with plans for next season's cottons in the air, we worked there at night; not from choice but because the days were too full to pause and make plans for more. Sometimes until late at night we bent over a table and labored over designs and their merits, often heatedly, always with conviction. And I was surprised when Homer suggested it would be better if we worked in town in the future. He could fix up a place in his building, he offered, and we would be just as quiet as at the mill.

"But, I can't ride all the way in every time we want to go over designs, Homer," I told him, wondering what prompted the suggestion. "I know you have to come to the mill, but August and I are here. This is where we put the designs into production. It really doesn't seem logical to change."

He still argued but he finally agreed reluctantly that I was right. And I thought no more of it.

Several nights later we worked alone under the single globe in the little room, the pine table before us littered with rough drawings of tentative designs. We had talked at first as we worked but then fell into silent abstraction as we became absorbed in our work.

There was no hint, no warning. I sensed no impending danger, as others claim to sense an event about to take place. It was not so with me. Feeling a draft against my ankles and believing the door had slipped off its latch, calmly I turned to close it and saw the figure that stood there.

He was a big man, the shoulders under the soiled white of the sheet sloping and powerful. Sickening horror knotted my stomach and swelled in my throat like poison. Below the sheet I saw—not aware that I saw—legs in wool khaki trousers and heavy work shoes, muddy and scuffed. And then, in the darkness behind the first figure, I saw the white-covered heads of the others, waiting along the narrow outside stair.

I must have made some sound. Not intelligible but enough to attract Homer's attention. He looked up from the design he worked over and across the table I saw his face as the blood slowly drained from it. I saw too the thoughts that flashed behind his dark, reasoning eyes with inconceivable swiftness. If it be false that a man's whole life passes before him at such a moment, certainly he views and weighs the meaning of innumerable factors before he reaches conclusion. I saw Homer weigh Marta, his love of life, his need to care for her, his past, and a hundred or a thousand memories at which I could not guess. In only a fraction of time the thoughts had run their course. Then, quite calmly, he went to the tall, powerful man in the soiled white sheet and spoke to him as if stating the only natural, reasonable conclusion.

"I'm the one you want here. I'll go with you."

He meant to protect me, to take whatever we faced upon himself and so save me from it. And he almost succeeded, because the big sheeted man grabbed his arm and wrenched it back, half turning toward the doorway as if to go down the stairs. But a voice called from outside, "Git her too. She's got it acomin' much as the other one."

"Now wait a minute," Homer murmured, "the lady has nothing whatever to do with this. I'm in charge here. I'm to blame. For anything . . ."

The big man, as if in revenge for the deception by which Homer had almost taken him in, struck him heavily across the mouth. There was a smear of blood on Homer's mouth when the hard, unclean hand came away, but the mouth itself was steady against the fear which he felt. He was afraid, and did not pretend that he wasn't. And, God knows, fear was a greensickness in me that choked and numbed and shamed me.

The big man flung Homer into the arms of one of his followers, and reaching across the table, pulled me toward him, tearing the shoulder of my dress. I hardly noticed, yet I did notice, as the big man in his soiled sheet with its clumsily cut eyeholes held my shoulders, that there was an honest, strong male smell about him. The smell of a man who works hard and long, mixed with odors of earth and fertilizer and feeds. I guessed he was a farm worker, perhaps a farmer in his own right, and it suddenly struck me as terrible that he should have the smell of honest toil that wrests food from the earth, yet be on his shameful errand.

Neither Homer nor I offered resistance as they led us down the steps to the millyard. Once I asked my captor what they would do with us and he called, "Show 'em what we fixed up, Lyle."

The white figure before us lifted his hand to show the broad, webbed belt dangling from the palm, like a belt from a farm machine, and I saw the rows of small brass brads pounded into its end.

Homer and I made no sound, and some change in the bodies under the sheets suggested disappointment.

"Won't kill you," one advised us. "Just teach you to be decent, God-fearin' folks. Not go carryin' on at night and runnin' roun' over the country. 'Tain't fitten for no woman."

Crossing the darkness of the millyard, held in a relentless vise by a massive hand, I became aware of horses nearby and surmised that these men, a dozen or so in all, had ridden up to the mill. Perhaps they would take us with them the same way, I thought with horror and disbelief. Yet in my mind the thought persisted that they could not be serious. Men . . . human, ordinary men . . . could not do this.

In the dazed chaos of fear and my struggle to seem unafraid, I did not know why suddenly we were free, why Homer was no longer pinioned between two white figures. I saw the result of the mill people's presence before I saw their dark, massing shapes that had slipped, by the hundreds, from their houses with uncanny quiet, circling the millyard until now Homer and I and our captors were walled and prisoned within their circle.

They had no weapons. They offered no violence in answer to violence. They simply stood, watching, their silence somehow more ominous than shouts or raised clubs and sticks.

The big man in the white sheet conferred uneasily with his hooded brothers, then faced the mill hands.

"Now looka here, you good folks," he began. But he was not allowed to finish. The voice of a man, a voice as anonymous for me as any hidden by sheets, interrupted and spoke in a heavy unhurried drawl of contempt.

"Seems like a mighty good time for you bed-sheet bastards to be clearin' out."

The men in white, uncertain and not swaggering now, again nervously conferred and, deciding that they were outnumbered, they strode with attempted nonchalance toward the bunched horses near the mill gate.

But their attempt to preserve dignity met with sudden, shattering disaster. The big man, mounting, snagged a toe in the hem of his shoddy regalia. He slipped, swayed off balance, and stumbling backward sat down with a painful thud. Scrambling to his feet, he clambered into the saddle. But the damage was done. A mocking storm of guffaws burst upon the heads of the hooded riders. Before the lashing scorn of mirth the horses broke into a frantic gallop and dashed through the lane the mill hands opened.

Even as I laughed with the others, I knew the Klansmen were no joking matter and my laughter not far from hysteria. Homer and I had been in luck. How the hands had learned of the horsemen in time to save us, I could not guess. Perhaps as they had known of the arrival of the machinery, as soon as Darty and I heard the wagons. I did not care what the explanation might be. It was enough that they had come and in time. It would be impossible to try to put my gratitude into words without seeming a fool, but I think that they understood. And Yancy Jackson, seeing that my terror lingered, paused to give reassurance. "Miz Jess, we wouldn't let them lily-white boys bother you none."

Whatever their reason for wishing to inflict punishment on Homer and me, the Klan did not return, and their reason for coming at all continued to elude me. The sins attributed to me by slanderous gossip and to Homer by bigoted prejudice might have inspired it. Or the suspicion and intolerance which steadily grew more ominous throughout the South. But when I suggested these reasons to Andrew, he shook his head doubtfully. To search for a reason, he advised, was futile and a waste of time. To expect reason of a mob was in itself unreasonable. I'd do better to put the Klan out of my mind and concentrate on Algernon Carr, who constituted a far greater threat than irresponsible Klansmen.

I did not reply that it took self-control *not* to concentrate on Algernon Carr, for his influence with the commission houses had hurt us. I had not been able to add to the fund I had saved toward the second note on the loan. Now, however, as my partnership with Homer began to show results, I was enabled to save again and at a rate, if I could maintain it, to assure the payment when it fell due. Though it would be a tight squeeze we might, if our luck held, win through.

But our luck did not hold, though through nobody's fault. Carrebee Mills, like hundreds of others, were caught in the maelstrom of the war which broke out in Europe and sent cotton prices tumbling frantically. The price of middling plunged to six cents; the enormous soft bulk of the cotton crop was blocked and, as it halted, choked the arteries of trade. The South's economy, supported on that vast, fleecy cloud, quaked in panic and the mouths of merchants turned grim.

The volume of Carrebee sales slackened to a meager, ruinous trickle that curtailed operation, and in spite of every possible saving, high operation costs and low sales forced us to slowed-up production, and not only did the increase I had promised the hands have to be postponed but the slowed production meant fewer hours' work. But when I explained that times were hard and Darty was careful to share out the reduced work fairly among them, there was but little grumbling. Far less than I received from Miss Camilla who, regardless of the explanatory statement attached to her check each month, accepted her own reduced income with acrimony. However, I was far more concerned for the loss to the hands, whose need was greater. I was depressed by the necessity forced upon me by the business slump and, as it continued, I faced the knowledge that unless things improved, and soon, the second note could not be met.

Eagerly I studied reports of meetings held by prominent Atlanta businessmen, with Algernon Carr a leading figure, to consider the emergency and recommend measures to ease it. From their deliberations came announcement of a plan to accept cotton warehouse receipts as collateral. They also advised Georgia farmers to raise more food products. Neither plan nor advice seemed, at least to me, to offer practical help, but I admitted I could offer none more effective.

Both newspapers and prominent businessmen agreed that business conditions were desperate, and I shared the prevailing despair. Only Homer seemed impervious to pessimism.

"Jessie, if we could sell your worrying instead of cottons, we'd make J. P. Morgan look like a piker. All right, so we got a little slump." He shrugged. "Nothing. A little sprinkling of late frost. Before you know it the sun will be back out again and business will sizzle."

"I only hope you're right, Homer. And that when it comes the mill will be here to feel it."

He raised his brows. "As bad as that, Jessie?"

"As bad as that, Homer."

He rubbed his chin, reflectively. Then with a gesture he tossed trouble into the air and banished the possibility of disaster. "Right. Things are bad. But before you know it that sizzle will be here. Already I can smell it cooking. And then *M'chayah!*"

"M'chayah?" Clumsily I repeated the strange word.

"It's from maybe the best language in the world. Yiddish. On the hottest day in July, you work all day and walk the five miles home, and get there. And on the back porch you take off your shoes and somebody hands you a pitcher of ice-cold beer and you take the first swallow . . ." He spread his expressive hands in a gesture that expressed complete and whole contentment. "That's *m'chayah!* And take my word for it, Jessie, pretty soon business picks up and booms, and you'll be feeling *m'chayah!*"

But business did not pick up pretty soon, and as I totaled the sum in the special fund of "Carr's money," which was how I thought of it, I felt panic jerk at the pit of my stomach. The total was little more than half what I must have. Unbearable as it had seemed to default on the first note and lose the mill, it seemed infinitely more unbearable now. It would make pointless the first victory.

It would leave Andrew crushed under debt that would take years to pay, it would mean Darty's savings. Homer, who had used his small reserve as well as gone in debt to raise his share of the partnership, would be pulled into the ruins. All the worry, all the weary hours of back-breaking work, all the faith and hope and planning would be swept ruthlessly away, wiped out, made meaningless.

Yet, one thing at least I had learned since that other time of desperation. I had learned to hide fear, learned to mask desperation. In a little closetlike room adjoining the mill office, I had arranged a dressing room with washbowl and pitcher, and one day unexpectedly catching sight of my face in the glass, I saw a stranger. The features were mine, the eyes the color of mine, but I saw nothing of myself. My face kept the secret of what I was, what I felt and thought, and I suddenly understood the secret faces that some men wear; why mine now was like theirs.

It would not help matters if I revealed to every hand, to Darty and Homer, Mitty, to Cade and Mady, that I was afraid. It was, I decided, just as well that the mask was there, so firmly set that even Mitty did not penetrate it. Sometimes she remarked that I looked a little peaked and tired, that a good night's sleep would do wonders for me, and I would agree and go to bed soon after supper, but not to sleep. Lying awake, my thoughts prowled the darkness in search of escape from failure that day by day closed in and tightened. Sleep would have been a surprise.

Often, shuttling from mill to Homer's place and back to mill again, I wondered why I persisted. The mill (and the South), still trapped in the slump, was in the doldrums. But invariably when my courage hit a new low the week end would come and from Hickory Hill and home I would gather strength to go on. Not that I could truthfully call home a place of peace and quiet. It was noisy with laughter and swift-running feet and doors that apparently could only slam, but I didn't mind. Poky's gurgling laughter and awkward stumbling feet, and the sound of Mady and Cade's singing on the front steps as they did lessons, could lighten my darkest mood.

On Sundays with Andrew and Homer and Marty, often Joel, the young man who taught the mill school, the house would run over. Adeline, who helped out at such times, roasted chickens or baked a ham, and we'd sit down to Sunday dinner. Great platters of vegetables out of Cade's garden; string beans, potatoes smothered in cream, topped off with Mitty's lemon meringue pie. On fair days after dinner we sat on the porch until sundown, then Andrew fetched the watermelons from under the porch and, rolling his cuffs back from the strong freckled hands, would cut them. Sometimes as we sat on the porch in the summer night a group of Negro serenaders would come up the hill to perch on the front steps and play and sing: "Weep No More, My Lady," "In the Evening by the Moonlight," and "Good Night, Ladies." When they'd passed the hat and eaten the cake or pie Mitty served them, they'd say good night and wander back down the hill, their softly strummed banjos and guitars fading with their voices. And I would return to the struggle next morning, my courage renewed.

It was then that I bought my first automobile, a Model T Ford, to carry me back and forth to the city. Moppet and the buggy I kept for the children and Mitty, for Mitty's awe of the Ford, which she called Jess's gas buggy, was invincible. "Anybody that tells me that contraption is safe can go roll their hoop," she sniffed.

One night, however, as we put out the lamps before going to bed, she announced, as casually as if for the hundredth time instead of the first, that next morning when I drove in to Homer's, she might as well go along.

I asked, "You aren't serious about taking a chance in my gas buggy—are you?"

"I am"—she was brisk—"and I don't want any backchat about it." Reaching into her apron pocket, she pulled out a letter brought from the mailbox yesterday, she explained, by Cade. From Miss Ad, she added, handing it to me to read.

Miss Ad's precise handwriting, signed *Your true friend—Miss Ad,* contained nothing except a brief *Mitty, please come. Camilla away.*

Returning the note, I said, "I suppose Miss Ad thinks now is a good time to see you, Miss Camilla being away."

Lips pursed, she moved her head in denial. "No, Jess. It means more than that. Ad's troubled. Or she'd never ask me to the house, for fear Miss Camilla would get wind of it. I figure Ad's life ain't what you'd call a bed of roses. Camilla treats her as if it was a brain she was lacking instead of a voice."

So next morning, when I waved at Mady and Cade and Poky and turned the Ford down the hill road, Mitty was beside me, her eyes betraying that she expected the Ford to take to the air any moment. Later we cut over to the Boulevard, and as we rode along the wide street the past was piercingly alive again, for this was the first time I'd come this way since the last time I rode it with Wes. Surprised, I saw how much the street—such a wonderful street it had seemed to me in those days—had gone down. Even the Carrebee house, which had always been so spruce and well-kept, had the tired down-at-heel appearance that neglected houses acquire. Yet it was handsome still and had not lost its air of comfort that to me had been its chief charm. The Dorothy Perkins roses were about to come to full bloom, and as I turned in the drive, their wafted fragrance brought back precious moments that would never again return. The summer day when coming home from town I saw Wes, back from Tybee, as he circled the house to the front. Tall, brown, beautiful Wes! I had known the moment I saw him. I hadn't recovered at Vestal Hall. I still was in love with Wes.

Now I turned in the drive and brought the Model T Ford to a stop behind a car already parked; so opulent, gleaming and handsome, my Ford was reduced to a chicken coop in the wake of an ocean liner. Mitty and I got out and stood looking about for a moment, seeking, as people inevitably seek in a place where they once lived, the part of themselves which, on moving, they feel they have left behind.

Before us the garden, uncared for, had become a miniature jungle, and in its midst stood the summerhouse desolate and forsaken. And it suddenly struck me as monstrous that inanimate as it was, incapable of living or feeling, it had survived, and the young boy Wes, with his passion for living and loving, had not.

Circling the house we went up the front steps as Miss Ad, hastening, came to meet us. When she and Mitty had laughed and hugged, Miss Ad's flashing fingers responding to Mitty's cheerful voice, she led us around the side porch to the rocking chairs behind the wisteria vines.

Then, their heads confidentially tilted, they had a long conversation; Mitty, as Miss Ad's fingers moved, repeating to me in a guarded voice what Miss Ad had to tell. I was forced to be on my toes lest Mitty's interpretation delivered in dots and dashes fail to fully interpret.

"Cissa's here" was the first news relayed, which was no news until it was followed by "to stay . . . left Syl . . . for good . . . won't go back . . . mean . . . no good . . . and broke . . ."

Word by word, phrase added to phrase, Miss Ad's fingers told off her story. Not pretty or happy, I thought as I picked up the words and strung them like somber-hued beads. Cissa drinking too much . . . quarreling with Miss Camilla . . . Miss Camilla egging her to go back to Syl . . . needs the money, she says . . .

Syl wanted her back. . . . Came every day to hound her. . . . Syl in the house now . . . his car in drive . . . but Cissa wouldn't go back . . . hates him besides . . . these days Syl not flush . . . worried about Purity League . . . if it does what it says . . . Syl out of business . . . first place they'd raid . . . that Sportin' House of his and Pet Belleau's . . . he'd be out in the cold for sure . . .

It went on, but now my attention was drawn by voices inside the house. Cissa's light and lilting still, yet unlike Cissa's somehow. The other flashing under and over hers like the swift-darting tongue of a snake. Its sound so like Syl Crowley himself, it inevitably invoked him. The cadaverous body in its beautiful suit, the arms like fleshless black sticks in the sleeves; the dead-white skin of the sunken face, and always upon it the shadow of smile—faint, ghostly—yet with a terrible vitality that rose from something corrupt at the source of his life.

Suddenly from within the house laughter rang out, not the normal venting of wholesome mirth but wild, edged with hysteria yet underlaid with vindictiveness. We sat up startled, then Miss Ad spoke with her fingers and Mitty relayed their message. "Don't worry . . . some of Cissa's going-ons . . . she needs to go to a place where they'll help her, poor thing . . . but Camilla won't pay . . . says let Syl pay . . . he won't unless Cissa lives with him again . . . she says she'll die first."

Footsteps came up the hall toward the door and Mitty's voice halted in mid-air. Then the screen door swung open and Syl Crowley, moving deliberately, almost lazily, and glancing neither to left nor to right, went down the steps and around the drive. I saw the face under the rakish brim of the hat in all of its naked fury, and it struck me anew that it wasn't to be believed that Cissa had married Syl Crowley.

Almost without volition I left my chair and went through the screen door to the wide, restful rooms that greeted me like old friends. At first I saw no one, but following the direction from which I heard tinkling glass, I saw Cissa. She stood at the dining-room sideboard pouring herself a drink. In her pale dressing gown, from where I stood she looked as she always had, with her head held high and the soft curve of her child's throat arched in arrogant pride.

I waited while she drained the whiskey, her head thrown back, then I went toward her. When whirling with swift suspicion she saw me, she laughed.

"Don't scare me like that, Jess," she scolded, the whiskey—obviously not the first—slurring her words. "I thought you were Syl coming back."

I asked quietly, "How are you, Cissa?"

She put her hand on the sideboard to steady her uncertain legs, then her beautiful eyes—that were beautiful still though blurred and bleak and unhappy—peered at me in their effort to focus.

"How am I?" she repeated, her mouth lifting cynically. "Well—how would you be if you had to let Syl Crowley get in your bed?"

I had no answer for that but, turning to pour another drink, she failed to notice. With the drink in her hand she unsteadily wheeled and faced me again, the crooked smile she gave me, friendly, incredibly sad.

"You don't know about husbands like Syl, do you, Jess? You married Wes. Did Wes ever hit you?"

"No, Cissa—no."

Her eyes clouded. "Wes was a good boy," she said softly, "good to me. Jess, did you love him?"

"More than anyone in the world."

She nodded. "Me too. More than anything—" Her voice trailed. "But you don' know 'bout husbands like Syl. That hit you"—her eyes closed and her face was suddenly bleak—"that would kill you if you got in their way."

I urged, "Don't go back to him Cissa—ever."

She opened her eyes. "No. Not ever." Suddenly she laughed. "Can't anyway. He's almost broke."

Puzzled, I asked, "But didn't he have a great deal of money when you married him?"

"He *made* big money. He and Pet had four whorehouses." Her laugh was scornful. "High finance. So many girls at so much a head."

I cried out, "Oh Cissa, why did you marry him?"

Her smile was wry. "You didn't know, did you Jess?"

"Of course not. How could I?"

She shook her head. "You never knew I married Syl—to spite Wes."

I was unbelieving and she laughed at me.

I said, "Oh! Cissa. And Wes loved you so. I know sometimes he didn't act as if he did—"

She interrupted gently, "I knew Wes loved me. Even when I came home from Europe and he had married you—" She broke off, asked, "Do you know what he sent me for a wedding present?"

"Why, we sent silver, didn't we?"

She was impatient. "Not you—Wes."

"I didn't know—" I began.

Her nod was very wise. "I thought so. Well, he sent me the damnedest clock. Horrible." She laughed. "I gave it to Syl for the whorehouse."

I said sadly, "Oh Cissa!"

She hardly noticed. "And not even a card with his name."

"Maybe Wes didn't send it," I suggested.

She poured another drink, looking back over her shoulder. "Oh, he sent it. Who else would write on a card, *What time, old witch?*"

I waited 'til she finished her drink, then I said, "Cissa."

She threw down the drink before she said, "What?"

"Why don't you go off somewhere where they'll help you stop . . . that . . . ?"

She held up the glass. "This?" she queried.

"Yes."

"I'll tell you why." She shrugged. "I'm broke. I've run up a lot of bills. Syl's broke and he'll be *really* broke if the damned Purity League smashes this setup. Mama—" She shrugged again. "It's the old story. I haven't anybody."

As if the whiskey had only just reached her mind and spread confusion through it, she looked across at me with a child's frightened eyes.

"I don't know what to do. I can't stay here with Mama nagging, nagging. I won't go back to Syl." Her voice sank. "And if I don't I'm afraid . . ." her voice lifted to the timbre of a child's, "afraid he'll kill me."

I soothed, "That's just talk. He won't."

She gazed at me an instant, then, arching her throat, laughed and laughed and, finally stopping, looked at me shaking her head.

"You don't believe he would, do you, Jess?"

"No, Cissa. I think Syl talks big."

"Then I'll tell you something. Syl would kill anybody on earth that kept him from having what he wants." She added, "That's why I'm scared, Jess. He wants me." She moved her head. "And I won't go back."

In the days that followed I could not keep Cissa out of my mind. As I worried over the continuing dearth of business with a wincing panic at the disaster toward which we marched, the bleak, haunted eyes and the lovely voice, slurred with liquor and wretchedness, would rise before me. And always this Cissa, who was Syl Crowley's wife, would revive another: the swift girl of exquisite insolence of that first Christmas at Miss Camilla's. Snow queen, I had called her, attended by the three graces. This changed, frightened Cissa revived another memory too. Another face, cynical and bleakly empty; another voice slurred and wretched. Wes. Wes, whom I had been unable to save or help, for all my love and desperate eagerness.

They were, I knew now, so terribly heartbreakingly alike, the two children who had spent so many hours alone, companioned only with servants in the big house and vast grounds. They resembled one another, I knew now, much more closely than I had realized; less in the slim, careless grace they shared than something beneath their surface beauty. For a second I had seen Wes's devil peer out from Cissa's eyes. And that I could not shrug away.

Thoughts of Cissa reminded me of yet another reason to dread failure. Cissa's income from the mill, though reduced, provided the only means by which she could be independent of Syl Crowley. At that thought I would start to pace the floor again. The mill must survive. Somehow I must hold it together until business took a swing upward.

Of this there was no indication, and in the gathering gloom, Homer's stubborn optimism was so isolated, so contradictory to the facts, that by contrast to the normal, it forced itself upon my notice. When he argued that the slump was temporary and would not last, I listened, and if I found his arguments no more convincing than before—I was convinced. For now I was grasping at straws.

He sat turned backward in a chair, his arms resting on its back, and faced me as he argued.

"War, Jessie, is waste. All war. Like that feller who struck a match to Atlanta once said, 'War is hell.' Hell is also expensive. War needs hundreds, thousands of things to keep going. This war in Europe will create a demand that makes any demand you ever heard of a piker. It's a pretty big war, I read in the newspaper."

"But it hasn't created demand, Homer. It's killed it. At least in Georgia."

"For the time being," he agreed. "Because everybody's uncertain. But the law of demand ain't changed. The demand will come. But we ain't ready when it comes." He shrugged. "So maybe we're stupid. Scared maybe. But we ought to be ready for it. Not stuff for soldiers, you understand. Not tents and towels and such, but goods to sell maybe to other countries that won't be able to buy them in wartime. Something we should get ready to sell, and do it fast."

Thoughtfully I admitted, "I don't say you aren't right. But it can't help me now."

The brown eyes regarded me seriously. Then, "Jessie, do you know what I would do this minute if I had a million in the cash drawer?" he asked, adding matter-of-factly, "Not that I expect to, mind you. But if I did, do you know what I'd do?"

"No."

He came to lean over my desk. "I'd buy up raw cotton and weave all the Carrebee fine-count goods I could turn out and wait for that demand."

He straightened and gave me a wise nod.

"It's a cinch, Jessie."

I shook my head. "It's too much risk, Homer. Too much chance of losing. Weaving cottons to stock, without an order in the place . . ." I shook my head again. "We'd be gambling with the very existence of the mill."

He threw out his hands. "So we gamble on a sure thing? Is that bad when cotton can't go down? From six cents a pound, how far can you dive, Jessie? It's got to go up, and cotton textiles with it. There's got to be a rise. The feller smart enough to be ready will get rich."

"It's too much of a chance," I said again, and he patted my shoulder consolingly.

"Maybe," he comforted. "So maybe I talk through my hat, Jessie. When it's your mill and your money for cotton, it looks different. What you think best, Jessie, you do with your mill and your money."

"I'd have to use the money I've saved to meet the next note at the bank. It would be like jumping off into space hoping I'd be able to fly. It doesn't make sense," I said stubbornly.

"No," he agreed. "It ain't sense to jump off unless maybe a bear is right behind you!"

Still unconvinced, I put it out of my mind when I went home at the end of the day. And during supper and afterwards when I watched Mady tuck Poky in bed and later talked with her and Cade and Mitty, not once did my mind revert to it. Yet, next morning when I woke to the jabbering of the jays in the hickory trees beyond my windows, I knew that Homer had won. I would buy up raw cotton, put the mill back to work, weaving Carrebee Cottons, and without as much as one order on hand. I was going to gamble on Homer's "cinch."

Darty ordered the cotton and when the bales thudded ponderously down from drays to the loading platform, he brought a fluffy twist to the office for me to see. He placed it upon my desk, combing the fibers with his blunt finger. The staples, he pointed out, ran at least an inch in length, and the color was good. If I could show him a prettier grade of cotton, he would personally eat a bale. If we found a better grade, I replied, we would weave, not eat it, and he almost broke into a smile.

When the mill, humming back into vigorous life, pulled the hands back on their jobs, our spirits received a lift which the facts did not wholly justify. And when Homer, blowing innumerable kisses to the ceiling, dubbed me Mrs. Napoleon of the cotton mills, I silently prayed that by buying the cotton and putting the mill on full production I had not prepared to meet my Waterloo.

The first Sunday after the mill had settled down to steady operation, I told Andrew of the job we had done, describing the risks involved and the possible gains. He must understand, I said, that my decision affected him too. He might never get back the money he had borrowed to lend me. I felt guilty, I admitted, because I had failed to consult him. But he shook his head. The decision, he said, was mine. He expressed neither approval nor disapproval, however, apparently feeling that since it was done there was no more to be said.

"Anyway," he said, "you made the decision and are ready to take the consequences. That's when you start to be a boss, Jess. Most people think the boss has a soft life because he can sit and look out a window or wander around the office. They don't know the difficulties that one decision may involve or how heavy it gets when you carry it on your back."

Glancing through the Sunday newspapers which he had brought out, he said, "You might find this interesting," and passed the paper over, pointing to a picture of Algernon Carr. Reading the story, I learned that he had been elected Chairman of Atlanta's Civic Purity League and in an impassioned speech had pledged himself and his organization to a vigorous and effective campaign against vice.

Having never heard of the Civic Purity League, I asked Andrew what it was. He explained that from its beginning Atlanta had been the Old South's "strangeling." Rough and ready and gusty, like a mining town with a lot of riffraff mixed in with decent folks. Unfortunately the riffraff rose in the world and got into politics. The result now and then got mighty questionable. Right now in Atlanta it wasn't too good. And the top of the barrel was planning to get rid of the rotten apples. Which led to the Civic Purity League. Algernon Carr, famous as a crusader against vice, was its chairman. "It might interest you to know, by the way," he added, "that he's planning to throw someone you know into a business slump that will make your troubles seem like a tea party."

Puzzled, I repeated, "Someone I know?"

"I'm speaking of Syl Crowley," he said. "His various enterprises, I hear, have been hard hit. Holy Carr has stirred up considerable indignation and a lot of Syl's colleagues are scuttling for cover."

"Because they are afraid of Carr?" I inquired.

"That's right," he answered. "It would seem a lot of people are afraid of Carr."

Leaning forward in my chair, my chin cupped in my hands, I mused. A lot of people afraid of Algernon Carr. It was true, I realized, but I wondered why? What drove him to be a man who aroused fear in others? And when they spoke of him with contempt—and some did—it was only another way of showing fear. As was hate. What made Algernon Carr arouse contempt and fear and hate?

I did not find an answer. I found only a riddle. And I realized that Miss Camilla, though more familiar and known better, was no more familiar, no better known to me than Carr. She too was a riddle.

"What makes them the way they are, Andrew?" I asked as if he should have been able to follow my thoughts, and then when he looked puzzled, I explained. "Mr. Poteat told Miss Camilla once that she belonged to the new ruling class of the New South," I said. "It was a long time ago. I remember he mentioned Algernon Carr's name, too. But that doesn't explain it, that I can see."

"I think Mr. Poteat meant that they are at the top of the heap and as a result they exhibit the traits of the whole, in a way. They are of the New South. But they're Southerners first, I suppose, and most importantly."

"But so am I. So are you."

"In a different way though. We're not as tied to the traditions and customs. We're not loaded down with a burden of dead ancestors and dead past. Carr and Miss Camilla are. They have as much family as anybody can claim with any basis except the lies they've heard from old maid aunts about great-uncle Henry's being descended from a king. But they are family and they have money. Camilla has always had it since she married Carrebee. Carr made it fast and hard."

I began, "But how does that explain . . . ?"

He interrupted quietly. "I'll tell you a little fable. Unfortunately, I'll have to mention the Lost Cause. I don't like to bring it up, because so many others never bring up anything else. But it's pertinent to the fable. Want to listen?"

I said of course, and he put his finger tips together and leaned his head back against his chair.

"Once there was a nation," he began, "and it began to grow great, but broke into two parts and fought a war."

"I know the ending, I think," I said.

"Nobody knows the ending," he corrected me. "Anyway, they fought a war, and like all war I suppose, it was a guilty war. Not that honest motives and admirable ideals were not held by adherents of both sides. But they were pretty well lost in the war. Lots of things are lost in every war, even ideals."

"It isn't the way I heard it," I said.

"It's the same story," he assured me, "but from a different point of view. As I said, it was a guilty war. One side, as it happened, was just learning to love the vice that made it guilty; the vice of the dollar. Not that all of them knew what was happening. But there it was. It was getting pretty widespread, as vices go."

"What was the guilt of the other side?"

"Much like the first, but a variation," he told me. "Pride. Pride in blood, in caste. One of the ideals of that war was that slavery was a crime—and God knows it was, but it got lost too. Anyway, the two guilts went to war and, as always happens, men died and people suffered, but the guilts grew strong. One side was defeated but neither guilt was beaten. But this happened. The penalty of the loser was that part of the nation, and those who were powerful in it and therefore assumed responsibility, were forced to assume both guilts. Dollar guilt and pride guilt. They still carry both and they're curiously congenial, by the way. They complement each other pretty well."

He sat erect. "I don't usually tell stories. And this one is an oversimplification, which is why it has value."

"But do you mean that Algernon Carr and Miss Camilla—?"

"Wear the double guilt?" he asked. "The guilt of dollar worship and the guilt of pride in family and in the superiority they give. Yes, I think both fit the bill pretty damned well."

"But you and I are Southerners too," I said. "Why don't we have the same guilts? Or do we, maybe, and just don't realize?"

He shook his head. "We don't. But that's because we're Southern in another way, one that Carr and Camilla have slight respect for. We're plain people. My father was a Scotch dirt farmer. Your grandfather was too, before he began to plant money and reap that kind of crop. We belong to the dirt." He grinned. "That's not even American. It's international. We don't belong to the past, where the pride began, and we were poor. We missed out on our chance at their double guilt."

"And you think that's why they are as they are? Because of the double guilt?"

"And for ten thousand other reasons, as a rough guess. But you'll find those two reasons among them, and they'll weigh heavier than all the others together."

The mill roared back into full production, the clashing looms unreeled yard upon yard of goods, the glumness of the mill hands lifted. Almost I envied them. My anxiety, rather than relieved by return to capacity production, was intensified, and the gamble I had ventured appeared foolish and hazardous. If Homer's predicted business upturn failed to materialize, if the goods we were storing in mounting bolts on stockroom shelves did not sell, the loss would make ruin inevitable. "Carr's money" had been used to buy the cotton and unless the upturn came—and before the note was due—the mill would go to Carr's combine.

A slight flurry of orders that arrived in the mail sent my courage soaring. But it was an extremely mild flurry, too slight to repay even a small share of the cost of the cotton. It was a sprinkle of rain when it needed a flood to keep the mill afloat, and with the cunning propensity peculiar to bad news I heard that others in cotton predicted that Carrebee Mills were about to go under.

It was Homer who informed me of these pessimistic predictions, gleaned, he explained, by friends in Wholesale Row who repeated to him overheard conversation. It was common talk according to Homer's report that Carrebee was taking a last-ditch gamble against fantastic and impossible odds; a situation that caused no surprise in cotton circles, the general belief being that there was little difference between the operations of a cotton mill owner and a cardsharp.

Hearing what they said, I told Homer I didn't doubt for a minute that they said a great deal worse. I added grimly that they probably were correct.

He was utterly cheerful. "When business booms, Jessie, they'll talk the other way. When we're raking in the money we'll be smart cotton operators."

"Business has to boom first," I reminded him wryly.

He nodded confidently. "Just keep listening, Jessie. Any day now, you'll hear that boom. Like Big Bertha."

Before his prediction came to pass I had a visitor. One totally unexpected. Seated at my desk, figuring up for the hundredth time the volume of business the mill must do in specified time if it was to meet the note, I heard someone enter the office and I turned expecting to see Darty or one of the mill staff, and instead saw Miss Camilla.

Elegantly dressed, poised and sure, I saw her again as she had been in the past; the creamy skin, the dimpled, plump hands and clear blue eyes unchanged. To my eyes she miraculously for a moment became the woman I had first seen in the room at the Kimball House, who had for a few moments stirred the hope that she was the mother of my illusive childhood fantasy. Quickly I had realized my mistake. But, hungry for love, I had been prepared to love her, had loved her, would now if allowed.

I did not know what my face revealed. Unprepared for her coming, it would be strange if she failed to perceive my shocked surprise. She, of course, was prepared and her confident self; incapable of doubting that she'd win any victory worth her while.

"You need be under no illusions," she said coolly. "I am here to talk business. A subject I assume we can still discuss."

When I replied, "Certainly, Miss Camilla," I envied her assured calm but knew I was still too far from the superlative actress she was to match it. Instead I suddenly felt gauche and young in her presence again and awed by her conviction of superiority.

I indicated a chair, and gracefully poised in it, she faced me, drawing off her gloves as she spoke.

"I assure you, Jessica, this is as distasteful to me as to you. Only one thing could have brought me. The thing we still have in common, however we feel toward each other."

"I think," I said, "that you have never known or know now my feelings toward you."

Her eyes widened as if with genuine surprise. "Whatever they were in the past, I am not mistaken about them now. Just as you know mine toward you. I certainly made them clear enough at our last meeting. And I am neither a weak woman nor one to change easily."

I gazed at her a moment. "Perhaps I am weak," I said finally. "Maybe I should hate you. But I'm not able to. I've felt bitter and resentful. Yes. But not even that—now."

Her little smile was knowing. "We see things differently." The throaty voice was calm. "I admit that I can hate."

"I'm sorry."

"You need not be. In any case, we waste time. I came to talk about business. Specifically about my monthly check from the mill. I can't support my home and my way of living on such an absurd sum. You lived in my home long enough to know that."

"Your check is prorated on your holdings," I pointed out, "after costs. Everyone's taking a cut. Business has been—and is—bad."

With a tinge of malicious dryness, she asked, "What? In spite of your noble experiments?"

"I don't consider them noble. I've tried to pull the mill out of the red."

"I'm afraid you're rather naïve," she said lightly, "to buy cotton in a slump; and running on full production without hope of selling the goods you produce isn't apt to get Carrebee out of the red."

"It was a chance I had to take," I said grimly. "If we win, the mill can go on and in sounder condition than for years."

"And if you lose?"

With a confidence I did not feel, I answered, "We won't lose. We're right."

She laughed aloud, her brusque, husky laugh a sound of contempt, not amusement.

"And I say you are wrong. On very sound authority. *I* still have friends, you know."

I ignored the implication in the words and she went on.

"I hear from reliable sources that the government intends to take every precaution to keep this country from involvement in the war in Europe. Trade with countries involved will be discouraged. Such a policy will prolong the slump—indefinitely. Even when the upturn comes —if it comes—cotton will be the last to pick up."

As she spoke I tried to conceal my consternation at the speculations her throaty, serene voice set in motion. She did know important people. It was likely she would have heard of policies to be adopted. She was friendly with those whose information was gained in high places. Undoubtedly her knowledge came from those "in the know."

". . . at least six months," she was saying, "before the upturn. Can you hold out six months?"

At the question, panic suddenly wrenched and jerked me to the point of nausea. But I fought it down, determined that she should not know the truth.

"Can you hold out six months?" she repeated sharply, her eyes intent on my face.

"I can try."

Her smile returned, a smile now of patient tolerance.

"You're a fool to lie to me! Don't you think I know? The note you must pay Algernon Carr? What you paid for all that cotton? To go into goods that will rot on your shelves? Do you think I can't see that you're green around the gills because you know you have failed?"

I did not answer, knowing it would be hopeless to pretend any longer. I asked wearily, "Did you come to say this to me, Miss Camilla? To fling it in my face?"

"I don't waste my time with silly scenes," she retorted. "I came because I hoped saving Carrebee might be more important to you than hating me, and"—as I started to speak—"I am not interested in how you feel. The mill is the question."

"Yes," I said, "the mill is the question." I met her eyes squarely. "If I couldn't save it and believed you could, I would turn control back to you any minute. So many depend on it for food and clothes and houses. They matter." I met her eyes again. "Could you save it?"

Relaxed and leaning back in her chair, she smoothed her gloves which she held.

"I wouldn't be here otherwise." She spoke with matter-of-fact simplicity that left no doubt of her certainty. Her blue eyes widening in the little trick they had, gave their usual effect of coming closer. "I told Wes, remember, that when you needed me I would come back. The mill was his and bears his name and I volunteer to do just that; though you did not ask it."

I listened, aware of a tiny ripple of smile hovering about her mouth.

"I would save the mill," she repeated. "But, naturally, with certain conditions. When I saved it and had it back on a sound basis you could not take it over again. I'm afraid I'm not quite that noble."

"If I let you take it, I would not try to come back."

She nodded approval. "I would have to be protected against that . . . er, possibility. It would not be difficult to arrange. You would make over to me a part of your stock. Enough, with my own, to give me legal control. Actually it's no more than fair. My husband established Carrebee. I carried it on."

When I said I would make over the shares to her I saw the hovering smile more definitely and it occurred to me that she kept her head slightly bowed to prevent my seeing her eyes.

"I will do what you ask," I went on, "if you save the mill. But how would you do it? I would have to know."

She shrugged, her husky laugh deprecating but no less sure. "It wouldn't be difficult for me. For you it would be impossible."

"Why—impossible for me?" I asked.

"Because you haven't . . . the right connections. The standing. I must speak frankly. You have no influence with the right people, no means of gaining concessions and consideration from those in a position to grant them."

"Who are they? Those people?"

"Generally speaking, a number. Specifically, Mr. Algernon Carr."

"Yes," I said, "to that extent you are right. I have no influence with Mr. Carr."

"Except that you"—she made a little move—"you annoy him. I seem to recall your telling me . . . had to do with that daughter of his who made such a fool of herself, didn't it? I suppose it left a bad taste in his mouth—your background and all. Thank heavens he likes me. A great deal, in fact. I made sure that he would years ago. I always had an idea he might be useful."

I glanced at her quickly but she either was unaware of how much she had revealed or was aware and not disturbed. Her eyes were as blandly innocent as a child's.

"Frankly, I've had several talks with him about the mill. He's most understanding. If I'm in control he'll give us an extension on the note coming up. Business conditions more than justify consideration, he says. And he'll give me a longer period in which to repay the balance."

I said, "I see," convinced that she told the truth, that Algernon Carr would grant the consideration she claimed. What I could not believe was his offering such liberal concession without demanding a return. He still was a banker, still the man who had formed the mill combine.

I said, "Naturally, such generous consideration would be granted on some sort of terms."

She looked at me as if surprised at the question. "Naturally. It is a mistake to accept something for nothing. Possibly you have yet to learn that."

I asked, "What are his terms?"

"He will take Carrebee Mills into the combine. We will belong to the organization and enjoy its benefits but preserve our independence. We'll have our own officers and so on, but we will be guided by the combine policy on wages, hours and so on. It will eliminate troubles with the lintheads too, for they'll know that all combine labor gets what they get so they'll be easier to handle. Then we'd receive increased consideration from the commission houses, as part of an organization controlling so great a volume."

"And how long would it be before the combine took over the mill?" I asked innocently.

"How long . . . ?" The blue eyes widened a moment before she snapped, "That would be most unlikely, with the advantage all mine."

"No"—I shook my head—"the advantage wouldn't be yours. He would never stop until he got the mill. He's wanted it all along because he doesn't have an Atlanta mill in the combine. And he needs one. He would never stop until he had you in a corner."

With a burst of sudden vehemence, she cried, "He likes me. He thinks I've got a good head for business."

"I don't doubt that for a moment," I said. "But neither do I doubt that he intends to get Carrebee. And keep it."

"How dare you say that about Algernon Carr? A man of integrity . . . high-principled . . . ?"

I stood up, calmer now than she. "I admit it," I said. "Once I wouldn't have. I thought he was without principles. I learned differently. He does have principles . . . of a kind. One happens to be that it isn't sound to be soft in business. He'd take the mill."

"Not from me!"

She had drawn erect in the chair, her face flushed, her fingers still mechanically smoothing the gloves.

"Not from me," she repeated.

"From anybody," I answered.

"I tell you I will save the mill. Isn't that the important thing?"

"Not if to save it, you throw it away."

"Then your promise to give it up was only your usual hypocrisy?"

I said, "If you could save it, I still say it. But if you save it by going into the combine, I won't let you do it."

She rose now and faced me, her face stony with anger; her eyes flaring like blue flames in a fire. "You little snip!" Her voice, deeper and rougher, was hoarse with her anger. "You fool, I at least would save it. You'll lose it before a month. Don't you see you've nothing to gain? You'll lose the mill to the combine, won't you? The day the second note falls due. Carr'll get it just the same. Can't you get that through your head?"

"At least he'll have to take it," I said. "I won't give it to him on a silver platter."

"If you would just listen to reason . . ."

I shook my head. "There's no use talking about it."

She started to speak but caught back the words. For a long moment she stood motionless, the anger fading from her face, her body releasing itself from tautness. Then she smiled gently, almost tenderly.

"My poor child," she said softly. "It isn't really your fault, is it? . . . that you see things as you do. I knew it . . . from the first. I should have warned Wes . . . instead I tried to be kind. I know now I should have told him the truth even if it made him hate me. It was my duty to tell my son that marrying you out of pity would lead to tragedy."

"Pity?" I was uncomprehending.

She still smiled. "A boy of his background able to marry any girl but marrying one out of the gutter? What other reason could he have had?"

"He could have, and did have, love for his reason. For whatever else I was or wherever I came from, I gave him love." After a pause I asked, "Did you, Miss Camilla?"

She stared at me bleakly a second and then gave her brusque, disparaging laugh.

"How noble of you! Quite the martyr, aren't you? But that's poor white trash for you. Pulling out all the stops!"

She turned and calmly strolled toward the door, casually and gracefully as if she crossed a fashionable room to greet a friend. Darty's face appeared outside the screen as she reached it and he, scowling his ferocious astonishment, automatically held the door to let her pass out.

Graciously she murmured, "Thank you, Darty," and went down the steps and out of my view.

The screen door whacked as Darty let it swing.

"What'd she want?" he demanded.

"The mill."

He snorted.

"She says," I told him, "that unless the mill's turned back to her, Carr will get it. And I'm convinced if she takes it back Carr will get it. It's the devil and the deep blue sea, isn't it, Darty?"

"Seems to me, however you play your hand, Carr wins."

I was incapable of pretense now and the mask I had learned to wear was shattered.

"It's likely, Darty, that you're right," I said.

That Miss Camilla reported to Algernon Carr the results of her meeting with me was a foregone conclusion. And I was human enough to feel a malicious glee at the thought of having outwitted his scheme to get Carrebee. On second thought I admitted that outwitting Algernon Carr benefited us little. It solved nothing so far as I was concerned. But it encouraged me to hope Homer's boom might arrive, and perhaps the same thought occurred to Mr. Carr. It perhaps occurred to him too that our heavy purchases of cotton which we were turning into goods at full production capacity placed us in a position to turn an extremely neat profit if there was a sudden spurt of activity.

There had been for a long time—and for a good many years would continue to be—a tradition of competition between mills themselves, a tradition not universally practiced but familiar enough to give rise to humorous tales of shrewd secret maneuvers by which one mill caused confusion in the operation of a competitor, even disrupted production.

I had heard vague references to these practices when I sat in on conversations with mill hands. Darty occasionally told me stories of the bygone and, as he suggested, hardier and more exciting days in the history of cotton milling. But not having had direct experience with anything of the sort, I would never have realized that deliberate damage was being inflicted on Carrebee. Even Darty could not have known so quickly, had it not been for Yancy Jackson.

One of the looms suffered a breakdown and Darty and I, inspecting the disabled machine, were told laconically by Yancy Jackson that there was something "right peculiar 'bout this here loom gittin' out of kilter." It was just too likely looking a accident for him to believe it was genuwine. Not a chance of pinning it on anybody—he shook his head regretfully—but it had been a right clever job of wrecking and by somebody who knew looms.

I had long ago been impressed by Yancy's uncanny sensitivity to the personalities and humors of machines, and I did not question his opinion. If he said the machine had been purposely disabled, it had, and as I returned with Darty to the office, I was experiencing a quiver of something not unlike apprehension. If the work should be obstructed now by sly violence to equipment, we would be seriously slowed down in producing the quantity of goods at which we aimed, possibly stopped. And if my reaction seemed unwarranted by merely one incident of malicious damage, it was because I knew how vital it was to have goods ready in case the market came back to life. Already I had gambled. But without steady production, I had already lost. If that happened—and it must not be allowed to happen—I would have nothing to sell except the raw cotton that waited, still baled, in the cotton shed. Even then I would have to wait until business picked up and cotton prices rose, to recover any part of my loss.

But, I told Darty Land when we returned to the office, I probably had an exaggerated idea of the harm that could be done us. He faced me from his swivel chair, his face creased with anger. A fellow who knew mill machinery, he snapped, could make plenty of trouble. Might be a good idea to post a few watches at night, he suggested, just in case.

"Put them on by all means," I told him. "Take every precaution."

Grimly glowering, he nodded.

"Any idea who might be behind it?"

I told him I was almost certain that Algernon Carr was behind it if, as Yancy Jackson believed, it had been deliberate.

Scowling, pushing out his underlip, he agreed. "Maybe. Don't know anybody else who'd go to the trouble. And Carr knows where we can be hurt quickest and surest. But who's behind it ain't important. Finding out who's doing it—is!"

That, however, was not easy to do. And though Darty Land and Yancy worked tirelessly, talking with recently employed hands, checking up on background and character, they unearthed no evidence that connected either new or old employees with the vandalism. Yet in spite of precautions, it continued. And then, as if the intentional damaging of machines infected the atmosphere of the mill, there was a sharp increase in the number of genuinely accidental breakdowns.

Now we were brought to realize that the hidden enemy did not limit his attacks to machinery, but was undermining the human force of the mill. First intimation of this came when Sandy Yeager, the work manager, appeared in my office to announce that he was quitting. When, astonished, I asked why, he said he had been offered another job.

"But now is the time we need you," I protested. "We depend on you to put the cotton in work so that our goods come off the loom as it should."

Sheepishly but stubbornly, he muttered he was sorry, and I shook my head wonderingly.

"When do you want to leave?" I asked.

"I promised right away," he answered. "I reckon I'm through, ma'am, when the whistle blows closing time."

"What will we do?" I asked, still amazed. "We have to have a work manager!"

He muttered again he was sorry, and then, in a sudden burst of words, explained that he didn't like leaving like this.

"You've been fair, Mrs. Carrebee, an' I got no complaint 'bout the job. But you see, ma'am, I been offered the same job someplace else and at so much more money I just can't turn it down. I've got to think about my family."

It was obvious that he felt guilt at leaving his job without notice, and I was curious as to the figure it took to triumph over his Scotch conscience.

"How much will you be paid in your new job, Sandy?" I asked, and he gave me a hopeful glance that told me if we could meet or even approach the offer, he would stay with the mill. But at his answer, his hope—and mine—faded.

"I can't meet it, Sandy," I told him. "And I don't blame you for taking it. But isn't that kind of pay unusual for a works manager?"

With genuine candor, he said it. He had never heard of a case before.

"I don't know what their setup is, Mrs. Carrebee. But if they're big enough fools to pay it, I can't bring myself to say no. I wish I could, ma'am."

Standing, I held out my hand. "Good-by, Sandy," I said. "And good luck in the new job. We'll miss you."

Grasping my hand, he thanked me miserably, assuring me of his regard, and that he'd been treated fair and square at Carrebee Mills. Then, turning abruptly on his heel, he clumped out of the office, as if overcome with fury, either at himself for being unable to resist the extraordinary pay or at others for offering it.

I sat in my chair again, gripped by a baffled frustration. First the machines, now the hands.

When Darty returned to the office, a few moments later, I told him of Sandy's resignation and of the pay he'd been offered. Darty heard me out with mounting fury that gave him the look of a malevolent gnome.

He stalked to the far corner of the office, then stalking back again, faced me. "Half-dozen families moving out of the village, too," he announced. "There'll be more leaving and we'll lose more of our key men, too. If it keeps up, you and me and Homer will be trying to run the blamed mill by ourselves. We're being raided."

"Raided?" I repeated, and he told me bitterly that it meant some other mill was systematically hiring away our hands with particular attention to skilled workers and supervisory employees whose loss would cause us most harm.

In a bleak voice that betrayed my tangled, hopeless thoughts, I said slowly, "And that's Algernon Carr too, isn't it?"

Darty nodded grimly.

"But how long can they keep it up?" I was speaking to myself as much as to Darty. "How many ways are left to fight us?"

With his back to me he stared out the window. "I don't know. But I'm beginning to feel like a sitting duck."

Depressed, I returned to my desk and tried to check the sheaf of cost sheets before me. When I realized that the figures on the sheets had no meaning, I pushed them aside and sat idle, and possessed by bleak fury.

My anger was not the explosive kind that finds release in a burst of hot fury but the anger of quietness, a black coldness, frozen and still inside me. Anger was sickness and I loathed it and the shame it left, like a scar; and the feeling that whatever dignity there is in a human being becomes petty and mean at its touch.

There had been times this past year when I could not avoid anger. For it seemed as if my life was a struggle so unceasing and bitter it was robbed of meaning or grace. On one side the hatred and enmity of Miss Camilla; and the other, hatred and enmity, no less intense, of Algernon Carr. The past months had been long and grim with conflict, months of nagging war, tainting with their bitterness the joy and goodness and love of my other life at Hickory Hill with Mitty and the children and Andrew.

There was no pleasure or zest in the combat now, no sense of reward in my efforts to make the mill sound and financially secure. Yet I must go on. If all was lost, how could I carry Hickory Hill or give care and comfort to those I loved? Even now, the mill devoured all it could get. Unless my gamble turned out well, I saw scant hope of victory. Sometimes I had the unpleasant sensation of hanging suspended above a chasm, knowing that the flimsy support to which I clung could any instant fail and plunge me into disaster.

How long I sat there at my desk, I did not know—until I became aware that darkness pressed its face against the windows and filled the office. The closing whistle had sounded, I realized, but whether minutes ago or an hour I was unable to tell, though Darty Land still bent over work at his desk; I wondered why he did not turn on his lamp. Night came earlier now and there was a chill in the morning and evening air. Autumn and weariness were much to blame no doubt for my depression. Tomorrow, after a good night's sleep, I'd have a more cheerful outlook. Now I must be starting for home. Mitty would have to wait supper as it was.

Still, I did not move but stared abstractedly through the window by my desk toward the mill buildings looming dim against the late glow of sky. I noticed a small blink of bright yellow on the roof of the cotton shed and wondered vaguely what it was.

I watched with only casual attention the odd little point of flickering brightness. It seemed to be slightly larger now, but the unsubstantial darkness made all shapes uncertain. I heard pounding feet run past the window where I sat and a hoarse voice that shouted a single word I did not understand; a mill hand calling to a friend, I thought. The brilliant fragment on the roof of the cotton shed was unmistakably larger now, I admitted idly, then felt a quick shock of apprehension for which I had no explanation.

"Darty," I said. Then, as absorbed in his work he did not answer, I spoke more peremptorily, "Darty, come here!"

I heard his grunt of annoyance and he crossed the office to stand behind my chair.

"What's that?" I asked. "See? On the roof of the cotton shed."

"Where . . ." he began in a surly voice, then gave a hoarse cough as if the wind had been knocked from him. I heard him cursing in a thin, blank voice of fear.

"What is it?" I demanded, then, before he answered—I knew. At the same instant, as if knowing that concealment now was pointless, the little light gathered and surged in a writhing, licking fury, high above the distant, darkening hills.

Darty said harshly, "More'n half the cotton still in that shed."

"The cotton . . ." I repeated, but he had jerked around and wrenched the door open, and I heard him yelling orders, and felt a sickening panic knot my stomach. If the raw cotton was burned or ruined, the mill was ruined too, and going down, would pull down all who depended upon it.

I followed Darty outside and, standing on the office steps, saw the flames at the far end of the grounds soaring triumphantly into the deepening, dark brilliance of the night. I saw an odd, incongruous star.

Darty sped toward the distant rim of mill grounds and cotton shed, and I followed. My chest ached and a hard sliver of pain pierced between two ribs, but, goaded by a spur of fear, I ran on, aware of the dark gathering of figures as mill people poured from their houses and ran as I did across the expanse of ground. A young man, nostrils flaring and neck cabled with strain, swerved past me and, recognizing me, paused.

"Go on," I gasped. "Hurry! Try to save . . . cotton!"

He hesitated, fearing I required help, and I heard my voice rail at him in shrill fury.

"Go on—for God's sake!"

He wheeled and sped away and I labored after him, telling myself that this too was the work of Algernon Carr. Proven or not, he was to blame and I knew it.

I was consumed by a gust of wrenching rage and then advised myself aloud that I had no time for anger now. "You can't take time for that," I gasped. "Not now. Later." I had come near enough to see that dark figures of men milled on the loading platform of the cotton shed, intangible black cutout shapes beating with brooms and sticks at tongues of fire. Lines of men and women were strung between the shed and water spigots and passed pails and buckets from hand to hand.

As I came in sight, I saw Darty forming another water line. But I paused neither to pay attention to buildings nor bucket lines until I reached the cotton shed. Here, Yancy Jackson had taken charge. Aided by a gang of the brawniest of the mill hands, he trundled out the bales of cotton, scattering them in the yard, with boys to protect them with brooms and croker sacks from sparks and brands.

All this I saw in a split second, the men moving in and out of the flaming shed, not noticing my arrival. I caught sight of Yancy's lanky figure rising above the heads of others as he gave directions in a composed voice, and with grunts and cursed panting more bales were levered onto loaders and rolled out into the night. How many bales must yet be moved, I wondered, before all the cotton was safe? Could they save all before the flimsy shed roof fell?

Clambering up on the platform, I looked about the stretch around me, now brilliantly aglow beneath the burning roof, and tried to count the bales yet unmoved. As I did, someone seized my arm, wrenching me around, and I saw Yancy's face.

"What in the name of God are you doing here?"

"The cotton . . ."

"We're taking care of the cotton," he snapped.

This was the truth. Only a few bales remained, and these were being moved slowly but steadily toward safety. I saw them reach the open air, in the moment after Yancy spoke.

"I got to get you out of here," he said, and unceremoniously jerked me toward the platform's edge. My dress caught on a bayonet of splinter from one of the timber supports, and I heard the rasping, tearing sound of the cloth and looked down at my skirt. A second later I was jerked violently from my feet and caught up under Yancy's arms, my feet hanging in space. I saw the slow, sagging tangle of flaming timbers and beams cascade to the floor and erupt in billowing clouds of haze shot with glancing sparks.

With Yancy's lean, hard hand a vise on my wrist, I was dragged a safe distance from the cotton shed and left to stand coughing and gasping in the cool fresh air of night. The flames leaped in a thin final crescendo of crimson, yellow and fiery white, projecting the mill and grounds vividly against the night for a moment. Then, with a rending sound of wood, the roof of the shed began a slow sprawling descent and sank upon its foundation, the fire dwindling swiftly upon its reduced bed of coals.

"Good it took the shed and left the cotton, Miz Carrebee," Yancy said at my shoulder.

"I know, Yancy. The shed doesn't matter if the cotton's safe."

Darty sidled over to us and stood looking me over with amused eyes. I became conscious of my smeared face, my smoke-blackened hands; and when I raised my hands to my disordered hair, a shower of gray ash flaked from it.

Darty's smile widened to a grin. "You look more like a linthead than any you got."

Before I went home he and Yancy and I inspected the bales of cotton. It had to be put under cover in case of rain, Yancy observed. He'd post a crew to stand watch tonight, just in case. With the exception of a couple of scorched bales, it appeared unharmed.

"I'd say we'll be able to use most of it, Miz Carrebee," he assured me.

"I hope so, Yancy," I answered. And when I had thanked him and all the others, I said good night and, dirty and weary, my body aching with fatigue, went to the parked Ford.

As I drove homeward, the car's head lamps making sickly yellow puddles that glided over the red road and clumps of roadside brush, I thought, "I can't worry about anything tonight. About being broke or losing the mill or Carr's damned note. Not tonight. I'm too tired to care. About anything."

But I knew it then for false comfort and untrue. For in spite of the throbbing weariness of my body, the twinging of every joint—I cared. I cared, not about being poor: I could even endure the loss of the mill if it was unavoidable. But I cared desperately about defeat. Cared desperately knowing I might learn tomorrow that I was defeated.

Steering the Ford along the dirt drive toward the carriage house, I noticed the strange car parked in the back yard and wondered vaguely who had come and what brought them, but as little concerned as with the appearance I must make with my torn dress, smoke- and cinder-stained, my hair tangled with ashes.

Climbing the back steps, I opened the door and went through the hallway toward the sitting room, searching for Mitty, wanting only a bath and bed.

At the doorway of the sitting room I paused, my eyes, smarting and inflamed by smoke and dazzled by lamp glow, obscuring the figure in the chair. In the next moment I knew, in spite of clouded vision, that it was Cissa. Cissa's slim body was unmistakable, even dimly seen. Before I could speak, Mitty was at my side, asking anxiously if I was all right.

"I'm all right," I told her wearily. "There was a fire at the mill. The cotton shed. But we saved the cotton."

Turning to Cissa, I said, "I'm glad to see you, Cissa. I've wanted you to come."

She answered with a quiet voice and a strange child's humbleness unlike her yet, I thought, like the Cissa I had always known—the Cissa who with crayons in a summerhouse had drawn a child's portrait of her sadness and loneliness. She was, I thought, like that Cissa now.

"There isn't anyone else," she said. "Just Aunt Ad and you, and Aunt Ad can't help. It's funny, somehow. In the end, nobody but Jess I could come to. You the only one I felt would care . . . really, I mean."

Suddenly she arched her throat and supported her head against the back of the chair, her hair shining against the dark background, her body shaking as if racked with ague. She was like a child, I thought, infested with night terrors, fleeing blindly to human contact.

I said, "Cissa, what is it? Tell me."

She controlled the spasm of shaking and asked through chattering teeth, "Can I have a drink?"

I brought it and her hand came up and taking it, carried it to her lips.

"Syl—" she said, "Syl. I must get home by ten . . . Syl . . ."

She said the name three times as if it were some dreadful rune, then was completely quiet.

I said, "Don't worry about Syl."

She looked up at me, her eyes wide, luminous, frightened. "I've got to. Syl does . . . terrible things, Jess. Ugly. . . . I've got to get away. Aunt Ad says she'll go with me. But . . . we have no money. Mama wouldn't let me come home unless I turned over my mill check." Her smile twisted. "Of course, she got all Aunt Ad had . . . years ago."

She was shivering again and huddled in the chair in desolate loneliness struggling with some horror that only she saw.

"I've got to get away," she repeated, looking fixedly not at me but at some point beyond the room. "If I don't . . . I'm damned." She added after a minute, "I'm damned anyway."

I tried to soothe her. "I know . . . I know."

She looked up at me again, a strange little half-smile, mocking yet pitiful.

"Poor Jess," she said softly. "You really think you do know, don't you?"

I sat down beside her and took her cold hands and held them tight.

"Cissa, how much money will you need for Miss Ad and yourself? We must get it at once."

She thought for a moment, then named it, and I held back the shiver that went through me. She said, "And you can send my mill check to me every month. I'd let you know where."

"I will," I promised.

"For God's sake, don't give it to Mama. I'd never see a cent of it."

I assured her I would not, and she continued to huddle in the chair, her eyes drifting about the room.

"Wes lived here," she said gently. "Wes was in this room."

She had spoken more to herself than to me, so I did not attempt a response. And after another period of gazing about the room, she added:

"I never came to Wes's house when he was here, did I?"

"No," I said. "We were sorry."

She got up slowly. "That's me." She tried to smile at me not too successfully. "Doing everything all backward." Her voice was a child's again. "Coming to see Wes and he isn't even here."

I said, "Can't you stay tonight?"

She shook her head. "No. No. Aunt Ad is alone. She and I . . . alone. She'll be glad to know you'll let us have the . . . money." She paused. "She told me to come to you. She said you . . . were good."

I tried to lighten our humor. I said, "I'm not as good as Miss Ad thinks."

She looked at me, a little frown gathering between her eyes. "Yes, you are good. Wes . . . told me that."

Her eyes surveyed her hands, which were tightly clasped in her lap. Unexpectedly she said, "I didn't have anything to do with Mama's trying to take the mill back. Or the gossip . . . I didn't feel like Mama. . . . I won't be glad when Holy Carr takes the mill." She suddenly laughed, a child's startled, delighted laughter. "That's what Wes called him. Holy Carr." She raised her eyes to meet mine clearly, not laughing, but oh, with such sadness. "I wish I could help . . . some way. . . ."

I thanked her for offering. It was kind of her, I said.

She looked at me, surprised. "No. Not kind, Jess. I'm not kind. I haven't been to you—ever. Or anyone—except one." She paused. "After you left the house the other day I was thinking of Wes—and you too—and I thought maybe if I tried somehow—maybe Wes would know—I tried—too late of course—but that's me—always too late."

She moved to the table for no reason, then said again and still vaguely, "I must go." But she didn't go. She stood by the table, her finger tips resting lightly, her eyes on her hand. Then they drifted to the *Journal* Mitty had left there. She picked it up and, glancing at the headline that seemed to jump out of the page, laughed bitterly. *Carr Pledges Clean Sweep of Notorious Night Spots.*

"Life is funny, Jess." Her lovely mouth curled. "I hardly know Holy Carr, but it's his fault that Syl is being so—so horrible. Why, today . . ." She closed her eyes as if to shut out what was too much to see. "He's afraid of Carr—afraid Carr will close that house of Pet Belleau's. If he does, Pet and Syl are out of business." Her face was suddenly ugly and bitter. "So he takes it out on me." She stared across at me. "For God's sake get that money to me quick."

"I will," I promised. "I'll go to the bank first thing tomorrow."

She left then and I walked out to the car with her, listening to her disjointed feverish talk of Syl and Carr.

In the car she leaned on the door to say, "Syl thinks he'll outsmart Carr yet." She laughed again then, and on the still night it was a desolate sound, so close to madness, I shivered.

"Ace in the hole. That's what he called her. Ace in the hole. She's sick . . . there in that whorehouse. He's keeping her there so . . . when they raid it they'll find her. Good joke on Holy Carr." The eerie laughter tinkled against the night. "Finding his daughter at Pet Belleau's . . ."

I asked swiftly, "Cissa, what are you talking about?"

Her face turned crafty, malicious. "But I trumped Syl's ace. I telephoned Holy Carr before I came here tonight. I told him if he went to Pet's at ten o'clock . . . he would find his daughter." How cunning her smile. "Then I called Syl, made a date so he wouldn't be there to stop Holy Carr—" Suddenly, desperately, hopelessly, she said, "Oh, Jess, if I run across the world I'll never get away from Syl."

Frantic with impatience, I forced myself to speak calmly. "You'll get away, Cissa. Tomorrow. I promise."

She said, "You're good, Jess," and started the car.

I said, "Be careful of the hill road. Wes smashed up on it."

She said slowly, "Wes, on the hill road." She moved her head. "No, Jess. That isn't where Wes smashed up."

"Yes it was," I began, but she stopped me. "No, Jess. I know. You see . . . I was there . . ."

Back in the house, I thrust my arms into the sleeves of my coat, calling to Mitty that I must go out for a while. If there were time, I thought, I'd stop at the mill and try to call Oakes—but there wasn't time. Ten o'clock, Cissa had said. I plunged outdoors again, hurrying toward the Ford. I was swinging it down the hill road, feeling the lurching skid of the wheels as they spun in the loose dirt of the slope.

A jostling thrust of memories crowded insistently from the past and forced their attention on me as I drove: Laura Lee, flushed with excitement, playing in the dusk a game with Oakes, Bucky and me at Ponce de Leon Springs, her taunting voice calling, "Catch me if you can. Catch me if you can . . ."

The taunting voice, thin and eerie, mingled with the humming wind against the car, flinging its dare, not at Oakes or me, but at presiding fate: "Catch me if you can . . ."

The hollow and Adeline's house slid into the watery glow of the swaying head lamps and then jerked back into darkness as I turned the Ford onto the road and headed toward Atlanta. As it clattered along, I was vaguely conscious that on verandas people ate ice cream, that young couples strolled along tree-shadowed streets, that life pursued its lazy warm-weather way remote from the room in Pet Belleau's house with its unfastidious bed on which Laura Lee lay sick.

The city had emptied when I reached it, and its dim, echoing streets were wrapped in a breathless heat. Each of the long-stretched ranks of yellow lamps held in its murky glow a frenzied, beating cloud of insects. Now I drove swiftly, the Ford's engine chattering against the quiet.

Then I came to the street on which stood Pet Belleau's house, once an exclusive section of the city, given over to sedately brooding houses that loomed up dimly from wide lawns. Now it was a dark street of surreptitious footsteps and windows that cast dim glimmers from beneath lowered shades and great magnolias that pooled shadow beneath their wide branches.

Set in spreading, careful lawns, rose the house of Pet Belleau, a vast structure of ancient dignity and excellent repair, and apparently the most circumspect of all its neighbors. It might have been the house of a dignified, well-to-do and respected family, too fond of memories in the house to leave them to strangers.

When I had parked the Ford a ways down the side street, I walked back, my hands ordering my hair as I went, with my handkerchief wiping the soot from my face. On the porch I found the bell in the dim light that came from a fanlight, and rang it. Immediately, as if waiting, a trim Negro maid opened the door, narrowly. "Please, sir, no vis'tors tonight," she said quickly. Then, her eyes adjusting to darkness, she saw me.

" 'Scuse me, ma'am, I thought you was just some more gennamen. Whut you wantin', ma'am?"

I explained that a friend of mine was here and, I had learned . . . ill. I wished to see her.

The door closed an inch and her face was wary. "Miz Belleau say, 'No vis'tors tonite,' ma'am. Ain't no sech frien' here anyway. Ain't nobody here but me and Miz Belleau."

"Then I'd like to see Miss Belleau."

The door closed another inch as she shook her head. "No vis'tors tonite, ma'am. On no account."

I thrust my foot into the dwindling crack of the door, groping feverishly for words that would get me inside before Algernon Carr arrived. . . .

I said, "Tell Miss Belleau I wish to talk with her about a matter concerning Mr. Algernon Carr."

Something—either the new authority in my voice or the name I called—galvanized her into action. With a final shove at the door, which my foot defeated, she darted up the broad stairs that rose from the big hall. When she vanished at the top I stepped inside and closed the door behind me.

I found myself in a spacious reception hall, gorgeously carpeted, richly paneled and mirrored. Through an archway on one side I glimpsed a ballroom, its dance floor agleam with wax, on the other a lounge, garishly overfurnished.

The maid spoke from the top of the stairs. "Right this way, ma'am," she said, and I went up the sweeping curve of stair to the second floor. She led me to the end of a wide corridor lined with doors and, pausing, knocked at vast double doors of carved wood. A woman's voice called, "Come," and opening the doors she let me pass and, withdrawing, closed them again.

"Just a minute." The same voice spoke authoritatively from an adjoining room.

I waited, I observed, in a room of dazzling cold brilliance and a chaos of tufted satin, gilt carvings and full-length mirrors. My stunned eyes wondered at the numerous white-draped tables that, lining the walls, bore an overwhelming array of cut-glass bowls and urns and vases, displayed as if set out in a shop for sale.

"What about Algernon Carr?" a voice demanded, and I turned toward the door and found Pet Belleau, in a satin dressing gown, surveying me from the doorway.

"Miss Belleau?" I asked.

"That's me," she said flatly. "Who are you?"

She was holding a lighted match to her cigarette, but the hand stilled when I told her my name, and let the light flutter out. "My God!" she said reverently. "You're Wes's wife." At my nod, she said quietly, "A fine boy! A gentleman. And they ain't many gentlemen I say that about."

I thanked her, and after a little she asked flatly, "What you got to say about Holy Carr, Miz Carrebee?"

I told her briefly, again aware of time. I had come to take Laura Lee away, I finished, before her father . . .

She broke in, "My God, if you knew how glad I am to see you. I've addled my brains about that girl. Told Syl he was messin' with dynamite. . . ."

"Why did he bring her here?" I asked, still finding what Cissa had told me hard to believe.

She shrugged. "Syl figures she'll get him a break if he plays his hand right. Syl don't let anybody kick him around without kicking back."

"I don't see . . ." I began.

"You don't have to," she told me. "All you need to know is there's gonna be trouble, and I'm clearing out. If you want to get the girl out, we gotta move fast."

"Then let's move fast, Miss Belleau," I said.

She nodded, and going to a desk, brought out a bunch of keys.

"This ain't my idea"—she shook the keys—"but Syl's. She's locked in on the third floor."

She led me up a second flight of stairs, and along a narrower corridor also lined with doors. At one she halted and, unlocking it, entered the room, her voice falsely cheerful.

"Now, honey, here's a friend of yours come to take you home."

Entering behind her, I saw the small room that was comfortable enough but with no touch of the opulent grandeur below. And from the bed Laura Lee watched my face with mingled uncertainty and hope. "Jessica!" The thready voice rose incredulously.

Dropping to my knees by her side, I lifted the thin body and pressed the head of dark curls close.

She said, "Jess," her eyes bright with tears of relief and weakness. "Jess—I prayed. Me, Jess. That somebody would come. I didn't know anybody to ask."

"It's all right now," I told her. "I'm here."

Holding her, trying to reassure with my arms and voice, I was heartsick for the lost Laura Lee: banished forever by this hollow-cheeked girl on the bed. Still lovely, though white and drawn, but changed. This girl was strange.

But even as I felt the strangeness and hated it, her eyes moved, and I saw a familiar light that had belonged to the other Laura Lee. And immediately they were one again. This Laura Lee only needed care and nursing and "fattenin' up," as Mitty would say, to be herself again.

"I've come to take you home," I told her, but she shrank suddenly away, her eyes darting about the room as if seeking a place to hide.

"Not home," she said. "Not to Papa—I won't go—I won't—"

"Will you go to my home, then?" I asked gently.

"Your home? Oh, yes! Please, Jess, yes."

I heard the restless rustling of silk and Pet Belleau's snort of impatience.

"If she's gonna get out before hell breaks loose," she warned, "we'd better hustle."

Laura Lee sat up fully dressed, I saw, even to slippers—evidence, I realized, of Pet Belleau's wish to be rid of her presence.

She brought a light coat from the closet and dropped it on Laura Lee's shoulders, and together we helped her to stand. Pet's wariness suddenly sharpened, and, motioning us to follow, she led the way down the narrow passage, a suggestion of intent stealth in the way she moved, the silk dressing gown swirling and billowing lasciviously behind her.

Compelled to move less swiftly by the weight of Laura Lee, who leaned against me, I followed. Once, irked by our slowness, Pet Belleau turned, her mouth thin, and made a peremptory gesture. As I tried to hasten in response to her anxiety, I was wondering what trouble she expected. Syl was with Cissa, and surely we'd be gone before Algernon Carr arrived.

It didn't matter, I told myself, that I understood nothing, though I felt, I admit, a natural female curiosity. But I felt something more, a gathering, heavy apprehension that was a stillness around me stifling the air.

At the top of broad stairs sweeping from the second to the first floor,

Pet Belleau paused and waited for us, looking over her shoulder until we came up with her. Then, jerking the yellow silk around the heavy, powerful thighs, she started down, with the intent wariness I had noticed before.

Down one step, then two, then three; but on the fourth she halted abruptly and I heard the sharp hiss of her breath sucked between red lips and saw her effort to regain self-command after the first second of shock. I heard, amazed, the good-humored, oddly masculine carelessness of her voice.

"Syl!" she cried jovially. "Thought you was having a late date tonight."

At the same instant she ordered retreat with a backward flip of her hand. But it came too late. Syl Crowley had already seen us. He stood in the arch between ballroom and hall, his thinness rigidly erect, his black-sleeved, sticklike arms grotesquely crooked by the hands that were thrust in coat pockets.

He surveyed us, not bothering to speak, but with the evil half-smile on his face his eyes moved from Pet to Laura Lee and on to me, and I sensed that he was the source of enormous and ungovernable violence capable of any destructiveness. He made me feel this without moving, without making a sound. Then he spoke, his voice almost the weak rasp of a mechanical toy.

"Get her back upstairs," he said.

He meant Laura Lee and, feeling her sag against me, I glanced down. She seemed unconcerned, as if weakness dulled awareness and protected her against shock.

Syl Crowley ordered again: "I said, get her back upstairs."

I saw the muscles move against the yellow silk between Pet Belleau's shoulders as she gathered defiance.

"Don't be a damned fool, Syl. You can't get away with this, and you know it. For God's sake, use your head. You can't bluff Carr or scare him. And he'd see to it that they'd string you up and set fire to you in the bargain."

He gave no sign that he heard the hoarse lashing voice. He still stood motionless, the evil half-smile on his face.

Pet Belleau's raucous voice held a hint of placation now. "If you're smart, you'll clear out like me, Syl. Set up somewhere else. Like me."

Syl spoke finally. "You can. You socked yours away."

"You know I'd stake you, Syl. We always got on. We could again. Just give up this blind, crazy idea. Listen to me for once. My God, don't you see? Even if you win, you lose."

His brows lifted, his eyes moved briefly to Laura Lee, then back to Pet Belleau.

"If you hold the trump, you're a fool not to play it," he said briefly.

She was shaken by quick fury. She snarled, "I'm coming down, Syl, and open that door and let this girl out of here."

He appeared to be faintly surprised, as if she suggested a feat obviously beyond possibility. "I wouldn't," he told her quietly.

I saw her hunched shoulders sag, and knew she was defeated. She wouldn't admit it, but the hearty raucous voice was edged with fear.

"Syl, look here, we can always get on, you and me—"

He interrupted her quietly. "Drop it. There isn't time."

"Time?" She asked it innocently, as if she didn't know. "What are you getting at?"

"He ought to be here soon now," Syl said. "That crazy bitch I married tipped him off to spite me"—he smiled, his evil mouth contemptuous—"and after a couple of drinks couldn't help bragging. That's why I came back." He added, his evil eyes cold upon me, "Good I did. Mighta lost my trump card."

I had managed to keep Laura Lee on her feet during this exchange. Now, feeling her body sag, I moved her toward the inside wall and braced her against it, with my arm supporting her weight. Her face hidden against my shoulder, she said petulantly, like a sleepy child, "Jess, I thought we were going to your house," her voice thready and thin.

"We will," I answered. "In just a little while."

I was far from certain that this was true. I had no inkling of what was to happen, or what Pet Belleau believed would happen. I was certain, however, that Algernon Carr, informed by Cissa, would come and that Syl hadn't wanted that yet. He wanted Carr's daughter found in Pet Belleau's house when it was raided. Perhaps to force Carr into granting immunity for his "business." Perhaps only to get even.

As I wearily waited and pondered I was aware that Pet Belleau had swept to Syl Crowley's side and murmured swiftly, tensely, a rush of unintelligible words. Then I heard Laura Lee's gasped cry, and thrusting past me she stumbled back up the stairs, hysteria on her face.

"Don't try to run away, Laura Lee," the deliberate, level voice of her father called scornfully.

I saw that the door of Pet Belleau's house stood open. The scarlet draperies in the hall shivered in the draft that swept past them and the Negro maid stood pressed back against a wall, her eyes white with fear.

The maid cried, "He just come bustin' through, Miss Pet!" But no one glanced toward her or seemed to hear her. We watched Algernon Carr, who stood within the doorway, his cold, still face surveying his surroundings with cold, deliberate contempt. Then they lifted and traveling upward found Laura Lee.

He raised his voice. "Come here, Laura Lee."

She did not answer nor did she move, but crouched on the stairs in desperate and helpless panic.

He moved toward the stairs, his face impassive, but Syl with a quick gliding motion went to the foot of the stairs. His quiet voice drawled, "Don't give any orders around here. This place belongs to me."

Carr, not glancing his way, said, as if answering a disembodied voice, "It won't when the Purity League gets through with it . . . and you."

Syl's quiet, taunting voice again: "I've got quite an investment here. And I don't expect to have it smashed up for your benefit."

"I have stated my intentions," Carr said. "And now I'll take my daughter and go. I have an engagement."

Syl said quietly, too quietly, "If they raid this place, the first thing they'll find is the daughter of Algernon Carr."

Carr, his eyes still refusing to see Syl, said flatly, "That makes not the slightest difference in the plans of the League."

"You're making a mistake."

"It would be a greater mistake if I allowed myself to be intimidated by the threat of a contemptible and despicable little crook who's unfit to walk on the street with decent men."

I saw the dull, bruised places of color that stung Syl's waxy cheekbones. He had married Cissa, Wes had said, because of his hunger for respectability. To be spoken to in this way rankled.

"If my daughter is here when we come, that's that," Carr said evenly. "We'll come just the same. A clean city has no place for a cheap hoodlum and pimp. And I've promised a clean city."

"I've warned you," Syl said. "I mean business."

"So do I. We'll hit you through everything we can find. We'll start with this house. We'll break it up and ruin it, and you won't stop us. You and no other cheap, common crook." His eyes lifted to Laura Lee's crouching figure. "Are you coming, Laura Lee?"

When she neither moved nor answered, he turned on his heel and walked deliberately toward the front door.

Syl said, "Just a minute."

Turning, but not looking toward Syl, Carr said levelly, "I've had my say. There's no point in discussing it."

He swung back to the door, and I knew Syl had been beaten. Not by force or intimidation. His attempted bluff had been called and he was left absurd and helpless. His face, poisonous white, writhed as if a decay of hatred was devouring his being.

"Maybe this will stop you," he said, still speaking quietly.

With the words, I saw the small deadly blue glitter in his hand, and heard the sharp, flat crack of the shot. Algernon Carr turned toward him, as if at last choosing to recognize his presence, his face wearing a look of casual surprise. As he turned, Syl Crowley fired five more times, the shots evenly spaced, each sound of exactly equal volume.

Gazing in fascinated horror at the body stretched on the brilliant carpet in the garish hallway, I vaguely heard Pet Belleau argue with Syl that now he would have to leave town, have to clear out, because he had let it be widely known he hated Carr. I heard her urging, threatening, pleading, knew that finally she went to her apartment and, returning, thrust a roll of bills into his hand.

He did not thank her. Nor did he give any of us who watched so much as a glance as he went to the front door. He picked up his hat from a chair, put it on, took his gloves.

Then he was gone. Wheeling, Pet Belleau addressed me.

"We got to get you and that girl out of here now. I knew she'd make trouble the minute I saw her."

I stared dazed at the motionless body, the face still superior as it gazed toward gauze-draped nymphs dancing in the ponderous gilt frame on the wall.

"What will you do . . . with him?"

She gave the body a casual glance, answering confidently, "Don't worry, I'll take care of that. It was only alive he spelled trouble. Come on, now, get out of here and take her with you. Don't waste no time, either. We wasted enough already."

She rushed me toward the back alley, helping me support Laura Lee. At the sidewalk we left her and went toward the Ford, I conscious of the policeman walking his beat with his casual night stick swung from his wrist. I heard Laura Lee's voice, trembling with hysteria but unfrightened.

"You don't have to take me to your house now, Jess. Now . . . I can go home!"

I turned the Ford into the drive that curved toward the turreted, balconied home of the Carr's and saw on the lawn the same iron deer with one foot forever lifted. A long, long time, I thought, since the day Algernon Carr stood above me on the side stoop and, looking down at me, said, "You are a very clever young lady."

Stopping the Ford under the portico, I asked Laura Lee, "Do you think you can walk? Or shall I ring for the servants?"

Her "No servants" was only a thread of voice, but with me helping and waiting, she finally was out of the Ford and we made the stoop, and then the side door. With my arm still circling her waist to give her support, my other hand reached and pressed the button set in the wall.

After a minute or so it was opened by a Negro woman of middle age, heavy, compact and efficient in her black dress and stiff snowy apron. She looked at us curiously and held the door carefully, not too wide.

"We wish to see Mrs. Carr," I said.

She tilted her head and her eyes were almost reproving.

"Mrs. Carr has retired for the night."

"We must see her, nevertheless," I informed her crisply.

Not an inch did she budge. "I'm 'fraid that ain't possible, ma'am. Mrs. Carr ain't well and Mr. Carr ordered she ain't to be disturbed under *any* circumstances."

I could feel Laura Lee's half-leaning figure weigh heavier and heavier upon me, so I spoke sharply to the Negro woman, who surveyed Laura Lee as she would a freak from a side show.

"It is imperative that we see Mrs. Carr. Open the door so we can come in."

She still hesitated, and I could not blame her if she feared to disobey the instructions of Algernon Carr, and I did not doubt that she feared him.

I told her, "This is Mrs. Carr's daughter."

She shrank back. "Then you mustn't bring her in this house, ma'am." Her alarmed eyes rolled in her face. "He told me if she ever come to the door . . ."

I cut in, "Don't worry about what he told you. She's coming in. Open the door so we can."

"Sweet Jesus!" she breathed. "Oh, sweet Jesus!"

"Give me a hand here. Miss Carr is ill."

With alacrity she took Laura Lee to her arms and easily, competently, half led, half carried her down the narrow corridor.

I asked as I closed the door, "Where can I find Mrs. Carr?"

"Upstairs in her room, ma'am. She ain't in bed yet. But *he* gave me orders, and he's a hard man." Then, not knowing she need fear that hardness no more, she breathed again, "Sweet Jesus!"

When, at the end of the corridor, we came to the foot of the stairs, I told her I would go ahead and prepare Mrs. Carr for her daughter's arrival lest it be too much of a shock. Which room was Mrs. Carr's?

She told me, and I sped ahead up the stairs and gaining the upper hall came to the right door and found it not closed, but standing ajar; and, in the deep chair before the fire, the delicate face under the nut-brown hair resting on the thin hand, I saw Mrs. Carr.

I went in quietly and held my voice quiet when I spoke.

"Mrs. Carr."

She lifted her head and, seeing me, rose swiftly from the chair, and at the awed questioning I saw in her eyes I wondered if somehow she knew whom I brought.

She came to me with outstretched hands. "Jess," she said softly. "Jess, you have come. I'm so glad."

Holding her hands tightly, I said, "Mrs. Carr, I brought someone . . ."

Her head moved quickly so she might look toward the door. "Brought someone? Who did you bring, dear Jess?"

I held her hands even more firmly, aware that her eyes searched my face. "Someone you've worried about so long."

The hands in mine began to tremble.

"Someone very dear to you and to me, who brought me here once to meet—her mother."

The blood drained from the thin face and her eyes questioned mine wildly.

"Is it Laura Lee?" the voice quavered, and nodding, I gave her her answer.

The hands trembled in mine like frightened birds. "Is she—you did not bring her home—dead?"

"No, no, no. She's been ill. She is still . . . but . . ."

But her eyes had deserted my face to stare toward the door, where the colored woman appeared, her arms about Laura Lee.

For a moment Mrs. Carr stood like one turned to stone and gazed at the thin figure as if she did not believe. Then Laura Lee, raising her head from the Negro's shoulder, looked at her from the door.

"I have come home, Mama," she said simply; and with a sound that expressed everything—the anguished years of not knowing, the joy of now knowing—the hours which one by one, each with its sixty minutes, had counted the endless time; all cried out in Mrs. Carr's wordless cry as with arms wide and reaching, she took Laura Lee into them.

After a little she and the Negro woman put Laura Lee to bed—in Laura Lee's own bed in Laura Lee's own room kept, her mother told her, always ready and waiting.

"Every night I've gone in and turned down your covers and wondered if, wherever you were, someone treated you gently."

Laura Lee stared up at her mother's face from dark, wide eyes that told nothing. I knew there was much she could have told; of the twisting, dubious way that led her to Pet Belleau's. But I suddenly knew she would never tell. She would laugh, she would make the years sound like a wonderful game—and tell nothing.

But now one thing she had to tell.

"Mama," she said, matter-of-factly, "you ought to know. Papa is dead."

Mrs. Carr's face stilled but betrayed no hurt, no emotion.

She asked quietly and with more wonder than shock in her voice, "Dead? How could that have happened? That he is dead?"

Laura Lee was still matter-of-fact. "He was shot by a man. When . . . I heard . . . I knew I could come home. I . . . I called Jess and she came and brought me."

Mrs. Carr stood above her, unmoving, her face expressionless.

"Why did the man shoot . . . him?" she asked, tonelessly.

Laura Lee's mouth curved scornfully. "You know that, Mama, as well as I. Papa was probably trying to punish him, too."

Her mother spoke slowly. "It had become an obsession. To punish, to inflict pain." She shivered. "I suppose that is my guilt, too." She asked a little later, "Where is . . . your father?"

Laura Lee said they would have to wait to know that, until they were informed. "We don't even know that he is dead. That is what we must pretend. It might involve innocent persons."

Mrs. Carr glanced at her sharply. "Are you sure it is true? That it is as you say?"

Laura Lee answered simply, "I am home, Mama. Would I have come if I hadn't been sure?"

For a space they stared at each other, Mrs. Carr's eyes questioning, Laura Lee's wide and dark—and unrevealing. Then, leaning, Mrs. Carr kissed her gently. "You are home, thank God. Home and safe. And now you must try to rest. Tomorrow, I'll have Dr. Gordon and we'll get you well and strong."

Sensing that she wished to have a few words with Laura Lee without the presence of outsiders, I said I must go, and told Laura Lee good night. But Mrs. Carr looked at me over her shoulder. "Jess, wait downstairs in the drawing room. I want to speak with you."

I went down the stairs and across the huge vaulted reception hall where I had first seen Laura Lee's mother. I had thought it such a wonderful hall that other time. Now it seemed less so, and I knew that, had I been wiser then, I would have known it expressed what Algernon Carr was—all outward ostentation.

I passed the Negro woman in the hall, where she was locking doors. I stopped to ask the way to the drawing room.

She pointed. "That way, ma'am."

Thanking her, I went toward it, recalling that I had never been in the drawing room. It had always been closed when I had visited Laura Lee and Oakes.

I opened the door to find the room dark, and I groped on the wall beside the door and, touching a switch, flooded the room not with brilliant light but one warm and amber, infinitely more charming than white.

I advanced to the center of the room and stood surveying it. What a vast room it was! I saw the tall windows (where had I seen such tall windows before?), I saw the teakwood tables, the delicate French chairs, their delicacy lost in the vastness—I saw the rosy carpet that stretched before me—seemingly past the windows—and onward into space. . . .

A strange confused sensation swept through me . . . a dazed sense of being dislocated from time and place . . . I thought I must be ill . . . to feel like this, and I felt myself slipping . . . I must not faint, I told myself . . . but I was slipping back into time. . . . I was a child again and this was the dream that all my life I had dreamed . . . my five-year-old self alone in the vast, many-windowed room where the ruby carpet stretching, stretching, glowed into limitless space . . . and I standing in it feeling . . . so small . . . so lost. Again, feeling the desolation sweeping over me, engulfing me until the vast, splendid room was filled with my desolation, my lostness, my aloneness. . . . I felt it around me now though not sleeping but awake. I thought dazedly, "But I am mad . . . I've never been here before . . ." and, reaching for reality, I said it again, but this time aloud.

"I've never been here before."

A voice from the doorway behind me spoke.

"So you did remember?"

Slowly turning, I faced Mrs. Carr, who stood in the doorway, her gentle eyes wide and with the same look of wonder I earlier saw in them.

I gestured. "I have such a strange feeling," I stammered, "almost as if I had—been in this room before." I added, "But I never have."

"You were here once," she said quietly, "just before you were three years old."

I looked at her, not daring to speak but inwardly sensing that this was a moment of no trifling consequence; my mind seethed in a confusion of surmise and wonder, of fleeting speculation.

I asked hesitantly, "I was here?"

She entered the room and quietly closed the door, then stood, her back braced against it.

"Your father brought you. He was Will Purefoy, which you undoubtedly know. He had kept you since—right after you were born until that day. Then he learned that he was to die and he brought you to me here—in this room—and asked me for God's sake to keep you."

Tall and pale but controlled, she continued to stand against the door . . . and impulsively I moved toward her; but, her thin hand lifting and forbidding me, I stopped where I was.

"You must wait and hear all there is to hear," she admonished.

"I could not keep you." Her voice rasped like an untuned string. "There was my husband, my children, Laura Lee barely a year older than you. I had to stand and watch your little feet walk out of my life . . . beside him. Later . . . I heard that he died in that house of his father's, and once when Mr. Carr was away I managed to slip out there to see Mathias Purefoy. . . . The house was empty, deserted . . . so I knew nothing . . . of you. I've looked into the face of every girlchild I've passed since that day. . . ."

Through my tears the haggard countenance wavered like a drowning face under water.

I asked, "You . . . are my mother?"

Not speaking, she bowed her head and, as if she could not bear to meet my eyes, kept it down.

"You must not call me by that name until you hear me to the end. You see"—she raised her head, the eager straining gaze of her dark eyes and the gentleness in every line of her mouth making a sharp contrast to the bitter voice—"I was no innocent girl seduced through ignorance. I was married and the mother of two children when I met Will Purefoy, so I haven't even the usual justification. I have none. In the years of my marriage every trace of lightheartedness, every pleasure in living, even the ability to laugh, had been worn down. Then I met Will. Young and handsome, and he laughed a lot. It was like coming out of a cave into sunlight. That was the year that Mr. Carr was sent to Paris to take charge of the office there. I was to follow with the children. When I found out what had happened—I delayed going one time after another and managed to—" She paused. "When I finally went, everything was over, here . . ." Then quickly, "Not in this house. There was a woman in

Atlanta then who 'arranged' such things in her own place. As soon as it was possible . . . Will took you away to that house of his father's . . . Hickory something-or-other, and I took Oakes and Laura Lee and went to Paris to join Mr. Carr. I thought he would never know." Her voice sank into silence and she stood, her face furrowed, as if thought made its way through the winding past. Then she said, her mouth curling, "But he found out. From me. He never rested until he pried confession from me, then held it over my head every minute of my life like a sword that might fall any moment."

Her head lifted and she said fiercely, "I'm glad he's dead. Glad!" With her hands over her face she waited until she was calmer. Then she took her hands away from her face and said abruptly, "Now you've heard all. I'm not proud of the part I've played, but you had to hear."

"You did the only thing you could do. . . ."

Her eyes were vague again as she surveyed the past. She shook her head. "No," she whispered, "I thought so, then. I know now, I've always known—if I had had more courage . . . but I knew nothing of courage, that sort of courage . . . no lady did. . . ."

I looked at the sweet face, weary and drawn, and it struck me how strangely events often pictured in the mind differ in actuality from the picture. Always in fancies concerned with finding my mother I had imagined her taking me to her breast and comforting me. Yet now it was I who desired to comfort; and going to her, I put my arms about her. "None of it matters now. We've found each other."

Her hand touched my cheek. "I found you years ago, my child. I've known since the day Laura Lee brought her friend in to meet me."

Wonderingly, I asked, "But how did you know?"

"When you came across the room toward me it was like seeing my young self approaching." Her lips curled. "He knew too."

Yes, I thought—he had known. I remembered how on the portico he had turned on the light and had stopped to regard me from the still, cold eyes; how he had said, "I think you are a very clever young lady." He had known; and now I knew why all these years he had hated me. To him I had been sin. The sin his wife had committed against him.

In the hours that wore on, from the early hours of night to the deep black of midnight, we sat in my mother's room before the fire and in broken confessions and answering words of comfort, with repetition that was not tiresome but a need, we nourished the bond which separation and longing had already established. And the questions for which heretofore I had known no answers were answered at last, and past and present joined. Yet—I realized—it could affect the aspect of my life but little now, and for this I was grateful; and I was glad that I had found that for which I had so tirelessly longed, too late to alter the face of my past. The past to which Mitty and Mr. Dolph belonged; and Mr. Poteat. Which held Wes and my wedding and honeymoon and hundreds of Parma violets; and Hickory Hill with its living and loving, despairing —and dying; and in Mady and Cade beginning to live again. No—I did not regret my past. It was my life and what it held was too infinitely precious to imagine any other that could have been half so good.

Yet, that other past had been a part of the actual one too. Vaguely, never materializing, but hovering just beyond reach and touch. I spoke to my mother of this; of the young man my childish imagination had chosen for the father image; of the recurrent dream of the vast room where the ruby carpet stretched, glowing, into space; of once hearing her laughter in a dream and waking to find it echoing in the room.

With her hand shading her eyes, she said quietly, "Who knows what remains indelibly imprinted on the baby mind? It's a question that has darkened every day of my life. I could not push out the memory of you standing beside your father, your hand in his, as he told me he was to die. I've told myself you were too young to realize the meaning of his words; or mine when I said I could not keep you. But your sad, wondering eyes have looked at me every minute of my life, and no matter where I was. They watched me as I walked along the street, and from the doors of small houses beside the railroad track, where children stood to watch the train I rode go by. I could not travel far enough to escape them. Then when Laura Lee . . ." She paused. "He said she was God's punishment for my sin. I hated God until I remembered that God was what he had never been: merciful and just."

"Perhaps you will be happy now," I told her gently. "You must try to be happy."

She shook her head. "I do not ask for that. I will not ask for what I fail to deserve. If I can know that my children are not cold or hungry or unkindly treated . . . I ask nothing more. I will not even complain because I must hold secret the fact that you are my child. So proud I would be to claim you! But you and I could gain no more than we have already—and others would be hurt. That I must not do. I've caused too much hurt . . . too much."

I told her not to think of it—that she had suffered most of all; and it dawned upon me that this was true, that it must always be true; that there is no hurt as searing and unceasing as the guilty knowledge that you have been responsible for the pain of others.

The night was almost spent when I drove toward Hickory Hill from my mother whom I had strangely and wondrously found. A rain had fallen during the hours we sat and talked, and the streets were shining and wet, the air freshened, and crowing roosters, winding a thread of hope into distance and bringing it back again, relayed their announcement of a dawn whose trembling promise they discerned, but I could not.

I was weary, and my body in clothes worn through many hours felt stiff with fatigue. As if, jostled and hectored by too many hours, their passing left it disheveled and untidy. Perhaps it was weariness that made me aware that my sense of fulfillment was transient and impermanent. That complete fulfillment was possible only with an end. And the end meant finished; and over and done with.

I was not yet ready for endings. Too much struggle and striving, too many hopes and plans, too much loving lay ahead. In this dawn hardly less dark than night, I was beginning again. There would be another beginning at tomorrow's dawn, and the next tomorrow's and the next . . . I still would meet many mornings and many beginnings.

In the first tenuous lifting of dark I made my way to Hickory Hill. Under the trees the shadows were pools of inky black and a fugitive little breeze stirred the trees to tremulous sighs and their splattering tinkle of raindrops on the upturned leaves below. With scant aid from my wavering head lamps, I guided the Ford surely in its clambering ascent up the hill road; the ruts and hollows as familiar as the palm of my hand. So many times from so many journeyings I had returned up it to Mitty and refuge. At its summit I saw a shadowy figure with a lighted lamp descend the high front steps. Cade or Mitty, I thought, as I got out of the car. But when I crossed the yard I saw that it was Andrew. Coming close, he held the lamp so he could better see and his eyes searched my face, concerned.

I said, "I have so much to tell, Andrew. So much! It will take a long time."

His face was strained, his mouth grim with worry. But he spoke quietly.

"It can wait 'til you've had some coffee. Mitty has a fresh pot on the stove."

Together we made our way to Mitty's kitchen; and when I saw Mitty's face I realized that the night, so short and crowded for me, had for Mitty and Andrew seemed a long and anxious time.

While we drank the black, scalding coffee I told them where I had been and of all that had happened this night. When I finished we sat silent, as if its strangeness and wonder transcended casual comment.

One question only did I ask of Andrew. Had he known all this time who my mother was?

He shook his head. "No, Jess. I told you all I knew, long ago. But knowing explains Algernon Carr's crusade against what he considered sin. Compensation for evil which his pride must keep hid, and convinced that before righteousness evil must be defenseless. He did not know that a Syl Crowley is never defenseless. His ruthlessness gives him weapons denied to an Algernon Carr."

He talked on, the steady voice reacting on my weariness like a crushing force. My head was nodding and my eyelids were pressed irresistibly down. Then vaguely, aided by Mitty and Andrew, I was stumbling up the stairs, was mumbling thick-voiced that I wasn't sleepy and I loved them both so much.

Nothing was changed, yet I felt a great change had taken place. By chance or fate—I could not know which now or even if the two were one—I was led by devious paths back to the hidden beginning, the secret entrance by which I had entered this world; and learned the explanation, so far as mortal creatures may, for my being. I could not reveal that beginning to the world, nor did I desire it. But at last I knew from what flesh and love I had come. And, knowing, I was freed of the bondage imposed by a riddle unsolved or a door for which we lack the key.

Speculating on the long years when that unsolved riddle, that unlocked door had shadowed my existence, it struck me as monstrous that the answer had lain so close—yet had eluded me. That since the day she watched Laura Lee's "wonderful Jessica" walk toward her, my mother had known me for her child, and by no word or action betrayed it. So easily the course of my life might have been changed if she had; and how faithfully I would have guarded that knowledge. And though the thought was free of blame or resentment, I did not forget that my mother had allowed me to walk out of that door—and her life—not knowing where I would end. That, Mitty would never have done.

This realization did not come to me immediately. Only after hours of thought and speculation, of weighing one possession against another, was I able to resolve clearly in my own mind how I felt. It was resolved as Mitty and I shortly after sat on the front porch in the summer's dusk and I exclaimed, rather suddenly as a result of my thoughts, that I could not do without her. Always before when I said the same thing, she had answered serenely that I wouldn't have to, that she wasn't thinking of going anywhere.

Now she did not give her usual answer. Instead she said matter-of-factly, "But you'll have to, one of these days, you know, dearie."

I glanced at her quickly, wondering if her words carried specific intent, for I had not been able to avoid the knowledge that Mitty was getting old. Her hair was snowy, her small figure smaller still. But the years had stolen upon her softly, as if even time understood that Mitty's gentle goodness deserved only kindly attention.

"You know," she went on placidly, "I've been thinking lately. How Andrew won't let you pay him for lawyering you and the mill, and you won't let him pay for all the food he eats here. And him seeming to be better for you than anybody I know, including me . . ."

I interrupted to tell her no one could ever be half so good for me as she was and had been always, but it did not budge her opinion.

"Since he's better for you," she repeated firmly, "and wants to be as good to you as I want to be, which is consid'able. And with you having a knack for loving and not likely to be happy 'less you're putting that knack to use, I can't help thinking lately that if I warn't around it'd be mighty consolin' to know you and Andrew . . ."

Kneeling beside her, I held her close and cried; not because some day I would lose her—her wisdom and goodness, I knew, would triumph even there. I cried for my love for her and because I could not understand how so small a body as Mitty's, with only one heart in its breast, could hold the enormousness of her love for me. Stroking my hair, she soothed me as she had when I was a child. Then, drying my eyes and smiling, I admitted that her thought was not wholly new to me or surprising.

"It isn't that I don't know all there is to know of Andrew's worth, Mitty. His steadfastness, his goodness, how faithful he's been—and how loyal. It's because I can't give less than all I have to give. I believe it will come and just as you want it, Mitty. But in time. There's plenty of time."

Lips pursed, she looked at me thoughtfully and shook her head.

"Well now, it's a quare thing about time. To young folks a year or two seems as long as kingdom come. But the older you grow, the faster time goes asteppin'. And a year's no more than an hour. Still"—she patted my hand—"a while longer won't hurt, if you don't forget that time can get out of hand."

She was right, of course, and time proceeded to prove it. And so swiftly that important events of today were thrust into oblivion by tomorrow's more important ones. The discovery of Algernon Carr's body in an isolated vacant field blazed in newspaper headlines for a few days, with the usual speculation on the guilty. The assumption that "Atlanta's underworld," in revenge for his vigorous fight to eliminate them, had "knocked him off" was generally accepted, and a drive for a fund was immediately started to erect a Carr memorial. In a statement through the press, a police official proclaimed the belief that in twenty-four hours the murderer would be apprehended and meet with swift justice. Before that happened, however, the announcement that Atlanta had secured the Sixth District Federal Reserve Bank not only stimulated business with new hope but pushed the mystery of Algernon Carr's death from the front page and out of the public's mind. Even the announcement that Algernon Carr's son had been made a vice-president of the City Bank failed to revive it.

By that time the boom predicted by Homer was beginning its dizzying upward spiral and I was too busy to have any awareness of time. For slowly at first, but with a faster and faster momentum, "Carrebee Cottons, Finer than Silk" impressed the merchandisers—that multitude of men and women who, their ears attuned to public demand, know, almost to an instant, when what has been no more than a murmur starts to swell to a mighty chorus.

The fame of Carrebee Cottons carried Carrebee Cotton Fashions along with them. Ready-made clothes of quality were for the first time singing the swan song of Atlanta's fashionable modistes and what was affectionately referred to as "my little dressmaker." And Otto, with that uncanny knowing of his, ignored the furbelowed "pretty" styles fashion proclaimed and presented to a nation of women, who had never heard the word "Casuals," a line of "Carrebee Casuals"; slim, unadorned cottons of impeccable fit and lines. The result doubled Homer's two dozen sewing machines, then tripled them; and his factory, unable to widen, began to grow upward two stories . . . three. . .

Busy as time was, it was prosperous time and fulfilling. If it was crowded with work, it was work that brought rewards. And though I had received, since Algernon Carr's death, only courtesy and patience from the bank, it was satisfactory fulfillment to pay off the loan and shake hands with Oakes. And later at Hickory Hill to drink, with Mitty and Andrew, a toast to a certain canceled document.

Now with each swift-passing day of time, the foundation of Carrebee Cottons was strengthened and broadened, and each day the chance of sudden disaster descending to sweep away our gain was a trifle decreased and by that trifle the foundation made more secure. We had accomplished much. And like a child who mulls over its treasures, I often counted those accomplishments. The houses and mill buildings painted. The grass spreading green in the village grounds; the gravel walks ribbon-trim. The schoolhouse where Joel Keddy, the young teacher, opened the wondrous door to knowledge heretofore closed to the mill children. Prices at the mill store fair and honest; the food at those prices of good quality. And the first resentment toward my rule of no children under twelve employed by the mill, dwindling with increased wages and at last wholly vanquished. Most of all I was proud of the warmth and friendliness of the mill hands towards me. For this had not been easily or quickly won.

Those years brought other reasons for satisfaction. The almost unbelievable swiftness of Cade's and Mady's growth, the glowing health in their faces, and through Joel Keddy's guidance their young minds reaching out hungrily. The chortle of laughter that burbled from Poky's throat as he stirred a doodlebug hole in the side yard, with a stick big enough to frighten a buffalo. And of course, there was Mitty. Never less loving, never less dear, her small hands never less busy as, rocking on the front porch, she darned stockings or let out a hem for Mady.

I was older now and no longer a dewy-eyed girl, and I often deplored a figure that failed to acquire the rounded curves deemed essential for beauty but remained too slim, I thought, and girlish. I consoled myself for that lack with the belief that with time I had gained wisdom—or at least enough to perceive how much there was I could never gain. And to accept without fretting the knowledge that I had changed and my life had changed with the years. Yet one thing remained unchanged.

I woke to find Mitty calling my name and the sound of my cry still echoing in the dark room.

"There, there, my blessed," she soothed when I started up. "A bad dream, I reckon." Then, pressing me back to my pillow again, as always she reassured me.

"What in the world do you dream, Jess, to make you cry out like that?"

I did not tell her. Nor would I ever tell her. So silly it seemed, and I a grown woman. For how explain the terror that in the dream mounted until it engulfed me—standing, a small child again, in the center of the vast splendid room, the ruby carpet stretching before me. And in the glowing vastness feeling small and lost and alone.

It was only a dream, I would tell myself. Yet I knew now it was more than a dream. It was the hurt of not being wanted that persisted still, perhaps would persist as long as I could feel pain. Each time it came I was reminded that even yet I did not belong, that in finding my mother I had not really found her, for neither her efforts nor mine could bridge the gap formed by dividing years. Reality had only shattered my dream of finding her. Now, still not belonging, I was stripped of my dream.

The war in Europe, everyone believed, would be over in a few months, and the world would go on much as before. But the sinking of the *Lusitania* opened our eyes. At a special session of Congress President Wilson asked for a declaration of war. And for the first time the Universal Draft Act, including men from eighteen to forty-five, was passed.

The war which to me had seemed tragic when, breaking out in Europe, it plunged the South into a business slump, now wrought far vaster havoc. It took Cade, just turned eighteen, first to a camp, then to a port, and from that port to somewhere in Europe. Time wore another face now, a threatening, frightening face that confronted us in the long stretches between letters, in which we greeted each day with the unspoken thought, "I wonder." Even when the letters arrived to be feverishly read and reread by Mady, Mitty and me, they did not hold the answer. For their dates were weeks old, and we slid them back into their envelopes, our faces grave, still thinking, "I wonder."

Where did time go? I worried, racing to the mill, then on to Homer's and back to the mill again. Check the goods Otto wanted for the new line: Had this order gone out? Or that? Would that special order from the big chain in the East be shipped on specified date?

Scowling, Darty reassured me. "Stop acting like Big Bertha," he growled. And at my blank look he explained, "That's the big seventy-five the Huns pulled out their sleeves."

"How can I stop?" I demanded. "With all I have on my mind?"

"You'd better slow up. You don't want to be too worn out to start in to struggle again."

"Struggle again?"

"Yep. The cotton business ain't reached heaven yet, though it might seem so. Watch it hit bottom again after the war."

If he thought to force me to "slow up" he missed his mark. It only sent me back to work harder. Thinking of Cade as I worked, thinking, "I wonder."

Now and then I dashed out in my car to sit in the room where the ruby carpet stretched into space and talk with my mother. Before each time I thought, Perhaps today we will break down the thing that divides us. We never did. She would talk of Laura Lee, who had gone to Europe with the Red Cross to drive an ambulance; of Oakes, who—unbelievably—was to marry Renette Colquitt. Telling me, she said, "A splendid thing for Oakes. The Colquitts are one of the very best—" Finding my eyes on her face, she broke off, then finished, "—such splendid people."

I ignored it, nor did I blame her. I realized that she, just as her husband, as Miss Camilla, was the product of her environment. And I think it was then that I began to realize that Algernon Carr had not been the determining factor when she let me walk out of her life. Then as now it had been the false gods the South served and would continue to serve.

When Mady told me she was to be married to Joel Keddy, the schoolteacher; with Poky would move to a small house near the mill, I stood shocked and aghast.

I cried out to Mitty, "But she's too young. She isn't—why, she isn't eighteen."

But Mitty was neither shocked nor aghast. "As old as you when you married Wes."

It was true, but for that very reason I could not accept it. I said wretchedly, "I've always thought if I'd been older and wiser . . ."

Her eyes were very gentle. "No, Jess. Wes . . . was a bent twig twisted out of shape long 'fore you came."

It was true, I thought. As true of him as of Cissa, who with Miss Ad drifted from place to place, fleeing as Wes had fled from a present which refused to return to the past.

I looked at Mitty through sorrowing eyes. "But, Mitty, they're all leaving us. We'll be—alone again. In this empty house." I shivered. "I don't like it."

"I reckon if you filled it up once," she said calmly, "you can again."

"But why—must it be like that? You fill it up and almost before you know it—it begins to empty . . ."

Holding the fragile corset cover she sewed for Mady's trousseau on her lap, she stopped her needle mid-air.

"Why, that's life, my blessed. A gathering in and a falling away. Over and over in my lifetime I see it. Big families—ma and pa with their sons and daughters together for years, then just like somebody snipped whatever bound 'em together—fallin' away one by one. Nothin' left but a bunch of tombstones with their names cut on 'em."

"Then what's the use of living if everything is to be lost?"

She went back to her sewing. "The use of living," she said firmly, "is living. And no better proof do you need than to see all those mounds in the graveyard. You come into the world from somewhere you don't know and you leave it for another somewhere you don't know. All you have is that little stretch of living between two not-knowings. And a body what is smart does all the living she can lest that little speck of living be wasted. And anybody who tells you different can—can just go roll their hoop."

I cried, "But what does that have to do with Mady getting married?"

"Just this, Jess. Mady's got a loving heart too. And if I ain't wrong she's aimin' to do a lot of livin'."

"But couldn't she *live* here with us for a while?"

" 'Twouldn't be the same. Livin' a life somebody else makes for her." She paused and her eyes looked out over the distant countryside. "Recollects you that day at Miss Camilla's when we had a talk 'bout 'gath'rin' the roses while it's May'?"

I said I recollected.

Her eyes came back to mine, steady and sure. "I reckon that's the way Mady feels," she said gravely.

Feverishly I plunged into plans for Mady's wedding and furnishing the little house, and a few weeks later she stood before the minister at Hickory Hill and, her beautiful eyes clear and unafraid, became Joel's wife. And when in a shower of rice they left in the small car which was Andrew's wedding present, Poky grinning delightedly on the back seat at the clatter produced by the tin cans he'd tied on its rear, I turned back to the house where Adeline "redded up," feeling a strange emptiness.

Later, with Mr. Poteat and Andrew, Mitty and I drank coffee and talked. Of my wedding day and the present Andrew had given me: Mr. Dolph and the cumbers; and in answer to Mr. Poteat's question I told how now and then the gypsy wagon dashed up the hill road and spilled Mr. Dolph and Lorny and the cumbers for a brief visit. Then I asked him about Miss Camilla.

Camilla, he said, was—still Camilla. Lived in that big house alone with Eula and Lem to look after her. Didn't seem to realize how it was going down. He dropped by . . . quite often, for he knew she must be lonely though she wouldn't admit it. Night after night she played solitaire in the sitting room—he smiled sadly—and always cheated herself.

That picture of Miss Camilla saddened me. Did he think she would mind, I asked, if I dropped by?

He considered it, his face, meshed with lines of defeat and dissipation, shadowed by his hand.

Then he said gently, "Camilla is a hard woman, my dear. She's never forgiven me for taking your side."

"But you go just the same," I pointed out.

"Yes. But I'm an old man. What she says to me doesn't hurt so . . . much any more."

Because he still loved her, I thought, he would cling though she scorned him. With new prescience I knew that had been his tragedy. In his search for something to replace what was lost, he clung to what had lost its right to hold him, irrevocably bound to what no longer existed. The Old South, his mad wife, now Miss Camilla.

Later, Andrew and his chauffeur helped him into his car—and he too departed. Then only Andrew was left. And when Mitty, saying she was "plumb tuckered out," had gone up to bed, he and I sat on the porch, the voice of the summer's night—the tree frog's chant, a mocking-bird spilling its music rapturously toward the moon—around us.

It was then that he told me he'd been called to Washington, to serve on the War Industries Board.

"But," he added quickly, "I'll be coming back often. It isn't as if I wouldn't."

I said sorrowfully, "So I lose you, too."

The freckled hand was reassuring on mine. "Not lose," he denied, "just lend for a while."

"I don't like it," I said stubbornly. "I don't like it at all!"

His hand raked his hair. "Don't like it so well myself. It's—it's a contingency I didn't expect. . . . I've had to get a young lawyer in to keep his eye on the affairs of Poteat, Whidby and Hardee."

"That's what you get for making such a reputation for yourself," I scolded.

"Yes," he said slowly, "it looks like that's . . . just what I get."

On the night he left I went into town and had dinner with him. We were very gay and laughed a great deal but I—and Andrew too—feeling sad and nostalgic. For we, with many others, were coming to doubt our earlier fatuous assumption that in three months the war would be over and everything the same. We were beginning to know that nothing would be the same ever again.

After dinner we walked along Peachtree Street, which was thronged with soldiers from Camp Gordon, the officers companioned by dashing girls, the buck privates usually in twos or threes or alone and with no girl at all, and I was touched by the lost, homesick look in their eyes. Like this Cade would wander lonely in a strange city. It suddenly struck me as monstrous that we should lift these boys from familiar lives and order, "Go make the world safe for democracy and for us," yet on the street pass them and never acknowledge their presence.

At the Terminal Station, on the same platform where he met me on my return from Vestal Hall, Andrew held me close for a moment and kissed me.

" 'Til the next time," he said.

I repeated, " 'Til the next time."

I stood waving among the many women and girls who watched their men go off to war. Mine, I selfishly gave thanks, was not, like others, bound for overseas or battle. Nevertheless there was little spring in my step as I returned up the long stairs and walked out to the Plaza to my car, a newer car and larger but not half so beloved as my first Model T Ford. To me that would ever be the most magnificent of cars.

Now, though I kept no less busy, I had the uncanny sensation that the orbit of my days had narrowed, and determinedly I tried to widen it. I would stop by Mady's, to find her engrossed in making puppets for the puppet show Joel planned for the mill children while Poky, supposedly helping, managed to deposit a great deal of paint in unlikely places. Standing above them as they worked, engrossed, on the floor, I thought back to another day when he had made free with paint and given me my design for Summer Rain. When he was older, I brooded, perhaps he would like design.

I left after a little, knowing they were hardly aware of my leaving. Their " 'By, Miss Jess" was automatic, abstracted, and though I told myself fiercely that this was as I would wish it, I had the terrible sense that I was no longer needed, that their lives like a widening stream had left the narrow cove of mine behind.

My visits to my mother met with no better luck. Deep in plans for Oakes' marriage to Renette Colquitt, she constantly paused as we talked to consult penciled lists. Now and then Renette would find me there, and I knew by the covert glances she sent my way that her suspicions of me were not allayed by my mother's "Laura Lee's dear friend—and mine."

Sometimes I had the sense of living in a trance, for whatever concerned one part of my mind, there was another part that existed in the past: my first days at Hickory Hill with Wes; afterwards Cade and Mady and Poky. The Sundays when Andrew and I sat on the porch or in winter before the fire and had our long, quiet talks.

No day had passed since his leaving that I had failed to turn over in my mind every memory I had of him. He, like Mitty, had given me "no countin' " love; he with his teasing, twinkling smile, though I realized now that many times he had not felt like smiling. All my years of unsureness and despair, of longings and fears, of expectant hopes shattered over and over—he had been faithful. Even when I forgot his existence, he had stood ready to help, to give.

May came hot and dry to an Atlanta whirling in the vortex of the preparedness program, with millions of dollars being spent on war plants and a frenzied demand for labor and supplies. And on a May morning of humid and stifling heat, Darty and I in the office discussed whether or not Carrebee would go on the double-shift night work which the war boom had started in many Southern mills. We decided against it. Carrebee would continue on single shift. We recognized the fact that the double shift lowered cost and at the same time doubled production, but we also foresaw the overproduction and glutted market which would inevitably result. Furthermore, the prestige of Carrebee Cottons was the result of our policy of not overloading the market—of keeping them at a premium.

It was close to one o'clock when I stepped through the office door and paused for a moment at the top of the steps to allow the breeze to whip through my hair, a welcome relief after the close airless office. Incuriously I looked at what appeared to be an ominous cloud hovering in the distance. Perhaps a thunderstorm would cool things off—

In the next minute my eyes narrowed, curious now. For what I had taken for cloud was like no cloud I'd ever seen. Then I understood. It was dense rolling walls of smoke, billowing and scudding before the breeze with unbelievable swiftness.

While I stood there a mill supply truck rattled through the gate and the young man at the wheel slowed when he saw me.

"Town's afire, Miz Carrebee. Started in a old warehouse on Fort Street and they can't stop it. Heading down the Boulevard now . . . and goin' a mile a minute—"

Before he completed his sentence I was down the steps and, running to my car, I was in it, swinging it through the gate. The Boulevard, he said. The Boulevard . . . and Miss Camilla alone in the house.

As I drove toward town the darkness deepened ominously, its density thrust by massive tongues of flame that shooting skyward carried flaming brands on their breast and flung them and black flaky soot and ashes like terrible snow. I heard the screaming of fire engines, the galloping hooves of their horses, the clanging of bells. And along the sidewalks I passed, the people poured in an unending stream. Mothers dragging small children by the arm, workmen deserting their jobs; old women, shawls about their shoulders, hobbling their way "to the fire."

At Howell Street two blocks from the Boulevard, we were halted by police, but not before I had seen the raging inferno of flame that was cutting across the city, and its direction. Reversing, I turned back a couple of blocks and swinging left, headed for Highland Avenue, planning to follow back streets until I neared Miss Camilla's. Driving, I kept my eye on the mountain of smoke and flame that two blocks away traveled parallel with me; that seemed to progress almost as fast as I, as if the long hot, dry weather had roasted to its taste a palatable dish for its greedy devouring.

At East Avenue I parked the car and, running, covered the few short blocks to the Boulevard, my way impeded by fleeing hundreds burdened with household gear. How foolish they were, I thought. The fire was blocks away; it would never reach here. Then the bedlam of terror—clanging bells and the voices of thousands, the smoke that filled my lungs, its acrid smell in my nostrils—was torn by a deafening blast, and another. I had no realization of what it was until a voice rising clear above the inferno said, "Blasting to stop it. It's leaping from house to house faster 'n a man can walk it. Be here before we know it."

At the Boulevard I paused and looked back up the street toward the fire and then, Oh God! I saw it. As far as the eye could follow, the homes on both sides of the street were monstrous torches. Fire curling through their windows, spewing from roofs, licking from doorways, its crackle and crashing an enormity of sound as if they were ground in a crusher of flame. Even in my brief pause the fire seemed to leap toward me with an unholy hunger and I was running again. But in the other direction toward Miss Camilla's. My breath tore at my throat and chest as the black, smothering smoke swooped down to blot out vision and air, then, lifted by an eddying breeze, thinned and shredded to reveal the flames that leaping forward, pursued me. And now I ran faster.

The house was safe. I saw its turrets and gables rising from the wide lawns where the Dorothy Perkins roses were budding, where the wisteria draped lacy lavender on the side porch. My sigh of relief was a knife of pain through my smoke-clogged chest. Miss Camilla was safe then. She'd had plenty of time. The fire was still a few blocks away. Even as I reassured myself, I saw the men who lurched through the door of the house loaded with household effects and clothing which they heaped hodgepodge on the lawn before they plunged back inside for more.

Then Miss Camilla came through the door, unchanged, assured, self-possessed, and without hurry descended the steps and crossed the lawn. Ordering one of the scurrying men to fetch a chair from the nearby heap, she directed him where to place it and seated herself calmly, and, face serene and head lifted proudly, she watched the men who, scurrying in and out of the house, might have played a fantastic game. To me she was a poignant figure, and in the holocaust of pandemonium and destruction, so alone. I crossed to her side. "Miss Camilla," I said.

She turned her imperturbable face. "Oh, it's you, Jessica." She spoke as formally as if we'd met at an afternoon party, then, turning back to the scurrying men, she forgot me.

"I'm tired of it, you know," she said, not to me but as if she merely gave utterance to her thoughts. The husky laugh then. "Of course, when Mr. Kimball built it back in the 'eighties it was the last word. But really it's quite tacky now."

I glanced at her, not comprehending. Then a scrap of overheard talk made everything clear. ". . . dynamite," someone was saying, "gotta clear a few of 'em out in order to stop the fire."

Now I understood.

"Those new apartments out on Peachtree are simply wonderful, I hear," Miss Camilla's husky casual voice began, but as a man waving a red flag dashed from the house it halted. I gazed avidly at the house. With its carvings and scrolls, its deviously set latticed windows, it rose like a great wooden castle, its pretentiousness mellowed into grace by the new foliage of tall trees and the Virginia Creeper that trailed over it. I remembered its vast lovely rooms where I had cried with joy and wretchedness. I remembered Wes coming to meet me with his certain, careless grace, the gleaming splendor of his first car in the driveway. . . .

If it held so many memories for me, what must it hold for Miss Camilla?

Instinctively I moved and put my hand on her shoulder, but her eyes turned to sweep me coolly and she shrugged away from my touch. "I was bored with it anyway," she said defiantly.

Whether she meant it so or not, it was her farewell. At the moment of her speaking the trembling earth was rent by an earth-splitting roar, the house shuddered as if shaken from within by a giant, then—but with what seemed incredible slowness—it was wrenched and twisted and flung upward with the thunder of doom. Turrets sagged and, collapsing, slid slowly earthward, shards of glass spinning madly, wisteria petals borne in a pale lavender maze on a mushrooming cloud, and nothing was left of the Carrebee house but a vast dust of decayed hours. Before it settled it made visible and terrible the twisted and broken shapes of living; the jumbled debris of the thousands of hours, the rent and jagged foundation demolished. And not wanting to see, I turned to go. And didn't go, but stood gazing off into the trees.

The house of the Carrebees was not wholly obliterated, I realized; nor would it be as long as the summerhouse remained. The summerhouse where small Cissa had scrawled, *Me . . . Cissa Carrebee . . . Me in the rain.* And where young Wes had carved, KEEP OUT . . . THIS MEANS YOU.

I was moved by the sudden desire to cross the lawn, to once more peer in its ghost-haunted space, but instead I turned and walked away, not looking back. Never again would I come to search and peer for the key to unlock a door to something sensed but never revealed. If its presence persisted, if it alone was indestructible, I would worry it no more. I would not return to scuff under its pitiful wreckage. I would let the past be past.

Yet, I told myself as I drove back to Hickory Hill, I had been guilty of just that. I had returned to the past to seek what was dead and gone, what could never be again, what—I was sure—had never had the perfection that memory bestowed upon it. Perhaps, I thought ruefully, I had learned less than I believed, was less wise than I imagined. Or perhaps there was not learning wide enough or wisdom deep enough to make me anything but what I was born, what I would be until I died: a Southerner.

Passing the mill, I decided not to stop. I would go home to tell Mitty of the fire and spend the rest of the day with her. I would get a little living out of living.

At the bottom of the hill road I stopped the car and reaching, took the mail from the rural delivery box. When I had glanced through it swiftly, I put it on the seat beside me, all except Andrew's letter. That I opened and, sitting in the car on the quiet road while in the distance Atlanta's great fire burned, I read it. It was brief—only a note. Due to a contingency, Andrew wrote, in the offices of Poteat, Whidby and Hardee, he was coming home for a few days. He thought he had better let Mitty know so she could get her hand "in" on spoon bread.

I slipped it back into its envelope and thrust it into my bosom, then, starting my engine, went up the hill road to Hickory Hill. And it was as if with every foot of the way my heart was lifted and lightened.

Andrew was coming home. . . .